FIRESTORM

FIRESTORM

Eleanor Liggens

Printed in the United States of America
ISBN 978-1-967279-23-4 (sc)
ISBN 978-1-967279-24-1 (e)

2025.04.25

This book is printed on acid-free paper.

Blue Ink Media Solutions
1111B S Governors Ave
STE 7582 Dover,
DE 19904

www.blueinkmediasolutions.com

This book is presented in loving memory of my big brother.

Booker Teleferio Hall
June 1952 – May 2012

A loving brother, a kind individual to all that ever knew him
and just a great all around human being.
I love you Big Brother

FOREWORD

The following story is based on the true experiences of the co-author, Booker Hall, during his tenure as manager of a Hot Springs Tourist Resort in Lolo National Forest in Montana. The names have been changed and certain characters and events have been dramatized.

Table of Contents

PROLOGUE

" *I*'m sorry, Mr. Newman, but as you know, we are experiencing severe budget cutbacks," the well-dressed man in the black business suit solemnly explained from behind his expensive mahogany desk. Over three-thousand jobs had to be eliminated and unfortunately, yours had to be one of them." He paused, with an unmitigated expression upon his face.

"But look Ron," Newman emphatically pleaded, "I've worked here for more than five years. You can't just cut my job like that." He snapped his fingers.

"I'm afraid I have no choice, Ken." Chambers calmly continued. "As of tomorrow you no longer work here. You'll get two week's salary in lieu of notice, but as of now, you are laid-off… laid off… laid off…"

Newman shot upright in bed and stared blankly into the darkness of the room. It took him several minutes to realize he had only been dreaming. But the scene, unfortunately, was no dream. The words laid-off reverberated in his mind like echoes through a deep canyon.

After five years, a $150,000 dollar salary with an important position as a public relations executive for one of the largest nuclear power plants on the West Coast, Newman, at twenty-nine years of age, thought he had it made. He lived in a $300,000 two and half bath, four bedroom house, with a two car garage, in an affluent suburban neighbor. He had a top of line 1980 Seville, three year old Cadillac, almost paid for. Expensive technology filled every room in the house with big screen TV's per bedroom, surround- sound with Bose speakers, a Crosley Record player with a diamond needle, leather furniture and much, much, more. As life was good, for what seemed like a never ending job,

Newman spent generously. Every month he held wild parties, every year luxurious vacations with different women abroad. Never did it cross his mind that he could be laid off. Those words again! This one single event, dramatically altered his life. He had no other choice but to sell his house, car, and worldly items, barely making enough to keep him afloat for 6 months.

With $17,000 dollars in his pocket, he moved to an apartment where he remained for 8 months trying to find a job. As months passed, money dwindled, Newman knew he had to act fast. One day, while sitting on the side of the bed contemplating his next move, he decided to call his sister in D.C. He asked if he could stay with her until he got on his feet. The reply was what he was hoping to here. He told her he would be leaving the next day. With less than $5,000 to his name, he knew he needed to act quickly before he didn't have enough money to travel. He asked his friends for help in transportation as he couldn't even afford to purchase a used car to make the trip, as it would further deplete his funds. Without fail, a dear friend gave him a 1967 light blue broken-down VW Bus. It moved, but not more than 50 miles an hour with gas pedal to the floor. So the journey would be long and tedious. Newman crammed all his earthly belongings into the bus and started on his journey.

As he drove around the winding roads on his journey from Montana to D. C., there was one thing he meant to do and never did. He wanted to spend a couple of nights at a beautiful resort nestled in the deep woods of Lolo, about 10 miles off the main highway. Newman knew he had nothing but time and decided to make a detour before continuing his travels.

Once he arrived there, he was in a quaint, sparsely, but beautifully furnished hotel room in the remote mountains of Western Montana. All of his earthly belongings in a beat-up VW Bus. Unable to sleep, he reached for the small clock that ticked methodically on the headboard of his bed. The lighted hands read 3:30 a.m. He tried to mentally convert Mountain Time to Eastern Standard Time.

"I'd better call my sister," he muttered aloud. "To let her know I made a short stop." He groped at the nearby nightstand for a phone before remembering that the woman at the check-in counter said that the hotel's only telephone was in her office.

He mumbled a profanity word under his breath and rolled his legs out of the bed. He grabbed his trousers, threw on a pajama shirt, and headed for the door. His room door open to the outdoors. A cool, crisp, gentle breeze greeted him as he stepped out in the morning air. Bright stars twinkled overhead as the roar of an eighteen-wheeler barreling down the highway punctuated the stillness of the night.

Just a few yards from his room was a small rustic log cabin. The words, *Resort Check-In* emblazoned in white neon lights were over the front door. He walked up the steps and pushed the wooden door open. The mature, middle-aged blonde woman with an hour-glass figure and piercing green eyes looked up from the receptionist desk as he entered. She was still dressed like a million bucks with a tight fitting black skirt and white blouse, with paten black pumps to match.

"Mr. Newman." She smiled, as he entered the office.

"That's right." Newman beamed, somewhat amazed she could remember him, especially considering all of the other guests that must pass daily through these doors.

"I need to make a call, and I remembered, you said the only phone on the premises was in your office."

"Sorry for the inconvenience," she somberly replied.

"Oh, don't worry. I couldn't sleep with so much on my mind. Besides, the brisk morning air did me good."

"Come into my office. You get a much better reception in here." Newman followed her a few steps to the back. She sat behind her huge beautifully designed oak wood desk and turned the phone toward him. "If it's long distance, I'll have to ask that it be collect."

"Sure."

Newman pushed the operator button. As he waited for the operator to answer, he couldn't help but notice the complete state of disarray apparent throughout the office. The desk was cluttered with papers and books of every size, shape, and description. Folded white bed sheets were stacked on the well-worn sofa across from her desk. Unopened mail lay scattered on a nearby end table. In a far corner of the room, a single stack of ledgers piled just a little too high, was precariously close to toppling over.

The operator finally came on line. Newman placed his call. The woman watched as Newman stood patiently with the phone pressed to his ear. She observed his tall six-foot frame, slender, yet masculine body and dark brown eyes. A truly handsome man, she thought, with his small fro and mustache trimmed to perfection on his top lip.

Seconds later, he dejectedly eased the phone down. "Line's busy," he volunteered.

"Well, feel free to wait," the woman insisted.

"Thank you. I will. It's important I make this call." Newman walked over to the sofa.

"Just push that stuff out of your way."

Newman set the laundry aside and eased into the deep cushioned sofa. The two sat quietly. He slowly eyed the log patterns in the ceiling, trying not to notice the sheer clutter that overwhelmed her office. Finally, the silence became too awkward for the both of them.

"So, are you just passing through?"

"Yes, I'm having a little car trouble." He didn't want to state the whole truth. "But, I'm on my way to D.C. and I need to call my sister to let her know I'll be a couple of days later getting there."

"Really? Won't you wake them at this hour of the morning?"

"Probably, it's Saturday. So they could go right back to sleep. I just don't want them to worry."

"I can understand that. You know… D.C. is filled with a lot of historical information. I've never been there. I'll have to try and make it someday."

"Maybe the owners might give you some time off and you could go one summer."

"Oh," she chuckled. "I don't think that's possible. You see, I am the owner."

"Really?"

"Don't sound so surprised Mr. Newman."

"It's just that… well, you were here when I checked in this afternoon. Now, here it is going on four in the morning and you're still here. I thought an owner would just hire someone to run the place, especially at odd hours like this. I mean you are still utterly, beautifully dressed, if I might add."

She sighed. "Thank you. But, I wish I could, believe me. I put in long hours because it's not just the hotel. I have a swimming pool, bar, restaurant, RV Park, horseback riding, golf, and that's just to name a few that I manage. They have to operate every day of the week. That's just the half of it. I simply can't afford to hire anyone to work nights. My husband and I even sleep in the spare bedroom down the hall. So as soon as I hear that little bell tinkle..." she smiled, pointing to the small silver bell hanging over the door in the outer office. "I just come a runnin'. You just caught me finishing up some overdue paper work. I try to get to bed around two in the morning."

"Sounds like you wear more than one hat around here."

"Sometimes I wear all the hats." Vicki smiled. "It's a challenging job, but then I've never run from a challenge in my life."

Newman was impressed by the tone of determination he heard in her voice and the defiant spark in her eye. She reminded him of the iron-willed matrons who commanded huge empires on night-time soap operas. While her empire was much smaller, it was, in fact, very real.

"And what do you do, Mr. Newman?"

He smiled. "Good question. Since we are being honest, I used to work in the public relations office for a big electrical power firm. Now, I don't know. I got caught up in a big company layoff. Lost my house, car, almost everything," he said dejectedly. "I've got some relatives in D.C. They've agreed to put me up for a few days."

"That's nice of them."

"Yeah, but I've always liked the wide open spaces of the Northwest, and I had heard what a beautiful place this was. So before I set sails to D.C., I also wanted to spend a little time here to relax and enjoy the view for a couple of days."

"Great."

"Besides, I'd really hate to live in the big city. I have my reservations."

The woman leaned back in her chair. "Are you serious about not wanting to leave the Northwest?"

"Certainly, but like I said, I have no place to stay."

"Yes, you do."

Newman looked perplexed. "Excuse me. Ahhh...? Where might that be?"

"Here at my resort."

His jaw dropped in amazement as he sat erect on the sofa. "Are you serious?"

"You obviously have lots of management experience. Look about you," she motioned around her office, "I could use some management expertise."

"I know, but—"

"Now, I couldn't pay you what you are probably used to making with that big corporation, but I will pay you what I can, and you could have your own choice of living quarters. The hotel is for the guests. I have dorms for single female and male employees and cabins for any families that work here."

Newman was totally taken back by the woman's blunt proposal. She was serious, there was no doubt. And depending on the charity of the relatives after living successfully on his own for so many years seemed almost humiliating. And the longer he stayed with them without finding a job, the more likely his visit would become increasingly strained. Working here would be nothing like working for a large corporation, but at least he'd be independent---making his own way.

"Thanks for the vote of confidence... Miss?"

"Victoria," she volunteered, realizing Newman didn't know her name. "Victoria Marshall, but please call me Vicki."

"Vicki," Newman smiled. "Thank you for your trust, but you hardly know me."

"You can't stay in this business long and not be a good judge of character."

"But I have absolutely no idea of how to run a tourist resort."

"There are only two rules to know. Rule number one, is keep the customer happy."

"And the second?"

"If the customer is unhappy, see Rule Number One."

Newman chuckled and shook his head. "I know this is the 1980's and you mean well, it's just that I don't think you've thought this through. There are bound to be problems."

"There are always problems in this business. That's what managers are for."

"I mean special problems."

"Why, because you're Black?"

Her bluntness caught him off guard, but she had addressed his major concern about staying there. He had yet to see another Black face in the seven hours he had been at the resort. These high mountain resort areas were home to some of the most die-hard, red-necked cowboys, loggers, and long-haul truckers in the state. Stories of area White supremacist groups made almost daily headlines. Living in this area, some people would probably question his sanity.

"Vicki, you know what this area is like. Most of the people here have never seen a Black man, let alone worked with one. Your crew would never work for me."

"They work for who I tell them to or they can find another job. Besides, if an old Polish warhorse like me, can get a decent day's work out of 'em, I know you can."

"Vicki, I just don't know," Newman countered. "I've never tried anything like this before."

She leaned toward him and smiled a confident sort of smile that made him feel a little at ease.

"That would make two of us," she said assuredly. "Look, I don't want to keep you, if you don't really want to stay. But, if you think you can face a challenge and a lot of hard work, I could really use you."

Staying at this Montana Resort did have its advantages, Newman thought as his mind began to race. The great outdoors versus the rat race of the big city. He'd be on his own again, rather than living off the charity of his relatives. Plus Vicki might be right, it would probably be the biggest management challenge of his life.

"Okay," he boldly announced. "I'll give it my best shot, and if it doesn't work out, I'm on my way to D.C."

"Sounds fair. I just know you'll love it here." She smiled. "Now about the money…"

"Don't worry. Whatever you pay the rest of the crew will be fine."

"Great! Why don't you just stay in your room, free, of course and I will get you started first thing later this morning when my accountant arrives."

"Okay, but I still have to make my phone call. They need to know I might take a few extra days in getting there."

Vicki set the phone near him. Newman picked up the receiver and started punching in the numbers.

Newman made his phone call and went back to his room, pondering the merits of his decision to stay. Even if the job worked out, resort management wasn't something he really wanted to do. The longer he stayed, the longer it would take him to get back into corporate management. But he did promise to at least give it a try. Perhaps, with Vicki's support, the job might even become a working vacation.

C H A P T E R

1

*I*t was only a few hours later, still early morning when Newman had donned work jeans and a sweatshirt in anticipation of his first workday. The bright morning sun was just beginning to peek over the majestic pines that surrounded the resort. This was his first look at the complex by morning light. Overall, it resembled a small frontier town in a Hollywood movie. To his right several yards away, was the service station. In front of him, also several yards away, was a log cabin-style restaurant. There were steady streams of thick white smoke from a small crooked chimney made of rock that appeared to have been designed that way. The chimney gradually puffed consistent spurts of little white smoke clouds into the hazy morning sky. Adjacent to the restaurant was a classic western style bar, it was already busy. Several eighteen-wheelers and other smaller vehicles were jammed into the parking area. A few feet from the restaurant you could see visible signs with arrows leading to the pool house that had to be, not far off in a distance.

Across the highway, off in a distance, was a narrow wooden bridge that spanned a gentle, rushing stream of water. On the other side of the bridge was a small general store sitting along an unpaved dirt road that led to the entrance of the RV Park. Several motor homes were already quietly parked there.

He stood surveying the scene when suddenly he heard his name called. "Kenny," the voice hailed.

1

Newman turned to see Vicki waving at him from the steps of the restaurant.

"I have set you up with my accountant, Lisa. Now, I want you to have breakfast with us. Come in and meet everybody."

Newman followed Vicki toward the rustic-looking building as she stepped inside. Upon entering the establishment, mixed voices and tinkling silverware permeated the packed dining area. Loggers, truckers, and early morning guests filled every table. Vicki walked passed a row of tables, stopping momentarily to chat briefly with a customer before making her way back to a long table near the rear of the room. There, seven men were seated, voraciously eating breakfast. Each man had a worn, rugged cowboy exterior, complete with Western-style boots, wide-brimmed hats, blue jeans, and John Deere ball caps.

Vicki made her way to the head of the table as each man continued to eagerly devour his meal.

"Where is this new head honcho?" One man asked without looking up from his plate.

"This is…" Vicki paused, "He was right behind me," Vicki said taking her seat, looking around. "He's going to join us for breakfast."

"Why you bringin' in an outsider?" One scruffy, unshaven cowboy grumbled between bites. "Carl can do the job, if you'd just let him. For heaven sakes Vicki, he's your son, ain't he?"

"No!" She snapped bitterly. "I won't ever put Carl in charge here again. Besides, you all know where I stand on that subject. Now case closed!"

"Okay, don't bite my head off. Where is this new boss man anyway?"

Newman had stopped in the doorway engulfing the picturesque establishment. Beautifully finished oak wood lined the walls with rodeo cowboys riding bulls. These were obvious events that had be held in prior years at this resort. The fourteen foot ceiling, lined with smooth log wood, angle shaped from the top to the wall. Each table seated four or more people with checkered white and light blue table clothes. Glass candles centered each table along with rolled napkins that contained silverware in them. Salt and pepper shakers were filled to the brim and country barbecue sauce bottles all sat center mass on each table. The fireplace was rock layered all the way to the crown with a huge opening at the base that maintained a real fire. This edifice could easily hold over two-hundred people. In surveying the room, he spotted Vicki waving her hand. He slowly moved in her direction. He stepped up to the breakfast table. Vicki stood and put her arm around his shoulder.

"Here he is gentlemen, Kenny Newman."

There was dead silence. Three mouths dropped in total disbelief. Three others just stared in amazement. The other man didn't look up from his food until several moments later. He froze in mid-bite. Newman smiled a forced, tight-lipped smile as he saw their faces slowly evolve from shock to anger. Vicki took her arm from his shoulder, pulled up her chair and sat down.

"Will you join us for breakfast Kenny?" Vicki motioned toward an empty chair.

Newman scanned the seven rankled faces. "Nooo, I'm not hungry. I'll catch a bite later. Right now I just want to get the lay of the land. Anyway, I will be talking to each of you individually later, so we can… how do you say… chew the fat? See you later Vicki."

He patted her gently on the shoulder and walked away. Seven pair of piercing eyes followed him as he left. Once out of sight, all eyes turned inchmeal towards Vicki.

"Do you know he's colored?" One man bitterly asked.

"I knew you'd notice sooner or later, Skeeter," Vicki chided.

"I can't work for no nigger, hell no! Vicki, no way."

"You will Matt, if you want to continue working here." She rose quickly from her seat, leaned forward with both hands on the table and then pointed her index finger menacingly at each of them. "I know this is going to be an adjustment for a lot of you, but you'd better make that adjustment, and make it fast. Because when he talks to you, it'll be just like me talking to you. And you all don't want to piss me off!" She observed their faces. "Do you!"

Seven quiet faces stared up at her.

"Ahhh…" Skeeter started to comment, then observed her stare down and became silent.

"Good! Now, finish your breakfast and get to work," she snarled. "The day's a-wastin'." She walked away without another word spoken.

Newman spent the first several hours trying to learn the layout of the area. Though the actual main compound encompassed only a few square yards, the total resort covered over forty acres, much of it wilderness. It was filled with hundreds of campsites, hiking and horseback trails that meandered deep into the wilderness. There was also a horse stable, an animal corral, and a gigantic open pasture filled with tall green grass.

Lewis and Clark had actually blazed most of the trails through this area. Newman started to empathize with them as he climbed huge rock formations and wandered down several hiking trails wondering what was around the next bend. He finally climbed a huge precipice over-looking the resort. His perch gave him a panoramic view of the entire area. Tall pines and tamaracks stretched as far as the eye could see, with only the meandering highway twisting through the otherwise-unspoiled majestic scenery.

Newman knew he had delayed his inevitable confrontation with the crew long enough and his self-guided tour of the resort was just a subtle way of trying to avoid the unavoidable. He made his way down the mountainside and walked over to the service station. He reached into his pocket and pulled out the list of names Vicki had given him. Dave Jackson managed the service station and Tim Jansen served as the mechanic.

Newman took a deep breath, then walked into the pump area. He saw a heavyset man in a dirty, tattered, oil-stained jumpsuit, pumping gas into a late-model Chevy sedan. He glanced up as Newman approached, then continued filling the car. Newman headed for the service station doorway.

"Hey!" The man called, looking up from his work. "Don't go in there!"

"It's okay," Newman casually replied. "I'll just wait inside until you finish there."

He yanked the nozzle out of the gas tank and jammed it back onto the pump. "I said don't go in there!" He vehemently insisted. "That's my shop and I don't need no…" he stopped in mid-sentence. "I don't need you poking around my shop telling me what to do."

He wiped his hands on his jumpsuit and collected the money before the car slowly pulled away.

"I'm not your enemy here, I'm just trying to be of assistance, okay?"

Jackson walked briskly past Newman into the service station and stepped behind the counter, Newman followed.

"Look," he angrily began as he rang up the sale. "I don't know why Vicki hired you, but I don't need you snooping around here telling me how to run this filling station. I and Tim have been doing fine. We don't need no help from the likes of you."

Just then a voice from the service bay interrupted their conversation.

"I've finished the brakes on the logging truck, Dave." The young muscular dirty-faced blonde kid stood in the doorway. He looked late teens, early twenties, wiping his oily hands on a paper towel.

Newman noticed the wedding band on his finger. "Hey young man, you should take off the wedding band if you are going to work on these vehicles. It could get caught up in something and you might end up losing a finger."

"Oh yea. You're right. I didn't wear it at all. But my wife, Barbara, keeps insisting that I wear it. So I forget sometimes." He removed the ring and placed it in his pocket.

"Well now, since you've finished the logging truck, start on the dump truck over there."

"What's wrong with it?"

"How in the hell am I supposed to know? Big Jake said it won't start. You're the mechanic, you find out why."

Tim seemed bewildered by Jackson's unusually harsh tone, but said nothing further as he stepped back into the service bay.

"Look." Newman calmly began, "No one said you were doing a bad job. But maybe, it's possible you can do a better one."

"And I suppose you have all the answers."

"Hardly, but with your help, we could at least agree on the right questions."

Jackson slammed the cash register shut. "Look you don't know the first thing about running a service station or a resort. In fact, we're all bettin' that you won't last the week here. This is White folks' country and you ain't got no business here. You ain't welcome! I don't know what Ms. Vicki was thinkin' about when she hired the likes of you."

Newman bristled at his suggestion that he didn't belong here. Jackson was obviously in no mood for friendly reasoning, so now it was time to put the gloves on.

"Now listen to me, you dime store bigot!" Newman snapped. "Like it or not, I'm here and I intend to stay. So get used to seeing my smiling face a lot around here. And as far as this being White folks' country? --- Well it ain't no more. There's a new face in town. You better get used to it." He and Jackson locked momentarily in a hostile stare. "We'll be seeing a lot of each other, Mr. Jackson."

Newman walked calmly out of the service station. He looked back over his shoulder to see Jackson still angrily eying him. Newman knew his initial meeting with the crew was going to be stormy, but he only hoped that he wouldn't have to repeat that scene with every single employee.

He walked over to the restaurant and stepped into the dining area. It was mostly empty. The lone waitress was leisurely wiping off the vacant tables, while the cashier was ringing up a customer's receipt.

There was a small path leading to the adjacent bar. He was not only surprised to find the bar open so early, but the music was blaring from the jukebox. It didn't have a familiar country twang, but rather had a more contemporary beat, music he hadn't heard since he arrived.

He stepped into the bar. Behind the long wooden counter stood a large heavyset Indian woman with two breast-length braids and a colorful band wrapped around her forehead. She was wiping the countertop in wide, sweeping circles. She glanced up as Newman entered.

"Hi, you must be the new manager." She beamed as Newman walked up to the counter.

"You seem to know me, but we haven't met."

"Oh news of your arrival traveled fast around this place."

"I've only been in this position for a few hours."

"Yea, but, you're unique. I'm Laura Sixkiller, the bartender." She and Newman shook hands. "Wow," she sighed, "a strong handgrip. A man should have a strong grip."

"Well, yours isn't too bad either."

"I know. I arm wrestle as a hobby. In fact, I'm the female arm wrestling champ for the state of Montana."

"Good for you."

Newman didn't really care one way or the other. He gently turned his attention to the modestly furnished bar. Behind the counter were four well-stocked shelves of assorted liquors and spirits. About sixty tables were scattered around the room, with little dishes of peanuts in the center of the white tablecloth. A billiard table sat in the center floor. Another wide square vacant area in the corner of the room was for dancing and a small band. A jukebox and a couple of pinball machines completed the furnishings. Newman sat on one of the barstools.

"So, what brings you to a place like this, Mr. Newman?"

"Ken, please… and it's a long story."

"Well, if there's one thing you'll find around here, is that everybody's got one."

"One what?"

"Long story. Nobody works here, especially for the long hours and low wages, unless they have a long story."

"By that, you mean…"

"A broken marriage or scrape with the law. You name it. It's either here or will be here."

"And how about you? What's your long story?"

Laura stopped wiping the bar. "The going wage for female arm wrestlers isn't too hot. So I came here for the tourist season."

"I take it then, you like it here?"

"Three hundred dollars a month, three meals a day, a roof over my head, and tips. What more could you want?"

"And Vicki, what about her? You like working for her?"

"Oh." Laura thought for a moment. "She's okay. She shoots from the hip a lot. She goes a lot with her gut instincts, which isn't bad, I suppose. But don't get on her bad side. I've seen what she can do to people who cross her."

"Really that bad, huh?"

"Let's put it like this. If she likes you, she'll move heaven and earth for you. If she doesn't, she'll rip you a new asshole, if you know what I mean."

"I'll keep that in mind."

"I wouldn't worry too much. Vicki made you her manager. She's never trusted anybody like that since… well, in a long time. So you must be on her good side. Besides we've never had a Black man here before. So, she apparently has a lot of confidence in you."

"Well…" Newman got up from the stool. "I told her I would do my best."

Newman glanced over his shoulder to see a petite young man with straight blonde hair that extended to the middle of his back. His soft, delicate physical features were accented by the dainty gait.

"Oh, you must be the new colored gentleman I've been hearing about," his soft high pitched voice greeted. "I didn't know you had company, Laura. I'll come back later."

"Oh no." Laura insisted. "We were through. What did you need?"

"Are you going to eat lunch back here or in the dining hall?"

"Back here today, Kelly. I've got to sweep this place out before two. I won't have time to make our usual scheduled lunch."

"Then I'll bring you lunch in here."

He turned and headed back toward the kitchen. Newman watched Kelly with measured disbelief as he left.

"Just who is that?"

"Oh that's Kelly, the Chef. Talk about weak handshakes, it's like shaking a dishrag."

"I can imagine. Is he…?" Newman rocked his hand slightly.

"As a three-dollar bill." Laura volunteered.

"That's interesting."

"Why, Mr. Newman?" She began coyly. "Don't tell me you are prejudice against gays?"

"No, no, it's just that with all of these macho cowboys, he-man loggers, and truckers around here, you'd think somebody like Kelly would be run out of town on a rail."

"Maybe, but for one thing, he knows his way around a kitchen. He can make clam chowder soup that'll bring tears to your eyes. It's sooo good. And if there's one thing these guys hate more than gays, it's bad food. Besides, when he dresses up, you'd swear he was a woman. You should see him in here some nights trying to pick up a boyfriend."

"Isn't that sort of dangerous?"

"He's gotten beat up several times. But then again, he hasn't gotten beat up several times, too, if you know what I mean."

"Spin the bottle and take your chances."

"I suppose…"

At that moment, the front door swung open, in swaggered a hefty-framed man, with a cowboy hat tilted back on his head. He had a protruding beer gut that drooped over the buckle of his gun belt. A .357 strapped low on his right leg. Trapped under his left arm were two money bags.

"Oh boy," Laura sighed. "Here comes Deputy Dog."

"Deputy Dog?"

"That's Curtis. He's our resident security expert," she said in obvious contempt. Curtis walked up to the bar.

"You must be the new guy Vicki hired?" He extended his hand. "Curtis Branin."

Newman accepted. "Ken Newman."

"Well, I don't know exactly what you're gonna do around here, but when it comes to safety and security, I'm you're man," he proudly announced. "I've got over fifteen years of police and security experience."

"I'm impressed. I'm sure there's a lot I can learn from you."

Curtis took one of the bags from under his arm and handed it to Laura. She turned and hit the *No Sale* button on her register. She removed all of the cash from the bag, placed it in the register, then closed the drawer.

"Being so far from town like we are, you can't afford to be lax on security. That's why I keep ole Herman here," Curtis patted his sidearm, "with me at all times."

"Herman?" Newman asked. "You named your gun?"

"Damn right. Cause if the time comes, Herman can sure do a lot of talkin'. See you later." Curtis headed for the restaurant.

Laura contemptuously eyed him as he left. "He's more dangerous than any robber could ever be."

"But fifteen years of law enforcement? He's got to be good at something."

"They kicked him off the force two years ago for being a fuckin' drunk. Big Jake just hired him because he couldn't get anybody else to take the job for the wages they pay around here."

"Big Jake?"

"Vicki's husband, Jacob Marshall. They call him Big Jake. He's about sixty, built like an ox, big muscles, and deep voice. He runs a logging operation up in the hills."

"Haven't met him yet."

"Oh you will. Believe me, you will. He doesn't let anyone stay here if he doesn't like them."

Not disturbed by the comment, Newman placed a check by the bar column on his notes. He had seen the gas station, bar, restaurant, and had only the pool, the RV Park and the stables remaining. He was also beginning to wonder about the highly unusual assortment of characters he was finding himself surrounded by—a gay chef, an Indian arm wrestler, a bigoted gas station attendant and a drunken ex-cop. All, being led by a Black, out-of- work public relations executive. Given this start, he couldn't wait to meet the rest of the staff.

Newman left the restaurant and drove over to the pool house. Steam from the hot springs drifted through the air. The mixed sound of splashing water, screaming children and other muffled voices were heard as he entered the building. One sign pointed towards the women's dressing area, the other towards the men's.

"What do you need?" A low voice growled. Newman turned to see a cowboy seated behind a counter, rows of clothes baskets were stacked neatly behind him.

"I'm Ken Newman." He walked toward the counter and extended his hand.

"I know who you are," the cowboy snapped. "I wanna know what you want."

Newman dropped his hand back by his side. "Just checking out the pool."

"Well, save yourself some trouble. I've been running this place for two years now, and I don't want your help or advice."

Newman could feel a confrontation rising. While he knew race was definitely a factor, this man's almost immediate air of defiance underscored an added tone of resentment.

As they faced each other, three women came through the front door.

"Is this where you pay for the hot springs?" One lady asked.

"Why yes it is. That'll be three dollars for each of you."

The woman handed the cowboy a ten. He reached into a money bag, handed her a one dollar bill. Then gave her three empty baskets.

"Just put your valuables in here and bring them back to the counter."

The woman grabbed the baskets, handed one to her friends, and they disappeared into the ladies' area.

"How do you keep track of how many people you have every day?"

"That's none of your business."

"It is if you can't keep an accurate count of the number of customers in and out of this pool every day. It's a golden opportunity to rip off the resort."

The cowboy slowly rose from his seat and leaned forward angrily over the counter. "You callin' me a thief, boy?"

Newman immediately stiffened. "No, I'm not calling you a thief, unless of course…"

The two men squared off like gunfighters at high noon, when suddenly a young boy in swimming trunks ran dripping wet past Newman up to the counter.

"Basket 19, please."

The cowboy broke his stare with Newman, he reached back, and handed the boy a basket. "Here you go."

"Thank you." He smiled, then darted back into the men's area.

The cowboy looked back at Newman. "Another time, another place," he calmly warned.

Newman waited momentarily, staring at him, then quietly turned and walked into the men's dressing area. He surveyed the room. There were only stalls and benches. Next, he stepped back out to observe the vast indoor Olympic size pool area of swimmers. There were people of all ages--just splashing, conversing and playing. Newman stepped out a side door and there was another pool, not quite as large. There were just a few people tanning under the morning sun on this beautiful day. However, the cowboy still eyed Newman with contempt, as he walked the vicinity.

By nightfall, Newman had visited every station at the resort and had come to the conclusion the task was more difficult than he'd first imagined. It would be bad enough trying to manage the place with the crew's cooperation, but without it, his job would be next to impossible. He wasn't even sure if Vicki was aware of the intense, blatant, and open hostility he was facing.

It was late night before he stepped back into her office. She looked up from her paperwork as he walked in.

"How's the first day on the job?" Vicki smiled, laying her pencil to one side.

"Oh," Newman sighed as he eased down onto the sofa. "It's going to have its moments, I can see that."

"Oh, don't let the crew get you down. It's just the first day. All they see is Black. Just give it some time."

"Maybe, I don't know. That guy over in the swimming area was ready to take a swing at me today."

"Carl?"

"I don't know his name. The conversation never got that far."

"Don't worry about him." Vicki quickly reached for her phone. "I'll take care of him right now."

"Don't!" Newman immediately insisted. "If I have to get you to step in every time I have a problem, I'll never get anywhere with these guys."

Vicki eased the phone down. "Have it your way. But, Carl used to be the manager here. So he might give you a little more trouble than the rest."

"Manager? Did you fire him or something?"

"Damn right I did."

"Then why is he still here?"

"He's also my son. That's the only reason he's still on the grounds, but he doesn't have the authority of a three-legged dog around here, and he knows it. If he's forgotten that, then I'll damn sure remind him."

"Then you have no objection to my instituting some sort of accounting system for the pool. Like, issuing tickets to the customers so we can keep an accurate tally of the pool traffic."

"Oh no. In fact, I've been trying to do something like that for a long time, so I could determine the correct amount of money being turned in from the pool. Right now, I'm totally at the mercy of whoever is on duty over there."

"Well, with your own son over there, you should be getting an accurate account of the pool sales."

She leaned toward him with a pointed finger. "I don't trust Carl as far as I can throw him and you shouldn't either."

Newman could see the mounting anger in her eyes. The mere mention of Carl's name triggered the same response as would a red flag to a raging bull. He thought it best to drop the subject for now. Although, he was curious as to why she so distrusted her own son.

"So where are you going from here?" She turned her attention back to the papers on her desk.

"Oh, the bar looks lively tonight. I think I'll drop by and see how Laura is doing, then call it a night."

"You have been up since six this morning. You must be exhausted."

"I am, but I haven't done this much physical labor in a long time. After sitting behind a desk for the past few years, it's actually been kinda fun."

Vicki laughed. "See me in a week and say that!"

Newman left the office and headed toward the bar. The parking lot was packed with vehicles as late-night cowboys and their ladies came and went. The twang of country music permeated the night air as laughter and mixed voices flowed from the bar. Newman pushed through the saloon-style double doors. The patrons were crammed onto the dance floor, whirling to the sound of the four-piece band on the alcove stage. Every table was filled with beer cans and half-empty alcohol bottles as the revelers traded talk and laughter.

Laura was working the bar feverishly, scurrying from end to end, refilling orders and wiping the countertop. Newman stepped up to the counter next to a cowboy nursing a half-empty beer mug. He looked at Newman, but Newman pretended not to notice him.

"What'll it be, soul brother?" The cowboy laughed. His breath reeked of beer. "You take a wrong turn somewhere? Ain't none of that Michael Jackson shit in here." He laughed loudly at his attempted humor.

Newman glanced at him, but chose to ignore him. "Laura!" He hailed, waving at her. She acknowledged him, poured another drink, and hurried down to Newman's end of the bar. "Looks like you need roller skates."

"Oh no, just another set of arms." She smiled. "What are you doing here?"

"Just came by to see if you needed anything. Maybe you could use another bartender on duty."

"Probably, but then I wouldn't make as much in tips. No, these folks came here to drink, and they know I'll get to them sooner or later."

"Well, you seem to have things under control. So I'll have one drink and call it a night."

"You bet. Whatta ya have Ken?"

The cowboy motioned to Laura. "Another round here," he slurred, pointing to his glass.

"Take care of him first Laura. I can wait."

Laura rushed over and immediately grabbed the glass. She turned, tilted it slightly under the draft dispenser, and pulled the lever. The golden fluid flowed to a frosty head. She turned again and set the glass in front of the cowboy.

"One dollar and fifty cents."

The cowboy began searching through the stack of ones on the counter in front of him.

"Hey!" He grew concerned. "Where's my $5? I'm supposed to have eighteen bucks here." He looked up at Laura. "I had $18 lying on this counter, now there's only $11."

"Sir," Laura calmly explained, "each draft is a $1.50, and so far you've had at least six. Out of $20 that only leaves $11."

"I ain't had no six beers," he bitterly complained. "You just took my money that was lying here." His tone grew increasingly hostile.

Laura also was starting to get riled. "You calling me a thief, Custer?" She angrily squinted her eyes.

"I know I had more than eleven bucks upon this counter."

"That's it Mister." She slammed her fist down. "You're through drinkin'. Get outta my bar!" She pointed toward the door.

"Not without my money, you thievin' squaw!"

Without hesitation, Laura's fist suddenly fired across the counter and landed solidly against the man's jaw. He reeled off the stool and fell back against several people before landing on the floor next to billiard table.

"Squaw that, motherfucker!" Laura yelled.

The man slowly grabbed the edge of the pool table and pulled himself onto his feet. The laughter and frivolity suddenly ceased as all eyes quickly shifted to Laura and the cowboy. Newman had never been in a bar fight before. While he didn't think Laura should tolerate racial insults, punching an obviously drunken man didn't seem like the best solution to the problem either. Maybe trying to reason with him might help resolve the matter.

"Excuse me sir," Newman politely began, stepping between Laura and the cowboy. "I think we can resolve this problem without further violence. How about we refund som…?"

The cowboy snatched a cue stick and mashed it against the billiard table. The stick exploded into pieces and the front piece flew wildly across the room. He brandished the broken cue menacingly at Newman.

"No squaw's gonna rip me off, sucker punch me, and expect to get away with it. Now step aside, nigger. This is between me and the squaw."

He pulled the cue back and swung at Newman. Several patrons screamed. Newman ducked just in time to feel the breeze created by the swinging stick, whoosh over his head. Instinctively, he jammed his fist into the man's abdomen. The cowboy doubled over, wincing in pain. Newman then jammed his knee up into the man's chin. The blow stood the cowboy upright. Newman quickly spun the man around, grabbed the back of his collar, and unceremoniously ushered him through the crowd and out the front doors.

As Newman returned to the counter, every eye in the saloon silently, followed him. The tavern was pin-drop quiet. Newman motioned toward the band several times. Finally the band leader started playing again, and the silence slowly escalated to murmurs and low whispers. Newman gradually eased onto an empty stool.

The man next to him looked up from his drink, but said nothing.

Laura smiled. "You seem to be pretty good at that."

"First time." Newman quipped.

"Oh, hang around here long enough and you'll get used to it. Every now and then, you'll get a drunken redneck in here just spoiling for a fight. It's important to take care of them convincingly the first time. That way you'll send a message to the rest of 'em that you can whip your weight in bobcats and that you won't be pushed around, especially in your own bar."

"Ahhh… Whip your what?"

"Kick ass. I forget that you're not from around here."

"I see. Anyway, you have a mean right cross."

"You develop one real fast in this business. And I thought you handled yourself rather well too." Laura quickly added.

"Fear." Newman joked. "The fear of being beaten to a pulp does wonders for one's self-defense capabilities, in fact…"

Unexpectedly a hysterical woman burst through the front door. "He's getting a gun! He's getting a gun!"

The patrons immediately quieted as everyone strained to see the woman. Suddenly, a shot rang out. The glass in a nearby window shattered, showering adjacent tables with jagged fragments. Screams of panic echoed through the barroom as everyone scrambled for cover. Newman quickly crouched. Laura dropped behind the counter. Newman hastily crawled over flattened bodies to reach the main door. He slammed it shut and dropped the iron bar bolt behind it. Abruptly, another gunshot rang out, producing another chorus of screams. Newman scuttled back behind the counter. He found Laura cowered behind the bar.

"We need a gun in here!" Laura was extremely nervous.

"Wrong. That's the last thing we need. What we do need, is a phone to call the police. Where is it?"

"We don't have one."

"What!"

"Vicki took it out about two months ago."

"Great!" Newman sighed in disgust. "Where's the nearest phone?"

"Next door in the café, but there's a locked iron gate separating the bar and the café after the café closes."

"Who has the key?"

"Vicki."

"That figures. Look, I've got to get to that phone. Sit tight. I'll be right back."

"Right…" Laura huffed. "Where am I gonna to go?"

Newman crouched low as he made his way out the back door. The night provided excellent cover, he thought, but it could just as easily hide the gunman too. While Newman hoped the gunman was still out front, the truth was, he could be anywhere. He considered notifying Vicki, but quickly dismissed the idea. He might just end up getting her killed. Besides, he was supposed to be the man in charge now, and this was as good a time as any to exercise that authority.

The back door of the restaurant was locked. He sighed an expletive. He looked around for signs of the gunman. Newman then picked up a rock, knocked out a window. Then carefully reached through the shattered glass to unlock the back door. He immediately flipped on the light switch and hurried into the dining room. He spotted the phone by the cash register.

He dashed to the phone, snatched up the receiver, and dialed 911. He waited impatiently for a reply.

The number you've reached is not in service," the female voice recording answered.

He jammed the phone down again. Then dialed. Again the recorded voice began its spiel. He slammed the phone down again and then dialed the operator.

"Operator," the bland woman's voice immediately answered.

"I'm trying to get the sheriff and this stupid 911 number doesn't work."

"Sir, are you kidding? This state doesn't have 911 service."

"No 911 service?" Newman was in disbelief. "You're joking?"

"If you want the sheriff, you'll have to dial direct. Would you care for the number?"

"If you'd be so kind." Newman sighed, exasperated. He memorized the number the operator gave him and dialed frantically.

"Missoula County Sheriff's Office," the woman's voice answered.

"I'm the manager at the Hot Spring's Resort up here in Lolo. There's a guy here shooting up the bar. I need police assistance immediately!"

"Is anyone hurt?"

"Not yet, but the night is still young."

"Can you describe the man?"

"He's average build, blonde hair, and Western-style hat."

"Sir, that description fits half the men in Montana. Could you be more specific?"

"No, I can't, Miss. Please just send help."

"What kind of gun is he using?"

"I didn't check. He was using it at the time." Newman was getting irritated.

"How about the make and model of his car?"

"Lady, listen," he growled. "I'm not applying for a loan. This is serious. Just send somebody, okay?" He slammed the phone down.

Newman didn't know who made him angrier, the cowboy shooting up the bar or the sheriff's department operator for treating the situation like a game show quiz. He made it back to the bar and found everything relatively quiet. Everyone had become more or less comfortable with their particular section of the barroom floor. But more importantly, no more shots had been fired. He crawled over to the stage and pulled down a microphone.

"Listen, everybody," Newman quietly announced. "I've called the sheriff. They're on their way. Just stay calm, stay close to the floor, away from the windows and everything will be okay."

Newman kept checking his watch as the seconds ticked into minutes and the minutes into hours. Still there was no sign of the sheriff. Panic and fear soon gave way to impatience, frustration, and boredom. The patrons grew increasingly restless. No more shots had been fired in the last several hours, prompting some of the bolder customers to take quick peeps through the window. The longer they waited, the longer the peeps, until finally people were peering boldly out of the windows.

"Look, I'd like to stay, but I've got a sitter at home. Besides, I think he's gone," one woman pleaded. "I really have to go."

"Me too," another man added. "It's been more than three hours."

"I'd really appreciate it if you all stayed to tell your story to the sheriff," Newman explained.

"We'd love to, but we can't, sorry," one man regretfully added. He removed the bolt and eased the front door open. All was quiet. A small group of people followed him out of the door.

Newman quickly bolted the door shut behind them and waited. Moments later, he heard the sound of engines starting as the cars drove away.

Another hour passed. Still, no sign of the sheriff. By now small groups of people were starting to quietly leave. Newman watched from the shattered window as each car safely departed. As more people left, more people developed the courage to leave. By 2 a.m., the bar was completely deserted, except for Newman and Laura. He was preparing to break on their third game of billiards, when a knock at the front door broke his concentration.

"Who's there?" Newman shouted.

"The sheriff."

Newman and Laura both chuckled. "One moment please."

Newman put his cue stick down and walked over to open the door. In the doorway stood an older man in a blue and gray uniform, Stetson hat, and Magnum pistol strapped low on his leg.

"Are you the man who called?"

"You mean four hours ago?" Newman snidely replied. "Why, yes I am. Come on in. We were just starting our third game of pool. Would you like to play the winner?"

The sheriff casually strolled into the barroom, carefully surveying the place as he entered. "Where are all of the customers?"

"They got tired of waiting for you and left," Laura volunteered.

"I mean, I can see being a few minutes late---even an hour, but you were... what?" Newman checked his watch. "Four hours getting here."

The sheriff casually walked over to the shattered window. "Actually, I was here about three and half hours ago," he remarked, examining the damage.

"Then why did you wait so long to show up?" callously, asked Laura.

"I came here looking to arrest a blonde-haired man with an average build in a cowboy hat," the sheriff calmly replied. "Not many men in here tonight fit that description. Did they?"

"I was in sort of a hurry." Sighed Newman.

"Maybe, but with just that information to go on, I couldn't just rush up here and shoot every average-build, blonde-headed white man in a cowboy hat, now could I?" Newman and Laura were a little perplexed. "I parked outside and waited for somebody to take a potshot at your window. And I waited out there for three hours."

"So you're telling me this man just got away?"

"Well, not exactly. There was a man matching your description sitting in a car parked outside. He admits to breaking a pool cue."

"And swinging it at me," Newman quickly added.

"Maybe, but he denies ever firing a shot in here."

"He's lying," Laura insisted.

"Did you see him?" The sheriff was emphatic. "Did anybody actually see him fire the shot that came through that window?"

"Well, we were all busy hugging the floor."

Newman was a little perturbed that he didn't let them know he was outside.

"And I didn't find a gun on him or in his car."

"He hid it obviously," Laura answered.

"Well, how about him taking a swing at me with that pool cue? Then there's the matter of the broken pool stick itself."

"If you want to swear out a complaint for assault, go ahead. I'll pick him up. You'll have to go to court and there'll be a trial. The whole process could take three or four months. And, if he's convicted and appeals… well then, of course, it will take longer. The cue stick is a civil matter. You'll have to sue him for damages in civil court."

Newman sighed in disgust. "What I'm hearing from you then, is that it's better to forget this whole thing ever happened."

"I can't tell you what to do, Mr.… ahhhh…"

"Newman."

"Mr. Newman, but those are the facts."

"I see." Newman shook his head dejectedly.

"You're fairly new to these parts, aren't you, Mr. Newman?"

"How can you tell?"

"Bar fights are a common occurrence up here. Liquored-up cowboys in for the weekend, long-haul truckers, and loggers make a pretty rowdy crowd. I suggest if you plan to stay in these parts, and especially if you plan to work in a place like this, you'd better learn how to handle these type of folks. We've been trying to talk Big Jake into letting us deputize some of his men up here. That way, you all can make an arrest, especially since we're more than thirty minutes away. Maybe you can suggest it to him again."

"Maybe, that's not a bad idea."

"Well, if you don't plan to press charges, I guess I'm outta here."

"I guess so Sheriff…"

"Bennett, Lucas Bennett. If you need me again, just call. Oh, and welcome to Montana, Mr. Newman."

"Thanks," Newman sighed as Bennett walked out the door. He turned to Laura as she stood by the pool table, cue in hand.

"Now what?"

Newman shrugged his shoulders. "I think I was about to break." He grabbed his cue stick and headed for the opposite end of the table.

C H A P T E R

2

The cold morning air blasted Newman's face as he removed the padlock from the front door of the log cabin-styled grocery store. He stood in the entrance, cradling a small wooden box and surveying the empty food shelves lining the walls and aisles. To one side of the store was an old cash register mounted atop a small checkout counter. Dust, dirt, and cobwebs covered almost every inch of the floor and shelf space. Newman placed the wooden box on the store counter and slowly walked down each aisle, stopping occasionally to place his fingers through the dust.

"It's a mess, isn't it?"

Slightly startled by the voice, Newman turned to see Vicki standing in the doorway.

"It's you. I just came by to see how much work it would take to get this place in shape for the summer tourist season."

"As you can see, it's going to take a lot of hard work. Practically a miracle."

"It's going to need a little work," Newman hedged casually.

"A little work? Boy, is that an understatement. This place needs a major top-to-bottom scrubbing and…" she walked over to a nearby food freezer and opened the lid, "it's got to be restocked. And all in time for the RV campers when they come through this summer."

"I'll get to it as soon as I can."

"Oh, don't concern yourself about it. Besides, you've got enough to keep you busy. I heard about your little incident last night at the bar. I already have someone fixing the windows, so you don't have to worry about that."

"Last night was an education, to say the least. By the way, why is there no phone in the bar?"

"Employees were making long-distance calls to their friends and family and charging it to the bar phone. But, it wasn't until I got that $600 charge to Sydney, Australia, that I decided the phone had to go. After last night, though, I think I'll put it back in."

"That would be great, we could just have the phone company to allow local calls only."

"I can do that. By the way Kenny, when you stopped by my office this morning to get the key for this place, I had these made for you." She tossed him a clump of keys. It had to be at least 20 or 30 on the ring. He snatched them out of the air. "An extra set of your very own. You have the keys to every room and establishment on these grounds. It's cheaper than continuously replacing broken back door windows."

"Sorry about that."

"Wasn't your fault. You did what you had to do. That's what I hired you for. If you see something that needs to be done, you have my permission to do it."

"Thanks for the vote of confidence, Vicki."

"Oh and another thing, this resort is huge. It covers over forty acres of prime land and we use every inch of it for something. I don't want you driving you're broken down putt-putt vehicle around. We have golf carts in the maintenance shed for getting around and for playing golf. You can go there, park your car and get one of those."

"Will do."

"Are you taking those tickets I gave you this morning over to Carl?"

Newman stepped behind the checkout counter and picked up the wooden box with the large roll of theater tickets.

"Yes ma'am. I intend to start the new ticket policy at the pool today. I've even got the ticket box right here for them to use." He placed the box underneath his arm.

"Good. Carl is over there right now, getting ready to open. Do you want me to come with you, just in case he gives you any trouble? He has a violent temper, and he can get pretty nasty."

"Thanks, but no. If I am going to have problems with him, then I'm going to have to handle them one way or another and by myself."

"Well, okay," she reluctantly agreed. "Use a carrot if you want to, but remember, I can provide a pretty big stick if you need one."

"I will remember that."

"Oh, Kenny if you have any questions about the business or your duties that we talked about this morning, don't hesitate to ask me. I want you to feel comfortable with what you're doing."

"Don't worry Vicki, you have my word. I will ask."

Vicki turned and walked out.

Newman left. Moments later, traded his VW Bus for a golf cart. With tickets in hand, headed for the swimming pool area. His stomach churned. The pool had been Carl's sole domain for years. How would he react to being told to change pool policy? And what about his violent temper? The more he thought about it, maybe he should have taken Vicki along, just in case.

As he neared the pool area, he heard splashing water as he opened the pool-house door. Carl stood on the edge of the deep section, shouting instructions at a young man bobbing in the water.

"No, no, Shay!" Carl angrily commanded. "You're taking too long down there. We open at ten, remember? Just get the big chunks of algae off the wall. I've got chemicals that'll get all that little stuff later."

The young man coughed and occasionally spat into the pool as he effortlessly treaded water heading in Carl's direction.

"Are you sure?" Shay sounded unconvinced. "Isn't the chemical spray broke?"

"Trust me, I've used it before. All you have to do is nigger rig the hose to the old spray nozzle, and it'll work just fine."

"Are you sure?"

"Yeah, I'm sure. It's just like having three niggers down there scrubbing those walls."

Carl glanced up and saw Newman standing at the opposite end of the pool. They exchanged acrimonious stares, but neither said a word.

Carl looked back down at Shay. He looked up at Carl and shook the water from his hair.

"Hey, better watch that nigger talk," Shay warned. "I hear we actually have one of them working around here somewhere."

"Don't bother me none." Carl sneered.

Newman walked over to Carl. "I want to talk to you." Newman announced coldly. Shay flinched startled by Newman's sudden appearance. Carl ignored him and walked pass Newman. "Carl," Newman repeated in a sterner tone, "I said I need to speak with you."

"Look, boy!" Carl turned to face Newman. The hostility in his voice was evident. "It'll have to wait until later, okay? As even you can see, I'm busy right now trying to get this pool open. So come back later, eh?"

"That's okay. I'll just leave these tickets on the counter." Newman flashed the roll in front of him. "You'll need them when you open the pool this morning." Newman turned and walked toward the check-in counter.

Carl infuriated, started after him. "Hey! What the hell will I need goddamn tickets for? This ain't no circus." Still defiant, "I don't know what my Ma told you, but I call the shots at this pool, not you. And I say, I don't need no damn tickets!"

Newman stopped and turned toward him. "Well starting this morning we will issue one ticket to each paying customer. You'll keep half and give the customer the other half. You will turn in the torn tickets when you turn in the money at the end of the day."

"You must be crazy. What is that going to prove?"

"For one thing, it'll give us some idea of how many people are using the pool on a daily basis."

"What the hell for? I could tell you that. But then Ma ain't never asked for nothin' like that before. Who wants to know that stuff?"

"I want to know." Newman sternly insisted. "Maybe we need to have longer hours or more people on duty or any number of things. But I won't know that until I find out how many people are using the pool. I just want the information."

"Information my ass," Carl growled. "Why don't you say why you really want to start selling tickets over here? You think I'm rippin' off the till, ain't that right?"

"I'm not accusing anybody of anything." Newman's voice was conciliatory but firm. "I'm just trying to implement a better accounting system for the pool, that's all."

His mounting anger flared. "Horseshit! Why don't you just come right out and say it. You think I'm stealin' from the pool. You're callin' me a thief, ain't cha, nigger boy?"

"I'm not going to stand here and argue with you." Newman floundered for a graceful way to avoid the escalating confrontation. "I'll leave these on the counter." He held up the tickets again. "I expect you to use them when the pool opens today."

Newman immediately turned and started toward the counter. Carl suddenly grabbed his shoulder and spun him violently around.

"I'm not through with you yet, nigger," Carl snarled.

Newman, startled by Carl's grip, whirled to see the rage in his face. He instinctively slapped Carl's hand away. Carl responded with a quick right cross to Newman's jaw. The blow sent him reeling backwards, trying to maintain his balance. The tickets went flying into the pool. Newman hit the deck, sprawled on his back. Newman felt the pain in his jaw. He hadn't been in a real fistfight since high school, and even then he lost. Now, he had to take on an obviously experienced brawler, even though his own boxing experience was limited only to what he had seen on late-night television. Suddenly, Carl appeared over him, still heaving mad. Shay retrieved the soaked roll of tickets from the pool and swam to one corner to watch the confrontation.

"Heard you're pretty good fightin' fallin'-down drunks, Sambo. How are you with real men?"

He immediately reached down and pulled Newman up by the lapels of his shirt. Newman struggled to his feet, trying to break the vise grip Carl had on his shirt. Carl reared and delivered another right cross. The blow turned Newman's head, but Carl's grip held firm. He drew back and blasted Newman repeatedly.

Shay's initial enthusiasm with Newman's beating slowly turned to a mild concern. Carl showed no sign of ceasing his relentless pounding upon Newman's face and gut. Finally his concern gave way to sheer panic.

"Stop Carl! Stop!" Shay screamed as he scrambled out of the pool. "You're killing him!"

Newman moaned. "Ahhhh…ahh…"

Carl let Newman drop to the concrete and continued unheeded. Shay rushed toward them. Just as Carl was about to strike another blow, Shay quickly grabbed his shoulders and yanked him back.

"That's enough!" Shay forcefully demanded, dragging Carl away. "That's enough!"

Carl struggled momentarily before allowing himself to be pulled away. Like a punch-drunk prizefighter, Newman's legs wobbled slightly as he struggled to stand and maintain his balance.

"Go on!" Shay warned. "Get outta here before he kills you!"

Newman watched momentarily as Shay struggled to hold onto a still-enraged Carl, who was like a mad dog on a straining leash. He felt a warm trail of blood oozing from his nose and lips as he gradually turned and staggered away from the pool house. He walked only a few feet before his senses had finally cleared. Though, he was still feeling his jaw for broken bones. He didn't know which assault felt worse---the one on his body or the one on his pride and self-respect. In extreme pain, Newman knew he couldn't let Carl get away with this and turned around.

He was about to open the entrance door when someone on the other side pushed it open and back into his jaw. He took a quick step back, holding his mouth shut to conceal what would have otherwise been a loud scream and an expletive. The small elderly woman, late sixties to mid-seventies, with silver-gray hair stood in the opened doorway with a small stack of freshly washed bath towels cradled in her arms. Newman sighed a bit of relief that it wasn't Carl.

"Excuse me," she automatically apologized. She froze with concern as she noticed the bruises on Newman's face. "What happened to you?" She stepped closer to examine him.

"It's nothing. I just fell on the concrete at poolside, that's all."

"You let me decide that. I'm a nurse…" She paused. "Or, at least I used to be a nurse. At any rate, I know how to treat cuts and bruises."

She ushered him back into the pool house. "Just step back in here and let me take a look at your face."

Newman scanned the area for Carl and Shay. They were nowhere in sight. She eased him down into a chair behind the check-in counter. She set the towels to one side, tilted his head back, and slowly began examining his face. She reached under the check-in counter and pulled out a first-aid kit.

"You said you fell on the pavement?" She was skeptical.

"That's right. You know how slippery the deck can get after it's been hosed down."

She took a quick glance around the pool and the concrete was dry, except for one spot where someone may have gotten out of the pool.

"I see. And how many times did you fall, Mr. Newman? Thirty or forty?"

He was surprised she knew his name. "Have we met?"

"I don't think so, but then I've heard all about you. How Vicki hired you to manage this place and everything. I'm Millie Peterson." She and Newman shook hands. "I'm the resident nurse, laundrywoman, part-time chef, minister's wife, and whatever other job needs to be done around here. I also run the resort gift shop."

"Mistress of all trades, uh?"

"Yes. And I actually master some of them too." Millie smiled. And like most elderly women she volunteered her life story. "I'm married to Reese Peterson. He is the resort minister. He also works with Vicki's husband, Jake, on his logging operation just north of here. Perhaps you've met my husband?"

"Not yet, but I'm sure I will."

"You'll enjoy meeting him. He's good people. And I'd say that even if he weren't my husband. In fact, we've been praying for some good people to come here and work instead of all these hobos, bums, and drifters. And God is starting to answer our prayers."

Newman chuckled grimacing from his bruises as Millie wiped the blood from his upper lip with gauze and placed pressure under his eye to stop the bleeding.

"I may be many things, Millie, but a gift from Heaven? I'm not so sure."

"Don't underestimate your value here, Mr. Newman."

"Ken, please."

"Ken, the Lord works in mysterious ways." She checked his nose and jaw for broken bones. "Everything appears to be in order and it seems as if the bleeding has stopped. If you wait here, I will go and get some alcohol and some ice to put on this cut under you eye."

Concerned that Carl may return before she does, "That won't be necessary, Millie. It'll be fine."

"Ohhhkay. But the swelling is going to get worse if you don't take care of it and that gash under your eye may get infected if not properly cleaned."

"I'll take care of it, I promise."

"Well, if you do, the swelling will go down in time. Some ice will help as well. Do try and be more careful in the future."

"I'll try." Newman smiled, rising from the chair. "Thank you for your attention. I hope I didn't stop you from something important?"

"No I was just putting some clean towels in my car that I washed from my room."

"So where were you before we bumped into each other?"

"In the pool laundry room. You see, one of my jobs is to keep the towels clean. So I come over here a couple of hours before the pool opens, I wash the pool towels, and I wash mine too."

"Well, I'm sure we'll see each other again."

"I'm sure we will, Ken." She put the first-aid kit back and threw the bloody gauze in the trash. She scooped up the towels and headed for the door. "Hopefully under healthier circumstances. Oh, would you like for me to wash your shirt, those blood stains won't come out easily if you leave them to dry?"

"No. I'll change it. Ohhhh, by the way, do you know where Shay and Carl went?"

"They stepped out back to get something for the pool. They should be back shortly, if you want to wait." She started to walk out the pool doors.

As the extreme pain pulsated around his face, Newman thought only a second before he followed the elderly lady out the doors. Now how was he going to explain his bruises to Vicki? But one thing was certain, he wasn't going to tell her the truth. This was only the first of what promised to be many more battles with Carl. He knew he would never earn his respect or anyone else's for that matter, if he called on Vicki to solve all of his problems. Besides, the problem with Carl had just become personal. Putting tickets in the pool area probably wouldn't stop anyone absolutely determined to steal from the till. However, instituting the ticket system was now more than just a matter of accounting—it was a test of wills.

He needed another roll of tickets and only Vicki knew where he could find one. He hopped in the golf cart and started up the path. The wind irritated Newman's cut underneath his eye. He went back to his room, changed his shirt and headed to Vicki's office. He soon reached his destination. He walked into her office only to find an attractive young female blonde sitting at the receptionist desk. She looked all of nineteen years of age.

"My gosh! Mr. Newman. What happened to your face?"

"Does it look that bad?"

She handed him a compact mirror from her purse. "Would you like for me to get some ice from the bar?"

Newman's eyes' were puffed, a three-inch gash sat under his left eye, his right jaw was swollen, and his lips had puffed up like balloons. He thought, that's not too bad.

"No… No thank you. I'll be fine. And who are you?" Newman mumbled as he handed her compact mirror back.

"I'm Lisa Meyer, Vicki's daytime receptionist. She's told me all about you. Welcome to the resort."

"Why, thank you. Have you seen Vicki?"

"She's over at the restaurant getting the lunches together for the logging crew."

"What time do you expect her back?"

"Oh, in a couple of minutes." The phone rang. Lisa answered it. "Hello… Yes… he's right here." Newman noticed she didn't answer the phone in a traditional manner, like—Ms. Marshall's office or Hot Springs Resort. Perhaps Vicki didn't care, so why should he. She handed the phone to Newman. "It's Vicki."

Newman placed the phone to his ear, but said nothing. "Ken?" Vicki asked.

"Yea."

"How are you? Say, I just came from the pool, and Carl isn't using the ticket system you were going to install this morning. Is there a problem?"

"Ahhhh… no. No… no problem. I just decided to postpone installing the system pending further study, that's all."

"Whatever. You sound a little muffled. You aren't getting a cold, are you?"

"No." Newman was keeping his sentences short as his lips were swelling.

"Say, would you be a dear and run some sack lunches up to the logging crew? I'm expecting some very important visitors in a few minutes and I can't leave."

"Ahhhh… yea, sure. I don't mind Vicki. But you know, I don't know where I'm going. I haven't been to the logging camp yet and I don't have transportation for that kind of terrain."

"You sure you aren't getting a cold, it's just a little hard to understand you." Newman was silent. "Look I know, Ken. Just ask Lisa for the keys to the truck and meet me at the restaurant."

"Okay." Newman handed the phone back to Lisa. "She said you have keys to a truck."

Lisa reached in her desk drawer and pulled out a set of keys. "It's the white Bronco out front in the lot."

Newman took the keys. He climbed behind the wheel and started the engine. As he backed out of the parking space, he knew his reluctance to take the lunches to the logging site was due more to his apprehension about finally meeting Big Jake, than any concern about possibly getting lost in the surrounding countryside. Five minutes later, Newman was in front of the restaurant. Vicki, Laura, and Kelly were standing there with sacked lunches.

As he pulled up and rolled down the window, Newman kept his hand over his lips. Vicki greeted him with one sack lunch in her hand.

"Here Kenny, this is for… you."

"Thanks." Newman placed the lunch sack on the passenger seat and kept his head down.

"What happened to your face, Kenny?" Vicki was concerned. Newman lowered his hand from his lips. "Ohhh, good grief. Who did that to you? It was Carl, wasn't it?"

"Let it be Vicki."

"He's fired!"

"No Vicki, please. If I am ever to earn the respect of those that work under me, I must handle the situation, not you."

"Alright, Ken. Did you put some ice on your face?"

"No, I want to remember for the rest of the day that I must deal with Carl and others like him."

Vicki sympathized. "Okay, it's your call. You say the word and he is gone."

"Got it. Now you were going to tell me where to take these sandwiches."

"Thanks Kenny, you're a doll for doing this for me. I really appreciate it. Even more so looking at your face. That's gotta hurt. You really should put something on that cut."

"Vicki please…" Newman was getting agitated.

Laura and Kelly placed several boxes filled with sacked lunches in the back seat and trunk.

Vicki gave Newman the directions. "Now all you have to do is just get on the highway as if you were going toward Missoula and make a right on the Spring Gulch Road. Then keep driving until you see their camp."

"It's that easy to find?" Newman wanted reassurance.

"It's that easy."

"Okay, Vicki."

Vicki backed away from the vehicle and waved.

Newman cranked up the truck and headed down the highway as she instructed, thinking about Big Jake. Big Jake's name rolled from everyone's lips almost with a religious reverence. The crew used his name when they needed final authorization to settle a dispute or when they needed the backing of unquestioned authority. "Big Jake said I could have this," one crew member would say, or "Big Jake said don't…" another would add. Once his name was mentioned, all other discussions and arguments ceased. Even Vicki, though she clearly ran the day-to-day operations of the resort, but dared not make a major decision concerning the complex without first consulting Big Jake. Newman knew their initial interaction would eventually have to take place. And though he did have Vicki's confidence, Big Jake's support was still absolutely vital if he was to have any success managing the resort.

He meandered through the hillside, bouncing over the rocks and potholes scattered along the unpaved dirt road. It snaked around rolling hills, rushing streams, tall green tamaracks, with an unobstructed view of majestic distant snow-capped mountain peaks. Finally, he could hear the faint sound of whirling chain saws and the distinctive crackling of fallin' trees. "Timberrrrr…" a loud shout echoed, followed moments later by the thundering crash of a fallen tree.

Newman rounded a bend and saw about twelve to fourteen men scattered throughout a densely wooded area. They were feverishly laboring to chop, cut, or saw down the towering pillars of timber that dotted the landscape. This was Big Jake's crew. Each seemed solely consumed with the task at hand. The consistent thud of the logger's axe as it repeatedly pounded against rugged timber, combined with the mechanical whirl of the chain saws, filled the air with an aromatic scent of freshly cut pine.

Newman pulled up alongside the cab of an enormous fully loaded logging truck.

"I'm looking for Jake Marshall." Newman called to the driver.

The young man slowly looked down at Newman. "He's on the cat," he casually answered, pointing toward a large tractor-forklift that was hoisting a huge log onto a waiting trailer.

Newman thanked the man and drove over to the loader. Behind the wheel of the machine sat an older graying man with the build of a professional wrestler. He was about six feet tall, and strapping, with muscles that revealed more about his profession than his age. His face was slightly wrinkled, but strong and determined. He handled the forklift with the ease and skill of a much younger man. The machine turned and twisted at his every command. If John Wayne had a brother, Big Jake Marshall would have been him.

Jake looked over to see Newman as he pulled to a stop beside his forklift. Jake stopped his machine and climbed down.

Newman got out of the truck and walked over to greet him. Jake removed his tattered work gloves and extended his hand. Newman shook his hand.

"You must be Ken," Jake greeted. His voice was deep and booming. "What happened to your face?"

"I fell, Mr. Marshall." Newman smiled slightly.

"How many times, Mr. Newman?"

"It's not that serious, Mr. Marshall."

"Then you need to look at your face again. Did one of our employees rearrange your face today? You should let Vicki know and she will fire him."

"I can take care of it Mr. Marshall and I told Vicki the same thing."

"Then enough said and call me Jake, please," he insisted, "everybody else does. Vicki's told me so much about you. She thinks you are a very special guy." Jake grinned.

"Well she's a very special lady. Very few women can run a business this size almost singlehandedly the way she has."

"I'm glad you feel that way. For months, I've been telling her to get some help and delegate some of the responsibilities. I've been doing what I can to help out, but this logging operation keeps me pretty busy."

"Well, I'm going to give it my best."

"And that is all I ask." Jake glanced over at the paper bags in back of the truck. "I see you brought lunch."

"Yes. Vicki said she was expecting important visitors, so she asked me to bring you all lunch today."

"Just hope Kelly made something that'll stick to our ribs 'til supper." He pulled a two-way radio from his belt holster. "Dean, sound the chow horn."

Moments later, a loud shrill horn blared through the area. The chopping and cutting noises ceased almost immediately. Bulky, muscular men were coming from all directions to the truck.

"Hey Jake, think we should finish cutting that baby down before we take a break." The logger pointed to the tree they were working on. "It's almost ready to go?"

"Can we eat first Jake? I'm starved," asked his partner.

"Stay here and eat guys." Jake reached in the back seat of the truck and grabbed a handful of sacked lunches. "Help me pass these out Kenny." Jake passed some bags to Newman.

Newman distributed the bags. "Hey I have a better idea."

Newman opened up the tailgate and pulled the boxes closer to the edge so the men could reach for the bags themselves. The men took their lunches and began to perch themselves under the trees in the vicinity.

Suddenly the ground began to shake violently. Newman struggled to keep his balance as Jake fell backwards against his forklift.

"Earthquake!" Someone shouted, as the other loggers began to scurry frantically from the trees, for open spaces.

As everyone fought to maintain their balance, just off in a distance, an unmanned bulldozer parked precariously close to a steep embankment wobbled momentarily. Then it slipped gradually over the side, tumbling end over end as it thundered down the hillside. Seconds later, the ground settled. Newman held firmly onto the truck's tailgate, while Jake clanged to the huge tires on his forklift. Able to maintain their balance, they stared at each other in awe of what just happened.

Jake yelled, "Is everyone alright!"

"Yeah!… Yea!… Yea!… Yeah! We're alright." Jake continued to hear until all men were accounted for.

"Wow!" Newman sighed. "Does this happen often around here?"

"Not that often, but often enough. Still, that was the strongest quake I've felt up here in the past couple of years."

Newman scanned the area.

"Doesn't look like too much damage was done, except for the bulldozer." Newman pointed toward the cliff.

Jake's head immediately turned to see the huge empty space where his bulldozer once sat. He pounded his fist angrily into the side of the forklift.

"Damn!" Jake murmured underneath his breath as he shook his head in disgust. "Now what do I do to move these logs? Even if I could retrieve the bulldozer from the bottom of the ravine, I still might not be able to fix it. And buying a new one, at this time, would be out of the question."

"If I can be of any help?"

"That's kind of you, thanks. But Vicki needs you more back at the resort. This is my problem. I'll take care of it. Let's just finish handing out these lunches so these men can get back to work. I'll check on that CAT tomorrow and see what can be done, if anything."

"Okay, I'll head back down and see how things are back at the resort."

"Good idea." Jake started to climb back on his forklift.

The men took their paper lunches and disbursed into little groups throughout the clearing. Newman started to climb back into the truck when abruptly the ground mildly swayed.

"Whoa!" Newman inadvertently exclaimed.

Several yards ahead of him, he noticed a partially chopped tree starting to slowly crack and topple. In its path strolled an inattentive logger fumbling through the contents of his brown bag.

"Hey!" Newman shouted. "Look out!"

The man continued to thoroughly examine the packaged lunch. Jake heard Newman's warning and looked around in horror.

"Mark!" Jake yelled. "Get the hell outta the way!"

Newman climbed out of the truck and sprinted toward Mark. The tree finally snapped and gave a thunderous roar as it came crashing toward the ground. Mark finally looked up. He dropped the open bag in frozen horror as the gigantic pillar rapidly bore down on him.

Newman leaped for Mark grabbing him around his shoulders and they both quickly rolled a few feet as the tree barely missed crushing them both. Newman slowly climbed to his feet. He brushed the dirt from his clothes as he gazed down at Mark.

"You okay?" Newman extended his hand. Still visibly shaken, Mark took Newman's hand and struggled to his feet. Jake rushed over, as did all of the other loggers.

"You both all right?" Jake calmly asked.

Mark looked down at his body. "Ahhhh... yeah. I guess so."

"We're both fine Jake compared to what could have been." Newman seriously noted.

"Good, if you're alright, Mark, then you and the rest of your men finish eating so we all can get back to work." Jake turned and headed back to his forklift.

"Excuse me Jake. It maybe none of my business, but with these aftershocks, it might be a wise decision to cancel the rest of today's work up here."

Jake immediately stopped in his tracks and turned coldly toward Newman. "You're right. It's none of your business! Not a chance," he ardently insisted. "You take care of things back at the resort. I'll run things up here. If I don't get this area cleared out before fire season, every tree up here could go up in smoke and I can't afford to lose one inch of lumber. Not now, not under the situation I'm in." He turned to face the rest of his men. "Eat up boys, we've got work to do."

As Jake headed angrily back to his forklift. One of his loggers caught up to him and asked, "Did part of the branches from that tree catch that fellow in the face?"

Jake only laughed. "Get back to work."

As Newman took his scenic tour back to the resort, he reached for his lunch that he had on the passenger seat. He opened his mouth for the sandwich and excruciating pain from his jaw prevented him from taking a bite. He put the sandwich down and pondered the situation with Big Jake. Newman arrived back at the resort a few hours later more uncertain than ever of his relationship with Big Jake. Was it now confrontational merely because he suggested that his crew discontinue work? It was only a suggestion. And how would Vicki react if Jake indeed had been angered by their exchange? But more importantly, why did he take such a defensive attitude toward what was obviously a routine safety precaution? Why was money so important as to risk the lives of his crew and himself?

When Newman walked in the office, the receptionist, Lisa was typing at her desk.

"Vicki around?"

"She had to leave, suddenly," she said without looking up from her typing. "Did you all feel the tremor up at the camp?"

"Yeah, everybody's okay though. Just a little shaken up a bit, that's all. How about down here?"

"A few nervous guess came by, but overall nothing major. We get those up here from time to time," Lisa casually smiled.

"And you don't know where Vicki went?"

Lisa stopped her typing and focused her attention on Newman. "Nope… My Goodness! Ken. Your face has swollen up a lot since I last saw you. You should let me get some ice for you."

"It'll be fine. No big deal. Has she been gone long?"

"About an hour ago she left with these two guys in expensive looking business suits. So I guess you are in charge until she gets back."

"In charge?" Newman stated aloud, in amazement. "Now just what is that supposed to mean? I haven't been here forty-eight hours yet. Like I know what's going on around here. What exactly does in charge mean?"

"I don't know. Just run things the best you can until she gets back. I guess."

"Just like that, huh?"

"Well, I can help you a little." Lisa volunteered. "I've been here for almost two years and I know where just about everything is."

"Good. That will help. She didn't say when she'd be back, did she?"

"Nope."

"Is this something she does often? I mean take off like this?"

"Not that often. Just every now and then."

Newman walked around her desk and peeked over Lisa's shoulder at her typing. He could tell by the numbered lines down the left side of the paper that it was some sort of legal document. Vick's name also appeared periodically throughout the text.

"Well," Newman sighed, "I guess I have little choice except to at least try to keep everything in one piece."

"Oh, Ken." Lisa shook her head. "It won't be that hard. I'm here until 6. If you have questions, call me."

Newman gave her a small pat on the shoulder. "I guess between the two of us, what can go wrong, right?"

He stepped around the corner into Vicki's office. Papers of almost every size and description covered her desk. Her wall was lined with family pictures and plaques awarded to the resort for various acts of community service. He eased into her big reclining armchair. Enveloped by the feel of the soft brown leather, he felt in total control. An aura of importance surrounded him as he slowly swiveled back and forth with his feet gliding over the deep shagged carpet.

"Ken?" Lisa's voice on the intercom broke his concentration.

Newman sat upright and pushed the intercom button. "Yes, Lisa."

"Big Sky Distributors are here to see you."

"Ahhh…" He cleared his throat. "Send them in." Newman sat back in the chair with fingers intermingled, with an authoritative appearance in posture.

A young man in a blue jumpsuit entered the office. "You're not Vicki."

"You're very observant."

"It's just that I have always dealt with Vicki."

"Well, she's out for the afternoon, so it looks like you're stuck with me."

"Okay." He pulled out a slip of paper and handed it to Newman.

Newman scanned the slip and shouted. "Four-hundred dollars and twenty-seven cents!"

"Due in full," the man quickly added.

"Well thank you very much. I'll see that Vicki gets this when she returns."

"No dice. It's due now, or I re-load the entire shipment of beer that I just finished unloading in your bar and take it back to town."

"We don't want you to do that. We won't have any beer for the weekend."

"Hey, that's not my problem. All I know is, that if I don't get the money, you don't get the suds."

Newman sighed. Vicki didn't tell him anything about this or anything else. What else was there that she simply had forgotten to mention?

"Okay. Tell Lisa at the front desk to write you out a check and…"

The man flashed a broad grin. Newman looked at him curiously.

"Did I say something funny?"

"Yes you did. The word check. You know that I can't take a check from you guys. This place is strictly cash only."

"Cash only? Any particular reason why?"

"Ask Vicki. She'll explain everything."

Newman pressed the intercom button. "Lisa, where does Vicki keep the cash?"

"In the safe behind her desk."

"Do you know the combination?"

"Don't bother, it's never locked. In fact, it's always open because she forgets the combination. Just pull the handle."

"Thanks." Newman whirled the chair around and pulled the handle on the safe door. It popped open. Inside were several small boxes of rolled quarters, nickels, dimes, and pennies. He counted the coins. "Only $153.25," he muttered. He turned back toward the deliveryman and showed him the coins.

The deliveryman shook his head. Newman ran his fingers over his mid-sized afro and then pushed the intercom button.

"Lisa, put down what you are doing. I need you to go to the gas station, the bar, the restaurant, and the pool and see if you can get a hundred-dollars from each till."

"Sure Ken, I'll be right back."

Newman sat back and reclined in the chair. "Just sit tight. Your money's comin'."

As he leaned back in the chair, he started to feel a small measure of pride about the way he handled this little problem. In fact, he felt that if Vicki had been there, she would have done the same thing. He was still puzzled though why Big Sky Distributors didn't take checks from the resort.

"Hey man, if you don't mind my asking. Were you in a boxing match today?"

"It's a long story and I don't care to talk about it."

"It just looks as if some ice would help that swelling."

"Thanks for your concern, but I'm fine."

Suddenly the phone rang. Knowing Lisa was gone, Newman immediately picked it up.

"Hot Springs Resort." He sounded with delight. "She's not here… I don't know when she'll be back. She didn't say… She didn't tell me… What do you mean you won't deliver the gas?… That's great." Newman breathed in disgust. "Thanks, that's just outstanding. And I suppose you all don't take checks from us either… Yeah, thanks." Newman slammed the phone down.

The deliveryman smiled. "When it rains, eh?"

Newman looked over at him unamused. The phone immediately rang again.

"Hot Springs," Newman tried to conceal the anger he felt. "Yes we have newlywed suites… right now? Well this is rather short notice, but I'll check." He reached for a large ledger book with the word Reservations imprinted on the front. He thumbed through the pages as he ran his finger down the category column titled Rooms Available.

"You're in luck. We have a newlywed suite open… Then I'll confirm you in the bridal suite… See you both in a couple of hours, bye." He hung of the phone. "Lisa better hurry up and get back here," Newman angrily muttered.

"Relax, man. You gave her four different places to go. I don't mind waiting to get all the money. My boss said bring the money or the beer back. He rather have the money." The man smiled.

Newman didn't share his sentiments. The phone rang again. He snatched it up. "Hot Springs Resort."

It was an hour late before Lisa returned. She had collected what was needed and the deliveryman was on his way. It was late afternoon before Lisa finally stopped buzzing the intercom for the seemingly endless parade of vendors, guest, and employees on the phone and marching in and out of the office, finally subsided. Newman lay slumped forward across the desk, his head resting in the elbow of his folded arm. Unexpectedly, there came a knock at the door.

Newman slowly raised his head, "Come in. It's open." He tried to sound fresh and alert. The door swung open. Millie stood in the doorway, holding a plastic covered tray.

"What time is it? Is Lisa gone?"

"Yes, it's well after 6, Ken. You missed dinner. I thought it might be because you didn't want anyone to see your face. And I brought some ice. It's in a cooler in my car."

"Things got a little hectic over here. And no thanks to the ice. I think the swelling has started to go down. So, how did you find me?"

Millie walked over and placed the tray on the desk. "I figured if anyone knew where you were, it would be Vicki. So I called and Lisa told me Vicki was out and you were here. So here I am with dinner."

"You've already taken care of me once today. If you keep this up, I will owe you my life."

"My pleasure. Now eat something." Millie removed the foil. Traces of steam rose from the juicy steak, string beans and the seasoned brown rice. "Does this meet with your approval?" She coyly asked.

Newman pulled the tray toward him to sample the rice. He slowly opened his mouth just wide enough to slide the rice through his teeth. His jaw still ached from the beating he took earlier that morning.

"Hmmm, good stuff," he mumbled between mini bites. "I can't believe that I actually forgot to eat something. You know when I first sat in this chair, I thought it was going to be a piece of cake. But you can get an ulcer back here real fast."

"It gets that way sometimes around here. That's why if you can't go to dinner, then dinner comes to you." Millie pulled out an alcohol pack and a Band-Aid. "Let me clean that gash under your eye. I would hate to see it get infected."

Newman sat back as Millie approached him. She ripped the alcohol pack and dabbed Newman's cut. He grimaced under the sting, but held still. Millie placed the Band-Aid on his cut and threw the litter in the trash can next to Vicki's desk.

"Thanks again Millie."

"That's what Good Samaritan's are for Ken."

Ken looked at his steak and realize it would be a task trying to put it down with a swollen jaw.

"I'll finish the rice and string beans, but could you take the steak back and label it for me. I'll get it from the kitchen, maybe tomorrow."

Millie pulled up a chair in front of Vicki's desk. "Sure Ken, eat what you can."

Newman accepted the challenge and tried to finish the rice and vegetables. While Newman ate, Millie began giving her opinion on how the resort should be run.

"Vicki's quite a woman to keep this place going for as long as she has, especially with the riffraff she's been forced to work with. That's why you really have been a godsend for her."

Newman placed his knife and fork down and leaned back in the chair. "Maybe then, you can clear up something that's been puzzling me. If she needed help so badly, what about Carl? He's her own son. Why doesn't she let him manage more of the resort?"

Millie leaned forward from her chair and whispered, "Don't tell anyone what I am about to tell you. If Vicki wants you to know, she will bring it up."

"My lips are sealed."

"They almost are. You really should let me get that ice from the car."

"No. Now, I'm listening, Millie. What happened?"

"Well, he did run the resort at one time. He was the only manager this place had for its first two years. In fact, Vicki would take long trips to Europe and the Orient, while Carl had the run of the place."

"And..."

"To make a long story short, he ran it into the ground. He spent money like a drunken sailor in a bar full of liquor and ran this place like his own private brothel. By the time Vicki realized what was happening and finally came back, he had almost depleted her entire cash account."

"She didn't set operating expenses or limit him to a budget? I'm no corporate genius, but, even I know that if she had only set Carl on budget, even he couldn't spend more than what was in the allotted account."

"She's no dummy. Of course she placed a limit on Carl's spending. But whenever he ran out of money, he simply forged her signature on the company checks. The more cash he needed, the more checks he forged. And since Vicki didn't know he was forging her name on her accounts, she naturally assumed she had more money in her account than was actually there. So she continued to travel until she went to get more money. And of course, there wasn't any left, because Carl had spent it all."

Newman sighed in awe. "Poor Vicki."

"Poor Vicki is right. Carl spent her right into Chapter 11. When she finally came back and took personal control of the resort, she fired all of the people Carl had hired. At least those who wouldn't work for three hundred dollars a month plus room and meals. And since Carl had enticed some real big executives to leave their jobs at other major resorts and hotels like the Hilton and the Holiday Inn, many of them couldn't get their old jobs back when Vicki took over. Man, did she ever make a lot of enemies."

"I'll bet."

"Now this place is only one step away from foreclosure and she's just hanging on by a thread. And Carl, well, she wanted to kill him."

"Who wouldn't after all that?"

"No, I mean kill him, in the literally sense of the word."

Newman suddenly appeared concerned. "You don't mean kill as in death, do you?"

Millie nodded her head. "Yes."

"How do you know?"

She hesitated. "Let's just say, I know. The only reason he's alive right now, is that he is her son. And he knows how to maintain the swimming pool better than anyone else that she can find for $300 a month, plus room and meals."

"Wow!" Newman sighed. "There is certainly more to this place than I first thought."

"No kidding. And after that, things started to really get bad."

"You mean there's more?"

"Much more. You really don't know what you have stepped into, do you?"

"Enlighten me further."

"Well…" Millie was abruptly interrupted by a voice from the other office.

"Is anyone here?" A man's voice hailed.

Millie rose from her seat and stepped into the receptionist area. A young woman in a bridal gown and a man in a black tuxedo stood in front of the desk.

"We called earlier about the bridal suite?" Newman overheard the couple and rose from his seat and scrambled around his desk into the outer office.

"Yes, Millie, I took the call." He and the groom shook hands. The groom and bride noticed his exterior facial bruises, but said nothing, as if they didn't want anything to spoil their joy. "Just sign them in," he pointed to the ledger.

As the couple started scribbling in the book, Newman pulled the key from the shelf and handed it to the groom. "Room 1451. Just pay when you check-out."

The groom smiled as he took the key.

Millie smiled and added, "Go out these doors, drive two blocks to the right and you should see your room number."

"Thank you," smiled the bride. The groom ushered his bride out of the office.

"Now..." Newman turned back to Millie. "You were going to continue with our conversation."

"Yes, like I was saying, Carl..." She began, then, unexpectedly stopped to examine the room key board. "Where is the other set of keys for the bridal suite?"

Newman looked up at the key board and noted the empty hook. "There should be another set of keys?"

"Yes, a spare. Did the other honeymooners check out today?"

"I don't know Millie. The register said they only wanted the suite for one day and they'd be out by today. I thought they would be out by 7 p.m. tonight."

"What about the other three bridal suites?"

"They were full. This is the one that said one day and that was yesterday."

"They checked-in on Thursday?" Millie asked for clarification.

"Yes, and since today is Friday, they should be gone."

"No, no Ken." Millie shook her head in horror. "That's in the hotel business. People who check in for one day on Thursday don't have to be out until 11 a.m. Saturday morning."

Newman stood dumfounded. "You mean there is another honeymoon couple in that bridal suite?"

They stared wide-eyed at each other for a moment, then, almost simultaneously, bolted for the door. Newman raced frantically across the grounds with Millie trailing him, until they saw the couple turn the key to the hotel door. Millie was behind Newman as he stopped in his tracks and tried to yell. But his lips were too sore and swollen to give out a huge cry. Bent over and breathing hard, he waited momentarily for Millie to reach him.

He mumbled, "Millie you call to them."

Millie was briefly out of breathe, but just as Millie opened her mouth, ear-piercing screams could be heard for miles around. As a matter of fact, the sounds echoed throughout the resort.

"After you, Mr. Newman."

Millie motioned toward the bridal suite with her arm. Newman stood up-right, cleared his throat, and then slowly proceeded down the road to the hotel room.

CHAPTER
3

As the days slowly turned to weeks, Newman gradually became more confident in his role as manager and his face had returned to normal. But more importantly, most of the crew were getting used to taking orders from him. In fact, they seemed quite content to accept his authority, while others did so grudgingly. Vicki's sole support for his decisions also was a key factor in their willingness to follow his orders.

However, despite that support, she still hadn't mentioned a word to him about the resort's Chapter 11 status or the reason she had fired Carl as her manager. Though he knew only part of the story, still he decided not to press the matter. She'd obviously tell him when she was ready. As for the rest of the story---the portion Millie never got around to explaining, he was certain Vicki would eventually tell him about that too, maybe. She still frequently disappeared on her sudden, unexplained business trips with the men in expensive three-piece suits. But Newman now felt, her absences weren't quite as traumatic since he had become a little more comfortable handling the resort's business affairs.

On this day, Newman stood in the kitchen's walk-in freezer inventorying the food supplies on the shelves. He left the door slightly ajar to allow a trace of warm air to enter. He had spent over an hour in the giant freezer when suddenly the door closed behind him. Darkness immediately descended.

"Hey!" He fearfully turned back toward the door. He quickly jammed the hand down, and to his relief, the door easily popped open. "Who closed the damn door?"

The kitchen crew turned to see him indignantly standing in the doorway. Kelly stood near a huge cast-iron stove, leisurely stirring the contents of a large simmering pot atop the range. He looked back over his shoulder at Newman.

"I'm sorry." Kelly gingerly smiled. "I didn't know you were in there." He walked over to Newman. "You can't get locked in there anyway. The doors will always open from the inside."

"Just the same, it does get very cold in there."

"Well...next time, let somebody know you're in there." Kelly mildly scolded. "I just saw the door open and I thought somebody had accidently left it open. If you're going to do an inventory, let me know. I can help out, you know."

"Sorry," Newman reluctantly apologized. "My fault. I should have asked you first before I entered your kitchen. It's just that some of the staff is taking a little longer to get used to me being here than some of the others, and..."

"You thought I'd throw you out of my kitchen just because you're colored."

"Well, it wouldn't be the first time someone has asked me to leave their shop, since I've been here. Some, more forcefully than others."

"Kenny you are welcome in my kitchen anytime." Kelly smiled, placing his hand on his hip. "In fact, maybe I can be of some help."

"Maybe you can at that." Newman agreed, stepping back into the freezer. Kelly followed. "How about a listing of the types of foods and the amounts we store in here on a weekly basis. It would be nice to know how well-stocked we are."

Kelly looked at him suspiciously. "Did Vicki tell you to do this?"

"No, why?"

"It's just that nobody's ever done an inventory in here before."

"Then how do you keep the kitchen stocked?"

"We wait either until we run out or are about to run out of something, then we drive into town and buy some more."

"But with an inventory you can measure how much food you use on a weekly basis and then buy that amount every week so you won't run out."

"Oh, I don't mind doing an inventory," Kelly said matter-of-factly. "I used to do them all the time. But when Vicki entered Chapter 11, she stopped buying food for the month or even by the week. Sometimes we'd just have enough to get by for that day. She just couldn't afford to buy bulk food anymore. Sometimes even when we were completely out, she didn't have the money to buy anything. So we made do with what we had."

Newman listened with resignation. For the first time, he was beginning to get a sense of the desperation Vicki must be feeling in her efforts to hold this place together, and to survive. Desperate people will sometimes resort to desperate measures.

"Well, I'll finish this inventory anyway," Newman sighed. "Who knows, maybe it just might be useful for something one day---for what? I don't know, but at least we will have done one, right?"

"Right," Kelly smiled. He turned to walk away, but stopped and looked back. "Mr. Newman?"

"Ken, everyone calls me Ken."

"Now, don't take this the wrong way," he quietly began, "but, like you said, some of the people here don't like you and…" Kelly awkwardly paused.

"Okaaay?" Newman urged, intrigued by what he might say.

"Well, I was just wondering. What's a nice colored man like you, doing in a place like this?" His question was both sincere and probing.

Newman caught somewhat off guard by the question, struggled for an answer.

"I… I really don't know, Kelly. Fate, I guess. But then, I suppose I could ask the same question about you."

"Why? I'm not colored."

"I know that, Kelly."

"Oh," he laughed. "You mean because I'm gay."

"I suppose there are probably more tolerant places in this country for both Blacks and gays than a Montana tourist resort surrounded by loggers, rednecks, and interstate truckers."

Kelly chuckled. "You'd be surprised how tolerant some of these guys can be behind closed doors, Ken. Oh, they rant and rave in public about how queer I am. They call me names and say bad things about me when they're around their friends, but when I'm alone with one of them, it's a completely different story. I know how the game is played, and I follow the rules. I take their abuse in public, and their apologies in private. I probably see more action around here in one week than you see in a month. So, I know when to keep my mouth closed and… when to keep it open. Ken you'd be surprised to know who ends up in my bed."

Newman smiled. "I probably would Kelly. But, everyone says you are an excellent chef, so what you do in private is really no concern of mine."

"Like they say, the way to a man's heart is through his stomach."

"And, obviously, to other parts of his anatomy as well, I guess."

Kelly said no more and they resume their food inspection. Kelly was very helpful and Newman did finish quicker with his assistance.

After the inventory, Newman left the restaurant and was climbing the steps to the front office when he heard Vicki's voice hailing him. He turned and waited. She rushed to catch up with him. They went up the steps together.

"You're a hard man to catch up with." Vicki puffed, slightly out of breath.

"You're looking beautiful as always. I didn't realize there was so much to do around here."

"Thank you for the compliment. I want you to know you are doing a wonderful job. That's not just me talking either. The crew is even commenting on how well you're doing. See? And you didn't think you could win them over." They stood on the front entrance talking.

"There are still some trouble spots."

"Listen. If you mean Carl is still giving you trouble---?"

"Vicki, I'll handle it, okay?" Newman sternly, but politely insisted.

"It's just that I don't want him giving you any trouble, especially since it seems everyone else is coming onboard with you being my assistant manager."

"It'll be fine."

"If it comes down to you leaving or him leaving… well, you get the idea."

"Don't worry. Before you know it, Carl and I will be sharing the same Ebony magazine."

'Ha!" Vicki laughed. "That, I'll have to see. I'm really sorry for leaving you as often as I do. But, some very important matters are coming up that need my urgent attention."

"That's okay. Lisa, your receptionist, has been awesome in keeping me straight and I'm learning new things about the resort business every day."

"Like when check-out time is." Vicki grinned. "Millie told me."

"That little old lady said she'd keep it to herself."

"You know Millie, nothing is secret with her."

"Well, that definitely was a honeymoon experience they'll remember for a lifetime."

Suddenly a loud angry voice boomed from inside the office. "You stupid slut," the enraged voice scolded. "How many times do I have to tell you?"

"What in the world is going on?" Newman asked aloud.

Newman and Vicki raced up the remaining steps and burst into the office. The receptionist's desk was vacant. The furious voice was coming from Vicki's office. Newman started for the door, but Vicki grabbed his arm and pulled him back.

"Just wait a few minutes." Vicki quietly cautioned in a calm, reassuring voice. "It's okay."

Newman was bewildered by her actions. They both stood placidly in the outer office and waited. Moments later, a balding middle-aged man came storming out of Vicki's office. He stomped angrily past them and out of the building. Newman watched as the man slammed the door behind him. He then turned to Vicki, pointing toward the door.

"What?… Who was that?"

"Shhhh!" Vicki cautioned in a low whisper. "That was Lisa's boyfriend. He regularly beats her up and abuses her like that. I've tried talking to her, but she says she loves him even though he treats her like a dog."

"Boyfriend! Lisa looks barely nineteen." Newman exclaimed in a whisper. "Are you sure that's not her father?"

"Trust me. Snake is too conceited to have children. Besides, children would probably take up too much of his drinking money."

"Snake?"

"That's what everybody calls him. He keeps a live boa constrictor in his house, uncaged, of course. It just roams around at will. I went over there once to take some paperwork to Lisa, and that thing came slithering out from under the sofa. I almost died from heart failure. I'll never go over there again. Let's just drop this for now. When we go into my office, just act like nothing happened, okay?"

Newman nodded his concurrence. Vicki slowly twisted the knob as she and Newman gingerly entered the office. Lisa sat at Vicki's desk, sobbing quietly as she brushed the tears from her eyes. Too their surprise, in the chair in front of the desk sat a huge, deep tanned skin man. He rose from the chair and stood what looked like 8 feet tall. He turned to face Vicki and Newman as they walked in. Newman was awed by the man's size of at least a three-hundred pound frame and all solid muscles. His unkempt beard, dirty, scruffy clothes, and faint, but detectable body order could only mean that he was a drifter. He, like the many other drifters Newman had met in the past several months, only wanted to work long enough to make enough money to get him to the next town.

"Vicki," Lisa beamed, trying to force a smile as she continued to dry her eyes with her hands. "This gentleman came by looking for work." She pointed at him. "I told him, he'd have to come back later and talk to you or Kenny, but he insisted on waiting."

"I see," Vicki looked up at him. "Well…" Vicki looked at Newman. "Will you discuss our employment opportunities with Mr.….?"

"Goliah," he sniffled, sounding tearful.

"Yes… Mr. Goliah. Mr. Newman here will speak with you in the outer office."

"I will?" Vicki eyed Newman emphatically. "I mean yes, I will speak with you in the other room, Mr. Goliah."

"Goliah follow you then."

He picked up the huge backpack propped against the wall and followed Newman out the door.

Newman's head slowly tilted back as he looked up to establish eye contact with the giant.

"I'm Ken Newman." He extended his hand, still quietly awed by the man's size.

His barrel chest surpassed the size of many professional wrestlers. He stooped slightly to keep his head from constantly bumping against the ceiling.

"What's your name again?" Newman asked, trying not to show intimidation.

"Goliah." He sniffled and extended his large hairy hand.

Newman's hand was like a two year old shaking the hand of a professional wrestler. Newman tried to give a firm hand shake, but couldn't. Goliah hands were massive. His almost painful grip left Newman jerking his hand back.

"Goliah, can I ask you a question?"

"You can ask Goliah anything."

"Why didn't you leave the room when you saw Snake arguing with Lisa? It was a private conversation."

"Goliah was there before man came."

"Why didn't you leave?"

"No one asked Goliah to leave." Goliah starting crying.

"Why are you crying?"

"Goliah felt bad for the girl. I wanted to help her, but she didn't ask for Goliah's help. I don't like mean people."

"I certainly understand that." Newman smiled to let Goliah know he did nothing wrong. "Do you really want to work here?"

Goliah wiped the tears from his eyes with his hands. He perked up from the question.

"Goliah strong! Me want to work here," he stated with much delight.

Newman realized with his childlike dictation and his nonthreatening demeanor, combined with his eagerness to please, served to give Goliah a certain charm. A charm that began to evoke more sympathy than fear of his mammoth size. In fact, he started to exude an aura of innocence that started to put Newman somewhat at ease.

"I can see that you are strong Mr. Goliah… ah, is that your first name or your last name?"

"Is only name."

"I see. Well, Mr. Goliah, what kind of work do you do?"

"Am strong." Goliah flexed his biceps that moved his shirt higher on his arms.

"I can see that. That's good, but what kind of work have you done?"

"Can pick up heavy things. Like this." He turned, stooped and in one swift motion, scooped the receptionist's desk up with both arms and held it up in the air with ease. "See?" He beamed boldly, hardly straining under the weight.

"I see, I see! You can put the desk down now." Newman insisted, trying to sound restrained.

Goliah eased the desk back down onto the floor with a thump. Vicki suddenly appeared in the doorway, visibly disturbed by the loud commotion. Goliah turned, saw her displeasure and looked back toward Newman. Vicki went back in her office leaving the door ajar.

"Well?"

"Well, what?" asked Newman.

"Do I get work?"

"If you will fill out an application, Mr. Goliah, I'll get back to you."

"No application," Goliah sternly insisted. "Goliah get job now or move on."

"Ken." Vicki overheard the conversation and quietly interjected. "We could always use another groundskeeper."

"Yeah," Goliah readily concurred. "I keep ground real good for you."

Newman hesitated. Vicki's practice of hiring people without background checks was beginning to concern him.

"All right." Newman conceded. "We'll see how you work out for a couple of days. Give me your name and social security number and I'll fix you up a room. We pay $300 a month plus room and meals."

"No, no room. Just money and food for Goliah."

"Do you have a place to stay in town?"

"No, but still no room. Goliah sleep outside, under stars."

"That's ridiculous," Newman sighed. "There's no need for that, Goliah. It's cold out there at night. Besides, we can give you a nice warm room."

"No!" Goliah was adamant. "No room! No put Goliah in room!"

"Okay, okay. You win. No room. There's an open pasture across the highway. Just take a few minutes to go over there, get settled, and meet me back here in about an hour. We're going to empty all the trash cans on the resort."

Goliah eagerly hoisted his backpack. "Goliah do good work for you. You see."

"I'm sure you will," Newman muttered.

Goliah left the office. Newman looked at Vicki and shook his head.

"And how do you explain that? No room to sleep in. Well, even if he doesn't want a room, I'm going to at least insist that he takes a bath."

"Kenny you'll find that all kinds of people eventually drift through here, some even stranger than him."

"That's hard to believe. Oh, sorry to interrupt you and Lisa. Were you finished talking to her?'"

"No bother. I heard the commotion in here and I just came out to see what was going on."

"Okay. I guess I'd better see that he finds a suitable place over there in the pasture to set up camp. I've met some strange people in my time, but him?"

Newman headed for the door and Vicki started back into her office when suddenly the collective roar of revving motorcycle engines thundered through the building. They both rushed to the front door and peered out into the parking lot across the way. Several dozen heavy-framed motorcycles were rapidly filing in, gunning their engines and racing circles around the parked cars. The riders all wore ominous-looking black leather pants and jackets, while others wore Nazi-styled helmets and carried large-caliber handguns strapped to their waist. Women in skintight black leather pants and spiked high-heeled boots clung to the waist of some of the riders as they filed vociferously into the parking lot.

"Boy, I didn't expect to see them this soon," Vicki muttered in awe.

Newman looked over at her. "Friends of yours?"

"Hell's Angels. They hold their national convention every year in Sturgis, South Dakota, and the quickest route for the northwest area bikers brings them right through here. These guys must be getting an early start on the convention."

"Great, Newman sighed in disgust. "Just what I need. Several hundred heavily armed psychopaths screaming around here on souped-up motorcycles. And look, they are all headed to the bar. Laura is going to be over there all by herself with an army of heavily armed, and soon to be very drunk, Hell's Angels. She'll probably be scared to death. How did you handle them last year?"

"Jake wasn't in the mountains logging last year, so he sort of kept them in line."

"He's in the mountains this year, so now what?"

"I really don't know. Like I said, I wasn't expecting them so soon this year."

Newman stepped over to the desk. "Well, that Sheriff Bennett is going to earn his money today." He snatched up the phone, dialed, and waited.

"Sheriff Bennett," the voice answered.

"Yes, Sheriff Bennett, this is Ken Newman up at the Hot Springs Resort."

"Mr. Newman. How can I help you?"

"We are being invaded by Hell's Angels."

Bennett paused as if he were waiting for Newman to further explain the problem.

"And…?"

"It would be nice to have a police presence up here to keep things from getting out of hand."

"We are not a security service, Mr. Newman. Have they committed a crime?"

"They all have guns," Newman explained. "Very big guns."

"You are in Montana, Mr. Newman. An unconcealed handgun is perfectly legal to carry in this state."

"You are joking?"

"Not in the least, Mr. Newman. Now you can forbid them to carry loaded weapons on your property, but until they've committed an offense, there's nothing I can do for you."

"Thanks." Newman sarcastically sighed. "As always, you've been a great help." He slammed the phone down.

"Do you want me to call Jake off the mountain?" Vicki sounded a little concerned.

Newman ran his fingers over his hair. "No… I'll try and handle this without him. I can't call him off the mountain every time I have a problem down here. Besides, if groups of these mutants are going to be pouring through here over the next couple of months, we're going to have to find a way to deal with them without calling Jake off the mountain every time they come through. By the way, where is that security chief of ours?"

"You mean Curtis?"

"And his gun, Herman."

Vicki checked her watch. "He's probably at the bar. But don't depend on Curtis to handle a real security situation like this. He's just here for show. Hopefully, if people see a man with a badge and a gun walking around, it will provide them with some sense of security."

"A scarecrow."

"Something like that. He's fine for telling otherwise-law-abiding tourists not to spit on the sidewalk. But, if you send Curtis over there to police those bikers, the best we could hope for is that they'll laugh themselves to death."

"Maybe, Vicki, but right now Laura's going to need some help to maintain order over there. Like it or not, he's all we've got. Let's just hope he has a little bluff left in him. If not, then Laura and I are gonna be in a whole heap of trouble."

"You go and see what you can do Ken. I'll finish talking to Lisa and see if I can call in some favors."

Newman left the office. Jumped in the golf cart and rode confidently toward the bar. Though his casual posture was meant to show the bikers that he wasn't intimidated by their presence, the sight of so many large caliber-handguns being so carelessly handled and cavalierly flaunted made him extremely nervous. Besides, if they even remotely suspected that he was afraid of them, he knew they would try to run roughshod over the entire resort.

As Newman approached the bar, several bikers laughed as they pointed at him.

"Hey check out the nigger," one of the other biker's sneered.

Suddenly another biker and his girlfriend clinging tightly to his jacket, gunned his bike and sped over to Newman. Newman slowed his speed. He menacingly, circled him, revving his engine with each pass. Newman tried to appear undaunted.

"Look!" The leather clad woman teased, pointing toward Newman. "A Negro. How quaint." She and the biker laughed.

Newman continued to drive easy toward the entrance way. He came upon another dressed in black skintight leather and spiked high-heeled boots. She was directing the parking order of the incoming motorcycles by pointing to their designated spots with a .44 Magnum.

Newman parked and confronted the woman. "That's not a flag you're waving there, lady," Newman warned, trying to put some authority in his voice. "Put it away, before you hurt somebody."

The woman stopped and slowly gave him a malevolent look. The other biker continued to circle him. Newman ignored the biker on wheels and stared the woman down.

"Well?" Newman forcefully asked.

The woman slowly flashed a tight-lipped smile. Put her finger in the trigger housing and twirled the weapon several times cowboy style. Then jammed the gun forcefully, into her holster. She turned and continued to direct the remaining bikers with hand gestures. Newman eyed her as he walked into the bar. It was packed with bikers. The regular customers apparently had either left or had been quietly urged to leave. Bikers now occupied every table. Nazi-styled helmets with the swastikas of the skull and crossbones emblems emblazoned on the headgear were resting on every table. It was apparent that drinking had commenced early with a varied assortment of beer cans, whiskey bottles, and wineglasses that were atop every table.

The atmosphere was wild and rowdy as the bikers and their molls crammed the dance floor. They were whirling to the beat of the country music that blared from the jukebox. Laura labored feverishly, trying to keep up with the frenzied demand for drinks. Frequently she would race out onto the floor to deliver drinks from her carefully balanced tray. Several bikers climbed atop their tables. They tilted their heads back, turned a bottle of Jack Daniels up to their lips, and began to gulp wildly as the onlookers tooted, cheered, and egged them on.

Newman spotted Curtis sitting on a stool near the end of the counter, eagerly watching the guzzling contest. He eased over to him.

"Curtis!" Newman shouted, trying to be heard above the near deafening ruckus. "I'm going to need your help to restore order in here."

"What?" Curtis asked, eyes still fixed on the contest.

"I said I'm going to need your help to try and get this bar back under control."

"Are you blind? Look around you. This place is totally out of control."

"You think?"

"Aw, hell Ken." Curtis casually chuckled. "They're just having fun. They do this every year."

"Look, Curtis, booze and loaded weapons aren't my idea of fun. Now are you going to help me or not?"

Laura suddenly scurried by with a tray of empty glasses. "Kenny," she sighed. "Boy am I glad to see you. A couple of those table said they weren't going to pay, and when I said they had to, that guy over there pointed his gun at me. A very big gun. Now I don't get paid enough to take this kinda shit. You either do something about these people or I'm walkin' right now." Her tone was emphatic.

Newman looked back over at Curtis. "Now will you help me?" Curtis hesitated. "Damn it, Ken! They ain't hurtin' nobody. What is it you wanna do?"

"For starters, I want to collect all of those side-arms and store them behind the counter. They can pick them up when they leave the grounds." Newman began discreetly pointing to the weapons strapped to their legs.

"Hell, Kenny, they know how to handle their guns. "Sides, what if they don't wanna give them up? You gonna take'em?"

"If I ask nicely, and if you back me up," Newman sternly insisted. "Hopefully, it won't come to that."

Curtis was reluctant. He shook his head dejectedly, "Oh, all right, Ken. I still say you're making a big deal outta nothin', but go ahead. Make your play. Me and ole' Herman here,"—he patted his sidearm, "will back you up."

"Good. Now I'm going to make the announcement that everybody has to turn in their sidearm. They are to write their name on a bar napkin, stick it in their holster, and hand their weapons to you, Laura. You keep them behind the bar and give them back only when they say they want to leave the grounds, not just the bar, okay?"

"Sure." Laura agreed. "Now how are you going to get everybody's attention?"

"There is a disconnect button for the jukebox behind the counter, isn't there?" Curtis volunteered.

"Ah, yes," Laura answered timidly. "But you're not going to…?"

"Oh yes I am." Newman turned back toward Curtis. "Okay man, look alive. Act like you have a little authority around here."

Newman eyed Curtis contemptuously as he meandered through the crowd toward the jukebox. Newman could almost see the fear in Curtis's eyes. It was apparent that his reluctance to confront these bikers stemmed more from his desire to appease them, than any special tolerance for their particular brand of fun. Curtis felt the need to control their access to weapons, simply wasn't warranted.

Laura walked over to the other end of the bar. She waited until Newman reached the jukebox. Once Newman was in position, she reached underneath the counter and turned off the power. The song slowed to garble and then to silence. The reaction was immediate.

"Hey, what the fuck?" The couples on the dance floor stopped in mid-step and looked around bewildered. All eyes turned back toward the jukebox and Newman.

"Hey, what gives?" One biker complained. "What happened to the fuckin' tunes, man?"

"May I have your attention please?" Newman politely announced, standing next to the darkened jukebox, trying to be heard above the grumbling. The bikers eyed him curiously at first, then with steadily increasing hostility.

"Did you kill the sounds, man?" One biker irefully pointed at Newman.

"I'll turn it back on in just a minute." Newman calmly began, trying to conceal the almost sheer panic he felt with an entire barroom of angry Hell's Angels staring at him.

"You'll turn them songs back on now, boy," an angry biker demanded. "Or I'll come over there and turn them on for you."

"Look everybody, we have a policy in this bar that you check your handguns in at the counter. You can pick them up again when you leave the grounds. Now if everyone will just write their name on a piece of paper and…"

"Fuck some piece of paper, Sambo." Another biker yelled. "You ain't gittin my gun."

The other bikers roared their concurrence. Suddenly one husky bearded biker rose from his seat. He stood at least six foot, three. His black leather vest was plastered with patches that read, 'Kill 'em all,' 'Blood makes the grass grow,' and other similar slogans. He swaggered menacingly over to Newman. Newman focused on his approach. The entire barroom was quiet. The biker stopped a few feet from him. They stared at each other momentarily, Newman's heart was almost in his throat as he tried to appear fearless.

"Bullshit!" The man sneered. He patted the Magnum strapped to his leg. "You want my gun, boy? You're gonna have to take it, and quite frankly, I don't think you're man enough. Now turn the music back on, and let these good, hard-ridin' folk get back to havin' a good time. But, I'll tell you what? When we need our boots shined, we'll call you. Meantime, get outta here while you still got your fuckin' teeth."

The other bikers laughed. Newman quickly surveyed the room. All eyes were on him. Laura had quietly retreated to the entrance of the walk-in cooler. She watched from a distance. So, Newman immediately began to search the crowd for Curtis. He was nowhere to be seen.

The bikers had called his bluff, but if for nothing other than his own self-respect, he had to play out the hand.

"If you won't surrender your weapons," he boldly proclaimed, "then you will all have to leave."

"Yeah?" Another husky biker asked. "And I suppose you're gonna throw us all outta here?"

The barroom burst with laughter.

"Never mind them," the biker continued angrily. "You throw me out."

The barroom immediately quieted.

"It's your call, boy. Either turn on the music or get your black ass kicked."

"The music stays off until you comply with the bar policy," Newman insisted.

"Then get ready to spit teeth, nigger."

Newman took a boxer stance and braced ready for the fight. As the biker drew back his fist, suddenly, a much larger hand shot out from the crowd and grabbed the biker's arm, freezing it in mid-swing. Goliah slowly stepped out of the crowd and spun the startled biker around.

"Ken, you need Goliah, help?"

The biker stared up at Goliah. Shocked that he was writhing in pain and agony as Goliah firmly held his arm in an ever-tightening vise. The crowd looked on with awe and silent gasps.

"Yes, yes, Goliah. I surely do." Newman withdrew from his stance and stood tall.

Goliah slowly forced the biker to his knees and then released his grip. The biker remained on his knees, grimacing in pain as he cradled his arm. Another huge biker quickly sprang from his chair, rushed over, and knelt to assist his friend. He looked up as Goliah stared down at them.

"You overgrown ape," the second biker cursed as he climbed to his feet. He drew back and blasted Goliah with a strong right cross to his stomach as he couldn't reach his face. Goliah didn't flinch, but stood firm. He looked down at the biker and smiled a broad grin. The biker gulped as he suddenly receded.

Goliah reached down, picked the biker up to face him, eye to eye level. Then, butted him in the head and threw him against the wall. He slithered down into an unconscious heap to the floor.

Infuriated by the brutal attack on their friend, several other bikers decided to assault Goliah. Seven or eight decided to jump him all at once. They leaped on his arms, one biker got on a table and jumped on his back, grabbing Goliah around the neck, while others punched away at his mid-section. They looked like ants on a piece of sugar. At that moment, Goliah became enraged and bikers flew from his body like bowling pins with a strike. When the dust settled, he was huffing, puffing, and standing tall. Looking for more, Goliah turned to confront the sea of silent faces. He had his arms and chest flexed like a body builder, showing his muscles to a panel judges.

"That's enough, Goliah!" Newman insisted. Goliah relaxed and stood by Newman. Newman breathed an inner sigh of relief as he looked out over the suddenly quieter, more cooperative crowd. "You all can just write your names on a napkin and use them as tags when you check in your weapons." He announced confidently. Newman looked behind the counter at Laura as she had gradually eased out from the entrance of the cooler. "The nice lady behind the counter will keep them for you until you get ready to leave the grounds." Bikers slowly began moving toward Laura placing their weapons with napkins on the counter for Laura to confiscate.

Goliah had tears forming in his eyes. Newman noticed his discomfort. "Here Goliah." He took him by the arm and sat him down by a nearby table until he finished with the bikers.

Quiet mumblings and complaints started amid the sound of unstrapping leather. The bikers continued to walk over to the counter and lay their weapons reluctantly on the bar. A small leather mountain began to grow as Laura began stowing the weapons underneath the counter.

"Once all weapons are put away and the bar is restored to order, I'll put the music back on. But first, put the overturned tables upright and chairs back in place and have your seats." Newman smiled at Laura.

Minutes later, Newman's instructions had been honored. He gave Laura a nod for the jukebox to resume play.

"Oh by the way, yawl enjoy your stay here at the Hot Springs Resort, yawl here."

Laura flipped the switch. The lights flashed on the jukebox and the record quickly reached proper speed. The bikers eased back onto the floor and were once again dancing and clapping to the music, though now in a slightly more restrained mood.

"Now I think you can collect from those guys who owe for drinks." Newman smiled at Laura as she placed a set of holsters under the counter.

"You know Ken, I think you lead a charmed life." Laura returned the smile. "I was certain I was going to have to get the Life Flight up here after that biker had finished with you."

"Oh? What is that? Is that a phone?"

"Life Flight is emergency flight recovery for near death victims. Cause I've seen these guys around before and they don't play. You were real lucky today. Believe me, Ken, most of these biker types are very dangerous backwoods psychopaths."

"Backwoods psychopaths? Come on now. Psychopaths? Some of these guys have national, possibly even global, potential."

"Don't say I didn't warn you."

"By the way did you see what happened to Curtis?"

"I didn't see him run. But my guess is, that's probably what happened."

"I just lost what respect for a law enforcement officer I thought he was."

Suddenly he felt a huge weight on his shoulder. He looked over at the huge hairy hand, then up into Goliah's broad face beaming down on him.

"Goliah no find you at office. Ms. Vicki say you over here. So Goliah come here."

"I'm glad you came here and I'm sorry you got in that fight. Are you still sad?"

"Yes, Goliah don't like to be violent. Unhappy."

Newman moved toward Goliah and stretch him arms around him as far as they would go.

"Goliah, you saved my life back there from those bad men and you've made me very happy." Newman smiled.

"Goliah, did good?" He smiled broadly.

"Goliah, did great!"

"Goliah, saved Newman's bacon today." Laura joked.

"Bacon! Goliah love bacon."

"No, no," Newman started to explain. "It's just a figure of… oh, forget it."

"Goliah, happy now. Come, we go empty trash cans like you said and get away from bad men."

Newman wanted to stay a little longer to ensure the bikers remained peaceful.

"Before we do that, are you hungry?"

"Goliah could use some food."

"How about breakfast?"

"Hmmm, yeah. Goliah love bacon."

"Great. We'll put that with some eggs. You like eggs too?"

"Goliah, love eggs. Lots of eggs and lots of bacon."

"You heard the man. Laura have Kelly cook a plate of bacon and eggs for Goliah. We will just sit out here at the bar for a spell."

Laura hollered at Kelly to whip of some eggs and bacon, while she wiped down the bar.

"Goliah, if some of these guys get rowdy again, I would like for you to bounce them out of here. Okay?"

"Goliah no bounce."

"Why not?"

"Need rubber to bounce."

Laura covered her mouth to restrain her laughter.

"Of course." Newman chuckled, slowly shaking his head. "Silly me."

CHAPTER

4

icki sat patiently at her desk as the two men in three-piece suits sat across from her. She listened attentively as one of the young men handed her a stack of papers.

"That's it," the man announced. "That's everything the government has against you."

Vicki took the stack and thumbed through the pages, stopping occasionally to read a few lines.

"I don't see it," she bitterly insisted. "Where's there case? Where's the evidence?"

"There's no smoking gun, Vicki, if that's what you mean. But those telephone transcripts, combined with what the FBI has on Carl, gives them enough circumstantial evidence to possibly convince a jury that you were involved. At the very least, passively involved in your son's counterfeiting scheme."

"But Carl had a good case for illegal entrapment, didn't he? I mean, if the government hadn't provided him with the paper and the plates to print the money, there wouldn't have been a crime in the first place, right?"

"True, but the government proved that Carl was predisposed to commit the crime anyway, so it would have eventually happened with or without their help. And since they were able to compile enough evidence to bring a conviction against him, that's why they're after you. They have enough circumstantial evidence to connect you to this entire mess.

That's why we have to keep your case completely separate from Carl's. I believe that's the only way we can convince a jury that you are just an innocent victim of your son's evil plans."

Vicki thought for a moment. "I'm just afraid that it's going to look like I'm a mother throwing her own son to the wolves just to save her own skin!"

"Look, Vicki," the other young man began. "We are your attorneys'. That's what you pay us to worry about. We'll take care of that. Carl's a big boy now. He made this mess, now let him take care of himself. Our goal is to keep you out of jail. We want to present you as the clean-cut, hardworking businesswoman who worked her way up from humble beginnings. That you single handedly raised a beautiful family, and who is now gallantly fighting to save her small business from foreclosure. So you had one rotten kid in an otherwise very successful family. There's a bad apple in every bunch. This one just happen to let its spoils rub off on you." He slowly rose from his chair and began to pace the room.

"And how about the contract for a hit man?" Vicki asked.

"That... If Carl doesn't bring up the matter of the supposed first one and since he can't prove it, I don't think he will. I don't foresee that as being a problem. And if he does, then we'll deal with it at that time."

"And how about the second hit man?" Vicki continued.

"We can explain that one as mere speculation. They have no evidence whatsoever tying you to that assassination attempt."

Vicki chuckled. "Boy, how do you explain contract killers as mere speculation?"

"Again, that's our job." The attorney stopped pacing and peered out the office window in deep contemplation. "That's what we get paid the big bucks for. We plan to parade an army of character witnesses across that stand, each one singing your praises louder than the last." He suddenly caught sight of Newman directing a small crew of workers emptying garbage barrels into a dump truck. "Who's that Negro?"

"He's my new assistant." Vicki was unsure of the reason for his question. "Why?"

"Is he literate?"

"Now, what kind of question is that?" Vicki countered defensively.

"Nothing racial, mind you. It's just that most of the people you have working here couldn't spell their own names even if you spotted them the first couple of letters."

"Well, Kenny has a bachelor's degree in journalism," she proudly announced.

"Really?" The lawyer seemed impressed. "Then what in the hell is he doing here?" He questioned as he continued to watch Newman direct the workers.

"It's a long story."

"I'll just bet it is."

"So what? I don't see what Ken has to do with the problem at hand anyway."

The lawyer turned to face Vicki. "Maybe nothing, but I was just thinking that of all the character witnesses we have lined up for you, none of them are Black."

"So?"

"Don't you see the possible impact a Black man testifying on your behalf could have on an all – white jury? Your commitment to equal opportunity, fair play, and all that good stuff. And by some miracle, if we were to get a few Black people on the jury, well…"

"Now wait a minute…" Vicki quickly interrupted, with a harsh tone. "Kenny didn't hire on here just to keep me outta jail. In fact, as far as I know, he doesn't know anything about my legal problems and I'm not going to drag him into this."

"Hey, don't get mad at me. I'm just trying to keep you out of the slammer, that's all," the attorney snapped angrily. "That's what you are paying us for, is to think of ways to keep you outta of jail. And I'm not overlooking any possibilities we may have of doing just that. And if he doesn't know about your problems, then I would suggest you tell him now, before your trial comes up. Because when it does, lady, you're gonna be front page news."

Vicki thought, sighed and bowed her head. Not another word was spoken.

As Vicki contemplated her attorney's suggestion for bringing Newman in to testify on her behalf, he was laboring with the grounds crew emptying the garbage around the complex. Ken watched as the last trash barrel was being emptied into the dump truck.

"Okay guys," Newman sighed. "That'll do it for this week. You all get washed up, grab some lunch and I'll meet everybody back here in front of the café in …" he checked his watch---"about an hour. We'll head over to the RV Park and put up those south side fence poles."

The crew brushed at their clothes as they tramped toward the restaurant. As everyone dispersed, Kenny called Goliah to the side.

"Goliah, you carried two huge barrels. You sure you can handle that and all the other hard labor we are going to be doing today?"

"Goliah, strong. Only need food to keep going. Be back in hour."

Kenny just nodded and followed him to the restaurant. Newman followed Goliah into the dining room. The tables were filled with the usual lunch crowd of long-haul truckers, local ranchers, and an occasional tourist. Voices mingled and silverware clanged as busy waitresses circled the tables with delicately balanced trays of food and drinks cradled carefully in their arms.

Newman was scanning the area for a vacant counter stool when he noticed Kelly and Goliah standing near the kitchen door engaged in what seemed like a very heated discussion. Kelly had one hand on his hip and the other finger shaking violently up into Goliah's face.

"You don't want lunch," Kelly angrily scolded, "you want your own supermarket."

Goliah stood patiently, calmly listening to Kelly's ranting.

"But Goliah need more food than just little bit on plate."

Newman walked up to both men. "Hey you two," he quietly began, "I can hear you both all the way out the door."

"Kenny," an exasperated Kelly sighed. "Maybe you can talk some sense into this overgrown gorilla."

"Goliah, not overgrown, just want more lunch."

"Lunch? Is that all this is about? Lunch?" Newman look at Kelly. "Feed the man his lunch."

"Okay," Kelly readily agreed. He handed Newman a slip of paper. "Here's the lunch order he gave the waitress."

Newman took the paper and began to read it. His eyes grew noticeably larger the farther down the page he read. He then looked up at Goliah.

"Ahhhh… two dozen?" Newman was in disbelief. "For lunch, today?"

"Scrambled." Goliah proudly smiled as he nodded.

"One whole ham, four loaves of bread, and a case of Diet Coke?"

"Goliah, have to watch weight. Don't want to get fat."

"Yeah, watch it skyrocket," Kelly muttered. He turned to Newman. "At this rate, we'd have to set up a special delivery purchase just for him. Not to mention, set aside half of the kitchen, just to cook his meals. It's crazy."

"No, Goliah take food back to camp. Goliah cook own food."

"So, you want to take these items back to your tent and eat there?" questioned Newman.

"Right, Goliah not eat here. Too many people stare at Goliah. Not feel wanted."

"Vicki said one serving per employee, per meal. Maybe seconds for the loggers, but that's it." Kelly wanted to be sure Newman understood Vicki's rules.

"Yeah, but, Goliah is providing his own room, so his lodging isn't costing the resort anything. We could probably make up the difference with a little extra food." He handed the slip back to Kelly. "Give it to him. I'll tell Vicki it was my decision."

Kelly reluctantly took the slip from Newman and huffed back into the kitchen. "Hell, at this rate, we'll be buying food supplies every goddamn day." He complained aloud.

Goliah eagerly followed Kelly. "Scrambled eggs to go."

Newman started back toward the dining area when the front door opened and in marched the loggers from Jake's crew. They each halfheartedly stamped the mud from their boots before they entered. Finally, Jake came in behind the last man. He saw Newman coming from the kitchen toward him.

"Ken," Jake greeted. "Gonna have lunch with us today?"

"I was about to grab a quick bite to eat, then head over to the RV Park and put up that South fence." At that moment, Newman noticed the loud, sometimes crude and obnoxious manners some of the loggers displayed as they approached the counter to order lunch. Their offensive behavior was unsettling to some of the lunchtime tourists. "I thought you guys ate up in the hills?"

"Normally we do, but the smoke from the North Ridge fire is beginning to get a little thick. It was starting to drift over the camp."

"Ridge fire?"

"On the ridge over on the Idaho side of the border. It's burning out of control about ten miles downwind. We're not in any danger here, but occasionally the wind will shift and bring thick white smoke clouds right over our camp. Sometimes you can't even breathe or see your hand right in front of your face. That's how bad it can get."

"Wow!"

"We also just got around to bringing that dozer in that fell over the side of the cliff that day you were there. It took all morning, but we finally got it over there in the shop." He sighed in resignation. "It's going to take a miracle to fix it."

"Don't worry, Jake. Tim seems like an excellent mechanic. And sometimes miracles have been known to happen. Oh and about the other day, if I stepped out of line by suggesting that you shut down your operation, I'm sorry. It was your call and I had no right to interfere."

Jake put his hand on Newman's shoulder and smiled.

"No, it's me who owes you an apology!" Jake shouted, trying to be heard over the raucous chatter of the dining room. "I shouldn't have snapped at you like that. Vicki would have killed me if she knew that I had. But the money from my logging operation is vital to the survival of this resort. If I can't get my logs to the mill…" He paused. "Say, let's have lunch. I'm starved." He called to one of his loggers. "Say Marty, have Kelly bring our lunch into the bar." Jake turned back toward Newman. "We can talk in private in there. Away from all this jaw-jackin'."

Jake ushered Newman through the dining area and into the adjacent bar. The area was quiet as the bar hour had not struck yet. The only noise that could be heard was the occasional cling, ding, or mechanical voice coming from the automatic prompters of the pinball machines. Jake pulled out a chair and sat down with the back of the chair to the front of the table. Newman sat across from him.

"Look Ken, Vicki tells me you're doing a great job for her here. That means a lot to me. I can't be in two places at once. A lot of times while I'm up in the hills, I worry about her down here."

"From what I can see, she does a pretty good job of taking care of things. Besides, I still have a lot to learn about operating a tourist resort."

"That'll come with time. But the important thing is that people 'round here are giving you their respect, even the people who came to me complaining about working for you when you first got here. Now they are telling me you're okay. Not all of them, mind you. But enough to let me know I don't have to worry as much when I'm up in the hills."

Newman chuckled. "That's ironic, because when I first got here, I had everybody pegged as racist rednecks. Now I'm starting to like some of them too. Again, not all of them are on my Christmas gift list but…"

"That's understandable. But it's important that you and the crew at least tolerate each other to get the work done, especially, during the next few weeks. Vicki's going to have to rely on you a lot more than she has in the past. I'd like to help, but my logging operation has got to come first. Every log I take off that mountain helps to keep these doors open. But together, I know we can pull this off."

"I'll do my best." Newman said confidently.

"She's a good woman, and she'll treat you right. Now, you'll hear a lot of bad stories about her in the coming weeks."

"Bad stories? From whom?"

"Mainly from people who are nothing but crooks themselves. But remember, the woman you work with every day---that's the real Victoria Marshall."

Suddenly three attractive teenage girls appeared in the doorway. They scanned the bar momentarily before spotting Newman and Jake. They walked casually over to their table. Though they obviously were just teenagers, their dress and demeanor denoted a maturity seemingly well beyond their years. Jake and Newman looked towards them as they approached.

"Look, ladies," Newman politely began. "The bar isn't open yet. And even if it were, I doubt seriously if you all are old enough to…"

"You must be Mr. Newman," the pretty young blonde excitedly blurted.

Newman was surprised that she knew his name. "Have we met?"

"I'm Kimberly Webster. Everybody just calls me Kimi." She extended her hand. "And this is Marcia Chapman." The pretty brunette wiggled her fingers hi. "And that's Angela McGinnis."

"Angie." The slightly overweight girl smiled.

"And what can I do for you young ladies?"

"We wrote to Mrs. Marshall last month about summer jobs here at the resort when school was out and she said she would hire us."

"She did?"

"Yes, isn't it great?" Angela beamed.

"I... I suppose." Newman uncertain, looked at Jake. Jake shrugged his shoulders.

"Well, here we are. Mrs. Marshall said you would put us to work."

"She did?... I see." Newman sighed. "What can you do?"

"I can wait tables." Angie enthusiastically volunteered raising her hand. Newman noticed the small silver bracelet on her wrist. She noticed Newman straining to get a better look at her wrist ornament and quickly eased her hand down.

"And I can swim," Marcia blurted, "look." She dug into her shoulder bag and pulled out a small red card. "I even have a current first aid card from the Red Cross. Mrs. Marshall said you'd need a Red Cross-certified lifeguard at the pool this summer."

"What are the three steps for CPR?" asked Newman.

"Check the victim for unresponsiveness, then call for emergency assistance. Two, push down in the center of the chest 2 inches-30 times. Pump hard and fast at the rate of 100 per minute, faster than once per second. Three, tilt the head back and lift the chin. Pinch nose and cover the mouth with yours. Blow until you see the chest rise. Give 2 breaths. Each breath should take 1 second. Satisfied, Mr. Newman?"

"I just needed to be sure. We are speaking of people's lives. So it's not a game. It's a job to be taken very seriously."

"I take everything I do very seriously, Mr. Newman." Marcia gave him a stern stare.

Kimberly quickly added. "And I can do dishes, clean rooms, and just about anything else that needs to be done."

"Okay," Newman blew out a short breath. "Well Marcia, go see Carl over at the pool. Angela go back to the kitchen and ask for Kelly. Tell him that I sent you. And Kimi, go tell Vicki that you want to clean her office."

"Wow!" Angela shouted. "Thanks Mr. Newman. We'll do a good job for you."

"I'm sure you will."

"Mr. Newman?" Marcia asked hesitantly.

"Yes."

"Well, like I told Mrs. Marshall, I live in Stevensville and I don't have a car, so I can't commute like the other girls."

"Sure Marcia. There's a vacant room in the women's dorm. I'll have somebody take you over there. When you get there, just make yourself at home."

"Thanks Mr. Newman, but we'll find it. Thank you." She gave a slight smile.

They all turned and scampered back into the dining area. Just then, Kelly entered the bar with carefully balanced plates in hand. He set the plates on the table in front of Newman and Jake. They were with filled with a huge steak and eggs. Then without a word, turned and switched his butt back to the kitchen better than some women he had seen at the resort.

Jake leaned over and smelled the aroma from his plate. "That man sure can cook."

"Yeah, he will make some man very happy one day." Newman shook his head and smiled. "I was just thinking, Jake. Those girls are some eager little beavers, aren't they?"

"How did you know if Marcia was telling you right?" questioned Jake.

"I spent seven years of my life in the Navy. CPR was a yearly certification we had to maintain while onboard ships."

"Oh, okay."

"Anyway, I hope the girls work out. Any extra added help around here is always welcome."

Jake didn't smile. "Trouble." He shook his head dejectedly as he dug into his food.

As Newman continued to consume his meal, he saw concern in Jake's face. "I don't understand, what kind of trouble could they possibly be?"

"Every year Vicki hires young girls like that---fifteen going on thirty. They've just discovered the opposite sex, and they're out to play like a child with a new toy on Christmas morning. It's usually their first time away from home and they think they are little adults, especially when it comes to booze and boys."

"So you're saying it's a mistake having them around?"

Suddenly, the sound of keys rattling in the front door caught their attention. They turned to see Laura stepping through the front door. "Well my first customers of the day." She proudly announced.

"Oh we aren't drinking." Newman explained, eating his food. "Jake and I were just having lunch and a little chat."

"Don't let me stop you," Laura admonished. She walked behind the counter. "The Miller-Lite-for-lunch bunch will be here soon. I'd better get ready for them."

Jake slowly rose from his seat, dabbing a napkin at his mouth. "I'd better be getting back to work myself. Those trees aren't going to come down by themselves."

"And I've got that fence in the RV Park to put up. Goliah is out there right now and I'd better get over there with some men to give him a hand. Although, I don't think he really needs one."

"Boy, that's one strong bird," Jake admired.

"Yeah, but he does have a way with unruly bikers." Newman smiled.

He and Jake shook hands. Newman stood by the table momentarily as Jake headed back to the dining room. He was puzzled by Jake's reference to people saying bad things about Vicki. What bad things would they have to say? Why would they say them? He was beginning to feel like he had walked in on the final act of a Broadway play and everyone knew how all of the pieces to the drama fit together, except him.

Perhaps Laura could shed better light on the situation. Newman walked over to the counter. Laura was washing beer glasses in a sink of running hot water.

"Laura?"

She looked up at him. "Yeah, Ken."

"Just what the hell is going on around here?"

Luara laughed. "Kenny you're the manager. If you don't know, how do you expect me to? I'm just the bartender." She set a steaming beer glass on a mat behind the counter.

As Newman watched her, "That glass isn't going to just dry by itself without spotting, is it?" Suddenly he noticed a loaded .357 Magnum. Newman confronted her about the weapon. "I thought all the bikers took their weapons. What is that?"

"It's my peacemaker." She proudly pronounced. "Now, when anybody steps outta line in here, I don't need Goliah and I don't need a phone to kick some ass. One look at this baby…" she pointed the gun in the air, "and that should take the fight right outta 'em."

"And what if it doesn't? Then what? Are you prepared to blow somebody's brains out with that thing?"

"If I have to. Yes."

Newman could see her determination and understood her reason for having the weapon behind the bar. But he felt that guns and liquor were still a bad combination, no matter how compelling the logic was for combining them.

"I wish you had talked to me before you brought that gun in here Laura."

"Why?"

"Because I can't allow people to carry guns in here, whether they be customers or the bartender."

"And why not?"

"If there's a gun in here, you're going to feel the need to use it at the first sign of trouble. When maybe, if you assess the situation, you could have found another way of dealing with the issue. If only the gun hadn't been there, you wouldn't have killed someone."

Laura odiously glared at him. "Oh grow up, Ken!" She began in disgust. "Just where do you think you are? Sunday school? You know what this place is like, especially now with the bikers here. Hell, you've had two close calls yourself."

"Yes, and both times the situations were resolved without gun play."

"But, how about the next time, huh? What's to say that next time when we need a gun in here, we won't have one?" She shook her head emphatically. "No way Ken. I'm not going to let you bet my life that I don't need a gun back here. This gun stays right where it is."

"Laura." Newman began apologetically. "I know how you feel, but I'm going to have to insist on no guns behind the bar."

Laura turned off the hot water and slammed the washcloth down on the counter. "Well Ken, let me spell it out for you. No gun, no Laura. No Laura, no bartender." Her tone was gravely serious.

Newman paused. He could see the defiance in her face, but he was equally resolute.

"Think about it Laura. Could you really shoot somebody?"

"To save my life… in a heartbeat."

"I don't think you could. But then, it really doesn't matter because I'm not going to let you keep that behind the bar."

"Fine." She grabbed the gun, jammed it into her purse, and hoisted the bag over her shoulder. "Me and my gun are leaving. Should you ever need our services, you know where to find us." She stepped from behind the counter and stormed out of the bar.

Newman watched in silence. He never actually believed she'd call his bluff. Now he was faced with the grim choice of either closing the bar for the day or rescinding his ban on handguns and chasing after Laura to beg her forgiveness. Neither prospect seemed appealing. Suddenly the front doors swung open. In stepped two muscular black-leather clad bikers. One walked over to a vacant table while the other one swaggered up to the bar. He spotted Newman standing near the end of the counter.

"Yo, barkeep," the biker yelled.

"Ahh… yes." Newman replied, trying to sound confident as he stepped behind the counter. "What will it be?"

"Whadda ya have on tap?"

"Ah… yeah. On tap?" Newman wavered. He tried to remember what "on tap" meant. "Let me see," he breathed, stalling for time.

The biker glanced over the counter at the draw handles, then looked back at his friend.

"Looks like Bud or Miller."

"Miller!" His friend shouted.

"A pitcher of Miller," the biker ordered.

"Miller, yes sir. Coming right up."

Newman turned and grabbed a pitcher from under the counter. He breathe a sigh of relief that the handles were labeled. He stuck the pitcher under the spout and pulled the handle.

The golden liquid flowed freely into the pitcher, partially filling it before slowly turning into a thick white foam. Newman carefully poured the foam out and began drawing more beer.

"You know, if you tilt the pitcher into the spout," the biker acrimoniously advised, "you won't get as much foam. But then, I guess a man with your extensive bartending skills knew that already, right?"

"I knew that," Newman insisted as he slowly tilted the pitcher under the beer nozzle and pulled the handle. "Just getting the air out of the line." He handed the pitcher to the biker. "That'll be…" He tried to remember the price of a pitcher of beer. "Three dollars," he guessed.

"How about some glasses?"

"Glasses! Yes, glasses. Coming right up."

Newman turned and grabbed a pair of glasses from the overhead rack and handed them to the biker. The biker looked at them, then handed them back to Newman in disgust.

"These are wineglasses," he was slightly irritated.

"Oh sorry, Newman immediately snatched the glasses back and replaced them with a set of hastily chosen beer mugs.

The biker slapped a five on the counter. "Put the rest toward a bartender refresher course."

He took the pitcher and glasses. He walked over to the table where his friend awaited him.

No sooner than the biker sat down, several tourist tramped through the front door. He wondered how he was going to bluff his way through this.

Three of the people found seats at a table while the man in the group strolled up to the bar. He smiled at Newman then pointed toward his table.

"A Bloody Mary, Vodka Collins, and a Screwdriver for the ladies and I'll take a Bud Lite."

Newman's heart sank. "Coming right up, sir. In fact, just have a seat and I'll bring your order right out to you."

Newman smiled, trying to conceal the total panic that was racing through his mind. He could make a Bud Lite, he thought in desperation, but what about the rest of those drinks?

The man returned to his group as Newman turned to face the liquor assortment shelves behind him. He had heard of these drinks before, but he never dreamed he'd actually have to make them. He began searching the cabinet for clues, when he inadvertently pulled out an unlocked drawer. Among the items inside were a corkscrew and a booklet entitled 1000 Commonly Asked-for Mixed Drinks. He snatched the booklet out and eagerly scanned through the pages. The drinks were listed in alphabetical order. He hurriedly found the recipe for the drinks he needed. He then pulled the necessary ingredients from the shelves and arranged them on the counter like a chef preparing a gourmet meal. Then, as if concocting a witches' brew, he began mixing the drinks carefully. He followed exactly the instructions listed in the booklet. Finally, he placed the obligatory paper umbrella in each glass, placed the glasses on a tray, and gingerly carried his creations over to the table.

He positioned the tray on the table, and each lady took her respective drink. "That'll be eight dollars." Newman guessed.

The man reached into his pocket and pulled out a ten, while the women began sipping on their cocktails. Newman waited with bated breath for their reactions. He fidgeted slightly as he imagined them violently spewing their drinks all over the table. To his surprise, they gently set their glasses back down on the table and casually continued their conversation.

"Keep the change," the man smiled. He handed Newman the bill, then popped the top on his beer can.

Newman took the money and gave an inner sigh of relief. His mixed drinks had passed the test of paying customers. This bartending stuff might just turn out to be a piece of cake, he smiled.

The progressing afternoon brought more tourists, truckers, and bikers, but Newman was gaining more confidence with each satisfied customer that left the counter. Though he kept his trusty little booklet nearby, most of the customers who came in, talked more than they drank. They didn't even seem to care what they were drinking, just as long as it contained alcohol and it at least, remotely resembled their favorite drink. The tips weren't bad either.

Then there was the incredible variety of people who passed through the bar, like the man with his three ex-wives all gathered at one table laughing and reminiscing old times. There was the retired Marine Corps Major, now headed to the biker's convention in Sturgis as part of a "Bikers for Jesus" group. There was the local television news anchorwoman and her station manager. Plus, two young women who had started out from Seattle several days earlier in an attempt to walk across the United States.

By now he had even found a price chart for the drinks, and to his surprise, he hadn't been too far off with his price guesses. And by now, he had mixed so many of the more popular drinks that he didn't even need the guide booklet anymore.

Newman was pouring the contents of a shot glass into a drink. He handed the glass to a young man in a T-shirt, denim jeans, and John Deere ball cap sitting across the counter.

"Four dollars and fifty cents."

The man handed Newman a five. "Keep the change." Newman took the bill and placed it in the register. "Hear you might be looking for a new bartender?"

"Why, you interested?"

"Me?" He laughed. "Not me. I'd drink you outta house and home. No, I'm part of Jake's logging crew. I drive one of his logging trucks and do occasional carpentry work around here, stuff like that. I just came down from the hill early, because I hurt my ankle. But it's nothing a good stiff drink can't cure." He held up his glass, briefly examined it in the light, and then gulped it in one swallow. He slammed the glass down on the counter and shoved the empty glass toward Newman. "Set up another one," he demanded.

Newman picked up the appropriate bottles and began mixing another drink. "You'd better go easy on that stuff, cowboy." Newman smiled.

"Atkins, Mark," he interjected.

"Well, this ain't water, Mark."

"Yea, tha' Tequila Twist. I know. It's the white man's burden. But I want to be good and plowed tonight when I go to bed. I wanna forget all about the pain in my foot as well as the fact that I work so hard all day for so little money. After Jake takes out what we owe him for our meals, logging, gas for our saws, and any bar tabs we might have, we don't have shit left in our pockets. Hell, some of us even end up owing him money."

"Well what kind of work experience do you have other than logging? Maybe you can find another job."

Mark chuckled. "Hardly, I'm also a carpenter, but I only have a tenth-grade education. What kinda job can I get with that sorta learnin'? Besides, before I signed on to drive Jake's logging truck, all he's ever had me do is his nigger work."

"Really?" Newman was jolted by his casual use of the work in his presence. "And what kind of nigger work did he have you do?"

"Oh, you know, sweeping floors, dishwashing, things like…" Mark then looked up at Newman and froze as if realization were a bolt of lightning. "Man, shit…" He blushed. "I didn't mean nothin' by that." He apologetically began. "It's just the way folks 'round here talk."

"Maybe, but not around me, okay? If nothing else, let's respect each other."

"Like I said man, I'm sorry. Fact is, I owe you my life and I never got a chance to say thanks."

"Your life?"

"Awhile back, up on the mountain, during that earthquake. Remember when that tree fell?"

"That was you?" Newman was surprised.

"Yep. Lots of guys thought you were just the kitchen help back then. We didn't know that Vicki had hired you to run the entire place."

Suddenly in through the front door stepped an extremely attractive tall woman with breast-length blonde hair, wearing a tight, well-fitting low cut black dress. All eyes in the bar turned to watch her as she stopped and slowly scanned the barroom like a feline on the prowl.

"Don't look now, Mark." Newman whispered. "But I think the rumors concerning Marilyn Monroe's death, was greatly exaggerated."

Mark glanced back over his shoulder to see the woman. He too found himself impressed by her beauty. He turned back around and took another sip from his drink. The woman stood in the doorway momentarily, then slowly made her way to the counter. Her shapely rear twisting in rhythm with each step. She came to the vacant stool next to Mark.

"Pardon me," she smiled at Newman. Her voice was low and sexy. "Is this seat taken?"

"Ahhhh… no." Newman stuttered. "It's all yours."

She looked seductively over at Mark. "Do you mind if I sit here?"

Mark stared at her for a moment. Shook his head and turned his attention back to his drink. The woman eased onto the bar seat and opened her purse.

"What will it be miss?" Newman asked in his professional bartender's voice.

She looked over at Mark sipping his drink. "I'll have what he's having." She smiled at Mark.

Mark acknowledged her. "Are you sure, lady? Tequila is a man's drink. You should probably order something more suitable for a woman."

"Make it a double… straight," she calmly replied.

Newman stared at her with a raised eyebrow. "Miss are you sure? That is pretty wicked stuff."

She pointed toward the counter. Newman gingerly placed the tiny goblet before her and dumped in two shots of the golden liquid. They both watched as she cupped the glass, uncertain whether she could actually handle such strong liquor. The woman quickly turned the glass up to her lips and downed the contents in one swallow. She slammed the empty glass back down on the counter.

Newman was amazed.

Mark extended his hand and smiled. "Tracy Collins," she confidently stated, shaking Mark's hand. "Just came in from the Big Apple."

"Ken Newman." He and Tracy shook hands. "And what brings you Montana way?"

"I wanted to get away from the rat race for a while. The rats were winning. Besides, this is beautiful country and I'd like to see it up close. Would either of you good-looking gentlemen care to be my guide?"

"Sure," Mark immediately volunteered. "I know this area like the back of my hand."

"Really? Then it looks like you're my man. Let's say we finish that bottle of tequila that I started and you can tell me everything you and I can do for fun together." She coyly smiled at him. She reached into her purse and slapped a $50 bill on the counter. "We'll take the bottle." Newman handed her the bottle. "Keep the change." She smiled as she eased off the stool and walked over to a corner table. Mark smiled, gave Newman the thumbs-up sign, eased off his stool and followed her.

Newman eyed them both as they snuggled close together and poured each other drinks. Suddenly his concentration was broken as another attractive woman stepped up to the bar. She leaned against the counter as Newman calmly walked over to greet her.

"What's your poison miss?" Newman smiled with the confidence of a seasoned bartender.

"I could go for a long screw driver." She whispered quietly.

Her request caught Newman by surprise. He wasn't sure he had heard the woman correctly. He leaned across the counter. "Excuse me, you need what?"

"A long, slow screw," she reiterated. "Are you deaf?"

"A slow screw? From me... Now?" Newman was startled by her apparent boldness.

"Yes, you're the bartender, aren't you?" Her voice denoted a mild irritation. "I'll be sitting in the far corner over there when you're ready." She pointed toward an empty table. "And don't take too long, eh? I wanna be back on the road in fifteen minutes." She turned and headed toward the table.

Newman stared at her momentarily, totally flabbergasted at her openly brazen proposal.

"She's not propositioning you." The burly man's voice called to him.

Newman turned to see the barrel-chested, tan-skinned man seated at the counter a few feet from him.

"I beg your pardon?"

"The lady was asking you for a mixed drink."

"She wasn't asking for sex? Are you sure?"

The man chuckled. "You apparently haven't been at this very long, have you? A slow screw is just a screwdriver with a shot of Slo gin, that purple stuff on the bottom row next to the Jack Daniels." He directed, pointing behind Newman.

Newman looked back over his shoulder at the bottle. Slo Gin was plastered in bold letters across the label. Newman looked back at the man. They both laughed. "Boy, do I feel foolish."

"Live and learn." The man quipped.

"Sometimes the hard way. Thanks… ah…?"

"Ridby. Bud Ridby." He and Newman shook hands.

"Newman. Ken Newman."

"So, how long have you been tending bar?"

"Counting today?"

"Yeah."

"Three and half hours."

"I would have never guessed." Ridby mendaciously chuckled.

"You could say the regular bartender and I had a non-meeting of the minds. So I was sort of pressed into service at the last minute, ready or not. But it sounds like you know your way around a bar."

"I practically grew up in one. I used to fight professionally. And to pay the bills between bouts, I tended bar as well as tossed out my share of unruly patrons from time to time."

"A bouncer and a bartender in one." Newman was impressed. "Well if you ever need a job, let me know."

"It just so happens, I am between jobs right now. In fact, I was on my way to Missoula to see a man about a bartending job."

"We can't pay much. Three hundred a month, a place to stay, and meals."

"Some cash and a place to stay. Boy that sounds like a deal to me."

"Great!" Newman beamed. "When can you start?"

"Oh, I don't know. How about right now? Looks like you could really use me."

Newman laughed. "Truer words were never spoken. Well, go over to the office, tell Lisa to put you on the payroll. Then come back here as fast as you can, before I make a total mess of things. And oh, I don't believe in guns behind the bar, do you?"

"Hey," Ridby confidently held up both fists, "with these, I don't need a gun or anything else."

"Great! Then hurry up and get back here. In the meantime, I'll try and make the lady's drink. Who knows, maybe the drink wasn't the only thing she wanted."

Bud Ridby chuckled as he climbed off the bar stool and walked away. As Newman watched Bud go out the doors, he realized he had broken his own serious concern of hiring without a background check. But he soon dismissed the thought for now, as his needs outweighed his precautions. He'll get around to it sooner or later. Bud Ridby seemed like a nice enough guy.

Meanwhile, the three young ladies Newman had just hired were making themselves comfortable at Marcia's new home away from home. Marcia pushed the room door open and carried her suitcase inside. Kimberly and Angela followed as they closed the door behind them. The girls carefully surveyed the sparsely furnished living quarters.

"Just your bare necessities, table, double-beds, chair, bathroom, desk etc…" said Angela.

"Where is the rest of the room?" Kimberly asked.

"Well it's not the Ritz. This must be a room just for the worker bees who are year round or temps like me." Marcia noted dejectedly as she set her suitcase on the double bed. "At least it's private and it shouldn't be too bad with a little fixing up." She walked over to the corner closet and hung up her clothes bag.

"You know you don't have to stay here, if you don't want to." Angela added. "Call me Marci. It sounds cooler than Marcia. I'm not at home now."

"Sure" both girls stated, simultaneously.

"I'd be happy to drive by and pick you up. Stevensville isn't that far from Missoula." Stated Angela.

"Thanks, but that's way too far for you to drive every day. Besides, I want to get out of my parent's house for the summer. They are talking about divorce. So I need a break from their constant bickering and fighting. This way, I'll be out of their hair, and they'll be outta mine."

"Besides, there are bound to be lots of cute boys here for the summer." Kimberly noted. "Now we have a place to throw a party and get as crazy as we want without anyone bothering us."

"I don't know." Angela said concerned. "I don't think that Negro will let us have male visitors here in the room since we are only sixteen. Besides, did you see the look on his face when he thought we were coming into the bar to buy drinks?"

"And he almost saw your medical-alert bracelet, Angela." Kimberly stated. "If they find out you are diabetic, they might not let you work here."

"Oh, don't worry about him," Marci chided. "We'll be making our own money, and with enough money, you can get anything you want. My father taught me that."

"I didn't even know they had Negroes in Montana," Angela wondered aloud. "Something about it being too cold or something like that. Anyway, I'll just take it off." She removed the bracelet. "That'll solve that problem."

"Don't worry about it," Marci sternly reiterated. "We came here to have fun this summer, right?" The other girls nodded in agreement. "Good. And nobody is going to stop us, right?"

"Right?" the girls agreed in unison, smiling at one another.

"Nobody." Marci quietly breathed with seriousness in her tone.

As the girls settled into the dorm and Newman stayed with Bud until late afternoon. He wanted to be sure Bud was not overwhelmed by the bar crowd. Newman, feeling confident Bud had everything under control, headed back to his room. As the brisk, cool air chilled his body leaving the bar, he knew the sun would be down soon and the temperature would plummet even further. He thought of Goliah out in the field without shelter. His concern lead him to grab some covers from the linen closet of the hotel, hop in the golf cart and check on Goliah in the field.

As the sun set, Newman's feet disappeared with each step he took through the tall, moist green grass that was ankle-deep. He cradled several woolen blankets under his arm to reach this man, that he almost can call his friend. But there was still much to learn about Goliah.

In the distance, he saw a small campfire flickering against the darkness. Why anyone would choose to live out here in the cold night air was a mystery. But then almost everything about Goliah was mysterious, to say the least. His strength bordered on the superhuman, but while he had the body of a giant, he had the mind of a little child. Where did he come from? How did he get here? Where was his family? Hopefully, Goliah trusted him enough by now to open up a little about his background. Maybe, just maybe, he would also provide enough information to at least fill out the employment application he had so far managed to avoid.

He tentatively approached Goliah's tent, treading softly, careful not to unduly alarm him. "Goliah." Newman called quietly. "Goliah? It's me, Ken. Are you home?" A giant hand pushed the tent flap back and Goliah poked his head through the opening.

"It's going to get a bit nippy out here tonight, so I brought you some extra blankets." He handed the blankets to Goliah. "You know you don't have to stay out here? There is a nice warm room with a hot running shower waiting for you back at the resort, if you want it."

"Thanks Ken." He smiled as he took the blankets. "But Goliah fine. Want to stay in tent no matter how fast shower run."

Newman chuckled. "Well suit yourself. But it does get pretty cold out here at night."

"Tent fine. Goliah no like being locked up in room."

"Locked up?" Newman was curious. "Why? You would have the key to come and go as you pleased."

"No!" He asserted his defiance. "No room! Rather freeze than be put in room."

"Okay, okay." Newman backed off. He could see the anger building in his face. Maybe this wasn't a good time to press for personal information. "I was just trying to make sure you were all right. Are you claustrophobic?"

"No. Just afraid of being closed in. But Goliah not freeze with extra blankets. Thanks Ken."

"You are most kindly welcome, Goliah. Oh by the way, I just want to thank you again for helping me out with those bikers. We haven't had any trouble with them since."

"Bad people!" Goliah huffed.

"I know, I know. Still, the situation was a little bit more than I could have handled alone."

"Goliah glad to help you, Ken."

"Well, goodnight." Newman turned, he noticed the lights in the general store windows. "Say," he thought aloud. "That place is supposed to be closed. No one's supposed to be in there." He turned back to Goliah. "Have you noticed anyone over at the store today?"

"Goliah not see nobody."

"Burglar's maybe?"

"You want Goliah to go see?"

"No, I'll check it out. It could be Vicki or somebody, but listen carefully. If you hear someone screaming his head off, you'll know it's me."

Goliah watched as Newman disappeared into the darkness.

Newman knew the last time he had visited the store, it was just a collection of cobwebs, old cans, and inch-thick dust. For Vicki to be cleaning here this time of the night would be highly unusual, especially considering that the store had been dormant all winter. Could it be that some drifter had broken in looking for shelter or a pilfered meal?"

He carefully climbed the steps, listening for sounds from within. It was quiet. He turned the knob. Surprisingly, it twisted easily in his hand. He pushed the door open. The little bell hanging overhead tinkled as he entered. As he surveyed the interior, he couldn't believe his eyes. The entire store had been cleaned. No, not just cleaned, it was spotless. The vinyl floor gleamed with a shiny new wax coat. The wooden shelves were neatly stocked with fresh goods. All the broken lights had been replaced and the fresh smell of pine, permeated the air. If a burglar had broken in and done this, maybe he could be persuaded to break into Vicki's office next. He picked up a can from the shelf and started to examine it, when suddenly a young woman dressed in sweats and carrying a broom stepped from the back room. She gasped as she looked up and saw Newman standing near the shelf. Newman turned in her direction.

"Look miss, don't be alarmed," Newman quickly consoled. "I'm the manager here. I just didn't expect anyone to be here this time of night."

"Oh," the woman breathed a sigh of relief. "You must be Mr. Newman. Vicki told me all about you."

"And who might you be?"

She pulled the sweatband from her head and extended her hand. "Beatrice Henderson. Please, call me Bea. It's what I've gone by all of my life. Vicki hired me and my husband John to run the store this summer."

"Mom?" A cute little red-haired girl emerged from the back room. She looked to be about ten years old. "Can I have…?" She looked up at Newman and froze.

"Candy," she pulled the little girl close to her. "This is Mr. Newman. Say hi."

"Candy shyly eased a finger in her mouth and began to fidget slightly. She smiled coyly, looking up at Bea for reassurance.

"Candy, that's a pretty name."

"Candice is her real name."

"And is John short for something?"

"Nope," Bea smiled. "Just plain ole John."

"Is he around? I'd like to meet him too."

"John and I worked on this place all day, trying to get it ready to open. He left a little while ago to look around. He should be back shortly."

"Good. I'd like to commend you both on the job you've done with this store. When I first saw this place, I thought I'd call the governor and try to get it declared a disaster area."

Bea smiled. "It was in pretty bad shape."

"Frankly, I don't recognize it. Are you and your husband magicians, by chance?"

"Heavens no. I'm just a simple schoolteacher, and John's just a plain ole stockbroker."

"Well, anybody who can pull off a miracle like this has got to know a little magic. Welcome aboard. Take it from me, this place is going to be unlike anywhere you've ever worked before."

"Believe me, after chasing twenty-five seventh-graders around all year long, nothing short of an atomic blast could faze me." She checked her watch. "It's been a couple of hours since John left. I wonder what could have happened to him."

"It's a chilly night. He might be holed up somewhere, getting warm."

"I hope so."

"Tell you what. You haven't seen much of this place yet, have you?"

"No. I've… I mean, we've been working on this store all day long."

"Let's go and look for him. I can sort of show you around. Granted, there's not much to see at night, but at least you'll get a lay of the land. Let's go. My ride is not far from here."

Bea thought for a moment. "Okay. I'll get my coat. Candy, lock the door behind us, and don't let anybody in unless it's Daddy. Tell him we went to look for him and that we'll be right back. We won't be long. Okay, sweetheart?"

"Yes ma'am."

Newman and Bea left the store and headed for the main complex. As Newman was pointing out the resort's various tourist attractions, Bea suddenly noticed a large woman frantically waving as she ran toward them.

"Ken," Bea tapped Newman on the shoulder. "That lady seems to be trying to get your attention."

Newman turned to see Laura running toward them.

"Kenny," she hailed. "I've been looking all over for you."

"Laura, this is Bea. Bea, this is Laura, our former bartender."

"That's what I wanted to talk to you about, Ken." She gingerly began. "I realize that it was wrong walking out on you today and if you don't want any guns in the bar, then that's fine with me. I'll leave mine at home from now on, I promise. I'm not fired or anything, am I?"

Newman sighed. "No, Laura. You're not fired."

"Then, who's that new guy I saw behind the bar tonight?"

"Bar?" There was a subtle, but noticeable note of concern in Bea's voice.

"Yes." Newman answered. "And a somewhat rowdy one at that. You seemed surprised."

"It's just that Vicki didn't mention anything about there being a bar here. When I think of resorts, I think of cabins and lakes and streams--that sort of thing."

"Well, here we have all that. But you can think of bars too, Bea." Laura added. "Now what about the new bartender, he's…"

"I'm sure you both can work out a schedule so that you two won't get in each other's way."

"Are you sure? I've seen him in action behind the counter, and he's not the kind of person you'd want to upset."

"Now what's that supposed to mean?" quizzed Newman.

"He's got a quick temper and I've seen him get violently upset over things that happen in there that I would just pass off as normal barroom antics."

"Like what, for instance?"

"Maybe you should go over there and see for yourself."

Newman looked over at Bea. "You don't mind if we swing by the bar, do you? This should only take a minute."

"Ahhhh… no," she hesitated. "Err… no. Stopping by the bar will be fine."

"Thanks. This probably won't take long."

Laura hopped on the golf cart and Kenny drove a few yards. You could hear the twang of country music. It filled the air as they approached the bar. Cars and pickup trucks jammed the parking lot. As one couple left, several others entered in a constant flow of revelry. The smoke filled air blasted their faces as Newman pushed through the doors. The three of them paused in the doorway, then slowly made their way virtually unnoticed into the midst of the crammed dance floor. The stage band swayed as the standing-room-only crowd laughed and danced to their country beat.

"Well," Laura shouted, trying to be heard over the clamor, "I see Kelly is up to his old tricks."

"What old tricks?" asked Newman.

She pointed to the corner table, where what appeared to be an attractive young blonde in a bright red dress was letting a half-drunken cowboy feel his shapely nylon-clad thigh.

"Is that…?" Newman incredulously asked.

"Yep. Whenever there are a lot of men around, you can always find Kelly right there, all dressed up and on the prowl."

"Do the guys know?"

"They eventually fine out, sooner or later."

"I guess so."

"Kelly?" Bea asked, only halfheartedly listening to their conversation as she anxiously scanned the bar for John.

"It's a long story," Newman sighed, shaking his head.

His attention turned to Bud Ridby. His experience as a bartender was apparent as he poured drinks, wiped the bar and chatted with the customers, all with the smooth motions of a virtuoso. His fluid movements and apparent ease of style were most impressive.

Newman turned to Laura. "Is that what you call a problem?" He pointed toward Bud. "Are you sure you're not just a little bit jealous?"

"Me? Jealous?" Laura huffed. "Hey, well look at that," she pointed back toward Bud Ridby. They watched as Bud gulped the contents of a small shot glass. "Now, even I don't drink when I'm on duty."

"You're right," Newman conceded. "The last thing we need on duty is a drunken bartender. But even so, he still seems to be cool and collected back there."

"Yeah, and some customers do feel offended if the bartender doesn't have a drink with them."

"Yea Laura, and after you finish not offending thirty or forty customers, you are more loaded than they are. I'll have a talk with him and explain that we don't drink while we are on duty here."

Suddenly, at a center table, a woman angrily shot up from her seat, slapped the face of the man across from her and then tossed the contents of her glass in his face."

"Hey baby," the man tried to explain. "What did you do that for?"

"My mother was the last person to touch me there, and you sure as hell don't look like my mother!"

"Just trying to be friendly." He smiled a half-drunken smile.

The confrontation continued unnoticed by most of the patrons, but Bud Ridby was closely monitoring the exchange out of the corner of his eye.

"Bud seems to have matters well in hand here," Newman noted as he watched Bud gulp the contents of another shot glass. "But his drinking does concern me."

"I'm right here, Ken. I can take over now if you want me to." Laura eagerly volunteered.

"No, that's okay. He's doing fine so far."

Newman glanced away from Bud to observe the crowd. When he did, he noticed Carl sitting at a table with a small group of cowboys laughing and drinking. He and Newman exchanged opprobrious glances. Carl then leaned toward his friends and whispered something. Then he pointed toward Newman. They almost simultaneously turned to see Newman, then looked back at Carl. He slammed his fist into his opened palm, then leaned back with his eyes closed as if he had been punched. The men roared with laughter as some of them glanced back over their shoulders to get another look at Newman.

Newman ignored Carl's gestures. "Come on Bea," Newman said. "We'll probably find John back at the general store." They started to leave.

"Wait, what about Bud?" Laura asked.

Newman turned to notice that Bud Ridby had left the counter and was vehemently arguing with the man involved in the confrontation with the young woman. Bud motioned toward the door as he and the man continued to quarrel. Suddenly, Bud yanked the man up from the chair and flung him violently to the floor. The barroom was silent as all eyes suddenly focused on the altercation. The man tried to get up, but Bud swiftly kicked him in the abdomen. The man grabbed his stomach and curled. Writhing from agony as Bud drew back and kicked him again and again, the man laid almost lifeless on the floor. Newman quickly became alarmed. Bud seemed to delight in delivering more force with each successive blow. Newman started to push his way through the crowd, trying to reach Bud. Just before Newman could reach him, Bud reached down, pulled the man up by the lapels of his jacket, and began hustling him toward the entrance.

"John!" Bea screamed as Bud sailed him through the front door.

Bud turned and calmly walked back to the bar as Bea bolted past him out the doors. Newman and Laura looked at each other bewildered.

"John?" They both said in unison. They rushed out after Bea. They scampered down the steps and knelt around John, while Bea cradled his head in her arms.

"Who was that crazy animal behind the bar?" Bea cried as she rocked John gently in her arms. "He almost killed my husband."

"Ahhhh…," Newman was at a loss for words. "He's ahhh… sort of our new bartender." He helped a still groggy John climb to his feet. "Let's get him back to the store. We can take a better look at him over there." Newman suggested. He pulled John's arm over his shoulder. "Just lean on me." John was slightly conscious. John's rubbery legs bent and buckled as he tried to walk.

Newman and Bea slowly ushered John onto to the golf cart. Laura climbed in too. Minutes later, they arrived back at the store.

"Right in here," Bea instructed. She led them into the back bedroom. John was muttering unintelligibly as Bea pulled the bedcovers back. Newman carefully eased him onto the mattress as Laura hoisted his legs on the bed. Bea sat beside him and began unbuttoning his shirt.

"Do you want me to get a doctor over here?" Laura suggested.

"No, I'll take care of my husband." Bea had tears in her eyes. "There's no need for that kind of brutality."

At that moment, Candy came from her bedroom. She saw all the people standing in the hallway of her mom's bedroom.

"Mommy!" Candy cried. Bea hurried from the bedroom.

"Honey…"

"Did you find Daddy?"

"Go back to your room sweetheart. I will be there in a minute."

Candy looked at Laura and Newman and did as her mother asked. Bea got a cold clean cloth. She sat by her husband's side and wiped the blood from his face.

"You know, you're right, Bea. There was no need for such a brutal beating. I'm going back there right now and give him his walking papers."

"No!" Bea insisted. "Please don't. Just let it be, please. I just don't want any trouble." She gently felt John's chest and rib cage. "Doesn't seem like anything is broken. He'll be all right."

"That's beside the point." Newman asserted. "If he'll go off like that on a customer, then there's no telling what he'll do to his fellow co-workers."

"Or his manager," Laura immediately added.

Bea rose from the bed. "Laura? Can I speak to Ken in private?"

"Sure. I'll be outside."

"No Laura. Why don't you go back to the bar and keep an eye on Muscles. I'll be back over there to talk with him in just a few minutes."

"You want me to walk?"

"Take the cart, I'll walk." He tossed her the key. Laura turned and left as Bea gently pulled the covers up on a still moaning semiconscious John. Bea closed the door to the bedroom so Candy wouldn't hear.

"I'm really glad Candy didn't see him. I really didn't want her to see her father like this again."

"Again?"

"John's an alcoholic." Bea began bluntly. "When he drinks, he becomes vocal, abusive, and violent. I didn't know that before we got married, or so help me, I never would have married him. But when he's sober, you couldn't ask for a better husband or father. I suppose you were probably wondering what a successful stockbroker and a schoolteacher were doing working here for three hundred dollars a month, plus room and board."

"Bea, whether I did or not, this is really none of my business. You don't have to tell me anything."

"But I want to tell you. Because sooner or later John's drinking usually causes a problem, not only for us, but those around us as well. So you really need to understand how two highly successful people ended up living in the back room of a log cabin store in the middle of the Lolo National Forest. John and I have been married for seven years and together we made over $195,000 a year." She readily continued as she slowly paced the floor. "We had two houses, three cars, and about $1,600,000 in stocks, cash, and other assets. And when Candy came along, I couldn't imagine how our lives could have been any better. John, at that time was a heavy drinker, but he always managed to keep it under control. At least, the drinking didn't impact our lives. But, I guess the pressures of the stock market started him to drink more and more. At least that's what I guess started him drinking to excess. Anyway, it started to show in his work with the absenteeism and the sick leave abuse. Sometimes he'd even show up for work drunk. Finally, they told him to find help or find another job. So he just quit."

Newman could see the agony in her face as she paced, talking almost to herself as she relived what must have been a nightmarish experience for her and her daughter. Tears formed in her eyes as she folded her arms in her chest. Newman reached to give her a tissue from the end table by the bed.

"You don't have to continue, Bea."

She took the tissue graciously and dried her eyes before a tear fell. John still laid unconscious in the bed. Bea continued.

"But even with John out of work, we still were able to manage for a while with my salary and dipping into our savings and investments. But the more money we lost, the more John drank. Finally, I went to the bank and found all of our money gone. John had withdrawn every dime we had and left me a note saying he didn't love me anymore. He said he wanted a divorce and was leaving me for this other woman he had met. Some former Ms. Washington State Apple Blossom or something like that. I came to discover that he had been having an affair with this woman for almost a year. I was an emotional wreck, but I had to try and go on for Candy. So what the bank didn't take, I sold. I sold the cars, the furs, everything. But it seemed John's new girlfriend was more interested in our million than she was in him. So when she got all of his money, she left him. And to make matters worse, she now claims that John is the father of her baby and she's suing us for child support. That's when he came crawling back to me."

"And you obviously took him back."

"He said it was the booze and Candy really loves her dad. So, yes, to keep my family together, I took him back. But I knew if we stayed in Seattle, around his old friends, he'd just climb right back into the bottle again. So one of my students who had been up here on vacation, wrote about this place for an essay assignment. They spoke about its beautiful surroundings and how much fun they had. So, I called Vicki about the possibility of bringing the family up here for an extended vacation. That's when she said she needed a couple to run her general store for the summer. Well, I jumped at the chance to get up here. I have always wanted to live among the mountains, the trees, the running streams and the wide open spaces. It just seems like everything is fresh and clean out here, away from the hustle and bustle of the city life. I wanted to give my family and our marriage a chance to heal as well as get John away from the city pressures and the alcohol."

"And you didn't know that we had a bar?" Newman sighed.

"It just never even occurred to me to ask if you had one. All I could see were the streams, the hills and the isolation. If I had known there was a bar up here, so help me, I would never have come."

"I understand your problem. Do you still want to stay?"

"We have no choice. We have nowhere else to go and very little funds."

Newman could see the frustration and the apprehension in her face. Though she had been through a horrible ordeal with this man, she still loved him. She loved him despite the agony he had put her and Candy through. Now, just when she thought the nightmare that had been her life was finally over, the sequel was more than likely, about to begin.

"Well, I'll do what I can to help." Newman quietly consoled. "And I'll leave word for the bartenders to take it easy on dispensing the booze when John orders from the bar."

"Thanks, Ken. I'd sure appreciate your support and understanding in this matter."

"Like I said earlier, it's none of my business. But pardon me if I'm out line, but have you ever thought of just leaving him?"

"A daughter needs her father," Bea replied almost automatically with all of the confidence of having answered that same question more than a hundred times.

"Well, I better get back over to the bar before Bud decides to brain Laura." He turned to walk out the door when Bea immediately grabbed his arm.

"Ken?" She pleadingly asked. He turned to face her. "I hate to ask, but could you stay awhile?" Her voice was meek and apologetic.

"Ahhh… sure, I guess. Why?"

"It's just that when John wakes up from one of his binges, he's usually pretty ugly and abusive. And I'd like for Candy to think that period in our lives is over. He doesn't usually get too nasty if someone else is around."

"Okay… sure." Newman paused. "Oh, why not. I can stay. We can take a look at your pricing charts while I'm here. Besides how much damage can Bud do in only one night behind the bar?"

Bea started to open her mouth. "On second thought, don't answered that," Newman quickly interrupted.

C H A P T E R
5

It was almost two in the morning before Newman finally left the general store. It was apparent from John's snoring that he was out for the night. Bea had quietly nodded off in a chair she had pulled from the back room to be by John's side. By the time he made it back to the bar, all of the patrons had left. Except, there were three ex-wives that were still laughing and talking over half-empty wine and beer glasses. Bud was busy wiping the countertop while Laura neatly stacked the empty chairs upside down on the tables.

"Kenny!" Laura hailed as he entered. "Great! You're just in time for cleanup. Grab a broom and make yourself useful."

"Sorry, but I'm beat. Just leave the floor till morning. Besides, you two look like you both could use some sleep yourselves."

"Not me," Bud smiled, running hot water over the stack of beer glasses piled in the sink. "I'm used to these hours. Why, in Boise, I once worked in an all-night bar, so this is a piece of cake."

Newman stepped up to the counter. "Were you that tough on the customers in Boise?"

"What are you talking about?"

"That drunk you threw out tonight. You were a little rough on him, weren't you?"

Laura pretended not to notice their conversation although she strained to hear every word.

"Oh, him." Bud chuckled. "Were you here for that? I didn't see you."

"Would it have made a difference? I mean, you beat that guy like he stole a chair out of the White House."

"If you were here then you saw what he did," Bud began defensively. He turned off the running water. "He reached under the table and put his hand up that woman's crotch. Now, as bartender, I don't have to tell you that it's my job to keep order in this place as well as see that the customers have a good time. And since you don't allow guns in here, I have to keep order with these." He held up both his fists.

"I understand, Bud. But as many times as you kicked that guy, you could have seriously hurt him."

Bud was beginning to resent Newman questioning his methods, and he was quickly becoming annoyed with this inquisition. "Look, you said no guns, right?"

"Right. I know."

"Well, my fists are the only other weapons I have to enforce order in here. Yeah, maybe I was a little rough on that creep tonight, but it sent a strong message to the rest of those yahoos to stay in line or else."

"Maybe Bud, but still that doesn't justify blatant brutality."

"Damn it! Ken." Bud pugnaciously insisted. "This ain't no social club. This is a country redneck bar in the mountains of Montana with the nearest law enforcement some thirty-five miles away. The bartender is the only law in this place. Damn it! Wake up and smell the coffee. You ain't in Kansas no more, Dorothy."

Newman stared into Bud's surly eyes. While Bud did have a valid point, it was apparent that he also had a violent temper. A temper that would either get him or someone else seriously hurt if left uncontrolled.

"Now you listen," Newman countered quietly but firmly. "I won't tolerate excessive brutality in this place, no matter what the provocation. Nor will I tolerate drinking with the customers while you're on duty. So no more drinking on duty while you're back there either, okay?"

"Got damn it, boy!"

Bud was now visibly irritate with Newman. "The customers expect you take a drink with 'em every once and a while, just to be sociable."

"The last thing I need back here is a bartender more juiced than the patrons." Newman's peeved voice retorted. "So if you can't handle that, Mister, then there are other bars in Missoula that I'm sure can use a man of your talent!"

Newman suddenly realized the intensity of their raised voices. He glanced around to see if anyone was watching them. Laura stood motionless, chair in hand, staring slack-jawed at them, while the man and his three ex-wives were all peering quietly in their direction.

"And as for you all," Bud pointed toward the table of four, "we closed at two, if you get my meaning. If you haven't drank it by now, you weren't meant to drink it." He turned and started for the door when he suddenly stopped and turned toward Laura, raising his finger as if to say something. Laura stood quietly awaiting his verbal blast. "And as for you, young lady…" he hesitated. "Oh… forget it."

As Bud turned to leave, he stepped right into the face of a man bolting through the front door. The man's face was wild, excited, and desperate.

"Sir, I'm sorry but we are closed for the night."

"Thank God you're open," the man blurted, almost out of breath as he stormed up to Newman standing by the counter. "Where's your phone? I gotta call for help! Those people are real hurt bad!"

"Now calm down," Bud consoled. "What people? Whose hurt bad?"

"Bout a mile and a half up the road going to Idaho." He struggled to catch his breath. "An eighteen wheeler… The driver musta' fallen asleep or something, but it ran off the road and down this cliff. I climbed a little ways down there, but it was too dark. You gotta help!"

"Laura!" Newman ordered. "Go to the office and wake up Vicki. Tell her what's going on and then call the sheriff. Bud, you stay here, get this place locked up and wait for the authorities. When they get here, bring them up to the crash site. "Mister," he pointed to the man at the bar. "Come on. Show me where this wreck happened."

"Can I be of some help?" The man had left his ex-wives at the table and rushed over to Newman. "I'm Raymond Scott, and I've got a four-by-four with a fender-mounted cable retractor and roof-mounted floodlights."

"Mister, are you in any shape to drive?" Newman was skeptical.

"Sober as a judge."

"Right… oh, okay. We'll take your jeep Mr. Raymond Scott. We'll need the lights. Come on, everybody. Let's get a move on." Newman commanded.

Bud watched as everybody raced for the front door, leaving him and the three women behind.

The man hopped into the back of the jeep as Newman and Scott hurriedly climbed into the front seats. Scott geared the vehicle and roared off. It took them several minutes to reach the crash site. The man pointed toward a darkened area along the side of the highway. Scott pulled to a stop at a fairly steep precipice near a bend in the road. The man climbed out of the jeep and ran to the edge of the cliff.

"It's down there," he pointed into the dark ravine. "I saw it go over right here."

Scott parked near the edge and cast his bright floodlights down the tenebrous hillside. Newman walked over and peered over the cliff. The pungent odor of diesel fuel filtered up to the road. He could see that the eighteen-wheeler split. The trailer lay to the left and the cab to the right. Further down the steep embankment was a long trail of grain, dotted with small scattered grass fires. Halfway down the hill, the huge grain trailer rested upside down, its wheels still spinning. Scattered grain covered most of the hillside, the overturned trailer had spread its contents over a wide area.

"I don't see any skid marks," Newman noted, surveying the road. "He must have driven right over the embankment."

"Probably fell asleep at the wheel or had a heart attack or something." Scott surmised, peering over the side of the cliff with Newman and the other man. "And it's a long way down there too. I don't see how anyone could survive that one."

"Well, I'm going down to check," Newman looked for the easiest path down the escarpment. "Maybe somebody down there got lucky tonight."

"Be careful," the other man called. "I smell diesel fuel. You'd better hurry."

As Newman placed a cautious step down the side of the hill, he found the footing slippery.

"Trying to walk on all of this grain is like trying to walk on marbles," he called aloud.

Several large trees had also been leveled as if the cab of the eighteen wheeler played pinball with the trees, bouncing from one tree to the next. There were small patches of grass and brush that burned like small flares flickering in the night. With each careful step, Newman's feet sank deeper in the soft brown grain. He used his hand to grip what bushes weren't burning to maintain his balance. Several yards down, the mammoth truck cab lay quietly on its side, driver-side out. The passenger side was impaled against a huge slightly tilted cedar tree that had almost held its ground against the impact of the collision. Fuel slowly ebbed from the huge twin fuel tanks mounted under the cab. The sight of the mangled, twisted wreckage was awesome, unlike anything Newman had ever seen before.

He gingerly walked around the front of the cab, climbed on the crumpled front bumper and peeped through the shattered windshield. He recoiled in horror. The driver's head had slammed through the jagged glass while his chest had collapsed into the steering column. Blood smeared the broken glass and most of the cab's interior. Newman's stomach churned. He started to feel queasy. He quickly turned his head away. His first actual encounter with death, and he wasn't handling it very well. To die such a violent and painful death seemed cruel even beyond the actual act itself. What had this man done in life that was so horrible as to deserve such a gruesome death? Newman thought he'd try once again to peer into the cab's interior. Perhaps he might find some evidence of what caused him to veer from the road. Suddenly, he noticed a slight stirring on the passenger's side of the cab. He strained to see into the darkness through the busted bloodstained glass.

The man was scrunched in the passenger's seat trying to move. He was miraculously alive. Newman scrambled for a closer view, but felt the cab move slightly as he adjusted his body to get a better look. The man was covered with blood. Whether it was his own or the driver's, Newman was uncertain. Now, how to get him out, was the question. With diesel fuel still profusely leaking from the ruptured tanks beneath the cab, time was of grave importance.

"Hey Scott!" Newman yelled. "I'm going to need your help. Bring a flashlight."

He scrambled around to the running board on the driver side. He pulled frantically on the driver's door. It was stuck, warped by the impact of hitting several trees on the way down. Newman tried again. It didn't budge.

"Ken?" A voice called from above. "Where are you?"

"Down here!" He waved, looking up at Scott.

Scott flashed the light in the direction of the voice and saw Newman standing at the cab door.

"What in the hell are you doing there?"

"There is somebody alive in here. But the door is jammed and I can't get it open."

Scott followed Newman's path and made his way down to the truck with the flashlight.

"Look in there Scott, he's still alive."

Scott stood on the running board and beamed the light in the cab.

"Good grief!" He sighed at the sight of the impaled man.

"The man next to him is alive," Newman called. "We've got to get him outta there!"

Scott climbed down. "Are you sure that's a good idea, Ken? That cab maybe unstable. If we try to do a lot of jerking on the door, the whole cab may slide further down this ravine. Not to mention, what if he has a spinal injury or something? We could paralyze him for the rest of his life."

"Take a big sniff, Scott," Newman impatiently commented. "This place smells like a fuel dump. If those tanks blow while we're all still down here, we all could be dead for the rest of our lives."

"Yawl need to hurry up. Those fumes are getting stronger." The man yelled from atop the cliff.

"I got an idea, Ken." Newman came closer to Scott. "Follow me."

Newman trailed Scott to the front of the cab. "What are you going to do?"

Scott climbed the metal twisted bumper and got on top of the hood. "Come on Ken. We have to hurry." He reached for Ken's hand and pulled.

Soon both men were staring at each other. "Now what Scott?"

Scott took the flashlight and began bashing the remaining broken glass in the windshield area. "This opening should be large enough to pull him through." He broke more glass. "The two of us should be able to pull him up the hill."

The man lay slumped backward, his body restrained by his seat belt. Newman reached in and unbuckled the strap as he and Scott struggled to pull the man through the opening. It took them several minutes to completely extract the man from the cab. Newman noticed a small black satchel on the seat next to him. He instinctively grabbed it.

"What's that?"

"I don't know Scott. It might be something he needs. It was just lying there, so I grabbed it."

Newman through the bag around his neck and cupped his arms under the man's shoulders. He lowered the injured man to an awaiting Scott in front of the bumper of the truck. Newman climbed down. He and Scott started dragging the man slowly up the hill. Scott and Newman traded positions dragging the injured man on the slick grain-covered hillside, until they had inched their way up the terrain. They could hear in a distance, sirens growing louder as they neared the surface.

Newman was about to take another step when suddenly a violent explosion rocked the ground beneath them. The blast knocked him off his feet as he struggled to maintain his grip on the injured man. Scott fell forward, landing face down on the grain-covered terrain.

"Wooooh!" Yelled the other man at the top of the cliff.

Newman looked down at the burning cab. Flames spewed from beneath the vehicle and illuminated the darkness below. Scott slowly pulled his dirt and grain spattered face out of the hillside and looked cautiously up at Newman. Finally they all reached the top of the embankment. Laura had arrived with the police, who had blocked off a section of the highway for the Life Flight helicopter. The chopper landed within minutes. The paramedics quickly strapped the man into the stretcher and were airborne.

It was almost four in the morning when Scott pulled into the resort parking lot. The police had dropped the man off at his car and had taken Laura back to her room. Scott stopped in front of his rented cabin.

Newman pulled the truck driver's bag from the backseat and climbed out of the jeep.

"Are you sure I can't drop you off back at your room?"

"Oh, don't worry about it Scott. The walk will do me good. Besides, you've got three women in there who are probably worried sick about you."

"Yeah," Scott chuckled. "If something bad happened to me, no more alimony checks."

"Anyway, you showed real courage on that hillside tonight. It's been good knowing you."

"You too, Ken, is it?"

"Yes, Ken." They shook hands.

"You sure I can't drop you off?"

"No, I'll be fine. I like the night air and I need to clear my head. I saw my first dead body tonight up close. I don't want to go to sleep right away with that on my mind."

"Yeah, I spent three years in Nam. You know, you never get used to it." Replied Scott.

Suddenly, loud angry voices blared from the cabin in front of them. "You bitch!" A voice roared. "You slept with him while we were still married."

"Well, you obviously weren't enough woman for him or he wouldn't have come crawling into my bed in the first place."

"You filthy tramp! Wait 'till I get my hands on that Raymond."

"Uh oh," Scott sighed dejectedly.

"Sounds like your ex-wives are reliving old times," Newman smiled.

"Both of you shut up!" The third woman's voice commanded. "Ray never loved either of you whores anyway," she sneered. "That's why he married me."

"Ken?" Scott asked meekly. "Ahhh… do you have another room I could rent for tonight? I don't think it's safe for me to go back in there. Maybe when they sober up later, in the morning I'll see what they remember."

"Hopefully nothing." Newman laughed. "Of course. I'm sure we can find something. Let's head back to the office and see what's available." He climbed back into the jeep. "Whatever possessed you to take three ex-wives out, all at the same time? You don't have a death wish or something, do you?"

"You have any idea of what three alimony checks can run a month? I thought maybe if I could get them all together, we all could make peace and they'd let me off the hook. This was supposed to just be an interesting little vacation for the four of us."

"The next time you decide to do something interesting, open an American flag concession in Iran. It would be a lot more interesting and a lot safer." Smiled Newman.

Scott laughed as he put the jeep in reverse and pulled out of the parking spot.

It was a restless night for Newman. He was unable to get the imagines of the truck driver out of his mind. He thought work could be his relief after four hours of trying to sleep.

At eight o'clock he had checked many common areas. By midmorning, Newman sat at Vicki's desk. His finger following a column in one of the ledgers, when he heard the front door open.

"Vicki? Is that you?"

"No, Ken. It's me, Lisa," she called from the outer office.

"Oh, Lisa. Thought you might be Vicki. She left a note saying she had an early business appointment this morning. So I'm kinda just filling in until she gets here. Could you step in here for a moment, please?"

"Right now, Ken?" She sounded hesitant.

"Yes, please."

"Ahhh… sure, Ken."

Newman turned a page in the ledger.

"What is it, Ken?" Lisa meekly eased over to the desk.

"This Coming Events Ledger," he began, still reading from the page. "Who's responsible for monitoring it? There are several events listed here that are just weeks away. I'd like to know what's being done to…" He glanced up at her and gasped.

Lisa didn't come close to the desk. She tried to conceal the extent of the cuts and bruises on her face. She had been viciously beaten. Her left eye had been completely blackened and was swollen shut. An assortment of other cuts and abrasions covered her face.

"My goodness, Lisa!" He quickly rose from his chair and rushed over to her. "What happened to you? You look like me a few weeks ago."

"It's nothing, Ken," she was defensive. "Don't worry about it. It's none of your business. And I can still work."

"Lisa, if someone is beating you, you don't have to just sit and take it. Whoever did this can be put behind bars. You could have been permanently disfigured or worse."

"Look. I'm twenty-two." Lisa appeared angry from his intrusion of her personal space. "I'm your secretary, not your daughter. I can take care of myself. Now, did you have a question or not?"

"I am just as worried about you as you were about me when my eye was swollen. Can I call for some ice for your eye?"

"No Ken! I'm fine. Now, did you have a question?"

Newman stepped back from her. The defiance in her eyes and her voice was unmistakable. Either she didn't want his help or was too ashamed or too proud to ask for it. Either way, there was nothing more he could do.

"Like I was saying," he walked back around the desk, "this Coming Event's Calendar---there are these two events here. One, this Brotherhood of Chosen Christian Soldiers and this Fourth of July Rodeo."

Lisa walked over to the desk and turned the ledger around. "The Fourth of July Rodeo happens every year and this Brotherhood group, I don't know. Some church group, I guess. Vicki normally handles those things."

"And this $200 for vet?"

"Oh that. There's a buffalo out in the pasture that they're going to kill and barbeque for the Fourth of July picnic. The two hundred is for the local veterinarian to come by and certify that the animal is fit to eat."

"I see. And this Christian Brotherhood group, do you know what denomination they are? Said's here that they have paid in advance and that they are expecting over four hundred people."

"They've never booked here before that I know of. But they did pay in advance, so I really don't see what the problem is."

"Neither do I, unless we aren't ready for them. I'll call them later, just to reconfirm their plans. They're in…" he checked the address on the ledger. "Hayden Lake, Idaho. Hayden Lake sounds like a peaceful little community, doesn't it? It also says here, that we'll provide a banquet room. Do we have a banquet room big enough to accommodate that many people?"

"Just close off the alcove between the bar and the dining room, as well as reserve the entire dining room for their meeting. Will that be all, Ken?"

"Yes, Lisa. Thank you. By the way, I didn't mean to pry into your personal life. It's just that, well… as a friend, I'm concerned about you."

"Don't be." She smiled politely. "I'm a big girl now and I can take care of myself." Lisa turned and walked out of the office.

Newman watched as she left and couldn't help but wonder what made her tolerate that kind of abuse. How could such an attractive and talented woman find solace in such an abusive relationship with a man twice her age?

He picked up the phone, scanned the ledger for the phone number of the Brotherhood of Christian Soldiers, and dialed.

"BCCS," the tart voice answered.

"Ken Newman from the Hot Springs Resort. I'm calling to confirm your meeting arrangements."

"You're not having problems with our meeting, are you?" The voice sounded concern. "We've already sent notices to all of our members to be there and we can't afford any last-minute changes."

"No, no, nothing like that." Newman reassured him. "I'm calling to see if there were any last minute changes in your plans."

"If there were, we would have called to let you know," the annoyed voice angrily corrected. "Now if all of the details are the same as we discussed earlier, I see no further need to prolong this conversation." The line suddenly went dead.

Newman held the phone away from his ear and stared at the receiver, slightly bewildered. "Gee, what a grouch!" He thought to himself.

"Christian my foot." He hung up the phone. He noticed the intercom light flashing and pushed the button. "Yes, Lisa."

"A Mr. Paul Grant is here to see you Kenny."

Newman paused. The name didn't sound familiar, and he certainly wasn't expecting anyone named Grant. "Send him back please, Lisa." Newman leaned backward in the chair and waited.

"Hi," greeted the well-dressed man in the three-piece business suit. "Paul Grant, United States Department of Agriculture, Forest Service." He extended his hand.

Newman rose from his chair and greeted the man. "Please," Newman motioned toward the chair in front of the desk---"have a seat." The man complied. "Now, how can I help you?" Newman eased back into his chair.

"I couldn't help but notice, is your secretary all right?"

"Oh she's fine. We get that every other week." Newman played it off.

"Every other week! There is a place for men who do that to women. It's called jail." Replied Grant.

"I totally agreed Mr. Grant. I tried to talk to her, but it's none of my business she so explicitly explained to me. Now what can I do for you?"

"I see. Well, I'm really looking for Mrs. Marshall, but I gather she isn't available. But, still this is a matter I probably should discuss with her."

"If you feel you have to. I can tell her you came by and maybe you can set up a time to meet with her later."

"No matter. Besides, I've heard that you are doing most of the decision making around here anyway."

"More rumor, than fact, I'm afraid."

"Nonetheless, as you may already know, there's been a large fire burning for some time on the North Ridge on the Idaho side of the Lolos." Stated Grant.

"I've heard Vicki's husband mention something about it a few days ago."

"I'm here to tell you it's no longer a range fire. It' been reclassified as a full-blown forest fire. Now your resort isn't in any danger. In fact, that's exactly why I'm here."

"I'm afraid I don't understand."

"Your locality and relatively safe position in relation to the fire, makes your resort an ideal location for a base camp."

"Base camp? Questioned Newman."

"Yes. You see, right now we are trucking men and supplies in from Missoula. By contrast, your resort is only ten miles from the fire. What we'd like to do is take that open land you have near the RV Park across the street and use it as a staging area for about three hundred men and their firefighting supplies. They'll bring their own food, sleeping gear, and living materials. All we need from you is your space. Not only are we prepared to pay you $240 a day for the use of the land, but our people are bound to use your pool, your restaurant, and bar during their off hours. The increased business would be priceless to your bottom line, I'm sure. And since we wouldn't be using anything you would normally reserve for the tourist, our impact on your resort's daily operations would be minimal at worst."

"Wow!" Newman sighed. "Extra income without the extra work. Sounds too good to be true."

"The offer is real, Mr. Newman. All I need is an okay from you and we are off and running. You are aware that the government pays thirty days after the receipt of invoice. So you won't see any of the funds until after the project is over. However, considering the magnitude of the fire, we could be talking about a substantial amount of money here Mr. Newman. So what do you say?"

Newman hesitated. "How soon do you need an answer?"

"As soon as possible."

"I see. Well, let me get with Vicki on this. Like you said, she really needs to be involved in any decision that materially affects this resort. But, I'm sure we can come to some sort of positive arrangement."

"Good, Mr. Newman." Grant rose from the chair. He and Newman shook hands. "I'll await your decision."

"It won't be long. In fact, I expect Vicki to be in sometime this morning."

"Good. I hope that handling such a large group like this doesn't present any special problems for your staff."

"I don't think so. We will have this huge religious convention of about four hundred people here when your people arrive, but it sounds like your people won't require any added housekeeping chores or meals. So if we don't know how to handle large gatherings now, we certainly will by the time your group gets here."

"Four hundred people, plus our crew, eh?… Boy, I guess that should be some lesson for your staff." Remarked Grant.

"Yeah, some group called the Brotherhood of Chosen Christian Soldiers. I guess they are coming here for a religious retreat or something."

Grant looked bewildered. "You mean the BCCS?" He questioned cautiously. "You invited them here?"

"Ahhh… yeah…" Newman hesitated. "Well, I didn't. Vicki did."

"That's the same group out of Hayden Lake…?"

"Idaho. Yes. I take it you've heard of them?"

"Of course I have. Haven't you?"

"Not really."

"They're that White supremacist group linked to that FBI shoo-out in Seattle a couple of months ago."

"You're joking?" a dumbfounded Newman, replied.

"No I'm not. It was in all of the papers."

Newman suddenly appeared concerned. "I musta missed that issue."

"They want to combine Montana, Idaho, and Wyoming into a single all-White nation separate from the rest of the United States."

"That wouldn't take much effort," Newman huffed.

"You're probably going to have every civil rights leader and anti-Klan group within a hundred-mile radius up here protesting this meeting, not to mention the media coverage. You're right. I guess after this little meeting, handling our three hundred smoke jumpers is going to seem like a piece of cake. I still think you should be commended though, for allowing them to meet here. I mean, as disgusting as their views are, this is still America. And everybody has a right to express their point of view. As I recall, they were thinking about trying to move this meeting to Wyoming, because nobody in the state of Idaho would host their meeting." Remarked Grant.

"We're just bighearted, I guess." Newman sighed, slumping dejectedly back into his seat.

"Well, I have to go. I'll be waiting for your answer. Have a nice day." Grant walked out of the door.

Newman sat back and pondered this latest crisis. Vicki must have known who these people were when she agreed to entertain their gathering, or did she? Did she agree to host the meeting merely for the money, or were there other reasons? And what of the participants? Armed fanatics ready to do battle with anyone who dared disagree with them? Canceling the event and refunding the money now seemed the only logical alternative.

As Newman pondered how to handle the BCCS, the pool was under siege from Marcia's aggressive life guard rules.

Marcia stood at the edge of the crowded swimming pool, watching three young children splash around in the shallow end. An occasional scream would grab her attention as some child would come screaming down the meandering waterslide. They would explode the water on impact, showering nearby swimmers with raining droplets. Her tight-fitting bathing suit revealed a well-developed young woman, seemingly much older than her sixteen years. The whistle on the long cord that dangled freely from her neck not only identified her as the lifeguard, but gave her an aura of authority she not only embellished, but took great pride in exercising.

"Slow down you two!" Marcia yelled. "Cut that out!" She commanded to another couple of kids while she paced the poolside pretending not to notice the admiring glances from the men and boys as she walked passed.

She walked over to her tower chair and climbed to her perch. Two muscle-clad young boys tanning nearby from the sun, raised their sunglasses and watched her bottom sway with each step she took up the ladder. Marcia pretended not to notice as she took her seat and peered out confidently over the pool.

"Do you see what I see?" One boy asked, his eyes fixed on Marcia.

"You mean just the most beautiful woman in the whole wide world."

"Now hold on there, Jay, I saw her first."

"It doesn't matter. She's going to be mine before the day is over."

"And just what are you going to do? Knock her in the head and throw her over your shoulder?"

"That's more your style, Martin. My style has a little more finesses, a little more savoir faire."

"And what exactly do you intend to do? Coax her down with a glass of white wine and a dinner invitation?"

"Watch and learn, little brother," Jay boasted confidently. "Just watch and learn."

He got up and waited for Marcia to look in his direction. She slowly scanned the entire area until finally his stare caught her attention. He waved and smiled. She nodded with a cold indifference.

"Hey! What's your name?" Jay called up to her.

"Now that's an original line if I've ever heard one," Martin muttered under his breath.

"Be quiet!" Jay whispered through the side of his mouth.

"Marcia," she blandly answered. "My friends call me Marci."

"Say Marci. Would you like a ride in my black Corvette?"

She hesitated, then glanced down at him and shook her head. "No."

"Couldn't we at least trade phone numbers or something?" pleaded Jay.

"Look," Marci was slightly annoyed. "You are about the thirtieth guy who has tried to pick me up so far today and I'll tell you exactly what I've told them---GET LOST!"

Jay resented her hostile rejection, but still his determination held firm---partly because he really did like Marci. But more importantly, he didn't want to admit defeat in front of his brother.

"Thirty guys, eh?" He challenged her assertion. "Well how many of them could do this?"

He stood on the edge of the pool with his toes slightly extended over the water. Then, from a standing start, he leaped, somersaulted, and pierced the water at a slight angle with only a minimum of splash. He surfaced seconds later, shaking the water violently from his hair.

"Hey!" Marci climbed down from her seat and shouted at two children near the other end of the pool, ignoring Jay. "Don't pull her under like that," she warned.

"Oh, hard to please, eh?" Jay swam for the side and pulled himself out of the water. Marci turned back toward him.

"Say, if you're going to dive off the side of the pool, then use the deeper end."

"You won't be able to see me down there." Jay took another diving stance. "Now watch closely this time."

He sprang high into the air, pulled his knees up into his chest, and somersaulted. He exploded into the pool as solid walls of water spewed high into the air, raining down on her and everyone else in the vicinity. Marci squirmed in a vain attempt to avoid the downpour. She bristled as she waited for Jay to surface. Seconds later, he shot to the surface and smiled up at her.

"Are you insane?" She scolded as he swam for the side and climbed out of the pool. "All of that water must have soaked your brain."

Martin looked on and smiled, shaking his head.

"Just you wait, Marci," Jay explained as he took another diving stance. "If that dive didn't impress you, this one certainly will." He stood with his back toward the water and his heels slightly over the edge.

"Oh no you don't!" Marci forcefully commanded as she raced toward him.

Suddenly Jay bent his knees slightly, then shot up and backward, somersaulting before he disappeared into another gigantic splash. She quickly turned again as another solid wall of water spewed up and drenched her. She shook the water from her arms and impatiently waited for Jay to resurface. However, instead of the usual seconds it took for him to reemerge, this time he took a little longer. Marci put her hands on her hips and drummed her foot, impatiently waiting for that smug grin to come crashing through to the surface.

Martin waited too. Still Jay didn't surface. "Don't worry," he called to Marci. "Jay is an expert swimmer. In fact, he's the captain of our high school swim team."

"He knows I'm going to kill him if he shows his face again," Marci bitterly insisted.

Seconds passed. Marci's concern began to grow. Suddenly, she dove into the water. Martin scrambled to the edge of the pool and eagerly watched as Marci remained under water for what seemed like an eternity. Finally she broke the surface, gasping slightly, her arm cupped around an unconscious Jay's chest.

"Jay!" Martin screamed. The crowd at poolside stopped and stared in their direction.

"Help me get him out of the water," Marci huffed, struggling to maintain her grip on Jay.

Martin hurriedly reached into the pool and helped her pull Jay's limp body up onto the deck. She scrambled out of the water, rushed over, and knelt beside him. A crowd had started to gather.

"I told him to dive in the deeper end of the pool," she explained as she tilted his head back. "He must have hit his head on the bottom and knocked himself out."

"Oh, my goodness'. Stated a stunned person in the crowd.

"Call an ambulance!" Marci commanded. "The rest of you stand back!" She shouted over her shoulder.

She pinched his nose shut and cupped her lips over his. She pumped several quick breaths into his mouth, then jammed his chest repeatedly with several quick thrusts of her opened palm. She hastily repeated the procedure until finally water bubbled and gurgled from Jay's mouth. Moments later, he started to cough and gag. Marci cupped her hand behind his back and sat him upright.

"You damned fool!" Marci scolded. "You almost killed yourself."

Jay coughed again before clearing his throat. He grimaced as he felt the back of his head. "What happened?" He feebly wiped the water from his mouth.

"You hit your head on the pool bottom when you dove in." Marci patted him softly on the back.

"Really?"

Marci looked around at the hushed crowd that had gathered. "All right everybody, break it up. The show's over. He's gonna be all right."

Martin came rushing back over to them. "Jay!" He excitedly exclaimed. "You're all right." He and Marci helped Jay to his feet.

"Like I said earlier, Marci," Jay smiled, clearing his throat. "I'm just dying to meet you."

The three of them looked at each other quietly for moment, then burst out laughing.

While the excitement subsided at the pool, the general store was having the final touches performed to it, getting ready for the big events coming soon for the summer.

Bea ripped open the cardboard box and began pulling the cans out and stacking them on the shelves.

"John?" She called. "Bring me that pricing gun on the back shelf, would please?"

John emerged from the back room, eating a sandwich. "It's not back there, honey." He answered between bites. "Maybe you left it somewhere else."

"Would you look again, sweetheart, please? I'm sure I saw it somewhere back there." John walked over to the cash register. "Babe, I'm eating right now. Can you wait a minute or maybe you can get Candy to look for it."

"She's not here. I enrolled her in school today."

"School? Here?" John sounded concern.

"Yes, I enrolled her today."

"Why school will be out for the summer in a couple of weeks. So what's the rush?" He opened the cash register and began thumbing through the bills.

"She's been out of school now for over two months, ever since we sold the house and moved here. What better way for her to meet friends her own age to play with during the summer recess, than to meet then now, while school is still in session. Besides, the bus stop is only a mile and a half down the road."

"You enrolled our child in public school," he said dejectedly.

"Of course. There aren't any private schools around here, and even if there were, we couldn't afford the tuition."

"Damn it, babe!" John bitterly snapped. "You know Candy has been enrolled in private schools all of her life. She's not used to uncultured children. That's why we pulled her out of the public school system in Seattle, remember? Being in classes with all those poor Black and illiterate children was causing her grades to fall. She was coming home depressed every day."

"I'd be careful what you say about Blacks around here," Bea warned. "The manager here is Black. Besides, I doubt if they'll be many Black children in Candy's class."

"And you think the children of these brain-dead hicks are any better? Besides, I don't give a shit what some spear chunker thinks. Vicki hired us, and as far as I'm concerned, we work for her and nobody else."

"Look John," she politely began as she climbed a small stepladder to reach an upper shelf. "Ken is a very nice person."

"Ken? You've met him?"

"Yes. He helped me bring you home that night… well, you know…" She struggled for the right words. "That night…"

"You mean that night when gestapo bartender nearly killed me. You know, I'm still not sure we shouldn't sue this place for every dime its worth." His voice grew angrier. "Or at the very least, have that fuckin' bartender brought up on assault charges."

Bea looked down on him and smiled, trying to console his ire. "John, it's over. Just try and forget it, okay? Say, why don't you help me with these cans, eh? We open for business in the morning. Don't you want our opening to be a big success?"

John turned his attention back toward the cash register. He pulled out a few bills and stuffed them into his pocket.

"Sweetheart?" She gently asked as he closed the cash drawer. "That's opening day change, dear. Where are you going with it?"

"Oh, don't worry. I left enough in the drawer for you to make change. I'm just a little low on cash right now. Just consider this an advance on my salary."

"And just what are you going to do with that money?"

"Oh, like I said, don't worry. I'm just going to unwind a bit, that's all."

Bea's tone grew more concerned. "You're going over to that bar again, aren't you?"

"Look," John began defensively. "It's not what you're thinking. I just need a few beers to unwind, that's all. The stress of getting this store in shape and moving here to Montana has gotten me a little jittery, that's all."

Bea slowly climbed down from the stepladder. "It's starting all over again, isn't it? The lying, the drinking, and the beatings."

"Now, now, Bea," he calmly consoled. "Don't go getting upset. Can't a man unwind every now and then, especially after a hard day's work?"

"Work?" Bea walked angrily toward him. "Work? What work have you done to help get this place ready to open tomorrow? You helped hang the drapes and put the money in the cash register and that's it. Candy and I scrubbed and waxed these floors and we cleaned and stocked the shelves. We worked like a couple of dogs to get this place in shape while you either slept one off or just didn't bother to come in until we were through working for the day." Her voice grew embittered. "Do you really want to know why Candy is in school today? To give her a break from the work, that's why. So she could attend school like a normal child instead of working all day while her father lies in bed passed out from alcohol. Public school? Ha! Candy's grades started failing when she started coming home every day and would either find you falling down drunk or you and I screaming at each other. Her grades only started to improve when her math teacher and our good friend Martha, who is Black, in case you've forgotten, started letting Candy spend nights over to her house. That's just so she wouldn't have to deal with our problems at home."

"Oh, so now everything's my fault, eh?" John became defensive. "Whose idea was it to move to this dump anyway? Away from the plays, the sports, the opera. And to where? Montana ---open air, clear skies, and blue waters, right?" He sneered sarcastically. "There's nothing here but hick cowboys and rednecks and I'm supposed to be happy living here selling insect repellent to the locals? Well, let me tell you something baby, after a $150,000 plus a year lifestyle, this is like dying and going straight to hell!"

"Our lifestyle in Seattle is over John. We lost everything--- everything!" Bea was adamant. "This is our new life now, and you'd better get used to it. We don't have much, but we are still together as a family, and right now, that's all we have. Please, John, don't destroy our last chance as a family," she passionately pleaded.

John looked into her determined face. While he had heard all of this before, he had never before heard that tone of finality in her voice. Usually her lectures were underlined with a glimmer of hope. "We can make it despite the odds and no matter the problems," she usually said, but that note of optimism was not in her voice this time. Her patience was wearing thin, and sooner or later she'd come to the end of her rope.

"Look, you're in no shape to talk when you are like this." John advised calmly. "I'll be back when you've settled down a bit. Then we'll talk, okay? I'm stepping out for a while. When I get back, we'll continue this conversation, especially the part about leaving Candy in public school." He headed for the door.

"John!" Bea screamed. He stopped and turned toward her. They stared silently at each other. "Nothing."

Bea shook her head in disgust. John turned and walked out. She quietly stared at the door for a few minutes. Tears swelled in her eyes and began to slowly trickle down her cheeks. She gradually fell to her knees and openly wept.

As the drama unfolded with John and Bea at the general store, Newman was curious about the bull that was for the festive rodeo in a few weeks. So he drove out to the open pasture where the animal was grazing.

Newman stepped up to the corral and placed one foot on the lower board of the wooden fence. He stood quietly and watched the buffalo gallop aimlessly around his enclosed domain with thundering hooves and an occasional blast of hot air from his nostrils. The raw power of the animal was impressive as it galloped from end to end of the paddock to the other. It was as if it were putting on a display of power for him. Newman felt as if the beast was trying to convince him of its primal desire for freedom and open spaces to roam---a desire frustrated by the confines of this corral.

His admiration of the animal was interrupted by the sound of an approaching vehicle. He glanced over his shoulder to see Vicki at the wheel of a topless jeep, bouncing its way over the rough terrain. Newman walked over to greet her as she pulled to a stop near him.

"There you are," Vicki smiled. "Lisa said you'd be out here."

"My goodness, Vicki, you look great in jeans, boots, and Stetson hat. I didn't know you had clothes like that. I'm used to seeing you in business attire. What's up?"

"I don't have to meet with my business associates in three-piece suits today. So what are you doing way out here?"

"I just wanted to get a look at our guest of honor for the Fourth of July rodeo. He's a magnificent animal. It's a shame to have to eat him."

"Well, just wait until you've tasted your first buffalo steak, barbequed to perfection," she said proudly. "You'll never go back to beef again."

"That, remains to be seen." Newman glanced at the beast still roaming the corral. "Seems like an incredible waste of a magnificent animal."

"Oh, don't get stuck on him. The Bison Range has hundreds of excess animals every year. So it's either eat them or let them starve to death, because there are too many of them on the range. Now, Lisa said you wanted to see me. It's not about the buffalo, is it?"

"No, actually it's not." Newman felt a little foolish developing such a quick emotional attachment to the bison. He was no different than the turkey on Thanksgiving Day. And he certainly felt no emotional attachment to the millions of condemned gobblers who graced holiday tables every year. "The main reason I wanted to see you, is that the Forest Service wants to rent the open space across from the RV Park as a staging area. They are going to make it a base camp for food and personnel to help fight the North Ridge Fire."

"Are we doing anything with it right now?"

"Goliah is living out there now, but other than that, no."

"Let's do it. Turning vacant land into money only makes good business sense, right?"

"My feeling exactly. I'll call Grant and set everything up."

"Good. Is that all?"

"Not quite." Newman wasn't quite sure how to address the topic of the BCCS. What if scheduling the group was a conscious decision on her part? "There's the small matter of that Christian Brotherhood meeting next week."

"Oh yes. I'm glad you reminded me," Vicki casually began. "You may want to get Millie and her husband to give you a hand on that one.

They are both evangelists and can probably give you some insight on how to deal with those religious people."

Newman was bewildered. "You honestly don't know, do you?"

"Know what?" Vicki was curious. "Have they changed their plans or something?"

Newman shook his head. "We should be so lucky. I don't know how to tell you this, but the BCCS isn't a church group."

"Really, what are they, then?"

"They are a White supremacist organization linked to armored car robberies, bombings, and even murder in Washington and Idaho."

Vicki laughed. "Who told you that?" She didn't believe him. "Somebody is pulling your leg."

"I called the FBI in Boise. It's true."

Vicki's smile quickly turned to a frown. "Ken, you've got to believe me. I didn't know. I got this call from their group president, and with a name like Christian Brotherhood, I just assumed… you got to believe me. I really didn't know."

'I know Vicki. I understand."

"There's only one thing to do," she said matter-of-factly. "Call them up, cancel the convention and refund their money. I don't want people like that running around my resort. If word gets out that I let those people meet here, no decent group will ever book with us again."

"I'm afraid it's not that simple."

"It's my resort. I can cancel any meeting I want to," Vicki sternly insisted.

"On what grounds? They have a paid contract with us. If we cancel them after they have sent out all of their announcements and made all of their plans to be here, we'll open ourselves up to a breach-of-contract suit. The possibility of them suing us, could tie us up in court for months with damage claims."

She thought for a moment. Additional litigation was the last thing she needed right now.

"What do you suggest?"

"We honor our obligations and bear the consequences. There's nothing else to do."

Vicki hesitated. "You're right," she sighed. "How could I have been so stupid?"

"It's called an honest mistake. We all make them."

"Yeah," she huffed. "but mine seem to always be just a little larger than most people's."

"It only seems that way." Newman sympathized.

"Well, you probably wouldn't say that if you knew all of the mistakes I've made."

"Nobody's perfect Vicki."

"Maybe. But I've certainly made more than my fair share, and probably now is a goodtime to tell you about some of them." Her voice became solemn and somber as if she were groping for the right words to say.

"You don't have to tell me anything Vicki."

"But I want to. Besides, you're going to hear about it anyway sooner or later. So I'd rather you hear my side of the story before you hear about it in the newspapers and rumor mills. You've been invaluable to me these last few months and in the coming days. The newspapers are going to be filled with a lot of stories about me as some kind of Ma Barker."

"This sounds serious."

"If counterfeiting five million dollars and attempted murder is serious, then it's serious."

"Wow!" Newman sighed. "You're kidding?"

"I wish I were," she quipped. "Hop in." Newman climbed in the passenger side. She geared the jeep. "I'll fill you in on the way back to the office."

"What about the golf cart?"

"I'll send someone out to get it."

As she drove slowly back to the resort, Newman was inquisitive. "How did you ever get involved in such serious stuff?"

"Carl." Vicki said bluntly. "All of my problems started the day I put him in charge. Boy, don't I wish I could go back and change things. You see, Carl was my manager. He ran the resort while I was away. I trusted his judgment and his honesty, after all, he's my son. So I gave him access to my checkbook and gave him the power to staff this place as he saw fit. So what does he do? He hires his girlfriend and personal friends to work here at outrageous salaries. More than that, he lured those high-priced chefs and managers away from other major restaurants and hotel chains, like the Holiday Inn and the Hilton. But the worse part of that is, he hired them at salaries higher than what they were making at their place. He spent a three-year budget in only year. So I stepped in and clipped his wings. I cut his staff in half by getting rid of that harem and the driftwood he had put on the payroll. I also gave him a fixed budget to work with by setting up a special account for him to work from. I cut him off from the rest of my money by placing it in accounts that could only be access by my signature. So you can imagine my surprise when I started writing checks on my accounts, only to find that I was broke, wiped out. It seems my trusted son," her voice had a bit of sarcasm, "had forged my name on all of my reserve accounts, and before I could stop him, I was flat broke."

Newman listened with bated breath. "You must have been devastated."

"Ha! Devastated doesn't even begin to describe how I felt. I never dreamed my own son would steal me blind. He'd be in jail right now if I had agreed to prosecute, but I was determined to get my money back from him. That's why he's out there in the pool, instead of behind bars. Now, Carl thinks I was mad enough to hire a hit man to kill him. I didn't of course, but I did have a quarter-million dollar life insurance policy taken out on him. He was the senior manager here, and after all, most major companies insure their top managers in case of their death or serious injury," she quickly added. "Yes, I could have used the money from his policy. But Ken, I'm not a killer and I certainly would never have had my own son killed no matter what he had done. So I banished him to the pool and took over daily operations of the resort myself. I had to file Chapter 11 and scale back operations to what you see now."

"Where does the counterfeit $5 million figure in?"

"To save on advertising, I decided to try and print all of our flyers and brochures in-house. So I brought this old printing press. Well, Carl got a hold of it. So he, along with this friend of his, Gary McDonald, decided to use it to make money the old-fashioned way."

"Print it?"

"Exactly."

"But I don't understand. You can't just print money like a newsletter, you need plates. You need the right kind of paper, the right kind of ink, and all sorts of stuff. You can't just pick that kind of stuff up at your local supermarket."

"You're right. They printed several batches of bills, and Carl tossed them all, because they didn't even remotely resemble real money. All this came out in Carl's trial."

"But if the money never got into circulation, how did Carl get caught?"

"Gary Mcdonald, his so call best friend, left and disappeared for a while. I thought he had found another job somewhere. But he came back a few weeks later and told Carl he had found a friend who could supply the right kind of paper and the proper plates."

"Really? Where did Gary find this friend?"

"The U.S. Treasury Department and the FBI."

"Ohhhh," Newman sighed.

"They supplied Gary with everything he needed to set Carl up. Carl never knew what hit him. They bugged my phone and monitored my calls and reeled Carl in like a prized marlin. But they never could implicate me directly in Carl's little scheme. Gary kept asking Carl to get me to help with their plans, but Carl never asked, and I never knew they were printing money."

"Sounds like one big mess." Newman took a deep breath. "But why if Carl and this Gary were such good friends, did he deliberately come back to set up Carl and try and implicate you in their money-printing scheme?"

"Gary McDonald was the senior manager at the Great Falls Hilton, $85,000 annual salary. Carl hired him for $100,000. So he quit his job, sold his house, and moved his family here to Missoula. When I stepped in, I slashed everybody's salary to $300.00 a month, until I could get this place out of Chapter 11, Gary couldn't get his old job back. So he blamed me for destroying his life. He stayed for a while, and I thought he had gotten over his anger. He apparently hadn't."

"So what have they got on you? Especially if there was nothing in the taped phone conversations to implicate you?"

"For one thing Carl and Gary kept the counterfeit plates in my safe. But you've been in my office, Ken. I never lock that thing, because I don't remember the combination. Anybody can put anything in there. But the FBI said they don't see how anybody could not know what is kept in their own safe or why anybody would leave their safe open for anybody to stick anything in there without their knowledge. To make matters worse, three days after Gary revealed he was an FBI informant, somebody planted six sticks of dynamite in the engine of Gary's car. He found it before the bomb went off, and now he's in protective custody."

"And I suppose everybody thinks you are the responsible culprit for the bomb?"

"Me or Carl. Though, the FBI thinks it was me since Carl has no money and the level of sophistication involved in placing the bomb, required the talents of an expert. Someone whom the FBI said, I not only had a reason to hire, but could also financially afford."

"Do they have any hard evidence linking you to anything?"

"No. Everything is strictly circumstantial. The plates in the safe are probably the closest thing they have to hard evidence, if you call it that. So a lot is going to come down to whether a jury is going to believe that I am the type of woman who not only would counterfeit $5 million, but also hire two hit men. One hit man to kill a government witness and another to kill her own son."

Newman sat quietly trying to comprehend the extreme seriousness and complexity of her situation.

"What do your lawyers say?"

"They've lined up an army of character witnesses who'll testify on my behalf, but what it really boils down to is who's more persuasive, the government or me." She took her eyes off the road for a few seconds, turned toward Newman to gauge his reaction to what she had just told him. "Well, Ken?" She asked matter-of-factly. "Do you still want to stay? I mean, if you don't, I totally understand. Even I have to admit, all of this is a bit much, and you haven't known me long enough to know if you can trust what I've said. So if this is a little more than you can handle, I'll understand."

Newman hesitated. "When does all of this go to trial?"

"Mid-August, but I thought it best to tell you now, before you read all of the wild pre-trial accusations in the papers."

"Hey… well, if I can be of some assistance, let me know. You call yourself a pretty good judge of character. Well so do I. I think you are a class act lady. So you can count on me."

Vicki smiled as she reclined in her seat, with her eyes on the road. "You don't know what that means to me, Ken. I can leave the daily operations to you, while I go to Great Falls and fight this thing." Her facial expression had a sense of calm as she continue down the unpaved terrain.

Minutes later, they arrived in the parking lot and stopped in front of the office.

I'll give this Forest Service guy a call." Newman climbed out of the jeep. "And as far as that Christian Brotherhood thing is concerned… well, we'll live through it, somehow."

"I'm sure we will Kenny. I'm going to the bar and have a drink." She started to drive toward the bar, when she suddenly stopped. "Oh Kenny?"

"Yeah, Vicki?"

"Thank you," she smiled.

Newman return the smile and walked into the office to make the call.

C H A P T E R

6

The evening bar crowd was relatively quiet, as soft, mellow strands of country and western music filled the air. Vicki followed Newman up the steps as he carried a case of beer into the bar and set it on the counter. Bud stood behind the bar, busily wiping the countertop. He looked over in their direction.

"Bud," Newman called. "Would you put this in the cooler for a Mr. Kiefer? Its dark beer, and it's already paid for, so just give it to him when he asks for it, okay?"

"Sure thing, Ken."

Vicki had taken a seat at one of the empty tables. Newman walked over to the table and pulled up a chair across from her. "Where did you pick him up?" Vicki whispered, noting Bud's overtly smooth manner.

"It's a long story. He's a good bartender though. He's got a short temper, but he's still a good bartender."

Suddenly a hand came seemingly from nowhere and slapped Newman forcefully on the back. The blow jolted him forward slightly. Newman quickly spun around. He found himself staring up at John. His alcoholic breath was blasting Newman directly in the face. Vicki watched, mildly amused as Newman tried to maintain his composure. John beamed his drunken smile down at him. His breath reeked of whiskey.

"Hey, Kenny, ole buddy." John grinned, rubbing his hand across Newman's back. "Let's have a drink."

Newman squirmed uneasily, glancing around to see if Bea was anywhere nearby.

"Ahhh… look, John," he began apologetically, "I don't have time right now. Maybe later, okay?"

"No, now, okay, soooul brother?" John slurred. "I really like you people. In fact, a lot of my best friends are nig… ah… I mean colored. Hey bro, I just want to buy you a drink."

Newman gently, but firmly, brushed John's hand aside. "Okay, but not right now." Newman's voice was firm. He turned back toward Vicki when John again laid his hand on Newman's shoulder.

"I wanna drink now!" John insisted. "You too good to have a drink with ole John-boy, eh?"

Newman was getting angry---very anger. He spun opprobriously in his chair and faced John. "Look, I haven't got time right now, okay?" He furiously insisted. He turned back toward Vicki. "Let's go somewhere else." He quickly hopped up from the chair and stormed off.

John looked around, thoroughly addled, as Newman arched past him. He look down at Vicki as she rose from her seat.

"Whadda I say?"

Vicki reached over and forcefully shook him by his shoulders. "Sober up, Mister!" She loudly commanded. She shoved him away and followed Newman through the alcove into the restaurant. She looked around the sparsely seated dining area and saw him sitting at a corner table, drumming his fingers angrily on the table. Vicki walked over and pulled up a chair. "Boy, I don't know why I hired them," she sighed. "They seemed like such nice people."

"Oh, his wife is." Newman quickly corrected. "But he's a drunken jerk." Newman insisted, pointing toward the bar.

"Look, Ken," she consoled, "I hope you won't let his off-color remarks get to you."

"Oh, it's not just him Vicki. I've been around enough dime store bigots in my time not to let him upset me. It's just that he's got a wonderful wife and daughter across the street, and he's putting them through pure hell with his drinking."

"That's not your problem though. It's hers, and if she had any sense, she'd leave him."

"She's doing everything humanly possible to hold her family together."

"I know, but there comes a point when you have to cut them loose and get on with your life. I know. Believe me, I know. My first husband was an alcoholic."

Newman looked rather surprised. "I didn't know you had been married before."

"Ron Snead was his name," she fondly recalled. "Dr. Ron Snead, MD. Met him in college. We got married after graduation. He opened a very lucrative practice, and I put aside my business ambitions to raise our three sons and our daughter. We had, what you might call, the picture perfect family, at least until he started drinking. He started coming home drunk, but I later learned he was drunk even when he was on duty. His fellow doctors just covered for him. So I didn't know he had a problem until... well, until it was too late."

"What kind of medicine did he practice?"

"Psychiatry." Vicki laughed. "Talk about physician heal thyself. The more he drank, the more abusive he became. He'd go to AA for a couple of weeks and everything would be fine. Then he'd fall off the wagon and make our lives a living hell again. But, he was my security blanket, so I put up with it... that is, until he started on the children and that's where I drew the line. I closed out our joint accounts, took the kids, left, and immediately filed for a divorce."

"Sounds like you and Bea have a lot in common. Where is Dr. Snead now?"

"He drank himself to death." She stopped and thought for a moment, as if just talking about the past brought on a sudden rush of very painful memories. "You know, I felt more relief than sorrow. My agony was finally over, but then so was his. It was like waking up from a very long and painful nightmare. I sold his practice, cashed in his somewhat sizable life insurance policy, and I went into business for myself."

"Good for you. But, it must have been hard with four children to raise alone?"

"It was at first. Some of my friends who were house wives, didn't mind watching the children while I worked days trying to get my business off the ground. They actually enjoyed being aunties as it gave them something to do during the day. As my hotel business grew, I became financially independent."

"So how did you end up with this resort if you were in the hotel business?"

"Well after several years of being in the business, Gregory was now 16 and he was helping me run the business. So I left him in charge of the business while I took a week's vacation here to unwind from the hustle and bustle of my every day grind."

"So is this where you met Jake?"

"Yes. Jake is everything you want in a man. He's forceful, yet gentle. Not to mention good-looking. He treated me like a queen that week I was here. So much so, that I came back several times just to see him. In our meetings together, he talked about how this place could use a woman's touch and the owner was looking to sell."

"Jake talked you into buying this place?"

"I saw it as an opportunity to be close to the man I love and still run a lucrative business."

"And you did quite well for yourself, from the looks of it all."

"At least in the beginning," she quickly added. "But this too shall pass, and when it does, look out world. I'm going to take the resort industry by storm, by… by…" Suddenly she clutched her chest desperately. Her eyes widened as she began gasping for air.

"Vicki!" Newman shot up from his chair and rushed over to her. "Vicki! Are you all right?"

"Water!" She gasped. "Water!" She began fumbling in her pants pocket and struggled to produce a small bottle of pills.

Newman quickly scanned the tables. He noticed a man casually reaching for his water glass. He darted over to the table and snatched the glass from his hand.

"What tha?" The man exclaimed.

Newman rushed back over to Vicki. He saw her fumbling with the small bottle of pills. He snatched them from her hand, ripped the top open, palmed a couple of the pills, and shoved them into her mouth. He then turned the glass of water up to her lips and watched her struggle to swallow. She was gurgling the water out the sides of her mouth.

"Is she going to be all right?"

Newman looked behind his back only to see the man whose water he had taken standing there.

"I'm fine," Vicki reassure, coughing, trying to catch her breath. "I'll be okay. It was just a mild heart attack."

"Mild?" Newman was puzzled.

"Yes."

Moments later, she slowly sat upright in her chair and gradually began to breathe normally.

"You gave us quite a scare there," Newman chided as he sat back down across from her. The other man returned to his seat. "Obviously this has happened before. So, how come you didn't tell me about your heart condition?"

"Haven't I burdened you enough?"

"After everything else you've told me? A heart condition is nothing, believe me."

At that moment, came a loud crash. Everyone turned to see the waitress sprawled on the floor surrounded by spilled food and broken dishes. Newman scrambled out of his chair and rushed over to her.

"Barbara?" He knelt down to assist her up. "Are you all right?" He cupped his hands under her back and helped her sit up.

Barbara grimaced slightly as she felt the back of her head. "I think I have a bump growing back here." She winced. "Geez, ohh that hurts." Newman helped her to her feet.

"Maybe you should sit down for a while."

"No, I'll be all right. I tripped over my own feet," she insisted. Barbara tried to walk, but her knees buckled. Newman caught her as she almost fell.

"Whoaaa… I guess I am a little woozy. I'm sorry Ken."

"Nonsense, accidents happen." He eased her into a nearby chair. "You're going home. I'm telling Kelly that you are through for the day."

"Kelly went home sick about an hour ago. Millie's back there cooking now." Spoke one waitress.

"Okay, I'll tell Millie. But you are definitely going home, my dear, and get some rest." Newman walked back over to Vicki. "I'm going to take Barbara home. I'll be right back. Will you be all right?"

"I'll be fine." She smiled. "Use the jeep." She reached into her purse and handed him the keys. "Guess today is your day to play doctor." Vicki quipped.

Newman smiled and walked back over to Barbara. He slowly ushered her to the jeep. Minutes later, he stopped in front of Barbara's cabin.

"Thank you." She smiled as Newman helped her from the vehicle and walked her up the steps to the front door. She pulled the door key from her smock pocket. "Would you tell my husband what happened and where I am?" She turned the key in the lock.

"You mean Tim over at the garage?"

"Yeah, the cute one. I have to remind him to wear his wedding ring to keep the girls off of him."

Newman nodded. "Sure. I'll head over there and tell him right now."

"He's trying to get the bulldozer that fell over the cliff during that earthquake working again. He's been working late every day this week on that project."

Newman headed back down the steps. "No problem."

When Newman looked back, he noticed Barbara had her ear to the door. She pushed the door open slightly as she heard voices and groans of ecstasy. Then suddenly she stopped, frozen in the doorway. Her eyes widened and her jaw dropped. She stood speechless, in complete shock. Unexpectedly, she turned and bolted down the steps. Newman watched her, puzzled, as she streaked past him. He went up a few steps, then slowly opened the door wider and peeped inside. There, in the middle of the floor was her nude husband, with both hands on his hips, straddling and giving full thrust, repeatedly to the raised backside of a naked Kelly, who was screaming harder, harder as he positioned himself for Tim's body. So engaged were both men in their sexual pleasure, that neither man noticed Newman in the doorway, until a slight breeze entered the room to cool their hot bodies. Both men felt the fresh air from the open door and turned simultaneously to see Newman in complete surprise. Newman closed the door immediately and went after Barbara.

On this same day about a hundred miles away. Business was brisk at the small secluded restaurant nestled scenically along the banks of the Coeur d' Alene, Idaho River. The tingling glasses and the mixed voices filtered out into the open air of the restaurant. So tranquil was the evening that almost no one noticed the three black-leather-clad figures as they strolled casually through the front door. The blonde women peeled off her metal-studded black gloves while her two companions slowly, almost simultaneously, pulled off their pilot-styled sunglasses. The two men adjusted their grips on the black leather shoulder bags, each carried slung over his shoulder. Compared to the business-styled dress of the other patrons, the three looked ominously conspicuous. Still they aroused little attention as the waitress stepped up to the trio and smiled.

"Table for three," she beamed.

"Naw, a table for three-hundred, honey." The blonde woman sneered.

"Geez," she shook her head.

"Of course three. How many do you see?"

She and the waitress exchanged hostile glances. "Follow me please," the waitress blandly instructed as she turned and started for the dining area. The woman and one of the men followed. The other man merely stood near the doorway. The waitress came to an empty table and gestured toward the vacant seats. She then noticed the third man still standing in the doorway. "Isn't your friend joining you?"

"He sure is," the woman answered. She quickly dug into her shoulder bag, produced a .45 and discharged a round into the ceiling. The customers screamed.

"All right!" The man near the doorway shouted. He reached inside his bag, produced a mini-machine pistol, and leveled it at the dining room. "We're just poor weary travelers passing through your fair city and we were wondering if you kind folks could spare a little change to help us on our way. Now my associates will be passing among you with their little bags. I want you all to deposit your watches, purses, rings, wallets, and anything else of value you'd like us to have and remember... God loves a cheerful giver."

The woman torpidly, anxiously panned the area with her weapon as she and her companion darted from table to table. Their black leather bags were held open as the terrified customers nervously dropped in their items of value. They had made their way back to the front of the restaurant when an elderly couple casually stepped through the front door. The woman immediately screamed at the sight of the gunman in the doorway. The gunman wheeled and leveled his weapon at the couple as they raced back out the door. He squeezed a short burst. The glass in the front door exploded as the man and woman jolted forward and landed face down in a pool of blood on the sidewalk.

Several women in the dining room screamed as the other two gunmen rushed to see the bodies lying on the pavement. The woman looked down at the two bodies, then back up at her companions.

"Had to be done," the gunman in the doorway calmly rationalized.

An eerie quiet fell over the restaurant.

"Yea," the other gunmen quietly agreed. "Guess so."

"Let's just get outta here," the woman calmly suggested.

They started out the door when the man with the Beretta suddenly stopped, turned, and fanned a long burst of gunfire across the ceiling.

The crowd screamed as they dove for cover under tables and behind chairs.

"We've got your purses and wallets, so we know where you live," he warned. "Remember that when the police start asking for witnesses." They gingerly stepped through the shattered glass and raced toward their motorcycles.

While pandemonium struck the streets on the banks of Coeur d' Alene, Newman was frantically trying to find replacements for Kelly and Tim, before their jobs would be sorely missed by those who would need to cover their shifts.

"Look." Newman impatiently began, "You're the third person I've been transferred to. Now don't transfer me to anyone else unless they can help me… yes, I can hold." He held the phone away from his ear and shook his head dejectedly.

Lisa peeped around the corner at him. "Hi," she smiled. "I'm back from lunch." He acknowledged her, then put the phone back to his ear.

"Well if Mr. Ravanna is there, can I speak to him?" He held for a moment. "Mr. Ravanna!" He greeted, relieved. "Hi, Ken Newman, Hot Springs."

"I know who you are, Mr. Newman," the polite, but bland voice on the other end replied.

"Good. Then please don't transfer me. I think I've talked to everybody in your department except the janitor."

"He's out to lunch," Ravanna quipped.

"Well, I'd just like to place an order for a mechanic and a chef, but everybody at Job Service treats me like I have AIDS or something."

Ravanna laughed. "It hasn't been quite that bad, has it, Mr. Newman? I take it that you are new there?"

"Yes, fairly new, why?"

"Let me be blunt and to the point, Mr. Newman. Your resort's history of late and nonpayment of its employer-related insurance premiums, coupled with the frequent complaints of bouncing payroll checks and poor labor practices, has left us with no choice but to stop referring applicants to your business."

"I see," Newman quietly acknowledged.

"In fact, just investigating the complaints concerning your resort has earned two of our staff enough overtime to finance a trip to the Hawaii Islands."

"You can't be serious," Newman bristled.

"I leave in six days." Ravanna coldly added. "Needless to say, we couldn't afford to keep that up. So we just stopped sending people to you."

"And how long has that been in effect?"

"Oh about, seven months now."

"I see, "Newman's voice was solemn.

"I understand your position, Mr. Newman," Ravanna added conciliatorily, "but please understand mine."

"I do."

"Now occasionally we do get extremely-hard-to-place applicants in here. I mean so desperate that they'll take anything. If I get any of these people, I'll send them your way, if you want them."

"Thanks," Newman said sarcastically.

"It's the best I can do."

"I'm sure it is. Well, thanks for your help."

"You're welcome, Mr. Newman, and aloha." Newman slammed the phone down. He turned to the safe behind him, pulled out two envelopes, and eased the door shut.

"Tim just called," Lisa's voice beckoned from the intercom.

"Okay, I've got their pay envelopes right here." He rose from his seat and stepped into the receptionist's area. "Where did they say they'd be?" He walked by Lisa's desk.

"They said they'd drop by and pick up their pay on their way out."

Suddenly the front door swung open. Barbara stepped into the office. There was a moment of eerie silence.

"Ken. Lisa." She solemnly greeted.

"Barbara." Ken replied, observing her actions.

Barbara walked past Newman over to Lisa's desk and placed her cabin key on the counter. "I'm moving over to the single women's dorm," she calmly explained. "I'd like to exchange this cabin key for a dorm room key." Her face was saddened, and her voice quivered.

"How's your head. You took a pretty nasty fall?" asked Newman.

"I'm fine, after seeing the shock of my life."

"Look Barbara," Newman consoled. "I know how you must feel."

"Really?" She snapped angrily. "Do you really know how I feel?" Her tone bristled with bitterness. "Has your husband ever left you for another man? Huh? Do you know what it's like for people to come up to you and offer you their sympathy, because your husband is a disgusting pervert? All the while, wondering what a lousy lay you must be, if your husband has to find love and comfort from another man?"

"Whatever Tim is Barbara, it certainly isn't your fault," Newman calmly explained. "His sexual preference was probably established long before you met him. Now I know this may not be the proper time to ask, but does moving into single women's housing mean that you aren't leaving?"

She chuckled. "And go where? Back to Mom and Dad and tell them Tim left me for another man? No, Ken, you still have a waitress, since that seems to be your biggest concern."

"If that's what you think, Barbara, then I guess you don't know me that well, do you?"

"I guess I don't, Kenny. I guess I don't." Lisa handed Barbara a new key. "Can I take the rest of the afternoon off? I need some time to move my stuff from the cabin to the dorm."

"Sure," Newman said confidently. He wasn't certain how he was going to cover her shift, but it was apparent that she needed the time off. Perhaps, not so much to move, but rather to reflect on what had happened and try to regain her self-respect. "I'll get one of the late shift waitresses to start early."

"Thank you," Barbara sighed. She started for the door. "I don't know how I could have been so wrong about Tim," she said mainly to herself. She closed the door behind her.

Newman turned to Lisa. "Where did Tim and Kelly say they were?"

"Packing, I suppose," she quipped, shrugging her shoulder. "I don't know."

"Well, if they come in while I'm gone, tell them I have their pay envelopes."

He walked out the door and headed for the restaurant, hoping, oddly enough, that fewer customers than usual would drop in today. It was a chore just to keep the restaurant going when it was adequately staffed. Now, without the Chef and short one waitress, a huge dining room crowd would be a disaster. Millie could probably handle a slow, steady stream of people, but should an unexpected tour bus or a succession of eighteen-wheelers suddenly arrive… well, he didn't want to even think about it.

He started up the restaurant steps when around the corner came a beat-up white pickup truck. The cargo bed was loaded with suitcases, carrying cases, and other assorted luggage. The truck pulled up to the foot of the steps and stopped. Tim sat behind the wheel while Kelly, in full dress and makeup sat like a regal queen at his side. Tim rolled down the window.

"Just on our way over to pick up our last pay," Tim smiled.

Newman walked back down the steps and handed him the envelopes. "It's all there, but you can count it before you leave."

"Naw," Tim grinned, stuffing the envelopes into his shirt pocket. "No need to do that. The talk around the compound is that we can trust you, so I think I will too. Say goodbye to Vicki for me."

"Sure and how about Barbara?"

"Naw, don't bother. I tried to talk to her, but she won't even step into the same room with me. I guess its better this way."

"You hurt her very deeply, you know?"

"Lord knows, I didn't mean to. It's just that I've always had these feelings. Somehow, I thought that marrying Barbara would help me get over them, but it didn't. Then I met Kelly and… well, you know the rest."

"Still, it was a bit unfair to Barbara, don't you think?"

"Maybe, but what was I supposed to do? Tell her, 'Hey! Marry me even though I like pretty gay boys?' I did love her Ken, but I just didn't feel complete."

"Perhaps you could stay a while and talk it over. She probably still loves you too. Perhaps, even if you can't be man and wife, you might be able to still be friends."

Tim laughed. "Stay? Ha! What do you mean stay? You don't know what it would be like for me if I stayed here with everybody knowing I was gay. I'm a good mechanic. A damned good mechanic, but nobody would notice that. The first words out of their mouths would be queer and fag. You don't know what it's like with people calling you ugly names, whispering behind your back, looking at you down their noses, threatening you, and making you feel like you just didn't belong here."

Newman chuckled. "You're probably right, I have no idea."

Tim paused to realize the irony in his statement. "Well, I guess you might have some idea," he hedged, "but, apparently, you are a much stronger man than I am to be willing to stay here and take this shit."

"That could very well be. I will say, that since you've been here, I've heard people who could only say nigger just a couple of months ago, now say Ken or even, God forbid, Mr. Newman."

"Maybe you could stay and change some attitudes too."

"Not me, and especially not with Barbara still here," Tim paused. "You know, I guess you and me are a lot alike in some respects."

"Everybody's a lot alike in some respect."

"In the years I've been here, I've used the word nigger on more than one occasion, and now I find myself on the receiving end of different words with the same meaning. I guess, I'm just as misunderstood as you are."

"Probably."

"And a nigger is just another human being that you haven't taken the time to get to know."

"That could very well be, Tim," Newman nodded in agreement.

"Well…" Tim leaned over and kissed Kelly while he shifted the truck into drive. "You continue the fight. Me and Kelly are outta here."

"Where will you go?"

"I don't know. We'll make it though." He reached over and squeezed Kelly's hand. Kelly smiled. Tim then extended his hand to Newman. "Don't take this personal, but from one nigger to another, good luck."

Newman smiled and shook his hand. "Bye Kelly," Newman waved. Kelly blew him a kiss as Tim drove off.

Newman watched until their truck disappeared around the bend. He walked on into the dining area. There were few customers during this post-lunch period, and the area was relatively quiet. Newman walked back into the kitchen area where he saw Millie slowly stirring the contents of a huge steaming pot. He stepped over to the simmering brew.

"Boy," Newman inhaled. "That smells good."

"It's my version of vegetable beef." Millie beamed proudly. "It's more on the style of Louisiana gumbo. I picked up the recipe while on missionary work down in New Orleans."

"It really smells good. Well, the reason I came over here is to let you know I gave Barbara the afternoon off so she could move her things into the single women's dorm."

"That's fine. I think I can manage without her for a while. It probably won't get too busy before the evening shift waitresses comes on duty anyway. I think Angela and I will be just fine. Besides, Kimi should be here in a couple of hours."

"Glad to hear that. Without Kelly here, I was really worried."

"Oh, we are much better off here without that heathen pervert. God told me he will start to bless this place more, now that he is gone. The more Christian people we have working here, the better off this place will be."

Newman looked at her skeptically. "God told you that?"

"Yes. Just before dinner last night. HE said HE would replace all the riffraff here with good, honest, hardworking Christian folks." She could see the uncertainty in Newman's face. "You don't believe me, do you?"

"Millie, it's not my place to judge another individual's personal relationship with the Almighty. If God talks directly to you and Reese, then you both are indeed fortunate. I will say, though, that for a heathen pervert, Kelly sure could cook."

"Be that as it may, I've better get back to work. I've got a lot to do before dinnertime."

Suddenly they heard a loud shout in the dining room. "Hot diggedy damn!" The elated voice screamed. "Five thousand dollars!"

Newman peeped into the dining room just in time to see someone slam down a newspaper, scramble hastily away from their table, and dart out the front door. He looked back at Millie, who seemed just as confused as he was. The customers stopped momentarily to see the commotion, then turned to resume their meals. Newman watched as Angela walked over to the vacated table, picked up the abandoned newspaper and scanned the page. Her eyes widened as they made their way down the page.

"Angie?" Newman called, noting her keen interest. "What's in the newspaper?"

She slowly walked toward him as she continued to read the paper. "One of the loggers," she muttered, her eyes still glued to the page. "He must have seen this and took off to collect the $5000 reward."

"Seen what?" Newman was curious. "A winning lottery ticket number or something?"

Newman took the paper from Angie and scanned the page. Suddenly his eyes widened. He shook his head in disbelief with each line he read. He quickly set the paper aside and hurried over to the cash register.

"What are you going to do?" Angie asked.

"Millie, I'm taking three hundred dollars out of here," Newman hastily explains as he stuffed the bills into his pocket. "You still have enough to make change, and I'll replace it when I get back."

"What's the problem?" questioned Millie.

"I'll let you know when I get back." He jammed the cash register drawer shut and bolted out the front door.

Millie walked over to the paper and picked it up. She immediately recognized the picture in the bottom corner of the page as Goliah's. It was a particularly unflattering mug shot with numbered lines in the background. Above the photo, the headline screamed, "Manhunt Continues for Escaped Mental Patient." She read the story of how Lewis Paul Zecevic, also known as Goliah, had escaped from the Montana Psychiatric Institute a month ago. He had been committed after being declared mentally incompetent to stand trial for the beating death of his stepfather. He was to be considered homicidal and extremely dangerous. The institute and the Montana State Police were offering a $5000 reward for information leading to his recapture.

Minutes later, Newman walked up to Goliah as he carried a huge trash barrel hoisted on his back over to a nearby truck. He set the barrel inside the flatbed and started to climb into the cab when he saw Newman approaching.

"Ken," Goliah smiled. "Have dumped all park trash. Now start on kitchen."

"Wait a minute," Newman quickly cautioned. "There's something I've got to tell you."

"Goliah work too slow?" He sounded concerned. "Goliah work faster, Ken. Promise."

"No, no, nothing like that," Newman consoled. "Your picture is in today's paper. By now, everyone knows you're from the institute."

Goliah's face immediately turned pale, then suddenly, to determined anger. "No!" He turned and pounded the truck's rooftop. Newman flinched. "No go back. Never go back!" He pounded the rooftop repeatedly. Then he suddenly stopped. He slowly buried his face dejectedly into the curve of his elbow. Newman nervously waited, unsure of what Goliah might do in this enraged condition. He watched as Goliah slowly turned to face him with pleading tear strained eyes and a saddened face. "Ken come to put Goliah back in cage?" He asked in a softened, more acquiescent tone. He stood quietly awaiting Newman's answer. Newman's nervousness vanished. He stared into Goliah's eyes.

His voice had the impassioned tone of a truly sensitive human being. This man was certainly no crazed homicidal killer.

"Nooo, Goliah."

"I like it here, Ken."

"I like you being here, Goliah. You're a nice guy and an excellent worker."

"Goliah, have to go now."

"Before you go Goliah, could you explain one thing to me? Why did they put you in the cage?"

"Man," he softly began, struggling with his words. "He marry my Mom, but him not real father. Real father die long time ago."

"So this man was your stepfather?"

"No, just man who married my Mom."

"Okay. Whatever."

"Not nice man. Call Goliah big and stupid. Him no want big stupid son. He drank, get drunk. Beat Mom. Beat me. When beat me, Goliah feel no pain. Goliah no fight back. But one day Goliah find him choking Mom. Try and stop. Man get gun to shot Goliah, so I hit man. Hit him too hard. Break neck. Police come and try to chain Goliah's hands behind back. Goliah say no. Done nothing wrong. Fight police. Big fight before they take Goliah to jail. Judge say be tested before go to trial, but Goliah no want to be tested. Want to be free. So break out and run."

"Sounds like you have a good case for self-defense, Goliah. Maybe you should go back and fight this in court."

"No go back!" He insisted. "No make Goliah go back… please?"

"No go back, Goliah. I'm not going to make you go back if you don't want to. But like I said, your picture is in today's paper with a $5000 reward notice. Now, human nature being what it is, you can just bet someone has already called the police and the institute."

"No let them take me Ken." Goliah sternly warned. "I'll fight!"

"And you'll probably in up getting hurt or hurting somebody. You know the world is bigger than the state of Montana and maybe you should try and see some more of it."

"Goliah run?"

"Run, is a pretty strong word. Let's just say, continue to explore. Just like you found us, there are other places out there to be found."

"Ken not try and stop Goliah?"

Newman chuckled. "Who, me? Try and stop you? Get real."

Goliah let out a huge belly laugh, then stepped over and enveloped Newman in a giant bear hug.

"The ribs!" Newman moaned. "The ribs!" He released Newman and started for his tent, when Newman called to him. "Say, aren't you forgetting something?"

Goliah stopped and turned back toward Newman. "No, Goliah have everything at tent."

"Three hundred a month, remember?" He reached into his pocket, pulled out the bills, walked over, and slapped them in Goliah's hands. "Don't spend it all in one place."

Goliah took the money and smiled. "Thanks Ken. You true friend. Hope to see you again." He turned and ran as fast as he could toward his tent.

Newman smiled. He thought he could give Goliah a better head start by taking him back to his tent. He climbed into the truck, picked up Goliah and took him to his campground. Feeling better about Goliah getting a head start, he drove back to the office.

Lisa was busy typing at the receptionist desk as he entered. He could hear voices coming from Vicki's office. Lisa looked up from the typewriter.

"Ken, Vicki's looking for you. She's in there with two new hires, and she wants you to meet them. So go right in."

"New hires?" Newman sounded skeptical.

"Yes. Job Service sent them up today."

"Job Service? You've got to be kidding."

"Nope."

Newman shook his head in disgust. He hesitated. After his conversation with Ravanna, he had serious misgivings about any applicants referred by Job Service. He knew how they felt and they were admittedly holding back the more qualified people. He was afraid to even guess what backgrounds these two had. He took a deep breath and knocked on her door.

"Come in," Vicki's voice called.

He walked in to see the two men and a small young boy about ten years old, seated in front of her. They turned to see him as he entered.

"Gentlemen, this is your new boss." She smiled and pointed to Newman. "Kenny, this is Wyatt Earp," pointing to the heavyset blonde man in Western-styled jeans, cowboy boots and with a long black plum extending from the rim of his tan Stetson hat.

The man stood as he and Newman shook hands. "Please to meet cha." He smiled broadly.

"Wyatt?... Earp?" Newman asked for clarification.

"That's the name ma pappy give me." He beamed.

"Well... ah... that's nice. Pleased to meet you, Mr. Earp."

Next to him stood an Indian with handsome features, rich brown skin, and shoulder-length shiny black hair, dressed in casual Western wear.

"And this is Andrew Rides," Vicki announced. "And his son, Daniel." Rides and Newman shook hands. The boy smiled. Though the boy also had dark features, his reddish hair and deep-blue eyes denoted his mixed racial background. Earp continued to eagerly smile while by comparison, Rides was more reticent.

"Mr. Earp is our new chef," Vicki continued, "while Mr. Rides has hired on as the new garage mechanic."

"Really?" Newman asked dubiously. He still remembered what Job Service had said about the quality of the applicants they would send him. "And what mechanical experience do you have, Mr. Rides?"

"I hold a master's degree in mechanical engineering from the University of Southern California in Los Angeles," Rides quietly answered.

The incredulous look on Newman's face was obvious as the two men eyed each other.

"And what brings you to Montana?"

"Just a change of pace from the rat race, Mr. Newman," he casually replied. "And how about you?" He stared Newman in the eyes. "Mrs. Marshall here stated you have a degree in journalism. What brings you to this neck of the woods?"

Vicki could see that their conversation was slowly becoming a verbal jousting match. "Well, they'll be plenty of time later for you two to get to know each other." She smiled. "In the meantime, let's get these gentlemen settled in, shall we? Wyatt can live in the single men's dorm and Andrew, you and Daniel can stay in Barbara's old cabin."

"Certainly," Newman agreed, picking up on Vicki's cue. "Andrew, go over to the garage and introduce yourself to Dave Jackson. He'll show you around over there. And, Wyatt, go over to the kitchen and ask for Millie Peterson. She'll get you started in the kitchen. Then come back here, and I'll get the keys to your rooms so you can go get settled in."

Both men started out the door. "I'll shore do right by ya." Earp smiled as he left the room. Rides quietly followed. Newman closed the door behind them, stepped over to Vicki's desk, and leaned over toward her.

"Wha… wha… what on Earth made you hire those two?" He whispered.

"We need to fill those two positions, and they seemed qualified to fill them."

"But they came from Job Service, and you know what kind of people Job Service is sending up here? People who can't get a job anywhere else."

"Yes, I know that. But it doesn't negate the fact that we need those positions filled."

"Well, did you happen to check the information on their applications? If that Rides has a degree from UCLA, I can fly a twin-engine jet. And that Wyatt Earp—if that's in fact his name, what's his background in?"

"He was a cook for twelve years at Deer Lodge."

"Deer Lodge? Well, at least he's had some resort experience."

Vicki hesitated. "Actually Kenny, Deer Lodge is the state's maximum security prison." She squinted as she awaited his reaction.

"Awe," Newman aspirated, "you must be kidding?"

"But I did talk to his parole officer," she quickly added, "and he said he was the best cook they've ever had on death row."

"Death row?… I don't believe this. While I have no doubt that he kept a little more than bread and water on the menu, what was he in for anyway?"

Vicki hedged a bit. "Murder one, I think... No, wait... it was murder two... no, no... it was two counts of murder one... yes, that's it. But, Kenny, he's paid his debt to society and he deserves a second chance. Besides, for $300 a month, we aren't going to get Julia Child in here. If it turns out that Earp can't cook or that Rides doesn't know a screwdriver from a hammer, we simply fire them and look for somebody else. That's all we can do."

"Great," he sighed dejectedly. "Well at least there's one good thing."

"Really, what?"

"Once word spreads that we now have a convicted killer as our chef, if his cooking does stink, no one is likely to complain."

"Kenny, you're so suspicious," she playfully chided. "Why, look at your own background. It's just as impressive as Andrew's. People are probably asking the same questions about you, that you are asking about them."

"But you know my background."

"I know what you've told me."

"I haven't tried to hide anything from you."

"That's not the point. Everybody needs a chance to start over, start fresh. Besides, in this business, and especially in the condition I'm in, you can't be too choosy. You have to be a good judge of character, and I pride myself on being one."

"Let's hope so. Because if you're wrong about Mr. Earp, I just hope we don't live to regret it."

Suddenly the front door burst open and an excited man's voice heaving with exhaustion boomed into the office. "Where is she? Where is she?" The desperate voice demanded.

"Who?" Lisa's voice echoed into Vicki's office.

"Vicki, who else?"

Vicki and Newman paused to overhear the conversation. "She's back in her..." Before Lisa could finish, the man tore past her and burst into Vicki's office.

"There she is!" He excitedly announced, pointing to Vicki as she looked up dumbfounded from behind her desk. Seconds later a uniformed policeman and a well-dressed middle-aged woman in a grey business suit stepped into the office behind him.

"Victoria Marshall?" The policeman asked.

"Yes," she answered hesitantly.

"I'm Theo Grambs, state trooper and this is Dr. Sandra Evans of the Montana Psychiatric Institute."

Newman immediately realized the nature of their business.

"We understand that you have Louis Zecevic employed here," Dr. Evans quietly interjected.

"Who?" Vicki was confused.

"Goliah," Newman volunteered.

"Oh, Goliah," she was relieved to know that their visit had nothing to do with her own legal problems. "Yes, we do. He's a fine worker too. Is there a problem?"

"He escaped from our institute a little over a month ago, and we came to take him back."

"My word!" Vicki sighed with concern. "He's not dangerous or anything, is he? He's been the perfect employee since he's been here."

"He's already killed a man, Mrs. Marshall," the trooper added.

"Goliah?" Vicki was in disbelief. "No, you must have the wrong man."

"Is it true that his stepfather tried to kill him and his mother?" Newman interjected.

"It kind of looks that way," the trooper agreed.

"Sounds like a case of self-defense to me." Added Newman.

"Maybe, but that's up to the courts to decide."

"And when does he go to court Dr. Evans?" quizzed Newman.

"As soon as he is declared mentally competent to stand trial and take part in his own defense."

"A year, maybe two…" stated the trooper.

"Or three or four or five," Newman interrupted. "In the meantime, Goliah rots in a cell while you all decide if he has enough intelligence to defend himself."

"Mr. Newman," the trooper sternly warned, "you are aware that aiding an escaped fugitive is a felony. If you know where he is, I suggest you tell us."

"Oh no you don't," the cowboy warned. "You ain't hoggin' in on my reward money, I know where he lives. Out there, in the pasture. I'll take yawl to him. That $5000 is gonna be all mine. Come on!" He hurried out of the office as the trooper turned and followed.

Newman looked over at Dr. Evans as she turned to leave. "He'll never go willingly."

"The police have tangled with Louis before. They've brought enough manpower for the job," she paused. "Look, I can understand your concern for Goliah, but under the circumstances, there is nothing I can do. We are only doing what we have to do, you understand?"

"Sure, Dr. Sandra Evans." Newman quietly smiled. "We all have to do what we feel we have to do."

Dr. Evans turned and left. Vicki shook her head dejectedly. "Poor Goliah. He really doesn't deserve all of this. Once they get him back to MPI, will you check on him and see if we can be of some help?"

"Oh, I wouldn't worry about Goliah. In the end, things have a way of working out for the best."

"I hope so. Except now we need another groundskeeper. Any ideas?"

"How about want ads in the local paper?"

"Not unless you want to be flooded with every resume this side of the Continental Divide."

"Well, how do you usually find workers?"

"Like I said, they usually find me."

Newman slowly strolled over to her office window. He could see the pasture across the highway. The small army of police were slowly climbing back into their vehicles as the cowboy, desperately pleading his case, struggled to keep pace with Dr. Evans. Visibly upset, with arms flailing and finger pointing, she stormed angrily out of the vacant pasture. Newman grinned.

Suddenly, from up the highway, he saw a canvassed army-style troop truck heading up the road. It was followed by another truck, and another and still another until a long caravan barreled up the highway toward the resort. The lead truck turned onto the bridge leading to the pasture just as the last police car sped away. He could see the U.S. Forest Service logo emblazoned on the door of each truck as it turned.

"Vicki," Newman quietly called, still watching the seemingly endless line of vehicles. "You'd better come see this."

She quickly pushed herself up from her chair and walked over to the window. She peered out the window. She slowly looked over at Newman, then back out the window. She watched as the trucks stopped at various locations throughout the open field. Men and women in green jumpsuits scampered off the back and began unloading supplies and setting up tents.

"We're being invaded," she muttered in awe.

"They didn't waste any time getting here, that's for sure."

They watched as a green sedan peeled away from the procession and headed for the front office. Vicki and Newman both hurried into the reception area to await the arrival of the person in the car.

Finally a car door slammed, footsteps clumped up the entrance, and the front door opened. Grant stood in the doorway and smiled. "I'm back," he announced proudly.

Vicki and Newman were both somber. Grant could see the serious look on their faces and that they weren't amused by his antics'. "Did somebody die?" He noticed their stone like expressions.

"Do you think you brought enough people?" Newman mendaciously asked. "There's only an army out there. Where's the Navy?"

"We'll never be able to handle a crowd that size," Vicki protested.

"Oh, relax," he consoled. "Like I said, we brought our own food, water, tents, shower trucks, outhouses… everything. We won't need anything from you but the use of the land." He handed Newman a stack of papers. "That's a copy of our agreement and pay schedule. Like I said, you won't even know we're here. This is probably the easiest money you'll ever make. Well, I've got to run. If you have any questions about your contract, call our contracting office. Leanna Clark is handling your account, her number is on those papers I just gave you. I've got to go and ensure things are set up properly. Don't worry. It'll be fine." He closed the door behind him as he left.

Newman looked over at Vicki. "Why do I worry when people tell me not to worry?"

"Now I know how the mayor of Atlanta must have felt right before General Sherman's visit." Commented Vicki.

"I'd better go to the restaurant and tell Millie what's going on. She just might have a couple of extra guest for dinner tonight."

Newman left the office feeling increasingly uneasy about this arrangement with the Forest Service. Even though Grant had stated three-hundred smoke jumpers, he thought Grant was just throwing out a number off the top of his head. He hadn't counted on so many people being involved in fighting the fire. Even if they did bring their own provisions, there was nothing stopping them from paying to use the resort facilities just like any other customer. What if they should all decide to use the pool or have dinner all at once… Newman relished the thought.

The dining room was virtually empty. Millie was sitting at an empty table, sipping on a cup of coffee. He could see Earp back in the kitchen, leisurely chopping a head of lettuce. Newman pulled a chair out and sat across from Millie.

"How's he working out?"

"So far so good." Millie smiled. "He knows how to make everything on the menu. He's fixed every order in a timely manner, and he said he didn't need my help, so I left. I've just been sitting here in case he gets in trouble, but so far, so good. We haven't been that busy, so I've been helping out on the floor. Two customers have even asked me to give their compliments to the chef."

"I'm glad to hear that, because it may get just a little busy tonight and every night for the next couple of weeks. The Forest Service smoke jumpers are arriving… and arriving… and arriving."

"Oh, dear," Millie sighed. "Maybe we should double the usual precooked portions for tonight. What do you think?"

"Triple them, would be a more appropriate choice. With you and Wyatt back in the kitchen, I don't foresee any major problems, especially if he's as good as you say he is. I'm going over to the women's dorm to see if I can get Marci to come over this afternoon from the pool. You are definitely going to need some additional floor help tonight. Barbara, Angela, and Kim aren't going to be enough."

Millie leaned toward him and whispered. "He said he's done time on death row at Deer Lodge."

"Ah… Yea," Newman hedged.

"I wouldn't count on him lasting the week," she said emphatically. "The Lord told me so."

"Well, Millie, the Lord works in mysterious ways."

"We shall see who is right, Mr. Newman."

"Alright Millie, I am not going to argue with you over such a trivial matter. But, what I am going to do is get you some more help over here for tonight."

"Who are you getting?"

"I'm going to check and see if Marci and some of the other women who worked the earlier shift wouldn't mind earning a little overtime tonight." Mille raised her coffee cup in agreement and watched Newman walk out the door.

Several minutes later, Newman had stepped through the doors of the single woman's dorm. He slowly surveyed the empty lobby. All was quiet except for the noise from the television set that softly played to nonexistent viewers. The chairs and flowers strategically placed throughout the lobby gave the area a quaint ambiance that reflected, in many ways, the personality of each woman who lived here.

The wooden balustrade led to an upper floor lined with individually numbered rooms. Newman was about to ascend the staircase when Barbara appeared at the top of the landing.

"Kenny," she hailed. "What brings you over her?"

"I was looking for Marci. Do you know which room she's in?"

"Number 4. Do you want me to check and see if she's in?"

"No, that's okay. You just settle in and get some rest. It's probably going to be very busy tonight. If you feel like working tonight, please come over to the restaurant."

Newman scampered up the steps and headed down to Room 4. He started to knock, but hesitated, as he heard the distinctive sound of a male voice coming from inside the room. He strained to hear more clearly. There was occasional laughter as the male voice would utter an expletive. Newman rapped loudly on the door. He could hear the sudden, almost frantic, scurrying inside. He knocked again.

"Marci! This is Ken. Open the door please."

"Okay," Marci called. "Let me get some clothes on. I'll be right there." Newman impatiently waited. Finally the door opened and Marci stood in the slightly cracked doorway dressed in her nightgown.

"Ahhh… Mr. Newman," she smiled. Running her finger through her hair. "This is a surprise. You don't normally come over here."

"You're right. I don't, because I expect the young ladies over here to be mature enough to look after themselves without someone looking over their shoulders twenty-four hours a day."

"And what is that supposed to mean?" She was trying to sound indignant. "I'm responsible enough to look after myself."

"Are you?"

Suddenly the pungent odor of a sweet herb scent flowed from the room. Newman took a couple of whiffs. "And what's that smell?"

"What smell?" Marci sniffed the air. "I don't smell anything."

Newman barged past her into the room. "I'm no authority on illegal drugs, but I do know marijuana when I smell it. It's illegal, you know."

"Look," Marci demanded. "You can't just come barging into my room like this. I have my rights."

"Really, Marci?" Newman reached over and snatched open the bathroom door. He walked in and ripped back the shower curtain. Jay, the young man whose life she had saved earlier at poolside, looked up. He was startled from his prone position in the tub. "No guest in the dorm without prior approval. Do you remember signing something to that effect, Marci?"

Marci walked over to the bathroom door and smiled as Jay climbed gingerly out of the tub. "He's not hurting anything," she casually explained. "Besides, I saved his life at the pool the other day. He just came by to say thanks."

"I don't care if you gave birth to him," Newman angrily insisted. "He's not supposed to be here in your room."

Jay calmly walked past Newman out into the living room. Newman followed. "Say, chill out, soul brother." He casually began, trying to sound smooth and relaxed. "Marci and I were just having a little fun. No harm done." He reached into his pocket and pulled out a rolled marijuana cigarette. "Here," he extended the joint to Newman. "Take a token. It'll mellow you right out."

Newman took the cigarette and examined it. "Say," Newman smiled in a calmer tone of voice. "This looks like good stuff. You got any more?"

"Hey, you bet." Jay beamed, excited at the possible prospect of Newman joining them. He reached into his pocket and pulled out a handful of cigarettes.

"Let me see those, Newman drooled. Jay handed the joints to him. "Is this all you have?" Newman beamed, examining the sticks.

"Yeah, but I can get more."

"You're gonna have too," Newman's voice changed abruptly. It was stern and serious. He stepped back into the bathroom and dropped the cigarettes into the toilet.

"Hey!" Jay angrily protested as he ran after Newman. He heard the toilet's ominous whoosh. He raced over to the commode just in time to see the cigarettes swirling into oblivion. He sighed in disgust. "Man that was over a hundred bucks worth of grass you just flushed."

"And another thing, Newman sternly warned. Keep your drugs outta this dorm! You read me, Mister?" He turned toward Marci, who was standing wide-eyed in the doorway. "And as for you young lady, if I ever catch you with drugs in this room again, not to mention a boy, you're gonna be on your way back home so fast, your head is going to swim. Do I make myself clear!"

She gulped. "Yes."

"Now, Mister," Newman looked back at Jay. "You know the way out."

Jay dashed pasted Newman out of the bathroom. Seconds later they both heard the front door slam. Newman and Marci stared quietly at each other.

"Is that all?" She asked defiantly.

"No it's not. They are going to need your help on the dining room floor tonight."

"Oh, Ken," she protested as she turned and walked back into the living room. "Do I have to after putting in ten hours over at the pool?"

Newman followed her. "It'll only be for a couple of hours, until I can get some added people in there on a full-time basis. Besides, Barbara's going to be a little late getting on shift tonight. She has to finish moving her things into her room over here."

"So I've gotta work overtime just because Barbara's husband likes it better with other men than he does with her, is that it?"

Newman was taken aback by her insensitive remark and opened his mouth to respond, but didn't. "Oh, just get dressed. I'll wait for you downstairs."

Minutes later, Marci jumped in the golf cart with Newman to make their way to the restaurant.

It was late evening, and the restaurant was a madhouse. Every table was packed. There was a relatively impatient waiting line meandering out the door, down the front steps, and almost into the parking lot. Kimberly, Angela, Marci and Barbara maneuvered hastily between tables and around the floor. Trays of food were delicately balanced on their open palms. Newman darted between empty table, quickly clearing the dishes and giving them a quick wipe before ushering in the next group of patrons. Periodically a bell would ding. Millie's shout of "Order Up!" would send one of the waitresses scurrying to remove a steaming hot plate resting on the kitchen window ledge. Once the waitress took the order off the ledge, she would hand Millie another order slip. Millie took the ticket and quickly shoved it over to Wyatt. "The Dinner Special, medium well!" She commanded. Millie took another plate, placed it on the ledge, and tapped the bell. Barbara almost instantly appeared and took the tray as she handed Millie another order. Millie shoved it to Wyatt. "Hot Springs Special!" She ordered. "Easy on the tartar sauce!" She quickly placed another plate on the kitchen ledge and tapped the bell. "Order Up!" Again she shouted. Marci whizzed by, snatched the plate up, and left still another ticket on the ledge.

Millie reached for another finished plate, but it wasn't there. She looked over at Wyatt as he sliced feverishly at a side of roast beef. Then suddenly, the fast, furious, and hectic pace of the dinner period had him visibly rattled. He fumbled with and frequently dropped utensils and often brought her order missing a required entrée. She looked into his face and could see the pressure slowly building. He started mumbling to himself and brutally hacked rather than sliced at the side of roast beef. "Cook this, Wyatt," she overheard him mutter as he repeatedly slammed the cleaver into the meat. "Cook that, Wyatt. Right now, Wyatt. Who the fuck does she think I am?" He suddenly looked up angrily at Millie and caught her staring at him. She forced a nervous smile and turned her attention back toward the dining room.

"Table for four?" Newman smiled, as he greeted the four young men in green jumpsuits standing in the doorway.

"Yeah, garcon. Something with a view," one of the men quipped in a mock French accent. They all laughed.

"Right this way," Newman invited, unamused. He seated the men at a vacant table and was preparing to take their orders, when Marci hurriedly walked up to him.

"Ken," Marci tapped him repeatedly on the shoulder. He looked at her, mildly irritated.

"Can't you see I'm busy?" He quietly scolded. "Can it wait until I take these nice gentlemen's orders?"

"Millie sad she wants to see you in the kitchen right now," Marci insisted. "She said it's important."

Newman sighed. "Okay. Will you finish this?" He handed her his notepad and pencil. "I'll be right back."

He walked back behind the counter and stepped over to the kitchen window. Millie had set another plate on the ledge. "Okay, Millie, what's wrong? Are the orders coming back too fast?"

"It's not the orders I'm worried about. It's Wyatt." Millie motioned back over her shoulder at him. "He's a rubber band stretched to the limit. He could snap at any moment."

"Snap? Like how?"

"How do people usually snap?" She appeared angry. "They just go!"

"You could be misjudging him. After all, this is only his first day."

"Well, why don't you just come back here and see for yourself."

Newman stared at her with quiet reservations. It was quite possible that she was overreacting. At least, he hoped she was, because with the size of this crowd, one cook back here would simply be overwhelmed. He walked back into the kitchen and quietly observed Wyatt for a few moments. The longer he watched, the more he too began to grow concerned with each passing moment. Wyatt grumbled aloud statements of violence and murder as he angrily jabbed at the roast. Then he bitterly hacked the cuts into pieces without regard to size.

Suddenly, Angela appeared in the kitchen window and set a plate of food on the ledge. "Say, Millie, could you get Wyatt to cook this steak a little more? The customer says it's almost raw."

Wyatt overheard the request as Newman had the kitchen door open. Wyatt suddenly slammed the cleaver into the wooden table. "No!" He shouted. Everyone flinched. Angela darted from the window. Wyatt yanked the cleaver out of the table, turned, and squared off angrily at Newman and Millie.

Newman flinched and let the door close. Millie recoiled in horror. "Look Wyatt," Newman cautiously began as Millie slowly eased for the door. "Put that thing down and let's talk about this."

"Talk about what?" He sneered. "How ole Wyatt can work just a little faster? Get more food up? I'm not gonna let you work me like a goddamn nigger."

Newman could see a blank, almost-distant gaze in Wyatt's eyes. It was as if Wyatt was staring right through him. He didn't know if trying to reason with him now, in this condition, was even a possibility.

Unexpectedly, the kitchen door swung open and Barbara barged in. "Say, what's the holdup on my baked salmon?" She complained. "What's going on back..." She froze in midsentence at the sight of Wyatt brandishing the cleaver. She screamed and bolted back out the door.

"Quick!" Newman turned to Millie. "Get outta here and call the police!"

Millie dashed for the door.

"No! Get back here!" Wyatt commanded. He lunged at Millie, swiping at her with the cleaver.

Newman scramble hastily around a nearby cutting table and quickly shoved it against the wall, blocking Wyatt's path. Several pots and pans fell from the table and crashed to the floor. Wyatt tried to scramble over the table as the door slammed behind Millie. He stopped and stared momentarily at the closed door. He then slowly turned and acrimoniously sneered at Newman.

"You think you're smart, don't cha, nigger boy?" He menacingly grinned. "Well, let's see how bright you are after I finish choppin' ya into a hundred tiny pieces."

He quickly sliced at Newman several times. Newman desperately ducked and dodged each deadly swipe. He frantically looked around for a weapon. He snatched down a large pot hanging overhead and squared off against Wyatt from across the main table. Several more overhead pots and pans came crashing to the floor. As Wyatt chased him around one end of the table, Newman quickly scrambled to another section, using his pot to bat away Wyatt's swinging cleaver.

Suddenly Wyatt scrambled over the top of the table. The move caught Newman completely by surprise. He instinctively threw the pot at Wyatt. The flying utensil blasted Wyatt's hand, knocking the cleaver from his grasp. It sailed across the floor and under the reach-in cooler. He glanced down at his suddenly empty hand, then back up at Newman.

Wyatt slowly grinned. "Hell, I don't need that thing to take care of you."

He torpidly stalked Newman, repeatedly punching his open palm. Newman slowly backed away until finally he was pressed squarely against the wall. Wyatt lunged at him and swung. Newman quickly ducked the wing. But Wyatt followed with a swift knee to the abdomen. Newman cradled his stomach as he doubled over in pain. Wyatt interlocked his fingers, raised his arms high into the air, and jammed his doubled fist solidly into Newman's back. The blow drove Newman straight to his knees. He tried to struggle to his feet as Wyatt raised his fist to strike another blow.

Suddenly a hand appeared seemingly from nowhere and caught Wyatt's arm in mid-swing. Wyatt looked back over his shoulder to see Rides, with a solid grip on his arm, smiling at him. Rides suddenly turned, twisted Wyatt's arm, and flipped him over his shoulder, judo style. The impact of the landing stunned him. He tried to struggle to his feet. But Rides calmly stepped over and jammed his foot forcefully into Wyatt's chest.

"Don't even think about it," Rides calmly warned.

Newman used the side of the stove to slowly pull himself to his feet.

"You all right?" Rides asked.

"Yeah… thanks," he moaned, still slightly bent over, cradling his stomach and trying to catch his breath. "Things were getting a little uncomfortable in here. Where did you learn to fight like that?"

"The Army, and where did you learn to fight? The Old Folks Home? It's okay to block a punch with something other than your stomach, you know."

"Yea," Newman grinned. He tried to stand erect. "I'll try to remember that. How did you know Wyatt and I weren't getting along back here anyway?"

"Well, first I saw Barbara come dashing outta here like the proverbial bat. Then, I saw Millie nearly run over a customer trying to get outta here. And when I heard the pots and pans crashing to the floor, I figured, either there was a serious problem back here, or that you had offered to cook dinner."

"Very funny," Newman smiled halfheartedly. "I hope your mechanical ability is as good as your sense of humor. Still, you didn't show up a minute too soon. Thanks."

"No problem."

I had Millie call the police. Could you take him over to the office and wait for them over there? There's still a dinner crowd out there that hasn't been fed."

Rides reached down and yanked Wyatt up on his feet. "Okay, Custer, let's move out, "he sighed, as he ushered Wyatt out the backdoor.

Suddenly, Millie and Jake burst into the kitchen. Jake stopped and surveyed the mess.

"What in blue blazes!" Jake exclaimed.

"Well, we have no cook, the kitchen is a disaster and we still have a dining room full of customers." Newman rationalized.

"We'll just have to cancel dinner for the rest of the night," Millie suggested.

"Oh no you don't," Jake warned. "We've got enough able-bodied people here to get this place back on track."

"But we don't have an extra cook, Jake," Newman explained.

"You may not have a cook, but you've got the best damned chef this side of the Divide."

"Who?" Newman and Millie said in unison.

"You're lookin' at 'em. Now let's get to work!" Jake commanded with authority of a general leading troops into battle. "Ken, work on getting' this mess cleaned up. Millie I'm gonna need some soup."

"But Jake, it'll take me at least a couple of hours to mix enough ingredients…"

"Hell woman," he growled. "There's a ton of canned soup back there. Just start ta openin' cans. Now move!"

Jake walked over to the reach-in cooler, quickly began removing steaks and flipping them onto the open grill. His fluent moves and ease of motion made it apparent that he definitely knew his way around the kitchen. He barked instructions and directions with the skill and confidence of a concert maestro.

Within minutes, the restaurant was back on schedule and running like a well-oiled machine. All of the orders had been prepared and delivered, and Jake, on occasion, even found time to leave the kitchen and personally deliver a meal or chat with a patron.

By midnight, the last customer walked out the door. Newman immediately slammed the door behind him. He bolted the door shut, leaned back against it, and sighed with relief. Millie rushed over and quickly flipped the closed sign in the window.

"Whew!" She sighed, plopping down in a nearby chair.

"I'll say," Newman agreed, walking slowly back toward the counter. "Jake, if you ever decide to give up logging…"

Jake stood at the cash register, punching in keys. "Well I had to cook for my logging crew in the early days, but no. I can't spend all day on the hill, them come down here and cook too. This was an emergency situation. I'm hanging up my apron just as soon as you get another cook in here. I just came over because Millie said somebody over here was trying to hack you to death Ken."

"I don't know what came over him." Newman shook his head.

"He was fine until that crowd rush hit," Millie explained. "Then all of a sudden, I guessed the added pressure just turned him into a wild man."

Most of the extra crowd came from that Forest Service crew across the street," Newman noted. "That story about them not being much trouble while they're here may not be exactly accurate. While they were paying customers, we aren't staffed to handle that kind of crowd every day."

"Oh, I wouldn't worry about that," Jake consoled as he counted the money in the register. "Most of them were just as frustrated with the slow service and the long lines. You can just bet that a lot of the people who came here tonight won't be back tomorrow. Besides, from the looks of the cash here, we've made as much tonight as we would have made in three nights. I know the North Ridge fire won't last forever, but with a night's take like this,"---he held up a fist of cash---"we might not want those guys to ever leave."

Suddenly a knock on the front door interrupted their conversation. Everyone looked at each other as they waited for an additional knock. It came.

Jake hurriedly stuffed the cash back into the register.

"We're closed!" Millie immediately shouted.

"It's me, Rides," the voice outside called. "And I've got the sheriff with me."

Millie walked over and open the front door. In walked Rides and Sheriff Bennett.

"Sheriff Bennett," Newman beamed. "Is this your regular beat, or do you just enjoy the pleasure of our company?"

Sheriff Bennett slowly removed his Stetson. "Mr. Newman, if I recall correctly. Wow! In the short time you've been here, you've had your bar shot up, you've been invaded by Hell's Angels, the state trooper said you all hired an escaped killer as your groundskeeper, and now a paroled murderer has tried to chop you up into little tiny pieces. Ah… how long do you plan to stay in Montana anyway?"

"Things will get better."

"For your sake, I hope so. Anyway, I've already taken Mr. Earp back to jail. I'm going to need a statement from you, Mr. Newman, about what happened here tonight."

"Is that all you came back for?" Jake asked. "That could have waited until tomorrow, couldn't it?"

"I suppose. But that's not the only reason I came back here tonight. There's a trio of bikers knocking over restaurants and tourist resorts throughout the Northwest. They've already killed three people in Idaho and two in Washington State, so they aren't trigger shy. Since you all will have a lot of bikers coming through here, I thought it best to come over and drop off some composite descriptions of them, just in case they decide to check out your resort."

Rides held up the posters. "Here they are, I'll leave a couple of these here and spread a few around the compound."

"Since this state doesn't have 911 service, just in case we do spot those robbers," Newman asked, "how long will it take you guys to get up here?"

"We'll be here as soon as we can."

"That's exactly what I'm afraid of." Newman sighed.

Bennett turned to leave, when he suddenly stopped at the door. "Oh, Mr. Newman." Newman turned to face him. "That man you tried to save in that truck wreck a few weeks ago, Rick Baddeley?"

"Yes."

"He died last night. I know how hard you all fought trying to save him, so I thought you'd like to know."

Newman's heart sank. To put that much effort---even risk his own life trying to save him and still he died. It didn't seem fair. He might have been killed in that explosion, and for what? The end result would have been the same had he just stood by and done nothing at all.

"Thank you sheriff." Newman exhaled.

"I told his wife what you did, and she wants to come by and thank you personally, if that's all right with you?"

"Ah… sure, Sheriff. That's fine."

"Good. Well, good night."

Millie started to lock the door behind him when Rides also turned to leave. Newman suddenly called to him.

"Andrew, wait a minute!" Newman turned back and pointed to Angela and Kimberly. "You two help Barbara clean up tonight, will you please? You both can sleep in tomorrow, but Millie," he looked over at her. "I'm afraid you've got breakfast duty in the morning, until I can find another cook. So get outta here, okay?"

Before they could answer, he and Rides walked out the door and headed for Rides' cabin. It was a cool and breezy early summer morning.

Small rocks and sand pebbles crunched beneath their feet as they walked along the poorly-lit, unpaved trail.

"I just wanted to say thanks again for pulling my chestnuts outta the fire back there tonight."

"Don't mention it Ken."

"Tell me something," Newman continues, "you are obviously a very talented man with some very impressive credentials. What brings you to a place like this?"

"I have my reasons. But how about you? I hear you also have a college degree. If anyone is outta place here, it's gotta be a Black man with a college degree. And of all places, at a tourist resort surrounded by White rednecks in a state with only about one hundred Blacks in its entire population. If anyone needed a background check…"

"Nothing personal, Andrew. It's just that I don't share Vicki's trust in hiring people, especially not after tonight."

"Oh, I don't know. She apparently hired you on instinct, and she did pretty well with that decision, didn't she? I mean, it just goes to show you that not everybody who comes here to work is a homicidal killer, right?"

"Point taken, but…" agreed Newman.

"My grandfather told me the story of the man who came home and found his wife in bed with another man. When the enraged husband angrily asked, 'What are you doing here in bed with my wife?' the man answered, "Everybody's gotta be somewhere.""

"Meaning?" Newman was unamused.

"Simply that, if you weren't here, you'd just be somewhere else. So you may as well make the best of where you are." They walked to the steps of Rides' cabin. "Oh, by the way, my son will be out of school for the summer, and maybe you can find something for him to do around here. He's a good worker."

"I'm sure we can find something to keep him busy."

Rides started up the steps as Newman turned to walk away. Rides stopped and called him. "Say, if you are interested in learning a little self-defense, I'm free tomorrow after six. It's about time you became a true Montanan, if you are going to stay here."

"Oh, I don't know," Newman hedged. "I still don't think fighting solves anything."

"Suit yourself. But I'm going to be out at the corral tomorrow after six anyway, so in case you change your mind, I'll be there. Besides, if you intend to stay around these parts and stay alive, you're gonna have to learn how to protect yourself."

"You know, fighting was one of those things my mother always warned me against." He pause reminiscing. "She said there was always a better way to resolve any dispute. Now it seems as if that's the only thing I've done since I've arrived. Before I came here, the only thing I've ever punched in my entire life was a time clock, and I even stopped doing that when I learned it might punch back. You see this face?" Newman pointed. "I'm a lover, not a fighter."

"Well, if you intend to stay up here, there are four things you're going to have to learn to do."

"And what might that be?"

"Ride, shoot, and fight."

"And the fourth? You said there were four."

"If you don't know what number four is, you're in worse shape than I thought."

"I got number four covered." They both laughed.

CHAPTER
7

A new day dawn on Newman. He knew after last night he needed more assistance to handle the waitressing and another cook. He had nowhere else to turn, but back to Job Services.

"So, I'm to understand that you have no one else you can send to fill the position," Newman concluded in frustration.

"Mr. Newman, I think Mr. Ravanna explained before he left on vacation that your resort's dismal pay record precludes us from sending any of our mainstream clients to you for employment. However, if I get any more special needs clients…"

"You mean any more homicidal maniacs?"

"Good day, Mr. Newman." The line abruptly went dead.

Newman slammed the phone down. He leaned back in Vicki's chair and breathed in frustration. The door eased open and Vicki walked in. She froze momentarily startled, seeing Newman behind her desk.

"Kenny, I didn't know you were here."

Newman stood up and pushed the chair back. "I didn't know you were coming in this morning."

"Oh, sit back down." She motioned toward the chair. "Anything I wanted to do can wait until later."

"Are you sure?"

"Positive. What were you doing anyway?"

Newman sat back down and pulled himself up to the desk. "I'm trying to get more waitresses, at least for the next month or so. But

165

most importantly, find a replacement for Wyatt, so Millie doesn't have to spend twenty-four hours in that kitchen. She was up half the night helping with dinner, and now she's over there cooking breakfast. Jake's coming in this afternoon to cook dinner, but he's been logging all day. Job Services won't send anybody up here unless they are either a crazed dope fiend or a serial axe murderer who once read a book on how to cook pasta."

"Oh, don't even bother with them, Kenny. Besides, I think I have the problem solved with the cooking."

"Really?" Newman's voice brightened at the news.

"Yep." Vicki smiled proudly as she sat in the chair across from him. "I didn't want to tell you before I knew for certain, but I got a call from him yesterday evening. And he'll be in this afternoon," she explained excitedly. "Isn't that great?"

"Ahhh… sure… but just exactly who is coming in this afternoon anyway?"

"His name is Nelson Adams. He was senior chef at the downtown Hilton, and he's won national awards for his soups and breads."

"Really?" Newman was impressed with the credentials. "And he's going to work here for $300 a month plus room and board?"

"He's worked here before, so I pay him $375 a month, but don't let that get around. "I'm in no position to give raises yet."

Newman leaned back in the chair and looked at her curiously. He thought to himself, if this man was the senior chef at a major hotel and could make award-winning dishes, why on Earth would he want to work here?

"If you had this boy wonder under wraps all along, why didn't you unveil him sooner?"

"He wasn't available before now."

"Vicki," Newman said with raised brow, "there's something you're not telling me about this guy. I mean, why would a chef of his stature want to work here?"

"Just wait until he gets here. You'll see. In fact, I know you'll love him."

"I'm sure I will." Newman blandly agreed. "Anyway there's another matter you need to look into." He turned a piece of paper around in her direction.

She scanned the paper briefly. "It's the monthly gasoline report. So?"

"Note the bottom row of figures."

Vicki read the numbers he had indicated. "I still don't see what you are talking about."

"The figures show that during May we bought 2,327 gallons of fuel. We sold 1,981 gallons and used 110 gallons for Jake's logging operation and in our own vehicles in-house. It shows we carried 150 gallons over into June, when we purchased 2,177 more gallons on the first of the month, which brought our tanks back up to 2,327."

"So?"

"That means there were 86 gallons of gasoline unaccounted for at the end of May. So I looked up the records for the last couple of months, and there's a discrepancy in every month-end report Jackson has submitted."

Vicki chuckled. "Oh, sounds like Dave needs to be a little more careful with his math, that's all. He only has a sixth-grade education, you know. Everything he knows about cars, he learned by actually working on them."

"Maybe, but what if he's guilty of a little more than simply bad accounting."

"You mean theft?" Vicki smiled, surprised. "Dave?" She chuckled. "Naw, he's been with me ever since I opened this place. Even so, I have to assume that everyone here has taken more than their monthly $300 allowance at one time or another. In this business, you have to assume that everyone steals from you. It's not a question of whether, but more of how much."

Newman shook his head. "I'm afraid I don't follow you."

"Listen," she casually explained, "nobody here works an eight-hour day. The average workday here is at least twelve or fourteen hours, with only one day off a week. I don't pay overtime, nor do I have any health or retirement benefits. Dave's labor at a regular gas station for example, would normally cost me at least $800 a month, and that's if he worked only eight hours a day with two days off a week. So if he stole, say, $200 a month plus his regular salary, I'd still be paying him less than $800 a month. So I'm still not losing anything by having him over there. It's only when he starts stealing more than he's worth, that's when I have to draw the line. Carl thinks he's getting away with the money. I know he's stealing over at the pool by not using those tickets, but I've got my eye on him too."

"And me?" Newman asked apprehensively. He didn't know if she considered him a thief or not, but the very thought, he felt, was an insult to the effort and the hard work he had put into this place so far. He wasn't staying here just to steal from her. "Do you think I'm stealing from you?"

"Only you know the answer to that question," she quietly began. Vicki leaned toward him. "I don't think you are, but it really isn't an issue. Your presence here has been invaluable to me." She struggled for the right words. "What I'm trying to say is, I can't place a dollar value on your importance here. Do you understand what I mean? Am I making sense here?"

Newman reclined in his seat, uncertain whether she had called him a thief or not. Somehow though, it didn't seem to matter. The essence of her message came through. He could see that she was genuinely concerned about hurting his feelings, and she anxiously awaited his response.

Newman shook his head and smiled. "Sometimes your logic is amazing."

She smiled with relief and rose from her seat. "Now, if you are through playing accountant, maybe you'll let me have my office back to make a few phone calls. There are people out there still trying to put me in jail, you know."

"Gotcha," he quipped as he rose from the seat. "I've still got to check on the preparations for that Christian Brother hood meeting Friday."

"Ken, I hope you know how sorry I am for scheduling that group here." Vicki sat behind her desk.

"Vicki, what's done is done. Don't worry about it."

"It's just that with a name like Christian Brotherhood…"

"I know. It sounds like a group you'd let your kids join."

"Anything I can do to help?"

"No. Andrew is putting together their sound and public address system. They are bringing their own satellite hookup to tie into some nationwide address to other nice little racist and bigots across the country. So it looks like we have everything covered. I need to meet this Nelson though, to go over banquet arrangements for this group."

"That Andrew is turning into a pretty handy guy to have around," she noted.

"Yea, especially after last night. But then, after Wyatt Earp, even Count Dracula would be a pretty handy guy to have around."

"Anyway, Nelson said he'd be here in time for lunch, so Millie can get some rest. You can meet him then. In fact, he might even be over there right now. He said he'd probably come in a little early to check out the kitchen. I'm sure you'd want to go by and at least introduce yourself."

She pulled some legal papers out of her desk drawer and began scanning through the pages.

"By the way, how is your defense coming?" Newman asked.

"Well, the trial isn't until August, so that gives me a couple of months to get things together. My lawyers say, I've got a good chance to beat this, but like they say, it ain't over 'till it's over."

"If I can be of any help," he offered.

"Thanks, Ken," she smiled. "I may take you up on that."

Newman left her office. Moments later, he was climbing the steps to the restaurant when a voice hailed him. He turned to see John waving and smiling as he approached.

"Say, Ken ole buddy," John smiled, slapping him on the back. Newman forced a restrained, tight-lipped grin. "Have you been by the store lately? Boy, I tell ya, Bea's really whipped that store into tip-top shape and it's ready for business."

"That's great," Newman smiled halfheartedly.

"And when Candy gets outta school for summer recess, she'll be able to work around here doing little odd jobs. I'm sure you can find something for her to do. She's great at gardening, and I noticed the flower beds around here needs a little work."

"I'll see what I can do," Newman replied nonchalantly. "I'm sure there is something around here we can find for her to do." He continued up the steps.

"Ahhhh…," John called after Newman as he climbed the steps behind him, "if she did work around here, I'm sure that would mean extra pay of course. I mean you can't expect the child to work for free, right?" He grinned.

Newman stopped and turned toward him. "Of course not." He smiled blandly. "We'd work something out."

"Of course," John quickly added. "I'm sorry to take up your time trying to get work for my little girl. You must have more important things to attend to. I wouldn't even ask were it just for myself, but I really need it for Candy and especially Bea."

"That's all right, John. I understand."

"I mean running this place is more than a one-man-job. I'm not saying that you're not doing a good job," he quickly added, "because you are. Yes siree, you're one of the best." He smiled. "But… well, I have a master's degree in business administration. I've been a financial advisor to some of the largest corporations in the region and I feel I'd be doing you and Vicki a gross disservice if I didn't offer you the benefit of my expertise. Hell, we can even haggle over an appropriate salary. I'm game."

"I'm sure you are," Newman sarcastically agreed.

"I can't let you Jew me down too much in pay though, but I promise to be reasonable."

Newman was startled by his choice of words. "Jew you down?" He needed clarification.

"Yeah," he readily continued, "I'm more than willing to bargain."

Newman was growing increasingly annoyed with John's presence. His motive for being here was obviously money. But that was Vicki's domain and she held the purse strings, tight.

"Look, I'll talk to Vicki about it, okay? Maybe we can work something out."

"Like they say, you get what you pay for."

"Ain't that the truth," Newman muttered under his breath.

"Say, I'd probably even settle for what you're making," John offered.

"Really?" Newman was a little irritated with John's badgering. "Then that should speed up the negotiations a bit. Because I'm making the same thing you are, $300 a month plus room and board."

John turned his head slightly in disbelief. "Who are you kidding? You mean to say that you're putting in these sixteen-hour days, managing all of these people and busting your ass, all for the same wages she pays everybody else? I don't believe you. But hey, if you don't want to tell me what you're really making, that's fine, but don't pull my leg."

Newman's patience snapped. "Look!" He snarled. "Believe what you want, but I have no reason to lie to you. Now if you'll excuse me, I'm busy." He turned and climbed to the top of the steps when John called to him again. "Now what, John?" He was visibly frustrated, not even bothering to face him.

"If you are telling the truth…" He paused. "If you are telling the truth and you are working for $300 a month, then you're a dammed fool." John started down the steps and headed back toward the general store.

Newman walked into the dining room. The lunchtime crowd of long-haul truckers, bikers, and the occasional spattering of midday tourists had just begun to file in. Newman walked back into the kitchen. He scanned the area. Though no one seemed to be around, the kitchen seemed different. It was neat and well organized, with everything seemingly in its proper place. The pots and pans were arranged in descending rows according to size. The dishes were stacked in neat little towers next to the range. The range itself, usually black with grease and burnt residue, gleamed with a silver sparkle that made it seem almost brand-new. The floors shined. The countertops were spotless. Newman surveyed the area in awe as he ran his finger slowly over the glistening tiled countertop.

"Looks pretty good, huh?"

Newman turned to see the distinguished-looking silver-haired, older man coming through the back door.

"Millie's an okay cook, but her sanitary requirements leave a great deal to be desired." He confidently beamed. "The trash I've thrown out of here this morning alone could fill a very large truck."

"Actually, in her defense, she hasn't always had the proper support staff to work with." Newman walked over to greet him. "I'm…"

"Mr. Newman," he quickly interrupted. "Vicki's told me all about you." They shook hands. "She's very impressed with your work. If you're half as good as she says you are, this place should run very smoothly this summer."

"Well, she's told me a lot about you too. Given your background and your qualifications, we are indeed very lucky to have you."

Nelson stepped into the walk-in freezer and remerged with a side of roast beef. "French dips are the lunch special today. If you get a chance, drop by and try one." He walked over to the prep table and began slicing the meat. Newman strolled over toward him.

"As far as authority goes," Newman began, "I'd like to leave the kitchen in the hands of the chef, especially in your case, considering your background and everything."

"Apparently Vicki hasn't told you how I want things run," he calmly countered, as he continued to slice the side of beef. "So, here are my rules. First, I only cook and prepare meals. I don't clean floors, wipe tables, and I don't do windows." Nelson's tone was tart and direct. "The way you see this place right now is the way I expect you," he pointed at Newman, "to keep it. How you intend to do it, of course, is your business. I also expect you to keep this place adequately staffed. However, if I don't like someone that you've hired, I expect that person to be fired on my command, no questions asked. If I don't like a waitress, either she goes or I go."

Newman was taken aback by his arrogant and abrasive tone. He listened with mounting resentment. "Is… is that all?" He asked sarcastically.

"Hardly. I expect you to keep this place well stocked. When I go to look for an item back in food storage, I expect to find it." He reached into his pocket and handed Newman a slip of paper. "Tell Vicki that's what I'm going to need before the day is out. How she gets it, is between you and her. Oh, and one more thing, the waitresses share their tips with me fifty-fifty. If it weren't for my great food, they wouldn't earn a dime in tips."

Newman shook his head. "I don't know about that one."

"Don't look so shocked, Mr. Newman."

"Disappointed probably is a better choice of words," Newman said emphatically. "Your attitude, especially toward the waitresses, is going to be a problem."

He set the knife to one side and turned to face Newman. "You're right. They probably won't like me. In fact, they'll probably hate me. But, like in the Army, they'll respect me. They'll do their jobs and they'll show up on time, in uniform. They'll share their tips with me because they'll respect me. Like you said, Vicki is damned lucky to have me here. Why? Because I am a class act, and as such, I don't have time to buy supplies, clean floors, hire the help, and all of the other mundane chores associated with operating a restaurant. If I am to concentrate on the world-class meals I am expected to prepare here, I need all those things taken care of prior to my entering this kitchen. The larger operations have special managers to handle those details. In an operation this small, I guess the job is all ours."

"Yeah," Newman huffed, "in addition to the thousand and one other things I have to do here."

Nelson shrugged his shoulders. "Life is tough in the big city, but we master chefs have a saying… if you can't stand the heat, you're probably in the wrong kitchen."

Suddenly, they heard the revved engine of a motorbike, coupled with yelling and screaming coming from the adjacent bar.

"What the hell?" Newman asked.

"Sounds like trouble in the bar, but then, that's not my problem, is it?"

"No," Newman breathed in resignation, "I guess it isn't."

He hurried out of the kitchen and raced into the bar. Once there, he saw a woman in her green Forest Service jumpsuit. It was zipped down to her waist, she was dancing topless in the stage band area, shaking her breasts in time to the jukebox music. Laura, meanwhile, was frantically chasing a man, also wearing a green jumpsuit. He was riding a small dirt bike around the barroom floor. The bare-chested woman looked down at Newman and smiled.

"We're not licensed for that yet, Miss," Newman chided. "Zip it up!"

Meanwhile, the man continued to maneuver the small-framed bike between the empty tables, breaking Laura's grasp each time she managed to grab him.

"Wheeeee!" He gleefully shouted, laughing as Laura continued to chase him.

"Stop, asshole!" Laura angrily demanded.

She looked up and saw Newman as he motioned her to steer the bike toward him. She started shoving tables in his path to block his avenues of escape. Finally, the bike roared directly toward Newman. Newman waited until the bike drew close enough, then pulled a table quickly into its path. The biker jammed the brakes, and the bike came to an abrupt stop. The rider gunned the engine repeatedly as he glared across the table at Newman.

"Okay, Mr. Knievel," Newman began politely, "playtime's over. Get the bike outta here. You can see what you're doing to the wood panels on the floor."

Laura came running over to help. "Boy am I glad you showed up, Ken," she breathed. "This idiot just rode his bike right up the steps and into my bar."

The rider looked over at Laura, then up at Newman. "Get that fuck-in' table outta my way," he scorned.

"If you'll get your fuckin' bike outta my bar," Newman calmly replied.

The rider chuckled. "Your bar?" He stood firm with a smirk on his face. "Since when did they allow niggers to own bars?"

"Probably the same day they let assholes ride dirt bikes," Newman countered. "Now, when I move this table, you're gonna ride out the same way you rode in."

"Really?" He sneered.

He slowly climbed off the bike. He eased around the table and strolled up to Newman. They stared at each other momentarily. The rider tried to move the table. Newman reached down to hold it in place. The rider suddenly turned and fired a blow at Newman's jaw.

"Kenny!" Laura screamed, as Newman staggered back against the counter. The biker rushed over to follow up on his attack, when Laura scrambled across the table to help Newman.

Newman struggled to regain his balance as the biker forcefully grabbed his lapels. He reared back to deliver another punch. Before he could strike another blow, Laura suddenly leaped onto his back and began flailing away wildly on the man with her clenched fist. He struggled to throw her off, but she held on with the tenacity of a bull rider.

Two more smoke jumpers casually entered the bar and caught sight of the wild affray. They immediately rushed over and attempted to pull Laura from the biker's back.

"Break it up!" One of them commanded as they both struggled to pry Laura's beefy arms from around the man's neck. The biker finally broke free as Laura continued to struggle with the two other smoke jumpers.

"Let her go!" Newman shouted. Laura eventually tore free of their grasp.

"What's going on here?"

"Your friend here has mistaken our bar floor for a dirt bike trail," Newman explained.

"Man," the biker protested, "I was just havin' a little fun, when this nigger here tried to…"

"All right, Sid, that's enough!" One of the smoke jumpers immediately interrupted. "Get that thing outta here and take it back to camp."

"Awww, come on, guys," he whined.

"Either you take it back or we will," the other smoke jumper coldly warned.

The biker looked at them both, then over at Newman and Laura. He shook his head dejectedly and muttered an expletive as he stepped back over to his bike. He shoved the table aside, climbed aboard the machine, and kick-started the bike. He gunned the engine several times, then shot out of the front door.

"Sid's really a nice guy," one of the smoke-jumpers explained. "It's only after he gets a little tanked up that he acts like a jerk. We've all just come off the fire line. Most of us are just gonna grab a beer and get some sleep before we have to go back in twelve hours."

"Well, if your friend is any indication of what we can expect from you smoke jumpers, maybe we outta just close the bar until your crew gets back on the line," Newman suggested.

"What's a smoke jumper?" Laura asked.

"They are sort of the Forest Service's answer to the Army's Green Beret," Newman quipped.

"We jump outta perfectly good airplanes into raging forest fires with only a backpack, a pick, and a shovel." Replied the smoke jumper.

"Even so," Newman added. "I'd appreciate it if you could spread the word over there for your friends to behave themselves when you're here in the resort compound."

"Sure," one smoke jumper agreed. "In the meantime, though, can we still get a beer while we're here?"

"I want a drink too." The topless smoke jumper staggered her way to the bar.

"After you put your clothes back on," admonished Newman.

"Of course." Laura smiled. "Have a seat at the counter, and I'll be right with you." All three fully clothed smoke jumpers stepped over to the counter and took a stool. Laura served the smoke jumpers at the bar.

She turned to Newman. "That was quite a spill you took," she was genuinely concerned. "Are you all right?"

"Sure," Newman groaned, feeling the side of his jaw. "I'm fine. But damn Laura, I'm tired of being everybody's punching bag."

"Face it, Ken," Laura quipped. "Mike Tyson you're simply not."

"Maybe, but it seems as if fighting's all I've done since I've been here." Newman walked over behind the counter. He picked up the phone and dialed. "You're right. I'm not a fighter, but maybe I'd better become one..." A voice came over the phone. Andrew? This is Ken... Are you still going to the corral this evening?... Ready when you are my friend."

While Newman was contemplating boxing lessons, John was on a mission. He stepped into the front door of the pool house amid the sound of laughter and splashing water. Carl sat behind the check-in counter, his face buried in a Western paperback. He peeped over the top of the book as John entered.

"Looks like a really tough job you've got here," John grinned sarcastically.

"Look who's talkin'," Carl snickered as he looked back down at his book. "Your old lady does all the work over there while you walk around all day long getting plastered over at the bar."

"Take it easy, huh. I just came over here to look around. Not to start any trouble."

"Don't start none and there won't be none."

John slowly strolled over to the poolside. He watched as shapely bikini-clad females tanned on deck, bobbed in the water, or were chased playfully around the deck by muscle-bound men.

"This is a neat job," John smiled. "Just sit here all day and watch the babes strut their tits and ass."

"Seen one set, you've seen them all," Carl blandly replied.

"Ever try and pick any of them up?"

"What's it to ya?"

"Come on," John calmly explained. "I know I couldn't work here all day without trying to get some sort of hard-on every now and then."

Carl slowly laid his book aside and looked over at John. "Why should you care? You have an old lady and a little girl over at the general store."

"Hey, even a man on a diet can still look at the menu, can't he?"

"Yeah but, are you sure you're even on a diet?" Carl turned his attention toward a dripping wet bikini-clad young woman as she approached the counter.

"Number 14, please." She smiled at both men.

Carl turned and thumbed through the clothes baskets behind him until he came to Number 14. It was filled with clothes, shoes, and other personal items. He picked it up and handed it to the woman. She smiled a little longer at John and disappeared into the women's dressing area.

John's eyes fixed on the woman's twisting rear as she exited. "My, my, my," he sighed. "Now that's what I call an ass. Did you see how she smiled at me?"

"You can forget it, John. Women who look that good aren't interested in pool jockeys or..." he motioned toward John. "Store clerks. Women like that want doctors, lawyers, and people with money."

"What do you mean people with money? Why your mother owns this whole place. You should be the man in charge here. I mean if you were, I'd just bet that the chicks would be all over you just like that." He snapped his fingers. "You've got more right to be calling the shots around here than that nigger your mother hired."

Carl looked at him, expressionless. "Listen," he coldly began, "What happens between me and my mother is none of you damned business, is that clear?"

"Say," John smiled as he walked over toward him, trying to defuse Carl's hostility. "I'm not trying to tell you or your mother how to run this place. It's just that I feel that a family business should stay in the family. All families have problems, but they don't bring in outsiders to run things." He paused. "Or another race."

Another young woman came to the counter asking for her clothes basket. "Here you are Miss." Carl gave it to her and she walked away.

"Maybe she just doesn't trust your management skills," John continued.

"What in the hell are you talking about?"

"Vicki, who else? That's why she doesn't let you run this place, right? She probably doesn't feel you have the proper education. But with my extensive management expertise as, say, your assistant or something, I could help you run this resort like a first-class outfit. Everything done with your approval, of course," John quickly added.

Carl slammed his fist down on the counter. "Damn it, man!" He whirled and angrily confronted John. "I don't know what your game is, fella, but stay outta my business, okay? If I need your help, I'll ask for it."

John quickly backed away. "Okay, okay, I was just trying to help you get back into your place as leader of this resort, but if you don't want to, fine." He stepped away from Carl and headed for the exit. He reached the door just as a beautiful blonde in a highly revealing bathing suit pulled it open. She smiled coyly up at him as she walked past. John's head turned to follow her. He smiled and shook his head. "I'm in love," he swooned. He turned and followed her back into the pool.

As John continued his roaming eyes in the pool area, Newman knew that he had to put his logic of negotiations with rednecks behind him and get with the standards of being a Montana Man, which was battle ready.

Newman's jeep slowly bounced its way over the uneven terrain. He could see Andrew Rides in the distance, his foot resting on the lower rung of the wooden fence, watching the buffalo gallop from one end to the corral to the other. Andrew looked back over his shoulder as Newman pulled to a stop next to him.

"I was just getting ready to leave when you called the gas station. Thought you didn't have any use for fighting."

"Let's just say recent events have forced me to reevaluate my position," Newman quipped as he climbed out of the jeep.

Rides turned his attention back toward the buffalo. "So, that's our Thanksgiving turkey," he sighed.

"Fourth of July turkey would be more accurate," Newman corrected as he pulled a small gym bag from the back of the vehicle.

"What a shame to eat such a magnificent animal. He should be roaming free."

Newman eyed him cautiously. "You're not thinking of letting him loose, are you?" He noted the solid expression of concern on Rides' face.

"Of course not," he bristled. "What made you ask that?"

"Mainly because I had the same idea myself a couple of weeks ago."

"Really?" Rides was surprised. "I had you pegged as being among the first to demand that animal's hide for the Fourth of July."

"Well, as far as I'm concerned, nothing takes the place of good old fashioned beef hamburgers."

Rides chuckled. "You really aren't from Montana, are you?"

"Nope. But then, that's the reason why I'm here, isn't it?"

"I guess, but still, I'd like to know what changed your mind."

"Let's just say, I've been shown the error of my ways and let it go at that, okay?"

"All right then," Rides agreed, stepping away from the fence. "Let's get started."

"Sure." Newman unzipped the shoulder bag. "Let me get into my gym clothes."

Rides stared at him in disbelief. "Gym clothes?"

"Aren't we going to go through some warm-up exercises first? And these are Levi's I have on."

"Sure. And the next time some drunken cowboy wants to separate you from your head, you can ask him to wait until you change into your gym clothes so you don't get your Levi's dirty." He took the bag from Newman and tossed it back into the jeep. "Listen, Ken. You've got to be able to defend yourself anytime, anyplace, and regardless of what you're wearing."

Newman looked over at the gym bag, then back at Rides. "Okay," he sighed dejectedly. "Now what?"

"Imagine I'm an attacker. Watch my eyes. No matter how an aggressor chooses to attack you, he'll begin with some sort of eye movement. Like a blink, a squint… something in his eyes will tell you when he's ready to make his move. When he does, then you make yours. Take a step backward," he illustrated. "You not only can see what he's going to do, but you can also see what you need to do, to counterstrike. Try to go for the groin or the stomach if you're after a quick kill." He crouched as he motioned toward Newman. "Let me show you. Try and punch me."

Newman hesitated. "Are you sure?"

"Go ahead!" Rides insisted. "Try and lay one on me."

"Okay," Newman reluctantly agreed.

He drew back and threw a halfhearted punch at Rides. Rides quickly sidestepped the slow-moving fist, pushed it aside, hooked his foot behind Newman's ankle, and pulled. Newman's legs shot out from under him. He reeled backward and landed with a muffled thud on the moist grass.

He looked up dazed as Rides stared down at him. "What's the big idea?" He complained as he struggled to his feet. "I thought we were only practicing."

"We'll either practice seriously or we won't practice at all," Rides bluntly answered.

Newman looked at him and gingerly shook his head. "Boy something tells me that this is going to be a long evening."

They began again. Newman attacked Rides, Rides countered. Repeating different attack positions, Rides showed Newman how to counter. As the night creeped in, Newman and Rides decided to call it a day.

"Do you need a ride back to the compound?"

"Naw, Ken. I'm going to walk back and enjoy the night air."

"Okay. See ya later."

Newman cranked up the jeep. Minutes later, he was back at the main office. He started up the steps to the office, staggering slightly as he used the hand rail to pull himself up the steps. He started to enter the office when he heard Bea calling him. He paused on the stairway and waited for her.

"Glad I caught you," Bea hailed. "I need to change this hundred for my cash register as soon as you… what happened to you?" She was concerned, as she noticed his soiled, tattered clothes and the bruises on his face.

"Oh, I'm fine," he beamed in pain, down at her. "Andrew was just teaching me a few self-defense techniques, that's all. What can I do for you, Bea?"

"I have no change at all, and I'm about ready to open the store. I'm also in kind of a hurry. Right now, Candy is over there all by herself, and I really don't want to leave her alone too long."

"Tell you what… just give me the hundred and get back to the store. I'll get your change and bring it over to you in just a few minutes."

"Thanks, Ken… oh, by the way, have you seen John? He said he was coming over to talk to you."

"Yeah…" Newman sighed. "We talked earlier. I don't know where he is now, though. But look, Bea," Newman continued compassionately, "if you and John need extra money, I'll talk to Vicki and see what she has to say about a small increase."

Bea looked at him, bewildered. "Extra money? Who said anything about extra money?"

"Well, from the way John talked, I was under the impression you both had decided you needed more money in order to work here."

"Is that what John told you?" Bea seemed baffled.

Newman could see the confusion on her face. "You mean you know nothing about it?"

"Believe me, Ken, John and I never agreed to ask Vicki for more money. I mean, we always can use more money, but I understand Vicki's situation. Maybe I should talk to him. Do you know where he is?"

"I have no idea, Bea. He left a couple of hours earlier. You'll probably find him back at the store."

"Probably," she smiled. "Are you sure you're okay?"

"Thanks. Bea. I'm fine."

She turned and walked away.

Newman headed on into the office. Lisa was on the phone. He could see the expression of concern on her face as she stared at his clothing.

"I'm fine," he whispered. "Is Vicki in?" He motioned toward Vicki's office. Lisa nodded her head. Newman walked back and knocked on the door.

"Come in," Vicki called. Newman pushed the door open. Vicki was on the phone as she beckoned him in. He eased the door shut behind him.

"Thanks... well look, I'll call you back later, okay?... Okay, we will... you too... Bye." Vicki hung up. She glanced up at him. Her mouth opened with surprise. "What happened to you?" She gasped.

"I'm okay, really," he quickly consoled.

"What are you doing to get so dirty... and beat up?"

"Andrew and I have just been practicing a few self-defense moves, that's all."

"Yeah, okay. But you two be careful."

"Of course. By the way, I've met Nelson Adams," he announced blandly.

"And? What did you think?"

"He's a rude, pompous, and an arrogant horse's rear."

"Wait until you see his bad points," she smiled. "But he does know his way around a kitchen."

Newman dug into his pocket, pulled out the slip of paper Chef Nelson Adams had given him, and handed it to her. "This is a little love note to you from His Highness."

She took the paper, scanned it, and smiled. "He knows I'm not going to buy half of the mess on this sheet. So, what he does, is pad the list with so much stuff that he can deal and bargain for what he really wants."

"I see you two have sung this song before."

"Oh, many times," she set the list aside. "He's a decorated Vietnam combat veteran. He commanded a flying horse unit."

"Air cavalry?"

"Something like that, but now he thinks he has to run his kitchen like an Army unit."

"That attitude is going to cause some problems."

"But remember, we need him over there. Besides, I can handle Mr. Adams. I always have."

"Oh, before I forget," Newman dug into his pocket and produced the hundred. "I told Bea that I'd bring her change for this."

"Safe's open." Newman walked behind her to the safe. "How's she working out, anyway?"

"She's a pure gem," Newman noted, counting the cash. "It's that husband of hers that's going to cause us a lot of grief."

"I know. In fact, were it not for that little girl, I would have gotten rid of them both a long time ago. I certainly would have hated to lose her, but don't forget, I was married to an alcoholic before I met Jake. They can drag you right into their living hell and Lord knows, I have enough problems. I don't need any more. Just keep me posted, will you? Like you said, she's a gem and I'd hate to lose her, but…"

"Sure, Vicki."

"Oh Ken, before I forget," She pointed to the brown leather satchel in the corner. "I didn't mean to open your bag, but I just saw it lying there, and I didn't know who it belonged to."

Newman walked over and picked it up. "Oh, this isn't mine. It belongs to that truck driver who got killed here a couple of weeks ago. I pulled it out of the wreckage. His wife is coming by to pick it up any day now."

"You mean it's not your bag?"

"No."

"Good," Vicki sighed. "Boy, I'm relieved. In that case, if I were you, I'd check the contents of that bag before I gave it back to his widow."

"Why? She's his next of kin. She's entitled to all of his belongings."

"Just look through the satchel before you give it to her." She rose from her seat. "I've got to go. You can reach me at my lawyer's office."

"Oh, one more thing. You look beautiful."

"Thanks Ken." She stepped from behind her desk and left the office.

Newman walked around to her chair and pulled the satchel over toward him. He unzipped the bag and lifted the top. Folded men's clothes and a pair of men's shoes were stuffed into the inside pockets. He removed the clothes and saw a few toilet articles and a thick brown envelope. He pulled out the envelope and removed the photographs and letters inside. One photo showed Baddeley dressed in black leather. His hands were bound behind his back, as a woman, also dressed in black leather, held a whip under his nose. Newman stared at the picture in amazement. He examined the next photo. Baddeley was chained nude to a bedpost with the same woman straddling him with a studded leather whip in her hand. Newman stuffed the photo back into the envelope, pulled out the letters, and read them. The letters told of the affection he had for the woman in the photos. He talked of how dull and boring his wife was and how he looked forward to his long road trips to get away from his family. He spoke of how these bondage sessions were the center of his life. He folded the letters, put them back in the envelope, and placed the clothes and the envelope back in the satchel. He closed the bag and set it beside the desk. Newman leaned back in the chair and thought. Did his wife deserve to know the truth about her late husband? Did she already know? And if she didn't know, did he have the right to withhold this information from her?

The intercom light flashed. Newman pushed the button. "Yes, Lisa?"

"Mr. George Peoples, Christian Brotherhood, on the line."

"Just what I need right now," Newman sighed quietly. "Thanks, Lisa, I'll take it." He cleared his throat and picked up the receiver. "Mr. Peoples, how can I help you?" Newman beamed as a voice came over the phone. "Yes, we know your meeting is coming up and everything will be ready. I'm personally seeing to it… Yes, I'm sure it will be your best one ever… no, I don't think meeting with you right now is such a good idea. I'm really busy… No… I don't think I can tell you everything

I'd like to right now… early Friday morning certainly is a much better time… yes. I look forward to meeting you too. It should be a memorable experience for the both of us… bye."

Newman hung up the phone. "Yes," he said to himself. "It should be a meeting neither of us will ever forget."

CHAPTER

8

*B*ud Ridby sat hunched over the lunch counter, scarfing down the few remaining green peas on his plate. He looked up as Barbara casually strolled behind the counter, coffeepot in hand, pausing to freshen an occasional cup.

"Hey, Barb," Bud called, shoving his plate toward her, "that was pretty darned good. Get over here and gimme another helping of peas?"

She stopped and glared over at him. "Is that as polite as you can ask?"

"Oh, come on," Bud sighed. "You're the waitress, ain't ya? Ain't gettin' my food your job?"

"For customers who know how to ask politely? Yes, it is my job."

The trucker sitting across from her gingerly dabbed his mouth with a napkin and smiled. "Well, miss," he beamed, "that was the best danged meal I've had in nine days on the road." He dug into his pocket, pulled out a ten, and handed it to her. "Keep the change. Your service was outstanding." Nelson watched the transaction from the kitchen window as the trucker eased off the stool and headed out the door.

"Thank you," Barbara smiled. She started for the register as she glanced over at Bud. "You see. Some people know how to treat a waitress." She rang up the sale and started to place the difference into her smock pocket when Nelson called to her. She looked back over her shoulder at him.

"Aren't you forgetting something, Barbara?" questioned Nelson.

She hesitated. "No," she replied. "Nothing that I can think of."

"Obviously you haven't talked to Ken since I've been here."

"What was he supposed to tell me?" quizzed Barbara.

"I require all of my waitresses to share their tips with me, fifty-fifty."

She shoved in the drawer and slowly turned to face him. "YOUR waitresses?… Require?" Barbara snarled, her hand resting indignantly on her hip.

"Listen!" Nelson sternly began. "Were it not for my excellent food, you wouldn't be getting one red cent in tips. And since I'm doing the cooking, I also deserve some of the money."

"I've worked as a waitress for more than eight years," she bristled, "and I've never met a cook so cheap, that he'd actually try and steal from the waitresses he works with."

"Chef, my dear," Nelson quickly corrected. "Chef. There is a huge difference. Secondly, you don't work with me, you work for me. And as such, you are subject to my rules as long as you are in this kitchen."

"Say," Bud casually interrupted, "don't be so rough on the young lady, eh? She's the best waitress you've got." Barbara glanced over at him, surprised by his sudden, unexpected praise.

"She is the best waitress I've got," Nelson agreed. "That's what worries me."

"What in hell is that supposed to mean?" She was visibly angry over the comment.

The sparsely occupied dining room glanced in their direction.

"Keep your voice down!" Nelson insisted. "You're making a scene."

"I'm making a scene!" She continued in her raised voice. "You stand there, try to rob and insult me, then you accuse me of making a scene?"

"Now calm down, Barbara," Bud consoled. "I'm sure Nelson didn't mean…"

"And just who are you to say what I did and did not mean?" Nelson bitterly interrupted. "If there's one thing I am, it's a man of my word."

Bud slowly eased off his stool. "Why you overstuffed, arrogant jackass. Just who the hell do you think you are?"

"Chef Nelson Adams," he announced proudly, stressing the word *Chef.*

"Well, somebody outta teach you a little manners," Bud sneered as he stepped behind the counter and started for the kitchen.

Barbara rushed over to Bud and held him back. "No, Bud!" She started pushing him away from the kitchen door. "I've got a better idea." She untied her apron and flung it back into Nelson's face. "You can handle today's lunch rush without this terrible waitress." She cupped her arm under Bud's and ushered him out of the dining room. "Thank you for sticking up for me," she smiled up at him.

"Anything for a pretty lady."

Nelson ripped the apron from his face and threw it to the floor.

"You're fired!" He bitterly shouted. "You hear me? You're fired!"

Barbara and Bud strolled casually into the bar ignoring Nelson.

As Bud and Barbara relieved their frustrations by walking away from Nelson, Lisa is just beginning hers with her estranged lover. Lisa sat at her typewriter, staring at the half-finished page in the carriage in front of her.

"Well," the gruff voice behind her barked impatiently. She wheeled to face Snake as he leaned ominously over her shoulder.

"I just don't know," she hesitantly insisted.

"What's there not to know?" Snake's voice was harsh. "You do all of her books and count all of her cash. If you juggle the books right, she'll never miss a couple of hundred here and there."

"Vicki's no fool," Lisa pleaded. "What if she catches me? I'll be fired, and then what? How will I ever get another job? She's been my employer since I was sixteen. I'll always have to use Vicki as a reference, and who'd hire a thief?"

"Damn it, Lisa!" Snake angrily snarled, pounding the desk. Suddenly, he paused, trying to regain his composure. She trembled. "Look, babe," he calmly continued, "you know we need the bread. That little she's paying you just ain't enough. You know I'd go back to work if I could, but my back still hurts from that accident. You wouldn't want me to go back up on that hill too soon and injure myself for good. Would you?"

Lisa shook her head meekly. "No."

"Well then. Take the money. Everybody else is. Hell Lisa, you don't think all of these people are content with their $300 a month, do you?" Lisa opened her mouth to say something, but Snake interrupted her.

"You don't think that nigger is busting his ass around here for no $300 a month, do you?"

"I make out the payroll," she quietly interrupted, "and his paycheck is the same as everybody else's."

"I'll bet," Snake huffed. "If it is, then I'll bet he's getting' his palm greased under the table. No matter. Either way, it ain't helpin' us none. Now you've been here for more than two years, and you deserve a raise… one way or another."

Lisa felt torn and distressed. Should she steal for the man she loved? What would happen to their relationship if she didn't? Snake was the only man she had ever loved, and while the relationship did have its problems, it was better than being alone.

"Well?" He seemed impatiently. She hesitated, then smiled at him.

"For you, darling," Lisa reluctantly conceded. "But not now. I have to wait for the right time."

"It's for us," Snake quickly corrected. "But don't take too long. Like they say," he smiled down at her. "Time is money."

The front door swung open. They both looked up as Vicki walked in.

"Snake!" She greeted, surprised to see him in the office. "How are you today?"

"Oh just fine, Vicki, and yourself?"

"I've had better days, and I've had worse too, so I'm not complaining. How's your back?"

"Still giving me trouble, but you know me."

"Indeed I do," she smiled a somber, tight-lipped smile. "Indeed I do." She turned toward Lisa. "Have you seen Kenny? I just came from the restaurant, and there's a problem over there between Nelson and Barbara he needs to look into."

"The last I heard, he was over at the corral with Andrew. Today Kenny said Andrew was going to teach him how to use a shotgun."

"A shotgun? First he's been giving Kenny fighting lessons for the past several weeks, and now he's teaching him how to use a shotgun?" Vicki expressed disbelief in Kenny's actions toward violence.

"I suppose." Suddenly, the boom of what seemed like distant thunder echoed through the office.

Vicki sighed. "Oh well. When in Montana… Tell him I'd like to see him---that is, if he's still in one piece when he gets back from over there. And I'm also expecting my attorneys in a couple of minutes. Just send them on back, will you?" She headed back to her office.

"Certainly, Vicki." Lisa smiled, looking up at Snake. He leaned forward and kissed her cheek.

Suddenly, another blast echoed through the air. As Vicki entered her office, she hoped Newman wouldn't shoot himself in foot. His diligent services around the grounds were priceless to her. Moments later, another blast and Vicki just sighed.

Rides held the weapon at waist level and squeezed the trigger. The shotgun recoiled violently as the blast again echoed throughout the grounds, but Rides held the weapon steady. He glanced over at Newman.

"The key," he casually explained, "is a steady grip and a controlled squeeze." He handed Newman the shotgun. "Remember, the pump loads the chamber, then squeeze, don't pull the trigger."

Newman took the weapon and cradled it firmly, but tentatively against his waist. "Like this?"

"Now just point it toward the mountain and slowly squeeze the trigger."

Newman pointed the shotgun toward a distant mountain and slowly pulled the trigger. It boomed. The recoiled yanked the weapon from his grip. Rides frantically dove for cover as the shotgun flew out of Newman's hand and landed on the ground a few feet behind him. Newman slowly glance down at Rides, who stared up at him, horrified. Newman looked back at the weapon lying on the ground, then down at Rides.

"I'm probably gonna need a little more practice, eh?" He said meekly.

"That's an understatement, Ken." Rides slowly dusted himself off as he got up from the ground. "I've got plenty of shells. Let's began again."

Rides had Newman practice for hours firing that shotgun.

"Look Rides, my fingers are getting sore. Can we do something else?"

"Of course, stay right there."

Rides left Newman sitting on the fence as he went to the stables. A few minutes later Rides rode up to him. He climbed down off the horse and walked over to Newman.

"This is one of the milder horses. If you're going to be a Montana Man we need to go all the way. Have you ever been on a horse before?"

"Piece of cake. I've seen how the cowboys do it on television." Newman boldly jumped off the fence and grabbed the reins of the horse and hoisted himself into the saddle. He sat there momentarily, trying to get the feel of sitting straddle the fidgeting, uneasy animal.

Rides stood next to the horse, holding the reins. "Now this is not a car," he sternly warned. "This is a living, breathing creature with feelings, sensitivities, and emotions. It can sense when you're not in control, and instead of you taking it for a ride, it will take you for one. Now hold the reins tight… Just like that… good. Now, to make it go left or right, just gently pull his head in the direction that you want him to go. To stop, just pull the reins straight back."

Newman looked down at him uncertain. "Ahhhh… How do you start it?"

"Just give him a gentle nudge in his side with your heels, okay? Now let's go for a brief ride. Just a few feet, and come back to me. Remember, just a gentle nudge in his side with your heels."

Newman gently nudged the horse. "Giddy up!" The horse didn't move. Newman tried again, but still the horse merely turned his head and looked aback at Rides.

"He's got a thick hide, Ken. You've got to nudge him a little harder to get his attention."

Newman forcefully jammed his heels into the animal's side. The horse suddenly reared, breaking free of Rides' grasp and bolted. Newman screamed. He clutched the reins with a vise grip as the animal fiercely galloped across the pasture.

"Not that hard," Rides quietly breathed. "Hang on, Ken!"

Rides ran after the horse and Newman, hoping he would reach them both before either one of them got hurt.

While Newman struggles with his daily practice of being a Montana Man, Bea is maintaining a busy general store. Bea placed the loaf of bread gently into the grocery bag. The man handed her a dollar bill. She rang the sale and handed him his change.

"Thank you." The elderly man smiled as he picked up his groceries. "You know, I must say, this is the cleanest I've ever seen this store. Me and the Mrs. pass through here every year on our way to see the grandkids. And this store usually looks so bad, I'm afraid to buy the few goods that you do have in here---that is, when there's actually something in here to buy. Needless to say, I'm impressed."

"Thank you," Bea smiled coyly.

"Lots of hard work. I can tell."

"You can say that again. Thank you and please stop by again."

"You can bet I will."

The man left the store just as Candy entered. She was followed by a well-dressed elderly woman with a broad friendly smile.

"Mommy!" Candy beamed as she enthusiastically darted around the counter and leaped into Bea's arms.

"Sweetheart!" Bea smiled as she scooped the child up in her arms. "How was the last day of school?"

"Great!" She smiled, holding onto Bea's neck. "We let these balloons go, and they went waaay up in the air."

"Sounds like you had a lot of fun, but how did you get home so soon? The school bus isn't due for another forty-five minutes."

The elderly woman stepped forward. "I brought her home," she said in a business-like tone of voice. "I'm Mrs. Hendricks, Candy's teacher."

Bea shook her hand. "I'm sorry." Bea blushed. "I was just so happy to see Candy that I just didn't see you standing there. I'm Beatrice, Candy's mother."

"Pleasure to meet you."

"Thank you for bringing her home, but she could have caught the bus just like she does every school day."

"Oh, it was the last day of school, and I was headed up here anyway. Besides, I wanted to meet you."

Bea was somewhat taken aback by her request. "Really? Why?" She slowly eased Candy to the floor. "Candy talks of you in such glowing terms, that you're almost a legend in class."

Bea chuckled. "Oh, you know how children are." She reached down and playfully touched Candy's nose. "Go wash up. Dinner will be ready in a few minutes." Candy trotted off into the backroom.

"I'd like to talk to you about Candy," Mrs. Hendricks solemnly continued.

"Candy?" Bea grew concerned. "What about her? Is she all right?"

"Oh she's fine. She's a bright, smart, an energetic child who has a wonderful academic future ahead of her."

"Then what's the problem?" probed Bea.

Mrs. Hendricks hesitated. "You see, I've been teaching in this system for over ten years, and I've seen a lot of kids come and go. I know what life is like for the parents who live up here in these resorts and logging camps. They come for the logging work or tourist season, then as soon as the work is done, they leave to relocate wherever the next job is. I understand that. But, I also understand the terrible toll this constant relocating takes on the children. They are afraid to form new friendships because they know they might have to leave the very next day. Or, they don't really care about their schoolwork because they figure they'll be gone before the teacher has to give them their first test. In fact, I've come to accept that as part of working in the school system here. That is, until I saw your daughter. Her enthusiasm, energy, and willingness to make new friends is something I haven't seen in my class for a long time. She hasn't just been biding her time, waiting for the summer recess, and not caring about her work. She threw herself into her studies and finished the year with outstanding grades."

Bea smiled. "She always has been a very bright child, but still, Mrs. Hendricks, I fail to see the problem."

"With this being the last day of school, I came by to see if you and your husband were planning to stay in the area for a while. At least, hopefully, you'll stay until the end of the fall semester. Your daughter has made a lot of new friends, and I'd like to urge you to enroll her in a good school wherever you go. Like that commercial says, 'A mind is a terrible thing to waste.' But in Candy's case, it would be a total disaster."

Bea was silent. She had never before heard any of Candy's teachers speak about her in such glowing terms. She now realized that Candy had come through the family's personal crisis a relatively healthy child.

She smiled, mainly to herself, for the job she had done in shielding Candy from John's drinking problems and basically holding her family together.

"Can I get you a cup of coffee, Mrs. Hendricks?"

"No, thank you. I have to be getting back." She started for the door. "Besides, I'm not used to coming up those winding roads. Going back down should be a bit easier."

"Well, don't be a stranger this summer. Bring the family up to swim or something. As a matter of fact, the Fourth of July Rodeo is this summer. Please try to make it."

"I will. That sounds like fun," Mrs. Hendricks spoke as she left.

John stepped through the front door just as Mrs. Hendricks was leaving. "How's business so far today, honey?" He nonchalantly asked, as he walked over to the cooler and popped the top on a can of soda.

"Great, babe!" Bea proudly beamed. "And the nicest thing just happened. Candy's teacher made a special trip up here to bring her home and tell us what a wonderful student she's been."

John pulled the can down from his lips. "Really? Was she selling anything like tickets to a raffle or ball or something, because if she was, I hope you had the sense to tell her *no*? We need all of the money we can get. We don't have a dime to waste on some backwoods country hoedown."

Bea's elation was soured by John's cynical assessment of Mrs. Hendricks's visit. "No, honey," she somberly began, "she just wanted to tell us what a great little girl we have and how she'd like us to reenroll her in school here this fall."

"Here?" John bristled. "Fat chance! Next semester, she's going to go to a school where the children lean more than how to chop down trees and slop pigs."

Bea could see that their differing view of Mrs. Hendricks's visit would only lead to a fight, and at this point, pressing the issue wasn't really necessary.

"Yes, dear," she quietly agreed.

"Good. Now that school is out, I want to get her started on some chores around here. She's old enough now to help earn her keep. This ain't like the good ole days when Daddy had all of the money, you know."

"Of course, dear." The doorbell tinkled, and Bea forced a smile to greet an incoming customer.

While Bea continued managing the store and dealing with her husband's depressing attitude. Vicki was continuing her quest to stay in control of her resort.

Vicki sat at her desk, carefully examining the papers in front of her. The two well-dressed men sitting across from her quietly observed as her finger carefully followed the numbered lines down the side of the typed legal paper.

"That's essentially the government's case," one of the men noted, pointing toward the sheet. "Basically, the most damning piece of evidence against you is the fact that the plates were stored in your safe. Were it not for that, they probably wouldn't even have a case."

"I never lock it," Vicki insisted, as she continued to read the page, "because I can never remember the combination."

"Be that as it may, they seem to feel that most people, even if they know nothing at all, know what's being kept in their own safe. And if you knew about the plates, then you had to have known about your son's counterfeiting operation."

"That's why this whole thing boils down to a question of credibility," the other man interjected. "Can the government convince a jury that you are a scheming, cold-blooded woman, capable of not only conspiring to counterfeit $5 million, but also, to kill a government witness as well as her own son?"

"Or can we convince them that you are a struggling businesswoman who simply relied too much on her own greedy son?" The other man interjected.

"That's why that list of character witnesses is so important. How about that Negro? Have you asked him yet, if he'll take the stand in your behalf?"

Vicki looked up from the paper. "No, I haven't asked him, although he did indicate that he might be willing to help."

"Then what are you waiting for?" One of the lawyers impatiently insisted. "Your trial is only two months away."

"I just don't see what possible impact his testimony could have in the matter. He wasn't even here."

"It doesn't matter when he got here. The point is, would a counterfeiter and a cold-blooded killer have the sense of fair play to hire a Black manager, especially up here in the logging hills of Montana? Your commitment to equal rights, fair play, and all of that good stuff just might win you some credibility points with the jurors."

"So you're saying I should use Kenny's color as part of my defense."

"I'm saying we are going to use every weapon at our disposal to keep you out of jail. We're pulling out all of the stops."

Vicki was momentarily quiet. "Can I think about it?"

"Don't take too long. We've got to make our list of names available to the prosecution so they can prepare their cross-examination."

"You know, Vicki," the other attorney quietly suggested, "we can always plea bargain. I know all of this hasn't been cheap for you, and a plea bargain would end the whole process. You might have to spend some time in jail, but again, we can haggle over something we all could live with."

Vicki became visibly angry. "Really, Mr. Ansell? And how much time can WE all live with? Are you going to volunteer to serve some of my time for me? Will you run my resort for me while I'm in the joint, huh? Don't worry about my bank account. Just keep me outta jail! That's all you're being paid to do!"

"That's what I'm trying to do!" Ansell huffed. "We're on the same side remember?"

Vicki noted the irritation in his voice. She suddenly felt a little remorseful about snapping at him. He was only trying to do the job she was paying him to do, but dragging Ken into her legal problems wasn't something that she relished doing, despite his offer of total assistance. She wasn't sure how long he would stay, if he were drawn deeper into her legal quagmire.

"Think about what I said," Ansell calmly suggested, as he pushed himself up from his chair. The other lawyer followed. "But remember, Vicki, you're in a dogfight, and in a dogfight you might have to do something you don't like to do. You can always express your regret after you've been found innocent." They grabbed their briefcases and walked out the door.

She had turned her attention back toward the legal papers on her desk when Newman poked his head in. She looked up at him.

"I didn't want to interrupt while you had company. Let me go change clothes first, and I'll come right back and help you with those kitchen supply estimates."

"Never mind those estimates, Ken. There's a problem over at the…" She froze in disbelief at the sight of his appearance. His clothes were soiled and torn, his right eye had almost swollen shut, and he had a rather large Band-Aid stuck to the bottom of his chin. "What happened to you?" She was in horror as she rose from her seat and made her way over to him.

"Oh, it's nothing," he consoled, downplaying the extent of his injuries. "I'll live. I was just practicing a few more self-defense moves with Andrew, that's all."

"Are you sure that's all?"

"Well," Newman hedged. "I also tried to sorta ride his horse."

"What horse?"

"You know, the one with the black spots."

"Charger?" Vicki was in disbelief. "He's the most difficult animal in the stable."

"Don't I know it," Newman nodded in agreement.

She sighed in frustration. "All right, but don't let Andrew get you killed out there. I know I'm not your mother, but I do worry about you, you know."

"You were starting to say something about a problem. What kind of problem?"

"Yeah." She made her way back to her desk. "There's trouble in the kitchen. Either Nelson fired Barbara or Barbara walked out on him—the story changes depending on who you talk to. The bottom line is that I can't afford to lose either of them."

"I knew Nelson's abrasive attitude was going to cause problems."

"Hopefully, being the diplomat that you are…"

"I'll go over there and see what I can do." He quickly interrupted.

Newman turned to leave when she called him. He turned to face her. Her lips formed to speak, but the words wouldn't come. She hesitated.

"Nothing," she quickly dismissed. "It's not important."

"You sure?"

"Positive. Go work wonders in the kitchen."

As Newman left, she wondered if Newman's testimony was really that 'do or die' to her case. Though she didn't want to admit it, asking Newman to be a character witness, just might mean the difference between freedom and jail.

Newman hurried back to his room, changed clothes, and headed for the restaurant. He knew discovering what actually happened in the kitchen was going to be difficult at best. With Nelson's inflated ego, everything was obviously going to be Barbara's fault. Newman clearly remembered Nelson's initial instructions that if he didn't like a waitress, she was to be fired, no questions asked. But Barbara was too valuable a waitress to fire. And even if he did manage to persuade Nelson to continue working with her, would she want to work with him? He could hardly wait to talk to either of them.

He stepped into the dining room. The evening crowd of smoke jumpers and other patrons had packed the tables to capacity.

Newman saw Millie behind the kitchen window placing orders on the ledge. Kimberly and Angela meandered between the tables with trays of food balanced on their open palms. He heard the familiar ding of the kitchen bell.

"Order Up!" Millie shouted.

"Millie? What are you doing here? Where's Nelson?"

"What happened to your face? You haven't been slipping on the poolside again, have you?"

"I'm fine. Where's Nelson?"

"Try the bar?" She snidely remarked. "That's his home away from home."

"The bar? Now?" Newman was in disbelief.

"Yes. He said the incident today with Barbara so stressed him out, he needed the afternoon off." Millie took another hard look at

Newman's swollen eye and the Band-Aid on his chin. "Do you want me to get you some ice?"

"It's nothing. You said the bar. I've got to talk to him."

Millie chuckled. "If he can talk. He's been drinking for the last couple of hours, and by now that drunken bum is probably flat on his face."

"Drunken bum? Who? Nelson?" Newman was surprised. "He seems so accomplished."

"You mean you don't know? Boy." Millie chuckled. "Where have you been?" She asked rhetorically. "Why do you think he can't keep a job at any of those fancy places he's worked for? He'd show up for work plastered out of his skull—that is, if he shows up at all. So they'd fire him. Then, Vicki would hire him back until he was able to find some other hotel that didn't know he lived in a bottle. He'd work there until he'd booze his way out of that job and end up right back here again. His story is like a broken record."

Newman shook his head in dejection. "We still need him around here though. I'll go see if I can pry him loose from his bottle." He turned and left.

"Good luck," Millie sarcastically called after him. "Better men have tried."

The slow twang of country music ebbed from the bar. Embraced couples packed the dance floor, slow dancing. Newman scanned the crowd for Nelson. Among the Stetson cowboys and girls in tight blue jeans and Western boots, he saw Bud and Barbara romantically entwined on the dance floor. He held her tightly as her head rested gently on his chest. He thought about how quickly Tim became a faded memory or perhaps being with someone else could help relieve the pain she was fighting so hard to suppress.

Newman excused a path through the maze of couples and made his way over to them. He tapped Bud on the shoulder. Bud looked back at him.

"Have either of you seen Nelson?" Newman shouted, trying to be heard over the music.

"Kenny, ole boy!" Bud grinned. "I didn't figure you for a country music fan... say, what happened to your eye?"

"It's a long story. I'm looking for Nelson. Have you seen him?"

Barbara looked up from Bud's chest. "That overstuffed lard head?"

"I know what he looks like. I just want to know if you've seen him."

"He's over there." Barbara said, pointing toward a corner table.

Newman followed the direction of her finger. He saw Nelson sitting alone in the corner with a half-empty bottle of Seagram's positioned in the middle of the table. He slowly rolled a small whiskey glass in both hands. He wobbled slightly as if he was going to fall out of his chair, only managing to right himself at the very last second. He didn't even notice Newman as he pulled up the chair across from him.

"Nelson!" He didn't respond. "Nelson!" Newman shouted louder. He reached across the table, grabbed and shook his hand.

Nelson slowly looked up at Newman. A slow broad drunken grin dawned his face. "I know you," he slurred, his head weaving slightly. He pointed his finger at Newman, "You're that super colored man that's going to turn this place into a woooonderful resort again."

"Nelson, you've had enough for one day. You've got to get up in the morning for breakfast."

"Enough?" He angrily insisted. He jerked his hand away. "Why, I haven't even started." He grabbed the bottle and poured another drink. Newman quickly rose from his chair, stepped over, and snatched the drink from Nelson's hand. "Hey! What sha doing?"

"You've had enough!" Newman slammed the glass down on the table. He grabbed Nelson's arm and pulled him up from his seat. "We're going home." He commanded, his voice straining under Nelson's weight. He struggled as he marched Nelson through the crowd and out the door.

Newman thought the cool brisk air of the night might help clear his senses. It was a long, cumbersome walk back to Nelson's cabin. Newman fumbled through Nelson's pockets until he found his cabin keys and opened the door. He guided Nelson into the living room, over to the sofa, and eased him down onto the tattered, sagging cushions. He looked around for the kitchen. Maybe he could find some coffee. The quaint cabin was modestly furnished. Above the fireplace was a photo portrait of an extremely attractive young woman with striking oriental features. Below the portrait were various military medals, all strategically placed along the mantel. He stepped into the dark ill-kept kitchen. The dishes apparently hadn't been washed in weeks and were stacked haphazardly in the sink. Empty beer cans littered the floor near the base of the trash can. Both cupboards were practically empty, and the only thing in the refrigerator was a twelve-pack of Rainer. On the counter sat a bowl of soggy old cereal soaking in stale beer. "Breakfast of champions," Newman muttered. He walked back into the living room. Nelson had passed out on the sofa. Newman folded his arms across his chest and walked out.

Newman went back to the restaurant to ensure the continuous flow of food and service was being provided to the customers. Millie had everything under control and the waitresses were handling the modest crowd with ease. Newman decided to go back to the main office to see if Vicki needed anything further from him as the evening was late.

When he entered the main office, no one was at the receptionist desk. Vicki's office door was slightly ajar. He knocked and pushed the door open gently. Lisa sat at Vicki's desk with several stacks of dollar bills scattered in neat little piles in front of her.

"Lisa." Surprised to see her there. He entered the room.

Startled to see Newman at the door, "Kenny! What are you doing here?"

"I thought you had gone home for the evening. I was looking for Vicki to see if she needed me for anything else. I know it's just midnight, but, I am going to call it a night, if she doesn't need me." He noticed the piles of bills stacked on the desk in hundreds, fifties, twenties and more.

"She is over at the bar and I told her I would help her close out the books for tonight."

Thinking nothing of the situation, as Vicki has probably done this many times before, leaving Lisa to close out the books.

"I didn't go in the bar. I guess I just missed her, because I was just at the restaurant. Well, if anyone needs me, I will be in my room."

"Thanks Ken, if anyone is looking for you before I leave, I will let them know. Oh, and you should put some ice on that eye. It doesn't look too good."

"Thanks Lisa, I will."

Newman turned and left the office. She hurriedly thumbed through the bills, scribbled some figures in a nearby ledger, set one stack aside, and picked up another stack of bills.

A couple of hours later, almost 3 a.m, Vicki entered the office carrying a large money bag and set it on her desk. "That's from the bar and the restaurant tonight Lisa." Vicki beamed. "Those smoke jumpers are really making a positive impact on our sales. I'll hate to see them go."

"Ken said they're like a herd of invading locusts taking up everything from the regular tourists." Added Lisa.

"Well as long as they pay, who really cares? Thanks for staying behind and counting this for me." Vicki checked her watch. "Boy, I didn't realize how late it was. I don't think I could stay awake another minute. Are you going to be able to get home tonight?"

"Yes. Snake's coming by later to pick me up. You just go on back and get some sleep. I'll have this all counted and ready for the regular morning deposit."

"Thanks, Lisa. Goodnight." Vicki headed into the back bedroom.

Lisa waited until she heard the bedroom door close. She got up from her chair and peeped down the corridor to make sure that Vicki's bedroom door was indeed shut. She then hurried back over to her desk and pulled out a stack of blank invoices. She had rolled one into the typewriter when the phone rang. She snatched it up. Lisa responded to the voice on the other end of the phone.

"She just went to bed. You might have woken her up." She quietly scolded. She peeped down the hall to see if Vicki's door was still closed. It was. "Of course, I'm waiting until she goes to bed. Whatta you think, I'm stupid?… Sorry, dear." Lisa's tone quickly became apologetic. "It's just that Vicki's been very good to me… you, dear, you know I'd choose you over my loyalty to her… Yes, dear. I remember how you showed me how to make false invoices… I'll have the cash with me tonight… Yes dear… pick me up in an hour… I love you too… bye." She slowly hung up the phone and eased into her seat. She stared at the invoice form in the typewriter carriage. She cleared her throat, sat erect in her chair, brushed tears from her eyes and started typing.

As Lisa contemplated her theft with serious remorse, Newman lay sprawled across his bed, sound asleep. Though he usually didn't get to bed until after the bar closed at two in the morning, Vicki had offered to stay up tonight and collect the closing receipts so he could try and get eight hours of sleep for the first time in weeks. He was in the process of rolling over when suddenly a frantic rapping at his door forced his eyes to flutter open.

"What… wha..tha… What is it?" He feebly called, still partially asleep.

"Ken! It's me, Barbara. We need you in the kitchen!"

Newman slowly sat upright and rubbed the sleep from his eyes. "Whatever it is, can't Nelson handle it?" He looked at his watch. "It's five in the morning."

"That's just it," Barbara pleaded. "Nelson isn't in the kitchen. He's in his cabin. I tried to wake him up, but he's too hung-over to work. I even tried to get Millie in here, but she closed last night and said she's too tired to cook breakfast this morning." Her voice was near panic. "The smoke jumpers, the loggers, and the truck drivers are all lining up outside, waiting for us to open at 5:30. What are we going to do?"

Newman yawned, slowly rolled his legs out of bed and wiped his eyes with the palm of his hand. He yelled through the door, "You head on back." He moaned. "Give me a few minutes to get dressed. I'll be right there."

"Hurry!" Barbara called. He heard her footsteps as she turned and scampered back down the steps.

Minutes later, he had thrown on some clothes and made his way over to the restaurant. He could see the small crowd gathering at the front steps. Some were engaged in small talk and many impatiently checking their watches, anxiously awaiting the 5:30 mark. Newman stepped through the back door into the kitchen. Barbara rushed over to greet him.

"Oh thank God you're here," she sighed. "What are you going to do?"

"Me? Whaddya mean me? I don't know the first thing about the kitchen." He walked over to the dining room window and peeped through the drawn curtains. The crowd outside was gradually increasing with each passing minute. "What did Nelson say to you this morning?"

"It wasn't a matter of what he said. He just came to the door and more or less moaned something about a hangover and went back inside."

"And Millie?"

"She said she can't make it in this early in the morning, after she finished cleaning up. She didn't get to bed until after three."

Newman was at a total loss. Nelson couldn't function in his condition, even if he did show up. Millie was out of the question and he didn't know the first thing about cooking. The only other option he had was to close the restaurant and wait until either Millie woke up or Nelson sobered up. He walked over to the phone.

"Who are you calling?" Barbara asked.

"Vicki. I'm going to tell her that we are cancelling breakfast this morning."

He held the phone to his ear and waited. A deep, gruff voice answered. "Hello."

"Ahhh… Jake… Is Vicki there?"

"She's asleep."

"Well, tell her that I'm going to have to cancel breakfast this morning."

"What on Earth for?" Jake was angry.

"We don't have anyone here, awake enough or sober enough to cook it."

"Where's Adams?"

"He's hung over."

The phone was silent briefly. "That drunken bum," Jake muttered under his breath. "Look Ken, I can't send those boys up on the hill without some food on their bellies. How about Millie?"

"She closed last night."

"Damn it!" Jake sighed. "Ken, I'd come over myself, but I've got to get up on the hill this morning. So, it looks like you've got to take over."

"Me?" Newman whined. Aghast. "Jake. I don't know the first thing about cooking, especially for this many people." He picked up a menu. "Some of this stuff, like a Denver omelet and a cheese quiche, I've never even seen before, let alone cooked."

"You can fry bacon and some eggs. Barbara knows how to brew the coffee. And the toaster is simple enough to operate. Just put the bread in and tap the button."

"So?" cried Newman.

"Well, that's the breakfast menu for this morning. Give them scrambled eggs, bacon, sausage, toast, and coffee." Answered Jake.

"What if they order something I can't make?"

"Then we are fresh out of it. Tell'em we are expecting another shipment in tomorrow."

Newman thought for a moment. "I don't know, Jake. Some of these guys aren't going to like this."

"Then tell'em there are three McDonald's forty-five miles up the road in Missoula. Now, will you at least give it a try?"

Newman sighed in resignation. "I suppose so." He hesitantly agreed.

"Good. See you in a few minutes."

Newman hung up the phone.

"Well?" Barbara asked curiously.

"Start some coffee brewing. I'll see what I can do about finding out where everything is back there." He motioned toward the kitchen. "You're now looking at Chef Newman, who's about to unleash his cooking on the world."

"You're kidding," Barbara smiled. "You don't know the first thing about cooking."

"Barbara, I wish I were kidding. Our menu this morning is limited to scrambled eggs, toast, and sausage only."

He hurried back into the kitchen, while Barbara scampered behind the counter and began filling the coffee urn.

Newman had seen the kitchen many times before, but now it looked more like a culinary jungle of pots and pans hanging from the ceiling. There were small towers of dishes stacked to one side, bowls, knives, forks and spoons of every size and description hanging everywhere. He pulled down a huge mixing bowl, then stepped into the walk-in cooler.

He emerged with an armful of bread loaves, bacon and sausage boxes. He set them near the range and began preparing his material. By 5:29, he had prepared several bowls of raw egg yolk, while a small mountain of bacon and sausage was sizzling on the grill. Barbara stood by the front door. Newman took a deep breath.

He waved his hand. "Unlock the doors Barbara."

Like greyhounds straining at the starting gate, the crowd poured into the dining room, quickly filling every available table and counter stool.

Barbara quickly darted from table to table. She was filling the preset coffee cups and hurriedly scribbling orders as she tried to explain the morning's highly abbreviated menu. She rushed the order slips back to Newman. Then, she snatched toast off the kitchen ledge and scurried back onto the dining room floor.

She stepped up to a table of three long-haul truckers. "What do you guys want?"

"I'll have your two eggs over easy," one trucker ordered, "hash browns, and a side order of ham."

"Sorry, sir," Barbara politely interrupted, "we're all out of ham and hash browns this morning."

"Okay then, I'll take a breakfast steak, medium rare."

"We're all outta breakfast steaks too, sir."

The other truckers looked up at her, exasperated. "I guess, first we should probably ask, what is it you do have?"

"We have scrambled eggs, bacon, sausage, and toast this morning."

The man thought for a moment. "Okay, I'll have the bacon and toast, but make the eggs sunny-side up." Barbara hedged.

"Sorry, sir. We're outta sunny-side up eggs this morning."

The man looked back up at her, slightly annoyed. "Let me get this straight. You're outta sunny-side up eggs, but you have scrambled eggs."

Barbara nodded her head. "Yes."

"Okay then, let me have the same eggs that you want to scramble, cooked sunny-side up."

Barbara was stumped for an answer. "Let me get the chef." She darted back into the kitchen. Newman was busy pouring another bowl of scrambled egg batter onto the grill. "Ken, there's some guy out front who wants to speak with you."

Newman hastily began scrambling the egg yolk. "Not now, Barbara. Can't you see I'm busy?" He was slightly miffed.

"But there are these guys out there at table 14 who have a question for you."

"Can't you handle it?"

"No. He wants to talk to the chef."

Newman looked over at her. "Oh," he huffed. He pulled off the apron and followed her out of the kitchen over to the men's table. Barbara moved onto the next table as Newman smiled down at the three stern faces glaring up at him. "How can I help you?" He beamed.

"You can start by telling me why I can't get my eggs sunny-side up. If you can scramble 'em, certainly you can make 'em sunny-side up."

"Ah… good point," Newman agreed. The man indeed had a good point, but Newman didn't want to start making eggs to order. He had a system going now with cracking a bowl of yolk, scrambling the eggs, and sectioning the contents onto the plates. He didn't want to interrupt that system and possibly risk falling behind on the orders that Barbara was taking. Even as he stood talking to these customers, he felt he was losing ground with other orders. "But, I'm breaking in a new cook," he explained, "and all he's learned to make so far are scrambled eggs. I'll start him on sunny-side up eggs tomorrow morning."

"Hell then, you make 'em!" One of the other truckers suggested.

"Oh, did the waitress mention that scrambled eggs were two dollars off this morning?"

Barbara overheard the statement and stopped scribbling in her pad as she glanced over at him.

The men's eyes lit up. "Really?" They were surprised.

"Yes, but it's today only."

"Okay," the men conceded, handling Newman their menus. Newman took the menus, handed them to Barbara and darted back into the kitchen.

They were now on a roll. The morning shift waitresses filed in and nothing could stop them. Order after order went through with ease.

By midmorning the smoke jumpers were on the fire lines, the loggers were in the hills, and only an occasional tourist drifted in and out of the restaurant. Barbara sat on a corner stool next to Bud, sipping on a cup of coffee. While Angela, who had come in several minutes earlier, was busy sweeping the dining room floor. Back in the kitchen,

Newman was casually sweeping the floor around the food prep table. He started to put the broom away when he heard Nelson's irate voice calling him.

"What have you done to my kitchen?" He angrily demanded.

Newman looked quickly over his shoulder as Nelson stormed into the kitchen. He examined a dirty dish.

"You don't mix egg yolk in a cake batter bowl!" He bitterly scolded. "And what's Barbara still doing here? I wanted her fired! Now you get outta my kitchen."

"What!" shouted Newman, perplexed to his anger.

"Before you destroy the place!" yelled Nelson.

"Uh-oh honey," Bud whispered, leaning over toward Barbara. "Looks like that asshole is still on the warpath. Let's get outta here before I'm tempted to punch his lights out again. I've got a bottle of Jack Daniels back at the cabin that's dying to be finished off." Barbara smiled. He ushered her off the stool, and they quietly eased out of the dining room.

Newman turned and confronted Nelson. "Now just one damned minute!" He bitterly began." Barbara and I have just finished running our butts off feeding over four-hundred people this morning, all because you were too hung over to show up for work. So don't come in here yelling about, 'your kitchen.' Had you been sober enough to come to work, I wouldn't have been in here messing up 'your kitchen' in the first place. And as for Barbara, she put in a first-rate performance this morning, so she stays. Besides, at least she was here. And as far as I'm concerned, a master chef who can't come to work sober, is the same as having no master chef at all, understand?" He slammed the broom against the wall and stormed past Nelson out of the kitchen.

"Hey, wait!" Nelson hailed as he ran after Newman. He caught up with him in the alcove. Newman stopped and turned to face him. Nelson stopped, then smiled. "You're right, Ken." He began in a calmer tone. "I should be thanking you, not throwing some childish temper tantrum. Thanks for covering my ass. You must think I'm some kinda hopeless drunk, don't you?"

Newman smiled and shook his head. "Nooo, I don't think you are hopeless. I do think that you are letting the bottle hold you back from the great career in cooking, that you obviously could have."

He laughed. "You know you sound like my daughter, Mi Ling. You must have seen her portrait on the mantel when you brought me home yesterday."

"I did. She is very pretty."

"Pretty? She's beautiful. I adopted her when she was just three years old, right before I left Vietnam. She was an orphan." Nelson chuckled. "I won her in a poker game, believe it or not, from the guy who ran the orphanage. She graduated with honors from MSU, and this fall she's starting med school at Johns Hopkins."

"Impressive."

"She's the only positive thing I've got to show for my entire life. You know… I started to adopt a Black child, but I didn't want it to grow up to hate me after it learned all about the bad things White people had done to Black people. You understand, don't you?"

"Why sure. I mean, had you adopted me and given me a decent home, good food, loving care, put me through college, and provided me with a chance to make something of my life, I'd probably hate your guts for treating me so well."

"Well, maybe I did place a little too much emphasis on the child's color, but, I don't know. After two tours in 'Nam, I just didn't care anymore. You meet friends, I mean good friends, Ken. The kind of friends you'd like to keep for the rest of your life, only to find out they were dead later that afternoon, or even the next hour or the next minute. So I didn't get close to anybody because I knew they might be dead or gone when I needed them. So I had a choice of either the bottle or the needle as my friend. I chose the bottle, because it was more acceptable than drugs. You didn't go to jail for having it, and my bottle was always there for me. That is, until I adopted Mi Ling. I felt so guilty about surviving the war, that I seriously thought about killing myself. So many men, better than me, deserved to live and didn't. But, Mi Ling, gave me a reason for living and she loves me like a daughter would love her biological father. Now she's all grown up. She just wrote and told me she's getting married. She wants me to give her away."

"That's great!"

"Only now, even she doesn't need me anymore. Now all I have left is my bottle. It's the only thing I know I can count on to be there when I need it."

"Ah… wrong answer," Newman quickly interjected. "Lots of men went to Vietnam and saw worse action than you did and still came back productive, well-adjusted members of society. So don't lay that on me. Besides, what is Mi Ling to do? Be dependent on you for the rest of her life? If you really love her, then be happy that she's making a life of her own. It's time you saw that bottle for what it is, a crutch. Something to hide behind when times get hard. But after you've sobered up, the problem is still there, isn't it?"

Suddenly Angela called to them from the dining room. "Say, I'm in here all alone, and the food isn't cooking itself, is it?"

"I'll be right there," Nelson called to her.

"Oh, and one more thing about you and Barbara…"

"Oh, that. She can keep her tips." Nelson smiled. "Besides, for a waitress, she's not too bad a person."

"You can tell her that." Newman glanced back into the dining room. "Where did she go?"

"I believe she left with Bud a little while ago." Angela added.

"That muscle-bound ox you hired as the bartender, he tried to punch me out." Commented Nelson.

"Bud? He can get a little tempered sometimes."

"A little tempered? If you don't watch him, he could kill somebody."

"Well, I'll go by her room later." He patted Nelson on the back. "And tell her it's safe to report back to work, okay?"

"Sure thing," Nelson smiled and headed back into the dining room.

Newman turned and headed into the bar. It was empty, except for a cowboy leaning over the jukebox, scanning the selections.

"Hey! Who put the Michael Jackson shit on the jukebox?" He yelled.

"I did," Newman bellowed without breaking a stride, annoyed at the cowboy. "Play it. You'll like it!"

He walked out the front door. The cool breeze felt good against his body as his heated temper subsided. He hopped into his vehicle. Newman headed back to the main office feeling confident about the way he had handled things. He also no longer felt intimidated by buffed up cowboys with Stetson hats. If there were to be confrontation, he was ready for it. Moments later, he arrived at the office. Lisa greeted him as he stepped through the door.

"There's a very upset lady waiting for you in Vicki's office."

Newman looked at her confused. "Upset? With me? Who is she?"

"Some lady. Says her name is Mrs. Ridby and that we stole her husband." Replied Lisa.

"Mrs. Ridby?" Newman hesitated. Bud's last name was Ridby. "Could she be Bud's… wife?"

Lisa shrugged her shoulders. "I don't know Ken."

He gingerly stepped into Vicki's office. An older, but still attractive woman in a well-tailored business suit immediately turned to greet him as he entered. She was stern faced and had a cold, businesslike demeanor.

"Mr. Newman?"

"Mrs. Ridby?" Uncertain he pronounced her name correctly, as he eased the door shut behind him. "How may I help you?"

"You can start by giving me my husband back."

Newman eased into Vicki's chair. He looked across the desk at the woman, slightly bewildered. "Your husband?"

"Your bartender, Bud," she angrily countered. "Don't play dumb with me Mr. Newman. How many Ridbys' do you have around here anyway?" She dug into her purse and flung a photo onto the desk. "That man!" She insisted with conviction.

Newman picked up the photo and examined it. It was a wedding picture of the woman and Bud embracing, as they lovingly fed each other a piece of wedding cake.

"Nice picture." He gave it back to her.

"Now, I don't know what he's calling himself, Bud, Buddy, or Bob, but whatever you say his name is, he's my husband. And I've come to take him to the hospital where he belongs."

"Hospital?"

"Yes. My goodness, don't you people run any kind of background checks on the employees you hire?" She was exasperated by the resorts hiring practices. "I swear," she sighed. "Bud's an alcoholic. He has a very promising career as a middleweight prize fighter if he can get a handle on his drinking problem. He was on his way to check into a treatment center in Missoula when he must have stopped in here for one last drink. And you guys gave him a job as, of all things, a bartender, for crying out loud."

"Mrs. Ridby, we didn't know."

"Did you ever try and find out anything about him before you hired him?"

"No. We really needed a bartender at the time, and Bud just happened to be there."

"Sure you did. And by now, he's probably had so much to drink, it's a small wonder he hasn't killed somebody. He's very violent when he gets drunk, or have you noticed that?"

Newman was growing concerned about Barbara. She was with Bud back at the restaurant, and they did, in fact, leave together. If Bud was as violent as his wife proclaimed, then Barbara might be in real danger. He remembered back to Bud's barroom attack on John. If that was an indication of what he was capable of doing while intoxicated, then Barbara might be in extremely grave danger.

"But what if Bud doesn't want to go into treatment?"

"He damn well better go. He's up on first-degree assault charges. This treatment is court ordered. He'd better be glad that I was able to find him before the authorities did. If the cops had found him, he'd be going to jail, rather than to the hospital."

"Well, let's go find him." Insisted Newman.

They walked over to Bud's cabin and knocked several times. There was no answer. Newman used his master key to enter Bud's room. It was empty. Since Bud and Barbara had both left together, neither was on duty. Since they weren't in the bar and his room was empty, there was only one other place they could be. He and Mrs. Ridby ran over to the single women's dorm. They raced up the stairs and hurried down to Barbara's room. As they approached the door, they heard screams, breaking glass, and other sounds of a struggle coming from inside.

"Help! Help!" Barbara frantically cried.

Newman twisted the knob. It was locked. He pounded on the door. "Barbara! Open the door! It's locked."

"He won't let me! You've got to help me!" She screamed.

Newman heaved his shoulder into the door. It didn't budge. He tried again as Barbara continued to scream.

"Do something! Use your key!" Mrs. Ridby frantically urged. "Sounds like he's killing her in there!"

"No time!" Finally, on the third try, the door burst open, exploding against the back wall. Bud with his shirt off and belt unbuckled, had Barbara forcefully pinned against the wall with one hand around her neck, while slapping her repeatedly with the other.

"Bud!" Newman shouted.

Bud ignored him and continued to flail away on Barbara.

"Do something!" Mrs. Ridby demanded. "He's killing her!"

Newman took a running start and leaped onto Bud's back. He grabbed his neck and wrestled him to the floor. Barbara quickly stepped away from them and ran, coughing, trying to regain her breath. Panic-stricken, she raced over near Mrs. Ridby and stood beside her. Trading punches, Bud gained the upper hand and forcefully shoved Newman against the wall and scrambled to his feet. He quickly kicked Newman in the abdomen before he could make another aggressive move. Bud immediately looked around for his prey. He stared wide-eyed over at Barbara. Then, in sudden shock, he caught sight of his wife.

"Jan!" He was surprised to see her.

"Buddy! What's wrong with you?" She was almost tearful.

Newman climbed to his feet and powerfully socked Bud in his jaw. Newman's punch only broke the trance Bud had on his wife. Being a prize fighter, Bud was unfazed by the blow to his chin and retaliated with a rapid right-cross to Newman's jaw and an immediate left hook to his abdomen. Newman fell to the floor. Bud looked down on him, angrily gritted his teeth, and then swiftly kicked him in the stomach again. Newman curled up in pain gripping his stomach as he laid on the floor. Bud started to kick Newman repeatedly.

"Buddy!" Mrs. Ridby screamed. Bud's focus left Newman and turned to his wife. He paused and stared at the tears streaming down her cheeks, then suddenly dashed past her out of the room.

Barbara immediately rushed over and knelt beside Newman. "Are you all right?"

Newman struggled to catch his breath and climb to his feet. "Yes… yes… I'll be all right. What set him off?"

"He wanted me to make love to him. We both had been drinking. I had a small glass, but Bud finished the bottle of Jack Daniels like he was drinking water. But, I wasn't drunk or anything. I said maybe later, but not right now, and he went crazy."

Mrs. Ridby frowned slightly as she overheard Barbara mention Bud had asked her to make love. "He's very violent when he's drunk. Sometimes he doesn't know what he's doing or saying." She looked at them both, as if embarrassed. "Well, I'd better go and find him." She quietly noted as she wiped the tears from her eyes and left the room.

Newman finally stood straight up, still clinching his abdomen. He stumbled to the door, leaning against the wall.

"Wait Mrs. Ridby, I'll go with you." He quickly called after her. "In his present condition, he could very well hurt somebody."

"Ken, who's that woman?" Barbara whispered.

Newman stood in the doorway and looked back at her. "His wife." He turned and ran after Mrs. Ridby.

"Wife?" Barbara quietly stated to herself.

Newman reached the outside porch, but there was no sign of them. He scampered down the steps and headed back to the main complex. From a distance he could see Mrs. Ridby searching the spaces between rows of parked cars. Newman ran over to her.

"Did you see which way he went?"

"No, when he's drunk, he's very hard to find because his decisions are based on impulse rather than logic. I just hope he didn't run off into the woods somewhere. If he's downed an entire bottle of whiskey, in his present state, he might die from exposure with his shirt off."

"If he's so violent, why didn't the authorities just escort him to the hospital themselves?"

"He's only violent when he's drunk. He managed to convince them that he didn't need an escort. But then again, I guess, even they didn't count on anybody hiring him as a bartender without first checking his background."

They finished searching the parking lot and started up the steps to the café when Millie came through the door, almost bumping into them.

"Excuse me," she smiled.

"No problem," Newman quipped. "We were just headed inside to see if we could find Bud."

"Bud? I saw him about five minutes ago. He was running toward the pool."

"Pool?" Mrs. Ridby asked excitedly. "Are you sure?"

"I know where the pool is," Millie continued, mildly irritated at the woman, "and I know Bud when I see him."

Newman and Mrs. Ridby hurriedly scampered back down the steps and into the parked golf cart and headed for the swimming pool. Newman burst into the pool house with Mrs. Ridby close behind. Carl sat behind the counter, his nose buried in a paperback.

"Have you seen Bud?" Newman asked frantically. Carl pointed toward the hot pool without looking up from his novel.

"He may still be in a fighting mood," Mrs. Ridby noted. "I'd better go in and talk to him first. If I need you, I'll holler, okay?"

Before Newman could answer, she disappeared into the men's dressing room. Newman impatiently waited.

"Is anybody in the men's dressing room, Carl?"

"There is nobody in there. Everybody is in the outdoor pool."

Suddenly, a loud terrified scream blared from poolside. The ear piercing sound startled the outside pool guests. Newman looked back at Carl, who looked up from his book. Both men bolted through the dressing room. Marci and others came rushing in. Newman and Carl reached poolside first to see Mrs. Ridby screaming, panic-stricken, at the sight of Bud lifelessly floating face down in the water. The slowly rising steam had enveloped his body in a scant haze.

"Call the Life Flight!" Newman ordered. Mrs. Ridby didn't respond. She froze, horrified. "Move!" Newman demanded.

She turned, startled, then bolted for the door. Newman pulled off his shoes and dove headfirst into the pool. He reached Bud and turned him over. His eyes were closed, and he wasn't breathing. Marci raced over to Carl while others watched in horror.

"Go with Mrs. Ridby, Marci and make sure she gets that call made." Newman shouted. Marci did as instructed.

Newman looked over at Carl. "I'll push him over to you."

He carefully guided Bud's limp body toward the deck. Carl reached in, grabbed Bud's arms and helped Newman hoist him out of the water. Newman scrambled out of the water and knelt down beside Bud. He checked for a pulse, started compressions, tilted his head back, pinched his nostrils shut, placed his mouth over Bud's, and began to breathe.

Fifteen minutes later, the Life Flight paramedics had landed. Newman helped them strap a semiconscious Bud into a stretcher. They quickly rolled him out of the pool house toward the waiting helicopter. Mrs. Ridby clutched her husband's hand every step of the way.

"Is he gonna be all right?" She nervously asked the doctor, trying to be heard over the whirling rotor blades.

"Don't know miss." She softly replied. "We'll know more when we get him back to the hospital. He's still alive thanks to Ken's CPR, but there's no telling how long he's been in the water. If he was in there for more than four minutes, we could have some problems. Like I said, right now we just don't know."

"Doctor what happened to him?" Newman asked.

"You said he had been drinking heavily before he entered the hot water. More than likely, the heat from the water caused the alcohol in his bloodstream to expand, choking off the flow of oxygen. He simply blacked out. Hopefully, you reached him in time. Now if you'll excuse us…" The crew hoisted the stretcher into the waiting chopper, then they climbed aboard themselves.

"I'm his wife!" Mrs. Ridby insisted. "Oh… okay…" the doctor conceded as she helped Mrs. Ridby aboard.

Newman watched, crouched slightly, fanning at the swirling dust generated by the helicopter as it slowly lifted off. Soon it angled its way skyward toward the distant mountains and finally disappeared into the clouds.

Newman observed, as the crowd slowly dispersed until finally only Barbara was left, standing all alone. Newman watched as she continued to stare into the heavens long after the helicopter had faded from sight. Newman quietly walked over to her, though she hardly noticed him.

"Earth to Barbara," he playfully announced. She turned toward him, slightly startled. "It's gone and it's not coming back."

"Oh, I know, Ken." She sighed. "It's just that I wonder why my choice in men seems to be so bad all of the time. Am I that unattractive?" She looked at him as if she expected an honest answer.

"How can you say unattractive, Bud wanted you."

"He was drunk."

"Yeah, he wouldn't have remembered a thing."

"Maybe I should have had sex with Bud, so just in my mind, I would know if I could still satisfy a man."

"That probably wouldn't have worked. Like you said, Bud was drunk and possibly wouldn't have remembered a thing."

"Perhaps you're right. You know, Ken. When I went back to my room with Bud, I just wanted to talk about Tim. After all, I just was getting to know Bud. I just needed to tell someone how I felt. But the more I talked, the more he drank, until the bottle was gone. I had never seen anyone down a bottle of Jack Daniels so fast."

"You don't have to explain anything to me Barbara."

"I know, Ken. Just let me get this off my chest." Newman listened tentatively. "After he finished that bottle he came over to the sofa and tried to undress me. I knew then he hadn't heard a word I said about my relationship with Tim. All he wanted was sex. It was never about me, the person, Barbara. So I started to leave and this blank stare came over his face and I knew then, this can't be good. And that's when he started to beat me and thank God you came when you did."

"Barbara…"

She continued. "I loved Tim. I loved him so very much. I met him here, right here at this resort eight years ago. We were both sixteen. He was my first and only love. We would talk about the things we like to do, the foods we loved to eat, and the places we wanted to go. We were going to save all our money from this place so he could open his own mechanic shop. We'd get a place of our own and have children someday. It was so romantic in the beginning. We must have walked every inch of these grounds, enjoying the beautiful surroundings. We'd lay in bed, evenings after work and hold each other intimately, until the next morning. We did this just about every day for six years. I should have suspected something then."

"And you never made love once from those moments you were alone with each other? I mean, didn't you want to?"

"Of course I did, very much so. But he would tell me we needed to save our virginity until we were married. At that time, I thought that was the sweetest thing. He said we would consummate our marriage on our wedding night. So I decided to wait patiently, until he asked me to marry him and he finally did, two years ago."

"What happened?"

"It was a beautiful wedding, Ken. We got married at a little church in Missoula and all of our friends and family came, even Kelly."

"Go on."

"Our honeymoon was spent right here. Vicki gave us the honeymoon suite for a week. That night, our first night, was the best night I had ever had. He was so gentle in every move he made and every touch of his hands on my body. I didn't know what to do for him, as he was the only man in my life. But, he made the night all about me. The next evening, he taught me how to satisfy him. We enjoyed each other so much, all I could think about during the day after we went back to work was getting back to the cabin and making love with my husband. For the first few months, everything was great and then he began to drift away."

"What do you mean?"

"After the first six months we couldn't get enough of each. But then the sex gradually started to fade. We made love twice a week, then once a week, then once a month, until not at all. So I became suspicious and thought that perhaps there was another woman. That's why I insisted he wear his wedding band to work. But, it wasn't another woman. Now we all know, it was Kelly. I guess I was a very poor student."

"This wasn't your fault, because you weren't skilled at making love. We all make choices. Tim knew long before you, what his commitment was going to be. He needed you to confirm his suspicions about himself."

"Why the relationship? Why the marriage?"

"He needed to be sure what he wanted. After he did all the right things with a woman and he still wasn't satisfied, then he knew."

"Oh Ken. When I saw them together…" She reminisced of that very moment. "It hurts. It hurts so badly."

"There's nothing wrong with you Barbara. You're a beautiful woman that any man would be proud to have by his side. But what you have to do, is give your life a little time to heal, be patience, and have some restraint. You're young. Stop trying to rush into another relationship. There's nothing wrong with being alone for a little while. And when the time is right, you won't have to chase love… it knows where to find you."

"And what if love never finds me?"

"Give it a chance. Love has a way of surprising you."

Barbara smiled. "Can a lady in waiting, buy her boss a cup of coffee?"

Newman motioned toward the restaurant. "After you."

She tucked her arm underneath his and they casually strolled back toward the restaurant.

CHAPTER
9

*R*ides stood on the top rung of the ladder at the entrance of the resort. He was holding one end of the banner as he glanced down at Newman.

"No. Higher," Newman instructed. "Just a little bit more… that's about right."

"You sure?" Rides asked emphatically. "I don't want to nail this banner in place, only to find out later it's still off center. Once I climb down, I'm not going to climb back up here."

"Trust me," Newman reassured. "It's perfect."

Rides carefully climbed down the ladder and walked over to Newman. Both men stood and gazed up at the banner.

"Positively disgusting," Rides admiringly noted.

"Now that you mention it, it does have that certain something that simply makes the stomach turn, doesn't it?" Newman agreed. "Brotherhood of Christian Soldiers---Knights in Defense of the White Race," the banner proclaimed. "I would just like to know who they're defending the White race from." Newman asked rhetorically.

"You and me," Rides interjected. "Who else?"

"Well, let's not forget the Catholics, the Jews, Hispanics, Orientals, gays, liberal Democrats, and left-handed mailmen with a lisp."

"Just say about 95 percent of the human race and get it over with. Anyway, what provisions have you made for their security?" inquired Rides.

"You mean other than simply hoping that everybody behaves themselves? Nothing. I just hope that everybody who shows up here today will respect everyone else's right to free speech. No matter how disgusting that free speech is."

Rides looked over at him as though he were totally amazed at his naiveté'. "Yea, right."

"Well? We can always hope. Let's head back to the office, finalize things and get some breakfast."

They both jumped into the golf cart and rode a bumpy trail back to the office. However, Rides didn't share Newman's optimism in brotherly love.

"Did you notify the sheriff?" questioned Rides.

"Yea, but he said he'd only come if somebody broke the law. He also suggested we hire a private security service for this event."

"Not a bad idea."

"With what money? Anyway, did you get the communication equipment and hookups all set up for the Master Race?"

"The cables are ready. They said they're bringing their own satellite dishes so they can link up with other White racist groups across the country—sort of a national hate convention."

"They're still paying customer, so we'll treat them like such. Unless, of course, they act otherwise."

As Newman and Rides arrive at the office, they see a well-dressed balding man walking towards them.

"Excuse me," he blandly interrupted. "I'm George Peoples, and I'm looking for Mr. Newman."

"I'm Newman," he politely greeted as he stepped from the cart.

People's face flushed as he froze, momentarily taken aback. "You're… you're… Kenneth Newman? The man I talked to on the phone?"

"I certainly am. Now how can I help you?"

"There must be some mistake," Peoples muttered, his eyes fixed solidly on Newman, "Boy," he sighed, running his hand nervously over his balding head. "I don't know about this. I spoke with Mrs. Marshall several months ago about organizing this event. And… well, I just didn't think there were any of you… I mean, no one said anything about… How long have you been here?" He finally blurted.

"If you are worried about my ability to handle your group, Mr. Peoples, then don't. Everything you asked for is in place, the hook-up cables are just waiting for your dishes, and the banquet room is all ready."

"That's all well and good," Peoples continued. "But you see…" He struggled for words. "What I mean is…"

"I know exactly what you mean, Mr. Peoples," Newman immediately interrupted. "This is your all-White showcase and you don't want it tainted by the presence of a Black man and an Indian."

"It's just that I don't think you two would fit comfortable around here during our meeting, that's all." George Peoples politely continued, "This convention is going to be Whites only, if you know what I mean. That's why we wanted this resort, or someplace like it. We figured it was out of the way and far from minorities and those protest groups. We just want a nice, quiet gathering, that's all. You understand."

"Certainly," Newman sympathetically agreed. "And I plan to see that you have a nice, quiet meeting, Mr. Peoples. While I promise, neither Andrew or I will apply for membership, we aren't going to go and hide in the woods either. Besides, if you want your communication gear hooked up, Andrew is the only one here with the expertise to do it. So, even if we don't like each other, let's respect each other, okay?"

Peoples sighed in resignation. "The equipment's outside in the truck."

Newman motioned toward Rides. "Andrew, go help this nice man get set up, will you? I'll see how Nelson is doing getting the meals ready."

Rides followed Peoples over to his truck. Newman got back into the cart and rode over to the restaurant to check on Nelson. When he arrived, Nelson was busy stacking dishes in neat little towers, then gently placing them on a serving cart.

As Newman entered the kitchen, he stepped up behind Nelson. "Any problems?"

"Yes, just one." Nelson replied without looking up from his work. "I think my food is too good to serve to swine like them." He gestured toward the banquet room.

"Now, now," Newman consoled. "They're paying customer, just like anyone else who rents the banquet room."

He reached over and began placing silver ware on the cart. "They aren't just like other paying customers. I would have expected you, of all people, to know that. You know that I have an adopted Vietnamese daughter? If she were here and they did one thing to hurt her," his voice grew embittered, "I mean just one thing…"

"All right, all right," Newman admonished. "Calm down, I get the point."

"I still can't believe that Vicki was so desperate for money that she actually booked these people." He turned and pointed a serving spoon at Newman. "Or that you let her. These people are nothing but a cancer under the armpit of humanity."

"I agree, but we do live in a democracy where everyone, even armpits, are entitled to their opinion."

"Save the civics speech for when these goons show up on your doorstep in sheets with burning crosses. Then, you come back and tell me about their right to free expression. In the meantime, make yourself useful and help me get this stuff over to the banquet room."

Newman grabbed one end of the table as Nelson grabbed the other, and they carefully rolled the cart out of the kitchen.

Meanwhile over in a distance, Carl watched from the pool area as cars began to fill the parking lot. Men and women in Nazi-styled uniforms, neatly pressed white robes, and business suits, climbed out of expensive cars and began streaming into the banquet room.

"Looks like it's going to be quite a show."

Carl looked back over his shoulder. John was standing behind him, peering out the window. "Where did you come from? Shouldn't you be over at the general store with your old lady? It's going to get very busy over there today."

"She can handle it. Besides, all of the action, not to mention all of the women, are over there." He noticed another group of white-robe-clad people climbing out of their cars. "Boy, if I were that Newman, I'd be as nervous as a one-legged man in an ass-kicking contest, don't you think? I mean, look at all those Klan boys roaming around."

"You never know. He might not scare so easy." Stated Carl.

"Only a fool doesn't know when to run. No, I think as long as these guys are around, we're probably gonna see a whole lot less of Mr. Newman."

Carl turned and handed John the money pouch. "Since you're over here, make yourself useful and man the fort for a while. I'm going over there and see what words of wisdom these guys have for us White folk. Oh, and don't let your fingers stick to the money in that bag. I'm coming right back."

By noon, the gathering was well underway. However, except for the unusually large number of cars in the parking lot, nothing else seemed out of the ordinary. No protest groups had gathered, and the few problems that did occur stemmed mainly from curiosity seekers trying to get a glimpse of the proceedings inside the otherwise-closed dining room. However two stern-faced men in white robes stood at parade rest on either side of the entrance and firmly steered any uninvited guest away.

Newman entered the back door to the kitchen and noticed Nelson with his ear pressed solidly against the serving-room door.

"Nelson!" Newman suddenly called silently.

Nelson shot up, startled, and quickly turned to face Newman.

"Kenny!" He sighed, relieved. "You scared the shit outta me. You shouldn't ease up on people like that."

"You shouldn't eavesdrop on things that don't concern you. Our job is merely to cater this meeting and see that it functions smoothly, just like any other meeting we'd book here. What they say or do is their business."

"Are you kidding? You should hear some of this drivel."

"I don't have to eavesdrop. I can just imagine what they are saying."

"Well don't just imagine. Stick your ear to the door and hear for yourself."

Newman had a good idea what they were saying. These guys were professional racists. They were, more than likely, using every vile racial and ethnic aspersion imaginable. However, the laughter and applause that filtered from the banquet room only served to heighten his curiosity. He would probably never again get this close to an actual Klan rally and stay alive. To get even a peek at the proceedings was sure to be a memorable experience. He hesitated, then eased closer to the door. Nelson stepped aside. He cracked the door ever so gently and peeked through the tiny opening.

On the makeshift stage was a seven-foot-tall television screen and two solemn faced white-robed men frozen at parade rest on each side. High above the screen on the wall hung an oversized Confederate flag. Huge stereo speakers were scattered throughout the room as the capacity, standing-room-only audience listened in quiet awe. Their eyes were riveted on the television screen as the balding middle-aged man in the neatly pressed white robe ranted and railed from his pulpit, with the energy and fervor of a fire-and-brimstone minister.

"So if you're not White Angelo-Saxon Protestant," he blasted, "then this message is not for you. I'm only talking to God's Chosen people. The darker races of the world haven't contributed one positive thing to human development. The White man brought us the trains, the airplanes, the telephones, and every modern invention you can think of. We must survive as a pure race if civilization itself is to survive."

The audience responded with thunderous applause. Newman scanned their eager, seemingly mesmerized faces with their eyes fixed attentively on the screen. Do they actually believe this? He wondered. Or, were they just here out of morbid curiosity, the way bad accidents draw a crowd--not so much, concern for the victims, but rather just to see what was going on.

Suddenly the door pushed back, slamming into Newman's face. Newman grabbed his nose and grimaced, trying to quietly conceal the pain.

The handsome, well-dressed young man noticed Newman behind the door writhing in agony. "Excuse me," he quickly apologized as he stepped over to him. "Are you all right?" Newman nodded his head as he continued to grasp his nose. "I didn't see you back here behind the door, but then again, I can understand why you preferred to stay back here. Are you with a protest group or something?"

Newman shook his head. "I'm Ken Newman, the manager here, and just who are you?"

He politely extended his hand. "Dean Walsh, Channel Eight Action News. I take it you haven't seen me anchor the nightly news... and please don't tell me you only watch Channel Two."

"Mr. Walsh, with my schedule, frankly, I've almost forgotten what television is. By the way, that's our chef, Nelson Adams," he pointed toward Nelson. They shook hands.

"For a while there I thought you were one of them," Nelson volunteered.

"Me?" Dean Walsh chuckled. "No, thank you. I just came back here to get a breather from that jerk on the screen. He should be committed, but of course, I can't say that in my story. Actually, I'm more interested in your story. If you're the manager, then you must have helped put this event together, am I right?" Walsh smiled.

"We treated it just like any other event that books here, if that's what you mean, yes. But this event was scheduled long before I got here. And to set the record straight, the owner, had she known who these people really were, would never have scheduled them."

"A Black man helping to sponsor a Klan rally. If that's not my story, then nothing is."

"Now wait just a minute," Newman insisted. "I don't want to be associated in any way with this group. You'll just have to find yourself another story. Why don't you wait for a protest group to show up or something? I'm sure they'll make a more interesting story."

"Protest groups?" Walsh stated in amazement. "What protest groups were you expecting?"

"I don't know," Newman fudged. "The NAACP or the ACLU or somebody."

Walsh chuckled. "The NAACP? In Lolo? You've gotta be kidding. Besides, what protest group is going to drive all the way up here, anyway? That's why these groups choose to meet in these remote locations. Besides, the average citizen here feels that the BCCS is your problem, not theirs. There aren't any protest groups here for the same reason that this state doesn't celebrate Dr. Martin Luther King Jr.'s birthday. There simply aren't enough minorities here to prod the local communities to speak out on civil rights issues. And no White person wants to step forward and advocate recognizing a King holiday and risk being ostracized by the rest of the White community."

"Even so Dean, I'm certain there are lots of fair-minded people in this state who don't agree with groups like this. The BCCS is only encouraged by the failure of these people to speak out."

"Of course there are lots of good, honest, people in this state who don't support their views." Walsh quickly continued. "No one in their right mind honestly believes that Montana, Idaho, and Wyoming will ever be designated 'White only' states. But most of the people who live here are WASP, the very people groups like the BCCS are claiming to defend."

"Defend? From what?" Newman asked.

"You obviously haven't been here long enough to understand. But a lot of people here, especially the farmers, are going through very tough economic times. People are losing farms and homes that have been in their families for years. They need someone to blame, something to fight. You can't fight declining farm prices and land values, but you can fight the people who are plotting to take away your farm and your house. Like the Jews who own the banks, the Blacks who threaten racial purity, and the list goes on. Most of the people out there in those chairs are really good, decent people who, just a couple of years ago, wouldn't have given a group like this a second thought. They are simply looking to fight for what they feel is being taken from them. They need a villain they can actually see and the BCCS is simply providing them with one. It's the same way the Nazi party seduced the people of Germany back in the '30's."

"Well, Mr. Dean Walsh," Newman explained, "there's your story. Why don't you just expose these people for the hatemongers they are?"

"Oh, we've run stories on this group before, but like I said, most Whites here don't feel directly threatened by groups like the BCCS. They see them strictly as a problem for minorities, so their ranting's just aren't news here. Besides, these groups not only thrive on fear and hate, they also need publicity. They'd not only welcome a media attack, but they'd just say that any attack made on their group was only a feeble attempt on our part to squash the truth. The truth, as they, of course, see it."

"But you forget," Newman quickly added, "that this group isn't just a threat to Blacks. They also don't like White liberals, White Catholics, White Jews, White gays, and any other category of Whites that don't fit their narrow definition of racial superiority. And until more responsible Whites step forward and denounce groups like the BCCS, and denounce them without the prodding of civil right organizations, they're going to feel that their message of race hatred and White superiority is, at the very least, tolerated here in Montana."

"Well, Ken, racial superiority isn't the real issue. Hell, if they actually thought you were racially inferior, you wouldn't have to eavesdrop on their meeting from behind the door. You'd be up there on that platform as exhibit "A" just to prove their point. The real issue has more to do with jobs, or why I'm losing my farm, or why my plant is closing—in other words, economics. Like I said, these are basically good, hardworking people, but just like in Nazi Germany, when times get hard, people need something or someone to blame. Groups like the BCCS tend to get their largest memberships during hard economic times."

Suddenly the back door swung open and Lisa peeped in. "There you are. Vicki's looking for you back at the office.

"Is there a problem Lisa?"

"A Mr. Grant from the Forest Service is over there…"

"Say no more. I want to talk to him myself." He turned back to Walsh. "Well, I've got to run. Besides, I think I've heard enough of that crap for one day."

"Crap, yeah." Walsh snapped his fingers, "Which reminds me why I came back here in the first place. Where's your bathroom?"

"Nelson will show you where it is. Have a good rest of the day Mr. Walsh."

Newman didn't feel Walsh understood where he was coming from. If some Whites felt these groups were unjust, they should stand up no matter what the economic situation was and let their voices be heard. Walsh felt the only reason why no one stood for justice is because of the economic situation that plague the community. Either way, nothing good was going to result from nothing being done.

As Newman followed Lisa back to the office. Vicki sat behind her desk as Grant sat across from her. Newman gave a slight knock on the door and entered. They both turned to see Newman come in.

"Kenny," Vicki smiled. "Mr. Grant here has been telling me how valuable your assistance has been to him while the firefighters have been here."

"Really?" He wanted clarification.

"Yes," Grant interjected. "The camp supervisor has had nothing but good things to say about you and your staff, and everything is operating just fine."

"Good. Then does that mean you all will be leaving sooner than anticipated?"

"Well," Grant hedged, "The North Ridge Fire crowned last night."

"Crowned?" inquired Newman.

"Jumped our fire lines from treetop to treetop. It's gotten kinda outta control." Responded Grant.

"Kinda?"

"Like I was telling Vicki right before you came in, we're going to be adding an extra one hundred firefighters to the base camp in the morning."

"You're kidding? One hundred more smoke jumper?" Newman was in disbelief.

"I was telling Mr. Grant about the increased business his people have brought us." Vicki interjected.

"Oh yes, and did you also tell him about the after-hour skinny-dipping, the fistfights, the dirt bike riding and the topless dancing in the bar. Let's not forget the sing-alongs around the camp fire at three in the morning. Or, my absolute, all-time favorite stunt, the twenty-four kegs of Bud Lite poured into the hot tub?"

"They spend twelve hours a day on the fire line and, well, boys will be boys. But we'll replace anything they break or damage while they're here, so just keep track and add it onto our final bill."

"Great!" Newman sighed. "In the meantime, by the time we finish repairing or replacing everything they break or destroy, we'll probably, just about break even."

"He's just kidding," Vicki playfully chided. "Aren't you, Kenny?" Newman was silent. "Of course he is."

"Whatever," Newman breathed. "Besides, I've got a group over there in the banquet room right now that makes your smoke jumpers look like Eagle Scouts."

"Oh yes," Grant recalled. "Those Christian Brotherhood guys are over there. How's that going?"

"Great so far. We've had no complaints. In fact, we've done everything for them except iron their sheets. Though, I suppose that's next."

"Well, I just want you to know that I think it's great that you're able to put aside your personal feelings and host a group like that. Not many people could." Grant checked his watch. "Hey, I've gotta run." He shook Vicki's hand, then turned to Newman. "Remember, you can bill us for any damages our smoke jumpers cause. If you have any questions, you can either call me at the office or call a lady named Leanna Clark in our purchasing department. She's handling your account."

"Is there a space on that bill for mental anguish?"

Grant chuckled. "I don't think so."

"Too bad. We could bill you for a fortune." Newman walked over and plopped down in Grant's chair as he walked out the door.

"How's Bud? Have you heard anything?" Vicki quietly asked.

"I called the hospital. He's out of danger. His wife will be checking him into an alcohol rehab hospital when he recovers."

"Poor Barbara. First her husband and now this."

"She'll bounce back. Everybody eventually does."

Suddenly, the door opened, and a slender older woman walked quietly into the office. Newman and Vicki turned to greet her.

"Where's Lisa?" Newman asked.

"There was no one outside. I don't mean to interrupt." The lady replied.

"Can I help you?" Vicki smiled.

"I'm Mrs. Baddeley," she meekly announced. "The state police said that I could find a Mr. Newman here. He has my husband's overnight bag?"

Newman immediately rose from his chair and extended his hand. "I'm Ken Newman." He shook her hand.

"The police told me that you tried to save my husband's life, and I just wanted to say thank you. I'll be eternally grateful."

"No problem. The bag is right here." Newman got up and went behind Vicki's desk and retrieved the bag from the safe.

"I'm just sorry that he didn't make it," Vicki volunteered.

"Even though he was gone on the road almost six months out of the year, he was still a good provider," Mrs. Baddeley, quietly began. "I never had to worry about the rent or any of the household bills or money for the kids…"

"Kids?" probed Vicki.

"Three. Two boys and a girl. They idolize their father. I suppose they always will."

"It's only natural for kids to love their father." Newman added.

"I suppose. But with him gone so much, I guess you only think of the good times and not so much the bad. But then, the bad times hardly seem important at a time like this."

Newman was shocked at her information, but didn't display his emotions. He handed her the satchel. She took it and clutched it tightly to her bosom.

"Thank you all again, so much." She somberly smiled. "It's good to know that there are still people like you left in this world."

"Good luck," Newman called. Mrs. Baddeley turned and left.

Newman sat back down in the chair. Vicki quietly glared at him. "Yes… I took the letters and the pictures out, if that's what you were going to ask." He quietly blurted.

"Good," she smiled as she eased out of her seat. She walked into the receptionist area. Newman followed behind her. "I didn't think you'd be so cruel as to leave them in there."

"It wasn't that I felt she shouldn't know. It's just that, I didn't feel it was my place to tell her."

As Vicki watched Mrs. Baddeley through the window. She noticed the cars still pouring into the parking lot.

"How's the conference doing?"

"Fine, so far. Andrew is keeping their communication dishes on line and Nelson did a fine job with the food. So everybody over there should be having a splendid time."

The front door opened and Peoples walked in. He looked at Newman and then over at Vicki and smiled. "Mrs. Marshall, I just wanted to tell you how pleased we are with the way you've handled our meeting. Everything has just gone beautifully."

"Thank you, Mr. Peoples, but actually Ken here, did all of the work," she commented, pointing toward Newman. "He deserves the credit."

Peoples turned toward Newman in a decidedly more somber tone. "Ah… yes. Mr. Newman," he quietly continued. "I suppose I should thank you and your staff for your hard work in sponsoring our little gathering. I know you don't think very highly of us."

"I'm sure the feeling's mutual."

"Oh no, really, Mr. Newman," Peoples earnestly explained. "We don't hate you people. It's just that… well, we just don't feel that you belong here. In fact, we know you'd be happier among you own kind. Just like we wanna be among our own kind. Surely you can understand that?" He asked as if he honestly sought Newman's approval.

"I guess, Mr. Peoples." Newman politely began, "I just have a problem with people like you, telling people like me, where I have to live and who I have to live with, in order to be happy. Now I know, it could simply be that you have the USA confused with the Union of South Africa. But, the last time I checked, the United States of America was a free country. And any citizen has the right to live anywhere and associate with anyone in this country they damn well please!"

Newman and Peoples stared at each other momentarily.

"Well again, Mr. Newman, Mrs. Marshall, thank you for your efforts on our behalf."

"You're welcome." Vicki said to him as he turned to leave. "Oh, Mr. Peoples," Newman hailed. He stopped and turned back toward Newman. "As meetings go, this one was a little dull, don't you think? For your meeting next year, may I suggest you book a conference room in Harlem or Watts or even Vatican City where your message can really be appreciated?"

Peoples quietly continued out the door.

"I'm sorry for having those people here in the first place."

Newman walked closer to Vicki and placed his hand on her shoulder. "Please," he consoled. "What's done is done. We'll know better next time." Newman got ready to leave when he noticed Carl out the window. "Look Vicki."

Vicki moved to the window. They noticed Carl heading back toward the pool area, his nose buried in a BCCS flyer.

"I should have known that those kind of people would hold an attraction for that no-good son of mine. My goodness." She sighed. "I just don't know where I went wrong with him."

Newman watched as Carl eagerly read the piece of paper. "We do the best we can, and that's all we can do."

"If he didn't know so much about running a pool, I would have given that job to someone else and fired him a long time ago, son or no son."

"Speaking of jobs, Bea's daughter, Candy, is going to be out of school for the summer. John wants me to find her a job around here, but I'm not familiar with the child labor laws in this state."

"Oh, don't worry about it. Just find her a small job somewhere and pay her five or ten dollars. In fact, you can have her start pulling those fireweeds out of my rose garden at the foot of the steps."

"Fireweeds?"

"Oh, it's that stuff that grows after a fire has burned through a forested area. Occasionally the wind will carry seedlings out of the burned area and drop them right into my prized rose beds, and weeds of any kind just don't belong in there. I would have her help out Carl over at the pool, but I don't want that sweet child to come anywhere near that man."

Newman snapped his fingers as if she had suddenly jolted his memory. "Which reminds me." He walked over to the desk, reached into the drawer, and pulled out a roll of theater tickets. "Carl and I have some unfinished business. See you later, Vicki." He bolted out the door.

He jumped in the golf cart and drove toward the pool area. Carl was just pulling up a chair behind the counter as he entered. Newman walked up to the counter and defiantly slammed the ticket roll down in front of him.

"Today, we are going to start issuing tickets to our customers," he boldly announced. Carl looked down at the roll then slowly back up at Newman.

"Say," he drawled. "This here…" he held up the BCCS flyer---"says people like you, ain't got no business telling people like me, what to do. Sides, I thought we settled this issue a couple of months ago."

"Settled? Hardly. Postponed seems more appropriate."

Carl tilted his baseball cap back slightly, got up from his chair and pulled his pants up on his waist. "Seems you need a memory refresher, boy." He strolled from behind the counter. Newman eased back slightly as Carl menacingly advanced. "Now, I'm gonna give you just five seconds to haul ass and take those goddamn tickets wit'cha before you have to eat'em."

Newman remained still. They squared off like first-round prizefighters. Newman carefully watched Carl's eyes. Suddenly Carl lunged as he swung, Newman quickly stepped back to avoid the blow. He countered with a swift kick to Carl's abdomen. Carl immediately doubled over. Newman quickly interlocked his fingers and slammed his combined fists down into Carl's back. Carl immediately fell to his knees. He suddenly grabbed Newman's ankle and pulled. Newman's leg shot out from under him as he reeled backward, landing hard on the concrete floor. Carl scrambled to reach him, but Newman countered with a swift foot kick to Carl's face before scrambling to his feet. Carl grabbed the counter-top and pulled himself up off the floor, gingerly feeling the warm trail of blood oozing from his lip. He glanced down at his blood reddened finger, then looked over at Newman, standing, ready for another round. He smiled a broad grin.

"See you learned a little from that filthy redskin," he snarled, "but it ain't enough to keep you from gittin' your ass kicked."

He quickly lunged and fired a powerful right cross at Newman. He ducked and countered with a swift upper cut that caught Carl squarely on the chin. He followed with a right that turned Carl's head and then a left that sent him reeling against the counter. He stood there, slightly dazed, and then slowly slithered to the floor.

Newman stepped around him, over to the counter, picked up the tickets and dropped them on the floor beside him. "Remember, one per customer." He casually advised, stepping over Carl and calmly walking out of the pool house. He continued back toward the office.

As he approached the steps, he looked back over his shoulder toward the pool house. A broad grin dawned his face. He leaped excitedly into the air and punched the sky. "Yeah!" He shouted to the world.

As Newman stood on the steps of the office celebrating his victory over Carl, he unexpectedly stood silent. Far, far, off in a distance he could see smoke coming from the trees. He wondered what was taking place at the base camp.

The two men in green jumpsuits stood leaning over either side of the oblong table, trying to hold down a flimsy piece of paper that fluttered slightly in the mild breeze. Faint traces of white smoke drifted through their outdoor encampment as they circled and pinned various locations on the paper. This area of the forest was normally alive with the vibrant sounds of the wilderness. The crisp, clean smell of pine used to be the norm. Now, the North Ridge Fire had turned this area of the forest into a wildlife ghost town with thick clouds of white smoke rolling in like a dense fog. Off in the distance, several huge air tankers lumbered slightly above the treetops, dropping thick clouds of reddish brown fire retardant on the raging fire below.

"We have containment along this perimeter," one of the men explained, pointing to a spot on the map. "If we place those four fresh crews on the southern flank, we can stop this baby from speeding farther south."

"That's not what concerns me," the other man interjected. "It's crowning north, and I don't know if we can cut the breaks fast enough with our current manpower to keep it from jumping the Montana state border. If it does, that whole section of forest between the border and Missoula is so thick, those trees will go like matches in a book. It might take weeks before we could get a handle on it again. So do we put those fresh crews in the south, where we know we can get control, or to the north, where we wanna get control?"

"We've got a base camp to the north that's right in its path. If we put all our efforts toward containment in the south, we just may lose our entire northern perimeter. I'll let them know what our decision is so they can be ready to evacuate just in case."

"Yea," the other man sighed, "but there's also a tourist resort up there. They're not going to be too happy about shutting down right at the height of their tourist season, especially since we aren't certain that the fire is going to jump. The loss of a summer's revenue could literally put them out of business. Besides, there is rain in the forecast. I'd hate to force them outta there, then suddenly have it rain."

"Well, they've been forecasting rain for the past couple days now and so far not a drop has fallen from the sky. Besides, I'd rather be safe than sorry. If we wait until the last minute, and that fire makes a sudden jump, who knows how many people might get trapped up there. Just the same, I'll hold off on a total evacuation order for now, but you better warn that resort, just in case."

"I've heard the owner is a stubborn old bird. What if she doesn't want to shut down?"

"Then you'd better tell that stubborn old bird, that if she doesn't shut down, she just might wake up one morning and find her goose cooked… literally."

Meanwhile, Newman had climbed down off his emotional high over defeating Carl and went to the restaurant. Once there, he surveyed the vacant banquet room. Empty plates, glasses, and assorted papers, littered the tables. He casually strolled over to one of the tables and picked up a leaflet. 'BE A MAN' the bold black heading proclaimed. Underneath was a white knight on a reared steed with a flaming lance pointed skyward. Captioned below in smaller letters read, "Jew Bakers Taking Your Farm? Niggers Taking The Jobs You Deserve? Too Many Of Them Next Door? Join Us."

Newman stared at the flyer momentarily, then slowly crumbled the paper tightly in his fist and released it. The paper ball fell quietly onto the floor. Suddenly, he heard laughter behind him.

"Ahhhh… hey, buddy," the voice jokingly hailed. Newman turned to see three young teenagers---two boys and a girl, all dressed in shorts and tank tops. They playfully burst into the room. "Yeah, you, soul brother," the young man with shoulder-length blonde hair called. His arm was tightly grasping the waist of an attractive girl. "Where's tha…

how do you people say?... tha happ'nins 'round here?" The others laughed.

Newman quickly grew irritated at the man's voice and demeanor. "The party's over for today kids. We'll be open tomorrow."

"Really, Okay." The blonde turn to his friend. "Let's go check out the bar." He turned back to Newman. "Say, bro... is your bar open?"

"Sure," Newman was trying to ignore their snide racial remarks. "You all have to show ID though, to get in."

"ID?" The young woman bristled. "We've never been carded anywhere else we've been. We're old enough to drink," she protested.

"Sure you are." Newman agreed sarcastically. "Sure you are."

"Ah... fuck this nigger man," the blonde boy sighed. "There are other bars along this road. Let's get outta here."

They turned to leave when suddenly, Newman raced over to them. He grabbed the blonde boy by the shoulders and violently spun him around. Then, Newman grabbed a fistful of his tank top and jammed him forcefully up against the wall. The boy's eyes widened as he stared horrified into Newman's snarling face. Newman's eyes seethed with anger. The girl gasped as the other boy looked on in a silent panic.

Newman kept the boy pinned against the wall, his chest heaving with anger. Neither said a word. Then Newman slowly released his grip and stepped back. The young man cautiously straightened his wrinkled shirt as he carefully eyed Newman. The boy was uncertain whether to trust his gradual retreat. He quickly grabbed his girlfriend's hand and bolted out the door. The other boy dashed after them.

Newman watched the door slam. He stared at the closed door momentarily, then walked over and sat at a nearby table. He rested his head dejectedly, in his palm. He sat quietly for several minutes before Rides casually walked in.

He slowly surveyed the area. "What a dump!" He commented in a halfhearted Bette Davis impression.

Rides continued to scan the room until he noticed Newman quietly sitting at a table with his chin propped. He walked over to him.

"Say, you don't know the proper temperature setting for storing ice cream, do you?" Newman didn't answer. "All week long I've been trying to adjust that ice cream display case behind the counter in the restaurant. If I adjust it too much, the ice cream freezes hard as granite, and if I don't adjust it enough, it comes out like soup."

"What am I doing here?" Newman asked, mainly to himself.

"Maybe if I call Baskin-Robbins," Rides continued, unaware of what Newman had said.

"Maybe those White supremacists have a point, in their own twisted sort of way."

"That's what I'll do," Rides said assuredly. "If anyone knows anything about ice cream, they'll know." He looked around the room. "Ken, where's the phone book?" Newman didn't answer.

"Why?" Newman still talking to himself.

"Ken?" He leaned closer to Newman. "Ken?" Newman didn't respond. "Earth to Kenny," he called, snapping his fingers in front of Newman's face. Newman startled alert as if awakened from a trance. "You haven't heard a word I've said, have you?"

"Ah... ah... yes I have," he said, struggling to regain his composure.

"Oh yeah? Well then, what did I say?"

"You said you were going to Baskin-Robbins for some ice cream and... and you needed the phone book to call them."

"Close... real close. Now, what's the problem?"

Newman paused, then looked over at Rides with a blank expression on his face. "What in the hell am I doing here?"

Rides sat down in front of him. "At this very moment or just in general?"

"Oh, you know what I mean. Why, you yourself once asked me the same question awhile back. Now I'm beginning to seriously wonder if this whole thing has been a big mistake and I'm hopelessly out of my element here."

Rides could see the genuine element of concern on his face. He knew that Newman was pondering this question very seriously. "What brought this on? Not those clowns in the bed sheets, I hope."

"Oh, they were only part of it. Just before you walked in, I jammed some kid up against the wall for calling me a nigger. It was like every slur and comment, all the evil stares and racial jokes I've endured since I've been here, had built up inside, waiting to explode. And when that kid said that word, it lit the fuse. Like the straw that broke the camel's back, I had, had enough. I wanted to tear his head off."

Rides laughed. "You actually jacked somebody up? I'm a better teacher than I thought."

"And that's another thing, before I started taking fighting lessons from you, I was more inclined to reason my way out of a situation. This is the second time today that I've resorted to physical violence. I honestly don't know myself anymore. Maybe I don't belong here. I need to be around people who don't tan, who watch Soul Train, listen to Michael Jackson, and read Ebony Magazine."

"Where are you going to find people like that in Montana?"

"My point exactly. Maybe I don't belong here."

"I know exactly what you mean," Rides quietly began, "which is exactly my point. If you want to leave, then, by all means, leave. But leave because you want to, not because you let a few narrow-minded assholes run you away."

"One of the first things I heard when I got here was, that this was White man's country. Now, don't get me wrong. I've heard racial slurs used as nouns before. But since I've been here, I'd never heard them used as adjectives. I've heard people nigger-rigging their equipment, having someone do their nigger-work, Jewing someone down in price… I mean some of these people could actually publish their own bigot's dictionary."

Rides leaned back in his chair and breathed a big sigh as he stretched his legs out under the table. "Did I ever tell you about the time I was stationed in Germany with the army?"

"No, but this isn't going to take all afternoon, is it?"

"There was this bar in the red-light section of Bonn called Soul Town. Nothing but Black GI's went there. In fact, for the first two years I was over there, it was declared off-limits by some of the Black GI's to all other racial groups. I mean like it was no big deal. The place wasn't really that hot, and there were better bars in other sections of town. But one day this Black major assembled this multiracial group of GI's and practically ordered us all down to the Soul Town Bar. It wasn't pleasant the first couple of times. There were some fistfights, and a lot of hard feelings. But every weekend, like clockwork, he'd take another mixed-race group of GI's down there. Until each week, there were fewer fistfights, fewer hard feelings, and about three months later, anybody who wanted to go in there, could."

"His objective was…?"

"The major said he wanted to make the point that the Army was just one color… green, and if the bar served one group of GI's, it had to serve them all."

"But this isn't the Army, Mr. Rides. Just because I'm their manager, I can't just order them to stop making racial slurs and comments."

"You still don't get the point, do you, Mr. Newman," he continued. "Just like that bar, this state is perceived as being off-limits to Blacks. Simply because enough Blacks haven't bothered to challenge that claim. If you stay, of course, it's going to be rough at first. Only because you've got a lot of preconceived notions to dispel. However, I'm sure you've noticed that, even just in the short time you've been here, some people have come to accept you more now than they did when you first came here. And next month, you'll get along with more people than you do right now. The point is, like my grandfather said, everybody's gotta be somewhere, and you have a right to live anywhere you want to. And the longer you stay here, the more they'll recognize your right to stay here. Every now and then, you need to just take a casual stroll through the Howard Beaches and the Forsythe Counties of this country. And that's just to remind the people who live there, that this is still the United States. So leave, if you want to, but if you let them run you away, then it only proves that they were right all along. You really don't have the right to live here."

Newman sat back in his chair and pondered Ride's words. To leave now would, of course, be the easy thing to do, but Rides was right. He wouldn't feel like he had left on his own, but rather, that he had been chased away.

"You know Rides…" Newman smiled.

"Well? Are you leaving?"

"Yes, I am… one day… maybe, but not anytime soon." His tone brightened. "Now, what's this about going to Baskin-Robins?"

As Newman's confidence grew from Rides' motivational speech, Newman thought church might do him good and he wasn't going to miss this Sunday. He decided he was going to join Millie and Reese in church service.

Millie buttoned the top button on her frilly white blouse as she checked herself carefully in the full-length mirror. It was a weekly Sunday ritual. As the minister's wife, she always appeared the epitome of conservative dress as she accompanied her husband to the dining room. It was always reserved every Sunday morning for Reese's church services.

Reese emerged from the bedroom in a dark flannel suit, a black tie, and a Bible tucked neatly under his arm. "About ready?"

"Just a few minutes," she answered, making a few last minute adjustments on her carefully coiffured silver hair. "How many people do you think will be there this morning?"

"Enough tourist, I hope, to make the collection plate worthwhile. For the past couple of weeks, between the handful of tourist and the two or three staff that show up, the collection plate hasn't even been enough to justify showing up. You'd think the smoke jumpers would come every Sunday to pray for their lives or their friend's lives."

Millie turned to him and smiled. "Honey, the work of the Lord is its own reward."

"You know that, and I know that, but tell that to Big Jake. Between what I make on the hill every day, what he charges us to rent the equipment for logging, since I don't have my own and the sodas we drink with the meals he feeds us, we hardly have any money left at the end of the month. What he puts in our pockets with one hand, he takes out with the other. That collection plate is the only way we're gonna make any money around here."

Millie walked over to him and smiled. "If they only realized how spiritually important we've been to this whole place. The riffraff she had before we came here, like those perverts Kelly and Tim are all being replaced by decent, God-fearing Christian people like Kenny and Bea. And it's all because our spiritual light has been shining like a beacon of hope in the night on this place."

"And don't forget that drunkard, Bud." Reese quickly added. "He got rid of them all, and it was only because of the high moral character we've brought to this place."

"And He's not through yet." Millie continued. "I heard Him say He's going to get rid of a lot more of these sinners and lowlifes before He's through."

"And that's not all. I heard Him say He's going to turn this whole place into a Christian retreat for His people with you as the director."

"Me?" Millie's was surprised by his comment.

"Didn't you hear Him? Right after dinner?"

"Honey, I was putting away the dishes."

"Anyway, you're going to have Vicki's job, and then we'll finally be able to staff this place with nothing but good Christian people." Declared Reese.

"Like Kenny and Bea. After all, they do come to service every Sunday."

"Certainly… Of course, they'll have to do what you tell them to do, but sure, they can stay. Vicki and Jake can stay too, but they'll have to undergo intensive Christian retraining to rid them of their materialistic desires." Reese checked his watch. "Come on, honey." He opened the front door. "We can't keep everybody waiting."

An elderly couple stepped gingerly up the steps of the restaurant and pushed the door open. Newman and Bea looked up as they entered the dining room.

"They said you'd be holding church services in here this morning. Are we in the right place?" The old woman asked.

"They told you right," Newman smiled as he walked over to greet the couple. "Come on in. We haven't even started yet. This is Beatrice Henderson."

"Pleased." Bea smiled as she rose from her seat and extended her hand. "Everyone calls be Bea."

"This is my husband, Norman, and I'm Emily," the old woman introduced. "We're on our way to Sioux Falls. We just wanted to give thanks to the Almighty before we continued on. We haven't missed a Sunday in church in forty years of marriage, and we didn't want to start today."

"Well, we're glad to have you here with us." Bea continued as she motioned toward the two vacant chairs in front of her. "We all consider ourselves friends here."

The front door opened, and a stern-faced Carl stepped into the room dressed in a blue Western-styled denim suit and a Bible tucked securely under his arm. He walked briskly past Newman and Bea and took a seat at an isolated part of the table.

Newman leaned toward Bea as he eased back into his seat. "At least, most of us consider ourselves friends here," he whispered.

Reese and Millie stepped through the front door and noticed the larger than-usual group gathered at the table.

"Tourists," Millie whispered through her smile.

"Yeah," Reese quietly noted. He smiled. "Might be a pretty good collection plate this morning."

The group quieted as Reese took his place at the head of the table. All was quiet as Reese opened the Bible and began his lecture.

Several more tourists wandered in before Reese finally concluded the service. He dismissed the gathering, took a place near the entrance, and shook hands as the congregation filed out the door. Carl quietly walked past him as Reese greeted a departing couple. Millie mingled with the remaining guest. She was explaining the ambitions and the expensive nature of their ministry. But the whole time she smiled at the guests, she was ever mindful of, but pretending not to notice, the rapidly filling collection plate sitting on the edge of the table.

Finally the room was empty, except for Newman, Reese, and Millie. Newman walked over to Reese and shook his hand.

"That was really one of your better sermons," Newman commended.

"I think everybody got something out of it." Replied Reese.

"Well, it's true. God does bless places that He wouldn't normally bless, solely because some of His children happen to be there." Added Millie.

"Oh, before I forget." Newman dug into his pocket and placed a $10 bill into the collection plate. "Hope this helps a little."

"Even the smallest gifts can do so much when employed to do His will." Reese smiled.

Millie stepped over and cradled the collection plate.

"Looks like a lot of people liked your sermon." Newman admired, noting the large number of bills in the plate.

"Well, the Lord loves a cheerful giver." Reese quickly added. He checked is watch. "Well, Millie and I better be going."

"Yeah," Newman agreed, looking around the dining room. "I'd better start getting these tables and chairs back in order so Nelson can open for lunch." Millie and Reese started for the door. "Good luck," Newman called after them.

The door closed and the dining room was quiet except for the faint motor hums of the freezers and coolers behind the lunch counter. He leaned, trying to push a table back into position, when a gruff voice called him from behind.

"I knew you'd still be in here."

He whirled to see Carl standing in the doorway. Newman stood alert and faced him. His muscles tensed as he prepared for a rematch of their earlier bout at the pool house.

"At least you had the decency to wait until after church, Carl." Newman's face was stern. "Can this round wait until later, or are you too busy this afternoon?" He wanted to avoid a scene with Carl, not so much for fear of fighting him again, but he knew Nelson wouldn't even try to start lunch until all of the tables and chairs were properly arranged. He didn't have that much time before lunch began. "Look, we've both just come out of church, and I really don't want any trouble with you right now, okay?"

Carl stepped inside and closed the door behind him. "Relax, okay? I just came by for another roll of tickets," he calmly began. "I ran out the other day. Vicki's not in her office, and you have the only other key."

"Oh?" Newman looked at him, somewhat startled by the innocent nature of his presence. "You mean you're not here to rearrange my facial features?"

Carl chuckled. "Heck no. Besides, since you've been taking fighting lessons from that Indian fella, you fight a whole lot better now, than you did when you first came here. And like you said, today is Sunday."

Newman sighed. "Boy, I knew Reese's sermon was good, but I never dreamed…"

"Reese is a jackass and a hypocrite," Carl blurted. "I have more religion in my big toe than he has in his whole body. His sermon has nothing to do with why I'm here."

"Then why are you here?" Newman was blunt. "You could have very easily open he pool this morning without those tickets."

"I know, but Mom… I mean Vicki, thinks I'm stealin' from her over there. She thinks I'm fighting the ticket system so I can continue to rip her off. Hell, if I wanted to steal, I could do it with or without those damn tickets. And though she doesn't believe me, I still love her. So if she wants tickets in the pool house, I'll put tickets in the pool house."

"I see." Newman checked his watch. "Well, you've got an hour before the pool opens, and I've got to get this dining room ready for lunch before…"

"Here," Carl volunteered. He pulled off his coat. "Let me help you. Two people can do this faster than one." He walked over to Newman. "Where do you want to start?"

Newman was flabbergasted. "Ah… ah… how about with this table right here. Just grab the other end."

Carl immediately complied, and soon he and Newman were pushing, pulling, and hoisting tables and chairs all over the dining room.

Newman chuckled as he strained with his end of a table.

"What's the problem?" Carl huffed.

"Nothing. It's just that, if someone had told me a couple of months ago that you and I would be working together like this, I would have asked them to take a urinalysis test."

"I'll admit, I ain't been one of your biggest fans around here."

"Is that ever an understatement? Ever since I've been here, it's been nigger that, nigger this. You and those Klan boys got along pretty good too." They set the table down.

"Well, I ain't over here to beg your forgiveness or nothin', but if you're willing to let bygones be bygones…"

"I'm willing to be friends with anyone who wants to be friends with me."

Carl leaned against the table. "See, all my life, I ain't never had much use for no nig—"He quickly caught himself. "I mean, colored people before. Hell, there ain't that many of you people up here to begin with. And those I did know, either worked for me or stole from me. When you came up here, I thought you were gonna do the same thing to Ma… I mean, Vicki. She won't let me call her mom no more. Anyway, I assumed when she finally caught your hand in the cookie jar, I'd be there to grab ya. Then maybe she'd even give me the pleasure of whacking it off." Newman walked over, grabbed a chair, and slid it under the table. "But during these last several month, I've seen how much she depends on you and how the people around here are startin' to like you too. So I figured you can't be all that bad." Newman picked up another chair and placed it under the table. "Besides, I thought maybe you could help me."

Newman stopped and looked cautiously up at him. "Help you?" Newman was stunned. "Help you how?"

Carl hesitated. "Get back in Vicki's good graces. She listens to you," he quickly added. "If you told her that I wasn't such a bad person, she might believe you."

Newman, threw up both hands. "Hey, wait a minute," he cautioned. "You give me credit for a lot more influence with her than I actually have. Whatever problems exist between you and Vicki, should be worked out by the two of you."

"How? She won't give me the time of day."

"Well, give her some time, maybe after her trial. You'll have to admit, you put her in a pretty difficult situation."

"Her?" Carl bristled. "I put, HER in a difficult situation?" He sighed and dejectedly shook his head. "Everybody talks about how bad I did my own mother. Nobody ever bother to ask what she did to me."

"Maybe it's none of my business, Carl."

"Well, Ken," he began emphatically. "I'm going to make it your business. Since you've chosen to stay here and work for my mother, she has obviously chosen to tell you her side of the story. So now, you're gonna hear mine as well, and you can feel fortunate because you're the only one who's gonna know the whole truth. And if you breathe a word of this outside these walls, I'll deny every bit of it."

Newman wasn't sure if he wanted to hear this. While he was willing to help Vicki run the resort, the last thing he wanted to do was get dragged into her legal quagmire. And hearing Carl's version of the story, especially if he revealed any previously undisclosed facts concerning the case, just might get him ensnared. But his curiosity was getting the better of him, so he did nothing to discourage Carl from continuing.

"Carl…"

"Shut up and listen. She once let me run the place," he confidently began, "just like you're running it right now. Except, I also had the purse strings too. While she was off globe-trotting around Europe and Asia. I was here busting my ass trying to turn this place into a world-class showcase. I wanted to run a world-class resort, not some flea-bitten hive like you see here. But I couldn't do half the things I wanted to do or hire the kind of quality people I needed to hire with the money she budgeted for me. She gave me a three-year budget, and I spent it in one. But I hired the best people, the best chefs, waiters, and bartenders in tuxedos… man, you should have seen this place," he admired, sounding proud of his achievements. "I mean this place had a reputation… you wanna see the news clippings?"

Newman shook his head. "That's ok."

"Then Ma calls from somewhere… London, I think it was, and said her accountant told her I was spending too much money. So she cut my three-year budget down to one year at a time and put the rest of the money in accounts that only she could sign on. There was no way I could maintain the class operation I had started on the money she left me. I risked losing everything. I had hired people away from places like the Holiday Inn, the Hilton, the Marriott… big names, Ken. I mean really big names. I needed that extra money she had put in those private accounts."

"So you forged her name."

"Damned right I did!" He said proudly. "I told myself it was for her own good, but yep, I forged her name on those private accounts until all of her money was gone. But, man, I was so close. Leaving her penniless wasn't my intent. I didn't know that was all the money she had left in the world. Just like she stashed that money, I thought she had other accounts stashed somewhere. But she wanted me to run a class operation, and I couldn't run one on thin air. Now everybody's got me pegged as some sort of monster who'd steal his own mother blind."

"I heard rumors that you had… how shall we say? A very nice car, clothes, and kept rather attractive company?"

Carl hesitated. "Well, maybe I did buy a few things that I felt a man who headed a major tourist resort should have. After all, I was putting in twelve and sixteen-hour days, while she was partying all over the world."

"But it was HER, money. You could have simply told her you needed the extra cash."

"She wouldn't listen. 'Cut back', 'Trim back' was all she'd ever tell me."

"Well, she must still love you a little, at the very least. Forgery is a serious felony offense. If she had decided to prosecute, you'd be in jail right now."

"Love me?" He laughed aloud. "I know how to operate a swimming pool better than anyone else she could hire at three hundred dollars a month. Besides, she actually wanted to have me killed."

Newman immediately remembered Millie saying something to that effect. But he had known Vicki now for more than half a year and nothing he had seen in her personality even remotely indicated she was capable of murder.

"I've heard chitchats to that effect," Newman casually began, "but I just don't believe Vicki is capable of having anyone killed, least of all her own son."

"Just don't cross her." Carl bluntly warned. "Don't ever get on her bad side. I've been there and it almost cost me my life." He looked quickly around the room to make sure they were alone. "This guy in a red Mercedes shows up one day and checks in for an extended stay. He drops by the pool a couple of times to talk to me, small talk, mainly. He wanted to know my habits, what I did for fun… that sort of thing. Lots of tourists do that, so I didn't think anything of it. But days later, strange things started happening to me. First, my chain saw exploded in my hand. Burned me real bad. The brakes went out on my logging truck. A stray hunter's bullet barely missed me while I was out logging and someone left a live electrical wire open over at the pool, while I was spray washing the deck."

"They all could have been freak accidents."

"That's exactly what they were meant to look like, I found out later Vicki had taken out a $250,000 life insurance policy on me. The policy paid double in the event of my accidental death. She was the sole beneficiary."

"Didn't you know about the policy?"

"No. The only way I found out was when an agent from the company showed up to have me sign some papers for a physical exam."

"Now, I don't know much about top corporate policy procedures, but it's not uncommon for companies to insure their senior executives in case they should lose them to illness or death. That way the company is compensated for the loss."

"But eight close calls in a three-month period? Come on, Ken. Do you know anybody that unlucky?"

"Well, if someone was really trying to kill you, they obviously weren't very good at it. I mean, if a professional hit man couldn't get you in eight tries…"

"He couldn't just come right out and kill me. It had to look like an accident for the policy to pay double the face value. Accidents are harder to stage than plain ole assassinations. That's why I felt I had to do something to get her money, so she'd call off the hit."

"Are you saying that's why you counterfeited those bills?"

"Damned right! I figured that if I could get her four million back to her and maybe print an extra million for myself, everything would be great. I'd be a millionaire, she'd be out of bankruptcy, and she'd call off her hit."

"But just how were you going to launder $5million? You couldn't just wake up one day a millionaire."

"That was the easy part. Just include the fake bills in with the real change you give back to the people who passed through here. Since they come from and go to all parts of the country, the fake bills wouldn't all turn up in any one spot."

"How did you keep the whole operation a secret from Vicki?"

"Oh, she knew," he nonchalantly replied. "She didn't know about it at first. She didn't actively participate. But Gary and I were up all hours of the night running that printing press. She had to have seen us when she made her rounds of the resort late at night. The money looked just like the real stuff too. Hell, it was the real stuff. The FBI gave us real plates, paper, ink, everything. That son-of-a-bitch Gary set me up good fashion. I guess he figured Vicki and I screwed him, so he was going to screw us. Besides, I kept the plates in her safe. Even though she never locked it, everybody else thought it was locked. So it was the perfect hiding place. She never asked where those plates came from and I never told her. She didn't want to know."

"She's a very trusting person, Carl. How do you know for sure that she knew what you both were up to?"

"Those freak accidents, they suddenly stopped just like that," he snapped his fingers, "right after we started our counterfeiting operation. Now, if you so much as breathe one word of this, I'll deny ever saying a word to you. I've caused her enough problems. I don't want to cause her anymore."

Newman seriously pondered what Carl had said. He was now trying to imagine Vicki in the lurid, sinister light Carl had just painted, instead of the brave, courageous, iron-willed entrepreneur, who was struggling valiantly to save her business that her evil son had ruined. Was it possible that the roles in fact, are reversed? Had Vicki deliberately withheld vital operating funds from Carl in order to finance her worldwide travels, forcing him to resort to desperate measures to try and do the very job she hired him to do? Was she capable of trying to have her own son killed? After months of seeing Vicki in the unquestioned role of heroin and Carl, as the evil villain, Newman was now, for the first time, beginning to have second thoughts as he struggled to resolve his ambivalence toward her.

"Why now, Carl?" Newman asked bluntly. "Why, after all of these years, are you just now trying to get back in her good graces? Especially if she is as bad as you say she is?"

"She's my mother above all else," he said somberly, "and, as you know, her heart is bad. I would hate for her to leave this Earth with things the way they are between us. She's made some mistakes, and I have made some mistakes. It's time to put those mistakes behind us and start life fresh as mother and son. Would you tell her that for me? She trust you. Considering the problems you and I have had, if you tell her I'm a changed person, she just might believe you."

"Carl, I don't know what I can do, but I'll do what I can."

"Thanks, man. I'd really appreciate that. Being friends again with my Mom, would really be great. You know, I've never had a nig… I mean a colored friend before in my life. You just change all of that."

Newman smile. "I'm glad to hear that. But, do you want to know something that could help that friendship along?"

"Tell me," Carl eagerly insisted. "You name it."

"Lose the 'N' word."

He laughed. "Oh, you mean…"

"Yea, that one," Newman quickly interrupted.

"Shucks, man. I don't mean nothing by it. That's just the way folks 'round here talk, that's all. Habit, man. You know how hard habits are to break?"

"I certainly do. But if this friendship is going to get off to a good start, that's one bad habit I strongly suggest you break."

"How?"

"Well, the best way I've found to break a bad habit is to substitute another one in its palace. So whenever you think of saying 'that word,' use another word in its place."

"Like what?"

"Like… like …" Newman struggled for a word. "Like Martians. Yea, there's one minority group that you can't possibly offend."

"You mean like in little green men?"

"That's exactly what I mean."

"Why, that's silly," he protested.

"No more so than that other word you've been using."

Carl thought for a moment. "Martians, eh?" He reluctantly agreed.

"Try it. You'll get used to it. Anyway, I'm glad we had this little conversation. You have definitely filled in a few more pieces in this awful puzzle." He surveyed the rearranged dining room. "Well, looks like we're finished here."

"Well, I guess we can go get those tickets now, eh?"

"Oh, forget'em," Newman sighed. "I'll tell Vicki it was a bad idea. Like you said, if you're really gonna steal from her, you aren't going to be stopped by a measly roll of theater tickets. Let's go."

They both started out of the dining room and stood on the front steps. When far off in a distance they noticed Mark and Tracy, stumbling, talking and laughing. They were trying to keep each other from hitting the dirt. They soon approached Mark's cabin. Newman and Carl were not surprised.

Suddenly, Mark winced, struggling to carry and extremely giddy Tracy in his arms, while twisting his key in the lock on his cabin door. He finally kicked the door open and carried her bridal-style into the cabin. He kicked the door shut, hoisted her into the bedroom, and dropped her like a dead weight on the bed.

"Tracy smiled coyly up at him. "Very good, cowboy," she softly admired, lying on the bed in a seductive pose. "Let's see what else you have?"

Mark stood by the bed side and hastily ripped off his shirt, revealing a well-developed six-pack abs, an extremely hairy chest and firmly toned muscled arms.

"Wow!" She drooled. "My kind of body."

"You ain't seen nothin' yet," he boasted, as he unzipped his pants and pushed them down to his ankles, revealing a very large hanging member.

Tracy crawled over to the side of the bed and gently cupped the rapidly swelling organ in the palm of her soft, delicate hand. "You're exactly what the doctor ordered," she softly whispered. She could feel him hardening in her grasp as she gently pulled him into the bed next to her. Their lips met as her free hand lovingly cupped the back of his head to maintain their seal of affection.

Half an hour later, an exhausted Mark had rolled over on his back and was staring quietly into the log cabin ceiling. Tracy gently snuggled close to him and ran her fingers gingerly through the waves of hair on his chest.

"That was good cowboy... very good." She smiled. "Let's do it again."

Mark glanced over at her, somewhat taken aback by her forwardness. He was used to being the aggressor in a relationship, and her efforts to supplant that role made him a little uneasy.

"What's the rush?" He calmly asked. "Are you checking out or something?"

"Not for another half hour or so at least." Tracey quipped. "So we've got time for one more."

Mark looked at her, astounded. "What!"

"Hey," she quickly added, surprised by Mark's reaction. "I was just kidding. I don't know when I'm checking out. I'm just here on vacation." She could see the uneasiness in his eyes and quickly sensed something else was bothering him. "Talk to me, cowboy," she playfully chided. "What's the problem?"

"Oh," Mark sighed. "It's just that something here doesn't make sense. I mean, a beautiful woman like yourself, driving a new Porsche with New York plates all the way to no man's land, and you end up in my bed. Then, the way you slapped that fifty on the counter back at the bar like it was nothing. I've gotta ask myself, why would a rich girl come all of the way to the mountains of Montana, to hop in the sack with a poor, dumb, uneducated logger like me?"

She looked up at him and chuckled. "You may be uneducated, but you certainly aren't dumb, are you?"

"Well? How about an answer?"

"Do I have to have a reason to sleep with you, or can we just enjoy it for what it is? Does everything we do, have to have a reason, cowboy?"

"That's just it. I did enjoy it. Can I look forward to jumping in the sack with you again, or is this it?"

"Let's just enjoy ourselves now, okay? And let tomorrow take care of itself. Tell you what cowboy," she quickly suggested, "let's drive up to Flathead Lake tomorrow, rent a boat, take a picnic basket and spend the day, just you and me?"

He hedged. "I don't know about that. I drive one of Jake's logging trucks, and I really can't afford to take a day off."

"Well then, can I hire you as my personal guide for, let's say… five hundred a day?"

Mark's jaw dropped. "Dollars?"

"No, silly," Tracy chided. "Coke cans… of course dollars. Now can we quit all of this silly talk and get back to some action?" She pulled his body close to hers. He slowly rolled over toward her and pulled the covers up over their heads.

Meanwhile, Vicki was sitting at the receptionist's desk reading a stack of legal papers when Newman stepped into the office. She looked up at him as he entered.

"Vicki!" Newman announced, surprised. "I didn't expect to find you here?"

"It's almost noon on Sunday. Where else did you think I'd be?"

"It's just that Carl said he came by earlier to get the pool keys and the door was locked."

"Carl," she sighed dejectedly, looking back down at the paper. "You had to bring his name up just when I thought the day was going so good. No wonder I didn't answer the door. When did you see Carl, anyway?"

"This morning at Church." Newman eased down into the chair across from her.

"Church?" She laughed. "Talk about closing the barn door."

"Vicki," Newman cautiously began. "don't be too hard on him. We had a long talk after services this morning. He sounds like he wants to turn over a whole new leaf, especially concerning his relationship with you."

Vicki laid the papers down on the desk, leaned back in her chair, and smiled. "I didn't think he could do it, but then, I should never underestimate that son of mine."

"Do what?" Newman was confused by the statement. "Snow you over. Especially, after that beating he gave you shortly after you first got here."

"I never said it was Carl who gave me that thrashing."

"You didn't have too. But just for your information, it was Shay who told me or confirmed my suspicion," she quickly continued. "There's little that goes on around here that I don't know about. If you had complained, I would have shit canned him that very day, but you didn't. So you said you wanted to take care of it yourself, so I let it be."

"Well you can see how things worked itself out."

"So what did he tell you Kenny? He probably told you about how I tried to kill him for the insurance money and how he only counterfeited the money so I'd call off this imaginary hit man."

"Vicki, I wasn't here, so, like I told Carl, I'm not going to take sides in this affair. Whatever happens is strictly between you and him. But if Carl is willing to admit his mistakes, maybe someday you both can at least be friends, if not mother and son."

"Ohhh, how touching," she quipped as she leaned forward and picked up the legal papers lying on her desk. "Remember my heart attack awhile back?"

"Of course. I gave you your pills."

"News of my possible departure from this world also spreads like wildfire, especially among people with a vested interest in my heath." Vicki turned the papers around toward Newman.

He read the bold-lettered heading. "LAST WILL AND TESTAMENT."

"And guess who's going to be cut out like a malignant cancer. Now, after I go through my will and finish deleting any and all references to Carl's name and he still wants to kiss my… and make up, then tell him we can talk."

The phone rang. Vicki snapped it up. "Hot Springs." She listened for several minutes. "Forty, are you sure?… Okay, thanks Ross for the warning." She eased the phone down and looked up concerned. "That was Ross over at the Lake Springs Lodge across the border, up the road. She said about forty bikers are headed our way. My goodness, Ken, what if that's the gang? The ones that are wanted by the FBI for holding up those resorts. What if they are in that group of bikers? I'll wake up Jake and tell him to get some men together."

Newman rose from his seat. "Vicki. Today is Sunday. How's Jake going to round up his men when they're all off today? Besides, they're loggers, not hired guns. This is a job for the police. They are trained to handle things like this. I'm giving Bennett a call." Newman grabbed the phone and dialed the sheriff.

"Kenny, those guys might take forever to get up here. I'm going to get Jake."

"So he can do what? If those murderers are in that bunch, the only thing you're going to do is risk getting him killed. Let the sheriff handle this!" He insisted. Newman dialed. "Hello?... Sheriff's Office?... Sheriff... this is..."

Nearly half an hour later, several sheriff's vehicles and SWAT unit vans had arrived at the resort with radios squawking and sirens flashing. Bennett had deployed men in flak jackets. Each man was armed with bulletproof vests, automatic weapons and high-powered rifles. He stationed them along the rooftops, behind trees, parked vehicles, and inside the buildings, behind the windows and doors.

Vicki and Newman watched from her office window as heavily armed officers in black took up prone positions at various locations along the highway.

"I'm glad you called me babe. Now, you two keep your heads down," Jake demanded, "or you're liable to get them blown off!"

Vicki and Newman both looked over to see Jake armed and ready with a double barrel shotgun at the front door. They both crouched under the office window and gingerly peeked over the ledge.

"How about the café and the pool, sweetheart?"

"They've evacuated them both already, Vicki. Now they're the professionals. Let them handle this," Jake insisted.

Seconds seemed like minutes. A tense, eerie calm permeated the area. Suddenly, over the ridge in the highway, appeared a sleek racing bicycle with small carrying bags hanging neatly on the rear of the bike. Its helmeted rider was hunched over the handlebars. He was followed by another bicyclist, then another and another. It seemed like an army of motorcycles came pouring over the ridge, coasting slowly down the incline in the road.

Newman and Vicki slowly rose from their crouched positions and stared out the window in shock and disbelief of the massive number of bikers.

"I didn't know so many traveled in one pack like that," Newman sighed.

Several cyclists quickly angled their bikes into the resort parking lot. As they were gradually surveying the area, they slowly brought their bikes to a complete stop. The sight of the flashing sirens quickly caught their attention. They noted the small army of highly armed police officers, each with an assortment of high-powered and automatic assault weapons trained at them. The bikers were in awe of the massive police presence that surrounded them, ready to fire at the smallest wrong move. Each biker quietly noted the extreme situation they were in and without hesitation, they slowly raised their hands high in the air.

"That was easy," Vicki sighed.

C H A P T E R

10

The smoke jumpers' base in Missoula resembled a military camp mobilizing for war. The firefighters clambered aboard Army style troop trucks and heavy-duty helicopters that slowly lumbered into the sky and angled toward the distant smoke-filled heavens. Two men in a parked jeep carefully monitored the frantic activity.

"Is that the last of the additional relief crews?"

"Yep, and they are all headed south across the Idaho border. We know we can stop it from spreading down there."

"Yeah, I know," the other man reluctantly agreed. "I guess that means we are also evacuating our base camp up near that tourist resort."

"Yea, that's right. I gave the evacuation order this morning. They are being relocated along the Southern Idaho border. They should be totally cleared out in the next couple of days."

"And how about the tourist resort? Did you order them to shut down as well? A sudden wind change could surround that whole place in a matter of hours. Given the rugged terrain in that area, we could never get enough rescue crews and equipment in there to evacuate everybody safely."

"Well, the owner has indicated that she's not going to close, no matter what. Especially, not at the height of her tourists season. Besides, we aren't even sure the fire will head her way. This whole evacuation is merely precautionary. And with the weather service forecasting rain for later today, this whole thing might all be for nothing. Besides, I hear she's already in Chapter 11. A shutdown like this could push her right over the edge."

"Hell, the weather service has been forecasting rain for the past several days. So far, not a single drop has fallen from the sky. And they aren't saying rain in what amounts. No, I'd feel much better if I knew those people were outta there."

"You're right, I'd sleep better too, knowing if that fire did come racing down outta those hills, innocent people wouldn't be trapped up there. I hear she's got a new foreman, who may be persuaded to see this problem, using a little common sense."

"Who's coordinating the evacuation of our people up there, anyway?"

"Grant, I think. Yeah, Paul Grant."

"Contact him. Tell him he's got twelve hours to persuade that woman to close shop. If he can't, then I'll issue a mandatory evac order and drag their butts' outta there kicking and screaming if I have to. They've got to clear out."

As the phone call was getting ready to come into Grant, Newman was continuing his normal duties of the day. Newman stood behind the counter at the swimming pool and accepted the clothes basket from an attractive bikini-clad young woman. She beamed a polite thank you and darted into the women's dressing room. Sunday afternoons were always busy at the pool, and today was no exception. Swimmers chased each other around the deck and children screamed as they careened down the waterslide. Marci sat confidently atop her elevated perch, casually monitoring the area.

Newman had finished hanging up the clothes basket when he turned to greet the next incoming customers. Mark and Tracy strolled arm in arm into the pool house, laughing and giggling as they stepped up to the counter.

"Hey boss man," Mark joyfully laughed, "you mean you actually do work around here?"

"At least until Carl comes down outta the hills with Jake's crew." He smiled at Tracy. "Are you keeping this guy outta trouble?" Newman chuckled.

"In trouble would be more like it," Tracy quipped. "Mark should be up in the hills with the rest of Jake's crew?"

"That's right." Newman noted. "Carl is up in the hills because that fire could come racing down outta those mountains at any minute. Jake wanted every available hand up there to fell as many trees as possible before the fire hits. In fact, I'm surprised he let you off today, Mark. I thought he'd have you drivers working overtime."

"Well," Mark fudged, "he didn't exactly let me off today. I'm sorta taking the next couple of days off. Tracy and me are going to spend a few days up at Flathead Lake."

"Can you believe he's lived here all of his life and he's never been there?"

"But didn't you have a contract with Jake to drive for him? I mean, he is gonna be a bit shorthanded without you, isn't he?"

"Ain't my problem." Mark confidently replied. "Besides, like you said, that fire may not leave him with any timber to cut anyway." He leaned over and kissed Tracy's cheek. "Let's just say that I got a better offer."

"Well, I guess it doesn't matter. Besides, apparently you two came here to swim, so here you go." Newman handed them both a clothes basket.

Tracy took her basket and kissed Mark on the cheek. "Last one in, as the saying goes." She darted for the women's dressing room. Mark watched until her well-formed rear had disappeared behind the door.

He turned back toward Newman and smiled. "Is that some woman or what?"

"She's quite a girl Mark."

"You know, we went out to Pier One last night. You know what a classy place that is, right? I mean, even the janitor's wear tuxedos. Anyway, I was scared to death 'cause I didn't know how I was gonna pay for the dinner and drinks. She just calmly whips out this Diner's Club Gold Card, and man, you shoulda seen those waiters fallin' all over themselves trying to serve us. I mean, it was unreal."

"Sounds like you two had quite an evening."

Mark paused and leaned closer to Newman. "We have had quite some evenings. You know, I think she's the one."

"The one what?"

"The one I'm going to pop the big question to."

Newman looked at him skeptically, slightly taken aback by his intentions. "Mark you hardly know her. What? I mean you've been dating almost a week, now?"

"I think I know all I need to know. She obviously loves me. She treats me like a king."

"And she's got money," Newman quickly added. "Would you still love her if instead of rich and beautiful, she were poor and ugly?"

"Yeah, sure… I suppose so. But even so, I still love her and she loves me, and that's all that matters."

"Well, if you are that sure, then go for it."

Mark took the clothes basket from Newman and handed him six bucks. "You know, I think I will." He darted off to the men's dressing room.

Newman turned to straighten the other clothes baskets when he noticed Grant and Vicki coming toward the pool. She smiled and waved. He acknowledged her by nodding his head.

"Kenny," she smiled as they stepped into the building, "I've been looking all over for you. Paul is back with some good news."

"Good news? Really? Is Grant's Army finally leaving?"

"Actually, we are," Grant volunteered. "That's what I came by to tell Vicki. Our camp has been ordered to evacuate as a precaution against being trapped up here in case the fire shifts directions and surrounds us."

"That's great!" Newman beamed. "Your people have done nothing but terrorize this place ever since they've been here."

"Mr. Newman," Grant politely began, "we try and keep tight reins on our people, but as they say… smoke jumpers will be boys."

"And that, of course, explains the two doors over at the hotel that needed to be replaced. The beer bottles from their after-hour skinny-dipping that we have to fish out the swimming pool every morning. And oh, not to mention the young lady who decided to bare her all in the bar several nights back."

"As I was explaining to Vicki, we'll pay for any damages our people cause. We have counseled some of our people on their inappropriate conduct. But they're just letting off steam. Remember, they're literally coming back from a war zone."

"Maybe, but that's no excuse for them to act like drunken sailors on shore leave. They're fighting a forest fire, not World War Three."

"You wouldn't say that if you actually saw what they were up against."

"You're right. I haven't seen the fire. But then again, they're trained to fight forest fires, I'm not."

Grant thought momentarily. "Are you free for the next couple of hours?"

"I don't know, why?"

"I'd like to take you on a little helicopter ride and show you the extent of the problem. I've tried to get Vicki to take a ride with me," Grant smiled over at her, "but she flatly refuses to go."

"No, thank you." Vicki readily concurred. "Standing on anything higher than a stepladder gives me the shakes. Besides, I don't care if the bowels of Hell are surrounding us, I simply can't afford to shut down this resort. I just can't, and I won't."

"Oh, I don't think so. I've got a lot of things to do around here."

"Oh, go ahead, Kenny," Vicki chide. "There's nothing taking place around here on a Sunday that urgently demands your attention."

"But Carl's not back yet. I'll have to wait for him."

"Don't worry about him. He's on a special logging project with Jake. Besides, I'll stay here until he gets back. Who knows, I may even get to see more of the pool funds now with him gone. Now, both of you get outta here."

Newman reluctantly stepped from behind the counter. And, with Vicki's continuous urging, followed Grant out of the pool house over to the smoke jumper's staging area.

It was the fear of flying more than any pressing workload that caused Newman to seriously dread this trip. Though flying had been a necessary part of his previous job, he had always boarded the plane as a reluctant passenger. That fear only became more pronounced as he approached the giant heavy-lift chopper. The side doors were open. Four men and two women in green jumper suits threw huge backpacks on board the craft, then climbed aboard themselves.

"He's just going to drop them off and come right back." Grant shouted, trying to be heard above the roar of the whirling rotor. "It's going to be a short trip, but it will give you some idea of what we are up against and why we wish you'd give some serious thought to evacuating the resort."

"Like I said, that's not my decision to make."

"Yes, but you can talk to her. Maybe she'll listen to you."

"And maybe she won't."

Both men approached the chopper with heads low. Grant pulled the passenger door open and helped Newman climb aboard. "Grab that handle inside the chopper and pull yourself in."

"Okay. Newman replied."

"You take a look around down there, then you decide," Grant yelled as he scampered aboard. He slammed the door shut, stepped back, and gave the pilot the thumbs-up sign.

The pilot acknowledged and pulled back on his control stick. Moments later, the pit of Newman's stomach began to sink as the ground grew farther and farther into the distance. Finally the chopper tilted and sped off into the distant hazy sky.

It was only minutes into the trip that the devastation produced by the forest fire became evident. Charred, smoldering trees spear for as far as the eye could see as billowing white smoke drifted lazily skyward. Bordering the blackened carnage roared and crackled a lapping wall of flames that seemed to stretch to infinity in all directions. Entire mountains and ridges had been burned away. The entire forest seemed a charred, desolate ruin. In a distance, he saw huge, lumbering aircraft dropping clouds of retardant. While other helicopters, fanned buckets of water across the desolation.

"Photos of Hiroshima didn't look this bad." Newman sighed in awe.

"This must be your first forest fire," the pilot calmly noted. "If it rains and the wind cooperates, we might just have this one licked. You should have seen this baby when it first blew or the one in Yellowstone two years ago. It was like flying into the jaws of hell."

"Where are we going now?" Grant asked. "Sector 40. All we have to do is drop these guys off about a half mile behind the fire line and head back in."

"You said this one is about licked. Does that mean it'll be out soon?" Newman asked.

"I said if it rains and the wind cooperates, we'll have it under control. Even so, it won't be completely out for several days after that."

"But you're about to get it under control, right?" Newman pressed.

"Yeah, unless the wind shifts and this thing takes off down the mountains toward Montana. Then we've got a whole new ball game." The pilot tilted the chopper again, and the craft angled off into another direction.

"Woooo!" Newman screamed. Feeling the uneasiness in his stomach.

Minutes later, the chopper slowly descended to a steady hover over a blackened hillside.

"Okay, ladies and gents." The pilot yelled over his shoulder, "Pack up and get out."

Newman looked with concern over at Grant. "They're not going to parachute from this distance, are they? They'll hit before their chutes open."

"They aren't going to chute outta here." Replied Grant.

"You can't be thinking of landing on that hillside?"

"You're definitely right there." Remarked the pilot.

"Well?" Newman impatiently awaited an answer.

"Just wait." Commented Grant.

From either side of the chopper, six ropes were pushed out of the opened sliding doors. The ropes extended some forty feet from the chopper to the charred hillside below. Moments later, the six smoke jumpers climbed out of the aircraft and began lowering themselves down the ropes like spiders on long strands of web.

Newman marveled at the seemingly effortless manner with which they dangled in midair with full field packs strapped to their backs, before slowly lowering themselves down to the surface.

"They must really be in great physical shape to do that," Newman admired aloud.

"Well, let's just say, who else do you know would climb out of a helicopter at forty feet into a blazing inferno with fifty pounds of gear, a pick, and a shovel?" quizzed Grant.

"Regular John Wayne's, they are." Newman quipped.

"We'd better get out of here. You've got to get back to the resort, and I've got to get back to town."

The pilot angled the stick, and the craft sped off in another direction. The whirl of the rotor thundered overhead, momentarily drowning out all other noises.

Suddenly the radio blared, "Mayday! Mayday! Fire team Delta, Sector 14, trapped on Ridge Nine. Need immediate assistance, over," the frantic voice announced. "Flames moving up all sides of the hill!"

"Base camp to Delta, rescue team en route. ETA fifty minutes. Mark your location spot by flare," responded the pilot.

"Delta team, 10-4 and out."

"How can they get a rescue team through all of that?" Newman was curious, pointing toward the distant flames.

"You simply evac them out by chopper, or airlift them out to the nearest road where they can be picked up by truck. Actually, we're closer to Sector 14 than anybody else." Grant noted.

"If we could get to them," Newman reasoned, "it would shave some time off getting them out of there. No telling how fast that fire is moving up the hill."

"I guess, but what do you have in mind? I can't have these guys land this chopper right in the middle of those trees. The best I can do is have them hover the treetops."

"Those six ropes back there. What if we were to let those ropes hang down to them and let them climb up?" asked Newman.

"Climbing down forty feet is one thing. Climbing up forty feet is another matter entirely," one of the pilots reasoned.

"But what if we have them tie the ropes around their waist, then lift them off the ridge? Then we could just carry then to the nearest road and let them hike out." Asked Newman.

"Ahh, I don't know," the pilot hedged. "Sounds risky. What if the ropes snap under their weight? They'd fall to their death."

"They could also burn to death in the time it takes another chopper to get there. At least mention my plan to the smoke jumpers on the ridge and give them the choice to say no." requested Newman.

The pilot looked over at Grant and sighed. He reluctantly picked up the radio and informed the base camp of Newman's idea. Before the base camp could answer, the trapped team overheard the conversation and enthusiastically endorsed Newman's idea. Moments later, the base camp gave their reluctant approval.

Newman and Grant climbed back into the cargo area and assisted the co-pilot in straightening the ropes as the pilot steered the aircraft toward the distant hills.

Minutes later, the pilot spotted the flare set by the endangered fire team. It glowed brightly from the densely forested hilltop. Meanwhile, lapping flames had engulfed the entire base of the hill and were rapidly climbing to the summit.

"Now I'll get just above the trees, and you can angle the ropes down to them."

"Good," Newman shouted back. "Let me know when you're in position."

"Team Delta to Chopper 4, we have you in sight," the radio squawked.

"The ropes are for you to tie securely around your waist," the pilot instructed. "We'll lift you off the ridge to a more secure area."

"Ten-four," the radio answered. "We copy."

Newman held onto the ropes to keep them from intertwining and maneuvered each rope carefully into position. The ropes dangled from the chopper like strands of fine web. The helicopter hovered motionlessly above the treetops as Newman and Grant struggled to angle the ropes between the trees.

Members of the fire team scrambled to grab the dangling strands. Newman watched from above as they began tying the ropes securely around their waists. Finally, they each flashed a thumbs-up sign at the chopper.

"They're ready to come up," Newman shouted.

The pilot acknowledged and slowly lifted the aircraft. Newman watched carefully as the ropes began to strain and slowly lift the men up between the trees. The fire crew members began to sway slightly in the breeze as they gradually emerged from between the trees below.

"They've cleared the trees," Newman announced.

The helicopter gradually rose and angled away from the hillside. The men dangled freely for several minutes before Newman suddenly noticed the strands in one of the ropes starting to unravel.

"Stop!" Newman shouted. "One of the ropes is starting to come apart!"

Grant scrambled to Newman's side of the helicopter.

"Look!" Newman pointed to the section of rope that was slowly popping apart strand by strand. "It's coming apart at the seams!" The rope strained under the firefighter's weight as one cord snapped, then another.

The pilot looked back over his shoulder at them. "I've got to set it down!"

Newman looked back at him in disbelief. "There's no clearing down there to land. You'll never make it!"

"That guy down there isn't going to survive a thirty-foot drop either, Mr. Newman," the chopper pilot countered. "I'll have to at least try and get as close to the ground as I can."

"Maybe if we tried to pull him up." Newman frantically suggested. "We might be able to get him aboard before the rope snaps!"

"No!" Grant insisted. "The rope might snap under the pressure of the pull."

"The rope might snap even if we don't pull. But if we don't do anything, he'll fall to his death!" shouted Newman.

Newman immediately grabbed the rope and pulled. He was straining with the weight as he tried to pull the thick strands aboard the aircraft. Grant rushed over, grabbed the rope, and started pulling as the pilot angled toward a distant clearing. The firefighter inched up toward the chopper as the aircraft angled closer to the ground. They finally reached the break in the rope just as it snapped. The man started to fall as Newman and Grant desperately grasped for the severed cord and held on for dear life. They grimaced and strained as they pulled back on the rope.

Meanwhile, the helicopter angled continuously toward the clearing. Seconds seemed like hours as Newman and Grant continued to strain holding onto the rope. The thick strands were slowly slipping from their grasp. Suddenly, his weight was too much for Newman and Grant, the rope slipped from their grip. Newman lunged for the last remaining inches before the final strands quickly slithered out of the aircraft. They both scrambled to the edge of the chopper to see the fate of the fallen firefighter. They peered down below and saw the man struggling to his feet as he untied the rope from his waist. They turned to each other and smiled. Relieved, as the helicopter hovered slightly above ground level for the other firefighters to release their ropes. Newman and Grant highfived each other and sat back on their seats, awaiting their ride home.

Back at the resort, Vicki sat behind her desk, listening with anger and impatience to the man in the Western-style suit sitting across from her. Jake stood nearby, arms folded, his ire raised.

"How?" The man unpassionately asked. "How can you continue to insist on sponsoring the rodeo with all this turmoil surrounding your place? Look, the rodeo is next weekend. You've got a raging forest fire almost on your doorstep. I read the papers. The Forest Service is thinking about shutting this place down."

"Like hell," Jake snarled.

"Even if you stay open, the bad publicity surrounding the fire, not to mention your own unfortunate legal problems, are bound to keep some people away."

"We've been doing fine so far this year, Mr. Haskell," Vicki calmly interjected. "There's nothing to say we can't continue operations here. People come here to swim and have a good time, not get involved in my legal problems."

Haskell shook his head and stood in front of her desk. "Damn it! Vicki, where are we going to set up the trailers and tents? The Forest Service has every inch of the spare grounds occupied with their men and equipment."

"They'll all be gone by next weekend, I promise," Vicki smiled. "You'll have all the space you need for your animals, horses and trailers."

Haskell sat back in his chair. "Maybe, maybe not. Now the Association has been checking into some alternate locations for this year's rodeo. In fact, most of the memberships feel it would be in everyone's best interest if the site were moved elsewhere this year. "

"Over my dead body," Jake growled.

"What my husband meant to say," Vicki calmly interjected, "was that we have a signed legal agreement with the Association. So far, we have done nothing to break that agreement. So if you breach your end, why we'll have no choice but to sue you for every penny you and the Association have. Do I make myself clear?" She politely smiled.

Haskell looked at her in dumbfounded silence and glared over at Jake. Jake nodded his head.

"Good." She rose from her chair and walked over to him. She gently pulled him out of his chair and escorted him toward the door. "Now don't look so glum, Jerry," she consoled. "I've never let you down so far, have I? And I'll come through for you again, you'll see. We'll have the biggest parade ever this year. Don't worry. I'll handle it." She ushered him out of the door, then turned and leaned against it with a big sigh. "How will I handle it, baby?" She asked, rhetorically. "That blaze has been burning for months, and they still haven't gotten a handle on it. And if they order us to evacuate, then what?"

"We stay put," Jake defiantly insisted.

"Right," she huffed. "And the Forest Service puts out an advisory saying don't come here, or you'll burn to a crisp. No one comes to the rodeo. It's the same as shutting us down."

Jake thought for a moment. "What if we could convince people that this place would be safe no matter what that fire did?"

"Ahhh," she laughed, "and how do you propose to do that?"

"Well, I'm no big-time firefighter, but I do know my logging. If I can clear a wide enough path between that fire and this resort, even if that blaze came roaring down the mountain, it would get right to that clearing and stop."

"A firebreak." Surmised Vicki.

"If that's what it's called, yeah."

"But, darling, you couldn't cut a wide enough path fast enough in time for the rodeo."

"Not cut, sweetheart, blow."

"Blow?" Vicki was hesitant. "You mean like with dynamite?"

"And blasting powder. In a week we could clear a five-mile-long path along either side of the highway. After we clear the debris, you'd have your firebreak."

Vicki sat in her chair and shook her head. "I don't like it. You're no demolition expert. You could get hurt or worse."

"Oh relax, woman." Consoled Jake. "What's complicated about setting a few charges, lighting a fuse, and hauling ass? In fact, I've got Carl and the boys up there right now setting the charges."

"Don't oversimplify matters. It sound dangerous. I know there's a lot more to it than that."

Suddenly the phone rang. She snatched it up. "Hot Springs Resort… Kenny!" She beamed. "Where are you?… I'm sure it is a long story. You can tell me all about it when you get back… About an hour? Okay, see you then… bye." She eased the phone down. "That was Kenny calling from the smoke jumper's base in Missoula."

"What's he doing there?"

"Oh, something about smoke jumpers on a rope. I didn't get the full story. He's on his way back now."

"Well, I'd better get back and see how those guys are doing." He turned to leave.

"Honey, I love you. I don't want to see you or anyone else hurt," Vicki pleaded. "I really wish you wouldn't."

"Look, that rodeo is one of the biggest moneymakers of the year. I'm not about to lose it."

"I don't want to lose you."

Jake stared lovingly into her eyes. "Babe, ninety-nine percent of the reason you even bought this resort is because I asked you too. And I'm not about to let you lose it. Now I'll take care of the firebreak, you take care of the rodeo." He stormed out of the office.

Jake made hast back up the trail. As he hurried up the road, he spotted Newman and Grant. Jake waved and zoomed past. Newman barely got his hand up to wave, before Jake had disappeared.

"Was that Jake?" Grant asked.

"I think so."

"He was in a hurry."

"Perhaps he didn't want to be away from his men too long."

"I guess."

Newman watched the trees whiz by as the car meandered its way up the mountain road. Though he didn't know why, the trip back to the resort always seemed to take longer than the identical trip to town.

"Well, what do you think she'll do?" Grant asked.

"Don't ask me. You know how adamant she is about not evacuating. I just don't know."

"But I have a legal evacuation order. She's got to shut down."

"And kill the biggest event of the summer season? And considering she's in a Chapter 11, this rodeo could make or break her."

"I realize that." Rationalized Grant. "But if we get several hundred people trapped and possibly killed up there, all because we didn't want to hurt her tourist trade… well, I'm sure nobody wants that."

"Let's just hope you can make her understand." Asserted Newman.

"Me?" Grant asked, surprised. "You're her manager, you've even seen the fire firsthand. By the way, that was a brave thing you did back there."

"Yeah, well, that was nothing compared to telling Vicki and Jake to shut down operations."

Grant pulled into the resort parking area and came to a stop in front of the office. "You break the news to her. I'll see how the smoke jumpers are coming along breaking camp, then I'll come back to talk to Vicki."

Newman climbed out of the car and shut the door. "Big deal," he huffed through the open window, "by then, the yelling and screaming will be over."

Grant smiled. "That's the whole idea." He sped off.

Newman started up the stairs when the door opened. Tracy stood in the doorway.

"Hi Tracy." Newman noticed a credit card receipt in her hand. "You're not leaving us, are you?"

"Fraid so," Tracy quipped.

"Well I hope you and Mark are happy wherever you go. And don't forget to write."

Tracy started down the steps. "Mark's not coming with me. I'm going back alone."

Newman looked at her, concerned. "You two didn't have a fight or anything?"

"No, he doesn't know I'm leaving. He went to the cabin about an hour ago. So I saw this as a good opportunity to leave."

Newman followed her down the steps to her car. "Tracy, if I'm out of line, tell me, but I thought you and Mark were hitting it off well."

"Too well," she hedged. "I didn't come up here to find a husband."

"Then why did you come, Tracy?" Newman candidly asked.

He knew it was none of his business, but he had always wanted to know why a sophisticated woman like her would even hope to find romance in a mountain resort of loggers, truckers, and cowboys. Especially, when New York reamed with executives straight from the pages of the Wall Street Journal.

"You've never been to New York, have you, Ken?"

"No, I haven't."

"You should go. If you think I'm attractive and affluent, you'll find ten more just like me around every corner. If you get tired of one, just move on to the next one. And men? There are men there, of course. Some of them think they are prettier than I am, while others are in such demand that they feel you should be honored if they call you once a month, if then."

"You and Mark have been stuck together like bubble gum to a shoe. Two weeks of fun and bye. Just like that. How is Mark going to feel?"

"I just wanted to see what it felt like to be with a man. No games, just muscles and sex, that's it. I read about the mystique of the Montana mountain man. It said they were big and strong. The Montana cowboys and loggers, shirts bulging with rippling muscles and sweat. All hunks with no commitment. Just raw animal passion. No brains necessary."

"Well, Mark has brains."

"And compassion, and wit, charm, so why? He's everything a woman would want in a man. That's why I have to leave." Newman watched as she climbed into her Porsche.

"Hey," he said, bewildered. "Run that by me again?"

"Look, Ken." She casually explained as she placed the key in the ignition. "He could never fit into my world. Three-piece suit, dinner jackets and tickets to the opera, and me? Well, Hee Haw, Merle Haggard, and Saturday night at the beer hall, just aren't going to cut it for me."

"Love always finds a way."

"Well, not this time." Tracy started the engine. Tears were forming in her eyes.

"Tracy don't you just want to talk to him before you leave like…"

"I'll write him a long letter when I get back to New York. Tell him good-bye for me, will ya?" She backed out of the parking spot and drove off.

Newman watched until her car was out of sight. He started to turn and walk back up the steps when he noticed Grant heading his way in an all-wheel-drive jeep. He suddenly realized that he hadn't told Vicki about the evacuation order yet.

"Kenny." He turned to see Vicki smiling at him from the top of the stairs. "When did you get back?"

"Just a little while ago. I was on my way to see you when I saw Tracy leaving."

"Yes, something about a new film production or something. She wasn't too clear. Well, how was your helicopter flight?"

"Interesting. Say, Vicki, I've got some…"

"Oh, look," she interrupted, pointing to the smoke jumper's camp. "Looks like they are almost all gone." She looked at Newman with excitement. "Maybe they'll be outta here sooner than expected. Wouldn't that be great?" She seemed to almost be talking to herself.

"Vicki," Newman began cautiously, "they're not just leaving, they're evacuating."

"Leaving, evacuating, same difference," she casually scoffed. "Just as long as they're gone and here comes Grant." She leaned toward him. "He's probably here to say good-bye. Kenny, be nice to him. You know, no comments about how the smoke jumpers made a mess of somethings."

Grant pulled to a stop at the bottom of the steps.

"Mr. Grant," Vicki smiled. "Looks like your people are almost gone."

Grant looked up at her. "Yes and so should yours."

"My people? What on earth for?"

"I haven't had a chance to tell her yet." Newman conceded.

"Tell me? Tell me what?"

Newman turned toward her with a somber face. "We have evacuation orders. We have to close and move."

Vicki stared at him in disbelief. "No, Kenny…" she shook her head, "no. I'm not closing up shop. I'd just as well give this place back to the bank if I closed now."

"You'll close anyway if this place is surrounded by that fire." added Grant.

"Then let the fire shut us down. I won't shut down on my own."

"You have little choice," Grant insisted. "It's for the good of everyone."

Vicki hesitated. Her frustration was evident. She looked back at Newman as if to ask his opinion. Newman was silent. "Well, let's at least wait and see how Jake's plan works."

"Jake?" Newman asked.

"What does he have in mind?" Grant questioned.

"He's going to take his logging crew and clear a path between the resort and the fire."

"A firebreak?" thought Grant.

"Yes." Replied Vicki.

"He can't do that on federal land. That's destruction of federal property. Besides, that could take weeks with the small logging crew he has. He couldn't possibly cut down that many trees in time."

"He's not cutting them down. He's using the dynamite from the old sawmill. You know, the stuff they use on log-jams. He's going to blast the trees for his fire break."

"No wonder he was in such a hurry when we saw him." Newman added.

"Vicki, those men are loggers, not demolition experts. Do they know how to use explosives?" Grant was concerned.

Vicki fudged, "Ahhh… I… I guess… I guess so."

Grant and Newman exchanged apprehensive expressions.

"They could blow themselves to kingdom come." Grant muttered.

"Vicki," Newman was anxious, "where did they go?"

"About two miles down the other side of the mountain."

"Hurry! Get in Ken." Newman scampered down the steps and climbed into the Jeep. "We've got to get there and try to stop them before somebody gets killed."

Grant geared the vehicle and sped off.

Jake's crew sat scattered among the timber, eating sandwiches and sipping on thermoses of coffee. Jake and Carl stood near the base of a tree and adjusted the straps holding the explosive to the bottom of the trunk.

"Do you think a stick per tree is enough?" Carl asked.

"More than enough." Jake tugged at the strap to insure its security. "We'll just use the long fuses on each of the sticks. Once this first stick goes, it will ignite the next fuse on the next tree down the line, like dominos. That should give us plenty of time after we light this baby to get the hell outta here."

"Yea, but which way will these things fall?"

"Who cares? We'll just bring in the loggers, clear out the debris, and we have our firebreak."

"But can we clear five miles in seven days?" asked Carl.

"We're gonna clear five miles in seven days," Jake said, determined.

He stepped back from the explosives. "Okay, that does it. Round up the boys. It's time to get this show on the road."

Jake turned and started up the hillside while Carl called to the rest of the loggers to check their explosives and head for higher ground. The men reluctantly rose from their earthen seats and began putting away their thermos bottles and pails.

One man took one last drag on his cigarette and carelessly flipped it into a pile of dried grass. The butt smoldered unnoticed.

"All right," Carl ordered, "grab your gear and head for the high ground. Jake's going to stay behind and detonate the primary charge. When he does, I want all of you outta here. Now move!"

The men complied, picking up their carrying sacks, tool cases, and other materials before climbing the nearby hillside. Jake waited and watched as his men climbed farther and farther into the distance. Suddenly he noticed a Jeep bouncing over the rough terrain, headed toward him. He strained to identify the occupants, until finally he recognized Newman and Grant. ' Now what in hell do they want?' He thought to himself.

Grant pulled up a few feet from Jake. He and Newman climbed out of the Jeep and walked over to him.

"What are you two doing here?" Jake asked bitterly. "I'm fixing to blast a hundred-yard-long line of timber here, and believe me, none of us want to be here when it goes."

"I'm going to have to ask you not to do that, Jake." Grant politely began. "You are destroying federal property. That's a felony, not to mention placing your life and the lives of your crew in danger. You don't know how to strategically place explosives."

Jake's anger mounted. "Now you just hold on. I'm not destroying government land, I'm saving my business. And I know all I need to know about explosives. You light the fuse and haul ass. Now, ain't no bureaucrat gonna stop me from clearing this area."

"But I have evacuation orders to shut you..."

"I don't care if you have a signed note from the Pope, this timber..."

Suddenly a violent explosion rocked the earth beneath them. They all looked up to see a tall pine tree being ripped apart at the base. Its trunk, ascended several feet into the air like a launching rocket before crashing violently to earth.

"What the...?" Newman exclaimed.

Suddenly the trunk of another tree exploded, then another, hurling the trunks several feet into the air.

"We gotta get outta here!" Grant yelled.

Immediately, they all made a mad dash for the Jeep.

"Move, move!" Jake insisted.

Grant climbed behind the wheel and geared the vehicle. The explosions became almost rapid-fire. Jake climbed into the backseat. Grant jammed the accelerator as Newman held on to the overhead roll bar. They bumped and weaved their way over the rough terrain. Grant frantically turned the wheel, trying to avoid the huge rocks and rotting logs strewn in their path.

One piece of falling timber barely missed their Jeep. The impact from yet another explosion almost flipped the Jeep, while still another tree fell across their path. Grant swerved as he slammed the breaks. The Jeep almost tipped over, but came to rest, tilting slightly on the fallen tree before righting itself.

Grant looked over at Newman, then back at Jake. "You guys all right?" He huffed, slightly shaken.

Newman slowly looked over at him, almost in a daze, his hands still with a firm grip on the roll bar.

"Fine," he gasped. "I'm… I'm fine."

Grant looked back again at Jake, who was holding tightly onto the backs of both seats. "What set them off?"

"I really don't know," Jake said, looking around at the debris. "We were standing near the primary ignition charge, and I didn't touch it," he wondered as much to himself as he tried to answer Grant's question.

They all got out of the Jeep to access the damage to the Jeep. "Jake you know better." Grant scolded. "Tree demolition is a skilled procedure. If done improperly, you could get yourself killed by trees falling the wrong way."

"Not to mention falling toothpicks," Newman interjected, picking at a small object that landed on his nose. Suddenly another object fell on his cheek. He wiped it off with his finger and examined it. "Say," he announced. "This isn't wood." He looked up into the sky and another drop of falling moisture kissed his cheek. "It's rain!"

Grant and Jake both looked up as raindrops were beginning to fall faster and faster, peppering their faces with tiny water droplets. Lighting squiggled across the sky, followed by a mild clap of thunder. Newman smiled.

Jake laughed with excitement. "Yes!"

"It looks like your pray has been answered," Grant stated. "Let's head back."

They climbed back into the Jeep. An hour later, the Jeep pulled into the front resort parking lot, amid a torrential rain. They hurriedly climbed out of the mud-covered Jeep and dashed for the front office door. Vicki anxiously greeted them as they ran in. She threw herself into Jake's arms as he stepped through the door.

"Honey, you're all right." Vicki put her arms around Jake's neck and kissed his cheek. "I heard the explosions, and I was so worried."

Now, now, woman." Jake consoled, slightly embarrassed by her open display of affection and attention. "I'm all right. In fact, everybody's all right. Look at you." He stepped back from her. "You're getting yourself all wet."

"Don't worry about me, I'm just glad you're all right. Did they tell you about the evacuation order?"

"Yes, and I told them we aren't going anywhere."

Grant held the phone to his ear. "That may not be necessary. This is the heavy rain they've needed to control that fire. Okay… I'll hold." Grant turned toward Vicki, Newman and Jake. "I'm sure there's enough moisture on the ground and in the air… wait." He turned his attention back to the phone. "Okay… right, got it… thanks." He hung up the phone. "Like I suspected, your evac order has been cancelled. The fire, for all practical purpose, is under control."

"About time." Newman breathe a sigh of relief.

"You won't be needing this." He reached into his pocket and pulled out the evacuation order, tore it in half, and tossed the pieces into the trash can.

"How about your people across the street?" Vicki asked.

"They'll be all gone in the morning. I know you want to set up for your rodeo, so I intend to make sure we're all out of here as soon as possible."

"Thank you." Vicki smiled. "And for that, you have two free tickets to the rodeo."

"Now the fire danger may be gone, but remember, you now have less plant life to absorb the rain. So flooding is a new problem you'll have to…"

"Goodbye, Mr. Grant." Vicki quickly interrupted. She grabbed his arm and hurriedly ushered him back toward the door. "See you at the rodeo."

"Goodbye, Mrs. Marshall, and you too, Mr. Marshall, and same to you Mr. New…"Vicki slammed the door behind him.

"Nothing, but nothing," she said matter-of-factly, "is going to stop the rodeo."

"Honey, I'm going to make sure all my crew got off that hill."
"Ok babe."
"God blessed us Vicki."
"You're right Kenny, so let's get to work."

For the next several days, she planned the activities of the rodeo like a person possessed. Everything else seemed to pale in importance. The problems with her trial and the fire had put the planning stage of the rodeo seriously behind schedule, but Vicki wasted little time in trying to put the event back on track. She spent hours on the phone with sponsors, media, as well as various groups and associations. She personally supervised cleanup crews. She had Newman travel to nearby towns and village with posters and flyers promoting the event.

The Rodeo Association had begun moving its stables, mobile home, makeshift animal barns, and livestock holding bins onto the grounds. Other crews were busy constructing the bleachers and stands for the rodeo arena. Livestock trailers gradually replaced the campers and RV's. Moos, grunts, snorts, and other animal cries echoed throughout the campgrounds.

Everything seemed to be falling in place. Newman stopped in front of the bar and climbed out of the Jeep.

"Hey, man," a voice called him, "where have you been all morning?"

Newman looked to see Rides approaching.

"Putting up these." He pulled out a full-color poster of a cowboy in full Western dress, riding a spirited bucking bronco. "I've been to every bar and café between here and Stevensville putting these things up."

Rides looked in the back of the Jeep and saw a huge stack of posters. "You're not finished, are you?"

"Nope. I just ran out of tacks, and I was getting low on gas. As soon as I get something to eat and gas up again, I'm, as they say so aptly around here, 'On the Road Again,' he sang to the tune of the Willie Nelson song. Newman looked around at the cowboys walking around the grounds and some had their saddles slung over their shoulders. "Boy, I haven't seen so many cowboys since I stopped watching Roy Rogers."

"And they all don't read Ebony magazine either, if you know what I mean. So watch your back."

"Hey don't worry. Since I've had your training course, I'm now a lean, mean, fightin' machine." Newman smiled.

"Don't get too cocky. With enough men, even Bruce Lee can get his ass kicked." Rides gently patted him on the shoulder and walked off.

Newman stepped into the bar. The dance floor was packed as Western attired men and women whirled to the country music blaring from the jukebox. Some of the patrons gave Newman a double take as he excused himself through the crowd and made his way over to the counter.

Laura had just set a drink in front of a man and was turning for the register, when she noticed Newman at the end of the bar.

"Kenny," she hailed, trying to be heard over the music, "it's a little too early for you to be drinking, isn't it?"

"Around here?" Newman laughed. "It's never too early to start drinking. But I just came by to see how your supplies were holding up. You know, your napkins, peanuts, swizzle sticks, that sort of thing. I'm heading back into town in about an hour or so, and I can swing by the wholesalers and pick up anything you need."

"Oh, I'm fine, Kenny. I think we have enough of everything."

Suddenly, a voice called her from mid-counter, "Hey, Laura," the gruff, angry voice demanded, "My glass is almost empty damn it! I told you not to let it go dry. I want more of that White Man's Burden."

Newman looked to see the drunk. "That's..."

"Mark," Laura interrupted. "He's been drinkin' like that ever since that woman, what's her name...?"

"Tracy."

"Whatever. She left, and now Jake's thinking about firing him because he hasn't been to work in a couple of weeks. He's just been hanging around until Jake's payday. Vicki offered him a job on the resort payroll during the rodeo until he gets paid, but he turned that down, too. And the way his bar tab is adding up, he's going to owe Vicki every dime Jake's going to pay him."

"Well, keep an eye on him," Newman cautioned, as he watched Mark down the rest of the drink. "If he gets to the point where he's totally out of control, cut him off and tell him to go home."

"Oh," Laura hesitated, "Mark's in a real ugly mood right now. I don't know if he'd go for that."

"Then tell him I said for you to cut him off. If he has any questions, tell him to come see me."

Newman left the bar and headed for the crowded restaurant. He was about to sit at one of the stools and order lunch when Vicki's voice hailed him from behind. He turned to see her approaching with an elderly man in a white lab coat.

"Kenny, Andrew said you'd be over here somewhere."

"I'm just going to grab a bite to eat, gas up, and put up the rest of those posters."

"Good, but in the meantime, would you mind running Dr. MacKenzie over to the corral? You know, where the buffalo is?"

Newman looked confused. "Is somebody sick or something?"

"Oh, no, I hope not. I'm the vet," Dr. MacKenzie volunteered, extending his hand. He and Newman shook hands. "I'm just here to certify that the animal in the pasture is disease free and ready for human consumption."

"So, today's the day," Newman sighed. "You're the priest before the execution, sort of speak."

"I guess." MacKenzie shrugged his shoulders. "But I've done this so many times. If you've seen one steak, you've seen 'em all. Buffalo or cow, makes no difference."

Newman shrugged his shoulders. "I guess not. Just think of him as slow roasting over an open-pit fire as you spread your favorite barbeque sauce over him. Makes it a lot easier to accept the inevitable."

"I guess." Replied Dr. Mackenzie.

Newman rose from his stool. "Well, let's get this over with."

He and Dr. MacKenzie walked out of the restaurant.

Mark gulped another shot of tequila and jammed the glass down on the counter. "Hey," he slurred, pointing to his empty glass. "I can see the bottom. Fill 'er up."

Laura tried to ignore him by continuously wiping the counter.

"Hey!"

Mark stood up, trying to attract her attention, but lost his balance and fell sideways from the stool onto the floor. The man next to him quickly stooped to help him up. Mark just brushed his hand away and struggled to climb back to his feet.

"Listen, partner," the cowboy smiled, extending his hand again, "don't you think you've had enough?"

Mark slapped his hand aside again. "You my daddy?" Mark slurred his words.

The cowboy angrily rubbed his slapped hand and eyed Mark in contempt. "I'm just tryin' to be friendly here, mister. I'm gonna excuse your slappin' my hand on account of you're drunk, but I ain't let too many men slap my hand of friendship and just walk away."

Mark staggered up to the man's face. "Oh, yea?"

Laura suddenly stepped over and reached at Mark from across the counter. "Mister, please," she politely begged. "He's really a nice guy. His girl left him a few days ago. You know how it is."

The man looked over at Laura, then back at Mark, a pathetic figure struggling just to stand up. He reached into his pocket, peeled out a bill, slapped it on the counter, and walked angrily away.

Mark sat back on the stool and shoved his glass toward Laura. "Fill it up!"

"No!" She was emphatic. "You've had enough."

"Listen, you ain't my mama. You can't tell me when to stop drinkin'. Now fill it up!"

"No, you can hardly walk. Besides, Kenny said to cut you off if you got too drunk."

"Ken?" He questioned aloud. "What's that nigger got to say about how much I drink?"

"Ken doesn't want to see you out of here on your ass," Laura said angrily, "which is exactly where you'd be right now if it weren't for Ken and Vicki."

"Well, somebody'd better teach that boy how to mind his own business. It may as well be me." He turned his bar stool around. Mark combed the bar for Ken. "Kenny boy!" The patrons sitting at tables looked in his direction. He stumbled off the stool and walked around the bar area. "Get set, Kenny boy," he muttered to himself. "I'm comin' to kick your ass."

As Mark scoured the bar searching for Newman, Newman pulled to a stop alongside the corral. MacKenzie climbed out of the Jeep and grabbed his medical bag. He saw Dave from the gas station standing near the corral gate holding a breeched single-barrel shotgun nestled under his arm.

"I see the executioner is right on time." MacKenzie quipped.

"Knowing Dave, he's been camped out here with that shotgun since yesterday." Newman muttered under his breath.

"Well, I've got some paperwork for this man to fill out," MacKenzie said. "It'll take a couple of minutes. You can stay and watch or come back and pick me up in about half an hour."

"I've got some more papers to pick up. I'll come back and get you later." Newman geared the Jeep and sped off.

Back at the restaurant, Mark was still on his quest to find Newman. He stormed into the restaurant and stood in the doorway, momentarily scanning the patrons.

Angie walked over to him and smiled. "Hi, you looking for a seat, big guy?"

"I'm looking for Newman," he growled. "Where is he?"

"Gee," Angie glanced around the seating areas, "I don't know. He was here not long ago." Inadvertently she looked out the window. "There he is," she announced, pointing to Newman's Jeep approaching the café.

Mark looked out the window. "I'm coming to get you nigger boy!" Mark yelled out loud. All the patrons heard him. He turned and stormed out of the front door. Seconds later, Angie looked over her shoulder at a small group of men that had quickly gathered at a window.

"Hey, what's going on?" Another patron asked one of the eager spectators.

"Fight," he immediately replied. His eyes were glued on Mark's determined march toward Newman's Jeep. "Twenty says he smokes the nigger."

"You're on," another agreed. "I'll take a piece of that." The men started eagerly digging for their wallets.

Newman pulled into the parking lot only to see Mark beckoning him. He angled the Jeep toward Mark and stopped several inches from him.

"What's up?" Newman asked with a smile.

"You know damn well what's up!" Mark snarled. "What gives you the right to cut me off from the bar? I'm a paying customer."

The smile disappeared. "Correction, you're a charging customer. You've got a tab there that's starting to rival the national debt. If you're not careful, you're going to leave here without a dime. Six months' work and still flat on your butt."

"You my daddy, eh, black boy? Suppose you're gonna tell me when to go to bed next, eh?"

"Somebody should. You're drunk on your ass right now, Mark. Go home and sleep it off."

"Drunk, eh? Well, get outta that Jeep. I can still kick your ass, drunk or sober." Mark staggered backward, raising his clinched fist at Newman.

"Then what? Say you kick my ass. Laura still is not going to give you a drink. Now you and I dueling it out here in the parking lot may make a nice sideshow, but it won't bring Tracy back. That is, what this is all about, isn't it? I mean the booze, the job loss, the anger?"

"You leave her outta this!"

"Why?" Newman climbed out of the Jeep. He could tell that the mere mention of Tracy's name touched a sore nerve that could either lead him to calm reason or explode in rage. "She's the reason you're drinking yourself to oblivion, isn't she?" Mark didn't answer. "Isn't she?"

"What if she is, damn it! I want to forget her, and I can do that in a bottle."

"You can also do it by finding somebody else. Look at this place. It's a supermarket of eligible women."

"You still don't understand, do you? I love Tracy. She isn't just another bitch to lay. I love her and her alone."

"Well, it takes two, doesn't it? She's decided to get on with her life. It's about time you do the same." Newman started to climb back into the Jeep.

"Damn it! Don't you walk away from me like that." He lunged and threw a wild roundhouse swing at Newman. Newman easily sidestepped the blow. He just grabbed Mark's arm and twisted it forcefully behind his back.

"Now you listen to me," Newman angrily insisted, "if you want to put on a show for everybody, fine. If you want to spend your last dime on whiskey, that's fine, too, but leave me out, understand? Yeah, it hurts, but if you haven't got the guts to lose at love, you shouldn't play the game." He shoved Mark away.

Mark fell. He struggled to his feet and dusted himself off. He took a couple of steps toward him. Newman squared, ready for a fight. Instead, Mark just stood there with tears swelling in his eyes.

"I love her, man." He shook his head somberly. "I really love her." Newman slowly relaxed.

"I'm sure you do," he gently consoled, "and she'll never know what a good thing she lost, will she?" Mark wiped the tears from his cheek.

"Say, I was headed over to the restaurant for a bite to eat. How about a cocktail on me?"

"A cocktail?" Mark was skeptical.

"Fruit cocktail, that is!"

Both men smiled. Newman threw his arm around Mark's neck and patted him in the chest. They both headed back toward the restaurant. Suddenly, there was a loud shotgun blast, followed moments later by a heavy thud. Newman shook his head sadly and walked up the steps with Mark for their cocktail.

CHAPTER
11

The drum major reared back and blew his whistle three times. He lowered his baton and the band behind him sounded a Sousa-style march as they stepped to the beat of the music. Cheering crowds lined either side of the highway, applauding the assorted floats and the decorated cars, while pretty girls in Stetson hats and tasseled Western wear, smiled. Their arms waving the metronomes, high astride frisky horses, or from the backseats of slow-moving late-model automobiles.

Jake smiled, while sitting astride his slightly unruly palomino, occasionally doffing his Western-styled hat at a pretty face in the crowd.

Several miles ahead of the parade, activities at the resort were in full swing. The grounds had never been so crowded. While, across the highway, the loudspeaker blared the appearance order of each rodeo contestant. By mid-afternoon, the resort had taken the appearance of a county fair, with small crowds at each attraction. The bleachers at the makeshift arena were packed to capacity.

Newman gazed out Vicki's office window and was awed by the throngs of people roaming the grounds.

"Is it like this every year?"

"Oh, no, sometimes there are more people," she casually answered.

"I guess a lot of them stayed home because of the forest fire scare." Stated Newman.

"Well, it's just as well. Even with the crews we have on duty, we'll be strained to meet the demands of a crowd this size."

"You were able to hire added part-time help, weren't you?"

"Yes, and Jake's logging crew is even helping out." answered Vicki.

"But still, Vicki, look at all of those people out there."

"Kenny, you worry too much. Everything will be all right. Just wait, you'll see."

The front door swung open. A young blonde boy wearing a Stetson hat and Western-style clothes stood in the entrance. Vicki looked up at the boy and smiled.

"Jeffrey!" She exclaimed. "Jeff, I didn't think you'd be back this year. What a surprise!" Vicki walked over to him as he stepped into the office and threw her arms around him. "I heard you were here today, but I didn't believe it, especially not after…"

"I know, Mrs. Marshall," Jeffrey interrupted somberly. "I hadn't planned on being back, but I changed my plans."

She looked over at Newman, who stood silently watching the two embrace. "Kenny," she smiled. "This is Jeffrey McBath, third-place all-around rodeo champion for all of last year and he's only fifteen years old."

"Please, Ms. Vicki." He blushed. "I'm sixteen this year. No point in makin' me out to be younger than what I am."

"Fifteen, sixteen---still that's a big accomplishment in such a short period of time." Vicki added. "Don't be so modest."

"It's a pleasure to meet you." Newman smiled, extending his hand.

"I've heard so much about you," Jeffrey said as they shook hands.

"Some good things, I hope." Newman quipped.

"Let's just say you're either liked or disliked by the folks around here."

"So what else is new?"

Jeffrey turned back toward Vicki. "I just came by to say hello. You were real good to Ma and me last year after…" he hesitated. "after what happened. Ma said I should come by and thank you again."

"That's really not necessary." Vicki consoled. "I just wish you had let somebody know you were coming. I thought you were skipping the rodeo this year."

"Like I said, my plans changed, Ms. Vicki, so let's just drop it, eh?" Jeffrey was getting defensive, and Vicki could detect the edginess in his voice.

"Well, you must be starving after your long trip here," Vicki smiled. "Have you eaten yet?"

"There's a line out the door of your restaurant," Jeffrey complained. "It's almost impossible to even get in there, let alone get something to eat."

"Oh, you'd be surprise what doors can be opened when you own the place." She turned to Newman. "Kenny, hold down the fort, I'll be right back." Vicki ushered him toward the door. "Have you ever had barbequed buffalo?"

Meanwhile, as Vicki entertained Jeffrey and Newman held down the office, at the corral, a livestock trailer was backing through the opened gate. Jake watched as the handlers positioned themselves on either side of the entrance. One man positioned the wooden ramp under the trailer, while the other one pulled the gate open. The enraged bull, trapped inside, occasionally rocked the trailer by slamming his body weight into the side of the cage. Finally, the angry bull came thundering down the ramp and into the corral. He charged the confines of the enclosure several times before stopping near mid-pasture, snorting and blowing.

Jake stared at the animal in awe. "He's still as mean as he ever was," he surmised.

"Nope, meaner," one of the handlers interjected.

Jake looked over to see one of the cowboys standing just a few feet from him.

"I know, because I feed him and take care of him. Most animals respond to care and kindness, but not this one."

"Why don't you just shoot him, and save everyone time and trouble." Jake angrily suggested.

"Shoot the Bone Crusher?" The cowboy was in disbelief of the comment. "No way! Why do you think people come to see these rodeos, anyway? The bull that can't be ridden. The Bone Crusher is what keeps the suspense in these events. Will this be the year someone finally rides the Bone Crusher? And the $100,000 purse really keeps the attention high, too."

"But that bull has already injured two men, one for life, and last year he killed that bull rider. What's his name?… Ahhh… McBath I think? Right here on these grounds." Remarked Jake.

"These are professional cowboys, Jake. They know the risk before they climb aboard these animals."

"But this is supposed to be a fun sport, not a matter of life and death."

"Jake, to some of these guys, professional rodeo is a matter of life and death."

Jake just shook his head and watched Bone Crusher gallop around the corral.

As the rodeo was in full swing and Vicki was entertaining a guest, Newman sat at Lisa's desk with the phone pressed against his ear. There came a knock at the door and a handsome young man in a black three-piece suit walked in. Newman looked up and motioned toward the man to wait. The man acknowledged.

Finally, Newman placed the phone down and turned to greet the man. "Yes, sir, what can I do for you?"

"I'm here to see Mrs. Marshall," he announced politely.

"I'm afraid she's not in right now. Can I help you with something?"

"Thank you, no," he firmly replied. "Perhaps you could tell me where I might find her."

"The last I heard she was headed for the restaurant. But really, she is quite busy today with the rodeo and everything. Maybe I can help you?"

"I hope she's not too busy to see her own son," the man casually replied. Newman paused as if to digest the importance of his statement. "You aren't Robert, are you?"

"No, I'm Gregory. But I can see she's been talking a lot about us."

"You can just bet she has." Newman rose from his chair, smiling and extended his hand. "I'm Ken…"

"Ken Newman," Gregory interrupted as he and Newman shook hands. "Mom's told me all about you in her letters. I just came down to see if it's true."

"True? If what's true?"

"That you can walk on water."

Newman chuckled. "Sometimes, I don't think even that ability would help much around here."

"You don't have to explain a thing to me. Before my private practice started growing, I used to help out down here during the summer. And I really needed eight arms just to try and keep pace."

"Well, if you have any suggestions on how to run this place, I'm open to them."

"I have one."

"Let's hear it."

"Convince her to quit."

"Quit?" Newman was in disbelief.

"Let the bank have this place so she can come and live with me or one of the other kids for a while."

Newman could tell by the passion in his voice that Gregory was serious.

"But Vicki has poured her heart into this place." Newman explained. "As her son, you more than anyone should know how much this place means to her."

"Look, I'm not telling you anything I haven't told her over a thousand times, and yes, she has fought her way out of some seemingly hopeless situations before in her first business. But she's not twenty-five anymore. Even if she succeeds in pulling this place out of bankruptcy, every dime's worth of profit she makes will go to paying off those lawyers she's hired to keep her out of jail. And the added stress, combined with her heart condition, on top of everything else, and you've got nothing but slow suicide."

"Then why are you telling me all of this?"

"You're the impartial third party. She trusts your opinion. I'm just a hysterical son."

Newman thought momentarily. "Have you mentioned this to Jake?"

"Jake," Gregory huffed. "How she ever got hooked up with that penniless cowboy, none of us will ever understand. No, I haven't talked to Jake. Mainly because I hold him responsible for getting her into this rat hole in the first place. And don't even mention, that, that no-good brother of mine, Carlton. Jake talked her into selling a profitable business in Oregon to buy this… this…" Gregory caught himself starting to rant and quickly regained his composure. "In other words, I really don't care to see Jake today or Carlton either, for that matter."

"I see." Newman decided not to press the issue. "Well, do you have your tickets to the rodeo? I'm sure Vicki has some extra ones around here."

"Oh, don't bother. Thank you, but no. The last time I took the kids to that rodeo, last year, in fact---some cowboy got his skull caved in by this bull he was riding. It was not a pretty sight, especially for eleven and twelve-year-olds."

"You mean somebody was killed in the rodeo last year?"

"A McBeth or McBride or…"

"McBath?"

"Something like that."

Suddenly Vicki walked through the front door. "Kenny, there is a case of beer that…" She stopped mid-sentence as she noticed Gregory standing near the desk. "Greg! "She exclaimed. She ran over and enveloped him in a huge hug. He gave her a big hug and a kiss on the cheek.

"I knew you'd come this year," Vicki beamed. "I just knew it."

"Have I missed a rodeo yet, Mom?"

"No, it's just that I know how you feel about this place and well…"

"Mom, you know I'd never let my feelings about this place come between us. I love you."

She smiled as she released her embrace. "That's good to know my son and I love you too." Suddenly as if realization were a hammer, "Oh, me, where are my manners?" She groaned. "Greg," she turned toward Newman, "I'd like you to meet Kenny Newman." She motioned toward Newman.

"Mom," Gregory gently corrected, "we've met already. Besides, from your letters I feel like I've known him for years."

"I just want you to know, Kenny's been like a godsend around here."

"I'm glad you've got somebody you can finally depend on."

"Well, I've always had Jake around, you know."

"Right." Greg said halfheartedly. "I know."

"Where are Paul and Amy?"

"In the car. I wanted to make sure you were here before I brought then in."

"Well, go and get them." Vicki said anxiously. "I want to see my grandchildren."

Newman was beginning to feel out of place. "I think I'll check on the pool crew." He suggested trying to excuse himself from the room.

"Oh, Kenny, there's a case of beer in the back of the Jeep and a brown bag on the passenger seat I want you to delivery to a friend of mind. He is in a trailer with a bucking bronco painted on the side. Would you be a dear and take them over to the barbeque pit area at the RV Park? I told the campers over there I'll bring it to them."

"Sure, Vicki." Newman quickly agreed, eager to leave this family gathering. "I'll take care of it right now."

He hastily left the office and climbed into the Jeep. As he started to back out, he heard the screeching sound of peeling tires on the pavement behind him. He quickly looked back over his shoulder to see clouds of black smoke billowing from the huge rear mag tires of the sleek black Corvette. He caught a glimpse of the occupants as they whizzed past. He recognized the driver as the same kid he had chased from Marci's room several months earlier.

The car stopped momentarily, then violently peeled off again, leaving thick, heavy clouds of black smoke and the pungent odor of burnt rubber in its wake. The car sped toward the RV campgrounds. Since Newman was headed in that direction anyway, he decided to reacquaint himself with the driver. He followed the Corvette to a spacious luxury mobile home parked in one of the wider spaces. Loud rock-and-roll music blared from within, as teenagers filed in and out. Many palming cans of beer.

The corvette stopped alongside the RV's entrance. The two boys started to climb out of the car just as Newman pulled up behind them.

"Gentlemen," Newman calmly hailed. They both looked back at him.

They looked at each other, then shook their heads. "What do you want now, man?"

"It's not against the law to drive off quietly in that thing." Newman said calmly, pointing toward the Corvette. "While you're on the grounds, in fact, I'm going to have to insist that you not burn rubber, okay?"

Both boys halfheartedly nodded their heads, then turned and headed for the door of the camper. A bikini-clad girl appeared in the doorway holding a can of beer. Jay took it from her hand and turned the can up to his lips. He then slowly crumpled the aluminum, looked over at Newman, then tossed the twisted metal onto the ground. They laughed as Jay followed her back inside the motor home.

As Newman started to leave he noticed Jeff McBath approaching the entry trailer for the rodeo. He knocked on the door of the expansive mobile home trailer and waited.

"Come in," the gruff voice from inside called.

Jeffrey pushed the door open and removed his black felt Stetson. He looked around at the neatly furnished room. The walls were lined with plaques and action rodeo photos. Trophies dotted the tables, and a pair of golden cowboy boots mounted as a centerpiece decorated the mantel. The heavyset man sitting behind the huge mahogany desk pulled the smoking cigar from his mouth and motioned toward Jeffrey to sit in one of the huge cushioned chairs facing his desk. Jeffrey complied.

"They said you wanted to see me?" asked McBath.

"Yes, son." The man smiled. "Do you know who I am?" The big man sternly asked.

"Raymond Rodgers. Why you're the president of the Western State Rodeo Association."

"Ray, everybody just calls me Ray. And I've heard about you, too. Why, in just a year, you've become the youngest ranked rodeo champion in the Association. Second or third, isn't it?"

"Third."

"Why, that shows determination and talent." Raymond smiled. He picked up his cigar and gave a puff. "When you consider that we cover Washington, Idaho, Oregon, California, and Montana, that's a great accomplishment, son."

"Sir, is this meeting about my achievements on the circuit, or is there another reason why you called me over here?" McBath appeared impatient.

"Actually there is another reason," Raymond slowly leaned back in his seat. "Son, I'll get right to the point. Now don't get me wrong, everybody understands how you feel about the death of your Pa last year and why you dropped outta high school to join the circuit. But frankly, a lot of people, myself included, don't think that a year is enough experience for you to try and ride a Brahma bull, especially one like the Bone Crusher."

"I could use the money."

"Sure, it'd be great if you did ride him and collect the $100,000 prize money and avenge your father's death. But, your father had eight years' experience riding animals like that. And if that bull hurts you or kills you this year, especially after killing your father last year, we're going to have to do a lot of explaining as to why we let a fifteen-year-old…"

"Sixteen," Jeffrey McBath quickly corrected.

"Whatever. Why we let a young boy out there in the first place to get killed by that one-ton killing machine. It'll be suicide."

"What you're saying is that you don't want me on that bull because if I get killed, it'll look bad for the Association, is that it?"

"No, that's not it." Raymond hedged.

"Then what's the problem?" His irritation began to surface. "You have to be at least sixteen and ranked in the top 5 percent of the riders to participate in every event, including bull riding."

"Damn it! Son. Nobody's sayin' you're not championship material. You've proved that. But think about what you're putting your Mama through. That bull took her husband last year. What's it gonna do to her if that same bull, takes her son?"

"Look, Mr. Raymond Rodgers," Jeffrey's voice was cold and firm. "I'm riding the Bone Crusher and nobody's gonna stop me. I may be only sixteen, but I can die at sixteen just as easy as I could at sixty. Besides, I'm as much of a man as any twenty-five-year old, maybe more. Age ain't nothin' but a number. It's what's in here," he pointed to his chest, "that really counts."

"Look son…"

"My Pa didn't leave us much when he died, so it's up to me now to look after the family, and I aim to do just that. Ma, she ain't got too much education and she's got her hands full bringing up my sisters. So

I'm bringin' home the bread. And I'm ridin' that bull. Now you can try and stop me. But I'll sue you so fast your head will spin. I'll end up owning this here fancy office." He pushed himself up from his chair and stormed out of the office slamming the door behind him.

Meanwhile, back at the bar, the cocktail waitress weaved through the noisy, crowed dance floor, carefully balancing a tray of drinks. Finally, she set the tray down on the table and positioned the drinks in front of the two men and the woman, each clad in black leather biker garb.

"That'll be eight-fifty, please," she smiled.

One of the men dug into his pocket, pulled out a fifty, and handed it to her. "Keep the change," he quipped.

The waitress's eyes brightened. "Gee, thanks, mister." She quickly stuffed the bill in her bra and moved onto the next table.

"Way to go, Rockerfella," the woman sarcastically whispered. "We're down to our last few bucks, and he's giving it away like it grows on trees."

"Relax, my dear," he admonished, reaching over to pat her hand. "Will you look at the crowd in this place? It's been like this all day long. Not to mention, the prize money for the cowboys. When we hit this place, it's not going to be for nickels and dimes like those other piss-ant resorts."

"Shut up!" The other man insisted. "What if someone hears you?"

"Look around. Who's noticing us? Besides, we did our last three jobs around Coeur d'Alene, Idaho. This is Montana. Those wanted posters they put out on us must be lining birdcages by now. So relax, the both of you."

"Okay, but this time let's do without the massive killin', eh?" The woman interjected.

"Baby, it's too late for that. We've already killed three people. So if they catch us, it don't matter whether we kill three or three hundred. We can only fry once."

The three sat somber momentarily. "When do we make our move?" The woman asked confidently.

"Relax, babe. Give the money a chance to accumulate. In the meantime drink up. In a little while, we'll head over to the rodeo and see if they've brought the cash in for the prize awards. Today's payday will be all we need to settle down and relax for a while."

As the bikers cased the bar, biding their time, Newman had delivered the beer to the barbeque pit area. Now he went to deliver the package as per Vicki's wishes. He stepped up to the red-and-white trailer with the bucking bronco painted on the side and knocked on the door.

"It's open." The voice barked from inside.

Newman twisted the knob and walked in. Past the small range and sofa sat a clown in full-color costume, red wig, and a big red ball nose. He was adjusting his makeup in a long mirror mounted on a dresser littered with makeup paraphernalia.

"Ahhh, excuse me," Newman said, gingerly stepping over the discarded shoes, clothes, and other garments scattered about the room. "I'm Ken Newman. Vicki asked me to bring this over to you." He held up a brown paper bag and handed it to the clown.

"Thank you," the clown smiled, taking the package. "And thank her for me, too, will ya?" He reached into the bag and pulled out a jar of cold cream.

"You'd think that as many times as I have taken this stuff off my face, I'd bring along a trailer full of cold cream. My wife, or rather my ex, used to see this stuff in my suitcase and wonder about me, if you know what I mean."

Newman smiled. "Yeah."

"How is Vicki doing, anyway? The last time I was here, she was into some heavy-duty action." He dipped a cloth into the cold cream and rubbed it over his face.

"I'm afraid she's still into heavy-duty action, as you call it. Complete with a bankruptcy and possible jail term in her future. I'd definitely call that heavy-duty action."

"That's rough, man. She's a nice lady. I met her at the restaurant one time when I came here. I was eating in my clown's uniform. So whenever I come, I make it a point to just say, hi."

Newman watched with curiosity as the man removed the cold cream. His curiosity soon turned to amazement as patches of black skin appeared on the clown's face.

"Either you're Black," Newman noted, "or you wear a pretty weird pattern of makeup."

He chuckled as he ran his fingers over his skin. "Nope," he quipped, rubbing his fingers together, "this don't come off. But then it ain't come off in the last twenty-seven years." He shrugged his shoulders. He extended his hand. "Allen Bendix." They shook hands.

"Kenneth Newman. Pleased to meet you."

"Yea, I've heard all about you on the grapevine."

"Well, I can explain."

"Actually, most of it was pretty good. You've actually earned the respect of some of these rednecks around here. I don't know how you did it, but more power to you."

"Thanks. And how about you? I didn't know Vicki knew other black people."

"I've only spoken to her in my clowns' uniform. I'm not even sure if she knows I'm black."

"Well, you don't find many Blacks in rodeo, do you?"

"You don't see many Black cowboys up here mainly because there aren't that many Blacks here in Montana. But down south or in New York State, why there's even an all-Black rodeo in Harlem that puts this one to shame." Added Bendix.

"Well, what are you doing in this one?"

"They needed clowns for this rodeo too. I go where I am needed. Unlike the contestants, we got a guaranteed paycheck, three hundred dollars a day. The cowboys get paid only if they place."

"Three hundred bucks? Forgive my ignorance, but why do they place so much importance on someone who just keeps children entertained?"

Bendix stopped in mid-stroke on his face and looked up at Newman. "You've never been to a rodeo, have you?"

"No, can't say that I have."

"Well, I'm not just some tap-dancin' Western-styled throwback to Steppin' fetch it out there, just to make the white folks laugh."

"I didn't mean to imply you were," Newman quickly added, afraid that he offended Bendix.

"Tell you what," he casually replied, "meet me back here in about… hmmm… let's say…" Bendix checked his watch. "three hours, right before the third event."

"Hey," Newman hedged, "look man, no offense meant. You have nothing to prove by me."

"Look, just be here, okay?" Bendix calmly replied. "I'm going to take you to your first rodeo, from a clown's-eye-point of view." Suddenly their conversation was interrupted by the pitched squeal of peeling car tires. Newman rushed over to the window to see the black Corvette spewing rocks, dirt, and other debris from its spinning rear wheels as the car sped off. "Those guys are going to kill somebody with that thing," Bendix solemnly noted. "They've been doing that all morning."

"Yep." Newman eyed the car until it roared around a corner, a thick dust cloud in its wake. "Well, if they want to race like A. J. Foyt, they won't do it on these grounds, not if I can help it." Newman turned and headed for the door.

"Where are you going?"

"To do something I should have done a lot earlier," Newman muttered as he left the trailer.

Bendix scrambled up from his seat and hustled after him. "Remember, fifteen minutes before the third event," he called. Newman gave him a thumbs up and drove off in the Jeep.

Minutes later, Newman was back in front of the huge motor home. The black Corvette was parked conspicuously nearby. Newman climbed out of the Jeep and walked up to the door. Music and laughter blasted from inside. Newman tapped several times on the door, but no one answered. He knocked again, but still no one answered. Finally, he took his fist and pounded repeatedly.

The door swung open. Both Angela and Marci stood in the doorway, each with a can of beer in their hand. Marci's blouse was partially unbuttoned. Her broad smile turned immediately to instant surprise.

"Ken… ahhh… er… what are you doing here?" asked Marci.

"Seems I could ask you both the same question," Newman said, climbing the steps.

He stepped past them and walked into the living area. The richly decorated spacious interior was packed with young teenagers dancing to rock music that blasted from the four huge stereo speakers scattered around the room.

"Marci maybe we should leave?" Angela questioned.

"He's not our daddy. I'm not going anywhere."

"May I have your attention, please," Newman shouted, trying to be heard above the laughter and the music. But the music volume was almost deafening. Newman meandered through the maze of twisting young bodies until he came to the stereo console. He reached over and carefully pushed the Eject button on the CD player. The abrupt halt to the music caught some of the kids still dancing momentarily, until they all finally looked over to the silent stereo.

"Hey, what gives? What happen to the tunes?" The angry voices from the floor growled.

"Look," he announced. "I manage this resort, and I need to talk with the driver of that black Corvette."

"Jay?" A girl's voice asked.

"If he's the driver, yes."

Newman scanned the angry faces. There were murmurs and grumbling. Finally, Jay emerged from the rear of the group.

"Yo," he calmly raised his hand. He put his hand defiantly on his hips and eyed Newman contemptuously.

"You've got to slow that car of yours down before you hurt somebody, especially now that you've been drinking."

"Listen, man," Jay defiantly replied. "Don't sweat it, okay? I can handle my car and my beer, so lighten up, eh?"

"Not on these premises, mister. Either slow it down or your party here is history."

"Hey," Jay held up both hand, "I don't have to take no shit from you, all right? Have it your way." He turned and motioned toward his brother Martin. "Come on, let's blow this place." They stormed toward the door as the rest of the kids followed him. Some called for him to stay. He turned and angrily pointed to Newman. "Not as long as Papa Nig there is around here." He angrily countered. "Marci, come on," he motioned toward her. Marci hesitated. She stared at Angela timidly, then back at Newman, and finally again over at Jay, who could see the uncertainty in her eyes.

"Fine, I don't need you." Jay stormed down the steps. "I don't need any of you."

He climbed into the Corvette as Martin climbed into the other side. Jay geared the car. The rear wheels dug violently into the earth, spewing rock and gravel high into the air as he roared off.

The kids stared at each other momentarily, then dejectedly filed back into the living room.

Angela looked over contemptuously at Newman. "Now look what you've done," she sneered.

Newman walked over to her and smiled. "Don't worry, something tells me that we haven't heard the last of those two. Besides, Angela, at your ages, should you and Marci even be drinking at all?"

"You may be my boss, but you're not my mother and we're not on duty."

"Yeah," Marci agreed, "you really know how to stick your nose in where it doesn't belong, don't you?"

"That's what they say." Newman smiled. "Well, I'd better get outta here before I get tarred and feathered."

Newman walked down the steps and climbed into the Jeep. He rolled the window down. "Still, young ladies, at your age, you shouldn't be drinking."

"Young ladies our age, shouldn't do a lot of things," Angela said as she turned to rejoin the others. She closed the trailer door.

Newman headed back to the office and pulled into a parking space. He was about to climb out of the Jeep, when suddenly, a car barreled in off the highway and screeched to a stop next to his Jeep. The driver scrambled out of the car and scampered up the steps.

"Hey," Newman called to him, "slow down. Where's the fire?"

"I've got to get to a phone!" He eagerly demanded. "Get help!"

"Get help for what?"

"About a quarter mile up the road," he heaved excitedly, "accident, real bad accident."

"Tell the lady inside to contact the rodeo's paramedics," Newman urgently instructed. "I'll get down there and see if I can help."

Newman threw the Jeep in reverse and spun out of the driveway. He had a sinking feeling in the pit of his stomach, but, no, the chances of the accident involving Jay were too slim.

He barreled down the highway. As he came to a slight bend in the road, he could see heavy black skid marks. He rounded the corner and immediately recognized the black Corvette. It had crossed the median and plowed at an angle into an oncoming car. The Corvette had caved in the driver's side of the oncoming car and rammed the vehicle into the guardrail, impaling the passenger's side into the twisted metal barrier.

Newman quickly climbed out of the jeep and ran over to the Corvette. He peered through the broken glass in the driver's-side window. Jay lay back in his seat, face bleeding slightly, struggling to unfasten his seat belt. Groping in agony.

"No, no," he groaned in a semiconscious state.

"Just relax," Newman consoled. "Help is on the way."

He looked over at his brother. The impact of the collision had forced his skull partially through the windshield. Blood copiously gushed from several massive breaks in his head. He was dead.

He rushed over to the other vehicle. The elderly man's chest was impaled on the steering column while the woman next to him lay back in her seat, blood streaming from a huge depression on her forehead.

Suddenly he heard a small cry from the car's backseat. He rushed to the rear door and pulled it open. On the backseat, strapped into a safety seat, was an infant baby girl. He reached in, pulled the seat out of the car, and examined the baby. There wasn't a scratch on her.

The blare of sirens ripped the air as a pair of ambulances screeched to a stop several feet from the collision. Paramedics scampered out of their vehicles, medical bags in tow. Newman met them in the middle of the road.

"There's one in the Corvette, and maybe one over here, too, but that's about it." Newman instructed, pointing at the cars. Two of the paramedics rushed toward the Corvette while the other two ran toward the other vehicle.

"Did you see what happened here?" One of the paramedics asked.

"No, I just got here myself, but from the skid marks and the angle of the impact, you can pretty well figure the rest."

The other paramedic pulled his finger from the woman's throat. "These two are dead," he said solemnly. "How about the baby in your arms?"

"Not a scratch on her," Newman proudly announced.

"Here, I'll take her. We need to check her out as well and notify next of kin to pick her up."

Newman handed the child to the paramedic. "How about the boys in the Corvette?"

He watched as they gently removed a delirious Jay from the driver's seat. They lowered him onto a stretcher and rolled him toward the ambulance. Newman walked over to the medics as they loaded Jay into the back of the ambulance.

"How is he?" Newman was concerned.

"We really can't tell for sure till we get him to a hospital, but just offhand. I'd say that other than a broken left foot, he'll be fine. Too bad I can't say the same for the guy next to him. He should have had his seatbelt on. It would have saved his life."

"That was his brother, Martin."

"The driver's breath will never pass a Breathalyzer test, either. He's just going to have to live with the fact that he killed his brother."

"Not to mention that couple," Newman somberly added.

"We'll take the baby to hospital and take the bodies back to the resort and wait for the sheriff and the coroner." Said the paramedic.

"I'll stay here and warn traffic around the wreck until the police get here." Replied Newman.

The paramedics carefully removed the bodies from the wreckage, loaded them on the ambulances, and sped away. Newman took the emergency flares from the back of the Jeep and placed them several yards in both directions of the crash site.

The police had an assortment of questions as well as the usual reports to fill out. It was several hours before he could get back to the resort.

By the time he made it back to the resort, the rodeo was in full swing. The stands were packed with hundreds of cheering spectators, and the announcer's voice blared from the various loudspeakers scattered around the grounds. Newman stood behind a barricade near the corner of the arena and stared up at the crowd.

"There must be over two thousand people here," Newman breathed in awe.

"Paid attendance was one-thousand-eight-hundred-ninety-three." The voice behind him added. "Not counting the rodeo riders and the people who sneaked in."

Newman turned to see Bendix standing behind him. He was bedecked in a bright red clown's suit, big round red nose, white gloves, and red rubber curled-tipped shoes, each with a tiny bell on the tip.

"Allen Bendix?" Newman was uncertain.

"In the flesh. I waited for you to show up."

"There was an accident."

"I heard. A real tragedy."

"How did you find me?" asked Newman.

"In this crowd? You're fairly easy to find, being the only grain of pepper in a sea of salt." Bendix smiled.

"And just when do you go on?"

"Oh," Bendix calmly smiled, "any minute now. Come on, let's get over to the bull pen."

"Bull pen? What on earth for?"

Newman followed Bendix through the crowd as they excused their way around the perimeter of the makeshift area.

"And now, ladies and gentlemen," the announcer's amplified voice boomed, "the third event of the evening. The most dangerous, death-defying competition of them all… the Brahma Bull ride, featuring the Bone Crusher."

"I thought they were going to have you go out to entertain the crowd nest," Newman mildly complained as they weaved through the crowd of cowboys and cowgirls on the sidelines. "They're just getting set for the bull ride competition next."

"Just relax, it's almost ShowTime."

Finally they came to an animal chute. A cowboy sat straddle a huge impatient snorting bull. He adjusted his grip several times on the rope strapped tightly around the restless animal.

"Where the fuck have you been?" The rider bitterly complained, looking down at Bendix and Newman. "I'm about ready to ride this thing."

"I'm here now." Bendix smiled. "Now, first up in the chute," the PA announcer continued, "on Black Lighting, from Stevensville, Montana, Bob Davis."

The cowboy astride the animal's back adjusted his grip one last time, then gave a quick nod to the man in front of the chute. The man pulled the gate open and the animal bolted out of the stall, violently bucking, twisting, and turning to the ahs and cheers of the crowd. The cowboy struggled to stay aboard the bull, his right hand in a death grip on the rope while his left, waved high above his head.

The ride lasted several seconds before the cowboy loosened his grip and quickly hopped off the animal's back. Newman watched as the cowboy hit the dusty turf and quickly crawled away from the wildly bucking animal.

"See you in a bit." Bendix smiled. He quickly vaulted one of the wooden barriers.

"Hey!" Newman called. But Bendix had scaled the other side of the barricade and bolted out on to center arena, yelling and waving frantically at the still violently bucking bull.

The cowboy had crawled to safety as the bull turned his attention toward Bendix.

"Get back over here!" Newman shouted. "Are you crazy?"

Bendix stared at the animal momentarily, then began making funny faces at the bull. The crowd laughed. Then suddenly the animal charged. Bendix held his ground, then suddenly turned and sprinted for a nearby plastic barrel. He looked back occasionally over his shoulder to see the ton of fury bearing down on him. He dove headfirst into the container only seconds before the bull lowered his head and rammed the receptacle. The barrel rolled several feet along the turf and came to rest sharply against the arena wall. The crowd gasped. A quiet hush fell over the arena. Moments later, Bendix crawled out of the barrel, stood, and waved at the crowd. They cheered.

Meanwhile, several other clowns stood in the animal's chute entrance, taunting the bull. The enraged bull finally turned and charged. The clowns waited until the bull was nearly upon them. Then they sidestepped the on-rushing animal. The bull's momentum carried it back into the chute, and the clowns quickly closed the gate behind it.

Bendix dusted himself, trotted back to the wall, and climbed back over the barrier.

"Well?" He huffed slightly. "What did you think?"

"I think you're insane. Is that why you asked me to come back here?" Newman was angry. "To watch you commit suicide?"

"You asked what rodeo clowns did. Now you know."

"I thought you passed out balloons and stuff to kids," Newman said in disbelief. "I had no idea you play tag with homicidal bulls."

"Our job is to distract the animal long enough for the rider to get away safely. I thought you knew that."

"Man, the closest I've ever been to a bull in my life has been a medium-well steak."

"It's really not that bad. You have to stay alert, but once you get the hang of it, it's like playing dodgeball with another kid. Maybe you'd like to try it one day."

"Ahhh… no, thanks. I'd probably choose a safer occupation, like javelin catching or something."

"You'd be surprised how even the most racist cowboy changes his views when he wants you to get a two-thousand-pound bull off his ass."

The sound of a chute door opening caught Bendix's attention. "Well, looks like I'm going to be needed in a few seconds. Enjoy the show." Bendix quickly climbed atop the barricade and waited as the bull and his rider violently twisted and jerked around the arena.

Outside, in front of the main trailer, an armored van pulled to a stop at the rear door. Two armed uniformed guards climbed out of the truck and proceeded to open the armored car's back doors. One guard removed two very large satchels while the other one kept a watchful eye on the surrounding area. They finally closed the doors and took the bags into the trailer.

"Its payday," one of the bikers driveled as he and his associates observed the transfer. "There's over a quarter million in each of those bags, and before the day is out, it's going to be all ours."

"When do we make our move?" The woman asked impatiently.

"Patience, my dear. The day is still young," the older biker cautioned. "Let's wait. We can hit the resort receipts and rodeo prize money all in the same afternoon. If we play our cards right, this may be the last job we'll ever have to pull for a long time."

"Well, what do we do now?"

"After all that drinking and this hot sun, I'm starving. Let's get something to eat."

The others agreed. They started for the restaurant.

Meanwhile, the crowd was applauding the latest bull rider as Bendix helped lure the animal back into his chute. Newman watched as Bendix and the other clowns seemed to enjoy teasing and dancing around the enraged beast as if participants in some deadly Western ballet. The work was obviously extremely dangerous, but they made it look so easy.

Bendix hopped on top of the barricade and smiled down at Newman. "Okay, Kenny boy, it's your turn to get out there."

"Not on your life."

Bendix watched as the next rider sat straddling his kicking, snorting animal, trying to adjust his grip on the rope.

"Oh, boy," he sighed as the chute master prepared to open the gate. "You ain't just whistlin' Dixie, pal," Bendix said in awe. "Somebody's gonna try and ride the Bone Crusher."

"What's a bone crusher?" inquired Newman.

"Just the biggest, baddest, meanest bull this side of the Continental Divide, that's all. Killed a man a year ago at this very rodeo. Crushed his skull like an egg. Wonder what brain-dead idiot is going to try and ride him this year."

"Probably the same kind of brain-dead idiot who's going to dance and wave in front of him."

"Point well taken."

Newman looked in the direction of the rider, but his hat prevented a clear facial recognition. For a moment, he thought it might have been McBath. In that instant, the chute swung open, and the bull tore out of the gate. The animal was ferociously twisting and snorting as it kicked and reared, thrusting its hind legs high into the air in a violent ballet of rage and fury. The rider held on the rope. The bull tossed him about like a limp rag doll. He swayed and turned with the animal until finally the sheer strength of the animal's motion began to toss him to one side.

Bendix began to grow concerned. He had seen this kind of trouble on a dismount many times before. As the rider tried to make his jump, the animal would make a sudden unexpected twist and throw off the rider's timing, causing him to land so close to the enraged animal as to endanger the rider's health or worse.

Suddenly, as the rider tried to dismount, his left foot snagged in the stirrup. The bull whirled the rider about like a dishrag. The crowd rose to its feet in silent horror. The bull continued to thrash about, turning its head, trying to gore the helpless rider.

Bendix positioned himself in front of the animal and began frantically waving his arms. The bull only glanced in his direction and continued to violently thrash about, savagely slinging his captive passenger.

Unexpectedly, one of the clowns charged the bull from behind, knife in hand, and slashed the rope around the animal's body. The rider fell free, but the bull reared, thrusting his horn into the rider's side as he fell. Bendix jumped frantically in front of the animal, waving wildly, trying to attract his attention, but the bull seemed intent on goring the helpless man on the ground beside him.

Other clowns soon joined the act, dancing around the animal. Trying to distract it. Bendix raced around to the rear of the bull, grabbed his tail, and pulled. The animal turned immediately to Bendix and snorted viciously. Bendix quickly released the tail and ran. The bull immediately charged him. Bendix reached the entrance, turned, and stood in the doorway, taunting the charging beast. The bull drew even closer, snorting wildly, locked in a thundering death charge toward Bendix.

With the charging beast just inches away, Bendix jumped. He grabbed the steel bar overhead and pulled himself above the charging beast, his legs locked tightly together, his feet pointed skyward.

The bull past safely beneath him into the chute as another clown quickly climbed off the fence, rushed over and bolted the gate. He then grabbed Bendix's legs and helped him lower himself from the bar. Bendix casually brushed himself off and waved to the cheers and applause of the adoring crowd.

He looked over at Newman. "What do you think of rodeo clowns now?" Bendix shouted with a self-confident smug.

"You're crazy. Why don't you take up something safe, like alligator dentistry?"

"Well, you haven't seen anything yet. Wait until you see the rest of the bull rides."

"No way," Newman countered. "Commit suicide if you want to. Me? I'll read about it, but I don't have to watch." He turned and started for the exit. "Just be careful out there, okay?"

"Careful? Why that's my middle name." Bendix smiled.

"I hope so," Newman muttered. As he climbed off the fence, he turned to see the wounded rider being placed in the ambulance. He hoped he would be alright.

Newman knew he needed to get back to work. He checked his watch. It was almost three. The rodeo would be breaking up in another hour or so, and most of the crowd would be heading to the restaurant for dinner. If the kitchen crew wasn't ready, the result would be pure chaos. He knew that Nelson would probably wait until the last minute before setting up, just in case the anticipated dinner crowd didn't show. He didn't want to have a lot of prepared food wasted. But if they did show, and the kitchen wasn't ready, the staff would be overwhelmed. He made it quickly back to the restaurant.

When he stepped into the dining area, the tables were filled with patrons talking and laughing over their meals. He also noticed several customers looking impatiently around for a waitress. He glanced around the floor, and no waitress was in sight. He waited. Newman grew increasingly concerned as no waitresses appeared to take the customers' orders. He hurried around the counter to the kitchen area where he saw Jake, Rides, Nelson, and all the waitresses engaged in an intense conference near the back door.

"Hey," Newman called, "is everybody suddenly on break now, or what? There are people out there who need attention."

"Where have you been, man?" Rides asked. "We've been looking all over for you."

"Why? Is there a problem?"

"I'll say," Nelson interjected as he thrust sheets of paper at him. The papers landed at Newman's feet.

As he picked them up, Newman examined each sheet. It was the composite drawings of the bandit bikers the sheriff had left several weeks earlier. "This is the notice of that group of bikers that's wanted for those resort hold ups."

"Now, go look at the customers at table eleven." Jake stated.

Newman stepped out of the kitchen, he looked cautiously, then eased over to the counter and peered across the dining room at table eleven. The three bikers sitting there were almost an exact match to the composites Newman held in his hand. He glanced at some other tables so as not to arouse their suspicion. He calmly walked back to the group.

"It could be them." Newman was unconvinced. "Let's suppose it is them, this is a matter for the sheriff. I assume someone has called him?"

"After that little escapade with those bicyclists, I doubt if he'd even come." Jake said. "Besides, it will take them over a half hour to get here, assuming they believe us. We could all be dead by then."

"If we're not going to call the sheriff, what else can we do?" Newman reasoned. "We very well can't take them by ourselves." He paused for agreement. There was only silence. Newman looked around at their quiet faces. "Come on?" He saw emotionless expressions. "If those are the right ones out there, they are seasoned killers."

Suddenly, Vicki came through the back door with a big grey blanket draped over her arm. "Kenny," she smiled, "we've been looking all over for you."

"Vicki do you know what they want to do?"

"I sure do." Vicki pulled back the blanket to reveal a Remington pump-action shotgun and a .357 magnum.

Newman stared in awe at the large-caliber weapons. "Come on, Vicki. There are dozens of innocent people in there. I mean, this isn't the OK Corral!"

"Look, Ken," Jake was getting impatient, "we all know what we've got to do. Either join in or get out of the way." Jake took the handgun, breeched it, checked the rounds, and pushed the cylinder back into the weapon. "Rides, Kimberly, Marci, Nelson, you know what to do. Vicki, you and Ken head back to the main office and stay outta the way. Take the waitresses with you."

"And leave you all alone here to do this without me? Not a chance." Newman countered.

"Look," Jake insisted, "I ain't got time to argue."

"Come on, Kenny," Vicki admonished, ushering him out the back door. "I know a way we can be of some help." Vicki turned to the waitresses, "Let's go ladies."

"How Vicki?" He continued talking as they went out the back door.

While Newman and Vicki escorted the other waitresses from the kitchen, Kimberly and Marci walked from table to table, handling irate complaints about the slow service and taking food orders. Finally Kimberly approached table ten. Before she went over to the biker's table, she looked over at Jake and Rides. Jake nodded to her. She took a deep breath, smiled, and walked briskly up to the bikers.

"Is everything all right here?" Kimberly beamed.

"You're slow as winter molasses, honey," the woman growled. "Don't expect a tip for service this slow."

"What my friend means is," the other biker calmly interjected, "a snail could have provided faster service." He sneered.

"I'm so sorry," Kimberly apologized as she collected their dirty dishes. "Our other waitress took sick, and we weren't able to replace her."

"Don't tell us your problem, dearie. But you got a problem on your hands with all these people in here. It looks like you can use more than one more waitress. About six would be more like it."

"Yes ma'am. And usually when a customer isn't satisfied with our service, the meal is free, and dessert is on the house. Just let me get the chef."

The bikers smiled. "Free desert," the woman stated with enthusiasm.

Kimberly turned and quickly disappeared into the kitchen. Moments later, Jake emerged in a white puffed hat, a towel draped over one hand and a covered tray balanced in the other. He walked over and set the tray down in the middle of the table.

"I'm Chef Jake." He smiled. "My waitress tells me you folks aren't happy with the meal."

"The meal was okay," the woman complained, "it's that the waitress was so slow."

"Good help, as the saying goes." Jake grinned. "But not only is your food on the house, so is dessert." He pointed toward the tray.

Their faces brightened at the mention of the free dessert. One of the bikers pulled the top off the tray. Underneath were three big slices of chocolate cake with a piece of paper sandwiched between two of the slices. The woman plucked the paper and read the note. She quietly looked at the paper, then slowly glared up at Jake.

"Well? What's it say?" One biker asked.

The woman was quiet.

"Well?" the other biker asked again.

"It says," she hesitated, "it says, 'Get up slowly and walk quietly into the kitchen or I'll blow your head off.' That's it."

"What?" The two men said in unison. They were all in shock. Jake slowly moved the tip of the cloth covering his other hand back, revealing the barrel tip of the .357.

"Is this some kind of joke, old-timer?"

"You see me laughin', dipshit?" Jake snarled.

The mood grew stern and serious.

"Look, old man, you don't know who you're messin' with. So we'll just walk outta here and forget this ever happened."

"Wrong, Jake confidently replied. "I know exactly who you are and I'd strongly appreciate it if you didn't leave just yet. There's also an Indian over by the cash register who says you can't walk outta here, not just yet."

They glanced over at the register. Rides stood there casually reading the newspaper. He eased the paper back slightly to reveal the dark, deadly hole of the pump-action shotgun.

"Like the note said," Jake calmly continued, "get up slowly and walk into the kitchen. I know you're all armed, but one false move by any of ya, and so help me, you'll be in hell before God knows you're dead."

They looked over at Rides, then up into Jake's cold, lined, determined face. Almost in unison, they slide their chairs back and pushed themselves up from their seats. Rides slowly backed into the kitchen. The woman followed the two men as Jake brought up the rear. Rides stood at the back door, motioning them outside. They followed Rides through the kitchen and out the back door. Nelson, Marci, and Kimberly were to resume functions in the restaurant.

Jake shut the door behind them. "All right, boys and girls, line up. Let's get friendly. Side-by-side, hands behind your heads."

They looked back at Jake, then at each other. Suddenly, Rides pumped the shotgun. The ominous click chilled the air. "I think the man meant today, boys and girls," Rides quipped.

The three lined up quickly, interlocking their fingers behind their heads. Jake walked over behind the woman and started pat searching her.

"Getting your thrills, old man?" She joked.

"You should look so good." Jake quipped. He found a bulge in her waist. "Either you're six months pregnant or..." he pulled out a .44 Magnum. "Such a big gun for such a little girl."

"There's a lot of scum out there."

"You're telling me," Jake added. "And how about you boys?" Jake continued, cautiously pat searching the next man. Jake reached into the man's trouser and pulled out a mini machine pistol.

"Squirrel hunting?" Jake quipped, examining the piece.

"Big squirrels." The biker commented.

"I'll bet." Jake shove the weapon into his trousers. He stepped behind the next man and carefully searched him. He found a .38 in the man's left boot. "Now we're all going to walk over to the office and wait for the sheriff."

Jake motioned toward the office with his handgun. "Move!" The trio hesitated momentarily, glancing at one another, then slowly began walking toward the office.

Rides and Jake carefully monitored the group as they walked for several minutes with fingers locked behind their heads. Suddenly, just before they reached the office, the woman's right leg buckled as her Stiletto heel twisted under her boot. She yelped in pain as she quickly leaned over to grab her foot.

"I think I twisted my ankle," she grimaced.

"You should learn to walk in those high-heeled boots before you wear them," Jake said.

"Let me give her a hand," one of the men offered and stepped over to help her. He positioned his body to shield her from Jake's view. She slowly pulled up her pant leg to reveal a big derringer strapped to the inside of her ankle. She slowly reached for the weapon and began pulling it from the holster. Suddenly, a blast echoed through the air. An explosion of dirt erupted near her foot.

She quickly dropped the weapon as all of them looked around, startled. Rides and Jake frantically scanned the area with their weapons pointed.

"How was that?" Newman shouted from the front office rooftop, his shot gun cradled against his cheek and still aimed at the woman's foot. Rides slowly walked over to the woman, reached down, and picked up the derringer.

"Not bad," he shouted, holding the gun up for Newman to see, "but you're still jerking the trigger, squeeze."

It was less than an hour before the sheriff arrived and arrested the trio. A small crowd had gathered to watch the police lead them into the back of a van and speed away.

"Good work," Sheriff Bennett smiled, turning to Jake. "You realize there's a $25,000 reward out for the capture of these yahoos."

"Well, I can't take all of the credit. These guys here did all of the work." Jake motioned to Newman and Rides.

"Well, I will make sure all three of ya get your fair share. You know Jake, I keep tellin' ya to let me deputize you and your boys. You'd be naturals up here. You know the area, and you wouldn't have to wait for us to get up here to have somebody arrested."

"And take your jobs away from you? No, thanks."

"But Curtis is a former cop, isn't he? Why can't you at least let me deputize him?"

"And let him shoot some tourist by mistake? A lawsuit is all I need. No, I'll just call you guys like we've been doing."

"Suit yourself, Jake. Well, thanks again for the collar." replied Sheriff Bennett.

As the last police car sped away, Newman headed back to the restaurant as the crowd that had gathered to watch the arrest started to disperse.

He stepped into the dining area on his way to the kitchen. Each table was filled. Kimberly and Marci darted hurriedly from table to table, delivering food and taking orders.

He started to enter the kitchen when suddenly the door opened, bumping him in the face. He stopped as Bea backed into the dining room with a basket of assorted dishes.

'I'm sorry," Bea immediately smiled. "I should have looked first."

"No problem. What's all that for?" He pointed toward the basket.

"This stuff is for the buffalo barbeque across the street. It's really going well. I just came over here because we ran out of clean dishes over there."

"Look, do they really need you over there? Kimberly and Marci could use a little help around here. Some of the other waitresses were a little shaken up from an earlier incident we had here and decided to leave."

"Okay, Ken. Let me run these back by the barbeque, and I'll come right back here."

"Thanks. Is Candy with John? Or is she working with you at the barbeque?"

"No, Ms. Hendricks, her teacher, came by and offered to take her to the rodeo. So she's enjoying the day. And if I'm not back by the time the rodeo is over, I know she's in good hands. She will take Candy back home, where John is mining the store."

"Great, cause we are swamped here. So please, as quickly as you can, it would be appreciated." responded Newman.

"Then in that case, I'll run this fresh set of dishes over to the general store and get John to run them over to the barbeque. That way I'll be back here in half the time. I won't be long." Bea smiled as she hurried out the front door.

She arrived on the steps of the general store only to find the entrance locked. "Be back in five," the crude handwritten sign hanging on the doorknob read.

Bea reached into her pocket, pulled out a set of keys and opened the door. The store was quiet. She set the dishes on the counter and started to write a note asking John to deliver the dishes she was carrying over to the barbeque.

Suddenly, she heard a faint laughter from the back room. She stopped and stood alert, straining to hear the noise. The faint laughter echoed again. Bea set the note aside and walked cautiously toward the bedroom. The giggling and laughter became more pronounced. She eased toward the bedroom door. It was partially cracked. She clearly heard a woman's giggle and John's husky laugh. She slowly eased the door open. Her face remained calm, as if she knew what to expect. John sat upright in the middle of the bed and a beautiful, younger blonde sat straddled his front. She gently bobbed up and down on him as they were entangled in a naked embrace. Bea stood quietly in the doorway as John's mouth was locked onto the woman's left breast as he cradled both breasts in the palms of his hands. Her head was tilted backwards, while her hands were tenderly cupped behind his head holding his lips to her breast. She was clearly enjoying the pleasure of her husband's body and vice versa as John made moans of sexual ecstasy. The woman eventually glanced over to see Bea standing in the doorway. She gasped quietly and slowed her motion on John. The two women stared momentarily at each other in a silent exchange. The woman smiled. Then lovingly, she turned her attention from Bea back to John and increased her effortless motion upon his body. While her well-manicured fingers gently stroked his hair, he continued his graceful motion of succulent indulgence upon her breast. Bea took a deep breath, eased the door shut, then turned and walked away.

C H A P T E R

12

A month later, it was now time for the inevitable, the courtroom was quiet, except for the neatly dressed balding man as he passed in front of the jury box gesturing passionately.

"It comes down to a question of credibility, ladies and gentlemen," the lawyer stated emphatically. "Can you honestly believe Mrs. Marshall when she says that it was possible for her son to produce five million in counterfeit bills right under her very nose, and her not be aware of it? Especially under the nose of a shrewd businesswoman like her?" He pointed toward Vicki. "Should you believe her when she said the plates were stored in her safe without her knowledge?" He paused and turned back toward the jury. "I think not. To even suggest that we, as reasonable people, believe that she didn't know what was in her own safe, stretches the imagination. As reasonable people, you, ladies and gentlemen of the jury, have no choice but to render a verdict of 'guilty'." He paused, then pointed collectively at them. "Based on the evidence you've heard during the last month and a half, you really have no other choice." He buttoned his coat and walked back to his table.

An eerie silence fell over the courtroom as the prosecutor positioned his chair at the table. He glanced over at Vicki, but she didn't notice.

The defense attorney pushed himself away from the table. All eyes followed him as he made his way over to the jury box. He stood there silently for a moment. Then he reached into his pocket, pulled out two pennies, and began tossing them around in his hand.

"Two cents," he quietly began, "two cents. We've all said it at one time or another—for two cents and a cup of coffee I'd leave you this instant. Or, how about, for two cents I'd take my fist and beat you senseless. Or the classic one, boy, I'm so mad with my wife or husband" he motioned toward a woman in the jury box, "for two cents, I'd gladly strangle him, or her as the case may be. But, of course, you never did. Why? Because the opportunity never presented itself and the reason why you felt the way you did eventually passed. And, of course, nothing bad happened. But," he quickly added, "what if, at that exact moment, someone came along and provided you with the opportunity to do what you felt like doing? What if at the exact moment you felt like strangling your wife, someone came along and provided you with the rope, the opportunity--the two cents. Now, we've got a different set of circumstances. Now you can actually act on what previously was only a fantasy. So did Vicki's son, Carl, want to print five million bucks? Of course he did. But based on the testimony you've heard, would there have been a crime committed at all had the FBI not provided the paper and the plates? Of course not. Were it not for the government providing the opportunity for the crime, there would never have been a crime committed."

Jake coughed and looked toward Vicki. He smiled and she returned a slight grin.

"Now, the choice before you is clear. You can either vote 'guilty' and give the government the green light to harass ordinary citizens, or send them a message they won't soon forget. My client is innocent. You have it within your power to strike a blow for the common man and his battle against government conspiracy. Vote 'not guilty', and tell the FBI where it can stick its two cents." He placed the pennies on the banister in front of the jury and walked away.

Murmurs and rumblings echoed throughout the courtroom. Vicki looked back over her shoulder at Jake. He sat in the front row, dressed as always in his Western-style suit and Stetson hat. He flashed her a smile and a thumbs-up sign. The judge banged his gavel several times and the courtroom slowly quieted.

"This court will come to order!" He admonished. "Jury, you've heard the evidence. Now you have to decide if Mrs. Marshall is guilty of conspiracy. Did she not only know of, but actually participate in her son's scheme to counterfeit five million dollars, or was she the innocent victim in an unlawful government plot? Good luck to you all. May God be with you. This court is recessed until the jury returns with a verdict." He banged his gavel. Everyone rose as he stood and walked out of the courtroom.

Jake stepped around the stream of people headed for the exit. He walked over to Vicki and enveloped her in a big hug.

"We'll whip this thing yet, babe," he reassured. "You just wait and see."

"I hope so," Vicki breathed deeply. "I really hope so." She turned to one of her attorneys. "How did we do?" A note of concern in her voice.

One attorney closed his briefcase. "A toss-up," he sighed, "that's the best I can say. I could see the doubt on some of the jurors' faces. They probably feel it's unlikely that five million dollars was being printed right under your very nose without your knowledge."

"But it's true," she insisted.

"I know Vicki, but did we convince them that a mother and grandmother was not capable of a criminal conspiracy? I still say we could have used that Negro of yours as a character witness."

"I told you to drop it and I mean it. He's too valuable running the place while I'm here. Besides, he wasn't even there when all of this happened. So let's leave him out of this."

"All right, all right, I'm on your side, remember?"

She turned back toward Jake. "I don't want to go to jail."

"You won't, baby. You'll see. You just wait and see."

"It's in the hands of the jury now." a tearful Vicki, replied.

"And God," Jake quietly added.

Back at the resort poolside, the crowd splashed and played in the hot mineral water as steam floated from the surface of the pool. Near the far end of the pool, a balding middle-aged man stood in the shallow end and surveyed the people splashing and swimming in the water.

Suddenly his attention became fixed on a small blonde-haired boy bobbing alone in an isolated portion of the pool. He smiled, then pushed himself off the pool wall and swam toward him.

While Newman expected things to be running smoothly around the resort, he sat at Vicki's desk, watching the television news. The anchorwoman began, "The jury has just retired to deliberate in the Marshall counterfeiting trial. Both sides expected a quick and favorable verdict in the case. As you may recall, Mrs. Marshall was arrested…"

Newman picked up the remote and turned off the set. Suddenly the door swung open, and Lisa stood in the doorway, a brown envelope cradled in her arms.

"Kenny!" She exclaimed, mildly surprised. "I didn't know you were here."

"Oh, Lisa," Newman rose from his seat, "I was just watching the news. The jury's out in Vicki's trial."

"That's right, her trial is supposed to wrap up today. How does it look?"

"I don't know. I wasn't here to watch the first of the news. So it's hard for me to tell what's going on."

Lisa stepped into the office and closed the door. "Vicki's had enough bad news lately. I hope the jury gives her some good news."

"I'll second that."

"Which is why I'm quitting now instead of waiting until she comes back to tell her."

Newman looked up at Lisa, surprised. "Quitting? Why?"

"It's a long story." Lisa began placing the envelope she was clutching on the desk. "But to make a long story short," she paused, as if to gather the courage to continue. "I've been stealing money from the resort."

Newman chuckled. "You can't be serious."

Lisa took a deep breath. "I'm afraid I am very serious." She pointed to the envelope. "There's most of it. About $3,000 I've spent, about another $2,000 over the past year or so. Tell Vicki I'll pay her back when I find another job."

Newman slowly rose from his chair and walked over to her. He could see the somberness in her eyes. "Why, Lisa?"

"To take care of Snake, I guess. At least that's what I've kept telling myself. But I guess the money was so easy to take. Snake said she owed it to us, because Jake disabled him in that logging accident a couple of years ago."

"So he's had you to steal what he thinks Jake owed him."

"Well at first. But it's been going on for so long. I don't think he'll ever want to stop as long as I have access to Vicki's money. So I've got to go before she fires me for being a thief."

"But Lisa, Vicki hasn't found out in all of this time. Chances are if you just stop, she'll never know you were ever stealing."

"Maybe, but I'll know."

Newman could sense the guilt in her voice. It almost trembled with regret.

"Why don't you take a couple of days and think about it?"

"No, please, Ken. I have to go. If I stop, Snake will beat me. When he gets drunk, he always beats me."

"It's none of my business, but why do you stay with him?"

"I needed him, I guess." Her voice became distant and uncertain.

"My real father abused me sexually when I was a child. I ran away when I was twelve. Snake took me in. I wondered the streets for a while, until I ran into Snake and he took me in. We've been together for seven years. It was innocent enough at first, but later we started sleeping together. He taught me how to smoke and drink. Since I had no place else to go, I stayed with him. After he hurt his leg up at Jake's logging camp, I stayed with him to nurse him back to health. He needed me, and I supposed I needed him. But I know now, I've got to try and make it on my own. So you see, Ken, I've got to go, if for no other reason than to regain my self-respect. Tell Vicki thanks for everything and that I'm really sorry." She turned and walked out of the office.

Newman followed her to the door and left it ajar. He turned, picked up the envelope and peeked inside. Several stacks of bills were banded together with a rubber band. He started to count the bills, when suddenly a voice called him from behind. He swung around, startled.

"Take it easy, guy," Rides said, "it's only me."

"Don't sneak up on people like that."

"Well don't leave your door open like this. Makes people think you are open for business. Besides, we have a serious problem."

"What else is new?"

"I'm not kidding. This makes all our other problems seem minor. You've got to come with me."

Newman picked up the envelope, placed it into the open safe, and closed the door. "Well, lead on. If I'm going to get bad news, I might as well get it all at once."

Newman followed Rides out of the office and closed the door behind him. Rides lead Newman to the tavern. They walked around the counter to the sink behind the bar. He turned on the tap and filled a glass with hot water.

"Before you taste it, sniff the steam rising from the glass."

Newman cautiously took the glass from him and gingerly took a whiff. His nose squinted. "Smells like… gasoline," he said in disbelief.

"Taste it." Rides urged.

Newman reluctantly tipped the glass to his lips and took a small sip. He immediately spit the sample back into the glass. "Tastes like gasoline," he said, amazed.

"It's in all of the bar water, and it's getting worse by the day in the kitchen, although it's not as bad in there as it is in here, yet."

"How about the water in the hotel rooms?"

"It's in there, too."

"How?" questioned Newman.

"Gas from the filling station is leaking into the fresh well water, probably through a rupture in an underground gasoline storage tank."

"Rupture?"

"Erosion, an earthquake, any sort of trauma could have caused the break."

"That could probably explain the missing gallons of gasoline I can't account for every month." Thought Newman.

"And while the smell is really bad in the hot water taps, because of the rising steam vapors, the fresh cold water is getting just as bad."

Newman was worried. If the guest were to discover there was gasoline in their water, they could check out so fast the resort would be a ghost town in a matter of minutes. Then there was the matter of the hundreds of civil lawsuits they would face. Not to mention, legal action from the county Board of Health.

"Can you fix it Rides?" Newman asked.

"Not without digging up all four of those service station gas tanks and sealing that rupture."

"How long would that take?"

"Ohhhh… bout a month, and that's with the station shut down, a backhoe, and at least two men."

"Then there is the loss of about three grand that the station makes a month." Newman paused. "I wonder what the health risks are from drinking gasoline."

"Well, I'm sure it's not recommended by the AMA, that's for damned sure. And I'll tell you another thing. My boy's not drinking any more water here. You and Vicki had better do something damned quick. Because I'm not going to stand by and watch all of these innocent people who come here for vacations get an unexpected fill-up with each glass of water they drink."

"Okay, okay, I understand. I feel the same way. It's just that Vicki has enough problems right now without this."

"This?" Rides was irritated. "You think this is the extent of her problems? I've had a chance to look around this place, and boy, have I been enlightened. This place is a repairman's nightmare. In addition to the gas in the water, over at the RV Park there's a busted sewer line. Raw sewage is just about to break the ground surface. The same is true for the sewer main under the bar. The big pool hasn't been drained since I don't know when. The bottom is lined with algae an inch thick. And just recently, she dries the hotel linen on an outdoor clothesline because neither of her industrial dryers work. Nobody's bothered to fix them. Plus," he quickly added, "the locks on most of the hotel room doors can be opened by a slight lift on the doorknobs. And all of this is just for openers."

I get the point, Andrew Rides." Newman was slightly annoyed. "This place needs a lot of work."

"No, you don't get the point, Ken Newman. This place didn't just fall apart overnight. You're looking at months, even years, of neglect. It's as if Vicki and Jake deliberately let this place go to hell in a hand basket."

"I'm sure they did the best they could."

"Let's be for real, okay? I know you like her and everything, but she's trying to stay out of jail. Those lawyers she's got don't come cheap. I dare-say those dollars that might have gone to maintenance are in her lawyers' pockets."

"Well, she can't run the resort from a cell block."

"Maybe, but I'm taking a sample of this tap water to the Board of Health. I'm not going to tell them where I go it from. But if they determine that the amount of gasoline in this water is dangerous, I'm blowing the whistle loud and long. Do I make myself clear?"

Suddenly the bar phone rang. Rides snatched it up. "Tavern, Rides… Yea, one second." He handed the receiver to Newman. "It's for you."

Newman gingerly took the phone. "Yeah!" He barked. He listened momentarily. "Okay, just wait. I'll be right there." He hung up the phone. "That was Marci. There's a problem at the pool."

"What a surprise." Rides muttered.

"We'll finish this later."

"Damned right we will."

As Newman left, Rides drew another glass of hot water and sniffed the stream as it rose from the glass.

As Newman parked, Marci met Ken at the pool's entrance.

"You need to talk to that lady over there," she said excitedly, pointing to a young woman frantically dressing her small boy.

Newman looked at Marci, then walked past her on into the pool. "Hi." He smiled at the extremely agitated woman. "I'm Ken Newman." He extended his hand. The woman stopped and looked up from dressing her son.

"Are you the one who's responsible for allowing perverts in here to molest my boy?" She scolded in sarcastic anger.

"Perverts?" Newman was more shocked than appalled.

"If I lived in this state I'd sue you and this whole flea-bitten operation for every dime you had. As it stands, I'll never come back here as long as I live."

"Ma'am please." Newman inquired. "What's the problem? Honestly, I have no idea what you are speaking of."

"Ask that creep with the bald head and the red-striped trunks. Who knows, you two might have a lot in common." She hurriedly ushered the boy out of the building.

Newman looked over to Marci, "Did you notice anything out of the ordinary?"

"I saw them together. The boy wasn't screaming. I thought they were together."

"Thanks, I'll talk to this man." Newman stormed the poolside. He scanned the pool for the bald man in the red-striped trunks. He spotted him near the shallow end of the pool. He had his head buried in the fold of his elbow. Newman rushed over to the man and knelt beside him.

"Hey!" Newman tapped him on the arm.

He slowly looked up at Newman. His eyes bubbled with tears. He stared pitifully into Newman's face. Newman was momentarily touched by the man's apparent remorse.

"I need you to step out of the pool please."

The man waited, then slowly hoisted himself out of the water and up onto the deck.

"Would you come with me please?" Newman pointed toward the exit. The man complied. Newman calmly followed him into the men's dressing room. The area was quiet and empty.

"I'll be frank," Newman blurted. "Did you molest a young boy who was in this pool earlier?" The man stood silently, his head bowed. "There's a woman out there who's understandably very upset. She said that you fondled her child. I think you'd better get dressed and leave before you force me to call the authorities."

The man nodded meekly and started to leave.

Rides appeared in the dressing room doorway as the man was departing. "Say, I'm headed to the health Department with a sample of the water. I just came by to see if you needed a hand."

"No, everything's okay now. That guy you just passed is some sort of child molester. Marci had a customer complain about him in the pool, but he's agreed to leave. So no, there's no problem."

"No problem!" Rides angrily exclaimed. "You just let a child molester walk out of here without calling the police and you say there's no problem?"

"Forget it Andrew. He's at the counter getting his stuff. He'll be outta here in no time."

"Outta here, hell!" Rides turned and disappeared into the counter area.

"Andrew!" Newman called and bolted after him.

The man was accepting his clothes basket from Marci. As she handed him his belongings across the counter, Rides ran up behind him and knocked the basket from his hand. He grabbed the stunned man's arm, shoved him, face-first, into the wall and twisted his other arm forcefully behind his back.

"Marci," Rides demanded. "Call the police. This scum's baby-raping days have just ended." Rides had one hand jammed into the man's back while he held the man's other arm twisted painfully behind him.

"Andrew!" Newman rushed over and pulled Rides off the man.

"Kenny, what are you doing?"

Rides protested as he struggled to maintain his grip on the man. Newman locked his arms around the struggling Rides. The man immediately grabbed his clothes basket, raced out of the pool, climbed into a late-model Porsche, and squealed out of the parking lot.

"Let me go, got damn it!" Rides angrily tore himself from Newman's grip. He turned and faced Newman, heaving with anger. "You realize that sick bastard will only go out and molest somebody else's child?"

"I know that. You think I wanted to let him go? The woman who made the complaint left ten minutes ago. If we did have him arrested, it would just be his word against ours. And in the financial shape this resort's in, do you think Vicki is willing to take on a libel suit?"

"Libel suit? Got damn it Ken! Is that all you can think about." Rides shook his head. "Ken, you don't have any children, but I do. And that just as easily could have been Danny in that pool. And so help me, had that been Danny, wild horses couldn't have kept me off that diseased animal. But, no, this place can't risk a libel suit to take on a pervert. Got damn! You act like you own this place. If he had molested your child, would you have worried about a libel suit? Huh? You know what, you don't have to answer that. Well, so be it, Ken." He reached into his pocket and pulled out a small vial of water. "But if the report comes back harmful, you don't have to worry about Vicki closing the resort. I'll personally shut this place down." He stormed out of the building.

Marci watched as Rides sped out of the parking lot. She turned to Newman, surprised.

"What's wrong with him?"

"Oh Marci, nothing. Just another fun day at the office."

Newman hopped in the golf cart and headed back toward the main office. He started to ascend the steps, when a voice called him from behind. He turned to see Snake running up to him.

"Say, man, you haven't seen Lisa around anywhere, have you?"

Newman looked at him with silent disdain. "No, man, I haven't."

"You sure, man?" Snake persisted. "I'm positive she was headed here when she left home."

"Well, I haven't seen her, Snake. Maybe she had some errands to run when she left."

"She packed all her shit," he complained as he followed Newman up the steps. "and she stole all of the money out of our bank account."

"God, I hate a thief, don't you, Snake?" He put his hand on the knob. "Look, I'm sure you'll find her around here somewhere. In the meantime, I'm busy, okay?"

"Ahhh, sure, Ken, sure. It's just that I miss her so. I'm sure you understand." Snake continued to follow Ken into the office.

"Sure." He smiled to himself. "I understand completely."

They stepped into the office just as the phone rang. Newman picked it up. "Hello… Angie?… Vicki's verdict?… Thanks." Newman hung up.

"Who was that?"

"Angie. She just called from the restaurant. She heard on the radio that the jury has returned and was about to deliver a verdict. Come on, we can watch from the tube in Vicki's office." They both rushed into Vicki's office. Newman turned on the set.

The female announcer began. "The jury has just returned with a verdict in the Vicki Marshall counterfeiting trial. Now for a live report, we go into the Municipal Building in downtown Great Falls…"

Inside the courtroom, the jury had begun to file in. Vicki was already sitting at the table. The district attorney and his associates stepped through the entrance, followed by an array of reporters and spectators.

Finally everyone was seated and the courtroom rumbled with anticipation.

"All rise." The bailiff announced.

A hush fell over the courtroom as everyone rose. The judge walked confidently into the courtroom and took his seat behind the bench. "Be seated," he announced. He turned toward the jury. "Have you reached a verdict?"

The foreman immediately rose. "We have, your Honor." Her voice was solemn and firm.

"Will the defendant rise and face the jury." Calmly spoke the judge.

Vicki and her attorneys gradually eased their chairs back and slowly rose to their feet. Vicki's eyes roamed slowly from juror to juror. Her heart raced as the foreman began to form her words.

"We, the jury, find the defendant, Victoria Marshall, guilty, as charged."

Rumblings echoed throughout the courtroom. The judge banged his gavel. "Order!" He commanded. The courtroom slowly quieted.

Jake stood in amazement of the verdict. The attorneys were melancholy with expressions of solemn disappointment outlining their faces. Suddenly, Vicki, from complete shock of the verdict, gave a large gasp and clutched her chest. Her attorneys immediately turned toward her and the judge rose quickly from his seat. Vicki slumped back into her chair and slowly slithered onto the floor. Jake rushed to her side.

C H A P T E R

13

*J*ake had alerted Newman of Vicki's medical situation in Great Falls. Newman continued to manage the resort as usual and reassure Vicki that things were under control.

"Don't worry about us on this end, Vicki," Newman explained, "You just take your time and get well. Everyone here says get well." He held the phone toward the group assembled in the office.

"Get well, Vicki. We love you. Come back soon," they shouted, almost in unison.

Newman put the phone back to his ear. "See? I told you. So don't worry about a thing, okay?… Oh, you know, we're just planning this fall's Annual Old Time Fiddlers Jamboree. I've just called everybody in to go over the plans for it. Don't worry, Vicki, we'll handle it. You just get well, okay?… Okay. Talk to you later… bye… okay… bye-bye." He hung up.

"Well, how is she?" Carl was concerned.

"She's recovering from a heart attack. The court bailiff saved her life with his CPR. Now she's going to stay in the hospital for a few days. Jake's with her now, but he's coming back tomorrow. Gregory will stay until she gets released from the hospital."

Carl quickly rose to his feet. "But she's not going to die, is she?" His voice trembled with consternation.

"No, Carl," Newman calmly replied, unimpressed with Carl's sudden display of emotion. "She's not going to die."

Newman was all too aware of the tension between him and Vicki. Carl's concern for her health was, at best, simply superficial. He just didn't want her to die without first including him in her will.

"Now, is everybody clear on their assignments for the Jamboree? You know, some of us with hotel rooms, like yours truly, of course, will have to double up or sleep in storage areas to provide added hotel rental space, but it's only for three days. We'll live through it. Questions?"

The room was silent.

"Good. And since there will be both indoor and outdoor concerts, Jake, Mark, and some of the loggers are going to build a temporary outdoor stage platform in the pasture."

"I'm also going to help set up the speaker system," Rides volunteered.

"Any problems?" Newman asked.

"Nope. Not yet anyway." A voice hailed from the employees.

"Great. If nothing else, then everybody go to work."

Everyone rose and started filing out of the office.

"Hey Jackson," Newman called as he was about to leave, "Could I speak with you a minute?"

Jackson stopped near the door and slowly turned toward Newman. His eyes rolled with anger and defiance. "Yea," he snarled, sliding his tongue over his lower lip.

"I owe you an apology for thinking you were stealing from the gas station till. I should have waited until I had all the facts. I'm sorry."

Jackson stood in defiant silence. "Is that all?" His tone was very cold.

"Yes, that's all."

Jackson angrily turned and left. Newman turned his attention back to the papers on his desk.

"Ken," a quiet voice called. He looked up to see Bea. They were alone in the office as everyone had left. Her solemn face looked down on him.

"Yes, Bea." Newman smiled, rising from his seat. "What can I do for you?"

She was nervous and hesitant. "Well," Bea quietly began, "I know this is a bad time, with Vicki being in the hospital and all..."

"Bea, if there's a problem..."

"I may have to leave," she calmly announced. "I know this is a bad time with Vicki gone."

"Bea…"

"God knows, I don't want to leave you with nobody to run the general store, but…"

"Bea, tell me what's bothering you, so I can help if I can."

She eased down onto the sofa. Newman could see the signs of distress in her face, as if she were here more for consolation than anything else.

"I am sorry, Kenny."

"Bea, you know this is the middle of the tourist season. The general store is one of the main business attractions of the resort. Replacing you and John on such short notice isn't going to be easy."

"Oh, it'll just be me and Candy. We'll be the only ones leaving. John will probably stay. At least he's not coming with us."

Newman sighed. "John?" He said matter-of-factly. "Now, it's none of my business, Bea, but does this mean you're finally leaving him?"

"Oh, but it is your business, Ken," she quickly interjected. "We've made it your business." Bea paused to gather her composure. "Oh, how I hate involving outsiders in my personal problems, but it's gotten to the point where I have no choice but to leave him. And you have every right to know why I'm leaving in the middle of the tourist season."

"Bea, you don't have to explain anything to me. I know why you're leaving him. I think it's a good idea."

"But I'm not one of those drifters who waltz in here for a few weeks, gets a paycheck, then waltzes out, Ken. I made a commitment to you and Vicki. I've tried to keep it, but lately John's only gotten worse. His drinking and womanizing have gotten to the point where I fear for Candy's safety. Last night he came in drunk, tore up the canned goods section of the store, then passed out behind the counter. I was so frightened. I locked Candy up in the bathroom all night."

"Bea. I know you'd like to handle this yourself, but maybe if I had a talk with him…"

"No, Ken, it's not your problem. Besides, he wouldn't listen to you anyway. He's been this way for several years now. When we left Seattle, it was to get John away from the liquor, the pressure, and the women.

To start clean up here in the wide open spaces. I realize now that you can't run from yourself."

The agony she was experiencing was readily apparent. She unconsciously wrung her hands as she seemed to talk more to herself than to Newman. He stepped from behind the desk and walked over to her.

"If there's anything I can do, anything." He emphasized. "Why didn't you just leave him a long time ago?"

"Believe me, I thought about it a hundred times, Ken," she cried. "Just please try and understand." She slowly climbed to her feet.

Newman looked down into her tear strained eyes. He smiled and gave her a big hug. She laid her head gently on his shoulder as he gave her several gentle pats on the back.

Suddenly the front door swung open. Newman and Bea looked up as John stepped into the doorway. He froze in midstride at the sight of Bea in Newman's arms.

John was in shock and visibly upset. You could smell the alcohol on his breath even though he stood several feet away.

"Let's go Bea."

They released from their embrace. John and Bea walked out of Vicki's office.

While Newman was trying to keep the resort functional, the water sample Rides took from the resort was being examined by the Health Department. The man in the white lab coat had his eyes buried in the lens of the microscope.

"Lou," a voice called him. He looked up from the instrument. "What's so interesting on that slide? You've been studying it for hours." Lou leaned back in his chair and sighed.

"Well, Greg, it looks like some kind of toxic substance mixed with water."

"Toxic?" thought Greg.

"Gasoline. Unleaded to be exact. I've been trying to double-check to see if there is another possibility." replied Lou. "Where did you get the water from?" asked Greg.

"Judy said some Indian brought it in."

"Lou, did she say where he got it from?"

"Nope. Just said he'd call back for the results in a few days." Lou noticed a concerned tone in Greg's voice. "Something wrong?"

Greg walked over to the table, a puzzled look on his face. "Our office has had two complaints about funny-tasting water so far this month."

"What?" asked Lou.

Greg picked up the phone and punched several numbers. "Yes, Judy, those two water quality complaints. Could you check and see where they came from?"

"Why the phone call Greg? Asked Lou.

He looked back at Lou. "Two complaints came in this month from people who tasted gasoline in their drinking water. Now, I'm not sure but…" A voice came back over the phone. Yes, Judy… Really?… Both of them?… Sure… Thanks." He hung up.

"Well" asked Lou.

"Both complaints came in against the resort up in the Lolos." Stated Greg.

"The one and the same."

"That low- life, hillbilly, redneck he…" Greg caught himself.

"Yeah…Jake Marshall," Lou remembered. "He pulled a shotgun on you one day, didn't he?"

"He says he didn't, but I know the business end of a shotgun when I see one. He dared me to shut down the fleabag soup kitchen he runs up there."

"Well, we may not have to shut the place down this year. I heard on the news where they found Vicki Marshall guilty of printing that five million in twenties. But, she had a heart attack before they could sentence her."

"Just the same, I think I'd better get up there and take a look around. High-octane drinking water may be just the beginning of the horror stories I'll find up there." Assured Greg.

As the two lab technicians contemplated their next move on the resort, Newman was putting a Band-Aid on the drinking water problem.

Newman staggered slightly as he struggled under the weight of the huge water cooler cradled carefully in his arms. He gently eased the container down onto the counter.

"Very good, Ken," Nelson Adams applauded as Newman breathed a sigh of relief. "Now how long do you think a twenty-gallon Igloo will last in the kitchen on a summer day like today? You may as well start getting another one, because between water for the customers and for my cooking, this twenty gallons is gone."

Newman was slightly miffed at Adam's apparent lack of understanding. However, he knew Adams was right. To keep the kitchen, the bar and each of the rooms in the hotel filled with gasoline-free drinking water, he'd have to assign someone full-time to transport water and handle the empty containers.

"Adams, I know this is awkward, but it'll have to do until I come up with something better, okay?"

"Tell Vicki to drill a new freshwater well."

"Well, I can't very well tell her anything while she's in intensive care, now, can I?"

"Look, Ken," Adams became conciliatory. "I know you're doing the best you can, but you're just putting a Band-Aid on a gushing wound."

"Hey, when a Band-Aid's all you've got." He shrugged his shoulders.

He turned and walked out of the kitchen and headed for the door. When suddenly, he heard the sound of someone frantically beating on the women's restroom door caught his attention. Newman stopped.

"Help! Is anyone out there?" The harried voice called.

Newman stepped closer to the door. "Miss, is everything all right?"

"No," the voice shouted back. This stupid doorknob keeps turning in my hand. I can't get out of this bathroom!"

Newman grabbed the knob. It twisted loosely in his hand, too. "Miss," he called, "push your knob in as hard as you can. Hold it firm, okay?"

The woman complied. Newman then grabbed the knob, turned it, and pulled the door open. Before him stood a strikingly attractive slender woman with shiny, bouncing black hair. She wore a well-tailored expensive white business suit with a matching bag tucked securely under one arm. She looked as if she belonged on the business end of Wall Street.

"Thank you, sir." She beamed politely in obvious relief. "I don't know how long I would have been trapped in there. I will have to point that out to the manager."

"Well, point no further, Miss…"

"Harrison, Colleen Harrison," she extended her hand.

"Pleased to meet you, Ms. Harrison. I'm Ken Newman. I sort of manage this place."

"Really," she made more a statement than a question.

"Don't seem so surprised. I'm not really that bad of a manager."

Colleen blushed, "Oh, don't get me wrong. It's just that I didn't know Vicki even knew any Black people, let alone, had one as a manager."

"Sometimes wonders never cease, do they?" Newman hadn't expected her to focus on his color so quickly, but then her reaction had become almost typical by now.

"I'll get that door fixed. Sorry for the inconvenience." Newman replied coldly. "Now, if you will excuse." He turned and headed for the door when Colleen called to him.

"Ken, wait," she walked briskly to catch him. Newman stopped and turned to face her. "Say, I didn't mean to come across like some closet racist. It's just that I've known Vicki for years. Never knew she had any Black employees, let alone a Black manager."

"Well now you know. So if you'll excuse…" He turned to leave.

"Wait." She grabbed him by the arm. Her persistence had become annoying. "This whole thing has gotten off on the wrong foot. Let's say we start over again." She extended her hand. "I'm Colleen Harrison."

A little shocked, Newman followed along. "Ken Newman." They shook hands. "Now if you'll excuse me once again, I really have an important job to do."

"I'll let you go on one condition," Colleen's voice was stern and direct.

"And what might that be?" Newman waited for her to continue.

"Have dinner with me tonight."

Stunned from the comment, "As you, a moment ago, pointed out the obvious. I'm Black. You don't want to taint your reputation."

"As I also pointed out a moment ago, I didn't mean anything by it. What time do you get off?"

Newman smiled. "You must be kidding."

"I've never been more serious about anything in my life."

"Colleen, you don't understand. See, Vicki's not here. "

"She's in the hospital, I know. I read the papers. But surely this place can survive without you for a couple of hours."

He chuckled. "You'd be surprised."

"You won't be sorry."

Newman hesitated in awe of her comment. The water problem would need his full attention. Then there were the little emergencies that always cropped up here and there. Then again, he'd been here for almost seven months without an evening off. Certainly a couple of hours away from the resort wouldn't be too difficult to manage.

"Six o'clock at the front office."

"I'll be there," Colleen smiled.

Newman headed for the office to get the Bronco keys and to raid the safe for more money to buy water containers. However, he knew he probably could not afford to buy all of the containers and water jugs he'd need to keep various stations supplied continuously with fresh water. And he felt uncomfortable spending so much of Vicki's money without her consent, especially while she was in the hospital. But safe drinking water was a problem that had to be solved.

As he approached the office, he saw Marci coming down the steps of the front office. Since she was his makeshift secretary, at least until he could replace Lisa, where was she going?

"Why are you leaving the office? What if a check-in or a visitor dropped by?" Marci looked at him, bewildered.

"Mr. Cameron is in there. I thought you knew."

"Cameron?" Newman wasn't sure what she was talking about. "Who the hell is Cameron?"

"He said he's Vicki's business partner. I thought you knew, Kenny."

Newman scurried up the steps past her and burst into the office. A distinguished-looking, middle-aged man with well coiffured hair and dressed in an expensive black-vested suit had the phone pressed to his ear. He looked up as Newman stepped into the office.

"And just who the hell are you?" Newman asked angrily. "And where do you get off running my secretary out of here?"

The man put his hand over the transmitter. "You must be Mr. Newman."

"I know who I am." Newman snapped. "It's you we've got questions about." The man leaned back in the chair and smiled.

"I'm Vicki's business partner, Mitchell Cameron. I own 49 percent of this place."

"Business partner?" Newman was skeptical.

"Here." Cameron smugly handed Newman the phone. "Ask her yourself."

Newman eyed the man cautiously as he took the phone and placed it to his ear. "Vicki?" He spoke gingerly. "It's just that you never mentioned him to me... well, not while you were in intensive care. Vicki I can... Sure, we can manage without Lisa for a while... We'll talk about the other problems when you get well, okay?... see you soon." He handed the phone back to Cameron.

"Okay, Vicki, I'll handle things on this end." Cameron smiled, leaning back in the chair. "Everything will be shipshape by the time you get well and come back... You too... bye."

Newman sat in the seat across from Cameron. He skeptically eyed Cameron as they both forced an obligatory smile.

"Sorry. Vicki never mentioned you to me."

"I'm afraid that's my doing." Cameron swiveled confidently in the chair. "You see, with her... ah, how shall we say, problems, I just didn't think it was wise to be publicly associated with her. You see, I own four luxury hotels in Washington and Idaho. I simply can't afford to have my business interest tainted with talk of counterfeit money, hit men and FBI wiretaps."

"What then brings you here?"

"Protecting my 49 percent investment. With Vicki in the hospital, I thought it wise to come up and oversee things---you know, just in case she takes a turn for the worse. Vicki and I go back a long way. She is very business savvy. So when she told me she needed an investor to keep her resort afloat, I was game. That was before I knew about all of this other mess. God, if I had only known."

"So you're here to see that we don't steal you and Vicki blind, while she's in the hospital. Is that it?"

"I wouldn't put it so bluntly, Mr. Newman, but Vicki and Jake haven't been here for the last few days. And well frankly, I was a bit concerned about my interest, yes. But I must say, your bookkeeping is rather impressive. I see you've given your expenditures and invoices matching numbers. So if I want to find out what this receipt for $42.50 is for, I just have to find the matching number over here in the invoice section."

"Yes Mr. Cameron. Just a trick I picked up, nothing incredible."

"Around here? Where the average worker couldn't spell 'dog,' even if you spotted them the first two letters? This is incredible, believe me. Don't underestimate yourself, Mr. Newman." He shook his head dejectedly. "How Vicki can stand to work with these dumb backwoods hicks, I'll never understand."

"Don't underestimate them either, Mr. Cameron. They've performed miracles around here with little or nothing to work with."

"Please, call me Mitch." Cameron sat upright in his chair. He and Newman sized each other up like prizefighters in the opening round. "Vicki has told me a lot about you, and frankly, I can't understand what a man with your talent is doing here. Don't get me wrong, I'm glad you are here. Heaven knows, Vicki would be up the proverbial creek without you, but surely a man with your education can do much better than this."

"I can spell 'dog,' if that's what you mean."

Cameron chuckled. "My point exactly."

"Let's just say I like a challenge."

"You may have bitten off more than you can chew here. It's going to take more than good intentions and determination to pull this place out of the fire."

"Time will tell... Mitch."

Cameron sighed, "You're probably right." He paused. "You know, you can take this any way you want to, but I've never had much use for nig... I mean colored people before. Except, of course, to work in my hotels or have them drag me in and out of court on one racial discrimination charge or another. However, I'm impressed with your work. It's rare to see a nig... I mean colored person with a college degree. Not enough to rush out and join the NAACP, mind you, but who knows. But if this doesn't work out for you, look me up. Maybe we can do lunch or something."

Newman rose from his seat and gave a closed lip smile. He had guessed Cameron to be a bigot. His rather candid admissions seemed ironically amusing. It didn't seem to matter whether they wore denim jeans, cowboy boots or drove a Mercedes and wore expensive sharkskin suits—a bigot's racial sentiments were all the same. Cameron had more in common with these 'backwoods hicks,' than he cared to admit.

"Rome wasn't built in a day." Newman quipped.

Suddenly the front door burst open. A young boy full of excitement burst into the room.

"Dad, I saw Scout at the stable, can I ride him?" Cameron looked over at the boy.

"Check with the stable hand. I'm sure you probably can."

"Gee thanks, Dad." The boy turned and raced out of the office.

"Some kid, eh?" He smiled. "That's Bradley, my oldest. He likes to come with me on my business trips. They're always fun for him."

"Well, I'm sure this trip will be no different." Newman checked his watch. "I've got to get rolling. There's a small problem that's got to be taken care of."

"Can I do anything to help?" asked Cameron.

"Prayer comes to mind, but other than that, no."

The phone rang. Cameron snatched it up. "Sure… one second…" He handed the phone to Newman. "It's for you."

Newman walked over and took the phone. "Newman here… Yes, the billing is correct… Well, I don't have time to discuss it now… Sure… Thank you… bye." He hung up. "The Forest Service. They terrorized us earlier this summer, and now they are questioning some of the charges on my invoice. I'll have to deal with that later. If you have questions, I'll answer them when I get back." He walked out of the office.

Meanwhile back at the bar, Laura was shoving a can of beer in front of Mark.

"Don't you think you've had enough beer?"

Mark slapped a dollar bill on the counter and pointed his finger angrily at Laura. "Listen, you just mind your own business." He fingered the can, turned it up to his mouth. Then placed it down on the counter. "Besides, Jake's not here."

"But isn't Carl taking over for him?" questioned Laura.

"Fuck Carl," he snapped. "That stupid jailbird son-of-a-bitch can't even print a decent twenty-dollar bill. Doesn't he know its Andrew Jackson, not Jessie Jackson, on the back of a twenty? We're up on that hill for ten hours a day, Jake or Carl working us like niggers, and for what? After Jake takes out for our food, our lodging, laundry…"

"And don't forget your bar tab." Laura quickly added.

"None of us have shit left over. We're just working to work, that's all. I haven't cleared but $500 in four months of working here. Hell, I may never go back up on that hill."

Laura shoved another beer in front of him.

"Hey!" Mark recoiled. "I didn't order this. Don't shove this beer at me. You're getting enough of my money as it is."

"Relax," Laura angrily countered. "It's paid for, so keep your shirt on."

"Paid for? By who?"

"That lady over there," she pointed to the woman at the small table in the corner.

Mark turned to see who Laura was pointing to. He immediately recognized her. It was indeed Tracy. She smiled gingerly and waved. Mark immediately turned and angrily shoved the can of beer back toward Laura.

"Take this over to the lady. Tell her she can just take this can and shove it up her…" he caught himself. "Just tell her I don't want it."

Laura looked at him, slack-jawed at his anger. She took the can and place it back into the cooler.

Tracy rose from her seat and slowly made her way over to the bar stool next to him. "Mark," she softly began, "talk to me, please?"

He turned angrily toward her. "Talk to you? Why? So you can tell me why you left without so much as telling me to drop dead?"

"Mark, if you'll just let me explain."

"You know, I almost fought Kenny over you. I wanted to drink myself into a coma, all because I wanted to forget you. But Ken wouldn't let me."

"Kenny's a nice guy."

"Yeah, but it wasn't just him I wanted to cream."

"Mark…" she was growing impatient at his persistent indifference. "If you want to hit me, go ahead, but you're going to listen to me."

"Why? So you can lie to me again?"

"You stupid jerk, you think you've been miserable? How do you think I've felt ever since I've been gone? I left because I was falling in love with you, but I didn't want to fall in love, so I ran."

"You could have at least told me that, before you just, up and left," he bitterly insisted.

"I didn't have the heart."

"Guts, you mean."

"Whatever you want to call it. But I realize now that I was wrong, and I want to try again."

Mark swirled on the stool to face her. "And how long do you plan to stay this time?"

Tracy laid her hand softly on his shoulder. "For as long as you want me cowboy. I've quit my job in New York and I've shipped all my belongings here to Montana. I'm in room 1123. I came back for you."

Mark shot up from the stool and stepped away from her. "Well you can just ship them all back. I want you out of my life, got it?" He stormed out of the bar.

Laura casually wiped the counter in front of her. "Sounds like he's really upset."

"I know, I know. I knew he'd be hurt. I didn't realize how much."

"He'll come around, you just wait."

"Not too long, I hope, or he won't see me or his child ever again."

"His child?" Laura was stunned.

"Yes. I'm pregnant with his child."

"Why didn't you just come out and tell him?" Laura insisted. "He needs to know. He'll want his baby."

Tracy's eyes followed Mark out the door. "It's my baby, too. If he wants his baby, then he'll have to want me too." Tracy turned and followed Mark out the door.

Laura just stood in awe of the latest gossip.

In the meantime, at the general store, Bea smiled as she handed the customer his brown paper bag. "Thank you for your purchase, sir."

She pushed in the cash drawer. The little doorbell tinkled as the customer left the store.

"Who was that?"

Bea turned to see John standing in the bedroom doorway, using his hand to prop himself up against the door frame. The other hand held a solid grip on the neck of a bottle of Jack Daniel's. His shirt was unbuttoned, his hair was mussed, his eyes were almost blood red, and his face was unshaven.

"It's just a customer, honey. Go back to bed." She forced a continuous smile.

"Customers, this time of night?" His speech was slurred. "Don't lie to me, Bea."

"I'm not lying to you, honey." She stepped from behind the counter and walked over to him. She placed her hand gently on his cheek. "Honey, it's only six in the evening. Please, go back to bed."

He ran his fingers through his hair. "Six! What the fuck! You let me sleep the whole afternoon? Where's Candy?"

"She's having dinner with Rides and his son."

"Wow, Bea. First a nigger with you. Now you let our daughter play with a redskin and his half-bred son. You're just full of surprises."

"John…"

"So what have you been doing while I was in here sleeping and Candy out of your way?"

"Honey, nothing but running the store," Bea insisted. "I didn't wake you because I knew you needed your sleep."

"Bullshit!" John angrily pushed her away. "You've been seeing that nigger Newman, haven't you?" He staggered past her over to the cash register.

"Honey, please," she pleaded. She rushed over to the counter. "That's not fair. I haven't seen Ken all afternoon. He's been in town."

"Oh yea?" He hit the 'No Sale' key. And the cash drawer popped out. He began pulling cash from the slots. "How do you know where he's been?" He stuffed the bills in his pockets. "I saw you two hugging in his office after the meeting this morning. Tell me what that was all about, eh? Eh?" He slammed the drawer shut. "You like'em dark now, eh!" He turned the bottle up to his mouth and staggered slightly.

"John! You've been drunk all afternoon. Your drinking is turning you into a monster. You've got to get help for the sake of our family, John. I don't know how much more I can take!"

John slammed the empty bottle down on the counter. "Meaning what? Are you going to leave me for your new nigger boyfriend?"

"John, what are you going to do with that money? It belongs to the store."

"It belongs to that counterfeiting jailbird, you mean." He stepped from behind the counter and headed for the door.

"Where are you going?"

"Don't you worry about it," John snarled, twisting the doorknob, "you'll find out soon enough, Ms. Henderson." He slammed the door behind him.

Even after seeing with her own eyes, John's adultery, she's maintained her allegiance to him. But he was becoming too unpredictable, drinking more and more each day. Her patience had worn thin. When was his drinking going to end? Tonight was going to be the night to end it all with John, regardless of her religious beliefs. She would now wait for John's return. She threw the whiskey bottle in the trash and continue working about the store.

As troubles plagued Bea, Newman was working diligently to keep clean water around the grounds. He staggered backwards into the bar, his arms wrapped around a huge glass watercooler.

Laura immediately rushed from behind the counter and stepped over to help him. "You know, this is why they make hand trucks." She quipped, as she cupped her hands under the container.

"Buy me one and I'll use it," he huffed. They carried the container over to the bar and set it down hard on the countertop. "Careful." Newman cautioned.

"How long do you plan to keep this up? Sooner or later you are going to have to drill a new freshwater well."

Newman breathed heavy as he leaned against the counter. "In the meantime, go easy on this one, will you? You've been going through this stuff today like…"

"Like water?" Laura smiled. Newman looked at her in momentary silence, then smiled.

"Go easy, eh? Say, wasn't that Tracy I saw here earlier today?"

"Yes, she's back."

"Does Mark know?" asked Newman.

"I'll say. And he's not at all thrilled over it."

"Can't say I blame him. After all, she did leave him without so much as a good-bye."

"Oh, and men don't do things like that?" Laura countered sternly. "At least she came back to apologize."

"Okay, okay." Newman threw up both hands in surrender. "Just making an observation. Besides that's their business."

"And the baby?"

Newman looked over at Laura, shocked. "Baby? What baby?"

"He doesn't know. Besides, it has to be his. Why would a woman with her kind of status want to trap a nobody logger, like Mark? Abortions are legal in New York, you know."

The bar door swung open. "So there you are," Colleen announced, stepping through the doorway wearing a stylish low-cut black cocktail dress and matching heels. "You know, I've been waiting hours for you to come back from town, and all the while you were over here."

Newman and Laura watched as she made a beeline to the counter. Every inch of her swayed with the grace and movement of a professional model.

"Looks like someone is in trouble…" Laura whispered in Newman's ear.

"I'm sorry." Newman smiled. "But I just forgot that you were waiting for me."

"I guess I didn't make a very good impression on you earlier today. Replied Colleen. And ahh… who is that jerk with the silver hair sitting at your desk?"

"That, my dear is a long story." Newman sighed.

"He has more hands than an octopus. Well…" she smiled at Newman, "are you ready to go?"

"That's right," he suddenly remembered, "we were going to town this evening."

"Don't tell me you forgot that too."

"Forget? Me? Of course not," he lied. "I just didn't expect you to be ready so soon, that's all."

"Well can we go now? I'm dressed and ready."

Newman eyed her from head to toe. "That you are. You look absolutely… Great!"

"Does that mean we can go now?" anxiously asked Colleen.

Newman didn't like the idea of leaving the resort, especially with both Vicki and Jake gone. But then, when would an opportunity like this fall into his lap again? How often did a rich, attractive woman literally beg to treat him to an evening on the town? Blow this chance and when would the next one come along? He hadn't gone out on a date since he's been there. Besides, Cameron was there in case any problems arose.

"Sure," he pounded his fist on the counter, "why not? Let me get dressed and I'll be right with you."

"No way, Ken. After waiting for you all afternoon, I'm not about to let you out of my sight." Colleen grabbed his arm and ushered him toward the door.

"If anyone asks, you haven't seen me, Laura." He called back over his shoulder.

"Sure, Ken, sure. Have fun."

As they were leaving the bar, Mark came trotting up the steps past them.

"Mark," Newman exclaimed, "congratulations. I heard you're going to be a father."

Mark stopped on the top step and looked down at Colleen pulling Newman toward the parking lot.

"Father? Just what in the hell are you talking about?"

"Ask Tracy," Newman shouted as Colleen put her hand over his mouth.

Mark waited momentarily, in disbelief. Then he scampered down the steps and dashed toward the hotel. Newman and Colleen watched Mark make a two-hundred yard-dash in ten seconds. As he entered the hotel parking lot, he noticed Tracy's Porsche parked in the last stall. He grabbed the railing, dashed up the steps and ran to the room on the end. He immediately began pounding on the door.

Newman and Colleen strolled to Ken's room as they watched Mark at the door.

"Who is it?" He heard Tracy bitterly snap inside.

"It's me, Mark, open up!" He urgently demanded. There was silence. "Come on," he insisted. "Open up or I'll break it down!"

"You've made yourself clear. Now why don't you go away and leave me alone."

"No way, Tracy. Not as long as you are having my baby."

There was more silence. Then he heard the chains unlatch while the knob slowly twisted. The door slowly opened and Tracy stood calmly in the doorway. She quietly looked up at him. "How did you find out?" Her tone was somber.

"Does it matter? I love you Tracy. That's all that really matters." Mark grabbed her tightly in his arms and kissed her passionately. He walked her back into the room and kicked the door shut behind him.

Newman and Colleen were still walking back to Ken's room as they noticed the door shut on Tracy's room.

"I think we know how that's going to end."

"Let's get you changed Mr. Newman."

Newman turned the knob on his room door. He opened the door for Colleen to enter first.

"Please, have a seat. There's the remote for the television. I will just hop in the shower and I will be at your beckon call."

Colleen fiddled with the television for about fifteen minutes, until she became restless. She casually walked around the room observing Newman's belongings and touching things haphazardly.

Newman wrapped a towel around his waist as he stepped out of the shower. Colleen called to him from the other room.

"Why did you do that?"

"Do what?" asked Newman.

"Tell Mark about the baby. If she had wanted him to know, she would have told him."

Newman began drying himself. "You don't know Mark. His pride is such that Tracy probably would never have gotten the chance to tell him. Never underestimate the pride of a wounded man."

"So you had to play the love doctor, right?"

"Hey, somebody had to."

"Well, there's another saying too, Doctor Love."

"Yeah, what's that?" Newman was cleaning the shower out.

Slowly the bathroom door eased open and Colleen stepped in. Newman turned, momentarily startled, to face her.

"Colleen!"

She gazed into Newman eyes, while one hand reached for the towel he had wrapped around his waist. He noticed her hand as she gently tugged on it. They both watched the towel drop to the floor. She admired his masculine body from bottom to top.

"Did you find something you like, Ms. Harrison?"

"Physician, heal thyself." She threw her arms around his neck and gently pulled his lips down on hers.

He slowly walked her to the bedroom, kissing her passionately each step they took. Once there, he gently rotated her body around and unfasten her garb. As the dress slithered to the floor, Newman slowly eased her beautifully curved, naked body onto the bed.

"I thought we were going out to dinner?" Newman asked as he gently brushed a hair away from her forehead.

"We are. We're just having desert first."

"I like desert." Newman smiled.

He centered himself above her body. He resume caressing her tenderly with his hands. He fondled the nipples of her breast and kissed her tenderly with his lips. He moved across her entire body with gentle kisses and loving touches with his fingers. As Colleen fell silently into his adoring motions of affection, no more words were spoken as the words were subdued by sexual moans of pleasure.

While Newman and Colleen were getting better acquainted, Bea's woos were continuing. The gun shop proprietor carefully laid the weapon down on the counter. "Now there's a beaut." He smiled. John picked up the handgun and softly stroked the long shining barrel.

"Yes, this is nice."

"Forty-four auto mag," the salesman gloated, noting John's obvious pleasure at feeling the cold hard exterior. "The most powerful handgun in the world. Dirty Harry wouldn't mind owning that one." He beamed.

"It looks like it could do the trick, all right," John weighed the gun in either hand.

"I guarantee it'll stop whatever you wanna stop."

"That's for sure," John laughed. "I need some protection for my wife and kid.

We live at that resort up in the Lolo forest. And a lot of strange people come through there."

"I'll bet," the gunsmith agreed. "Well, you can't go wrong with this baby. Just the sight of it will stop a man dead in his tracks."

John eased the weapon back down onto the counter. "I'll take it," he said confidently, "and a box of ammo."

"Wise choice." He started ringing up the sale. "Cash or charge?"

"Cash. Oh, will I need to go through a waiting period or something? I really need it today."

"Don't worry. This ain't one of those wimp commie states where a man can't own a gun without a lot of paperwork. Just sign this piece of paper." He shoved the form toward John. "Says you're not an ex-con or mental case, or nothin', are you?"

John scribbled his name on the paper. "That, I'm not," he smiled as he handed the paper back to the salesman, "but, for the sake of argument, would it make any difference if I was?"

"Ah, probably not, just as long as you know how to use it."

"I'm going to practice shooting cans." John smiled.

"Cans? That's a waste of good .44 ammo. You can get a smaller-caliber ammo for target practice."

"No, these cans are special types of cans." He paused, "Mexi-cans, Puerto Ri-cans, especially Afri-cans…" The salesman stared at him, concerned momentarily, then smiled. Then, he and John both broke into spontaneous laughter.

Far away from John or Bea, Newman sat across the dinner table from Colleen, the plate in front of him, almost empty. "I can't remember when I've had a dinner quite that good before." He smiled.

"I pride myself on having nothing but the best," Colleen coyly replied. "The best clothes, cars… company. I hate to sound like I'm bragging, but I did without for so long as a child. I promised myself I'd always have the things I wanted as an adult. And so far, thanks to my restaurants and hotels, I can afford them."

"Don't feel bad bragging. It's a poor dog who won't wag his own tail."

She chuckled. "Quaint but accurate. And how about you? What have you been wagging your tail about since you came to the Hot Springs?"

"Oh, there have been some small achievements."

"You know, if you came to work for me…"

"Thanks for the offer," Newman quickly interrupted, "but I'm going to stay where I am, at least for now."

"Suit yourself, Ken. But tell me, you don't honestly think you can rescue this place from the halls of bankruptcy court, do you? Even if Vicki doesn't go to jail, she'll be completely broke in six months, maybe less. And with her legal fees, along with everything else, she probably won't have the cash to stay in business past the end of the year."

Newman watched her as she carefully nursed her wineglass, rolling the goblet between her soft, professionally—manicured fingers. Her confidence was apparent. What wasn't apparent was how he fit into her plans, or even what those plans were. "Is that what this is all about? You need a manager for your hotels?"

"Please, Kenny," Colleen eased the glass onto the table, "give me enough credit to simply ask you outright if that was my purpose for asking you out."

"But I'm sure a women with you obvious worth can attract the attention of a lot of men with your resources."

"I'm my own woman, Kenny. I don't need a man to provide things for me. Since I'm free of that need to attract wealthy men, I can concentrate more on interesting men, regardless of their financial status."

"Is that why I'm sitting here? You find me interesting?" Newman was skeptical.

"Oh, very. And I don't just mean because of you color, although finding a Black man in these parts is very unusual. I'm also interested in why you think you can pull that resort out of the fire. I know you said you like a challenge, but I think you're in over your head. I mean, if you pull this off, it'll rank right up there with Iacocca's turnaround at Chrysler."

"Oh, I wouldn't go that far. It will be a challenge, no question. But, I've never had a challenge quite like this one before and probably never will again."

"So all of this is just a challenge for you? A little test to see if you can pull off the impossible."

"Something like that."

"And let's say you do succeed. Then what? Vicki's back in the saddle, and what do you get out of all this? Her thanks?"

"Maybe, I really don't know. But then that's a bridge I'll have to cross once I get to it, right?"

"Right," Colleen readily agreed. "And I also know we are wasting a good evening with business talk. There's a dance club I know in the Southgate Mall that is simply fantastic."

"It's your dime," Newman quipped.

She raised her finger. "Check, please."

Her conversation about the resort had raised his curiosity as to her interest in him. But the evening was young and Newman's first night out in months. Newman dismissed the conversation for now and was ready to party.

While Newman was enjoying the evening with Colleen, Bea stood on the second rung of the small stepladder removing cans from the box and placing them on the shelf. She reached for another can when the doorbell's tinkle caught her attention. She looked back over her shoulder as John entered the store.

"Honey, where have you been?" Bea asked more out of concern than curiosity.

John didn't answer her. He marched past her and disappeared into the back room. His small package nestled securely under his arm. Bea watched the back room entrance momentarily, then climbed down from the ladder.

"John?" She followed after him. She came to the closed bedroom door. She stood there, bewildered, then knocked. "John? Honey? Is everything all right?" No answer came. She knocked again. "John?"

She raised her fist to knock again when suddenly the door swung open and John stood silently in the doorway. He glared down at her with a look that bordered on rage. Bea had seen him angry before, but never like this. The blood in his eyes had swollen to the point where he looked like a different man---a dangerous man. Now would not be a good time to let him know of her departure with Candy, she thought.

"John, is anything wrong?" Her voice trembled slightly, but she tried not to let her fear show.

"Wrong? Why should anything be wrong?" His tone had a bit of sarcasm.

"It's just that you left here early this evening in such a huff, and with all of that money in the register that you took for whatever reas..."

"Is that what you're worried about, the damned money?"

"Honey, that isn't our money," Bea pleadingly explained. She slowly moved closer toward him, forcing a smile to hide her mounting apprehension. "It belongs to the resort, and we're not thieves, honey."

"Thieves?" His anger was mounting. "You work in this place from eight in the morning until eleven at night for only three hundred bucks a month and you call me a thief?" John emphasized the word 'me.' "That convict who owns this place has been working us like niggers since the minute we got here, and she's using a nigger to do it." He laughed aloud. "Working like a nigger for a nigger. Boy, how did we fall this far?" He asked rhetorically.

Bea had seen these episodes of his rage and self-pity before, but never with such an intensity. It was as if he was trying to laugh and cry simultaneously.

"Honey," she softy began, "we knew the terms of living here before we even moved here, remember? And Vicki and Ken have been nothing but nice to us. How can you say such horrible things about them?"

Surrre," his voice had a bit of sarcasm. "Ken has been real good to you lately, hasn't he?" He turned and stormed into the bedroom, reached under the mattress and retrieved a brown bag.

"Now, what's that supposed to mean?" Bea's tone became angry. She followed him into the bedroom.

"Oh, don't lie to me. I saw the two of you today after the meeting. Him holding you like a long-lost lover or something."

"That's not true!" She angrily insisted. "I was just upset, and he was consoling me, that's all."

"Damn it, woman!" He spun toward her, pointing repeatedly at his chest. "That's my job. I'm your husband. Consoling you is my job. Mine! But no, you find more comfort in the arms of that… that… spear chunker than you do your own husband!"

"Husband?" Bea began, enraged. "Husband? When was the last time you acted like a husband? Someone I could lean on when I felt depressed and lonely. Between your drunken episodes and your mistresses, you're the reason why I'm depressed. After we lost everything in Seattle, this was supposed to be our new start, but you haven't changed a bit."

"I'm trying." He bitterly insisted, "But you won't give me time."

"Time? How much time do you need, John? How many times do I have to forgive you for beating me after you've sobered up, or listen to your 'never again' speech after I've caught you laying with some bimbo in my bed John… my bed!" She paused. "I've had enough! I can't take this anymore!"

He watched the anger on her face, her features strained as she vented frustrations she had held in for years.

"So when do you and Newman plan to leave together?" John asked matter-of-factly.

"For the last time, there's nothing between Ken and me," she replied sternly, more incensed than angry by his accusation. "But if I were to leave you, it wouldn't be for another man. I have to think of Candy. She can't grow up constantly exposed to your drunkenness and womanizing."

John sneered. "I'll never let you take my daughter away from me."

"I will, if you leave me no choice, John."

John tore open the package he had tucked under his arm and produced the .44 mag. "You won't take Candy and live." He brandished the weapon menacingly, waving it cavalierly.

Bea's eyes widened. Her jaw slackened as she stared in horror at the huge gun in John's hand.

"Where... where did you get that?"

"Oh, that little withdrawal I made earlier today from the cash register. It's a beaut, isn't it?"

Bea was genuinely terrified. John at his worse never use a gun. And the glee with which he displayed his prize caused her a level of concern she had never experienced before.

"Honey," she calmly began, trying to suppress anxiety in her voice, "put that thing down before you hurt somebody."

"Like who?" John voice was menacing, "You, maybe?" He pointed the gun at her. She flinched. He pointed the gun toward the ceiling. "Or your boyfriend, maybe?"

Bea turned and bolted out of the room. John dashed after her. She managed to reach the counter, but john lunged, and grabbed a handful of her hair. She screamed as her head jerked back. John jammed her head into his chest.

"Don't run from me, baby," he angrily sneered. "Don't you ever run from me." She grimaced in pain. "I'm your husband. Now..." He marched her over to the telephone. "Call Newman. Call Newman over here, now. Tell him you need consoling." He said sarcastically. "That should get him over here real fast."

"What are you going to do?" Bea's voice trembled.

"Never you mind your pretty little head. Just call him!" He picked up the phone and shoved it to her ear. "Now dial."

"But John, Newman is not..." she hesitated.

"I said dial!"

Bea gingerly pressed the buttons. Seconds later... "Is Ken there?... He's not?" Bea's voice brightened at the news. "No... don't transfer me... I don't want to hol..." A few seconds later... Mr. Cameron?"

"You still want to see him," John whispered into her ear.

"Ahhh... I'd like to see Ken when he gets in the offi..."

"It's urgent," John whispered.

"It's urgent." Bea repeated. "No thanks, Mr. Cameron. Just Kenny, but thanks for the offer anyway."

John took the receiver and slammed it down. He shoved her toward the door. "Lock it and turn the 'closed' sign on." She complied. "Good. Now come here and we wait."

"Candy will be home soon."

"If you're dead by the time she gets here, she'll die too."

Bea, knew at that moment, John had lost it. How was she now going to reason with a crazed man?

As Bea was trying to figure out how she was going to reason with a demented human being that was no longer the husband she once loved, Newman was still on his exquisite date with Colleen.

He effortlessly guided the steering wheel of the Mercedes with one hand. The other hand gently grasped Colleen's shoulders with her head resting softly in his chest. The stereophonic beat of Prince's latest album pulled through the car's speakers. His body unconsciously weaved to the beat.

"I see you like Prince," Colleen said, examining her nails.

"How can you tell?"

"Because I don't think you've stopped moving since I put the tape on."

"Well it's not every day I get to drive a Mercedes with quadraphonic sound and hold a beautiful woman in my arms." He leaned down slightly and kissed her forehead. "Besides, I hear so much country and western around that place, I'm actually beginning to remember some of the lyrics."

"You're the manager. Just put some soul songs on the jukebox. Assert your authority."

Newman chuckled. "Then you really want to see a riot, don't you? Especially on Saturday nights when all the good ole boy loggers, truckers and cowboys gather in mass. I played a Michael Jackson record for Carl once. He said he sounded like he had his pecker caught in his zipper---his words."

"In college, my best friend's roommate was black. She had all of those soul records—you know, Brook Benton, Sam and Dave, just every big soul name of the '60's and '70's. She was always playing those sounds on the stereo every time I came over to see Trish. Well, needless to say, soul music wasn't too popular in my parents' household. But the more I listened to it, the more I liked it. Now I have a music collection that would rival a soul music radio station. Who knows, maybe the same will happen with you and country music."

"No way," Newman emphatically insisted. "Why would I?"

She looked up at him. "Trish's roommate was the same way. It's as if, even if she did like it, she wasn't going to admit it."

"I guess probably the only thing I have against country music is that Carl and people like him, like it," Newman sighed. "I can remember as a kid climbing aboard this white man's truck to go to work in the tomato field one morning. And he goes, 'All right, let's get the niggers in the truck, we ain't got all day,' he said in a mockingly deep voice. Hank Williams just blasting from his truck radio. And to this day, every time I hear that song, I think of that man."

"Guilt by association."

"Something like that. Like trying to see a Confederate flag as just a historical symbol instead of a racist banner. Especially, when those bikers and truckers come in here with it flying from their vehicles."

"Well, get used to seeing that Confederate flag. Some of these people will give up their firstborn, before they give up their stars and bars."

Newman rounded a bend and the flashing Hot Springs road sign became visible from the road.

"I still say we could have stayed out later." Colleen chided as she sat upright in her seat. "This place can survive one night without you. How did they manage before you came here?"

"With Vicki in the hospital, I just don't feel comfortable staying away too long. Besides, I don't know Cameron that well. There's something about him I just don't like. But this isn't the last I intend to see of you. There will be other nights, right?"

"Of course, but…"

Newman turned into the parking lot. "No buts, but I'll tell you what. Let me check in at the office and see how things are going. If everything's okay, I'll meet you over at the bar for a few hours. We can dance to some country music and go back to my place for some more desert, okay?"

"Yes. I did enjoy desert very much this evening."

Newman stopped in front of the office. "Now this shouldn't take long." He smiled, got out of the car. He leaned through the passenger window and kissed her.

"Hurry back. I'll wait right here."

Newman scampered up the steps. He stepped into the office to find Marci seated at the receptionist's desk, facedown and her head resting comfortably on her elbow.

"Huh, hummm. I'd like a room," Newman loudly announced.

Marci immediately shot up, startled momentarily, reaching aimlessly for the papers on the desk. She then looked up at Newman.

"Kenny," she smiled with a sigh of relief, "you scared me."

Newman smiled. "Well, I didn't mean to interrupt your nap. Where did Cameron go anyway?"

"He's over at the bar."

"Great. So I guess there's nothing really exciting going on."

"Nope. One of the few nights where the whole place is quiet."

"Good. No messages or anything?"

Marci searched among the papers scattered around the desk. "Just that Forest Service lady called again, Leanna Clark. She left these messages for you." She held up several slips of paper.

"Oh, don't worry about it. I'll call her back tomorrow. I'm going to the bar. I'll be back here in a couple of hours to close up. You can hang in there until then, can't you?"

Marci giggled. "Sure, Kenny, sure."

"Okay, see you in a bit."

He turned to leave when she called to him. "Oh, Ken, I almost forgot, Bea called. She sounded kind of strange."

"Did she say what she wanted?"

"No. Just that she really wanted to see you tonight. I past her to Cameron, but she insisted on seeing you."

"Boy," Newman sighed. "It's probably that sleazebag husband of hers." He said under his breath. "Okay thanks Marci. I'll drop by the store before going to the bar. Then I'll come back and relieve you. Think you can stay awake that long?"

"I said I could, Kenny," she responded a little irritated. "Gee whiz." "Okay, okay," Newman said, backing out of the door. He walked down the stairs and got in the drive side of the car.

"Something's come up. I've got to go to the general store for a few minutes. Let me drop you off at the bar and wait for me there. This shouldn't take too long."

"It'd better not, or I'm coming after you, mister. That's a promise." Newman drove to the bar. Colleen leaned over and kissed his lips. "There's more where that came from." She smiled as she climbed out of the car. He watched as Colleen made it safely into the bar.

Newman was about to head for the general store when he noticed Candy and Danny laughing as they sprinted toward the swimming pool.

"Hey! Kids," Newman hailed as he approached them. "Where are you two headed in such a hurry?"

"I was racing her to the hot pool," Danny breathed, smiling excitedly.

"Well slow down, you two. You could both hurt yourselves. And by the way, isn't it past both of your bedtimes?"

"Dad's at the pool," Danny volunteered.

"And Mom told me I could hang out with Danny until Mr. Rides close the pool tonight." Candy added.

"You talked to her?" asked Newman.

"Yeah, I called her about an hour ago."

"Is there a problem at the store?" quizzed Newman.

"No, she didn't say anything about a problem when I asked her if I could hang with Danny. She just told me to hurry over here to the pool with Danny."

Newman hesitated. Maybe the reason she wanted to see him wasn't that serious and could wait until tomorrow. Colleen was waiting at the bar, and while it was getting late, the night was still relatively young.

"Want a ride, it's a good ways down the road."

"No thanks, Mr. Newman. We are racing each other. I know I can beat Candy."

"Alright Danny. Don't you two stay out too late, you hear?" Newman admonished.

"We won't," they replied, almost in unison. They both darted toward the pool.

Newman smiled, shook his head, and then continued on toward the General Store. He stepped onto the porch and noticed the 'Closed' sign in the window. He checked his watch. It's too early for the store to be closed, he thought. He opened the screen door and twisted the doorknob. It was locked. He knocked twice. "Bea!" He waited for an answer. "Bea!… It's Kenny." He waited. Suddenly he heard the knob unlock, and the door eased open. Newman was puzzled by the door's partial opening without anyone being there. He gingerly pushed the door open wider. By the glimmer of moon he saw Bea sitting in a chair across the room, whimpering uncontrollably. Her hands were behind her back, and tears streaming down her face.

He rushed over to her. "Bea?"

Suddenly the door behind him slammed shut. Newman whirled. John stood in front of the door with one hand behind his back.

"Ken." John turned on the lights.

"John?"

John smiled menacingly, "Glad you could make it, Kenny boy. I was beginning to think you weren't going to show up."

"Newman turned to Bea. "What's going on here? I heard you wanted to see me."

She looked up at him. Her eyes were red from her prolonged crying. "He made me call you. He said if I tried to warn you when you came through the door, it would be the last words I speak," Bea sobbed. "I didn't want to, Ken, believe me, I didn't."

Newman noticed that she didn't rise from her chair, and her hands were constantly behind her back. He peered behind the chair to see her hands bound at the wrist with pantyhose.

"What the…?" He instinctively reached to untie her.

"Uh uh…" John cautioned, "None of that."

Newman looked up to see John leveling the handgun at him. Newman froze, his eyes rooted on the black hole of death staring him directly in the face. He opened his mouth to speak but couldn't form the words.

"Honey, please put the gun down." Cried Bea.

"I went through a lot of trouble to tie that knot," John said casually, "so leave it alone."

"John what are you doing?"

"Heard you got lucky with that whore tonight." John smiled as he stepped away from the door.

"What luck?" Asked Newman.

"The very night I plan to blow you away, you almost missed it because you're out getting a piece of ass." He chuckled. "Just as well. I haven't seen you with a woman since I've been here. For a while I thought you rode sidesaddle---that is, until you started taking an interest in my wife here." He pointed the gun at Bea, then back at Newman.

"Look, look, John," Newman's voice trembled. "I don't know what you're talking about."

"Oh, don't you now." Newman could see John's delight in his total control. "Where's that confidence? You know, like when you told Bea to leave me. Get rid of the drunken bum." He mocked in a halfhearted imitation of Newman's voice. ' I'd leave him if I were you.' Isn't that how you put it after the meeting earlier today? Oh yes, I heard every word. Leave me? For what? For you? Do you really think I'd just sit back and let Candy call you daddy? I'd see her dead and buried first."

"John, I'm not leaving you," Bea shouted through her sobbing. "You don't have to do this."

"Oh, but hone, I do. You see, I've seen the way super nigger here seems to always be around every time we have our problems. Before I lose you and Candy to him, I'd rather see you, me, Candy, but especially you, Kenny boy, dead. You understand me? Dead… dead… dead!" His voice was intense with anger.

Newman slowly stepped away from Bea. His proximity to her could only further enrage John. The initial shock of seeing the gun was starting to wane. He began to realize that these could easily be his last moments on earth unless he did something, and fast.

"John, look," Newman calmly began, "whatever problems we have, I'm sure they can be worked out without that gun."

"You really think so?" His voice reeked of sarcasm. "Do you really think I could convince you to leave my wife alone if I put this gun down? You think I can convince you to stop telling her to leave me?"

"Stop it, John!" Bea shouted. Her fear was slowly giving way to an anger and frustration that bordered desperation. "Don't drag Kenny into our problems!"

"I didn't, you did. Every time we'd have a fight, you'd run straight to him."

"That's not true," Bea angrily countered, "and you know it! I've tried to work out our problems with you, but every time we take a step forward, sooner or later you take two steps backward. The beatings, the booze, the other women, John. I saw you! I just saw you yesterday in bed with some blonde half your age. The way you were making love to her sickened me to my stomach. It hurt me! It hurt me so bad, I turned around and I walked out. Do you understand how indignant I felt? I had to talk to somebody. I was going insane, John." She looked over at Newman. "I'm just sorry it had to be you, Kenny." She turned her attention back to John. Bea's voice turned soft and serene. "If you're going to kill somebody, John, then kill me. I'd never leave you, but I don't know how much more of this I can take. Put me out of my misery, because I can't tolerate the beatings and the adultery anymore. Kill me. Kill me John."

John was silent. Her words had struck like a hammer. Pangs of guilt began to gnaw at his conscience. But he stood firm. "Aw, cut your whining, Bea." He countered, asserting himself. "You haven't had it that bad."

"Then what are we doing here at this place? You son-of-a-bitch! How did we lose a $260,000 house, a Mercedes, a BMW, all of our bank cards and over a million in cash? And tell me, John, why is that former beauty queen suing us for child support? If I haven't had it that bad? John, you've put me and Candy through hell."

"Then why haven't you left before now?"

"Isn't it obvious, I still love you. As bad as it's been with you, I can't imagine life without you. Candy adores you, and I wouldn't take her away from her father."

As Bea passionately pleaded with him, Newman watched as John's anger gradually began to subside, even as he seemed desperately trying to hold onto it. For the first time during this whole ordeal, he seemed more interested in Bea than himself.

"I've tried to do better, honey, you know I have." His tone softened. "I agreed to come here with you, didn't I?"

"You did, and I know you're trying, baby, but you've got to put the gun down. If you kill me or Kenny, any chance we might have for a future will be all over. And think of Candy. Her father will be in jail, and I'll be dead. Who will raise our daughter? She needs her father and her mother."

John looked at her quietly. His arm was beginning to tremble slightly from the fatigue of holding the gun. He turned his attention from Bea back to Newman. He caught Newman's quiet stare. Suddenly, his arm stiffened and his resolve suddenly hardened.

"It's too late. Kenny here just can't wait to get out of here and call the police."

"Look," Newman quickly added, "put the gun down, let us walk out of here, and as far as I'm concerned, tonight never happened."

"Sure, sure. You'll say anything now."

"John listen," Newman pleaded, "no matter what you think of me, I've never hated you as a person. I've hated some of the things you've done, but I've never had anything against you personally. Candy's a sweetheart and I know you love Bea and your daughter. I'd take no pleasure in seeing you in jail. Your family needs you more. Let's just call this a bad nightmare, okay? And when we all wake up, it'll be over."

Suddenly several small knocks echoed at the door. "Mom, Dad, let me in."

"It's Candy." Bea gasped.

"What's it gonna be, John?" Newman quickly stated.

John looked frightened and confused. "Quick," he pointed to Bea, "untie her."

Newman scrambled over to Bea and fumbled momentarily with the nylons. Seconds later, Bea's hands dropped to her side. She began massaging the stiffness from her wrist.

"Honey, take her back over to the pool for a moment."

Bea rose from her chair and hurried for the door. "Come on, Kenny, let's go." She called as she turned the knob.

"No!" John quickly interjected. "Newman stays."

Bea turned toward Newman, "John, Kenny said he'd forget tonight ever happened. Now I'm not going to leave him here for you to kill him."

"Mom!" Candy's voice cried louder. "It's getting cold out here."

"Go get the kid, Bea!" John commanded. "Ken and I have some unfinished business to discuss."

"What kind of business?" Bea insisted. "Mom!" Candy cried.

"Get out of here! Now!" John shouted.

"Go on, Bea." Newman motioned toward the door. "I'll be all right."

"Don't be so sure," added John.

Bea hesitated. Newman motioned again for her to leave. She hesitated again, then turned and opened the door.

"Mom!" Candy sighed. "I've been waiting forever for you to open the door."

Bea scooped Candy up in her arms. "Sorry, honey." She kissed her on the cheek. "Mommy's been busy. We're going back to the pool for a while, okay?"

John closed the door behind them. "She's quite a woman." He smiled.

"Quite." Newman agreed. "Now, what's this unfinished business?"

John leaned casually against the door, the gun pointed toward the floor. "You know, I still don't know how I got such a good woman."

"John…" Newman was growing impatient.

"Despite all the shit I've put her through," he continued almost to himself, "she still loves me."

"Great that you realize that, John."

"But she's right about one thing. I have put her through hell. What with my affairs, gambling, drinking, you name it. And I want to stop, God only knows how I want to stop---the drinking, the whores. I want to stop, Kenny," he insisted, "you know?"

"Yes. I know John." Newman nodded in agreement.

"But I can't. I can't stop drinking. When I see a nice-looking woman, I can't help but try and get her into bed. And you know, I'm going to continue to make her cry for the rest of her life. And she's right. She won't leave me. She comes from one of those 'till death do us part' families. You know the kind, no abortion, no divorce, no sex, till you're thirty-five." He chuckled. "And she deserves better. Candy deserves better."

"Let her help you." Newman admonished. "She's got all the patience in the world."

"You're right. But I don't. She may believe in me, but I don't believe in me anymore. She could soar like an eagle, if she weren't tied to me. She could give Candy the life she deserves, if only I weren't around."

Newman was growing concerned over the tone of his conversation. Now his concern wasn't so much for his own well-being as it was for John's.

"John, Candy loves you. She needs you in her life."

"She's young, Ken. Kids are more resilient than you think."

"John," Newman's voice was in near panic, "listen, just put the gun down and let's talk."

John quickly snapped the barrel up to his temple. "Till death do us part, man. I love her so very much. Now, finally, I've got a chance to show her."

"John, no!" Newman lunged toward the weapon.

Several yards away from the store, Bea stood quietly with Candy in her arms when the deadly report of the .44 ripped the calm night air.

"Noooo!" Bea screamed.

It was well into the early morning when the police began taking down the crime scene tape. The red and green flashing sirens illuminated an otherwise dark, drizzling morning. Only a few die-hard observers remained of the several hundred on-lookers. Many of whom, had crowded the perimeter of the police barriers that were set up hours earlier. The coroner hauled the black vinyl bag out of the store and sped off into the night.

Bea stood solemnly as the slight drizzle soaked her clothes, Candy hoisted in her arms, asleep on her shoulder.

Newman stood next to her, Colleen's arm wrapped tightly around his waist as a policeman in a transparent plastic rain gear stood between them, notepad in hand.

"I think I have all of the information we need for now," the officer politely surmised, flipping the pages on his notebook. "You'll both be around if I have any more questions, right?" He looked over at Bea. She stared quietly at the general store.

"Yes, we will," Newman quickly interjected. The officer noted the empty glaze in Bea's eyes. He turned back to Newman. "Is she going to be all right?"

Newman looked over at Bea as she slowly, methodically patted the sleeping Candy on her back.

"Yes," Newman insisted, "she'll be fine. We'll take care of her."

"Okay, then I'm through." He tipped his hat to Bea and walked off.

Newman cupped his arm around Colleen and walked over to Bea.

"Bea," he said softly. She didn't respond. "Bea," Newman said a little louder.

She looked startled over at him. "Candy needs to go to bed, don't you think? She looked down at her sleeping child.

"Let's go to the office, get a key to one of the hotel rooms, and get some sleep. We'll deal with this in the morning, okay?" She quietly nodded. "The car is right over there. It's open."

She started to walk away, then stopped and turned back toward Newman. "Kenny…" Bea hesitated.

"I understand," he smiled.

She turned and headed for the car.

Colleen looked up at him and smiled. "You're quite a guy, you know that?"

"It's been on helluva night babe." Newman sighed.

"I'll bet." sympathized Colleen.

"You haven't lived until you've looked down the business end of a .44."

"Well, maybe I can help take your mind off of tonight."

"Oh really. And just how do you plan to do that?"

"Let's have desert, all night long. My treat." Colleen gently pulled his lips down on hers.

"My kind of woman." He ushered her back toward the Mercedes.

C H A P T E R

14

The Bronco pulled to a stop in front of the front office steps. Jake hopped out of the driver's seat and walked around to the back of the wagon. Vicki stepped out of the passenger's seat and surveyed the grounds.

"Well," she sighed, "at least it's all still here."

"You mean, you're still here," Jake corrected as he pulled the luggage from the back gate. "That heart attack could have killed you, you know. The doctor wants you to take it easy for the next few days."

"Take it easy," Vicki huffed as she hurried up the stairs, "I've got sentencing pending. I've got to prepare my appeal. And as good as Kenny is, I can't expect him to do all of my work for me."

She opened the door and gasped. Above the entrance was a long white banner with black lettering. "Welcome Home Vicki."

Newman emerged from the back room. "Vicki," he beamed, "we knew you'd be back sometime today, but we didn't know exactly when. So some of us just put up that banner in case we weren't here to see you when you got back."

Jake appeared in the doorway, a suitcase in each hand, and disappeared into the back room. "Well, are you all right? I heard on the news what happened here last night at the general store."

"It wasn't a pretty sight, but I'm no worse for wear. It's Bea and Candy I'm worried about. I haven't seen her all morning and I'm worried about her."

Vicki walked over behind the desk. "Why don't you go and check on them in a few minutes. Now, what was Lisa's problem?" She began fingering through the papers and folders.

"Seems as if Snake had her stealing money from you. She just didn't want to continue, so she brought back about three thousand dollars and quit. That way Snake couldn't make her steal from you anymore."

Vicki shook her head in disgust. "Poor Lisa. I knew all along that skuzzball was making her steal from me, but she never stole more than she was worth to me," she sighed. "She didn't say where she was going, did she?"

"Just someplace where Snake couldn't find her."

"And neither can I, probably. What else?"

Newman paused and took a death breath. "Well, I don't know how to tell you this, but there's gasoline in the drinking water." He expected a startled reaction from her, but she merely picked up a stack of papers and continued to read through them. "Vicki," he reiterated. "There's gasoline in our fresh water well."

"Okay, Kenny, I heard you," she answered slightly coarse. Then she caught herself. She laid the papers down. "Look, Ken, don't worry about it. Say, did you know that the Indians once used oil and water to cure pneumonia?"

"Great," he sighed. "All we have to do now is require that everyone who checks in here contracts pneumonia first."

Jake emerged from the back room. "Honey, your stuff's in your room. I've got to get up to the hill and see how those boys are doing with Carl in charge for the last couple of days. I'm almost afraid to go up there."

"Okay, honey," Vicki replied, her attention still fixed on the papers in front of her. "Have a good afternoon."

Jake pulled the door open, and Bea stood in the doorway.

"Oh, Jake," Bea appeared startled. "I didn't know you had made it in."

Vicki quickly stepped from behind the desk. "Beatrice, come in, please."

Newman walked over to her. "I was just coming by to see you."

"Please everybody," Bea smiled, almost embarrassed, "don't make such a big fuss. I'm okay, probably better than I've been in a long time. I'm now actually going to get on with my life."

"Good for you," Vicki smiled.

"That's why I came by to tell you all that I'm leaving. I know this is a bad time for you, on the tail end of the summer season and all, but I just can't work in that store anymore. School's only a month away, I want Candy to get over this as soon as possible."

"She's young." Vicki placed her hand on Bea's shoulder. "Children are tougher than you think."

"How is she taking it?" Newman asked.

"She cried all morning, but then what else would you expect? I told her that her father was killed protecting me during a holdup attempt. That's the only story she'll ever hear."

"Where are you headed?" Jake asked.

"Back to Seattle. John's parents are driving down to get us. I've cleaned the store from top to bottom and restocked the shelves. So it's ready to go for whoever you find to replace me."

"You didn't have to do that." Vicki consoled.

"But I wanted to. You all have been very kind to me and Candy, and John," she quickly added. "I don't want to leave like a lot of the other people who come here---get a paycheck, then leave."

"You'll always be welcome here." Vicki smiled and hugged her.

Newman then enveloped her in a big hug. "Take care of yourself." He smiled.

"Nobody else will. Good-bye everybody." Bea turned and walked out the opened door.

"I'm going up on the hill, honey." Jake followed her out the door.

Vicki walked back behind the desk and eased down into the chair. "That's some woman," she noted, picking up another stack of papers.

"Vicki, now back to the water. I've been hauling fresh drinking water to the bar and kitchen for drinking and cooking, but that's not going to solve the problem."

She was silent briefly as her eyes followed the words down the page. "Un-huh."

"Vicki," Newman insisted, slightly miffed at being ignored.

"What?" She snapped, looking up at him.

"The gasoline is in the water. What are we going to do about it?"

"I don't know right now, Kenny. I just got back, remember? Let me catch up on what else is going on. We'll talk about it later."

"Vicki, what other problems could we possibly have that's more important than the possible poisoning of our guests?"

Vicki slammed the papers down on the desk. She glared up at Newman with a sudden burst of anger he had never seen in her before. "Kenneth," Vicki sternly began, "I own this place, not you. I set the priorities at this resort, me!" She pointed confidently to herself. "I was managing this place long before you came, and if you don't like my rules, there's the door!" She pointed.

There was an eerie quiet as she and Newman stared at each other momentarily. He had seen her use that tone before with other people, but never with him. Newman turned to leave when the door opened, and a young man with a briefcase stood in the doorway.

"Vicki Marshall?" The man asked.

"I'm Vicki Marshall. Who's wants to know?"

"Greg Redman, Missoula County Health Department. Can we talk?"

"I was just leaving," Newman quipped. "I'm sure you two have a lot to talk about." Newman walked past him and shut the door. He had almost made it to the golf cart, when he heard Vicki hailing him.

"Kenny, wait, please?"

Newman stopped and waited impatiently. "How do I tell you I'm sorry? You've been a godsend, Kenny. And you didn't deserve to be talked to like that. I'm sorry, but in the past couple of weeks, I've been convicted of a crime I didn't commit, I almost died, I lost Lisa, and now Bea. I've got a sentencing coming up, and now you tell me I need ten thousand dollars for a new fresh water well. I just don't know what to do. I need you here, though. Would you stay... please?"

Newman stared at her coldly, then smiled. "I was just going to lunch."

Vicki beamed. "Great! But first could you take care of that Redman fellow?"

"But, Vicki..."

"Thanks, Kenny," she interrupted as she backed away from him. "I'll send him right out. Oh, and whatever you do, don't let him taste the water. We'll talk about it as soon as he leaves, okay?"

"Ahhh… sure, Vicki."

Vicki disappeared back into her office and Redman appeared on the steps and walked over to Newman.

"Good afternoon, I'm Greg Redman." He and Newman shook hands. "Missoula County health. You must be Mr. Newman."

"Ken, please."

"Please to meet you. Let me get right to the point. This is just a routine surprise inspection. We conduct one on every public eating establishment throughout the year to make sure minimum safety standards are maintained. While some restaurants would argue, we are actually just here to help."

"I understand."

"Really? Mr. Newman."

"Yes."

They both climbed into the jeep and headed for the restaurant.

"Then maybe you can explain that to Vicki's husband."

"Jake?" asked Newman.

"Yeah, the last time I was here, I found so many violations, that I threatened to shut this place down. When I came back for my re-inspection, he pulled a shotgun on me."

"A shotgun?" Newman asked as they ascended the steps of the restaurant.

"Double barrel."

They pushed the door open and walked in. The sound of tinkling dishes met them at the door. Greg Redman glanced around the crowded dining area.

"Looks like you're doing a brisk business," he noted.

"It's Vicki' notoriety. Counterfeiting may put you in jail, but the publicity you receive is priceless."

Redman placed his briefcase on the counter and pulled out a long white form.

"I'll be going down this list, noting the deficiencies as well as the time the inspection starts and the time each deficiency was noted. That's so you'll be able to compare yourself to other restaurants in your same category. Shall we begin?'

Newman nonchalantly stepped behind the counter, trying to conceal the anxiety he felt over the inspection. The kitchen had a lot of deficiencies that he could see, even with his untrained eye. To a veteran inspector like Redman, it was bound to be a disaster. Well, at least now he would know the problems to correct.

Redman peeped into the dishwashing room where a newly hired dishwasher was scrubbing plates over a mound of suds. He looked up as Redman entered, then turned his attention back to the dishes. Newman stood in the doorway and waited.

"Who's that?" The voice over his shoulder asked.

Newman turned to see Nelson peering at Redman over his shoulder.

"That's the health inspector," Newman replied casually.

"Health inspect…!" Nelson exclaimed.

"Shhhh," Newman quipped.

"Health inspector," he whispered. "Got damn it, Ken! Why didn't you give me some warning?"

"Because I didn't get any. Anyway, it's too late to go scrambling now. He's here. Let's just take our lumps, correct our mistakes, and pass on re-inspection."

"Say you." Redman re-appeared back into the kitchen.

Nelson dashed away. "Yeah." Ken responded.

Redman walked closer to Newman. "I meant the other guy. Was that your cook?"

"Yeah, that was Nelson."

"What happened to that other guy? Well… I guess it was a guy."

"Oh, you mean Kelly. He's not here anymore. Ahh… it's a long story."

"I'll just bet it is. Well, for starters, you don't have a third sink."

"Third sink?"

"Wash, rinse, disinfect. Every public eating establishment has to have that third sink. I've been through this before with Vicki." Redman sounded frustrated.

"Well, go over it with me."

He reached into his pocket and pulled out a small packet of bleach. "This or a mild bleach will do. But a third sink is mandatory." He walked past Newman. Newman turned and followed him.

Redman observed Nelson and the kitchen crew as they labored over sizzling frying pans and boiling pots. "Everybody has hairnets." Redman was pleased.

"Yes," Nelson volunteered. "we always wear them whenever we work in the kitchen."

"Sure…" Redman sarcastically acknowledged. "Sure." He walked over to the counter and examined a blender. "This will have to go."

"Whadda ya mean, go?" Nelson asked.

"Household appliances can't be used in commercial application," he blandly answered and moved on. Nelson looked at Redman menacingly as he passed him.

Redman noted the watercooler on the counter. "Why is this here?"

Newman and Nelson were both silent. "It's distilled water for cooking. It makes the soup taste better." Newman hastily explained.

Redman looked at Newman skeptically. "Okay."

Redman kicked the bottom box in a stack of boxed potatoes. "These need to be on a pallet off the floor, in case of flooding, you know."

"Of course," Newman agreed. He followed Redman through the kitchen, through the storage room, and on into the bar. Redman scribbled on his sheet almost continuously.

Meanwhile, a shiny black Lincoln town car was making a slow, deliberate tour of the RV Park. The well-dressed elderly man at the wheel closely observed the various RVs scattered around the park. The middle-aged woman next to him impatiently checked her watch.

"Haven't we seen enough yet?" The man complained.

"No Franklin, I want to get a good, solid look at this place. Forty acres of wide open spaces, fresh air and pure mineral spring water. And I might be able to pick it up for a song."

"But, Nina," Franklin complained. "This is so far away from home. I don't know anything about the Lolo Forest."

"Don't you worry about a thing, baby." Nina consoled. "I'll take care of everything."

They rounded a bend in the road.

"But I really like what I see, so I think I will stay here just a little bit longer. Now what's that woman's name again?" asked Franklin.

"Vicki Marshall," Nina replied. "Why do you ask?"

"It's just that I'd hate to meet the woman again and not even remember her name, especially if we're going to take her resort from her." They both laughed.

"I'm beginning to like this place, fresh air, open spaces. This place does have a lot of potential." Smiled Nina.

"So did the Hindenburg," Franklin huffed.

"We could wait until it falls into bankruptcy?"

"No Nina. We'll have too much competition if that happens. Let's wait and see if she goes to jail and then make her an offer."

"You're too smart for your own good, Frankie, baby. That's why I love you."

"That's how the rich, stay richer my dear."

They both smiled and continued their own personal excursion of the resort.

As potential buyers of the resort cased the surroundings hoping for Vicki's demise, Newman was still entertaining Redman with his inspection. Redman sat on the bar stool. He scribbled a few notes on the paper, then handed it to Newman while Laura stood at the far end of the bar, engaged in conversation with a customer.

"Any questions on the evaluation so far Mr. Newman?"

Newman examined the paper, trying to decipher the scribblings on the page. "No, I think I understand perfectly. I'll have a whole new resort ready when you come back to re-inspect."

Redman chuckled. "Not exactly, but it couldn't hurt. This place needs some close attention. You know, this used to be the best restaurant in the whole Bitterroot."

"Well, I'll do my best to get these problems taken care of. Who knows, maybe we can get it back to its former glory."

"Good luck. I'll be back in forty-eight hours, and we'll have another look." Redman sighed. "Boy, all that walking around has made me thirsty."

"I'll get you a soda from the restaurant." Newman volunteered.

"Hey, that'd be great. Diet anything will do."

Newman hurried into the dining room, pulled a large paper cup from the dispenser, and watched the liquid pour into the cup. He turned and carefully carried the cup back into the bar. He looked over to see Redman standing behind the sink, the water running and the steam rising. Newman almost dropped the cup. He thought he had successfully steered Redman away from the contaminated water.

Redman looked up at Newman as he entered. "Are you planning to offer a free lube job with a fill-up of drinking water, Mr. Newman?"

"That wasn't very nice, sending me for a soda just so you could examine our water. You could have simply asked."

"And got another line of bull, like special water for the soups? No, thank you. I had hoped you'd be a little more candid with me about this, but you chose not to do so."

"What did you want me to tell you? We have unhealthy drinking water? We are taking care of the problem."

"From the smell of this water," Redman took a whiff of the steam, "not very well. I'm taking a sample of this water back to the lab. And, judging from the smell of this water, I'll have no choice but to issue a closure order for the entire resort."

"But there's fresh, drinkable water in all of the rooms and in the kitchen for cooking." Newman sternly protested.

"And how about bathing? Anyone showering in this water will come out smelling like a service station. Not to mention, the health hazard should anyone inadvertently swallow this water during their shower? No, I'm sorry, Mr. Newman, but I can't let this place operate with such a severely contaminated water supply."

"But we're working on it."

Greg Redman snapped his briefcase shut. "I'll be back day after tomorrow. "If gasoline is still in the water, I'll have no choice but to have you close the doors." Newman sighed. "You can take me back to my car now."

While Newman took the blows from the Health Inspector, Vicki was doing the same with her attorneys. The two men in three-piece business suits sat across the desk from Vicki, briefcases opened on their laps. One man handed Vicki a set of papers. She took them and began scanning through the contents.

"Well, that's it," one of them sighed. "You have been officially sentenced."

"Three years!" Yelled Vicki.

"Don't get too excited. Two and a half years-suspended," The other man quickly added, "so that's just six months of actual jail time. Plus you get a third off for good behavior. You'll spend it at a minimum security women's prison up near Helena. There are no bars, no towers, and with good behavior, you could be out in four months, tops. Not bad for someone convicted of counterfeiting five million dollars."

Vicki flipped to another page on the report. "You make it sound like I've just won first prize on a game show or something." She tossed the papers on her desk. "What have I been paying you two over fifty grand for?" Anger echoed the room.

"You paid for good legal representation and you got it."

Vicki pounded her fist on the table. "I paid you two to get me acquitted. Hell! If I wanted to go to jail I could have managed that myself and a whole hellava lot cheaper, I might add."

"Four months in what essentially is a country club. Vicki, considering the charges you were facing, I consider you extremely lucky."

"Lucky! Mr. Ansell?" She leaned forward in her chair, "You call going through life with a prison record, convicted of a crime I didn't commit, lucky?"

She looked at them both angrily. They sat in subdued silence. She then sat back, unconsciously strumming her fingers on the desk. "Okay, gentlemen, what's our next move?"

The two attorneys looked at each other, then back at Vicki. "Move?" Ansell asked.

"Yes, my appeal." She pushed the papers toward them. "I'm not going to take this crap lying down. So, what's our next move?"

Ansell cleared his throat and loosened his tie. "Vicki, can I speak candidly?"

She chuckled. "A lawyer asking if he can speak," she remarked sarcastically. "Sure, why not."

"Vicki like you said, you've already spent over fifty thousand dollars on your defense. Now you don't have to be a genius to figure out how you are financing your defense. You don't have to be a genius to see the effect it's having on your resort. A prolonged appeal will only further drain your financial resources and saddle you with further legal and financial burdens. Not to mention, the added burden of keeping this place afloat. Four months in jail, all your legal problems will be over, and you can get on with your life."

Vicki listened in silence. A quiet hush fell over the room as they awaited her response.

"Are you through?"

"Quite."

"Good. So I only have to say this once. I'm not spending a single night in any prison. I don't care how cushy. Not four months, four days, or even four seconds. My children and grandchildren will not have a convicted criminal for a grandmother. I'm innocent. I will fight this to my grave. Now if you two won't take my appeal…"

"I didn't say that, Vicki."

"Good. Then let me know when you've started the paperwork. Until then, gentlemen, I have a resort to run." The lawyers clicked their briefcases shut.

"We'll be in touch," Ansell announced as they both rose from their seats.

"I'm sure you will and, yes, gentlemen, cash in advance, as usual, for your services." The two men briefly glared at Vicki in amazement. Then turned and walked out the door.

Newman and Rides stood near the bottom of the front office steps. Rides scanned through the Health Department's report.

"Whoa," he sighed, flipping through the report, "has Vicki seen this?"

"No, I was on my way to show it to her, but I recognize that Porsche over there." Newman motioned toward the black car parked near the entrance. "Her lawyers."

Rides agreed. "Heaven knows, that car's been here enough times to qualify for its own private stall."

"I know how important her legal briefings are to her."

"But if she doesn't deal with this," Rides held up the report, "she won't have a resort day after tomorrow." The front door opened, and the two attorneys filed down the stairs. "Looks like Mutt and Jeff have taken her for all the dough they can today." Rides commented.

"Well, I certainly hope they left her with enough for a new freshwater well. If not, she won't be able to make a dime from a resort that's been shut down."

"Not to mention our resulting unemployment."

"Kenny!" A voice hailed him. He turned to see Colleen dressed in a black bathing suit and heels. She ran up to him and kissed him on the lips. "I haven't seen you all day. Are you avoiding me?"

"Of course not sweetheart and I must say you look stunningly beautiful today."

"Thank you. Are we seeing each other today?"

"I've just had one fire after another to put out this morning."

"Are they all out?"

"Not by a long shot Colleen."

"Well there's another fire burning in my room."

"Can I put your fire out later today?" smiled Newman.

"Only if you promise."

"I promise."

Kenny and Rides started toward the office.

"Before you go, Kenny baby," Newman walked closer to Colleen. "I also wanted to go to a movie this evening, that is, if you can get away."

"I'll see. No promises, I don't know if I'll be done that early, but I'll try, okay?"

"Sure." Colleen leaned forward, wrapped her arms around Kenny's neck and kissed him passionately. "Well if no movie, I just have to look forward to you putting my fire out."

She turned and headed for the pool. Her well-formed rear twisting and straining the fabric of the bathing suit with each step, captivated Newman and Rides.

"You both can put your eyes back in their sockets now." They both turned and looked up, mildly startled to see Vicki standing at the top of the stairs.

"Vicki." Rides beamed. "Ken here was just protecting good customer relations."

"I'm well aware of Ken's interest in Colleen." Vicki added, peering down at Newman, "Is it serious, Kenny?"

"I only met her a few days ago. But right now I have to say, she has my full attention." Newman was slightly embarrassed to admit strong affections, for such a short period of time.

"Come on in you guys." They followed Vicki up the steps. "You know Ken, as always, it's good to go slow on any new relationship." She admonished.

"Yes, mother," Newman replied, miffed.

"Oh, don't take it personally, Kenny. But I think she has a few years on you. Eleven, if I am not mistaken."

"I'm not counting Vicki. I like her."

"Relax Ken, I've known Colleen for much longer than either of you. I met her when I started my hotel chain a while back. Besides, I didn't call you in here to check on your love life. How did the things go with that health inspector?"

"Well, ah… not good." Replied Newman.

"How not good?"

"Very not good." added Rides.

"Come on into the office. Apparently we need to talk."

"I'll say." Newman took the report from Rides. Rides headed back toward the gas station. Vicki stood atop the steps and looked down at the rose bed at the base of the steps.

"That fireweed is still in my rose bed."

Newman looked down at the bed. "It's hard to get rid of. I had Candy pull those weeds several weeks ago."

"Well, they need to be pulled again. They don't belong in there. They distract from the beauty of the roses."

"I'll get someone on it again." Newman followed her into her office.

Far, far away from the Lolo Resort, it was nearly 2:00 p.m. in the afternoon, Southern California time. Elizabeth Van Der Horn nervously checked her watch as she paced the blue plush-carpeted office of her lavishly-furnished seaside condominium. She puffed almost unconsciously on her cigarette until finally she angrily jammed it out in a nearby ashtray. She folded her arms and continued to nervously pace the floor. The roar of the ocean lapping at the beach several stories below ebbed over her balcony. Finally, the mild ring of her phone startled her. She raced over and snatched up the receiver before the first ring had faded.

"Hello."

"Ms. Van Der Horn?" The man's voice on the other end cautiously asked.

"Who else did you expect? You're late. You said one-thirty. Have you found them?"

"First, I said around one thirty, and no, we haven't found them. But we do know he bought a used car in Lewistown, Idaho. When he filled up, he asked the attendant for directions that would indicate he was headed for Montana."

"I want him found, you understand? Or I'll hire another agency, do you understand me?"

"We've done everything reasonably and professionally possible to find your husband and your son."

"Ex-husband, "Ms Van Der Horn quickly corrected. "I just want my Danny back. I want to see Andrew behind bars." she angrily demanded. "Now I'm flying out for Europe in the morning. You have my number there, don't you?"

"Yes we do."

"Day or night. Call me. Finding a ten-year-old mixed-blood Indian boy and his father shouldn't be that hard, especially in Montana." She jammed the phone down.

As Ms. Elizabeth Van Horn had private detectives scouring the US for Rides and Danny, Vicki was trying to keep her resort from closing down. Vicki listened in chagrin as Newman carefully explained the results of the Health Department's inspection.

"As bad as the inspector was, we can rectify most of the problems very easily, except for the well water."

Vicki sighed. "Was the inspections really that bad?"

"After our score fell below forty, he simply stopped grading. But like I said, if we don't correct that well water problem, everything else is academic." Explained Newman.

"Even if I had the $10,000 to drill a new well, we couldn't get it done in two days. We'll just have to ask for an extension."

"To do what, Vicki? If we don't have a plan to deal with the gas—a plan they'll believe---they wouldn't give us an extension. Especially, if it meant continuing to operate with gasoline in the freshwater supply."

"Well, I'm not going to let them shut us down, that's for sure."

"You may not have a choice."

"Last year Jake stood them off with a shotgun. I didn't approve then, but if that's what it takes..."

"Vicki, the Sheriff's Department has shotguns, too. Besides, that's not going to accomplish anything, particularly with either you or Jake sitting in jail on assault or attempted murder charges."

"I'm not going to just sit here and let them take away my whole life, Kenny."

Suddenly a knock at the door interrupted their conversation.

"Yes?" Vicki called.

"It's me Andrew."

"Andrew, can whatever it is wait? Kenny and I are trying to resolve a very important problem."

"Okay, Vicki. But when you're ready to hear a solution to your gas problem, let me know."

Newman and Vicki stared at each other momentarily. Newman scrambled out of his seat and snatched the door open. Rides stood in the doorway, a smug grin on his face.

"What took you so long? I knew you would come up with something. Get in here." Newman sounded excited.

He stepped into the office and eased the door shut behind him. "Now I was just thinking..." Rides began.

As Newman, Rides, and Vicki discussed strategy to save the resort from a complete shutdown, the local government employees were trying to figure out the expense charges of the smoke jumpers. The sound of clicking typewriter keys, meshed with the mechanical whiz of high-speed printers, zipped back and forth across endless streams of computer paper to analyze financial data given to them from the resort. At times the noise seemed to drown the consistent chatter of mixed voices. People darted from desk to desk in the open workstations like bees between spring flowers.

At one of the stations, one young woman sat across from another woman as she pointed to the piece of paper on her desk.

"Leanna, can you explain this item to me? Thirty thousand dollars for a one-ton dump truck?"

Leanna turned the paper around and examined the item. "Oh, that's simple. The smoke jumper's base said they needed it to haul food and fuel into the hills during that North Ridge fire up in the Lolos."

"But why buy it? We could have just rented it and save the government the annual maintenance cost of keeping that dinosaur in shape. It's just going to sit in some garage until next summer's fire season."

"Apparently the smoke jumpers don't want to wait until next year for us to get competitive bids from every single truck vendor this side of the Divide, before they can get a delivery truck." Replied Leanna. "This way, they'll have a truck when they need one."

The woman leaned back in her chair. "Well, you've been in Forest Service purchasing long enough to know how the competitive bid process operates."

"I know exactly how it operates, Ava. That's why I don't blame the smoke jumper's one bit." Leanna smiled and shoved the paper back toward Ava.

"How close are you to closing that whole North Ridge account?" questioned Ava.

"I have everything done except for that account with the Hot Springs Resort. Seems the only person there who can sign for any payment has either been in court or the hospital."

"That's, that Vicki Marshall woman, isn't it? I read about her in the paper yesterday." Stated Ava.

"She was convicted of printing about five million in twenties or something like that." Asserted Leanna.

"Talk about making money the old-fashioned way." Remarked Ava.

"But the person who submitted the expenses is some guy named…" She opened the file folder on her desk and ran her finger down the page. "Newman, a Kenneth Newman. He's listed a couple of expenses here that I don't think we can pay."

"Expenses?" thought Ava.

"Yea, like, well here." Leanna pointed to a paragraph on the page. "Seems some smoke jumper rode a dirt bike into their bar and damaged $300 worth of wood floor paneling. There's another bill here for $400 to drain their hot pool, when the smoke jumpers dumped twelve kegs of Bud Lite into the water."

Ava chuckled. "Sounds like they had a great time."

"Even so, these are expenses that should be covered by private insurance, not government reimbursement."

"Well Leanna, call him and straighten it out."

"I've tried, but he's never there to answer my calls, and no one bothers to return them."

"Now what? That account should have been closed three weeks ago."

Leanna sighed. "I'm going to have to go up there, I guess. That way, they'll have to deal with me, one way or another."

"Ah, hey, I don't know if that is a good idea, Leanna. First, they are counterfeiting money, then they had that suicide up there a couple days ago. Doesn't sound like a place I'll be visiting any time soon."

"Awe, Ava. Where's your sense of adventure."

"Certainly not at Lolo. Oh, by the way how is your transfer to Alaska coming?"

"Slow, very slow. I send my prayers up every night. So one day, Ava… one day."

Leanna placed the papers in a folder and planned her trip to Hot Springs Resort.

Back at the resort, Newman, Vicki and Rides were executing his plan to save the resort from total shut down. Newman stood ankle-deep in a pool of stagnant water as he strained the wrench, turning the valve on the water pump. Rides and Vicki observed.

"How are you doing down there?" Rides called from above.

Newman looked up. "Fine. I just love standing in water up to my ankles at eleven o'clock at night."

"Well, it's either this or get set to find another job when that health inspector comes back."

"I've got a date with Colleen tonight."

"Had a date," Rides corrected. "We'll be here till morning, easy."

"Well, Vicki can you tell her where I am. We'll just have to take a rain check on our movie."

"Sure Ken. I'll head back to the office now and give her a call." Vicki left.

"How long did you say Rides?"

"I'm going to help too, Kenny."

"Really?"

"Well, at least we're not alone. I've got the preacher and a couple of other guys up here in the pipe chase. So once you get the water turned off, we'll be ready to rock and roll."

"Just don't forget I'm down here. Ankle deep, is as deep as I care to get."

"I'm on it Kenny, my man. Not to worry."

While Newman was ankle deep in stagnant water. Colleen was waiting patiently for Newman to arrive and spend the evening with her. Fully dressed in heels and tight fitting jeans, Colleen's impatience of waiting for Newman lead her to go on a search for her man. She headed straight to the main office.

Vicki peered over the top of her glasses as she sorted the papers on her desk, when suddenly the door opened. She looked up to see Colleen.

"Kenny, I thought…" Colleen stopped in midsentence as she spotted Vicki sitting behind the desk. "Oh, I didn't know you were back, Vicki. I thought Kenny was in here."

Vicki leaned back in her chair and peeled her glasses off. "Apparently, but he's not here."

"Well, do you know where he is?'

"He asked me to call you and let you know that he's working."

Colleen checked her watch. "This time of night?"

"It's a very important project."

"How long will he be?"

"Now that, I really don't know, Collen. Why don't you go back to your room and paint your nails or something." Vicki's tone showed irritation.

"Do you know where he is?"

"Maybe you should just wait until he gets through with his job. At least some of us know how to work."

Colleen could sense the irritation in Vicki's voice. "Now, now Vicki, I know we've had our differences in the past, but I'm willing to let our bygones be bygones."

"What are you doing here, anyway?"

"Vacationing."

"Really? Or could it be you smell blood, especially with my resort in bankruptcy and me in the hospital near death from a heart attack."

"Vicki, Vicki, Vicki," Colleen huffed, "I'm shocked you'd make such an accusation. You know me…"

"Oh, I know you all right," Vicki interrupted, rising from her seat and placing both hands on her desk as she leaned forward. "That's why I wouldn't trust you as far as I can throw you. And since Kenny knows where all the skeletons around here are buried, his knowledge would be invaluable in any bid to establish the true value of this place in a bankruptcy court, don't you think?"

Colleen was quiet for a moment. "I don't have to stand here and take this," she huffed.

She turned to leave.

"That's right," Vicki added. "And that's why I don't want you dragging Ken into our problems."

Colleen walked back to her desk. "Kenny's a big boy now. My interest in him is none of your business. He doesn't need Mama Vicki to hold his hand, so back off!" She bitterly demanded. Colleen turned and slammed the door.

Vicki listened as her footsteps descended the stairs. A car door opened and slammed shut. The engine roared, and the car peeled out of the parking space.

Vikki eased back into her chair. She picked up the phone, tapped in several number, placed the receiver to her ear and waited.

"Hi, is Forester there?… Have him call Vicki… Vicki Marshall, he knows me."

She put the phone down and reclined confidently in her chair and smiled.

It was midmorning, Newman and Rides were still checking the valves on the water pumps outside of the restaurant. He strained to tighten a valve when Danny called to him.

"Dad? Are you going to eat breakfast or what? Mr. Adams said he can't hold the breakfast line all day."

Rides gave another twist on the wrench as Newman stood by. "Tell Nelson to go ahead and kill the breakfast line. I'll grab a bite at lunch. This valve's got to hold or there will be water everywhere. They'll close the resort and we won't have a home if this doesn't work."

"Then maybe we can go back to San Pedro, eh, Dad?" Danny pleadingly asked.

He stopped and turned angrily toward Danny. "No!" The boy was frightened by Rides' sudden, unexpected burst of anger. He could see the look of horror on his son's face. Rides immediately smiled. "I mean no, son," he said in a softer tone. "We can't go back home for a while."

"But when will we see Mom again?"

"I told you, she would call us when she gets back from Germany. Until then, we'll just tour the country, just like I promised. You like it here, don't you?"

"Ahhh, sure, Dad..."

"Good, and you've met new friends, right?"

"I miss Candy."

"You'll meet new friends, I promise. Now go ahead, you're cleaning the pool today, right?"

"Yeah."

"Did you have breakfast already?'

"Yeah, Dad."

"Then go on to the pool and I'll see you later." He gave Danny a big hug. "I love you, son."

"I love you too, Dad." Danny turned and ran toward the pool.

Rides watched him until he disappeared around a corner. He shook his head, smiled and turned back toward the water pump.

"Wow, Rides. I didn't know you were married. I just assumed you were a single father."

"Ex-wife. It's a long story."

They diligently continued to work a few minutes more, taking turns with the wrench until they were satisfied that the problem had been resolved.

"Well, you'll have to tell me about it sometime, but right now, I am going to get washed up and pay a visit to someone I owe a movie to."

"Sure Ken, she seems like a nice lady, enjoy."

Newman headed straight to Colleen's cabin suite which was secluded, cozy, and spacious from the rest of the resort. He knocked gently on the door and stood there with his shirt half button from the top, leaning with both arms on the sides of the door.

"Hey baby, guess who?" He called through the door. "I hope you're not mad at me for last night. I want to apologize for yesterday."

Colleen came to the door with nothing on.

Newman smiled. "I missed you baby."

Colleen sniffed the air. Whooo, you stink."

"I know. I was hoping you would take a shower or perhaps a bubble bath with me."

She pulled Newman in the room by his belt buckle. She closed and locked the door.

"I just want you to know these past few days with you have been incredible. I find myself thinking about you as much as I think about the things I have to do around this resort."

"Shhhhh... baby." She put her forefinger to his lips. "Let Colleen take care of you."

She helped him undress and took him by the hand. Colleen turned the water on. She pulled him into the shower. Newman faced the spout and leaned against the wall with his arms raised letting the warm water run down his body. Colleen grabbed the soap from the shower cup. She stood behind him and began to lather his back. Then she went from his shoulders and under his arms with the soap to his frontal exterior. Seconds later, Newman turned to face her. He immediately placed his arms around her waist and with a slight show of strength pulled her body close to him. He kissed her lips and caressed her breast lovingly in his hands. He soon left her lips and continued kissing her cheeks, down to her neck and then her breast. His hands began to roam her entire body. His fingers tantalizing her inner self. She exploded with moans ecstasy. Moments later, Colleen gently pushed him back and began to lather his lower front once again. As his lower extremity grew to Colleen's delight, Newman couldn't take the sensual pleasure anymore. He took the soap and dropped it in the tub. He wrapped his arms around her waist. Kissed her passionately under the warmth of the water as it rinsed the soap from their bodies. He soon stepped out of the shower, picked Colleen up in his arms. Carried her to the bedroom. He gently placed her on the bed and resumed kissing her passionately all over her body. Small screams of ecstasy echoed throughout the room. Then Colleen wrapped her arms around his chest and pushed him to the bed. The roles were reversed. She gently kissed and fondled his breast, soon moving to the lower extremities of his body with the warmth and juiciness of her tongue, leaving Newman begging for more. Moments later, Newman climbs back on top, giving Colleen the same pleasure once again. Soon she reaches for Newman and he gently moved inside of her. Each delicate motion of force inside her, increased her desire for more. "Harder!" She screamed. Newman's pace and thrust intensified. Screams of sensual pleasure from both of them, filled the room. Minutes later, Colleen relaxed and smiled. Newman laid beside her. She rolled over and lay her head on his chest.

"Thanks for desert." Smiled Newman.

"Apology accepted." Beamed Colleen.

He kissed her on the forehead and fell fast asleep.

As a new day dawned, Newman and Rides had worked diligently to get the gasoline out of the water. Until finally, two days later, it was time for Redman's return. Early that morning, Newman nervously checked his watch.

"Relax," Vicki admonished. "I'm sure you and Andrew took care of the problem with the gas."

"It's just that I've always hated inspections. Ever since I was in the Navy waiting for the Captain to come and look over my uniform. It was always a nerve wracking experience. And with so much riding on this one…"

"They won't shut us down, Kenny. They just won't." Vicki turned the page on the report in front of her. "I've been looking over your listing of the bands for the Labor Day Country Music Jamboree. Ahhh…"

Newman paced from Vicki's office to the reception room, peering out of the window, looking for the health inspector.

"Ahh… what?" Newman looked back at her.

"The Jamboree on Labor Day, I'm changing the order of the bands that are scheduled to appear."

He walked over to the desk. "Vicki, I've already sent out the notices to all of the bands involved."

"Don't worry, I'll send out new ones. Oh, don't worry, there's nothing wrong with your order of bands. It's just that, I think I can do better."

"Oh," Newman sighed, "whatever, Vicki."

"And we'll need lots of additional help, you know, for the bar and the kitchen."

"Sure, but, Vicki, don't you think we need to cross this bridge first? If we don't pass this inspection, there won't be a Jamboree."

She looked up from the paper. "Kenneth, you want to know how I can think about planning for Labor Day? Because I won't allow myself to think that the Health Department will shut us down. You've got to learn to think positive, too."

The door suddenly swung open, Greg Redman stood in the doorway.

"Mr. Redman," Vicki smiled. "Kenneth here has been waiting for you. He didn't think you'd ever come."

Redman smiled. "Wild horses couldn't keep me away, Mrs. Marshall."

"Well, Kenny, don't keep the good man waiting."

Newman turned and headed toward the opened door. Redman started back down the steps. Newman followed, closing the door behind him. Rides watched from the restaurant window as Newman and Redman approached. Newman caught Rides peering out of the window. Rides flashed him a thumbs-up sign and smiled.

"I must tell you, Mr. Newman, that the water we tested contained enough gasoline to make it too toxic for human consumption." Redman explained as they entered the restaurant. "So our first order of business will be to test the water. If it doesn't pass, then the rest of the inspection won't even be necessary, understood?"

"Perfectly," Newman replied confidently.

Newman followed Redman into the kitchen. Nelson and the kitchen crew watched in anxious anticipation as they turned on the hot-water faucet. Steam floated up from the downpour. He leaned forward and took a sniff. The gasoline aroma that was so pungent only two days ago was gone. He turned on the cold water tap. Hot water poured from it too.

Redman stood upright and stared at the twin streams of hot water pouring from the faucets, "Ah… Ken," he pointed to the faucets, "there's no cold water."

"No, it's all hot mineral water. The same water we use to fill the pool."

"But you can't drink or cook with hot mineral water." Remarked Redman.

"That's why we're still leaving the watercooler in the hotel rooms and here in the kitchen. We're filling those with cool distilled water delivered by truck every day. But we are piping hot mineral water to the showers and the toilets."

"But you still have no fresh water on tap."

"You mean we have no gasoline-filled water on tap, and that's the bottom line." Replied Newman.

Redman looked back at the twin steams of hot water pouring from the faucets. "Okay," he sighed, "you've gotten rid of the toxic water. That's what we asked you to do. So let's see what the rest of the place looks like."

Newman breathed an internal sigh of relief and turned to follow Redman to the next station in the kitchen. When Redman's back was turned, he gave a thumbs up to Rides. Rides smiled.

While Rides made sure the water passed inspection at the bar and restaurant, Danny stood at poolside, spraying the deck with a high-powered steam of water. The pool was quiet, except for the powerful water jet bouncing off the red-squared brick surface. Danny had almost finished spraying the deck when a voice broke his concentration.

"Hey!" The young boy hailed. Danny looked up to see a young boy about his own age, dressed in swimming trunks calling him. "Is your pool open?"

"Sure, it's just that most people don't show up until after eleven o'clock."

The young boy checked his watch. "Oh, is it still okay to swim then?"

"Sure. There's no lifeguard on duty. I think its three dollars to swim, but I'm sure you can go swimming. You can swim, can't you?"

"Ahh… like a fish." He walked toward Danny.

"Are your parents here, too?" asked Danny.

"No, just me and my two brothers. We were just passing through and saw your Hot Springs Resort Sign and decided to take a swim here before we moved on. I've never been swimming in hot mineral water before."

"You'll enjoy it. I go swimming in it every day."

"That must be neat to work here every day. How did you find a neat job like this?"

"We just asked. My Dad and I both work here."

"Really?" The boy looked excited at the prospect of finding possible employment at the resort. "You wouldn't know if they are hiring for other jobs here, do you?"

Danny turned the water nozzle off. "I don't know. Vicki, she's the owner. She just lost her bookkeeper and storekeeper lady. She might be looking for somebody to fill those spots."

"Really? Oh, by the way, I'm Toby Johnson." He extended his hand.

"Danny Rides." The two boys shook hands.

"I'll go tell my brothers. Who knows, maybe we can get jobs here, and you and I can be friends."

"I'd like that." Danny beamed.

"Great. My brothers are waiting in the car. I'll go and tell them. I'll be right back."

Toby turned and ran back into the pool house. He dashed out the front door and walked over to the passenger side of the black BMW parked directly in front of the pool house.

"Are they open?" The young man in the passenger seat asked.

"Yes, but the cashier isn't on duty yet. Its three dollars to swim," Toby replied, "and they also might have jobs here."

"What kind of jobs?" The handsome man in his mid-twenties, sitting behind the steering wheel, asked.

"A bookkeeper and a storekeeper." Toby replied. "Some lady named Vicki does the hiring."

"How interesting," the man behind the wheel contemplated. He thought for a moment. "Look, you two go swimming. You both should know the routine by now. I'm going to talk to this Vicki lady. If we play our cards right, we'll all have jobs here by nightfall."

Toby raced back toward the pool, while the other young man got out of the car, stared at the driver, slammed the door and followed Toby.

Meanwhile, Redman and Newman stood at the base of the front office steps discussing their findings at the restaurant.

"Well, Mr. Newman, I must say, I'm impressed."

"Really? Mr. Redman."

"Yes. Oh, not so much with the condition of this place. But for your ability to hold it together with enough spit and bailing wire to get it just within the borders of passing inspection. My hat's off to you."

"Is that a compliment?"

"It's an observation, Mr. Newman, strictly an observation. Like I said, believe it or not, you and I are both on the same side. I'm sure both of us want to see the public served in a healthy environment."

"Of course."

"Then take pride in your victory today, Mr. Newman, but you haven't a hope in hell of winning the war."

Newman could see the sternness in his face as if he were telling him something that had been on his mind for a long, long time.

"I'm afraid you've lost me."

"Then open your eyes, Mr. Newman. This place is rotting from the foundation. What you've done today is to merely give it a reprieve, not commute the sentence. You are a good administrator, but you've been made captain of the Titanic after it hit the iceberg."

Redman reached into his briefcase, pulled out a sheet of paper, and handed it to Newman. "Here's your Department of Health Certificate to operate for another year." Newman took the certificate. "Post it in the usual place."

He turned and walked to his car. "Oh, Mr. Newman." Redman opened his door, "this is Vicki's and Jake's mess, not yours. Jump ship before it's too late." He climbed into his vehicle and drove off.

Newman watched his car as it sped down the road and around the distant bend. He thought momentarily about Redman's words, but the certificate he held in his hand was like a monument to his hard work and leadership. The resort would survive. He grabbed the handrail, bolted up the stairs, and burst into the office. Vicki was sitting at her desk, laughing with a well-dress, handsome, silver haired, middle-aged man seated across from her.

"Oh, excuse me. I didn't know you had company, Vicki."

"Nonsense, Ken, come in. Come in." She beckoned. "We got it." Newman beamed, holding up the certificate. "We got our certification from the Board of Health."

"Great!" Vicki exclaimed. "I told you to think positive."

"Yes, I guess positive thinking does work, doesn't it?"

"Oh," Vicki remembered. "Where are my manners? Forest, this is Ken Newman, my manager."

Forest stood up and shook Newman's hand.

"Ken this is Forester McClain."

"How do you do?" "He owns the Bitterroot Valley Hotel chain along with his wife...Colleen Harrison McClain." Smirked Vicki.

Newman was silent and expressionless. He stared at Vicki, wondering why she let Colleen's marriage be a secret, when she knew he was enjoying the pleasure of her company.

C H A P T E R
15

*N*ewman slowly backed the aging dump truck to a stop onto the grassy mound. The truck wheezed as he set the air brake. He climbed out of the cab and walked around to the back. In the rear of the truck, standing knee-deep in a load of dirt, were two young men in blue jeans and T-shirts.

"Okay, guys," Newman hailed, "we've got to cover this mound with dirt to keep the raw sewage from seeping to the surface."

He opened the back panel and lowered the gate. The two men grabbed shovels, scrambled out of the truck, jammed the shovel blades into the mound and tossed the dirt onto the grass. Newman also grabbed a shovel and started tossing spades of dirt onto the mound. A Bronco pulled to a stop alongside the trail and honked. Newman looked over to see Vicki waving at him. He jammed the shovel blade into the ground and walked over to meet her.

"You asked about the cost of replacement pipe for the underground sewer line."

"Yeah, and…" stated Newman.

"I was able to get these quotes." Vicki handed him a slip of paper.

Newman quickly scanned the slip. "Well as soon as Andrew gets through measuring the length of the busted pipe, we can figure out how much we need. In the meantime, Redman said if we can keep the raw sewage from breaking the surface, we'll still comply with health regulations."

"Why don't you let them handle that?" Vicki insisted, pointing to the two workers shoveling dirt.

"Three people can get it done faster than two, Vicki."

"You can come back and have breakfast, you know."

"I know, but I'd rather stay here." Insisted Newman.

"Colleen is over there," she said softly, "and she still wants to talk to you."

"No way!" Newman insisted. "She's the last person I want to see."

"She does want to at least talk to you and explain things."

"Why? So she can lie to me again? No, thank you. I'd much rather stay out here with this crap," he pointed to the mound, "than to listen to anything she's got to say. And why didn't you warn me Vicki?"

"Like you told me, I'm not your mother. Sure you won't change your mind?"

"Positive," he said emphatically. "Now, I've got to get back to work." He turned and trotted back to the work site.

Vicki geared the Bronco and headed back to her office. She pushed her door open to see Colleen seated at the reception desk. She was neatly dressed, legs crossed and fingers interlocked across her lap. Her thumbs were twirling in a nervous anger around each other.

"Are you applying for a job as a receptionist?" Vicki quipped, closing the door behind her.

"You just couldn't mind your own damned business, could you?" Colleen growled.

"Whatever in the world are you talking about?" Vicki coyly asked.

"You know damned well what I am talking about." She pushed herself up from the chair. "There's no way Forest could have known where I was. You called him, didn't you?"

"So what if I did?"

"My relationship with Ken was none of your business."

"Everything that goes on at this resort is my business," Vicki continued. "And don't tell me your interest in Kenny is just some short-term fling. I've known you too long, Colleen. Forester is rich, handsome, and white. The three criteria I know you require of all your men and Kenny strikes out on at least two out of the three."

"Oh really? And what are you now, his mother?" She huffed. "My interest in Ken is strictly my business, do you understand?" Colleen pointed to her chest. "Mine!"

"Maybe, but now if you want to get inside information on the conditions of my resort, you'll have to look elsewhere."

Colleen laughed. "This run-down old fleabag? I wouldn't waste a dime on trying to take over this dump. You'll be broke by the end of the year, anyway. If I really wanted this dive, I'd pick it up in bankruptcy court. Unless, of course, they've hauled you off to jail first."

Vicki was seething with quiet anger. "If you've finished, your husband's waiting for you at the bar. I suggest you not keep him waiting. Or would you rather I go meet with him and explain how you've been vacationing at my resort?"

"Be careful Vicki, you're treading on thin ice. Don't forget how crude I can be. If you thought our grappling for hotels was ruthless, I can make your court situation seem like child's play. So don't mess with me."

The two women stared angrily at each other. Colleen stormed past Vicki and out of the door, slamming it forcefully behind her.

Several hours later, Newman had parked the dump truck back at the garage. He and his two workers were seated at the counter eating lunch in the busy, crowed restaurant. He even contemplated having a mid-day drink. He left his plate and walked over to the bar. Just as he started to get Laura's attention, he soon dismissed that thought, thinking of all the work he had to do later in the day. How could he be so depressed as to let the relationship with Colleen lead him to having a drink while on duty? He returned to the restaurant. Newman stirred aimlessly at the peas on his plate, almost oblivious to the mixed sounds of voices and tinkling silverware in the background. Even though he had been with many women prior to Colleen, most of them were just one night stands. Colleen had been his only affair so far this year with a woman. Now, to discover that she was married was a blow from which it would take him some time to recover.

Suddenly a hand on his shoulder broke his concentration. He looked up into the face of Forester McClain.

"Newman," Forester announced.

Newman stared into his face startled, "Ahhh... yes... can I help you?"

"My wife's told me all about you," he casually stated.

Newman's throat lumped. "She has?"

"Yes," he smiled, "and I'd like you to join us in the bar for a drink."

"You would?" Newman was confused.

"Sure, come on. We've got a chair waiting for you at our table."

Newman thought for a moment. "No thanks, but I can't, because..."

"Nonsense," Forester insisted. "I haven't had a chance to really get to know you. My wife has told me wonderful things about how you helped her when her car broke down. She told me how you took her to Missoula yourself, for the replacement parts."

"Really?" Newman asked matter-of-factly, beginning to get the gist of Colleen's confession to her husband.

"Tell her it was no problem. I'd do the same for any of the guests."

"But she thinks it's special, and frankly, so do I. And I'd feel honored if you'd join us for an afternoon drink." Newman opened his mouth to protest. "Please?" Forester asked, almost begging. "It would mean so much to the both of us."

Newman shook his head and sighed. He pushed his plate away and rose from the stool. "All right. But I can't stay long. I've got a lot of work to do."

"Sure." He put his arm around Newman's shoulder as they walked from the dining room into the bar. Country music ebbed from the jukebox, barely heard above the voices of the sparsely-occupied tables scattered around the room.

Forester McClain ushered Newman over to the table near the corner. Colleen sat in one chair, nursing a wineglass. She watched uneasily as Forester and Newman entered the bar.

"Honey, look who I have here." Forester beamed, giving Newman a couple of hefty pats on the back. Newman, too, smiled uneasily. "He was going to have lunch all by his lonesome, but we won't hear of it, will we, honeybee?"

"Of course not, dear," Colleen agreed. "Won't you sit down, Mr. Newman?" She motioned toward a chair.

"Please, Mrs. Harrison, I mean Mrs. McClain." He pulled out a chair. "Call me Ken."

"Harrison is my maiden name," she smiled.

"I must have seen it on your check-in card, Mrs. McClain, my mistake."

"I tried to get your attention when we noticed you at the bar. So I followed you. Like I was telling Colleen here," Forester began as he and Newman adjusted their chairs. "It's not often you find people willing to help complete strangers when they are away from home. When Colleen's car broke down, it was just a stroke of luck that you happened along."

"Just plain luck." Newman agreed.

"Why don't you let me get you a drink Ken?"

"No thank you. I have lots of work to do."

"Very well. You see, me and Colleen, well, we had this fight." He turned to her. "It was my fault, honeybee, I'm sorry, I was a jerk, I know." He turned to Newman. "But she got mad and left the house and didn't tell me or Dana, that's her daughter…"

Newman looked over in quiet astonishment at Colleen. She briefly acknowledged his glance, then looked back down at her wineglass.

"Anyway, neither one of us knew where she was." He turned to Colleen. "I called all over the place honeybee and no one knew where you were. So we were getting a little worried. Thank God, Vicki called and told us you were all right. I was about ready to call the police." He laughed and looked at Newman. "Wouldn't that have been a riot? Me, thinking she's lying in a ditch somewhere, and all the while she's lying here, in a hot tub."

"Yeah…" Ken gave a halfhearted grin.

Forester reached over and pulled her lips onto his.

Newman watched as the two of them kissed. He started to squirm uneasily in his seat. "Well, you lovers have a lot of catching up to do. So I'll leave you two alone and get back to work." He rose from his seat.

"Please don't rush off on our account." Colleen insisted.

"Really?" Newman glanced at her in amazement. "Thanks… but I have to go."

"Well, at least give us a chance to return the hospitality." Colleen insisted. "Why don't you come visit one of our hotels as our guest?"

"Yes, yes." Forester agreed. "That's a great idea, honeybee."

"I don't know." Newman hedged. Backing slowly away from the table. "They keep me pretty busy around here."

"Nonsense." Colleen insisted. "I have some VIP cards out in my car. Let me get one for you. In fact, I'll write our home number on the back so you can call us before you come. That way we can make special plans for your arrival."

"Oh, honeybee," Forester complained, "no use in traipsing all over the parking lot, just write it on a napkin."

Colleen looked at him and smiled. "But sugar plum, can you imagine the look our cashier will give him if he tries to check in with a bar napkin? Just stay put, honey, I'll be right back." She rose from the chair and kissed Forester on the forehead. "Come on, Mr. Newman… ah, Kenny." She stepped from around the table---"Let's walk to my car." She looked back over her shoulder. "I'll be right back, babe." She followed Newman out of the bar.

Newman stepped briskly, looking straight forward, but Colleen kept pace with him stride for stride.

"For a minute back there, I thought it was going to be another John and Bea situation with your husband. He was so insistent that I join you both at the table, that I thought he may have had a gun in his pant leg, going to shoot us both."

"Why?"

"You really have to ask that question?"

"Don't hate me."

"I don't hate you honeybee. I'm sure you would have told me about your husband and your daughter and your married name sooner or later. They just probably slipped you mind."

"I don't know what Vicki told you."

"Nothing actually. She never said a word about you."

"She seems to think that I'm some sort of corporate Marti Hari, trying to seduce you for the vast corporate secrets this place holds."

"This has nothing to do with Vicki. But it doesn't really matter what either of us thinks now, does it?"

"It matters to me what you think, Kenny. I really like you. That's a fact."

"You knew I was falling for you and you said nothing." He paused and thought… "I guess turnaround is fair play, because I used to be a player. I have had more women than you can imagine. But, at least I told them all I wanted was a good time. But there was something about you Colleen that stimulated my mind and emotions, such that none of the other women I had could compare to what I had with you. But you… you played with my heart like a toy, something you pull out when you want to play with it and put back when you're done. Another blissful night with you and you would have been two kisses away from me telling you how much I loved you."

"Kenny… I…"

His tone changed as she was about to speak. "If you just wanted a good fuck, any of these blonde haired, blued eyed cowboys would have tripped over their pants to get you in bed. It wouldn't have been very hard."

"I didn't want them, I wanted you."

"Your husband seems to want you too."

"That drunken bum." Colleen shook her head. "I left that night because I found him in bed with one of our maids. He hasn't been faithful to me since our honeymoon."

"Sounds like you're upholding the family tradition. You decided to get even, eh?"

"No, nothing like that. I just wanted to get away from him. I needed to think."

They reached her car. It was parked several feet from the entrance to Vicki's office…

"Think about how you could get even with good ole Forester, eh?"

"No Ken. So when I give you this card, I want you to call me. We had a good thing going, Ken. It doesn't have to end." Newman shook his head in amazement.

"I don't believe this. You just don't quit, do you?"

She opened the car door, sat behind the wheel, and leaned over to open the glove compartment. She found a pen and her cards. "I'll put my private number on the back of this card."

"So all the beautiful evenings we had together were just for revenge against your husband?"

"No, Kenny. At least it may have started out that way, but things changed."

"Sure it did. You weren't interested in me as a person. So, why didn't you just ask me to screw you since you were just curious about black men and didn't need or want a commitment? At least then I would have understood your motive for wanting to be with me and I wouldn't have poured any emotions into this relationship." Newman watched her as she scribbled on the back of the card. Colleen ignored the question.

"I still want to be with you. I like making love to you."

"You mean having sex. There's a difference."

"Oh Kenny."

"Oh Kenny hell. You just needed a black man to get even with your husband, right?" Newman paused. "Am I right Colleen?" No response came. Was she Black?"

"Who?"

"The maid your husband screwed. Was she Black?"

She sat upright, looked up at Newman, and then silently gasped. "Ahh…"

Newman noticed the slightly stunned expression upon her face, then glanced back over his shoulder. Forester stood near him. "I didn't hear you walk up behind me."

"It's just that you two were taking such a long time. I thought you had run into problems or something."

"No, dear," Colleen curtly corrected. "We weren't having problems." She stretched her card to Newman.

"You know I can be a very suspicious son-of-a-bitch." Forester softly spoke.

Newman plucked the card from Colleen's fingers and crumpled it in his fist from the sight of Forester and placed it in his pocket. "I'm quite sure you can be, Forester. I'm sure you can be. In fact, you two were made for each other. Have a good day. I have work to do."

He turned and headed back to the office. Forester looked at Colleen, she shrugged her shoulders. "What?"

As Newman walked up the stairs to the office, he just shook his head in disbelief of the conversation he just had with Colleen. When he opened the door, he stopped cold. A handsome young man in designer glasses and blow-dried blonde hair looked up from the reception desk.

"Who… Who?" Newman stuttered.

The man rose from the chair and cordially extended his hand. "Rodney Johnson. You must be Mr. Newman."

Newman skeptically shook his hand. "What are you…?"

"We haven't met." His voice was smooth and polished. "I'm Mrs. Marshall's accountant."

"Accountant?"

"Yes. I've also heard a lot of good things about you, too. I look forward to working with you."

"Ahhh… sure, you bet. Have you seen Vicki around anywhere?"

Johnson pointed over his shoulder. "She's in her office."

Newman walked past him and knocked on Vicki's office door.

"Come in," she called.

Newman opened the door. He saw Vicki sitting at her desk, writing on a sheet of paper.

"Kenny," she began, "how is that sewage problem over at the RV Park coming?"

"Oh, it's okay for now. It's going to need ongoing attention." He eased the door shut. "Who's the golden haired boy out at the front desk?" He whispered.

"Oh, him? That's Rod Johnson. He's my new accountant."

"Really? Where did he come from?"

"He says he's from Idaho. He worked for an accounting firm in Clarkston before it closed. He was on his way to Helena with his two brothers when he stopped in here for a swim. We got to talking. He mentioned that he was an accountant. I mentioned that I needed one. It was just a stroke of luck."

"Yea," Newman ran his fingers over his hair, "did he say what firm he worked for in Idaho?"

"No, but, Kenny, don't give me that old line about checking backgrounds. I didn't check yours, did I? Besides, Ken, this isn't some big Wall Street job in New York with some big salary and hundreds of people applying. For room and board and three hundred bucks a month, nobody's gonna lie and cheat to get a crack at this job." She chuckled.

"With my reputation lately, it's a wonder Rod doesn't want to check my background."

"You're going to let a perfect stranger do the financial book keeping? We have hundreds, sometimes thousands of dollars a day coming in here and you're going to let a total stranger handle the books? Come on Vicki. What are you thinking?"

"Yes. You know I can be a good judge of character sometimes. Look at him, he's cute. How dangerous can a face like that be?"

"Whatever, Vicki," Newman sighed in resignation.

"Not only is he our accountant, but his younger brother Nicholas has agreed to run the store until we can find somebody else. He also has a younger brother about Danny's age who's going to help Danny at the pool in the morning. They've agreed to work just for the spare room in the back of the store, sort of three for the price of one."

"That's just great! Doesn't something smell fishy about that whole situation, Vicki? Look, they were on their way somewhere, they stop in here and now they are all staying. Com'on, there's something wrong with that picture."

"Relax, Kenny, I've been at this for years. I'm a good judge of character."

"Okay, well I hope he works out." He turned to leave. On the other side of the door, Rod quickly pulled his ear away and quietly tiptoed back to his desk. Newman opened the door and walked back into the reception area. He stood for a moment by the door. Rod was at the desk, fingers dancing effortlessly over the typewriter keys. Newman paused, impressed at the continuous rhythm of the clicking keys.

"Wow," Newman noted, "you're pretty good."

"Somebody had to fill in when my secretary called in sick," Rodney quipped, looking at Newman without breaking stride.

Newman walked out of the office. As the door closed, Rod stopped typing and pulled the sheet out of the typewriter. He examined the jumbled typing of alphabet gibberish on the page. Smiled to himself, balled up the paper, and tossed it in the trash can.

Meanwhile, Jake and his logging crew were working diligently cutting and loading logs onto trucks to get the mountain cleared to make profits for their load. But one truck was not moving and Jake wanted to know why. Jake left the logging camp so angry, speeding his jeep around the bend to get to the resort that he almost turned the truck over. When Jake stepped into the bar, the anger on his face was apparent. He scanned the bar, stopping briefly at each face before walking slowly up to the counter.

Laura noted his swagger and the force with which he yanked off his logging gloves. She stepped over to his section of the counter and forced a smile.

"Jake," Laura beamed, "you're down from the hill early."

"I can't move all of my fuckin' logs," Jake growled, "because that no-account driver walked off the job."

"You mean Mark?" Laura asked.

"Is there another no-account driver around here you know of?"

"You do know his girlfriend came back from New York and they are going to have a baby?"

"Look, I don't care if he found the crown jewels of England, I've only got three licensed drivers for those logging trucks, With him gone, a third of my trees can't get to the mill every day. Do you know what that's costing me?"

"Jake," Laura began calmly, "you can't make Mark work on the hill if he doesn't want to."

"We had a contract, damn it!" He pounded the countertop. "I was counting on him for the rest of the timber season."

"Well, he's not here right now, Jake."

"I was under the impression that he came here to belt down a few with that old lady of his. Well, I'm just going to wait right here for his ass. He's bound to show up sooner or later." Jake walked over to a corner table and waited.

As the rest of the day went by, Toby was helping Danny with the pool. They finished their chores, now Toby and Danny were going to make the best of the rest of the day by hanging out together. Toby and Danny were tromping through the woods along a well-worn hiking trail. They pushed an occasional branch out of their way as they followed the meandering path through the trees.

"Are you sure you know how to get back to the resort?" Toby asked as he followed Danny along the trail.

"Oh, sure, I've been on this trail hundreds of times. We'll be home before you know it. I'm really glad your brothers were able to get jobs here. Now we can play like this all the time." Smiled Danny.

"Yea, being around my brothers all the time gets to be boring after a while, they're always talking grown-up stuff."

"Like my Dad and Mr. Newman. Now that your brother is running the general store, maybe we can play over there sometimes."

Toby suddenly grabbed Danny by the shoulder and spun him around. "No!" He emphatically insisted. Danny looked at Toby, visibly shaken by the sheer determination on his face. Both boys were silent. Danny was afraid to speak. Toby slowly pulled himself together. "I mean, with my brothers there and everything, it wouldn't be such a good idea." He quickly released his grip on Danny's shoulder.

"Sure… ah… ah… that's okay." Danny agreed, uncertain of what to make of Toby's violent reaction. "We're almost home. We'd better get going." The boys continued slowly down the trail.

Meanwhile, Rodney Johnson was taking a break from the receptionist desk to grab a bite to eat. Rodney sat at the lunch counter slicing at the piece of steak on his plate. Nelson strolled behind the counter, coffeepot in hand, touching up an occasional coffee cup along the way.

He tipped the pot at Rodney's cup, but Rod held out his palm. "No, can't afford to get wired around here. Too much coffee clouds the brain."

"You the new bookkeeper Vicki hired?"

He extended his hand. "Rodney Johnson. My friends call me Rod."

"Welcome aboard, Rod." Nelson beamed. "I'm the chef. Hope you like it here."

"People seem to be friendly enough, and there's plenty of work to keep me busy, so I can expect to get along just fine here."

"Good."

"Say… ah, Nelson. What's the story on that Newman guy?"

"Whaddya mean?"

"Well, it's a bit odd for a, well you know, Negro to be hanging around these parts, don't you think?"

"Ah, Ken? He's okay. Vicki and Jake are behind him, so I guess he's all right."

"But don't you think the crew around here would rather work for a White man?" quizzed Rodney.

"Probably at first, but everybody's use to Ken by now."

Suddenly a logger came over to Nelson with an empty plate in hand.

"Boy, Nelson that was good turkey and smashed potatoes. Got any more?"

"Just head on back into the kitchen. Barbara will fix you up."

The logger disappeared in the kitchen.

"Is that a common practice? Letting the crew have seconds?" Rodney calmly questioned.

"Sure. Those guys put in a full day up on the hill. They need their food."

"Three hundred a month, plus room and three meals a day. Not three and a half meals, not four meals, three, just three. In the future, no seconds unless they pay the menu-posted price," Rodney sternly instructed.

"Says who?" Nelson huffed angrily.

"Don't get upset, Nelson. Part of my job as accountant is to not only track cost, but reduce them where possible. Now you do want to see Vicki recover from bankruptcy, don't you?"

"Of course, but..."

"No butts. Multiply all those seconds by the number of crew eating every day of the week. You can see how the food costs can pile up." Rodney pushed his plate away. "No more free seconds." He spun around on the stool and walked away.

Nelson watched him leave with a raised eyebrow and tilted head.

As the day progressed, Mark and Tracy were enjoying their day just being together. They decided to stop in the bar and have a drink before they continued their stroll around the grounds. Mark pushed the bar door open for Tracy and walked in behind her. He briefly surveyed the nearly filled tables before spotting a vacant table near the jukebox. He pointed toward the table and ushered Tracy toward it.

He pulled her chair out, then proceeded to sit down himself.

"What'll it be, honey?" Mark sweetly asked.

"Orange juice. I'm drinking for two now." Tracy gently patted her stomach.

Mark smiled. He started to rise when a man's hulking shadow slowly eclipsed their table. Mark looked up to see Jake's stern, angry face peering down on him.

"You ain't been up on the mountain in the last few days," his deep barrel voice growled.

"Oh." Mark was momentarily startled. "Jake, I didn't see you come up. I told Carl I quit. You were in Great Falls for the trial, so I didn't get a chance to tell you."

"We had a contract," Jake countered. "Now how am I gonna get them logs off that mountain?"

"You're a bright man. You'll think of something."

Jake's teeth gritted as he took a firm grip on Mark's shoulder. "Don't push me, boy. You're just a hair's breathe from spittin' teeth."

Mark looked down at Jake's mammoth hand resting squarely on his shoulder, then back up at Jake. Mark knew that even though Jake was more than thirty years his senior, his lifetime of swinging an ax made him stronger than most men his age. Taking on Jake in a fistfight wouldn't be an easy victory by any means.

"Hey, Jake, listen," he calmly began. "Have you met Tracy? She's going to have my baby."

"Ma'am," Jake politely acknowledged her. He turned back toward Mark. "Now we had a deal. You were to haul logs through the end of October. Now what am I supposed to do? A third of my load is still up there."

"Jake, I'm sorry, but I need a break from that mountain. Tell you what. Even though I won't drive for you anymore, I'll still help you finish that outdoor Labor Day Jamboree platform."

"Don't bother, mister. I don't need your help. In fact, you take your break at another lodge. You ain't welcome here."

"Jake, you can't make me leave here. I'm living with Tracy now and she's a registered paying customer."

"Now you listen, and listen well, boy." His voice trembled with anger. "This is my resort, and you leave when I say you're gonna leave." He turned toward Tracy. "No offense, miss." He turned back to Mark. "But I don't care if you're staying with the Queen of England. I want you packed and out of here by this afternoon."

Mark stared up defiantly at Jake, but Jake didn't flinch. "Hey, whatever you say, big man," he agreed, throwing up both hands.

He pushed his chair back from the table and extended his hand to Tracy. She pushed her chair back. Mark escorted her out of the bar.

Meanwhile, after Rodney finished laying down the law to Nelson, with no seconds on meals for anyone unless they pay, he contemplated how he was going to run the resort. He walked into the general store. The little bell tinkled as the door swung open. The customer thanked Nicholas as he pushed in the cash drawer. He flashed a forced smile. The man took the bag and walked past Rod on his way out.

Rod eased the door shut. "You're getting pretty good at this storekeeper stuff," he quipped.

"Nothing to it." Nicholas smiled. "Just let them walk in and pick out their shit, and they give you the money, cash."

"Yea, it's basically the same way over there in her office. They just bring me the cash from the bar, pool and the café. It's a piece of cake."

"No problems?" probed Nicholas.

"None to speak of. Everybody's gives me a clean bill of health, except that Newman guy. He could be a problem."

"We've taken care of problems before."

"Yes, but I want to wait a little while. He's the only Negro in this whole place. Most of these people don't like Negroes, especially telling them what to do. I've got an idea. Maybe if we play our cards right, we won't have to get rid of him. We can get these ignorant rednecks to get rid of him for us." Rodney looked around the store. "Where's the kid?"

"Oh, he's out playing with that half-breed boy up in the woods somewhere." Replied Nicholas.

"Well, I've got to be back in the office at ten tonight for the late receipts. In the meantime, I'm going to bed for a couple of hours. Then I going to implement some more changes I thought about, especially in the pool area. If the kid comes in before I leave, tell him where I am when he comes in." Rodney hesitated. "Say, by the way, how old is that little half-breed boy?"

"Ten, nine, shit, I don't know."

"Fine out for me, will you? He's a nice looking kid."

Rodney disappeared into the back room.

While Rodney rested, Newman was concerned about the pasture and sewage pipes bursting. Newman walked back to his vehicle with a shovel slung over his shoulder. He had finished one section of ground in the pasture where the raw sewage was threatening to break the surface. Though it was covered, it certainly would not hold for long. This was going to be an ongoing project with no end in sight. He started to drive back to the office, when he saw Mark hammering on the skeleton outline of a platform stage in another section of the pasture. Newman waved at him.

"Hey Kenny," Mark hailed, looking up from his work. He climbed down from the platform and headed toward Newman.

Newman stopped. Mark walked out of the pasture still carrying his hammer. "Where are you going with that thing?" He pointed at the hammer.

"Away from here," Mark said assuredly. "Jake told me to clear out. I'm just trying to finish a few last-minute details on the stage before I go."

"Why?" asked Newman.

"Actually, it's partly my fault. I won't work for the wages he's been offering me in our contract. But then I don't need to anymore. Tracy has enough money for the both of us."

"So you're going to be a kept man for a while, eh?"

"You bet. No getting up at five in the morning, no busting my ass every day for nig… ah, I mean slave wages."

Newman chucked. "You're at least trying."

Mark smiled. "It's hard after years and years of saying that word."

"You know, like I told Carl one day, the best way to break an old habit, I've found, is to replace it with a new one."

"Like what?"

"Well, whenever you feel like saying the N-word, substitute another word."

"You mean like Pollock?" asked Mark.

"No. I told Carl to use a word like, say, Martians. That's a good one. There's one ethnic group that shouldn't mind being slandered."

"Martians, huh?" Mark grinned.

"Try it for a while. See how it works."

"Okay, you've got a deal."

"Where are you and Tracy going? Do you know yet?"

"Naw, Tracy's got all the money, so she's gotta figure that out."

"Boy, I hope for your sake this relationship works out."

"It will," Mark confidently replied. He paused, then looked at Newman, perplexed. "You don't think it won't?"

"You've heard of the Golden Rule, haven't you?"

"Do unto others?"

"No Mark, he who has the gold makes the rules, or in this case, she."

"So you're saying that since she has all the money, she can tell me what to do whether I want to do it or not."

"And with Jake as your last employment reference…"

"My chances of finding another logging job would be shot to hell. And logging's all I know." He pondered Newman's words. While his growing dependence on Tracy had begun to concern him, he still didn't want to face the possibility of their relationship falling apart. Without her, he would have absolutely nothing. "You think I should stay on and drive for Jake, don't you?"

"Your call, Mark. But this is late August. Logging season's over in October. Why burn bridges needlessly?"

"But I ain't workin' for the wages he wants me to. Besides, I'm living with Tracy now. And she's paying for our room and meals."

"I think Jake's pretty desperate for a third driver. You two can probably come to some sort of an agreement." Stated Newman.

Mark chuckled. "You know, I think he is desperate at that. Can I ask you a question?"

"Sure."

"And I want a straight answer."

"Of course."

"Tracy and me. What are our chances? I mean, like she's, you know…"

"She's opera and champagne, and you're football and Miller Lite."

"Something like that."

"Mark, when two people love each other, nothing else really matters, does it?"

"I guess not. Well…" he tossed the hammer in the air and grabbed it. "I'd better get back to work on that platform. I've got a long way to go before I finish." Mark trotted back toward the pasture.

Newman geared up his vehicle and headed back to the resort.

When Newman arrived at the bar, the jukebox blared, and the evening crowd had filled the stools and the tables. Couples were dancing between the opened spaces. Newman stepped over to the end of the counter, and Laura came over to greet him.

"How are things going?" Newman tried to speak over the music and the laughter.

"You mean since you said we can't pour drinks freehanded anymore?"

"Since I said what?" Newman stared at her confused.

"Since you said we had to use shot glasses, instead of pouring our drinks freehanded."

"But I never said no such…" Newman was perplexed.

"Well, the long-time customers don't like it. I don't like it either." Laura complained.

Newman shook his head. "Now, run that by me again. What did I say?"

"That guy, the new guy, what's his name?"

"Rodney?"

"Yea. He said pouring freehanded wasted too much money and from now on, I'd have to measure the booze by a shot glass. I've been bartending for eight years now. I know how much to pour."

"I'm sure you do, Laura," Newman calmly replied. "I never told Rodney to tell you how to pour drinks. It's all some kind of mistake, honest. You can pour drinks any way you like."

Suddenly, a stern angry voice called his name. "Newman!"

Newman turned to see one of the loggers storming toward him. "What's this crap about you paying for seconds? I've been eatin' my fill ever since I've been on this crew. Now you and Vicki come up with this shit? Well, I ain't payin'. You can take your food and shove it up your ass for all I care."

Newman sighed in confusion with his eyes wide open. "Now, now, what are you talking about?"

"You know damn well what I'm talking about. Nelson told me you said we had to pay for seconds."

"I did no such thing." Newman's anger mounted.

"Well, Nelson said…"

"Well Nelson's wrong! Let's go talk to him." He turned to Laura, "Excuse me."

Newman stormed past the logger and marched into the dining room. Nelson stood behind the register, counting change back to a customer. "Thanks and come again." Nelson smiled. The customer clinched the bills, turned and walked away.

"Nelson!" shouted Newman.

Nelson looked up at Newman.

"What's this I hear about everybody paying for seconds?"

"Yea. Didn't you tell Rodney to tell me to start that?"

"Rodney…" Newman breathed in disgust. "No, Nelson, don't charge anybody for seconds. I don't know where he got that from, but he's mistaken. Give the money back if you've taken some away and see that these guys get full, okay?"

"Sure, Ken. I thought…"

"I know, I know."

Newman wasn't sure what was behind all of these sudden rule changes, but he knew he hadn't discussed any policy changes with Vicki. And he didn't think Rodney was that arrogant to simply implement them on his own, or was he? Only one person could clear up the confusion and he was going to see her right now. Kenny marched into the office.

Vicki looked up from the papers on the desk. "Kenny." She beamed. "I want you to look at these plans that Rodney drew up for opening a snack bar near the pool. Why, the sales from drinks and sandwiches alone could average three grand a month."

"Rodney's been a busy little beaver lately, hasn't he?"

"Yes." Vicki said excitedly. "He's got a lot of good ideas about saving money."

"Like no free seconds at chow and shot glasses at the bar?"

"He mentioned something to that effect."

"Vicki, these people don't work nine-to-five, eight-hour days around here. Sixteen and eighteen-hour days are common. Everybody here works six days a week. Seconds on chow is a bargain compared to the service they provide."

"Well, I told him to discuss any policy changes with you."

"Rodney Johnson didn't. And I've had people ready to tar and feather me for policy changes I had nothing to do with."

"I'm sure he meant well."

"Sure," Newman sarcastically agreed. "I'm going to have a talk with him."

"Don't be too hard on him. I really hope he works out. He's got a lot of good ideas, and he does have leadership potential." Newman seemed uneasy.

"Vicki, boy, I don't know. Something about those brothers makes me very uneasy."

Vicki smiled. "Why, Kenny, you're not afraid of a little competition, are you?"

"Of course not," Newman countered. "If he can help out around here, then more power to him. It's just that he seems to want to step in and run things his way."

"Well, like I said, I hope he works out. You said earlier, everyone here works long hours. And if my accounting serves me accurately, that evening you had with Colleen was the only day off you've had since you've been here. It'd be nice to have somebody fill in for you a day or two so you can get out of here once in a while, wouldn't it? All work and no play, so the saying goes."

Vicki was right. It was fun to get away from the resort for a while. He had become so involved in putting out the daily fires around the grounds that he had forgotten how much fun an evening on the town could be. If nothing else, he had Colleen to thank for that. But still, it wasn't that sharing the management responsibilities was as troublesome to him as sharing those duties with Rod. His whole demeanor made him feel uneasy, though it was nothing he could quite put his finger on, at least not just yet.

"Okay, Vicki, you win, but I still need to talk to him to prevent these misunderstanding from occurring again. Do you know where he is?"

"At the pool. Don't get mad, but I think he had some ideas for improving productivity over there, too."

"Boy," Newman sighed. "I can hardly wait to see what they are."

Newman left Vicki's office trying to remain calm. His anger was heightened by the fact that Vicki said she told him to discuss any policy changes with him before implementing them. The fact that Rodney chose to ignore her and change policy anyway made Newman even more suspicious of his intentions. Changing policy without discussing them first with him was a point he would have made an issue of with Rodney, were it not for Vicki's desire for Rod to "work out."

Newman opened the pool door. The sound of splashing water and mixed screaming voices echoed from inside. Rides sat behind the check-in counter. He looked up from his paperback as Newman entered.

"My, my," Newnan noted, "aren't we hard at work."

Rides looked back down at his book. "Is this Bug Andrew Day? First that other asshole, and now you."

"Asshole? What asshole? Rodney?" asked Newman.

"He came in here with an ink pad. And spoke about some crap, about stamping the back of the pool patron's hands so we can keep track of how many customers come into the pool and at the same time cut down on theft."

"Well, that idea may have some potential."

"Come on, Ken. If you wanted to rip this place off, you could just take the money without stamping anybody's hand. No one is going to come over here and measure the amount of ink left in the pad and compare it to the number of customers in the pool."

"So what have you done with the ink pad?"

Rides nodded toward the wastebasket. Newman peeped over the counter to see the ink pad resting atop a pile of crumpled papers in the trash can.

Suddenly, the pool entry door opened. Rod stepped in with his head down, writing in his notepad.

"Poolside looks pretty good. I made a few notes on improving..." He looked up at Newman and Rides. "Oh, Ken, I didn't see you. I was just looking around the pool to see where we could be more efficient."

"Of course," Newman sarcastically agreed.

Rodney walked over to Newman. "I've just been looking around the resort to see ways to cut cost."

"Like charging for seconds at the restaurant?" Newman added.

"I meant to talk to you about that, but I couldn't find you."

Newman could see the nervousness in Rodney's face as he struggled to explain his actions.

"Listen," Newman calmly began, "I can appreciate your desire to cut coats, but around here we work as team. You have some good ideas, then we can talk about them. But let's communicate first, okay?"

Rodney laughed, "Sure, Ken. It's just that I get a little excited when I see ways to cut waste. But you're right. You're the boss and I really need to clear things with you first."

"We'll clear things with each other, how's that?"

"Sounds good. Hey, well I have to go, but I'll remember to communicate." Rodney smiled.

He pushed the front door open and left. Rides shook his head as he looked up from his book.

"If you believe that line, I've got some swampland in Florida I can let you have real cheap."

"What's that supposed to mean?" Newman asked.

"The guys' after power, Ken. It's written all over his face. He's out for one thing and one thing only... Control. I spent four years in the Army. Those kind of guys you can spot a mile away."

"Yea, but I don't want to come across like some power-hungry dictator either, afraid to entertain new ideas."

"It's not you I'm worried about, Ken." Rides had a voice of concern. "Rodney really worries me. He's not just power hungry... he's dangerous."

"Oh, come on." Newman was in disbelief. "He looks to be a twenty-three year-old accountant. How dangerous can an accountant be?"

Rides just smiled and returned to reading his book.

Rodney walked into the general store and eased the door closed behind him. He leaned back against the door momentarily and stared dejectedly up at the ceiling.

Nicholas looked up from the cash register as Rodney walked in. He noticed his demeanor. "Problems?"

"It's that fuckin' Newman," he sighed. "I swear that… that nigger is going to cross me one day and boy, look out."

"We still can take care of problems the old-fashioned way." He reached under the counter and pulled out an M-16 automatic assault rifle.

Rodney's eyes widened in panic. "Put that thing away!" He rushed over to the counter and snatched the weapon from Nicholas. "What if somebody sees you with that thing?"

"Then it's just their bad luck," Nicholas calmly added.

"You idiot. Fuck this little gig up, and so help me…"

"Ahhh, don't threaten me, Rod. And call me Nick. I'm a man, not some boy to be called Nicholas." Anger flowed with each word spoken. "You need me too much to do the shit you don't have the stomach for. Like that nigger. Nobody's gonna notice a missing nigger. Not in these parts. And with him gone, the manager's job will certainly be yours. Now stop fussing at me and let me fuck em' up!"

"He's not just another drifter. I keep telling you that. Besides, he's the only nigga up here. They would miss him. Let me do this my way, okay? I'm almost her co-manager now, so don't blow it. If I need stronger measures, you'll be the first to know." Rodney looked around the store. "Where's our little brother?"

"He's in the bedroom where he's supposed to be."

"Good. Now you put this thing away." He shove the rifle into Nick's arms. "And don't pull it out again unless I tell you to, understand?"

"Yeah." Nick reluctantly nodded his head in agreement. Angered over that fact that he treats him like he's an idiot, instead of an equal. "Let me take care him. What if we made it look like an accident?"

"Don't get impatient, my friend. Rest assured, I'll gradually ease him out. But one thing is certain, Newman is leaving here, one way or the other. I got this Nick. Right now we need brains, not brawn. Let me take care of it."

Rodney disappeared into the back room. Nick followed him with his eyes, in disgust.

CHAPTER
16

*R*ides watched as several huge RVs lumbered into the parking lot. Many of the gargantuan motor homes measured over thirty feet long and had several rows of rear double wheels. Some even had long banners streaming from the sides of their vehicles. The Singing Harrison Family, and the Wailing Washington's, proclaimed some of the banners, as the RVs stopped in front of the office. The occupants climbed out, all dressed Western style, clutching banjos, guitars, and other music instruments.

An attractive older woman in a Western-style blouse and calico skirt climbed out of an extremely long expensive RV. "Howdy," she beamed as Rides approached. "Can you tell me if the RV Park is open?"

"Yes ma'am, it is right across the road," Rides pointed, "but aren't you all a little early? I mean the Labor Day Jamboree isn't until next week."

"Sugar," she confidently began, "we've been comin' to this thing for five years now. If there's one thing we've learned, the early bird gets the best RV space." She elbowed him gently in the ribs, then patted the side of the RV. "So just show me where to register this baby."

"Well, you can pay either at the manager's office or over at the general store."

"Honey, then take me to the manager's office." She hooked her arm under his. "Nothing like meeting the folks at the top, my daddy always says."

Rides walked arm and arm with the woman until they came to the bottom of the front office steps. "Just walk right up there and ask for Ken Newman or Vicki Marshall. They'll fix you right up."

She gave him a peck on the cheek and headed up the stairs. Rides smiled. She opened the door to see Newman leaning over the receptionist desk, reading a paper.

"Excuse me," she smiled. "I'm looking for the manager."

Newman looked up from the paper. "You've got him."

"Really, sugar?" She was surprised.

"Really."

"We're here for the Labor Day Jamboree, and we need a space for our RV."

"You're here a little early, aren't you? Labor Day isn't until next weekend." Responded Newman.

"We have a thirty-two-footer."

"Boy, you don't need a space," he sighed. "You need a football field."

"Now you understand why we are here so early."

Newman reached into the drawer and pulled out a slip of paper.

"Fill that out." He handed the paper to her. "And just bring it back when you get ready to leave."

She took the paper and began filling it out. "We're gonna have to rent two spaces from you, darlin'. And, as always, we'll pay cash."

"Vicki will like that."

"Where is the sugar plum, anyway?"

"Nina!" Vicki screamed.

Newman turned to see Vicki standing near the doorway.

"Vicki! Nina shouted. The two woman rushed to meet in the center of the office and embraced each other.

"I knew you'd be here." Vicki said, patting Nina repeatedly on the back.

"Wouldn't miss it for the world. You know that."

"Did you bring the monster RV back with you again this year?"

"You bet. Between all my family's music equipment and costumes, we brought a ton of stuff." Nina walked back over to the desk. "You know last year we had our RV broken into…"

"Well, don't worry. This year we'll have our own security force on patrol. Nobody will dare come near that monster of yours again."

"Great!" Nina beamed. "Well, drop by sometime. You, too." She pointed toward Newman. "We'll be practicing our music all week long over there."

"Sure will, Nina. Did Franklin come with you this time?"

"Nawh, sugar. You know that husband of mine is like a couch potato. He's at home like always." Vicki smiled as Nina walked out the door.

"Ken that was Nina Thompson. She owns the Thompson Department Stores."

"What's this security force of which you speak?" Newman asked bluntly.

"Oh, didn't I tell you? I'm going to reissue Curtis his badge and gun." Newman sighed in disgust.

"Oh, Vicki, for crying out loud, not Deputy Dog."

"Now, Kenny," Vicki consoled. "He's a former police officer."

"Former is right. I'll never forgive him for deserting me that day I faced those bikers. Besides, he's just as likely to shoot off his own foot as capture a bad guy."

"I'm sure it won't come to that. Trust me, I've sponsored this thing for the past five years. Other than that incident last year with Nina's musical equipment, every Jamboree has run as smooth as silk. Curtis will be no more than a scarecrow, that's all. I promise."

"Okay, Vicki, I just hope no problems crop up that Curtis has to take care of."

"Speaking of problems, I want you to come back here and take a look at something."

Newman followed her back into her office. Vicki stepped behind her desk and turned an accounting ledger around to face him.

"There are the café, pool, bar, and general store receipts for the past two weeks."

Newman looked at the ledger momentarily. He looked back up at her. "So?"

"Now look at the numbers for the previous two weeks."

Newman looked back down at the ledger. "Oh, looks like a drop in business for the last two weeks."

"Have you notice a drop in business?"

"Not really, but just because we have people here doesn't mean they are spending the same amount of money from week to week."

"No, but it could also mean that someone's fingers are sticking in the till."

"Somebody's stealing?"

"Possibly, I don't know. But the only people who have had access to the receipts have been you, me, and Rodney. And in the last two weeks, it's just been me and Rodney."

"You don't think…"

"I don't know what to think," Vicki quickly interrupted. "Now I expect a little thievery, but not more than the individual is worth to me."

"Well, Vicki, you said you don't have proof. I don't want to accuse somebody of stealing without proof. I already made that mistake once."

"Neither do I, but what I'd like for you to do is count the nightly take before Rodney gets over there to collect the receipts. We'll then see how well Mr. Johnson's numbers match yours."

Suddenly the bell on the front door tinkled.

"Sounds like we've got company." Uttered Newman.

"Hope it's not Rod. He's supposed to still be at lunch. I haven't finished looking over these books yet."

"Well, don't worry, I'll see who it is." Newman walked into the front office to see an attractive well-dress woman with long reddish brown hair, briefcase in hand, waiting at the front desk. "Can I help you?" Newman smiled.

"I'm looking for Kenneth Newman." She quickly smiled.

"I'm Kenneth Newman."

"Leanna Clark. U.S. Forest Service Contracting."

She and Newman shook hands. "How can I help you?"

"I'm trying to wrap up our account with you all covering the period when our smoke jumpers stayed at your resort."

"Terrorized our resort, you mean."

"Semantics, Mr. Newman."

"Ken, please. No one has called me Mr. Newman since the Navy."

"Ok. To the point in hand. Some of the claims you've listed in your billing, Ken, aren't covered by government liability. Your own company's insurance should cover a lot of the expenses listed on your report. When the smoke jumpers were on their own time, they were just like any other tourist."

"Other tourist didn't ride their dirt bikes on our barroom floor and fill our pool with twenty-four kegs of beer."

"They weren't your typical guest, I'll admit that. But still, Mr. Newman, ah… Ken, your private insurance carrier should be responsible for any damages to your resort."

"Well, have a seat Leanna Clark." Newman motioned toward the chair. "Let's hash this out. You want to clear your books. We'd like to get paid."

Leanna hoisted her briefcase onto the desk and popped it open.

As Newman wrestled with Leanna over the financial reimbursement of the resort, Vicki had called Curtis to let him know she needed his expertise in security during the Jamboree Gala events. Curtis was excited about being reinstated to protect the resort. He didn't let a minute go by in preparation for possibly serious encounters with law abiding citizens.

The deadly report of gunfire echoed throughout the deep woods. On a distant log, the long line of glass bottles burst, one after another. When the last bottle finally exploded, Curtis holstered his weapon.

"Alice," he called over his shoulder, "bring me another box of ammo out of the trunk, will ya?"

The shabbily dressed middle-aged woman reluctantly climbed out the driver's side of the worn tattered station wagon. She walked around to the opened tailgate and pulled out a box of cartridges.

"Curtis, which ones do you want, the rifle or the handgun?"

"Damn it, woman. Do you see me out here with a rifle? I need the .38 rounds."

Alice put the box she held in her hand down, picked up another box, and started toward Curtis. "How do you expect me to know which ones you want? You ain't used either gun in over six months."

"That was when Vicki took my gun and badge because I didn't help Newman throw out those bikers awhile back. But now she needs somebody to protect them visitors during the Jamboree, and I aim to be ready."

She handed him the box of bullets. "But, Curtis, you ain't carried a gun since before the summer. And you ain't fired a gun at nobody since you left the police force in Missoula."

He emptied the shells from his chamber and began pulling rounds out of the box. "That was then honey. That's why I'm out here practicing." He continued as he jammed round after round into the breeched chamber. "With a little practice, I'll get my old shooting form back. Then, you'll see, they won't laugh at ole Curtis no more."

"Honey, I just don't want to see you get hurt, that's all."

"Just let me get a little more practice, honeybun. When I get through here, boy, they will have to respect Curtis again." He squeezed the trigger and again the deadly report echoed through the forest.

Back at the office, Vicki was questioning her own judgment for hiring Rodney on the spot. Vicki's right fingers danced over the numbers on the calculator as her other index finger followed a line of numbers down the side of the ledger. The discrepancy from the prior weeks before Rodney appeared and when he started handling the books was such a significant difference. She just couldn't ignore the numbers. She needed to know the truth. Suddenly a tap on the door broke her concentration.

"Come in." Newman stepped in.

"Say, it's past eleven. I've already locked the pool. Here are the day's receipts." Newman set a money bag on her desk. "It's already counted. I counted it three times so there would be no mistake in the numbers and a tally sheet is in the bag."

"Good." Vicki grabbed the bag, zipped it open, and fingered through the cash. "I'll take the receipt out, give it to Rodney to count and see how your two totals compare."

"In his defense Vicki, we have been getting along better these last several days. Like you said, he has a lot of good ideas. Besides, having an assistant isn't such a bad idea."

Vicki peeled off her glasses. "Remember what I said about stealing more than you are worth? He hasn't been here a month and already I see a huge drop in sales. If he is stealing, I don't think Rodney is worth what he might be taking."

"If he's taking anything," Newman added quickly.

"Listen, there's a big crowd over at the bar tonight, with the early Jamboree arrivals and all. Be a dear and bring me a portion of the cash in the register over there. I'd like to at least see some of it before Rodney counts it."

"Oh, Vicki," Newman consoled, "don't be paranoid. I'll get the cash, but I'm sure Rodney is trustworthy."

"Well, what changed your tune? Several days ago, you were ready to run him out of town on a rail."

Newman sighed, "It's been kind of nice having an assistant around. No more sixteen-hour days."

"Well, maybe I am being too harsh, but in my business you can't be too careful, especially when the obvious is apparent. Just bring me the cash, will you?"

Newman pulled the door open. "I'll be back in a flash with the cash," he quipped. "Besides, with a bar filled with country music, believe me, I won't hang around very long." He closed the door behind him.

Vicki gave a slight grin and resume calculating the receipts.

Minutes later, Newman parked in front of the bar. The blare of laughter and live country music echoed through the cool moonlit night.

The parking lot was filled to capacity as cowboys, cowgirls, and couples locked arm in arm, raced between their cars to get into the bar. Newman approached the base of the steps to find Angie and Marci standing there arguing with Curtis.

"Oh, no you don't," Curtis angrily demanded. "Now both of you get out of here before I carry ya both off by the seat of your britches."

"What's the problem?" Newman asked.

"These two tried to buy a six-pack from the bar," Curtis bitterly complained. "Laura threw them out. Now they're trying to bribe people to go in and buy the booze for them."

"That's before sheriff stupid here," Marci scolded, pointing to Curtis, "came along and threatened to have us both arrested"

"Minors consuming alcohol is not per..." Curtis insisted.

"I know, I know," Newman concurred. He turned toward Angie and Marci. "Look," he calmly began, "I'm afraid I'm going to have to side with Curtis on this one. You know we could lose our liquor license if either of you are caught in that bar. Besides, what are you two doing out this late at night?"

Marci shook her head as she put her hands on her hips and looked up at the night sky. "Geez, Kenny, we're not babies. We've both tasted beer before. Besides, it's almost time to go back to school. We want to have one last summer fling just like you grownups."

"Probably so," Newman agreed, "but you won't get any beer out of this bar, young ladies. Drinking is a very bad habit that kids your age shouldn't get into. Remember what happened to your friend Jay?"

"Aw, Kenny," Angie whined, "you're acting just like our parents. Besides, we're not driving."

Newman walked past them on up the stairs while Curtis escorted the girls away from the base of the stairway. Newman opened the door and the full brunt of the music blasted him in the face. The floor was packed with dancing, whirling couples. Newman excused his way through the crowded dance floor. He had almost reached the counter when a woman's shrill voice hailed him. He turned to see Nina meandering through the crowd to reach him.

"Kenny." She smiled grabbing his arm…"glad to see you could make it. How do you like my family band?"

"It's real nice." He shouted, trying to be heard over the music and laughter. "It's not quite my cup of tea, but everybody seems to be having a good time and that's all that really matters."

"How about dancing with me?"

"Can I take a raincheck?" Newman hedged. "I'm on an errand for Vicki. Besides, I wouldn't know a two-step from the foxtrot."

"Shucks, honey, that ain't no excuse," Nina playfully countered. "I'll teach you."

"Really," he insisted. He suddenly spotted Rodney sitting at the counter with two cases of Miller Beer stacked before him, peeling off several bills from a huge cash roll.

"See that guy over there who looks like he just won the state lottery." Newman pointed toward Rodney. Nina followed Newman's finger down the counter. "That man loves to dance. Just ask him and he'll keep you dancing all night long."

"Really?" She huffed sarcastically.

Newman motioned toward Rodney. Nina squinted playfully, then slowly started toward Rodney. Newman stepped behind the counter and walked over to the register just as Laura was about to ring up a sale.

"And just what do you think you are doing?" Laura asked defensively.

"Removing some of your cash," Newman replied. He hit the 'No Sale' button, and the cash drawer eased out, slowed by the mound of bills Laura had crammed into the trays. "And from what I can see, I arrived none too soon." He began pulling some of the cash from the drawer.

"Well, leave me enough for change, and bring me back some small bills. Tonight's a real busy night."

"I can see," Newman concurred, quickly scanning the bar. "How's it going? Are you short of anything?"

"No, not really. But I find it odd that Rodney Johnson got here just two weeks ago broke as Job's turkey, and now just two weeks later, he's flashing a roll that could choke a horse."

Newman wrapped a rubber band around the bills in his hand. "Laura, the man not only drives a BMW, he's also an accountant. Besides, nothing said he had to be broke when he and his brothers came here."

"Still…"

"Still nothing." Newman quickly interrupted. "Leave Rodney alone. He can drink whatever he can afford." He shoved the cash drawer back into the register and stepped from behind the counter.

Nina eased next to Rodney as he sat quietly on the bar stool. He turned the glass up to his mouth, then set it down on the countertop.

"Buy you a drink, if you'll dance with me." Nina smiled.

Rodney slowly looked over at her. "I buy my own drinks, lady."

"You have a problem with being sociable?"

Rodney shoved the glass out of his way. "Lady I am sociable." He wrapped his arms around his two cases of beer. "See ya around." He eased off the stool.

Newman headed for exit when he noticed Leanna standing in an isolated corner of the bar, nursing a small glass. She looked apprehensive as a cowboy approached her. She politely waved him away.

"Didn't know you were a country music fan," Newman shouted as he walked over to her. Leanna turned and looked up at him.

"Ken," she was slightly startled. "I didn't see you come up."

"Been here long?"

"No. I've rented a room here for the night. After all, it's Friday night and I've never been here before."

"Well, have fun, and I hope you like to dance because an attractive woman alone in this bar is nothing but a challenge to every cowboy in this place."

Leanna smiled and Newman left out the front door. He geared his vehicle and left to deliver the cash to Vicki.

Meanwhile, outside the bar, Rodney had tucked a case of beer under each arm and was meandering through the rows of cars on his way back to the general store when he heard a young girl's voice whisper his name. He turned, startled, to see Angie and Marci standing beside one of the parked cars.

"Don't sneak up on me like that," he scolded. "Why aren't you two in bed, anyway?"

"It's Friday night, Rodney, and everybody's up having a good time. Why do we have to be in bed?" asked Angie.

"Because you're both kids, that's why."

"Look," Marci pleaded, "have a heart, Rodney. We've been trying all night to get somebody to buy us some beer. Nobody will, and neither Curtis nor Kenny will let us in the bar."

"Super nig strikes again, uh, girls?"

"Yeah, well we were wondering if you'd go to the bar and buy us a six-pack of Bud Lite." Commented Angie.

"We've got the money." Marci unfolded her fist, revealing several crumpled twenty-dollar bills. "This should cover it," she added. "And you can have what's left."

Rodney looked at both girls, then down at the money. "You're both serious, aren't you?"

They eagerly nodded their heads. "Yeah." They spoke in unison.

"Here," he handed Angie one of his cases of beer and snatched the money from Marci's hand.

"Gee, thanks." Angie beamed, cradling the slightly heavy box.

Several car rows away, Curtis looked up just in time to see the transaction by the light of the parking lot lamppost.

"Son-of-a-bitch," Curtis cursed under his breath. He started trotting toward them. His holstered gun was flopping methodically at his side with his protruding belly bouncing rhythmically over his buckle.

While Curtis tried to chase the trio for illegal distribution of liquor, Leanna was trying to enjoy herself in a crowded bar. This was not her forte, but still it was something different she had never experienced before.

Leanna took another sip from her glass. She scanned the bar for an empty seat, but there still weren't any. She turned to leave, when suddenly a man's alcoholic breath blasted her in the face.

"Say, sweetheart," he grimed down at her. His elbow was propped against the wall slightly above her head, "you look like you could use some company tonight." His presence was forceful and over bearing.

"Leanna forced a smile. "I'm fine, really."

"Nonsense. You're standing here like a wall flower." He took her glass. "You're poison, lady. Whatta you drinkin'?"

Leanna grew annoyed. "Ah… ah, water," she finally blurted. "Lemon water."

"Lemon water?" He was dumfounded. "What kind of drink is that for a lady?"

"Mister, please!" She pulled away from the man's advances and was about to run for the door when she heard her name being called. She looked in the direction of the page to see Newman hailing her.

"Leanna, Sis," he called. Newman reached her as the cowboy looked on, bewildered. "Sis, I've been looking all over for you."

The cowboy looked at Newman, then back at Leanna. "Sis?"

"Yeah, Mom and Dad are outside in the car waiting for you, and here you are, socializing. They're ready to go back to town." Newman leaned toward the cowboy. "You know how sisters are," he whispered.

"Sister?" doubted the drunken cowboy.

"Ahhh… yes…" Leanna added, picking up on the cue. "How thoughtless of me to keep the family waiting. Sorry, brother dear, I'm ready to go." She leaned toward the cowboy, "You understand, don't you? Family calls."

Newman took her by the hand and ushered her out of the bar. They stood on the steps in the cool crisp air under the star-filled night sky.

"I suppose I should thank you for rescuing me back there. I thought you had left."

"Oh, don't mention it. I just came back to give the bartender some change, and I saw you in that wrestling match with Tex back there."

"Do you think he believes that you and I are really brother and sister?"

"Oh, who cares? By the time he figures it out, you'll be safely back in your hotel room. Good night, Leanna." Newman started down the steps when she called to him. He stopped and looked back up at her.

"If it wouldn't be too much trouble, would you walk me back to my room? I'm really uncomfortable walking alone in the dark."

Newman chuckled. "Sure, just one of the many extra services we provide here at the resort." She descended the steps and slowly strolled with Newman toward the hotel. "Does your boyfriend know you're spending the night up here with an army of sex-starved cowboys?"

"No, but then I don't have a boyfriend for precisely that reason. I travel a lot in my job. I like to feel I can spend time wherever I want, with whoever I want to, with no one to answer to."

"Free spirit."

"Something like that. Besides, I'm not really looking to get serious with anyone right now."

"A woman of adventure?"

"Well, sort of. I want to know what's around the next bend. I guess that's why I've applied for a position that's open in Alaska."

"Alaska?" thought Newman.

"Yes. I've never been there before, but it's a state that seems rife with adventure, and I'd like to see it." specified Leanna.

"Well, good luck. Sounds like a bold move."

"And you, Ken? You're obviously not opposed to bold moves and adventure either. This has got to be one of the boldest adventures I've ever seen anyone undertake. Is there a secret heart somewhere waiting in your life?"

"No. I thought there was, but it turned out to be a false alarm. So I guess, like you, I've put off finding someone special, at least for now anyway."

"Two brave, adventurous spirits," Leanna noted.

Suddenly a voice called them. Leanna jumped, clutching Newman's arm. Newman turned. Curtis stood a few feet behind them, breathing heavy.

"Damn it, Curtis!" Newman shouted, "What are you trying to do? Scare us to death?"

"Sorry, but I'm looking for those two girls," he huffed.

"What two girls?"

"Angela and Marci. They bought a case of beer from Rodney, and when I tried to take it from them, they took off like jackrabbits. I lost 'em somewhere over here. You haven't seen 'em, have you?"

Newman sighed, "No, Curtis, we haven't. You mean you're out here chasing around in the dark, after two kids, just because they bought some beer?"

"This is serious, Ken. Selling liquor to minors is against the law. Vicki could lose her liquor license over this."

"Whatever, Curtis," Newman sighed. "If I see them, I'll talk to them, okay?"

"Right, Ken. In the meantime, I'm going to have a talk with that Rodney. He's got no right selling beer to those little girls."

"That's right, Curtis." Newman sarcastically agreed. "Go get 'em."

Curtis immediately turned and waddled off.

Leanna, still clutching Newman's arm, watched Curtis leave. "Who... who... who was that?"

"That, my dear, is the Hot Spring's answer to Quick Draw McGraw. Living proof that you don't need brains to carry a gun."

They watched until he disappeared into the distant night. Leanna looked down at her arm, still entwined with Newman's. She immediately snatched it away.

"I'm sorry," she said, a little embarrassed, "I had no right to do that."

"Did you hear me complaining?"

"Some brave, free spirit," Leanna dejectedly added.

"Tell you what. It'll be our secret, okay? On one condition."

Leanna looked at him skeptically. "What?"

"Labor Day weekend, I'd like you to be my guest for the Jamboree."

"Country music? But I hate country music."

"Really? So do I. It should be great though."

Leanna thought for a moment. "Can I have a couple of days to think about it?"

"Sure. I know it's not every day someone who hates country music invites you to a country music jamboree, but as they say, misery loves company."

She laughed as they continued toward the hotel. Once they arrived at her hotel room. The evening was still young.

"Would you like to come in for a while?"

"No, I am going to check with Vicki on some matters we discussed earlier this evening. But I will take a raincheck, if that's okay?"

"Of course, see you tomorrow, perhaps?"

"I will try to make sure you do. Goodnight."

Leanna closed the door with a smile and Newman headed to the main office.

Meanwhile, Rodney had made his way back to the general store. He set the case of beer down on the counter.

"Where's my case?" Nick bitterly asked.

"I sold it."

"Sold it!" Nick huffed.

"What gave you the right to sell my beer?"

"Relax. You can have my case. Besides, I can afford to buy two or three cases for what those two stupid little bitches paid me for one."

"What stupid little bitches?"

"Those two girls that work at the pool and the café." Replied Rodney.

"Oh, those two. Yeah," Nick agreed, "and I'm going to fuck that little Angela before we leave here."

"You and your crude taste," Rodney sneered in disdain. "Where's Toby?"

"In the bedroom."

"Good. Why don't you put the 'Closed' sign in the window? That way you can drink your beer and I can relax in peace in the backroom."

"Sure," Nick agreed. "Whatever you say."

Nick walked over to the door and flipped the card in the window. Suddenly, he saw a man with a tin star gleaming from his chest and a sidearm strapped to his hip approaching from the shadows.

"Rod!" He called, almost in a panic. "Come here. Now!"

Rodney casually walked over to the window. "What is it?"

"Look!" Nick pointed toward the approaching figure.

Rodney was startled to alertness. "Fuck!" He sighed. "It's the cops!"

"How'd they find us?" Nick asked in a panic.

"Who gives a shit? We've gotta get outta here… fast!"

"But how? They probably have the place surrounded."

"Get the guns! Climb out of the side window and make for the car. I'll get the kid and meet you in the back!"

"Man, forget the kid." Shouted Nick. We've got to move… Now!"

Rodney reached and grabbed Nick forcefully by his lapels. "Now listen. Since when do you give orders?" He angrily demanded. "Get the kid and put him in the fuckin' car… now!"

Both men stared angrily at each other. Nick tore away and scampered into the back room.

Curtis ambled casually toward the general store, his holster swaying with the bouncing motion of his bloated hips and buttocks. He heard several car doors slam, but thought nothing of it. Moments later, an engine revved and tires squealed. He kept walking, even as the outline of the BMW emerged at a high rate of speed from behind the store. It swerved onto the road and headed straight for him. Curtis recognized Rodney's car and could see his face behind the wheel by the gleam of the cars' headlights.

He froze in horror as the speeding car bore down on him. He waved frantically, crossing both arms in front of his face, in a desperate attempt to wave the vehicle off. Instead, the headlights exploded to bright as Rodney floored the accelerator. Curtis shielded his face from the blinding light and instinctively leaped to one side. The vehicle sped by, barely missing him. His weight carried him like a huge wrecking ball, crashing through the wooden handrail. He crashed with a big splash into a shallow creek below. He landed with a thud on his back. Momentarily stunned, as the cool rushing water swirled around him. Curtis lay there momentarily, then slowly climbed to his feet just in time to see the BMW swerve onto the highway and speed out of sight. Curtis watched as his Stetson hat floated leisurely downstream. He mumbled a curse word, then tromped through the water and climbed up the hillside.

While Curtis was recovering from a near death experience, Vicki's fingers tapped methodically on the calculator. She then hit the 'Sum Total Key'. The number immediately illuminated, and she smiled. "Now that's what a Friday night bar take should look like." She beamed with pride.

"Well, it's not every weekend we have live music, especially a band like Nina's. Her band's not that bad," Newman commented, sitting across from Vicki.

"Why, Kenny, does that mean you are finally acquiring a taste for country music?"

"Oh, I hope not."

"Just give it time. Before you leave here, you'll be humming country tunes in your sleep."

"God forbid."

Vicki chuckled and handed him huge stacks of bundled bills.

"Now I want you to go and put this back in Laura's cash drawer before the bar closes."

"Put it back??" Newman was confused. "She barely has room for the money still in her drawer."

"Well, take her a money bag or something, but I want it all back in there before Rodney collects the cash when the bar closes tonight."

"Vicki, he was over there at the bar tonight and probably saw me collect some of the money."

"Good. When you put this money back in the drawer, he'll think the bulk of the cash has already been collected. If he reports more than you've got there, fine. If he reports less than that, well, we'll know we have a problem."

"I still think this is a waste of time," Newman sighed, rising from his chair.

"I hope you are right, Kenny."

"Oh, by the way. I cleared up those problems we had with the Forest Service. Looks like you can expect a check for $7,500 from them in about two weeks."

"Great. When did you find that out?"

"I saw Leanna over at the bar tonight."

"Oh, Leanna, is it?" Vicki coyly asked.

"Oh, relax. At best we're just friends, nothing more. Besides, after my last venture into the world of romance, I think 'just friends' is about all I can handle right now." He turned to open the door to leave only to find Curtis standing in the doorway, fuming with anger and dripping wet.

"Curtis!" Newman was dumbfounded.

Vicki rose from her seat and hurried around the desk. "Are you all right?" She was deeply concerned.

"Yes, ma'am." Curtis nodded, shaking the water from his arms.

"When you use the hot pool next time, Curtis," Newman joked, "take your uniform off first."

He eyed Newman with contempt.

"What happened?" Vicki asked.

"That Rodney Johnson and his brothers tried to run me over."

"Rodney?" Vicki was in disbelief.

"Yea," he eagerly continued, his voice slightly raised. "I was on the bridge going to the store. I saw Rodney give one of those girls a case of beer."

"Rodney?" Vicki asked. "He knows they're underage. We could get in big trouble over that." Interjected Vicki.

"I was on my way to tell him to stop, when their car comes roaring out the back of the store and nearly runs me over. I had to dive into the creek just to avoid being killed."

"You sure it was Rodney?" Vicki had her doubts about Rodney, but why would he try to hurt Curtis?

"Positive, Vicki. I know that fancy car when I see it. I tell ya, something ain't right about them boys."

"Curtis, you go get into some dry clothes," Vicki consoled.

"What about Rodney?" asked Curtis.

"I'll take care of Rodney. Now go home and change before you catch your death."

Curtis reluctantly turned and headed out the door.

Vicki looked at Newman. "Well, what do you think of that?"

Newman peeped around the corner to see if Curtis had left. "Sounds like he got drunk, fell in the creek, and just needed to explain it."

Vicki shook her head. "Nooooo… He didn't smell like he was boozed up. Besides, he had his gun. Curtis knows how I feel about him drinking while he's armed. No, there's something more to it."

Newman checked his watch. "Well, when Rodney brings the receipts by tonight, you can talk to him."

"I'm usually sound asleep by eleven. The bar doesn't even close until after two in the morning." responded Vicki.

"I'll talk to him in the morning then. I'm sure there's a logical explanation for all of this."

"Ok Ken try and get a good night sleep."

Vicki headed toward her room in the back, while Newman left through the front door.

Not long after Curtis had explained the curious event that surrounded his uniform being soaked, the front door to the general store slammed shut. After careful deliberation of who they tried to run over in the dark, Nick and Rodney had returned.

"You're an asshole," he railed at Nick. "You're nothing but a fuckin' asshole."

"All right, all right," Nick angrily countered, laying the automatic rifle on the counter. "That's enough outta you. How was I to know that was only that buffoon coming over here. He had a badge on." He pointed to his chest. "You know, like the real ones wear? I'd rather be safe than sorry."

"But now, he's probably told everybody in the complex we tried to run him over."

"So what the fuck did we come back here for? We should be halfway to Wyoming by now." Firmly replied Nick.

"Because we can make a killing in this place. In just two weeks I've managed to keep almost $3,000. I've got access to every cash register in this resort. I'm just not going to walk away from this kind of money."

"Even if it means going back to the slammer?" questioned Nick.

Rodney pulled the .45 pistol from his belt. "Hey, Toby!" Toby immediately appeared in the bedroom doorway. "Take this and put it under my pillow." He gave the boy the weapon. Toby dejectedly took the gun and walked back into the bedroom. "Like you said, that guy is the town clown. Nobody takes him seriously. If he says we tried to run him over, we'll say we just didn't see him. We were in such a hurry to get our little brother Toby to the hospital in town, we just didn't see him on the bridge."

"And they're supposed to buy that?" Nick countered in disbelief.

"If you sell it right."

"And just what was this life-and-death illness Toby is supposed to have?"

"Leave that to me. By the time I'm finished, not only will Curtis be over here apologizing for being in our way tonight, but I just might finally get that cute little half-breed boy over here to check on his sick little friend. Now, let's get some rest and call it a night." Smiled Rodney.

While the incident to Curtis was not considered as a real threat by Vicki and Newman, no substantial consideration was made to find out what actually happened. The weekend went on as planned. Everyone involved enjoyed themselves. However, Leanna had to return by Sunday to be ready for work on Monday. It was early Sunday morning before Leanna arrived back at her midtown Missoula apartment. She set her suitcase on the floor and plopped down in the bed. Before long, she found herself fast asleep. Hours later she awoke and noticed the telephone answering machine by her bed blinking. She reached over and hit the playback button. The machine began repeating the various messages she had received. Several minutes into the playback, she recognized the voice of her best friend.

"This is Ava. Where have you been? I've tried calling you all day long on Saturday and no one answered. If I don't hear from you before

I go to bed today, I'm calling out the National Guard by Monday morning."

Leanna chuckled, then picked up the phone, punched in several numbers and waited.

"Ava, it's me. I'm in one piece, so you can relax, okay? When I got in today, I was a little tired. I laid down to rest before listening to my messages."

"But you're usually not a late night, weekend person. I was just worried."

"I went up to the Hot Springs to close that account. Instead of driving all the way back in the dark, I just spent a couple of nights and came back today."

"Spent the weekend?" thought Ava.

"In my own bed, thank you very much."

"So here I am worrying about you, and you're out partying the nights away."

"Oh, I wouldn't say that exactly, though I did use the hot tub."

"Oh, really."

"Yes, and I even went to a country music bar." Grinned Leanna.

"Oh, really?" Ava's tone expressed excitement. "Meet any nice guys?"

"Sort of. He's the manager. He even invited me back for this coming Labor Day weekend."

"Are you going?"

"I might."

"Oh, really?" Ava's voice brightened. "Must be some guy."

"Yes. We had a few hours together this weekend. Oh, did I mention that he's Black?"

"Oh, really," Ava's voice took a decidedly somber tone.

"Yea."

"Boy…" Ava sighed. "I didn't know there were Black people up in the Lolos."

"Well, there's at least one." Noted Leanna.

"Are you going to go?"

"I don't know. I've got a week to decide." Said Leanna.

"You know, interracial dating can be dangerous up in those parts."

"Down in these parts, too," Leanna added.

"Well you always said you had a sense of adventure. Do you think he's worth the effort?"

"I don't know. There's only one way to find out, though, isn't there?"

"Just be careful where you tread. The grass isn't always greener on the other side." Warned Ava.

"No. But I'll never know, unless I try to find out. I've some unpacking to do. I will see you Monday morning. Goodbye." Leanna hung up.

As Sunday evening went, Monday morning arrived. Newman was trying his best to maintain supplies for the Jamboree.

Newman held the phone dejectedly to his ear. "I understand we're on a cash-only basis." Newman explained. "But I've got the cash right here. Just send the deliveryman up. I'll give him the cash before he unloads one single tray of hot dog buns… Prepayment?… What's the difference between me driving all the way into Missoula to pay him and paying him when he gets there? I've got the cash right here." Newman held a money bag anxiously in his other hand. "No… well you think about it." Newman said angrily. "I've got five-hundred bread orders here. If you want it, then you'll get your buns up here." He slammed the phone down.

Vicki emerged from the back room carrying several small slips of paper. "Who was that?" She noted the look of exasperation on Newman's face.

"Oh, Woody over at Central Bakery. He wants me to come into town and pay for the order before he'll send a bun delivery up here."

"Did you tell him we had the money in full?"

"Of course. He said rules were rules for cash-only customers. You know, we could probably make out cheaper if we went into town and just bought the bread from a wholesaler. We'd have to rent a truck, but in the long run, it would be worth it, don't you think?"

"You can try it and see."

"It would solve one problem." Newman noted.

"Speaking of problems. I have the receipts from the bar last night. Rodney collected them early this morning."

"Did you ask him about Curtis?" asked Newman.

"I haven't seen him. He just left the money and the receipts on my desk." Vicki handed him the receipts. "Compare them. Remember you put the money back that you had already counted. Is it more or less than what we already had?"

Newman studied the slips. He stared at them in momentary silence. "Oh, boy." Newman sighed. "I had a few more choice adjectives, but 'oh, boy' will do for starters."

"What?"

"According to this, the total take for last night was $500 less than the sample we counted and put back in the till."

"Now, I can understand possibly not making any more money for the remainder of the night, but losing money that we'd already made?"

"How does he get the register receipts to match the cash he turns in?"

"Oldest trick in the book, Ken. He simply rings up a new receipt to match the amount he plans to turn in."

"So, he is stealing." Newman breathed deeply.

"No question. He's got to go… today," Vicki insisted. "I can tolerate a little theft, but not on this scale. At this rate, he'll have enough to open his own resort."

"When do you plan to fire him?"

"Me? I thought maybe you could fire him. I mean, you being the manager and all. You know, tell him it's not working out or something like that."

"But Vicki, you hired him."

"So? I made a mistake. Sometimes I take a chance on someone and I'm wrong. That happens."

Suddenly, the front door burst open, and Danny raced excitedly into the office.

"Slow down, young man." Newman admonished.

"Sorry Kenny. I just need the keys so I can get in and clean the pool this morning."

"Doesn't Toby Johnson pick those keys up in the morning?" Vicki asked.

"He burned his arm real bad last night, so he won't be working today."

"Really?" Vicki asked.

"Yeah, I talked to Rodney this morning at breakfast." Explained Danny. "He said they had to rush him to the hospital last night."

"Really?" Newman asked.

"Yeah. He said he'd like for me to go over to the store later and see how he's doing. So I'm going over there this morning before I go to clean the pool, if that's okay?"

"Sure, sure, Danny." Newman insisted. "Go on. And give Toby our best." Newman reached into the desk drawer and handed Danny a set of keys.

"Thanks, Kenny." Danny grabbed the keys and darted out the door.

Newman turned to Vicki. "You know, Toby getting burned could explain why Rodney may have almost run Curtis over. If my brother were badly burned, I might accidentally run over somebody too, trying to get him to a hospital."

"That still doesn't excuse the stealing. No, I want them all out of here today. I'll leave it up to you as to when and how to tell them."

"Well"… Newman pushed himself from the desk…"if there's one thing I learned in corporate offices, it's get your firings out of the way first. Otherwise, it'll hang over the rest of your day like a dark cloud. Besides, it'll probably take them several hours to pack." He stepped from behind the desk and walked over to the door. "Oh, I'm expecting a call from that girl from the Forest Service. If she calls, tell her I'll call her right back."

"Sure Ken." Vicki sat behind her desk and looked at the receipts shaking her head. Moments later, Newman climbed into his golf cart, but decided to have a bit of breakfast before he headed to the general store.

Meanwhile, Danny couldn't wait to see his friend Toby. In just two weeks they felt like the best of friends. Danny ran toward the General Store. He rushed up onto the front steps and pushed the door open.

"Toby," Danny called.

Nick stood behind the counter counting the cash in the register. He looked up as Danny entered.

"Hi, Danny. Toby is in the back bedroom. He's been asking about you. Go on back." He motioned toward the opened doorway.

Danny hurried into the back hallway. He looked down the empty corridor to see Toby emerging from a bedroom door. Danny noticed the huge white gauze taped to Toby's lower right arm.

"Toby?" Danny exclaimed.

"Shhhh…" Toby held his finger to his lips. Toby shook his head from side to side. "Rodney's asleep." He eased the door shut.

By the time Danny had reached the General Store, Newman was on his way there to fire them all.

Minutes later, at the main office. Vicki sat at the reception desk, her glasses perched on the tip of her nose, pressing one key at a time on the typewriter. She started rolling the paper out of the carriage when Curtis suddenly burst excitedly into the room, his gun drawn. Vicki shrieked at the sight of him brandishing the weapon.

"Curtis! Have you gone mad?" Vicki screamed. "Put that thing away!"

"Rodney…" Curtis asked, "Where is he?"

"He… he's at the store. My goodness, Curtis, even if you think that he did try to run you over, that's no reason to shoot him."

Curtis holstered the weapon. "Vicki," he excitedly began, "Rodney and that Nick fellow aren't brothers. They're escaped convicts."

Vicki gasped and her jaw dropped. "Convicts? Are you sure?"

"Yeah, the Oregon State Pen. Those two broke out a month and half ago."

"Now how do you know all this?"

"I got to thinking about them trying to run me down last night. So I called their license plate in to a buddy of mine who's still with the sheriff's office. The car is stolen. It belonged to a CPA in Yakima, Washington, named Rod Johnson. He's been missing for three weeks."

"My goodness." Vicki sighed somberly. "Did they…"

"Kill him?… They haven't found a body, but the police are pretty sure they killed him."

"How about Toby?" quizzed Vicki.

"They don't have any record of a little boy, but Thomas Hansen, the guy we call Rodney, is a convicted child molester and murderer.

The one we call Nick Johnson is really Nick Holland, doing time for murder one and drugs."

Vicki gasped, "Oh, Curtis." She cried. "Kenny's gone over there to fire them. You've got to do something!"

"Yes ma'am. Can I take the Jeep?"

Vicki reached in the drawer and handed him the keys. "Hurry."

He obediently replied and darted out the door. Vicki ran to the window to see Curtis hastily waddle off toward the Jeep, clutching his holster to keep it from flopping against his side.

Off in a distance the sound of approaching sirens became more and more pronounced. Newman thought the sirens he heard were for an accident that may had occurred up the road. His main thoughts were how he was going to break the news easy without confrontation. He continue his ride to the store, oblivious to Curtis or the reason for the sirens being so close.

Curtis saw Newman just crossing the bridge heading for the store. He blew the horn and yelled out the window.

"Ken!"

Newman didn't respond. He was almost upon the store. Curtis crossed the highway just in time to see a line of speeding police cars rounding the bend. Curtis slowed down. He waited until the lead car was plainly in sight, then motioned for the driver to follow him. He then continued on toward the store.

Inside the store, Nick kicked in the bedroom door, an Uzi machine gun cradled in his arm.

"Hey, wake up!" Nick demanded.

Thomas Hansen, *alias Rodney*, struggled to sit up in the bed.

"What?... What's the problem?" Hansen stammered, still groggy.

"Cops, lots of 'em. I saw 'em out the window. They know we're here."

Hansen immediately scrambled out of the bed. Nick tossed him the Uzi. Hansen snatched it out of midair. "How..."

"I don't know, but hear those sirens?" The chorus echoed through the store. "I saw that fat fucker Curtis leading 'em right straight to us."

Hansen looked solemnly up at Nick. "Where's Toby?"

"Forget about Toby. We're under siege."

"I ain't goin' back to the joint." Hansen said quietly.

"Hell, with that murder in Washington, we'll get the chair for sure. It's either die now or die later."

"I'll take the back side." Hansen volunteered. "You take the front. Anything that tries to come through that front door dies."

Nick hurried out of the bedroom, knelt behind the counter, and pulled a clip-fed assault rifle from the lower shelf.

Newman climbed up the porch steps, then turned to notice the steady stream of speeding police cars headed his way. He also noticed Curtis racing toward him, waving frantically.

"Ken!" Curtis called.

Newman waited momentarily. "What do you want, Curtis?"

He spoke as if annoyed. He grabbed the knob and twisted. He started to push the door open when Curtis leaped upon the porch and tackled him. His weight carried both men over the side, just as a burst of automatic weapons fire riddle the front door with bullets.

The police cars screeched to sudden stops at various positions around the store. Uniformed officers scampered out of their cars and took prone positions around the store. Weapons were drawn and aimed at the building. The sound of breaking window glass dinged from the store window onto the porch. Seconds later, a long barrel of an automatic rifle pointed through the remaining broken glass and began firing. Car tires popped like balloons, windshields were shattering one after another. Bullets riddled the side doors and hoods of the police cars until they looked like Swiss cheese. The police responded with volleys of shotgun and small arms fire. The shots peppered the wooden cabin leaving holes in the edifice. The sound of cans and broken bottles hitting the floor left no doubt that bullets were destroying the inside of the store. A fierce gun duel had erupted. The exchange of gunfire had both men trembling with fear.

Vicki anxiously watched the battle from her window. Suddenly, Rides bust into the office. "What the hell's going on over there?" He was unnerved by the gunfire.

"The so call, Johnson brothers. They are really escaped criminals."

"What?"

"Yeah, and now they are battling it out with the police."

"Oh, my God. Danny's over there!" Panic gripped his heart. "I've got to get to him!" Rides turned and bolted for the door.

Vicki immediately grabbed his arm. "You can't go over there," she insisted, holding his arm tightly. "Listen to that gunfire. You'd be dead before you got within ten yards of that place."

"Damn it! Vicki, my son's over there. He's in danger, and I'm going to get him!"

He tore his arm away from her and snatched the door open. Standing in the doorway was Danny and Toby, both breathing heavy and almost out of breath.

"Danny!" Rides screamed with joy. He knelt down, snatched Danny up in his arms, and pulled him tightly against his chest. Toby quietly looked on.

Curtis huddled on the ground next to Newman as bullets whizzed overhead. "What the hell is going on here?" Newman asked, scared and bewildered.

"Vicki hired two escaped killers as our accountants."

"The Johnson brothers?"

"Yeah, now shut up and keep your head down."

The shooting raged for nearly twenty minutes before the firing from inside the store began to subside.

Moments later there was silence. Newman and Curtis lay perfectly still. All was quiet. The police then slowly, carefully, inched their way closer to the store. Curtis and Newman remained huddled on the ground. Two officers took positions on either side of the front door, while other policemen took up various positions under the windows and at the back door.

The two officer at the front door nodded to each other. One officer then pointed his shotgun at the lock, then pulled the trigger. The blast exploded the lock. They kicked the door in and waited.

Seconds later, they both charged into the store. Two blast rang out. Then there was silence.

Several hours later, the large crowd that had gathered around the police line had begun to slowly dwindle. The coroner had loaded the last body into the ambulance as police car radios squawked and uniformed officers roamed the area around the store.

Vicki watched the activity from her doorway, while Newman stood at the foot of the steps.

"First John's suicide and now those two." Vicki said quietly. "That store has had more deaths in this one year…"

"Well, before I left, I saw inside the store. There are bullet holes everywhere. It's really in bad shape. By the way, what happened to Danny and Toby?" asked Newman.

"Danny is with his father. Toby went with the police. His real name is David MacKinnon, a runaway from Walnut Creek, California. Those convicts picked him up in Portland. That convict we knew as Rodney was sexually abusing him."

"Why didn't he just run when he had the chance?"

"Apparently, when they killed that CPA in Washington State. They said they'd tell the police David helped, if he tried to run."

"Poor kid." Newman sighed. "How did he and Danny get out of the store before the shooting started?"

"David, the little boy, said Nick burned his arm last night to provide an excuse for trying to run Curtis over. Apparently, Nick saw his badge and gun and thought he was a real police officer. It seems Hansen also had a sexual interest in Danny. But, David didn't want Danny to be abused the way he had. So he helped him escape this morning while Rodney, or whatever his name was, was still in bed, asleep."

"Poor kid," Newman shook his head. "I hope he can get his life back together. And by the way, where's Curtis?"

"He's over there, helping the police, where else?"

"I owe him an apology. He saved my life."

"He can have his moments."

"Oh, and Vicki"… Newman looked up at her…"before you hire any more accountants…"

"Yea, yea, I know."… Vicki acknowledged. "Check references." She sighed.

CHAPTER

17

As the gun battle between law enforcers and convicts had subsided, the Jamboree was revving up. The RV Park was packed with mobile homes of various shapes and sizes. Crowds lingered around some of the mammoth vehicles laughing, talking, and engaged in impromptu sing-alongs. People carrying guitar and trumpet cases walked back and forth across the highway between the stage platform in the park and the main resort complex. The parking lot was also packed with cars and trucks as the twang of varied country songs echoed throughout the compound. The entire resort had taken on a carnival atmosphere. An occasional tourist would scamper up the steps of the bullet-riddled general store, only to find the front door boarded up with a sign, 'Closed' for remodeling, nailed across the front. A huge crowd had gathered around the outdoor platform while a band in rhinestone-studded Western wear wailed from the stage. Couples danced and whirled on the dry green grass. Festivities were in high gear.

Newman sat at a long table outside the front office along with two other temporary young workers handing tickets to the small line of people who had gathered in front of them.

"Harry and Betty Rice," the cowboy in front of Newman laughed, hugging the woman next to him.

Newman scanned the list in front of him. His finger followed the line of letters in alphabetical order down the column. "Rice," he announced, "here you are." He pulled a couple of tickets from the box

443

on the table and handed them each one. They took the tickets. He then ushered the woman away from the table.

"How's it going?" Newman looked up to see Vicki standing in front of him.

"Ticket sales are brisk, very brisk."

"Yes, and after we pay the bands, figure in the three-day receipts from the hotel concession, the bar, restaurant, and other activities we should clear a tidy profit." Vicki smiled.

"Three day," Newman sighed dejectedly, "three days of nothing but country music."

"Oh, relax, Ken," Vicki patted him on the shoulder, "you'll have a good time too, I promise."

"Sure, Vicki," he skeptically agreed, "sure." Newman looked back down at his listing as another person walked up to his desk.

"Name please?" He asked without looking up from the list.

"Clark," the woman said.

"Miss, I really need a first name if I'm going to find your…" he looked up to see Leanna smiling down at him…"ticket. Leanna! What are you doing here?"

"You did invite me back up for the weekend, didn't you?"

"Yes, but when you didn't call, I thought…"

"Well, I'm here." Smiled Leanna.

"So you are." Newman looked over at Vicki. "Could you ah…?"

"Go," Vicki nodded…"I'll cover for you."

"You sure? If you got something else to do… I…"

"Go," Vicki reiterated, placing her hand on the back of his chair. "You two have fun."

Newman rose from the chair and stepped around the table. He and Leanna turned and walked away.

"Glad you could make it," he quietly began, "This is going to be a long weekend. I hope you can at least tolerate country music."

"I'm not a country fan, but if you live here long enough, you sort of develop a tolerance for it. It's just that I didn't realize there would be this many people here. I rented the last hotel room, or so Vicki told me."

"Probably so. The staff had to give up our hotel rooms to free all rooms for the guest. Most of the staff has doubled up, but I just made a bed in the back of the bar storage room. It's not the Ritz, but at least I don't have to share it with anybody."

"Why that's horrible."

"It's just for the weekend. Besides, no one can find me back there. It's probably the only place where I'll get some peace and quiet."

Leanna chuckled as they strolled across the highway over to the RV Park. "I heard about what happened at your general store." She noted the bullet riddle structure. "It must have been scary to have those kind of people around and not even know it."

"When you realize what they did and what they could have done, you're right. It is scary."

They strolled over to the crowd that had gathered around the stage platform. People were swaying and clapping to the music of the band. They turned and strolled along the path winding through the RV Park. Rows of RVs lined either side of the path, many with awnings overhanging the front entrance. Outdoor barbecues dotted the areas between the RVs, as did spirited volleyball and softball games.

"Any word on your transfer to Alaska?"

"No. While I've never been to Alaska before, I know its beautiful country. But still, sometimes I'm not really sure that I want to go," Leanna said uncertain.

"Why? Sounds like a great adventure."

"Yeah, but it's a long way from home and it's a place to be without any family or friends."

They came to a small bench next to a massive RV. A softball game was in progress in the adjacent vacant lot.

"What happened to that adventurous spirit?"

Leanna eased down on to the bench. "It's been tempered with a sense of reality."

Suddenly a softball came rolling over toward them. Newman looked up to see several people chasing the ball. He picked it up and tossed it back toward them. A man grabbed it, turned, and tossed it back toward the playing field.

"Thanks." He smiled, turning back toward Newman.

"No problem."

"What's for dinner tonight? Do you all know?" The man asked, smiling.

"Beg pardon." Leanna asked, bewildered.

"Ahhh… you two are with the Mattington family reunion, aren't you?"

Newman and Leanna looked at the man, then at each other. They both chuckled.

"No, I'm afraid not." Newman said.

The man blushed. "I'm sorry. It's just that this whole area has been leased for our family reunion. Everybody who wanders in here, well, we just assume they are family. You're welcome to join us anyway as my guest." He extended his hand. "Eric Mattington."

He and Newman shook hands. "Ken Newman, and this is Leanna Clark. I'm the resort manager."

"Really?" Mattington beamed. "Well, you are a man definitely well worth knowing. If you decide to join us, you're welcome."

"Thank you." Leanna smiled as Eric trotted back to the game. She and Newman looked at each other and laughed. "Family reunion?" They expressed disbelief of the comment. "Do we look like we're related?"

"Probably not. Husband and wife maybe?" They looked at each other momentarily, then shook their heads. "Naw!" They said almost in unison.

"You know Ken, I really enjoyed your company last weekend when I was here."

"The feeling was mutual. That's why I am so glad to see you. It seems we have so much in common, especially with country music."

Leanna laughed. "Yeah."

As the sun beamed down on them sitting in the open field, they were getting over heated.

"Want to grab a drink back at the bar?" asked Newman.

"Only if its lemon water."

"I meant water, but lemon water it is."

She and Newman strolled from the field. Newman inadvertently brushed her arm. "I'm sorry." Leanna grabbed his hand and squeezed.

Newman smiled and maintained the grip. Once they reached the main grounds, they noticed Vicki. She stood on the front steps, a guitar cradled in her arms while Nina stood next to her.

"Vicki!" Newman hailed. "I thought you were passing out tickets. Do you need me to go back there and help out?"

"No Ken. Everything is under control. Enjoy your day. I'm just having a little fun with Nina here."

Newman and Leanna continue their quest toward the bar.

Nina and Vicki resume their tasks at hand.

"What were you saying Nina?"

"Now, just let the neck rest in the palm of your hand," Nina instructed as she helped Vicki to position the guitar. Vicki struggled to comply with her instructions.

"Like this?"

"Yes, like that. Now strum softly."

Vicki ran her fingers gently over the strings and produced a few disjointed notes. "Oh, Nina," she sighed in resignation. "I'll never learn this."

"Don't give up so easily sugar," Nina consoled.

Suddenly, the door swung open. Tracy stood in the doorway,

"Vicki," Tracy announced cheerfully, "there's a call for you."

"Saved by the bell." Vicki smiled, handing the guitar back to Nina.

She followed Tracy back into the office. "I really appreciate this, Tracy… I mean you're helping out in the office until I can find a permanent replacement for Lisa."

"Oh, no problem Vicki. Since Mark's decided to stay until Jake's logging season is over, I will do anything I can to help out around here."

Vicki snatched up the phone, "Vicki Marshall," she listened tentatively, "Yes…" Her look turned to immediate frustration. "And why not?… No… Appeal that if you have to… Don't worry about the money, I'll get it!" She slammed the phone down.

Tracy appeared concerned. "Can I help with something?"

"No, no, not unless you personally know a circuit court judge."

"Beg pardon?"

"Nothing. Just thinking aloud. Say, I'm going to step back into my office. Would you ask Nina to come back and see me, please?"

"Sure Vicki."

Vicki disappeared into her office, with a sad, dejected look on her face.

By late evening, the crowd around the stage platform had swollen to several hundred. While the bar was packed almost beyond capacity with Western-dressed revelers dancing to the country beat. Newman stood behind the counter. He was serving drinks at a furious pace. Waitresses in skimpy cowgirl uniforms meandered through the crowd with trays of drinks perched delicately atop their opened palms. Newman planted a can of beer on the counter and took a bill from the customer. He turned to the register to ring up the sale only moments before Laura came to the counter.

"We're going to need another keg before long." Commented Laura.

"We're going to need a truckload of kegs at this pace." Newman noted. "Don't worry, I ordered enough beer to fill an ocean. It's only a matter of how fast we can shovel it out."

Laura deposited the cash and turned back to greet another customer.

Newman placed several bottles of beer and mixed drinks on a waitress's tray. She turned and waded back into the crowd.

"Bartender," a woman sitting at the counter hailed. Newman turned quickly in the direction of the voice. He stopped and smiled as he noticed Leanna sitting at the end of the counter, gingerly waving at him. He acknowledged and made his way down to her.

"How long have you been sitting here? I thought you went back to the hotel after I decided to stay and help Laura with this crowd."

"Oh, about half an hour. I came back to see if you were still back there." She smiled, nursing a small glass. "I thought you said you'd be off at ten." Leanna checked her watch. "What happened?"

"My temp bartender hasn't shown up yet. I can't leave Laura back here by herself, not with this crowd."

"Bartender!" An irate customer yelled.

"I'll be right back." Newman patted her hand and headed back down the counter.

Leanna sat patiently. She was carefully nursing her drink when a cowboy, palming a can of beer in one hand, swaggered over to her. He propped his elbow on the counter next to her.

"Hey baby." She squinted as his alcoholic breath blasted her in the face. "Let's say you and me light up the dance floor?" Leanna fidgeted, trying not to show her disdain.

"No, thank you." She forced a polite smile.

"What's a matter, baby? I ain't good enough for ya? Eh?" His anger was visibly displayed from her resistance.

"Maybe later, okay?"

"Ain't no later baby. You and me are here now! Wadda drinkin'?"

"Lemon water," Leanna volunteered, slightly frightened of the cowboy's advances.

"Hell lady, that ain't no drink." He turned to Newman, "Hey, barkeep!" He slammed his hand down on the counter. Newman hurried down to greet the man.

"Yes, sir?" He smiled.

"Two slow screws for me and my lady friend here." He put his arm around Leanna's shoulders and pulled her close. Instinctively, she struggled to push the man away, but his grip held firm. "Say baby," he slurred, "I'm just trying to be sociable."

"Say buddy…" Newman calmly began, "the lady doesn't want to be bothered, okay? So give it a rest, eh?"

"What?" The cowboy had difficulty hearing over the music.

The cowboy continued to grip Leanna. "Excuse me, sir," Newman pressed. The cowboy stopped, then slowly turned toward Newman and glared at him from across the counter.

"Look boy," he growled, "you… you just stick to pouring the drinks, eh? Stay outta things that don't concern you." He turned back toward Leanna. "Now baby, why you don't…"

"Look, mister," Newman insisted, "the lady says she doesn't want to be bothered."

The man turned toward Newman. "Sambo, listen…" the cowboy snarled. "this is white folks' business. Get yourself some watermelon or something and keep quiet."

He turned to Leanna again, puckered his lips and pressed then toward her.

Newman lunged across the counter and collared the man, pulling him forcefully into the counter. The cowboy brought up both arms and broke a bottle on the counter. Newman released his collar. The nearby patrons scrambled to get away from the exploding glass.

"Okay, Sambo," the cowboy sneered, heaving with anger, crouched and ready to fight, "let's see what you know."

The area grew quiet as he and Newman confronted each other.

"Look, I don't want to fight you. You're drunk, I'm sure we can talk…"

"Come on, nigger!"

The crowd gathered around the cowboy to see the impending fight.

Suddenly Mark stepped out of the crowd, grabbed the man by the shoulder and spun him around. The cowboy turned only to see a streaking fist rocketing toward his face. The blow sent him reeling backward against the counter. The broken bottle in his hand hit the floor. He fell between two stools and slowly slithered to a sitting position on the floor, eyes closed and head tilted to one side.

"All right, folks, show's over." Mark grimaced as he kissed his knuckles. Everyone slowly started back toward their tables.

"Friend of yours, Kenny?" He looked down at the man.

"What did you do that for?" Newman was irritated.

"Well, excuse me," Mark apologized sarcastically, "but from where I stood, it looked like he was getting ready to carve his initials in your chest."

"I was going to try and handle this without violence."

"Sure you were. Is that why you reached over the counter and nearly disrobed my man here?" He pointed to the unconscious man on the floor.

"Listen, Mr…" Leanna interrupted.

"Atkins, Mark, ma'am." Mark tipped his Stetson hat. "At your service."

"Mr. Atkins, I'm afraid Kenny was merely trying to assist me in repelling this gentleman's advances. Ken asked him nicely, but he just stared at him like… like…"

"He was a Martian, or something?" Mark interrupted.

"Very funny." Newman glared.

"I take it you two know each other." Mark surmised, pointing toward them.

"We're friends." Leanna volunteered, as if to dispel any notion of any serious romantic involvement.

"Well, Kenny, I suggest you and your friend here leave before sleeping beauty recovers from his nap."

"I can take care of myself," Newman said defiantly. "Besides, I can't leave Laura back here by herself."

Mark walked over to the counter and leaned toward him. "Listen, Ken, it's not a matter of being afraid. Rednecks always travel in packs. I know. I used to be one, remember? And before long, his buddies are going to come looking for him. And when he wakes up and tells his buddies what happened, they're gonna wanna tap dance all over your face."

"Hey…" Newman protested. "but you're the one who decked him."

"Look, Ken, all Tex here remembers of me is the design on my class ring. All he knows is that some Martian-lovin' cowboy decked him, and with all the cowboys in here tonight, he wouldn't know me from the man in the moon. You, on the other hand…"

"I get the picture." Newman interrupted.

"Hey, I'll take over for a couple of hours. When he comes to, he'll look around for you awhile, then give up and go home."

"What do you know about bartending?" Newman challenged. "It takes months of training to really be comfortable back here."

"Oh, just leave me the cheat book in your back pocket and I'll do just fine."

The cowboy on the floor began to stir.

"Let's go Kenny." Leanna insisted, grabbing his hand.

Mark stepped behind the counter. "Go on, you two. Enjoy the night."

Laura hurried over to them. "Will somebody please give me a hand here?" She impatiently insisted, scurrying along the counter.

"Go on." Mark insisted. "If we need you, we'll call."

Newman slowly walked around the end of the counter. Mark plucked the small booklet from Newman's back pocket. Leanna slid off the stool, and she and Newman excused their way through the crowd and out the door.

They slowly strolled hand in hand back along the moonlit trail toward the hotel. Newman paused and pointed at some stars.

"See that constellation over there?"

Leanna looked skyward. "Yeah."

"Know what that's called?"

"I have no idea."

"Me neither."

They both started laughing and gazed into each other eyes. Newman leaned slowly toward her lips. Just in case she decided not to kiss him, she could resist. But instead, to Newman's delight, she placed her arms around his neck and they kissed passionately. As they released from their embrace, Leanna started to walk away.

"Hey, wait." She turned toward Newman. "That was nice."

Leanna didn't acknowledge his comment, instead she changed the subject as they continued their walk. "What was all that business about Martians between you and that Mark Atkins?"

"It's a long story. Let's just say an old dog is trying to learn new tricks."

"Learning new tricks… is that why you agreed to tend bar for a country music audience?"

"No, Laura just needed help, that's all."

"It's just that I've never been accosted by a drunken cowboy before, and to be associated with a barroom brawl…"

"Hey, I'm sorry," Newman interrupted, mildly irritated at her apparent scolding. "I didn't intentionally put you in that situation. I certainly didn't plan to have a confrontation with that man back there."

"Okay, okay," Leanna insisted, stopping at the base of the hotel. "I just didn't understand why you took me in there, that's all. I just want you to know that beer and bars aren't my idea of a good time."

"That's one of the reasons I asked you to wait for me in your hotel room."

"You were taking too long. I came this weekend to have a good time with you and bars are not it."

"Really? Then what is?" Newman walked closer to her trying to resume where they left off only moments ago.

"No Ken, I don't want to move too fast."

"Then tell me, what's your idea of a good time?"

"Oh"… Leanna thought for a moment…"A movie, a quiet evening, good company, Yahtzee."

"Yahtzee?" questioned Newman.

"It's a board game."

"Sounds complicated."

"Not really. It's played with dice and scorecards. You add up your score at the end of each game, and whoever has the most point's wins."

"Okay." Newman shrugged his shoulders. "I understand it already."

"It's not that hard. Come on." Leanna grabbed his hand and pulled him up the stairs. "I have a board game in my room. I'll show you how to play."

She pulled him down the corridor until she came to her door. She produced her key. Pulled him into her room, closing the door behind him. Neither of them was aware of the peering eyes from the window several rooms away.

As Newman was about to learn a new board game, Mark and Laura were keeping glasses full. There was never a short order for drinks. The barroom was in full swing when the two cowboys stepped up to the counter. They stopped to notice the man still slumped between the stools. His ragged cowboy hat was pulled down over his face. They looked at each other, smiled, then leaned over to assist the cowboy.

"Hey, Mole," one man called, kneeling beside him. He straightened Mole's hat on his head. "Wake up," he commanded, gently slapping his face. Mole began to groan and grunt as he stirred awake.

"Damn it!" The other man cursed. He leaned over and both men helped Mole to his feet. "Send you over here for one bottle of Jack Daniels and what do you do? Pass out drunk."

Mark watched the exchange while trying not to seem interested.

Mole felt the left side of his jaw. "Drunk, hell," he moaned. "I was sucker punched."

"By who?"

"Shit if I know. Somebody just spun me around and hammered me while I was arguing with…" Then, as if recollection were a hammer, he spun quickly around and eagerly searched up and down the bar. "That nigger," he insisted, leaning over the counter to get a clear look behind the bar.

Mark casually walked over to him wiping his hands on a washcloth. "Yes sir, can I help you?" He smiled.

"That nigger that was back here. Where'd he go?"

"Nigger?" Mark asked innocently. He looked under the counter, "No. I don't see any nigger back here." He held up his index finger. "One minute, I'll check." He called to Laura. She came down to his end of the bar. "Say, this gentleman seems to have misplaced a nigger. You haven't seen one around here anywhere, have you?"

Laura thought momentarily, "No… wait a minute, maybe I have." She stepped over, raised the lid on the ice chest, and peered inside. "Nope. If we had any, they'd be in here. I like to keep 'em on ice, you know." She dropped the lid.

Mole looked at his friends. "Fuckin' comedians," he muttered. "Oh, come on. If there is a spear chunker in these parts, he shouldn't be too hard to find." They all laughed, turned, and walked away.

Meanwhile, Leanna tossed the dice onto the game board and waited until the cubes rolled to a stop. "Three of a kind," she smiled, as she recorded the score on her game sheet of paper.

"How do you do that?" Newman sighed, looking on in amazement.

"It's all in the wrist," Leanna gloated.

"But why does this game take so long? We've been at this for two hours, and we're only halfway through."

"What's your rush, Mr. Newman? Stay here and fight like a man."

"Well, now that its halftime, let me run back over to the compound just to see how things are going."

"Do you have to?"

"It won't take long, I promise."

Leanna pushed the board game aside dejectedly. "I wonder how they did it."

Newman looked at her curiously. "Did what?"

"Got along here before you came."

"Now what's that supposed to mean?" Newman was defensive.

Leanna rose from her seat. "Ken, its two o'clock in the morning, and you've been up since five this morning. Now I've seen people put in eight, ten, and sometimes even twelve hours a day, but twenty-four? Maybe the reason they can't do without you around here is because you won't let them do without you."

Newman pondered her words. She had hit so close to home that she actually caused him to reconsider going back to the resort just to prove her wrong. Though he had been putting in many long hours, he still wasn't sure if his importance to the resort was due, in large part, to his insistence that he be involved in all the resort activities.

"You know you're right." Newman agreed. He sat back down at the desk.

She pulled up her chair. "Get set to lose," she sneered.

He reached for the dice when suddenly a knock at the door broke their concentration.

"Who can that be?" Leanna whispered. She pushed her chair away from the table, walked over to the door.

"Maybe Laura or Mark."

She opened the door. "Can I help you?" She greeted the tall heavy set man standing in the doorway.

"Yes." He beamed politely. "I'm Reverend Peterson. Is Kenny in?"

Newman rose from his chair and walked to the door. "Reverend Peterson." Newman had stepped up behind Leanna. "How did you know I was here?"

"HE sees all," he replied, pointing toward the sky, "and so does my wife, who happened to see you two from our window down the hall." Peterson smiled.

"Is there a problem?"

"Not really Ken, it's just that there was such a large crowd at the bar tonight that Vicki kept the restaurant open later than usual for some after-dance munches. Well, they sort of made a small mess of the dining room, and you know how Nelson is. He won't start breakfast in a dirty kitchen. I was wondering if you could give me a hand for a few minutes."

Leanna looked at him somberly.

"Ahhh… sure," he agreed. Newman turned to her. "This shouldn't take long with two of us. I'll come right back and we'll finish our game."

"Sure," Leanna smiled halfheartedly.

He kissed her on the forehead and left with Reverend Peterson.

Leanna watched momentarily while they walked down the corridor and headed for the main complex. She then peeked down the hall to see the curtains close shut. She turned and eased the door closed.

"She seems like a really nice girl." Peterson casually noted as they started up the restaurant steps.

"She is."

"Now, I know it's none of my business or anything, but you've been one of the best Christian examples we've had here."

"I'm no saint."

"Compared to some of these drunken heathen loggers and cowboys, you are." He countered. "Don't underestimate yourself. In addition, well," he hesitated, "I think you know the Bible's position on sex between unmarried couples."

Newman looked at him, amazed that he would make such a statement. "You mean me and Leanna?"

"She's an attractive girl, Ken. Temptation can be strong."

"Well, I'll do my best to fight it." Newman assured as they entered the restaurant.

"It's only your eternal soul." Petersen quietly added.

It took them nearly an hour and a half to restack the chairs and to sweep and mop the dining room floor. Meanwhile, the bar crowd had begun to dissipate. Most of the crowd was walking and in many cases, staggering to their cars or across the highway to the RV park.

Reverend Peterson locked the restaurant door. "I'm calling it a night." He sighed with fatigue. "The door will lock behind me as soon as I go. You can exit through the bar and see how Laura is doing before you go to bed."

Peterson pulled the door shut as he left. Newman turned out the lights and headed to the bar.

Laura was darting from table to table, picking up empty bottles and glasses. The bar was virtually empty except for an occasional cowboy, his head buried in his elbow face down on the table.

"Laura," Newman noted, "how did it go tonight?"

"Well, she deliberately hesitated…"they didn't drink us dry, but it wasn't from a lack of trying. We also blew a fuse on one of the stage lights, but Andrew came by and he's fixing it. Other than that, it's been relatively quiet since you left."

"Where's Mark?"

"As things slowed down, I told him I could handle it. So he left about an hour ago."

"Okay, well, I will help you finish things up in here."

"Thanks Ken."

Ken grabbed a dishcloth and wiped down tables while Laura continued removing empty cans and bottles from the tabletops.

In the meantime, in the front parking lot, Mole's two friends were pawing and groping over two girls they had managed to entice into the backseat of their well-worn station wagon. Mole finally walked up to the front passenger's seat and leaned into the opened window.

"Damn it."

"What's wrong, Mole, honey?" One of the women asked coyly, with a cowboy's hat buried between her breasts.

"Ah… he's got nigger on the brain," the other man volunteered, pushing his girlfriend aside as he turned angrily toward Mole.

"I know that nigga is still here."

"Look, we searched the pool, the bar, the restaurant, and the RV Park, looking for some darkie who you say sucker punched you. We ain't seen no sign of him. Now let it rest. If there was a nigger here, he's probably long gone by now. So just get your ass in this car so we can get outta here." He turned his attention back toward his girlfriend. "So we can get it on," he sniggled as he jammed his hand quickly up her thigh. The woman screamed playfully.

Mole appeared thoroughly disgusted. He slammed his hand against the door. "I'm going to check that bar one more time."

Newman picked up the last chair, turned it upside down, and carefully set it atop a table.

"Thanks, Ken." Laura smiled, pushing the wide-angle broom across the floor. "I realize you didn't have to do this."

"Don't mention it. You'd do the same for me at three-thirty in the morning, I know." She didn't answer. "Did Andrew get the fuse box fixed? We're going to need it for tonight's concert."

"He said he had to find the proper fuse size, but that he'd have it fixed before tonight's concert."

"Well if you've got things under control here, I'm going back to Leanna and finish our board game."

"Board game? At three-thirty in the morning?" Laura was skeptical. "Sure, Ken, tell me anything."

"Really! A board game." Newman insisted. "She's got this weird game called Yoo-hoo or something, and we're halfway in the middle of it."

"Well, by all means, don't let me keep you away from you're…" she cleared her throat and winked, "board game."

"Actually, after about three sets into it, you can understand why they call it bored."

Mole casually stepped into the bar, mildly frustrated at not being able to find Newman. Neither Newman nor Laura noticed him as he walked in. Nor did they see his eyes light up with amazement at having finally found the elusive Newman.

"There you are!" Mole shouted, almost as if he were relieved to discover that Newman really existed.

Newman and Laura both turned to see him.

"You ran off before we could have our powwow, boy," Mole sneered. He reached into his pocket and pulled out a switchblade. The knife made an obvious click as he brandished it threateningly at Newman. "Come on, boy," he goaded, waving the knife menacingly, "let's see what you're made of."

Newman and Laura both watched as Mole's face beamed with excitement as he nervously fondled the knife handle.

Suddenly a hand grabbed his shoulder and spun him around. He whirled just in time to see a fist rocketing toward him. The impact of the blow sent him reeling against a table. He knocked over the stacked chairs as he lay sprawled on his back unconscious at Newman's feet.

Newman looked down at the cowboy, then slowly up at the doorway. Rides stood in the opening, massaging his fist, grimacing slightly.

"One of our creditors, I presume." Rides quipped as he stepped into the bar. "You know this guy?"

"It's a long story." Newman sighed.

"Well, spare me the details. I just came back to replace the fuse in the box, then I'm going to bed. It's almost four in the morning."

"You're right." Newman agreed. "I'd better go tell a certain lady good night and hit the hay myself. And since I'm sleeping in the bar storage room, I do mean hay in the strictest sense."

"Go ahead Ken," Laura said, sweeping around Mole. "I'm not opening this place until eleven in the morning anyway. I need to get some sleep too."

"How about sleeping beauty here?" Newman asked, pointing toward Mole.

"Don't worry," Laura volunteered, "I'll make sure he gets outta here." She brandished her broom. "Either walking or on a stretcher."

"Oh Ken, go out the back door of the kitchen. I saw some cowboys outside, they maybe friends of his."

"Thanks."

Newman did as Rides instructed. He walked back to Leanna's room and knocked. She answered the door in her night robe. "I didn't think you were coming back tonight."

She smiled, trying to fight back a yawn.

"Something came up that took longer than I expected. So why don't we finish our game some other time. I've got to get some sleep, too."

"Sure." She smiled. "I understand." Newman turned to leave. "In fact, you can spend the night here instead of in that dirty old storage room if you like?"

Leanna's blunt suggestion took him aback.

"Are you sure?"

"Sure. It's a double bed. We're both adults, and when I say sleep with me, I mean sleep, in its most elementary interpretation, understand?"

Newman smiled. "In the shape I'm in, I couldn't do anything else but."

She stood behind the door and opened it wide. As Newman walked in, she eased the door shut behind him. The opening between the two curtains in the window a few doors down also eased shut.

Newman didn't hesitate. He quietly eased onto the bed and within minutes, he was sound asleep. Leanna gazed upon his handsome face and masculine exterior and wondered why he took her seriously.

Leanna didn't sleep well. She was thinking about the man she had sleeping in her room. Her thoughts of a relationship between the two of them plague her all night long. Not being able to sleep, she rose early and went to the restaurant alone. Leanna sat at the table in the dining room scanning the breakfast menu when the waitress casually walked over to her table.

"Decided yet, ma'am?" She was blunt.

Leanna smiled at her. "Your Denver omelet looks very good. Would you recommend it?"

"I don't know, ma'am," she blandly replied. "I just serve it. I don't eat it."

"Your Denver omelet, please."

"Anything to drink?"

"Coffee. You do drink that, don't you?"

The waitress glared coldly down at her. She plucked the menu from Leanna's fingers, turned and walked away. She stepped behind the counter and placed the order on the kitchen ledge.

"Mile high chicken," she shouted back to the kitchen.

"One mile high comin' up." Nelson automatically replied.

Another waitress walked up to the window ledge. "Say, isn't that the girl who spent the night with Ken?" She whispered.

"Yeah," the other waitress coldly replied. "I've got a friend who has the room next-door to hers. She said she could hear her screaming, 'Yoo-hoo' all night long. Ken must be an animal."

"You know what they say. Those people have real big ones."

"Still, that ain't no reason for no self-respecting white woman to go around being no tramp like that."

At that moment the door swung open. One waitress turned in that direction. While the other one continued eying Leanna.

"Shhh, here comes Kenny."

"Huh?" She looked in the direction of the front door to see Newman entering the restaurant. "He probably forgot to pay her for last night." They both laughed.

Newman saw Leanna sitting at a table reading the morning paper. He walked over and slid into the seat across from her. "How come you just let me sleep in?"

Leanna lowered the paper to the table. "You were sleeping like a newborn. You obviously needed the rest."

"But I have work to do."

"You got several extra hours of sleep and guess what? This place obviously survived without you. Don't look so disappointed."

"But where did this come from." He reached into his pocket and produced a note that read, 'Vicki wants to see you.'

"Your reverend friend came by and knocked on the door. I told him that you were in the bed asleep and that I'd leave the note for you instead of waking you up to read it."

"He saw me in bed? With you?"

"Of course."

"Oh my." Newman sighed, leaning back in his chair.

"I don't see what the problem is."

"He probably thinks that you and I had sex together."

"So what?" said Leanna.

"By now, thanks to that bigmouthed old lady of his, your reputation around here is now just slightly above that of the town whore."

She leaned across the table toward him. "Ken, do you honestly think I'm going to lose any sleep over the impressions a bunch of racist rednecks have about me? We didn't have sex together. But even if we did, it would have been nobody's business but ours."

"But still…"

"But still nothing. I think, if the truth be known, that you're more concerned about your reputation than mine."

"Mine?" Newman became defensive.

"Yes. For months now, you've been the tireless Christian worker leading this ragtag band of ruffians on their journey back to respectability. Now, comes along this whore who entices you into sin, at least in the eyes of the reverend and some of your friends."

"That's ridiculous."

"Oh, yea? We'll see. Especially when I come back next week."

"Next week?"

"Sure. You didn't think you'd get out of finishing that game of Yahtzee that easy, did you?"

"No?" Newman hesitated.

"I can come back again, can't I?"

"Sure, I'd love to see you again." Newman emphatically replied.

"Good, then it's settled. If I'm going to lose my reputation, then by god I wanna do it in style."

The waitress walked over, unceremoniously plopped her plate down in front of her, turned, and left in a huff.

"See?" Leanna noted. "They're starting to like me already."

"Are you sure you want to put up with this crap?"

"Are you sure you want to put up with it, Mr. Newman?"

"I'm game if you are." He sighed.

"Good. Are you going to have breakfast with me?"

"No. I'm going to see what Vicki wants. She's never called me this early in the morning before."

"Maybe she's going to warn you against sleeping with me, too."

"Not likely." Newman rose from the table. "You be careful, young lady."

"I'll be fine." Leanna quickly added, "Take care of your business with Vicki."

Newman walked over to the office still concerned about Leanna. Her cavalier attitude toward the hostile feelings her presence had generated could leave her vulnerable to possible physical assault. But even more troubling was Vicki's note to him. It wasn't so much the fact that she left it, as it was the message's vague nature. To merely say she wanted to see him at six in the morning, without given a reason only added to the misgivings he felt about seeing her. He knocked on her office door. She beckoned him to come in. She sat behind her desk, casually flipping through papers, in a subdued, depressed mood. He had seen her in these moods before, but not quite this somber.

"Vicki," he gingerly asked, "is something wrong?"

"Sit down, Ken." She motioned toward the chair in front of her desk. Newman pulled up the chair and sat down. "You've put a lot of hours and sweat into helping me keep this place afloat, and I just wanted to say thanks."

"Is that what this is all about?" He was surprised.

"No. It's just that I wanted you to hear what I have to say from me and not through the rumor mill."

"Sounds serious."

"I've never walked away from a fight in my life and the battle to keep this resort and stay out of jail are both no exceptions. But I've come to the realization that I can't do both. The circuit court denied my appeal, and it looks like I'm going to have to mount an all-out fight before the State Supreme Court. And to do that I need cash, more cash than I have right now. And just from a physical standpoint, I can't run the resort, fight bankruptcy, and finance a Supreme Court fight, all at the same time. So in order to get the cash I need to eliminate the bankruptcy problem, I've decided to put the resort up for sale."

Newman stared at her, momentarily speechless. "Ahhhh…"

"I know I gave you my brave speech about fighting back from disaster and saving the resort, and I'm all too aware of the hours you've put into keeping this place going. I just didn't want you to hear about my plans to sale the resort secondhand."

"I see." Newman said somberly.

"You realize that new owners usually bring in their own management team."

"That's the way it usually works." Newman quietly agreed. "Well, when do you plan to put the place on the block?"

"It already is." Vicki said matter-of-factly. "I've even got a potential buyer."

"Really? So soon?" Newman was surprised again. "Who is it?"

Suddenly the front door opened, and Nina came barging in with her nose buried in a thick report.

"Vicki, darling. About this sale price on the gas station…" Nina stopped in midsentence when she noticed Newman seated in front of her desk. "I'm sorry, sugar. I didn't know you had company."

"Kenny, you know Nina, of course."

"Sure, of course."

"Well, she just might be the new owner of this resort."

Nina smiled as Newman looked on in total amazement.

CHAPTER
18

*L*eanna cradled the phone between her cheek and shoulder as she leafed through the report on her desk.

"No sir." She calmly explained, "That's not what the proposal says. I have it right here in front of me… Yes sir, I'm aware of the provisions and you certainly are right. We are calling for one thousand pounds of fryers… But sir, if you'll read the adjacent clause, those are frozen fryers, not live chickens… No, sir, I won't, but if you kill them and freeze them, I'll certainly consider it. Good day." She slammed the phone down.

"Temper, temper."

Leanna looked up to see Ava walking over to her desk. "Oh, just another deranged vendor. Apparently, he got hold of our proposal for 1,000 pounds of frozen fryers for the smoke jumpers training base. He offered us 700 live chickens, but we'd have to kill them and freeze them ourselves."

"Did you tell him this is the Forest Service, not Holly Farms?"

"Ava, I didn't tell him half of what I wanted to tell him."

"Speaking of telling, you didn't tell me how your three-day weekend went up at the resort."

"Oh, there's nothing much to tell, really. We relaxed in the hot tub, we went horseback riding, and we danced till the wee hours of the morning."

"Really, wow! Sounds like you had a good time."

"Well, that's what I wanted to do, anyway. What I ended up doing was getting involved in a bar fight, and I probably set the virtue of white womanhood back some one hundred years."

"Oh, yeah. That's right… you went back to see that colored manager they have, didn't you?"

"Black, Ava, Black. We aren't in the '50's anymore, dear."

"How did it go?"

"Okay, I guess. I think he likes me, although he worked most of the time I was up there with him. So we never really spent that much quality time together, but when I go up next weekend…"

"You're going up there again to see him?"

"Sure Ava. He's really a nice guy, and I like him."

"Have you told your mother yet?"

"No, but eventually I will."

"Leanna, how do you think she'll take it?"

"She'll probably freak, but so what? She's not dating him, I am. Besides it's not like I'm dying of cancer or anything. I'm just dating a guy I like. What's the big deal?"

Ava fidgeted slightly as she returned to her seat. She and Leanna had been best friends for years, and she had always felt secure approaching her on any subject… that is… any subject except this one.

"Leanna," she timidly began, "I know this is none of my business…"

"Since when has that stopped you from saying what was on your mind?" Leanna reassuringly smiled.

"Now, I'm not a racist or anything…"

"But?" Leanna quickly interjected.

"I don't think a racially mixed couple would be welcomed in Missoula or anywhere else in the entire Bitterroot area for that matter. For one thing, there aren't enough color… eh, black people here for you to be friends with. And a lot of the whites will be indifferent at best. Most will be downright hostile at worst. You two are doomed to have problems."

"And racially compatible couples don't have problems?" Leanna rationalized. "So in addition to the usual set of problems couples face, we'll have one more problem to deal with."

"And what if you get married and have children? They'll have problems, too."

"Whoa! Who said anything about marriage? We haven't got that far yet. So what if we did have children? So what? In addition to deciding whether to have sex before marriage, taking drugs, and whether they'll be popular in school, they'll just have one more problem to deal with."

"And your mother?" asked Ava.

"She'll probably be angry, just as she was when I went to MSU instead of U of M, and the time I went to the prom with Harvey Chapman instead of George Westinghouse. George wanted to be a doctor, and Mom said he'd make a better date than Harvey. But, like all of those other times I did things she didn't like, she'll get over it."

"And if she doesn't?"

"Then I'll have to deal with that if it happens."

"You sound so sure of yourself."

"I'm not. Like any other potential relationship. I don't know what's going to happen in the future. But I do know, I will never find out, if I don't ever give it a try."

Suddenly the clanging wheels of a pushcart rolled up to her desk. Both women looked up to see a young man standing over a tray cart filled with envelopes and packages.

"This one's for you." He smiled, reaching into his basket. He pulled out an envelope and handed it to Leanna. Leanna read the return address as the boy rolled the mail cart away.

"It's from Alaska," she noted, examining the envelope.

"Well, open it." Ava urged impatiently.

Leanna tore the end of the envelope and removed the contents. Ava eagerly watched her as she read the letter.

"Looks like this whole conversation has been for nothing." Leanna said quietly. She looked up with growing excitement in her eyes. "I got my promotion, and I'm going to Alaska." She announced excitedly.

As Leanna was rejoicing over the news of her long awaited promotion. Newman knelt beside the rose bed, carefully pulling the fireweeds from among the roses. This was about his fourth attempt to remove this stubborn growth from the bed. It seemed every time he tried to remove them, they grew back stronger.

"Having fun down there?"

Newman looked up to see Nina smiling down at him.

"I didn't know you had a green thumb."

"I don't." Newman climbed to his feet brushing the dirt from his hands. "It's just that this has been an ongoing battle ever since the fire this past summer. And no matter how hard we've tried, we just can't seem to get rid of them."

"Then why don't you just leave them alone? If they're that determined to stay, they simply shouldn't be removed."

"I guess you're right. It's just that this is Vicki's prize rose bed, and she's put a lot of effort into it."

"Kind of like this resort, eh?"

"I guess," he agreed nonchalantly.

"Look, Ken." Nina started down the steps. "I know you aren't all that thrilled with the possibility of me taking over this resort. You and Vicki seem to work well together. But if you're concerned about losing your job, then don't be. I've seen you work around here, and the workers respect you. If you can hold this operation together with these low-caliber workers, just think of what you can do with some money and a first-class crew."

Newman smiled. "Thanks for the vote of confidence, Nina, but you don't understand. It's not the job that I was after, it was the challenge of doing something I'd never done before in a place I'd never been before. Helping Vicki bring this place back from the brink of death when everybody else said it couldn't be done… that feeling of accomplishment is worth more than any money can buy. Anybody can run a resort with the proper financing and top-notch personnel, but to accomplish what we did, with what we had, is something I'll remember for the rest of my life."

"I admire your spirit of adventure. However, I hope you will consider my offer. I'm sure we can agree on a salary to your liking. I haven't made her an offer yet, so take a few days to think it over, okay?"

"Sure, Nina. Maybe we can agree on an offer I can't refuse."

"Just call me the Godmother, sugar." She patted him on the shoulder and walked away. Newman knelt down and resumed plucking the fireweeds.

The front door opened, and Mark stood in the doorway, holding Tracy's hand. He gave her a kiss. "Honey, I might work a little late. Vicki and I are going over some figures."

"Okay, babe," Mark smiled…"but don't stay too late, okay?"

"I won't," she readily agreed.

Tracy closed the door. Mark started down the steps and noticed Newman in the rose bed at the bottom of the stairwell. "Gardening now?" Mark joked.

"In case Vicki sells the resort and Nina fires all of us, I'll need to do something to make a living."

"Who's kidding who? I was just in the office, and I overheard Nina telling Vicki she'd love to keep you as her manager."

"Yeah, I know. She just told me."

"Why don't you climb out of that rose bed and walk over and get some lunch with me?"

"Sounds good to me." Newman brushed the dirt from his pants.

He and Mark started casually walking toward the restaurant.

"Well, are you going to stay?"

"I really don't think so, Mark. I'm not really interested in this kind of work. I kind of got wrapped up in Vicki's efforts to save this place. I don't know why, I just did. But now that she might be leaving, I don't think there is any reason for me to hang around."

"If you go, then good luck." Mark extended his hand, "I mean that." They shook hands. "I guess I haven't met many Black people in my life, but of all the ones I could have met, I'm glad I met you first."

"For a redneck, you didn't turn out too bad either." Newman smiled. "How about you and Tracy, are you both going to hang around?"

"I don't think so. Tracy wants to start her own business in Spokane, and besides, I'm going to be a daddy soon."

"That's right. Boy or girl. Do you know?"

"Boy," Mark said emphatically, "definitely a boy. She wanted a girl, but boys don't get pregnant when they turn fourteen."

"Good point."

"And how about you and that nice young lady I saw you with Labor Day weekend. She definitely had some class about her. Plus, she seems to have more than one working brain cell, unlike some of these amoebas floating around here."

"Leanna? Yes, she is nice, but boy, I don't know. Seems like she's really interest in me and I could really get interested in her but…"

"But what?"

"There are so many differences between us. Seems like we're from two different worlds."

"You're a Martian and she's not."

"Among other things."

"Seems like a couple of months ago, I had the same problem and a wise old sage had some helpful words of wisdom for me."

Newman chuckled. "In the future, if you see a wise old sage, run like hell."

"If you love each other, everything else will eventually fall in place, right?"

As they stepped into the restaurant, Nelson came running over to them. "Ken, Ken," Nelson excitedly began, "is it true that Vicki is going to jail and leaving you in control of the resort?"

Newman looked at the excited Nelson momentarily, then over at Mark. "It's going to be a long day."

While Newman and Mark discussed their future at the resort over lunch, Rides was still trying to put Band-Aids on major issues to keep the resort running smooth.

Rides scampered up the office steps and entered to find the front desk vacant. "Is anybody home?"

Tracy poked her head out of Vicki's office. "In here, Andrew. Vicki will be there in just a minute. We're adding some figures together right now."

"Sure, I can wait. But, just tell Vicki that I'm going to get the filter pump for the pool. I'll pay for it and she can give me the money back later when she has the time."

"Sure." Tracy smiled. "I'll tell her." She disappeared back inside the office.

Rides turned to leave when the phone rang.

Tracy poked her head back outside the door and asked. "Be a dear and get that for us Andrew."

"Sure." Rides walked over to the desk and snatched up the phone. "Hot Springs Resort."

"Hello, this is the Daniel Train Agency, and I have a $20,000 cash award for a Mr. Andrew Rides-at-the-Door. Could you tell me if he's there?"

Rides' face grew pale with panic. He froze, the phone still to his ear. "Ahhh…" Words couldn't form quickly enough for a response.

"Hello?" The caller asked.

"Ahhh… no, there's no one here by that name." Rides nervously replied.

"Well, he might be using the last name of Rides or Door. He'd really hate it if he missed out on this $20,000 cash reward."

"He's not here," Rides insisted. "Good-bye." He slammed the phone down.

"Who was that?" Tracy called.

"Oh, nobody. Just a wrong number."

"If you hold on Andrew, Vicki said she will get the money for you."

Rides watched Tracy go back into the office. He immediately rushed out the front doors.

Back at the restaurant, Newman was trying to simplify things for Nelson about the resort not belonging to him no matter what happens with Vicki.

"So you see, Nelson," Newman explained. "Vicki is trying to sell the resort to Nina to get the money to keep from going to jail."

Nelson leaned on the counter, his chin propped on his palm. "I'm glad you cleared that up. Rumors have been flying around here ever since word of the sale leaked out."

"Well, put out the straight scoop, will ya? Before wild rumors spread all over the compound." Newman admonished. He looked around the sparsely filled dining room. "Did you see where Mark went?"

Nelson quietly pointed toward the bar. "Where else?"

Newman left the restaurant and headed to the bar. Mark was sitting at the counter talking to Laura in the otherwise empty bar. Laura looked up as Newman entered.

"Kenny," she smiled broadly. "Come on in." She motioned him toward the bar. Newman skeptically walked over to her, unsure of her sudden burst of affection.

"I know you don't drink this early in the day, but can I get you a Coke or something?"

"Ah… I guess so," Newman agreed, gingerly approaching the bar.

Laura reached under the counter and produced a can of Coca-Cola. "How does it feel to own your own resort? You know, I've done a pretty good job here, haven't I?"

"Laura." Newman held up his hand to stop her.

"You know. I've always thought you were a great guy to work for."

"Laura! Enough! I don't own this place. Vicki's trying to sell it to Nina Thompson."

Laura looked stunned. "You mean she's not giving it to you before she goes to jail?"

Newman shook his head. "No. I'm sorry."

She eased the Coke can back under the counter.

"Hey! What about my Coke?"

"Buy your own can. Seventy-five-cents-cash, buster."

"How soon they turn." Mark jokingly noted.

Tracy suddenly appeared in the tavern doorway. Mark and Newman turned to greet her.

"Honey!" Mark smiled. "I thought you and Vicki would be tied up all morning working with those figures for the resort sale."

She walked over to them. "We are, dear, it's just that Andrew came by for money to buy a filter pump for the pool, but he left before she could give it to him. Vicki told me to find him and give him the money, but I can't find him. I thought he might be over here."

"I'll find him and give it to him." Newman volunteered. "He's probably working on a project somewhere."

Mark grabbed Tracy around the waist and pulled her close to him. She halfhearted pulled away.

"Not now, silly," she playfully protested. "I still got work to do." She gave him a brief kiss on his lips. "That'll have to do for now, okay?" She turned to Ken and handed him the envelope. "Tell him there's $300 in there. Vicki said to let her know if he needs more. She'll give it to him later."

Newman took the envelope from her. "I'll find him. He's got to be around somewhere."

Newman left the bar in search of Rides and Tracy followed Newman out the door. Mark turned back to Laura and began another conversation.

While everyone was diligently contemplating their next move with the resort up for grabs, Reverend Peterson and Millie were praying for the right move to make, since the resort was up for sale. Reverend Peterson knelt quietly, his head bowed and hands clasped. Millie stood quietly a few feet behind him, her head bowed and fingers intertwined in front of her.

Several minutes later, he rose, crossed himself, and turned toward Millie. "Aren't you through yet?" He coarsely asked.

She crossed herself and looked up at him. "Now I am. How many times do I have to tell you that Father sometimes talks to me longer than he does to you?"

"That's only because you are so hard of hearing that He has to repeat everything He tells you."

"That's not true." Her feelings were emotionally shaken by the comment. "That's a terrible thing to say."

Peterson walked over to her and gave her a big hug. "Just kidding, darling. You can't do God's work without a little sense of humor." He slowly released her. "What did he say about Kenny?" He started walking toward their living room.

"He's been committing fornication with that girl. He's no longer morally fit to manage this resort. And with Vicki going to jail, this place is going to need a new leader. And I can't think of anyone better qualified than you."

"You know, Father was telling me the same thing. But have you heard the news? When she goes to jail, she's going to leave Kenny in charge. She might even give him the whole resort. How can he lead this place while he's wallowing in sin?"

Millie sighed as she eased down on the sofa. "You can't be a leader without moral character and it's obvious that Vicki doesn't have it, what with her crimes. And with Ken sleeping with that jezebel, he can't provide the moral leadership this place needs, either. And you're right, you can."

"Maybe we can talk Vicki into leaving it to us."

"Why would she do that?" asked Millie.

"We're good Christian people. What other reason do you need?"

"You're right, honey. It never hurts to just ask."

They both smiled at each other.

As the Peterson's are contemplating electing themselves as the new resort managers, Newman walked up the steps to Rides' cabin. He noticed Rides' car packed to the ceiling with household belongings. Normally, he would be out around the grounds, performing some chore. So finding him here, this time of the day was very unusual. He knocked on the door.

"Andrew!" No one answered. "Andrew!" He turned the knob, and the door opened. Newman peeped in. "Hello?"

The cabin was nearly vacant except for a few color portraits of Indian chiefs mounted over the fireplace. Rides appeared in the bedroom doorway, holding a box nearly overflowing with packed belongings. He paused momentarily to gain recognition of the intruder in front of him.

"Ken, you startled me. I didn't hear you come in."

Newman looked around the near-empty cabin. "Is there a garage sale or something going on?"

Rides walked past him and set the box on the dining room table. "Look, I know this is sudden, but I'm leaving. It has nothing to do with you or Vicki. In fact, I heard you bought the place. Congratulations."

"No wait, why the sudden departure? I thought we were friends? I'm at least entitled to an explanation."

Danny appeared in the doorway with an armful of towels. "How about these, Daddy?"

"No, leave those white ones here. Just the colored and print towels, son."

Danny darted back into the bedroom.

"Great kid, isn't he?" Rides noted.

"Sure is," Newman agreed.

"He's my whole life. I tried to tell his mother that, but she doesn't think I really love him as much as I do. His voice grew somber, and his eyes became distant as he spoke. "I met his mother when I was a Captain in the Army, stationed in Germany. She was a West German ambassador's daughter and very beautiful, of course. She only knew of the Native American from the cowboy movies she had seen on West German television. Well, we got married, and we had Daniel. But then things started falling apart. She felt Rides-at-the-Door was too Indian, so she asked me to shorten it to Rides. I loved her, so I went along, although I felt I was denying part of myself in the process." He paused, almost tearful.

Newman listened intently. "Go on."

"Well, when I got out of the Army, I took a job with this electrical engineering firm and brought her to the states. She didn't have to work… her father saw to that. Her sole concern was Danny's welfare. I wanted to teach him about his native culture and heritage. To her, if it wasn't European, he didn't need to know it. That and a few other things led to our divorce. She got custody. I got to see him every weekend. Still, I'd teach him the ways of my people, the Flatheads. She found out and got so angry she made plans to move back to West Germany. I'd never see Danny again. So one day I cleaned out my savings account, picked up Danny for my usual weekend visit, and we've been running ever since."

Newman was speechless. He could only imagine the impact such a life on the run was having on Danny. "What does he think happened to his mother?"

"She left and went back to West Germany. That's what I told him. And that's how it's going to stay for a while."

"Then why run? She doesn't know you and Danny are here."

"She and her father hired this private detective agency to track us down, and they are good, I mean real good. They have dogged me across this country, and they know that I am here."

"How do they know that?"

"They called today. They said they had a cash award for me. But when they said Rides-at-the-Door instead of just Rides, I knew they were working for my ex-wife."

"What kind of life is this for Danny?"

Rides paused momentarily. "It's a life with me, his Indian father," he replied confidently. "That's all that matters."

"How long do you think you can keep running?"

"As long as it takes," he said emphatically, "as long as it take."

Newman stepped over and embraced him in a hug. "Good luck my friend," he said, lump-throated. He backed away and they shook hands. "I'll always remember everything you taught me."

"I hope so. I'd hate to think all that training was for nothing." Rides smiled. Danny reappeared in the doorway.

"Daddy, that's everything in the bedrooms."

"Go wait in the car son."

Danny immediately complied with his father's instructions.

Newman dug into his pocket and pulled out an envelope. "Here." He placed the envelope in Rides' hand. "Take this."

Rides opened the envelope and fingered through the contents. "Hey, I can't take this."

"Go ahead. Something tells me I won't be able to forward your last paycheck to you, so take it."

"You sure?"

"Positive."

Rides folded the envelope and placed it in his back pocket. "Thanks. Well, I've got to go."

"Drive carefully."

"Always." Rides grabbed Newman's shoulder briefly, then walked out the door.

Newman fought back tears as he waited. He heard the car door slam, the engine start, and the car pull away.

He looked around the empty room momentarily, then dejectedly walked out of the cabin. He stepped out just in time to see the car turn around the bend and then out of sight. So emotionally hurt from losing a best friend, Newman decided to have a small drink of coke from the restaurant to drown his sorrow.

As Newman entered the restaurant, his mood was somber as he stepped through the front door of the dining room. It was empty except for Millie who stood behind the counter trading conversation with Reese as he swiveled casually on the counter stool.

Millie looked up as he walked in. "Kenny!" She hailed. "You're just the man I wanted to see." He walked over to her.

"What's the problem?" His voice reflected a sense of sadness. She looked at him, concerned with his obviously depressed tone of speech.

"Is something wrong? You sound like you just lost your best friend."

He stared at her, startled by the surreal truth in her statement. He forced a smile. "No, I'm fine. I guess I should be asking what your problem is."

Millie held up a menu. "I was just telling my husband here that we have all this stuff listed on our menu. Yet we don't have half the ingredients to make the dish. Here, look," she insisted, pointing to an item and handing the menu to Newman, "our dieter's dish. Says here we serve it with cottage cheese."

"There's not a single container of cottage cheese back there," Reese interrupted. "I know, because I wanted some." He tittered.

"And that's not all," Millie continued, "look here…"

"I get the idea," Newman interrupted, easing onto the counter stool next to Reese. "Where's Nelson?"

"Where else?" She huffed. "In the bar, getting plowed. Honestly, Ken, I'm getting sick and tired of covering for that drunken heathen. He hasn't been to one of Reese's sermons since he's been here, and if anyone needs to have his soul saved…"

"I get the message." Newman coldly interrupted. He handed the menu back to her. "I'll see about getting you more supplies."

"And while you're at it, maybe you can do something about getting us another waitress too," Reese commented.

"Really? Is something wrong?"

Millie nodded toward the corner. "Look over there." Angie leaned, angled over the table, her legs wobbling uneasily as she struggled to steady herself.

"She's been like that all evening." Millie sneered. "If she's going to work here, at least she aughta be sober. One slobbering drunk back here is enough."

"Maybe you should send her home to sleep it off." Newman suggested.

"Maybe you should fire her and send her back to Mom and Dad so they can foot her booze bill." Reese advised.

Newman swiveled around on his stool. "Angie?" She didn't respond. Newman noticed how she struggled to stand erect, then turned uneasily and faced him. Her eyes were glazed, and her legs trembled. "Angie?" Again, no response. Newman genuinely became concerned.

She took a step, then slowly slithered to the floor in a heap. "Angie!" Newman screamed. He leaped from the stool, rushed over, and knelt beside her. "Angie?" Newman called, hoping the sound of his voice would awaken her now slumber. She didn't respond. He propped her head. He felt her pulse. Her skin was cold and clammy.

"Don't worry about her," Reese casually commented. "You should just let her lay there until she sobers up. It'll serve her right reporting for duty in this condition. Smell her breath. She probably smells like a brewery."

Newman leaned forward and inhaled near her mouth. "Smells like she swallowed a bottle of nail polish remover," he noted, surprised.

"Nail polish?" Reese echoed.

Newman momentarily pondered the smell. Suddenly he sprang alert. "Quick!" He pointed to Reese. "Get the Life Flight up here… now!" He cradled her limp body in his arms.

"She's just drunk." Reese opposed the suggestion. "No point in dragging that helicopter all the way up here for a drunken waitress. Just let her sleep it off."

Newman struggled to his feet with Angie in his arms. "She's not drunk! Now call!" Her appearance mounted serious concern. Newman thought back to his military training. "Millie, I need a Coke."

"A Coke?" Millie was confused by the request. "Not a cup of hot coffee?"

"Damn it! Get me a Coke or anything with sugar in it," he bitterly commanded.

Newman rushed her over to the counter and laid her gently on the surface. Millie handed him a glass of soda while Reese dialed the emergency number.

It was several minutes later, as Newman heard the methodical whirl of the helicopter rotors outside in the parking lot. Minutes later, the paramedics had Angie strapped to the gurney.

"Kenny," she meekly muttered, holding tight to this hand.

"Relax, Angela," Newman gently consoled. "This nice young lady's going to take good care of you." He smiled, pointing to the young nurse next to her.

"What… what happened?" Angie looked around, confused.

"That's enough talk," the nurse softly commanded. "We'll take it from here."

Newman gently patted, then released her hand as the medics wheeled her out of the dining room.

"She is a minor," the nurse noted. "We will need to contact her parents."

"I know." Newman handed her a slip of paper. "Here's their number. Will she be all right?"

"She's coherent, that's a plus," the nurse sighed. "We'll have to get her sugar level stabilized, but that shouldn't be too hard. How did you know she was in a diabetic coma?"

"I smelled her breath for alcohol, and I smelled nail polish remover instead."

"Ahhh!" She reasoned, "Acetone breathe, very good. Too often people mistake a diabetic coma for intoxication because the symptoms are so similar."

Newman glanced over at Millie and Reese as they watched him. "Don't I know it."

"Hey, well I've got to run. I'll keep you posted." The nurse dashed out of the door.

Newman stepped over to the window and watched as the chopper slowly lifted off and angled toward the mountains.

"I didn't know…" Millie somberly began. Newman looked back over his shoulder at her. "I actually thought she was drunk."

"Well, maybe if you were a little less judgmental and a little more compassionate, you could avoid these kind of mistakes. Excuse me." Newman walked away.

Reese and Millie were left staring at each other, dumbfounded.

C H A P T E R
19

ark struggled to hold his end of the huge box while Newman strained to hold the other end. "Take your end more to the left," Mark instructed, his voice straining. Newman complied. "Let's just ease it down." They gradually lowered the box until it hit with a mild thud on the concrete floor. Mark huffed and puffed. "Boy, what's in this thing, a dead body?"

Newman blew. "No, close though. It's a filter pump for the swimming pool. The old one was just leaving too many impurities in the water."

"Now with Andrew gone and everything, who's going to install it?"

"Oh, the company's sending someone out tomorrow. It's just that we save a seventy-five-dollar delivery fee by bringing it out ourselves."

Mark shook his head. "Boy, it's too bad about Andrew leaving so sudden. Must have been a death in the family or something like that."

"Yea, something like that."

They both started out of the pool house.

"By the way, have you heard anything about Angela?" Mark asked.

"Her mother called to say she's home now. She's not coming back to work. She's just going to stay home and be a high school student for a while."

"Well, at least she's okay. Say, if Nina buys the resort, have you decided if you're going to stay?"

"I really don't know Mark. I don't think so. This place is not just a job, it's an adventure."

"Boy, isn't that ever original?"

"Seriously, I didn't come here for the job. I was just trying to help Vicki meet the challenge of pulling this place out of the fire."

Mark opened the door for Newman and followed him out of the pool house. They drove toward the main office.

"If you don't mind me asking," Mark began, "if she had succeeded, what was in it for you? I mean, I've seen you put in some long hours, but also put up with shit that the average white boy wouldn't put up with. You get $300 a month plus room and board, just like everybody else, yet, you worked like you have an investment here."

"For one thing, I'm not your average white boy." Newman chuckled. "And you're right, I don't have any claim on this place except for my $300 a month and room and board. But you know Vicki, her sense of mission can be infectious. Had she succeeded in pulling this off, it probably would have been, to coin a phrase, one of the greatest comebacks since Chrysler."

"And you would have helped to engineer it."

"You betcha. And you can't place a price tag on that sense of accomplishment."

"Well, after the baby's born, Tracy is going to open up her dress shop in Spokane."

"And how about you? You're not cut out to be a househusband."

"Maybe not, but I can see being a kept man for a while." Mark smiled. "I mean it's a tough job…"

"But somebody's got to do it." Newman interrupted.

As they reached the parking lot, they noticed Tracy coming down the steps of the front office. She saw Mark and Newman walking her way. She waved to greet them.

"Hi, babe." Mark smiled as Tracy walked up and kissed him.

"Well," she sighed, grabbing Mark around the waist. "The deed is done," Tracy somberly announced.

"What deed?" Mark asked, confused.

"You know, the sale of the resort. Vicki and I have finished the figures on the net worth agreement, the creditors have all agreed to the sale, and Nina has accepted the terms. Everybody has signed the contract except Vicki."

"Why hasn't she signed?" Newman asked.

"Something about proofreading the contract, but I expect she'll sign it sometime today. Oh, by the way"… she turned toward Newman… "She wants to see you."

"Me? Did she say what for?"

"Nope."

Newman wondered, what so concerned her, that she wanted to see him on such an important occasion as this. He headed toward the office.

Tracy turned back toward Mark, "So, this is almost the end of Vicki's reign as queen of this resort. It's almost like the end of an era."

"What with the problems she's got, you'd think she'd be relieved, even overjoyed, to get this nightmare off her back."

"You'd think so Mark, but actually, I've never seen a woman more depressed. It's as if she doesn't want to let go."

Newman soon reached the office and knocked once on her door.

"Come on in, Kenny," she quietly beckoned.

Newman entered to see her leafing quietly through the huge document on her desk. She shoved a nearby envelope toward him. "That's for you."

He picked up the envelope and fingered through the cash inside.

"That's for the pump you bought and a little extra for all you've done around here."

"Vicki, this really isn't necessary."

"Yes it is. I'm glad you gave that money to Andrew. I just wish I'd known that he was leaving. I would have given him more. He was very valuable around here."

"He knew that Vicki, and I'm sure he would have appreciated the thought."

"Did he say anything about trying to reconcile with his ex-wife over Danny's future?"

"Nothing positive, just a couple of vague promises."

"Too bad. That's a good boy and he deserves a better life."

Newman walked over and sat down in front of her. "Speaking of lives, what does yours look like now? I saw Tracy, and she said that you and Nina had come to terms on the sale."

"Sale? Robbery is more like it. They put people in jail for what she's doing to me. But I guess a bad deal is better than no deal at all."

Vicki dejectedly looked down at the documents in front of her. She picked it up and weighed it carefully in her palm. "All I have to do is sign this, and it's all over. Nina gets the resort, my creditors get paid, I get a little cash, but after my appeals are over, I'll probably be penniless, and I may even still have to go to jail."

"Maybe with the resort out of your hair, you can concentrate more on your defense and you won't have to go to jail."

"I've never lost at business, Ken, never. When I bought my first hotel, a run-down dump in Eugene, Oregon, they said I'd never make it. I turned it into a profitable chain within three years. When I sold it and bought the Crown Plaza in Great Falls, they said it would be a mistake. I was able to sell it for three million in five years. When I bought this place, I knew it could be a showplace. If only that no-good son of mine hadn't…" She caught herself in midsentence. "Life is full of maybes."

"When you give it your best, that's all you can give."

"Are you staying on with Nina? She promised me there'd be a place for you here, if you wanted it."

"Thanks, Vicki, but I think I'm going on to DC. I have relatives there who have been expecting me since the first of the year. And this has been without a doubt, the longest side trip I've ever taken."

She chuckled. "Yea, well I think I've earned myself a long trip, too. Someplace where I never have to hear the words bankruptcy, Secret Service, or FBI again."

"I think you've earned it too, Vicki."

"And how about that nice young lady I've seen you with? Does she know you're thinking about leaving?"

"No. But she's coming up tonight to spend the weekend. I'll mention it to her then."

"You two have been seeing each other for over a month now. Seems like a shame. You two seem so happy together."

"She is a very warm loving person," Newman agreed. "But I don't know if we have enough in common to build a strong relationship."

"If you stop comparing skin shades and see what's in your hearts, you may find you have more in common than you think."

"It's not the skin color. I'm just not sure she looks at me that way. But, I'll give it some thought. Ahhh… When does Nina officially take over?"

"As soon as I sign this document. She is going to make her grand announcement during her band's live performance tonight."

Newman rose from his chair. "Knowing Nina, it should be quite a show. In fact, I'd better get over to the bar and help Laura set up for it."

"Fine. Will you find Tracy and ask her to come back here? I want her to answer all my calls for a while. I don't want to be disturbed."

"Sure, Vicki."

Newman closed the door behind him as he left.

Vicki stared at the document with a glazed, dejected look on her face. She turned the document to the last page and eyed the line for her signature. All that she had worked so hard for, for so many years, was about to be gone with one stoke of the pen. When she started to sign the document, the pen trembled in her hand.

The evening grew late, the Friday night crowd had packed the parking lot as usual. However, in the center of the neatly parked rows of cars, sat Nina's huge RV, large neon signs mounted on each side boldly flashing Thompson Department Stores. Inside the bar, the country tunes blared from the band onstage as the packed crowd danced and whirled to the Western beat.

Nina watched the crowd, clapping and smiling as Tracy and Mark stood beside her.

"How come she hasn't signed the dammed thing?" Nina cursed, still trying to maintain her smile as she clapped in time to the music.

"I don't know. She let me go over two hours ago," Tracy answered. "I'd been taking her calls all day. She had locked the door and wouldn't let anybody in."

"Damn it, I can't announce my ownership until she signs the contract. I don't understand. She's had all day. Where's Ken? Maybe he can see what her holdup is."

"When I left the office, his girlfriend had just come in for the weekend. He's helping her check into her room."

"He'd better get over there and talk some sense into her before she blows the whole deal." Mark added.

As the discussion heated up about Vicki, Newman was following Leanna up the hotel steps, struggling slightly with her suitcase.

"Are you staying the weekend, or the month?"

"Just a few essentials," Leanna continued down the corridor. "Yahtzee board, Trivial Pursuit, and of course, that old standby, Monopoly."

"I see."

Leanna opened her door. As she and Newman started to enter, Newman noticed Millie coming down the hallway.

"Millie!" He waved as she approached. "I'd like you to meet my girlfriend, Leanna Clark. Leanna, this is Millie Peterson, Reverend Peterson's wife."

"Leanna," Millie acknowledged blandly, but politely.

Leanna could feel the icy, self-righteous manner of her presence.

"Will you two be attending the announcement at the bar tonight?"

Leanna turned to Newman. "What announcement?"

"Vicki's selling the resort. Nina Thompson is buying it, and Nina plans an announcement tonight at the bar." Added Newman.

"I normally don't attend functions at bars, but my husband and I feel Ms. Thompson may need a strong Christian hand to guide her through the transfer period."

"Leanna will be staying the weekend, so we'll get a chance to drop by your husband's church services."

"I hope so Ken," she coldly replied. "I truly hope so." She continued down the walkway. Newman eased the door shut behind them as they walked into the room.

"Hypocrite," Leanna muttered.

"What?"

"I said hypocrite." Newman tossed her suitcase onto the bed. "She's so full of her sense of holiness that Mother Teresa would probably have to beg her for forgiveness. I wouldn't attend her church if it was the last one on earth."

"I think you're judging her a little harshly."

"I don't think so. Besides, it's not only me she disdains. To merely be here with you, only proves that I'm a fallen woman. You, on the other hand, have yielded to temptation. Hence your fall from grace is definitely more serious."

"What temptation?"

"Sex. Isn't that all we've had since we met?" Leanna opened the suitcase and began removing the contents.

"I still think you're misjudging Millie."

"It doesn't matter. It is really none of her business what we do. I doubt if she is going to lose any sleep tonight over how I feel about her."

Newman sat in the chair across from her as she darted between the closet and her suitcase. "Do you want to go to the bar with me to hear the announcement?"

"After my last experience over there? Not on your life. I'll read about it in the paper, thank you very much. How is the sale going to affect you?"

"Nina's asked me to stay on, but I don't think so. She's got the cash to hire anyone she chooses."

"Then have you thought about what you'll do?"

"Probably go on to Washington, D.C., like I had planned before I got sidetracked here."

"Oh," she replied. "Then I guess it's probably just as well that my promotion in Alaska was approved."

"Really!" Newman was excited and stood up. "That's great news, isn't it?"

"Sure is," Leanna replied, trying to sound confident. "I've been applying for that job for nearly a year and a half."

They both were silent. They were trying to avoid the question that both of them wanted to ask. Did this mean the end of their relationship? He knew how much that promotion meant to her, and asking her to give it up just so they could stay together seemed out of the question. Even if she agreed to give up her promotion, he wasn't sure if he wanted to stay in Montana. Would she quit her job and follow him to Washington, D.C.? Not likely.

"Looks like we have a questionable future," Newman blurted.

She looked over at him as if his remark had broken the barrier for discussion.

"Do we?"

"I mean, you're going to Alaska, I'm going to D.C. You can't get more questionable than that."

"Do we really care for each other that way?"

"Leanna, I know we haven't known each other very long, but somehow I feel like you and I... its fate. I have never felt this way about anyone before Colle..." He paused. "You aren't married with children are you?"

"What?"

"Don't answer that."

"I feel the same way, Kenny."

"So what are we going to do?"

"You know, there's nothing really keeping you here. Other than your family, there's not really anything waiting for you in D.C. I realize family is important, but you've lived without family being nearby when you were in Washington State, didn't you?"

"What's your point?"

"You know, Alaska really isn't a bad place to live."

"You mean follow you to Alaska?" He paced the floor in deliberation of her words. His tone was a little harsh. "Are you serious?"

"It's just a thought," Leanna added, sensing his obvious disbelief and his underlying hostility. "It was a bad idea. I'm sorry."

"Leanna," he began pacing the floor again, "What will I do in Alaska? I hate cold weather, and I hear its dark six months a year."

"Partially true. It's no colder there in the winter than it is here in Montana and it's never dark all the time... there's twilight in the evening, during the winter months."

Newman paused, moved by her rationale. "You know," he softly began, "you could come to D.C."

"It's a nice place to live, but moving there would mean resigning my job and waiting for an opening with the Forest Service there. If there were an opening. In the meantime, both of us would have to depend on your relatives for support."

"Well, let's just stay here."

"Let's just drop the subject for now." She insisted in frustration. "We may not have much of a future, but what we do have is very real here and now. Let's just concentrate on that, okay?"

"But…"

"No, buts. I'm here, you're here. We're alone. Forget the silly old announcement at the bar. If someone comes banging at the door, we're not in, agreed?"

"Agreed." Newman smiled. "Now what do you want to do?" Leanna smiled. "If you don't know, you're probably right, we don't have much of a future."

"It's just that, the last time I tried to kiss you, you didn't seemed to want me too."

"That was almost four weeks ago. At the time I really wasn't sure you felt about me the same way I was feeling about you. I didn't want you to think I was easy."

"And now…?"

"Now I know that our feelings are mutual."

Newman smiled. "And no, let's play Ya Whooo?"

"Yes, I do want to play… with you."

"And I you, Ms. Clark." Newman walked over to a CD player he had placed in her room. He pushed the button and Marvin Gaye's Sexual Healing echoed the room. "May I have this dance?"

"What, no country music?"

"Not this time, Ms. Clark."

Leanna smiled. Newman stepped close to her and gently pulled her into his arms. They began to slow dance across the room. As they gazed into each other's eyes, their lips met in a seal of affection.

While Newman was getting better acquainted with Leanna, Nina nervously checked her watch. It was almost midnight. The barroom was still going strong, but she had expected Vicki to be there by now. She wanted to make the announcement jointly with her, but if Vicki didn't want to take part in the announcement, that was fine, too. However, Nina still needed the signed contract to move forward.

"Nina!" She turned to see Jake, in a blue Western-cut suit, Stetson hat, and shined cowboy boots, standing next to her.

"Jake," she greeted, "I'm waiting for that wife of yours to get over here with that contract."

"I saw her about four hours ago. She was still reading it. I told her I was getting dressed for the evening, make a run to the hills to check on my men and come back here."

"What was there to read? We've been over it more than a hundred times. She's just stalling."

"Now hold on," Jake growled defensively. "Vicki ain't never welched on a deal in her life, and I don't think she's gonna start with you."

"You don't suppose she decided to keep the resort, do you?"

"Maybe, but whatever she does, you can bet she'll shoot straight with ya."

Tracy tapped Nina on the shoulder. "I'll go see what's keeping her."

"Tell her if she doesn't get over here this minute," Jake jokingly threatened, "I'm comin' over and draggin' her out of that office myself."

"That should get her over here real fast." Tracy smiled.

"You want me to go with you babe?" asked Mark.

"No, honey. I'll be right back with Vicki."

"Ok. Then I'll have another drink for the both of us." Mark smiled.

Tracy made her way through the crowd, out of the bar.

Minutes later, Tracy had reached the main office. The reception desk was vacant. Everything was still in place, just the way she left it.

"Vicki!" Tracy called. No one answered. "Vicki, they're waiting for you at the bar." Still no answer.

Tracy walked back to her office and knocked on the door. "Vicki!" She twisted the knob. The door was locked. "Vicki, I know you're in there." Tracy called confidently. She knocked gently on the door. Still silence.

She walked behind the reception desk and pulled the main key from the rack of keys on the wall, then returned to Vicki's office door. "Vicki," she inserted the key in the lock. "Jake said if you didn't come this minute…"

She pushed the door open and looked up from the lock. She froze in horror. Vicki sat slumped over her desk. "Vicki!" She dashed over to her desk and pulled her upright in her chair. She remained limp, her lifeless eyes staring blankly at the ceiling. Tracy checked for a pulse on her neck. There was none. She reached for the phone and dialed. Without hesitation Tracy hopped back into the Jeep and headed for the bar in sheer panic.

Suddenly, Tracy burst into the bar and frantically shoved people aside trying to get to Jake and Nina.

"What's keeping Tracy?" asked Jake.

Nina wondered to herself. "Tracy's been gone for over fifteen minutes Jake. If Vicki changed her mind, boy…"

"Relax, woman," Jake interrupted. "I know my wife, and if she has a problem, she'll let you know." He turned from Nina and continued to drank his beer and listen to the country music.

Nina turned and noticed Tracy making her way through the crowd. No Vicki in sight. Tracy finally reached them, almost out of breath.

"What's wrong Sugar?" Nina asked. "Is Vicki with you?"

"She's dead!" Tracy blurted excitedly. "I found her dead!"

Jake overheard Tracy over the music. "Who's dead?"

"Vicki. She was dead at her desk."

Jake dropped his glass and tore through the crowd for the exit. "Call an ambulance!" He shouted.

"I already did." Tracy responded. She started to get Mark at the bar.

"Did she sign the contract Tracy?"

Tracy looked back at her. "What?" She was unsure of Nina's question.

Nina bolted after Jake. "Check to see if she signed the contract!"

While the news of Vicki's death was spreading throughout the resort, Newman and Leanna had slowly danced their way to the bed kissing each other the entire time. As the music continued to play, he began unbuttoning her blouse as she unbuttoned his shirt. He looked up from their kisses and muttered, "Millie Peterson, eat your heart out." He gently eased her down onto the bed and playtime began.

He held and kissed her breast passionately as she cupped the back of his neck softly, holding his head as he roamed her body. She released small moans of sexual pleasure. The time mattered not, as they kissed and caressed each other, seemingly lost in their passion. They would stop momentarily and smile at each other. He then would lower his lips slowly back down onto hers, and the kissing and caressing continue.

Moments later, she gently pulled away from him. He gazed down at her as she smiled up at him. Though there was silence, it was as if the thought of completing the act of making love had occurred to each of them simultaneously.

"Enough foreplay, I want you Mr. Newman."

He slowly climbed off the bed, stood up and began unzipping his pants and let it drop to the floor. She lay on the bed, smiling at him, fumbling with the zipper on her skirt. Newman began to assist her in removing her skirt, when a frantic banging began on the door.

Both instantaneously looked at the door, startled by the noise. Leanna held her finger up to her lips. "Shhhh," she whispered, "they don't have to know we're here."

Newman froze, hoping the banging would go away.

"Kenny, it's me. Tracy. Vicki's dead."

Newman looked at Leanna, startled. He put his pants back on, ran to the door and snatched it open.

Tracy stood in the doorway, tears streaming down her face. She began rambling-rapid-fire.

"Kenny, it's awful. She was just sitting there. I checked her pulse. She wasn't breathing or anything… I got Jake and…"

"Slow down, Tracy. What happened?"

"It's Vicki. She's dead."

"How?"

"Heart attack at her desk."

Newman scrambled back to the bed, grabbed his shirt and stepped into his shoes. "Let's go." He buttoned his shirt as he followed Tracy out the door. "Where's Mark?"

"Back at the bar. He's squeamish about death."

At the front office, a large crowd had gathered around the building. Parked in front of the entrance was a green Forest Service vehicle with a flashing yellow light twirling atop the cab. Newman frantically pushed his way through the crowd. Tracy followed close behind. A uniformed

Forest Ranger stood on the steps of the building. He blocked Newman's path as he came charging up the steps.

"Let me in!" Newman insisted.

"I'm sorry," the Ranger politely, but forcefully insisted, "no one but immediate family."

"I'm the manager of this place." Newman angrily persisted.

Jake opened the door and stepped out onto the front porch. "It's all right," he told the Ranger. "Let him in."

The Ranger stepped to one side as Newman bolted up the stairs.

"There's nothing you can do, Ken." He began somberly, "These guys are from the range station at the Idaho base camp up the road. They heard the radio call to Missoula General and came over. The medics said she's been dead for several hours. There's nothing anybody can do. It was a massive heart attack. They say she must have went quickly."

Newman sighed, as his throat began to lump. "Is there anything I can do for you?"

"Not for me. What you could do is take these keys." He pulled a clump of keys from his pocket and handed then to Newman. "Go open up the kitchen. Put on some hot coffee and doughnuts for these people. A lot of them know her, and they said they just want to stay for a while."

"Sure, Jake." Newman took the keys and slowly descended the steps. Tracy followed.

It was almost an hour later before the coroner's wagon arrived. A small group of people gathered at the dining room window to watch the long black vinyl bag being loaded into the station wagon. Still, others sat somberly at various tables scattered around the dining room. Some nursed a slowly cooling cup of coffee, while others just sat quietly. A calm silence in the air. Leanna and Tracy walked from table to table, quietly refilling coffee cups. Newman kept an eye on the dwindling supply of donuts that slowly vanished from the various trays scattered around the dining room.

Leanna walked up to Newman to get another pot of coffee. "Are you ok babe?"

"Thank you for helping out. I'm fine. Here's that coffee."

Newman turned to set a fresh tray of pastries on the counter, when he noticed Nina staring quietly at the coroner's wagon as it backed out of the parking lot. He poured a fresh cup of coffee and took it over to her.

"Here," he handed her the coffee, "maybe this will help."

Nina looked over at him, then took the cup and smiled. "Boy, this is awful," she sighed.

"Yes, I know." Newman agreed. "It's an unexpected loss."

"I'll say," she quietly stated. "She didn't even sign the contract." She shook her head in despair.

She watched the station wagon turn onto the highway and speed down the road. Nina looked back over at Newman, who was staring quietly at her in disbelief at her apparent insensitivity.

"Nina how can you think of business at a time like this?"

"Oh, don't get me wrong, Ken. Of course, I'm saddened by her untimely passing, but the reality of the situation is that now the future of this place is up in the air."

"I don't see why. The creditors and the bankruptcy court agreed to your buying the resort. So instead of buying it from Vicki, you buy it from the creditors."

"That's true, were it not for a small matter of Mitch Cameron, Vicki's partner."

"Vicki never told me about him. I thought she and Jake owned this place."

"No. Jake never wanted anything to do with this resort. But the owner was selling and when he met Vicki, Jake talked Vicki into buying the resort. He saw it as an opportunity for her to get this place fairly cheap and for them to be together."

"So how does Cameron come into the picture?"

"Vicki had about ten million in assets with her hotel business. The owner wanted seven million for the resort. Vicki didn't want to dissolve practically all of her assets to buy the resort, so she called some of her associates who may have wanted in on the deal. She asked me, but, I'm all over the place and wasn't interested at the time. She asked Colleen. She wanted the controlling fifty-one percent, and she asked Cameron and he agreed to forty-nine percent of the business. I am telling you Ken, Vicki had this place running like a well-oiled machine. Everyone was on salary. She had three chefs for evening dinners. Waitress were in cowgirl uniforms. Live bands after seven. She was making an annual profit of two mil for over five years. They were doing so well that's when they decided to take a two year vacation and enjoy the fruits of their labor. So she let her son handle her assets while they were gone. That's when everything came crashing down. Vicki used her half of her remaining funds for Carl's bail and trial. And she used Jake's funds and her money, what was left, for her own trial. Now here we are at this given point in time."

"So how does Cameron just move in like he has?"

"There's a clause in her partnership that states in the event of a partner's death, the other partner inherits the deceased partner's interest. Since Vicki had the controlling interest, she didn't need that weasel's permission to sell. But now, he's got her controlling interest as well as his own. Since he wasn't involved in our original contract, he's not bound by any of the terms."

"In English please. What are you saying?"

"I'm saying that Cameron owns this place now. Since he is under no immediate pressure for cash like Vicki was, he may very well scrap the entire agreement. Keep the place or try and renegotiate a new deal. A deal that very well may not include you staying on. To be frank, Cameron isn't a big champion of equal rights, if you get my meaning."

"I know, he told me."

"Then you know why I was really hoping she had signed that contract. I could have kept my pledge to her and see that you had a spot here… if, of course, you wanted it. I believe Vicki was innocent of everything. The only thing she was ever guilty of, was trusting her son."

"Sure," Newman sighed skeptically, "sure. You don't have to save face with me."

"Listen, you may think ill of me for standing here talking business while Vicki's body isn't even cold yet. But that's the way the game is played from up here," Nina said matter-of-factly. "You view death only as to how it affects your balance sheet. You mourn too long and you get run over. Believe me, if it were me in that wagon and Vicki was standing here, she'd be talking the same way. Pity is strictly for losers."

Newman's disdain for her suddenly peaked. Even if she were right, her cold, callous attitude so soon after Vicki's death left him wondering if she weren't completely devoid of any human compassion.

"Well, especially for Vicki's sake," he said sternly. "I hope to hell you're wrong."

Nina said nothing further. She could see the compassion and sympathy Newman had for Vicki. Her corporate-like attitude was not striking home with him.

It was nearly four in the morning before everyone had left the restaurant. Newman locked the door. He and Leanna made their way back to her hotel room. Newman lay on the bed and stared blankly at the slowly revolving ceiling fan. Leanna sat quietly, her chin propped dejectedly in her palm on the table. She could see Newman's chest slowly rising and falling as he gave an occasional sigh.

"You've got to get some sleep. You've been up all night."

"I can't sleep," he answered somberly.

Leanna rose from her chair and walked over to him. She eased down on the bed beside him, reached over, and gently placed his arm around her neck as she placed her head gently upon his chest.

Late morning, came quickly for Newman. He quietly left the hotel room, leaving Leanna asleep on the bed. The crisp morning air signaled the onset of fall. He didn't know what Jake's plans were for handling the business matters for the next few days. He thought he'd check in with Jake to at least see what he could do to assist him.

He buttoned his brown leather jacket and headed for the office. The parking lot was sparsely filled with a few cars and several eighteen-wheelers scattered about the grounds. Nina's RV was still parked in the middle of the lot. Newman saw her standing in front of the RV, scraping the morning frost from the windshield of the RV.

Newman walked up to her. "Hey, those things are supposed to defrost themselves, aren't they?"

"You'd think for the price I paid for this thing, it would do more than defrost itself. But the defroster has been broken for months. I keep putting off getting it fixed."

"I'm going by to see Jake and see if I can be of some help."

"Oh, you don't know, do you? Jake's up in the hills with his logging crew."

Newman was surprised. "Really?...Nina. Who does he expect will make the executive-level decisions necessary to run this place with him up in the hills?"

"Jake's not authorized to make executive decisions concerning this place. His name was never on the deed. The only one who can do that is Cameron."

"Really? Well, Jake should at least be here until Cameron can be notified and can get here."

"Boy, you really haven't heard. Cameron's already here. He flew in this morning on his private jet, no less. He's in the office with Tracy. He's trying to make sense of the disaster in there, that Vicki called an office."

"Really? Well, I've met Cameron before." Newman started to walk away. "I need to at least see what his plans are."

"Ken, Cameron is an asshole. Don't expect anything other than the behavior of an asshole from him."

Newman was unsure of what Nina meant. Even though he was a bigot, business was all he seemed interested in. Considering that Nina was intentionally vague, it led him to believe that she knew something she either couldn't or didn't want to tell him. He headed to the office with a twinge of reservation. This was the first time he had walked into the office with someone other than Vicki sitting behind the manager's desk. Being the business man Cameron was, surely he would need his assistance until he could hire his own replacement.

Newman soon entered the office to find Tracy sitting at the reception desk. Her fingers were dancing swiftly over the typewriter keys. She stopped and turned to greet Newman when he entered. "Kenny!" Tracy smiled. "I've been wondering where you were. Ever since Mr. Cameron arrived, things around here have been going crazy."

"Well, why didn't somebody come and get me if you needed me over here? Usually nobody has any reservations about pulling me out of bed at awful hours to come to the office to help solve a problem."

"Cameron hasn't told you?"

"Told me what?"

Suddenly, Cameron emerged from Vicki's office grasping a stack of papers. "Tracy, what is this mess?" He asked angrily, shaking the papers at her. He noticed Newman standing at the desk. "Kenny!" He smiled broadly. "I heard you had been up all night, so I didn't want to disturb your rest."

He handed the papers to Tracy. "I want to say thanks for all the help you were to Vicki," he somberly began. "She often told me what an asset you were and I'm sure she'd want you to know that."

"Thank you." He could almost feel the patronizing tone and the hesitance in his voice, the way he seemed to be building up to something. The way a rejection letter begins with glowing tributes, before finally telling you to seek employment elsewhere. "Well, what's you game plan?" Newman asked confidently.

"I'm not selling the place, that's for damned sure. And certainly not for the price Nina tried to get it for." Cameron chuckled. "I'm going to see if I can raise the value of the place a little and, who knows, maybe even get out of debt. If not, I'll just unload it piece by piece for what I can get."

"Well, if I can help, let me know."

Cameron put his hand on Newman's shoulder. "You know, I'm glad you brought that up, Ken. Like I said, you've done a great job here for Vicki. But… well, for what I want to do, I'm going to need someone with a little more extensive hotel management experience. Your back ground is public relations, right?"

Newman nodded. "Yes."

"So I'm going to hire a new manager here in the near future so I can get the expert help I'll need to turn the place around. In the meantime, Millie has agreed to fill in the manager's slot until I can hire my new manager."

"Millie?" Newman was totally surprised.

"Yes. Reverend Peterson's wife. You've met her, haven't you?"

"Yes, but…"

"She's in Vicki's office right now helping me make sense of Vicki's filing system. You've been back there, haven't you? It's a nightmare."

"I'm sure it is."

"So just leave any keys you might have with Tracy here and"… he paused and thought for a moment…"You're not receiving any special manager's salary, are you?"

"Nope." Newman replied matter-of-factly.

"Just checking." Cameron smiled. He turned to head back into Vicki's office, then stopped and turned back toward Newman. "Give that pretty young lady you've been seeing a big kiss for me, huh?"

"Ahhhh… sure thing." Newman paused. "How did you know about Lea…"

"Boy, I tell ya, when Millie told me about you two, I could only be proud of the progress this country has made in race relations. Why, just a couple of years ago, if a white woman and a colored man shared a room together, they'd be run outta town on a rail or worse, you know?"

"Yes, I know." Newman blandly replied.

He turned to leave, then stopped again, "Say you don't think I replaced you as manager because you're sleeping with a white woman, do you?"

"Perish the thought." Newman sarcastically replied.

"Good. Like I told you earlier, I'm not a big NAACP supporter or anything, but I don't have anything against you people."

"That's comforting news."

"So you just go on back. Take the day off and report back here in the morning. By then I'll have your new assignments all figured out for you."

"Thank you," Newman smiled. Cameron turned and disappeared back into Vicki's office.

Newman quietly watched the closed door, then shook his head in disgust. "Yea, nigga work." He muttered.

"I'm sorry, Ken." Tracy said quietly.

"Hey, don't worry about it. You're not responsible for the stupidity of others." Newman consoled. He walked over to her desk. "He just gave me my exit cue."

"You're leaving?"

"You don't think I could work for a man like that, do you?"

"I guess not." Tracy sympathized.

"I guess after Vicki died, my welcome here died, too. It's ironic, but I do believe had she not chosen to fight her conviction and had taken her four months in that minimum security prison, she'd be alive today." He picked up the phone and punched in seven numbers.

"Who are you calling?"

"Yes," he answered, speaking into the phone, "when is you next bus to D.C.?... I see. And the one after that... and how much is a one-way ticket?... Thank you." Newman put the phone down.

"So," Tracy sighed, "you're leaving."

"Got to. My job's finished here."

"You know you've got some final money coming. Where do you want it sent?"

"Tracy, keep it. Something tells me that by the time Cameron gets through here, it won't even be the $300 I would normally get. So, keep it." He stretched out his arms to her. Tracy came from around the desk and gave Newman a kiss on the cheek and a strong hug. "Good luck to you and Mark."

Tracy patted her stomach. "If it's a boy, his name's gonna be Kenneth."

Newman smiled and walked out the front door. As he stood on the front steps, he scanned the area and reminisced about all the events that had taken place and the people he had met. He took a breath of fresh air and exhaled. He descended the steps and went back to his hotel room to tell Leanna his decision.

EPILOGUE

few days later, after the funeral, Newman and Leanna were ready to leave the resort and start their individual journeys. Leanna repeatedly struggled to close the car's trunk until finally the latch locked and the lid stayed down.

"Say, is there room for this?" Leanna looked down to see Newman holding up a small black-and-white television set.

"Bring it on down," she called skeptically, checking the space in the backseat of her car, "but I'm running out of space down here."

"I guess I shouldn't have sold by VW Bus. But I didn't think it would make the trip and the more money I had in my pocket when I got to D.C. the better off I thought I would be."

"No problem. We'll make everything fit."

"Well, I've got another box up here, and I'd like to get it in there if I can." Newman walked back into the room.

"Okay, I'll try to squeeze it in but remember, this is a Rabbit, not a pack mule."

Newman folded his shirt and laid it gently into the suitcase. Leanna walked in and surveyed the room.

"Other than that night lamp, is there anything else you want to take?"

Newman locked the latches on the suitcase. "This should do it." He strained picking up the suitcase. "I'll drop the room key off on the way out."

Mark suddenly appeared in the opened doorway. "Tracy said you were leaving." They turned to see him leaning casually against the doorway. "Not without saying good-bye, you're not." He walked over to Newman and grabbed his hand, pulled him closer and gave him a hug.

"Thanks Mark. I'm going to miss you too."

"You know, when you first came here, I didn't know what to make of you. But in the past few months… well, it's been good knowin' ya." Mark smiled.

Suddenly, Nelson appeared in the doorway, almost out of breath. He had a roll of toilet paper in his hand. "Ken, boy," Nelson huffed. "Boy, when I heard you were leaving, I didn't want you to leave without saying good-bye."

Newman stepped over to him and shook his hand. "Don't poison anybody while I'm gone."

"Hey, you know me. I could serve horseshit in such a way to make you ask for more." Nelson handed Newman the roll of toilet paper. "So the staff wanted to give you a going-away present, but since you're leaving so soon after the funeral, for us to find a card or anything, this is the best we can do on such short notice."

Newman took the roll and slowly pulled the sheets. "Good luck from the gang at the bar, signed Laura. Take care of yourself, Marci." There were also good-bye wishes from the crew at that gas station and the maids at the hotel. He carefully rolled the tissue back up. "Thanks, Nelson. This is the first time anyone's given me such a unique farewell present." Newman smiled. "But I will always cherish this, because I know that this was done with much love."

"Kind of symbolizes all the shit we've put you through since you've been here." They all laughed. "Where are you headed?" Nelson asked.

"D.C. I've got relatives there."

"How about you Leanna?" asked Nelson.

"No, I won't be making the trip with him."

"Too bad. You two belong together." Nelson noted.

Newman and Leanna looked at each other, then smiled.

"We'd better get going." Newman said, checking his watch. "I've got a bus to catch."

Everyone followed Newman out of the room and down the steps to Leanna's car.

"Boy," Nelson sighed, noting the luggage piled onto the back seat of the car, "how are you going to get all of this stuff on that bus?"

"Oh, don't worry, Leanna's going to ship this stuff up to me. All I'm carrying to the bus is this." Newman patted his suitcase and tossed it onto the backseat.

Leanna climbed into the car and closed her door. Newman stood in the opened door, talking and shaking hands. Leanna leaned over toward him.

"Say, if you want to catch that bus…"

"Look, guys…" Newman reluctantly explained.

"No need to explain." Nelson interjected. "Have a good trip."

Newman climbed into the car and closed the door. Mark ran over to the car door. "Jake wanted me to tell you good-bye for him and thanks for everything. You know he's not one for emotional goodbyes. You saw how solemn he was at Vick's funeral and he loved her a lot more than the affection he actually displayed. He has a lot of respect for you Ken. He also told me to give you this." Mark handed him an envelope. Newman looked inside and gasped. "It's the reward money for your help in capturing those bikers. Plus a little extract for all the effort and time you put into keeping things together."

"Kenny the bus." Leanna stated.

"Thanks Mark."

"Good luck, buddy." Mark stepped away from the door.

Leanna geared the car and slowly drove away. Newman could see his friends waving good-bye as the resort was gradually disappearing in his rearview mirror. Many times he had left the resort en route to Missoula, and each time he returned. Seeing the resort fade in the background for the last time provoked more of a sense of sadness, tempered with relief. Though, while the battle to save the resort wasn't won, at least it was finally over.

Minutes later, Leanna and Newman held hands as they waited near the boarding gate of the bus terminal. The terminal bustled with activity as passengers scurried back and forth.

"Now you have my address in D.C. to mail all of my luggage to."

"Yes Ken."

"And you have enough money for the shipping cost."

"Don't worry. I've got everything I need to get your luggage to D.C. I also have your number in case anything goes wrong."

He struggled for things to say to her. Not so much to try and remember forgotten details, but rather to hold on to her for as long as possible before boarding time.

"You will write, won't you?" Newman was somber.

"Sure," Leanna gingerly answered. "And once I get to Alaska, I'll drop you a postcard every now and then or at least until one of us gets tired of writing. Or perhaps, you might meet someone else in D.C. and, as all long-distance romances eventually do, it will die with the passage of time."

"That doesn't have to happen with us."

"Sure. Ken, sure," she unconvincingly agreed.

"Come with me to D.C." He emphatically insisted.

"Shhh! We've been all through this. There's no reason to rehash it here. When you get settled in D.C. and if you want to take a vacation, say in Alaska, look me up, okay?" Leanna smiled, trying desperately to hold back the tears swelling in her eyes.

"All aboard! Greyhound through service to Cheyenne, with connections for Chicago, Pittsburgh, and all points east. Now boarding in track seven. All aboard, please!" The intercom voice blared.

"Hey," she gulped, "that's you."

"Yea," he reluctantly sighed. "Hey, you know there's a lot of opportunity in D.C."

"Go. You're going to miss your bus," Leanna reluctantly urged. Newman picked up his suitcase and joined the slow, but steady line filing aboard the bus. The smell of diesel fumes and the constant roar of the engine filled the boarding area. The driver stood beside the entrance, collecting tickets from each passenger as they boarded. He smiled politely as he took Newman's ticket.

"D.C.?" He asked rhetorically.

"Yeah." Replied Newman.

"You'll change in Chicago. You've got a long ride ahead of you, mister." He handed the ticket back to Newman.

He picked up his suitcase and looked over at Leanna who stood beside him. They both were silent. She then leaned towards him and he put his arms around her. They kissed each other passionately.

The driver watched them momentarily as the people behind him began to grow impatient. The driver finally, loudly cleared his throat. Newman broke away and carried his suitcase up the steps. Leanna watched as he made his way toward the center of the bus. He threw his suitcase onto the overhead rack, and took a seat near the window. They waived, made faces, and mouthed messages to each other while the passengers continued to file aboard.

"This seat taken?"

Newman looked over to see an elderly woman looking down at him.

"No, ahhhh… no…" he stuttered, caught by surprise.

The woman climbed into the seat next to him. Newman returned his attention to Leanna.

"Your girlfriend?" The old woman asked.

"Beg pardon?" Newman turned toward the woman.

"That pretty girl you're waving to down there. Is that your girlfriend?"

"Ahhh… yes. Yes she is."

"I could tell. You two seem like you're really in love. I'll bet she can't wait until you get back from your trip."

He looked back out the window at her and waved. "It's going to be awhile before we see each other again."

"Oh, that's too bad," she said matter-of-factly. "I guess sometimes that can't be avoided." She sighed, "But if there's anything I've learned this past seventy years, is that true love is too precious to be apart for too long. You might not ever find it again."

She took her seat, reached into her purse and pulled out a paperback novel. She opened it to the bookmarked page, reclined, and began reading. Newman watched her motions and thought momentarily about her words.

The driver helped the last passenger aboard, then climbed aboard himself. He closed the door and slowly backed the huge vehicle out of the parking slot. Leanna watched as the bus stopped, then slowly pulled forward. It stopped again at the curb, the left blinker signaling an impending turn. The bus sat at the curb for what seemed like an inordinate amount of time. Suddenly, the door whizzed open, and Newman stepped off the bus, suitcase in hand. The door closed, and the bus turned down the busy street as Newman walked back toward the terminal.

Leanna watched slack… jawed from the boarding area as Newman walked up to her.

"What is your problem?" Leanna demanded in astonishment.

"You." Newman dropped the suitcase and gave her another passionate kiss.

She pulled back from him still in amazement. "What are you doing?"

"Clean socks. I realized I don't have enough clean socks for a three-day trip to D.C."

"Are you insane? You can't get another bus out of here until tomorrow."

"I was thinking. I've seen D.C., it's big, has lots of people, and paid parking. I hate paid parking. I'm in the mood for a change of pace, in some place quiet and remote, like Hawaii. Or, hey!" He snapped his fingers. "How about Alaska?"

"You mean you're willing to come to Alaska with me?" She beamed with excitement.

"Sure, why not? I'll invest in some long johns and a snow sled, and boy, I'll be set to go."

"Well, save that bus ticket. It'll help pay your airfare up there, when I go."

"Won't the Forest Service pay for my ticket?"

"Get real, Ken. What am I going to tell them? To pay my boyfriend's way to Alaska?"

"Well, if not your boyfriend's, how about your husband's? Won't they pay your husband's fare?"

"Sure, but…"

"No buts."

"Ahhhh… is this a proposal?"

Newman put his arm around Leanna's waist and ushered her back toward the terminal entrance.

"Of course it is."

"Well, isn't there supposed to be some flowers or an engagement ring, or a bended knee, or something?"

"Just say yes." Smiled Newman.

"Okay, yes, I'll marry you, but if you think you're getting off the hook for the flowers and the ring, you've got another thing coming, mister."

"Let's say, I turn my ticket back in, we go to your place so I can unpack, call my relatives, and tell them I've been sidetracked again."

"This time to Alaska." gleamed Leanna.

"This time to Alaska." Affirmed Newman.

They both smiled and gazed into each other's eyes. Newman broke the trance.

"They're gonna love this one," he said, tongue-in-cheek. "And maybe we can finally complete what we tried to start back in the hotel room."

"I don't know. They were pretty skilled at finding you back at the resort. What if they track you down and knock on my door while we are… you know?"

Newman opened the terminal door for Leanna. "In Alaska, we'll let the bears get 'em."

Leanna smiled. He followed her into the terminal and the door closed behind them.